Books by Jack Weyland

Novels

Charly
Sam
The Reunion
PepperTide
A New Dawn
The Understudy
Last of the Big-time Spenders
Sara, Whenever I Hear Your Name
Brenda at the Prom
Stephanie
Michelle and Debra
Kimberly
Nicole

Short Stories

A Small Light in the Darkness
Punch and Cookies Forever
First Day of Forever

Nonfiction

If Talent Were Pizza, You'd Be a Supreme

Weyland

PepperTide

A New Dawn

The Understudy

Brenda at the Prom

Kimberly

FIVE COMPLETE NOVELS BY BEST-SELLING AUTHOR

Jack Weyland

DESERET BOOK COMPANY
SALT LAKE CITY, UTAH

Library of Congress Catalog Card Number 94-72305

ISBN 0–87579–864–0

Printed in the United States of America

10   9   8   7   6   5   4   3   2   1

Contents

I.
PepperTide

II.
A New Dawn

III.
The Understudy

IV.
Brenda at the Prom

V.
Kimberly

PepperTide

JACK WEYLAND

Deseret Book Company
Salt Lake City, Utah

PepperTide

CHAPTER ONE

When I was fourteen years old, my father announced he had a deal going that would make us all rich. He always had deals on the fire, and it seemed we were always just about to get rich. This one required him to go to Mexico for a few days. He gave me fifty dollars for groceries, put me in charge of my younger brother and sister, threw a sleeping bag in his old pickup, hugged the three of us, and drove away.

That was eleven years ago. It was the last we heard from him until six months ago.

"I have a person-to-person collect call for Jimmy Pepper from Hank Pepper. Will you accept the call?" the operator asked.

"You must have the wrong number," I said.

"Jimmy? It's me—Dad. I saw you on Johnny Carson last week. You were so funny—I died laughing."

"Will you accept the call?" the operator broke in.

"What?" I mumbled, feeling stunned. ". . . I guess so."

". . . Like I said, you were so funny. Even my barber said so."

"Who is this again?"

"It's Dad."

"Where are you?"

"Buffalo, Wyoming. I work at a carwash."

A long silence. "Why did you call?"

"Just to say hello."

"Oh sure. Well, nice hearing from you . . . call again sometime."

"Wait. The reason I never came back . . . I was in jail in Mexico. When I got out, I didn't know how to contact you . . . not till I saw you on TV last week."

"Do you need money, is that why you called?"

He said he didn't need any money.

"Ryan's dead," I said.

There was a long silence. Finally he said, "I heard about it. It was too bad. He was a good boy."

"How do you know what he was? You weren't around to find out."

A long silence. "Can you and Jill come see me?"

I wiped my forehead. "Hank, I'm having a hard time with this. Give me your number and I'll get back to you."

"Who was that?" my wife asked after I'd hung up.

I stared at the phone, worried it might strike again. "My father—he's alive. He wants Jill and me to go see him."

"Are you going?"

"I don't know." I left the house for a walk, trying to fight the flood of memories. Somewhere in my mind a dam had broken, unable to take the strain any longer.

There were three kids in our family. I have a sister, Jill, sixteen months younger, and a brother, Ryan, three years younger.

When Dad left, we were living in a small rental house in Cheyenne. The front door opened into the alley, the only house in town that did. The address was 319½ Holcomb. As a boy, I remember resenting the ½, as if it meant we weren't good enough to merit a whole number. Once I tore it down from where it was tacked on a tree in front of the house, but Jill told on me and I had to put it back.

Both our parents were originally from Utah, but after they were married they never returned. Hank had little use for religion or relatives, both of which were in too plentiful supply in Utah.

There's been a parade of mothers and foster mothers running through our lives. Our real mother died when I was eleven, a victim of a hit-and-run accident along a gravel road near Cheyenne.

Our second mother was a woman Dad met in a truck-stop cafe when he was driving truck. It was less than a year after Mom died. Her name was Joan. We woke up one morning to find a woman rattling around in the kitchen, complaining about the mess. Dad walked in, tucking in his shirt and carrying his shoes and socks, and more or less off-handedly announced, "Oh, this is your new mother."

"We don't want a new mother," I said.

He shrugged his shoulders and sat down to put on his shoes. "Don't matter what you want. You got one, and you better obey her if you know what's good for you."

She made good hash browns and liked to watch TV, but more than anything I remember she looked on the grumpy side of life. If you said it was a nice day, she'd tell you it was going to rain.

We didn't get along very well with her. It wouldn't have been too bad if Dad had been around to smooth things over, but he was still driving for a moving van company. He drove all over the country. We loved it because each time he returned, he'd bring gifts from wherever he'd been. Once he went all the way to Maine and brought back a lobster frozen in ice. We loved to hear him talk about the places he'd been.

I'm not sure exactly what went wrong between him and Joan, or whether they were actually even married. About a year after she'd been there, a man started to drop by and pick her up at nights while Hank was away. She always said she was going to a movie, but there were only two movie theatres in town, and they changed movies once every two weeks, but she was gone four times a week.

When Dad got back from a long trip, they got into an

argument that lasted late into the night. I tried to stay awake to listen, but finally fell asleep.

The next morning she was gone.

"Where's Joan?" Ryan asked.

"Gone," was all Dad ever said about it.

For a while he quit driving so he could watch us. He got a job as a dispatcher for the company. Either it didn't pay much or he didn't like sitting at a desk, because by the time I was fourteen he'd quit.

After that we didn't know what he was doing. He'd be gone for a few days, then suddenly appear with lots of money. It was great when he came back, because he'd take us out for pizza and buy us things. Once he bought us new bicycles, and another time, fishing and camping gear. He'd stay home a week or two and then be gone again. At first he paid a lady to come and stay, but I told him he might as well save his money, that I could cook as well as that lady, who always made casseroles with noodles and cream of mushroom soup. It was years later when I finally realized why most women would rather fix casseroles than just about anything.

That's why he left us alone on that last trip.

We got along okay at first, but after three weeks, with him already two weeks late, I started to wonder.

One day we were playing in an old junk car that perpetually sat in our front yard, which, because the house faced the alley, was everyone else's backyard. To us, the car was a wonderful toy, rich with the smell of mildew and rotting orange peels and grease. In that car we had chased and been chased by outlaws. Sometimes it was even a plane or a rocket.

Ryan was sitting on top of the car eating a peanut butter sandwich while Jill and I played "Famous Actress." It wasn't that much fun for me, but she liked it. She was a famous rich actress, and I was her chauffeur. She'd spend hours rummaging in an old trunk in the basement, where Dad had put Mom's clothes. Then she'd come outside, her face smeared with makeup. She'd get in and order me to take her to the Empire State Building.

While we were playing, I looked back and saw a neighbor lady from across the alley standing at her fence and staring at us long and hard. She'd come to empty her garbage but had already done that. She just stared at us. Then without a word she shook her head and left.

The next day after school a woman came. She said her name was Miss McCormack and that she was a caseworker from the county. For a while I thought she meant she worked in a canning factory. But that isn't what she meant at all.

I couldn't figure why she came, because all she did was sit and look. We were watching TV and having our usual peanut butter sandwiches and milk. She sat on the couch in front of the TV, but didn't seem very interested in the show.

"I can change the channel if you want," I said.

"No, that isn't necessary. Is that your supper?"

Seeing she was a woman, I figured she wouldn't be happy about that being our supper. "In a few minutes," I said, "I'm going in the kitchen and make a nice casserole."

"May I see the kitchen?" she asked.

Before I could say no, she was in there opening cupboards, writing things down on her clipboard.

We had plenty of peanut butter. Once while Hank was working as a dispatcher, he heard about a wrecked semitrailer load of peanut butter. He bought several cases at a good price. Due to various disasters in the trucking industry, our basement was usually full of good deals.

"Do you get paid to do this?" I asked, watching her open the refrigerator and write something down.

"Where's your mother?"

"In heaven," Ryan said proudly.

She wrote on her clipboard.

"We have a stepmother though, and she'll be back any day," I said.

"Where is she?"

"She went away with a man," Ryan said.

Miss McCormack started to write that.

"She didn't either," I interrupted. "She went to visit her sick aunt, but she'll be back any day now."

"How do you know?" Miss McCormack asked.

"She died," I said.

"Who died?" she asked, her pencil ready to pounce on my words.

"My stepmother's aunt. That's why our stepmother will be home any day now. She has no reason to stay there. Tomorrow—she'll be back tomorrow. Won't she, Jillsy?"

I winked at her in our own special code. "Tomorrow," she agreed.

"Then who's that man she always goes to the movies with?" Ryan asked.

"Ryan, go watch TV."

Ryan left.

"And where's your father?" the lady asked.

"Away on business, but he'll be back on Friday. What do you call your job?"

"I'm a social worker."

"What do you write on the paper?"

"My impressions."

"Impressions of what?" Jill asked.

"Of the conditions here," Miss McCormack said.

"We don't have any conditions here," Jill said.

Miss McCormack opened another cupboard—full of peanut butter. There were grocery stores with less peanut butter than we had.

I thought it strange she left before *Gilligan's Island* was even over.

The money Dad left was almost gone. We were down to five dollars. I had a paper route that brought in a few dollars a week.

The next day I was in the kitchen working on an old lawn mower engine Dad had brought home for me once. I liked to take things apart and try to figure out how they worked. I didn't always get them back together, but the engine didn't work anyway, so it wasn't like I was wrecking anything.

Since we ate all our meals around the TV set in the living room, we weren't using the kitchen table for anything. It became my workbench for taking the engine apart.

There was a knock on our back door, which most people thought was our front door, because it was the one that faced the street, or rather faced the house in front of us, which faced the street.

I answered it, thinking it might be the lady with the clipboard again, but it was a guy my age. He asked if my name was Jim Pepper, and I said, "What if it is?" He said his name was Kevin Gallagher. That didn't mean anything to me. He mumbled something about being a president. That made even less sense to me.

"You don't look like any kind of president to me," I said.

"I'm the teachers quorum president."

"I don't want to be no teacher," I grumbled.

"You're supposed to be."

"Who says?"

"God." He was very nervous. He cleared his throat and looked like he was going to either cry or sneeze. "I'm supposed to talk to you. Can I come in?"

I shrugged my shoulders. He followed me inside and sat down on a stool and watched. To tell the truth, I enjoyed making him nervous. I banged the wrenches and grunted a lot like I was a mechanic and knew what I was doing.

He sat there stiff as a board. I noticed he was wearing corduroy slacks.

"Are you a Mormon?" he finally asked.

"Maybe I am," I said, remembering a baptism long

ago at my mother's insistence. I dropped a wrench on the floor. He jumped at the noise.

"You could be in our scout troop."

"Why'd I want to do that?"

"We go camping and fishing."

"I don't care about none of that."

"We learn to do things."

"What kind of things?" I figured I had him, that he'd say something dumb like how great it was to learn to tie knots.

He looked at me for a second, then said, "We learn to fix engines."

"Yeah?" I said, suddenly interested.

"Tomorrow night we're starting a new class on auto mechanics. We have a mechanic in our ward who's going to show us some things. I'll come by and get you."

I'd always figured that if I could ever get that engine working I'd rig it up to my bicycle. But the way I was going, I'd never fix it.

"I might go," I said as negatively as I could.

In a way I figured he was just talk, but he really did come by to pick me up. When we got to the church, he introduced me to Bishop Townsend, who shook my hand and said he was glad I could come.

The bishop introduced me to the scoutmaster. In his uniform, he looked a little like an overweight Jolly Green giant. But once I got to know him, he turned out to be okay—he just happened to like scouting.

There were about 15 other guys in the troop. Not all of them were going to learn about car engines. In fact, Kevin and I were the only ones. I wondered if Kevin hadn't created this whole engine mechanics course on the spot just to get me to go to church with him.

We went to Olson's Garage, and Mr. Olson showed us a lot of things about engines and tools. "When you get a car, make sure you always lock it when you leave, or somebody'll come and steal it. Happens all the time."

"How can they start it without a key?" Kevin asked.

"They hot wire it. So remember to lock up."

The conversation drifted to carburetors.

Afterwards we washed up and went back to church. The bishop asked if I'd had a good time.

"It was okay," I said, trying to sound unimpressed. But when I thought about what I'd have done at home, it was ten times better than that.

The next day we ran out of money. I went out and collected from everyone on my paper route. I found that you can collect from the husbands at night if their wives aren't home, and then collect from the wives the next day. But it wasn't stealing, because I was marking it all down in my book. I just figured it was like paying in advance.

That night we went through our couches and chairs, searching between the frame and springs where money can drop. We found a couple of dollars that way. And we turned in some pop bottles at the store.

The next night I sent Ryan through the neighborhood going door to door, saying he was on a treasure hunt and needed three pop bottles. Jill and I followed with an old wagon to put the bottles in.

I rode my bike to the airport, where there's a fountain where people with nothing better to do throw pennies and nickels and make a wish. I'd made a small rake at home so I could get the money without having to go wading. I got over three dollars that way.

On Saturday morning, while Ryan and Jill watched cartoons, Kevin came and asked us to go to church with him the next day. I didn't really want to go, but he said that after church his parents said it would be all right for us to come to supper. I jumped at the offer.

I don't remember much about the first time in church except in priesthood meeting, Kevin ran the whole show as far as the quorum went. He got up and welcomed everybody and said who'd take care of fixing the sacrament. He told them about me, saying I was a mechanic, and just what their quorum needed for their summer cycling trip.

Mostly I remember the food after church. We ate everything they had, and then, since we were still hungry, Kevin's mother fixed some scrambled eggs. They asked about Dad. I said he'd be back on Wednesday.

Monday after school, Miss McCormack came again, this time with a man. She called him Mr. Ackley. He had on a gray western suit and a bolo tie. I figured he just wore that stuff so people would think he was a regular Westerner—but I could tell he really hated Wyoming. He never spoke directly at us, and when he said anything to her, he talked quietly as if he were telling secrets we weren't supposed to hear.

"Is your father back yet?" Miss McCormack asked.

"Not yet, but he phoned yesterday. He had a little trouble with his truck, but everything's fine now. He's in Omaha now and has to make a delivery in Minnesota. Then he'll be back."

"Hmm," Mr. Ackley said.

We all sat down in the living room. Ryan was watching TV, and Jill was in the basement trying on dresses again and experimenting with eye shadow and rouge.

"We'd like to look around," Miss McCormack said.

"What for?"

"We'd like to evaluate conditions here."

"Is that all you people do?"

Miss McCormack started for the kitchen. Mr. Ackley followed.

They weren't too happy about the jumble of engine parts strewn on the kitchen table. "This is a pigsty," Mr. Ackley said to her.

She opened the refrigerator for him to look in. Green mold was growing on one of Joan's casseroles. He shook his head. "Deplorable," he whispered to Miss McCormack.

Then Jill swirled into the kitchen, unaware of our company. She had eye shadow and rouge all over her face and was wearing one of Joan's old low-cut dresses about four sizes too big. She looked ridiculous. When she saw Mr. Ackley and Miss McCormack, she screamed and ran out again.

"Who was that?" Mr. Ackley whispered.

"The twelve-year-old," Miss McCormack replied.

"Almost thirteen," I added.

"She looks like a tramp. I recommend foster homes as soon as possible."

"Hey, look," I interrupted, "Dad is coming back on Thursday at the latest, and we got cases of food downstairs. We just don't happen to keep it in the cupboard."

I ran downstairs, got the last case of beans, and lugged it back to the kitchen. "Look at this," I said, "our whole basement is full of food." I didn't think they'd go downstairs to find out, seeing they'd have to step over part of the lawnmower engine to get there. It was a lie about there being more food downstairs, but I figured it was just as wrong for them to barge in with their clipboards and start making plans about shipping us to other homes.

"Who could we use?" Miss McCormack asked.

"How many children are there?" he asked.

"Just the three."

"The Johnson family could take one, Rosettis will take the girl, and Palmer might take the oldest boy."

I figured I had to shout to get them to hear me. "My dad said we could definitely expect him by Thursday. See, what happened was his manifold went out on the truck, and that caused his Bendix spring to break. He explained it all to me when he phoned me last night."

I rattled on, using words I'd learned at Olson's Garage. Mr. Ackley didn't seem to hear me, but finally Miss McCormack said, "He says his father is coming back on Thursday."

"I guess we can wait till then," he said.

They went to the car and wrote on their clipboards and then drove off. I knew they'd be back.

I knew what was coming. They were going to split us up and put us in three different homes, homes where we'd have hot cereal for breakfast and casseroles for supper. They wouldn't know that sometimes Ryan would wake up crying for Mom in the middle of the night, but if you went in and touched his forehead for a while, he'd fall asleep again. They wouldn't know that Jill didn't like corn. It didn't matter how often you said it was good for her, she wouldn't eat it—not plain, not creamed, and not on the cob. There were things about them only I knew, and if we were separated, we'd stop being a family. I couldn't let that happen. Dad put me in charge, not them.

I'd told so many people that Dad was coming home on Thursday that I almost believed it myself. But when Thursday morning came, I knew we had to do something or we'd wind up in foster homes, and be visited every week by Miss McCormack, not because she cared about us, but because the county was paying her to evaluate conditions.

I got Ryan and Jill up early. While they were eating their toast and peanut butter, I turned off the TV and told them what was going to happen to us if we didn't leave town. "They want to put us in different homes. If they do that, maybe we'll never see each other again."

Ryan looked like he was going to cry.

"Hey, don't worry, I won't let 'em do that, but we've got to leave town today. How'd you like to go to California?"

"Is that where Dad is?" Ryan asked.

Jill looked at me to see if I'd lie.

I would. "Yeah, he's there. He wants us to come and meet him."

"I'm supposed to do a report today for school," he said.

"Bring it with you. You can give it in California when we get there."

We went downstairs and got our camping gear and packed some food in our packs, plus a hatchet, matches, and a flashlight, along with our clothes. Then we took ropes and tied everything to our bikes.

We left about eleven that morning. On our way out of town I stopped at a few places and collected on my paper route.

The night before, when I'd thought about us leaving, I'd pictured us catching fish and eating berries and trapping animals for food on the way to California. But things never work out the way you picture them. We had to go slow because the chain on Ryan's bike kept coming off. Finally we had to take it in to get it fixed. So by three in the afternoon, we were still in town, surrounded by motels and fast-food stores. There were no trees to chop and no fish and no berries.

When the wind blows in Wyoming during the day, it's one thing, but at night in October, that's another thing entirely. If you don't know about Wyoming wind, you don't know what it's like to have nature ticked off at you. Just before dark we stopped at a city park. There were several McDonald's boxes lying around, and some other paper stashed in a trash can. We burned them to heat our can of pork and beans. We ate quickly. The beans on the bottom were burnt, and the ones on top barely warm. They tasted terrible. To make our meal a little better, I ran and bought fresh apple pies from McDonald's. Then we went to a shopping center and walked around until it closed.

It was a cold night. To keep warm we zipped two of our sleeping bags together, and all three of us crawled into it. It was tight but warm. Jill's hair tickled my nose.

We fell asleep.

Sometime during the night, we woke up with a flashlight shining in our eyes. "What are you kids doing here?" a cop asked.

"We're sleeping out," I said. "It's okay with our parents. We do it all the time."

"You can't stay overnight in this park."

We put on our shoes, rolled up our sleeping bags, and threw everything back into the packs.

The cop stood and watched us, then walked over to his car and picked up the mike for his two-way radio.

"I just found three kids sleeping in the park. You got anything on any runaways?"

"Run!" I whispered sharply to Ryan and Jill.

He saw us leaving. "Stop!" he called out.

Jill fell down. I stopped and helped her up. She put her arm around me while we continued across the street. I could hear the cop starting his car.

We ran through McDonald's parking lot, across another street, through one yard, along a fenceline for a while, and then into another yard. We found a garage door open and ran in and quietly closed the overhead door and waited.

There was a small window on the garage door. I kept watch. Jill quietly opened the door to the station wagon parked in the garage, and she and Ryan crawled in the back.

The police car passed the street twice, shining his spotlight on everything as he passed. After a few minutes, he quit circling the block.

I left Ryan and Jill and went back to see if I could find our gear. I saw the cop packing everything into his trunk. He parked behind a building to wait for us. After a few minutes, he tired of his game and drove away.

I went back to the garage. We stayed there until it began to get gray outside.

California seemed a long way off.

* * * * * * * * * * * * *

In the morning we slipped out of the garage and went to McDonald's for breakfast—Ryan and Jill needed the assurance of the familiar plastic and cardboard and Ronald McDonald to make them feel at home. There wasn't much money left, so I told them I wasn't hungry.

All the time they were eating, I kept telling them about California, and about the beaches and oranges, and about going swimming any time we wanted.

They believed me.

By the time we were through, we were feeling good again. I had a plan. We'd walk to the truckstop on the edge of town and tell them about Dad, how he was a trucker too, and because truckers stick together, one of them would give us a ride to California. We bundled up and started walking, but we had to stop every few blocks to warm up because of the wind.

It was almost noon by the time we got there. We sat at a booth and ordered two bowls of chili. I figured I could just eat some crackers and get by.

After we finished one tray of crackers, I went to another table and asked a trucker if we could have his. He nodded his head.

"My dad's a trucker too," I said. "You ever heard of him? Hank Pepper's his name."

"Can't say I have."

"He drives for Mayflower, goes all over the country. He went to Maine once. Where you going?"

"Oregon."

"Can we get a ride with you?"

He looked at Jill and Ryan. "Running away from home, huh?"

"Gosh, no. See, our mom moved there, and she wrote us a letter and told us she'd finally gotten an apartment, and said we should move out with her."

"But she didn't send any bus money?" he asked.

I paused. "Well, sure, but it got stolen from my locker at school."

"Phone her and she'll send some more."

"Well, that's just it, because I can't remember where she said she moved to, so we don't know how to contact her."

"What town in Oregon did she go to? You can call the police and they'll find her for you."

"That's just it. I don't remember what town in Oregon it is."

"Then it wouldn't do any good for me to take you there, would it?"

"Oh, once we got to Oregon, we'd know."

I paused, and he grinned. "Gotcha," he said, his toothpick waving in his mouth as he talked. He got up and paid his bill and left. I made sure he didn't stop at a pay phone and call the cops before he left.

Another trucker finished his meal. I sent Ryan over for his tray of crackers.

A few minutes later I looked out to see a cop car pulling into the parking lot near an outdoor phone booth. The first guy we'd talked to stepped out of his truck to talk to him.

"Let's get out of here!" I pulled Jill and Ryan with me, through the kitchen and out the back door.

We ran full speed to the end of the parking lot and into a vacant lot.

We kept moving. Finally I saw a large water drainpipe, tall enough to walk through if you bent over. It went underneath the highway. I found some wooden crates we could sit on, so we went in and rested.

We waited till dark. It started to snow. I decided on a plan. We went back to the shopping center.

"Look for a car either with the keys in it or else unlocked," I said.

"What for?" Jill asked.

"We're going to steal a car," I said.

"We are?" Jill asked.

"Somebody's not going to like that," Ryan said.

"If the caseworkers get us, we'll never see each other again. Do you want that to happen?"

He shook his head.

"All right then. Find a car."

We started walking slowly through the parking lot.

"Here's one that's not locked!" Ryan yelled.

"Quiet!" I whispered loudly.

We hurried to the car and looked in.

"But there's no keys in it," Ryan complained. "You need keys."

"I'll hot wire it," I said.

"What does that mean?" Jill asked.

"For crying out loud, Jill. Don't you know what hot wiring means? It means you start the car without keys."

I had Ryan and Jill keep watch while I got in the car. I stared at the dashboard and wished I knew what to do. I tried to start it without the key, but it wouldn't work.

After a few minutes Jill complained. "It doesn't look like you're doing anything except staring."

I decided hot wiring must involve something under the hood. I stepped out and after struggling for a few minutes finally got the hood open.

I stared at the engine. There were so many parts.

"Why don't you do something?" Jill asked.

I looked at her.

"You don't really know how to hot wire a car, do you."

"It's different with a Ford," I said, slamming the hood shut.

"It's okay. I'm glad you don't know how."

I felt like a failure.

She put her hand on my shoulder. "Hey, it's okay. Don't worry so much."

I felt better. She could always do that to me.

There was no place to go except home. When we got there, we didn't put on any lights because we were afraid the cops or Mr. Ackley would be checking the house, looking for us. The house was cold, and the furnace didn't work. I figured somebody'd turned off our gas. We paddled around in the dark until all the blinds were shut, then pulled the TV set into the bedroom, where the three of us huddled together and ate peanut butter and beans and watched TV till we fell asleep.

I was the first to wake up in the morning. I unraveled Jill's hand on my arm, and Ryan's leg from on top of me, and looked outside. It had snowed a couple of inches during the night.

I looked at Jill. She was the prettiest girl in the world, but I never told her that. For one thing, she was always a pain when we were younger, because she always told on me. The first words she ever said, according to our mother, were "Dimmy did it." Mom told us that whenever she said that, I would turn to her and scowl and say, "Dumb dumb Dill."

That morning I pictured myself protecting her and Ryan from life's harsh realities. In the end, they were the ones who saved me from self-destruction.

Ryan woke up. "I like all of us sleeping together," he said.

"Yeah, but we can't do it all the time," I said.

"Why not?"

"Because Jill's a girl."

"So what?"

"It's just not done." I looked at Jill sleeping. "You're too young to understand."

"Let's wake her up," Ryan said.

I picked up my pillow and dropped it on her head. She mumbled something and rolled over on her side.

"Ryan," I whispered, "now you do it."

He hesitated.

"It's okay, go ahead." I said.

He did. She awoke and sat up. While she yawned, I tossed a pillow at her. She picked it back up and threw it at me, then jumped at me and knocked me down on the bed and sat on me and started hitting me with the pillow. I was laughing so hard I couldn't fight back.

"Ryan, help me!"

"How?"

"Hit her with the other pillow!"

Never in his whole life had Ryan wanted to hurt anyone. When we were very young, Mom would give gold
stars to the child who was the most obedient that week. I
never got the gold star. Jill got it some of the time, when
she was not hanging around me, but mostly Ryan got it. I
used to call him Gold Star.

Now he had a problem. He could help me only by hitting Jill with a pillow.

"Ryan! Please!" I giggled.

He hesitated, then picked up the pillow and hit Jill
with it, knocking her off me.

"All right you two!" she yelled, laughing at the same
time.

What a mess we made. By the time we were through,
the pillows had ripped and there was a cloud of feathers
every time we hit each other. But we didn't care anymore
about the house.

Sometimes your mind takes a picture and freezes it,
along with all the emotions and textures of a moment.
There is such a picture in my mind of the three of us
standing on the bed giggling uncontrollably, feathers
floating everywhere. Jumping on the bed, holding hands
in a circle.

The last of a family circle.

After we'd scattered feathers all over, the bed frame
broke from too much jumping. We sat on the mattress,
now on the floor, and ate peanut butter with a knife out
of the jar and watched Saturday cartoons.

About ten o'clock a car pulled up. I looked out and
saw Mr. Ackley and Miss McCormack coming up the
walk.

"Get dressed!" I ordered, turning off the TV. "We'll
have to run for it."

I'd already dressed, but they scurried around in their
pajamas hunting for their clothes among the rubble of
feathers.

"Hurry up!"

There was a knock at the door.

Jill found her things and ran into the bathroom to change. Ryan stood there in the middle of the room, looking dazed.

"What's wrong?" I asked him.

"I can't find one of my shoes."

The knock became louder.

"For crying out loud! Where did you put 'em last night?"

"I don't know."

"Hurry up! If they catch us, they'll throw us in jail!"

I frantically helped him look for his shoe. While I was moving the mattress, I accidentally bumped part of the frame, which collapsed even further, making a loud crash.

"We know you're in there!" I heard Mr. Ackley shout. "Let us in!"

Jill came in dressed.

"He lost one of his shoes," I told her. "Try to find it, while I go stall 'em."

Mr. Ackley was pounding on the door.

"Just a minute," I shouted.

I took as long as possible to open the door a crack, but I left the chain on.

"What do you want?" I asked Mr. Ackley.

"Is your father here?"

"Yeah—he got in late last night. You know that Bendix gear I was telling you about, well, wouldn't you know it, it went out again on him. I asked him about it, and he said, it's just something that happens on some models of Mack trucks, especially that particular model . . ."

"We want to talk to him."

"He's sleeping."

"Well, can you get him up?"

"He doesn't like to be woken up when he comes back from a long trip."

"When will he be awake?"

"This afternoon sometime."

"Can you unlock the door?"

"I'm not supposed to let strangers in the house."

"I think you're lying about your father being here," Mr. Ackley said.

"If you want to wait in the car, I'll let you know when he wakes up."

"We're going to the police," Mr. Ackley said. "They'll be able to get him up."

"Wait, don't do that. I'll go see if I can wake him up. It may take a while though."

I walked slowly down the hall until Mr. Ackley couldn't see me, then ran into the bedroom. Ryan was still standing there, one shoe on, and Jill was on her hands and knees feeling inch by inch for the shoe.

"Forget about the shoe! Go out the back now! And hurry! I'll meet you by the tree fort in a minute."

I watched them leave, then walked back to the front door.

"My dad says he doesn't want to see anybody for a while. He's sick. He says he's been throwing up all night. He's afraid you might catch it."

"You're lying," Mr. Ackley said.

I shrugged my shoulders. "Okay then—but don't blame me if you come down with it. I'll go get him."

I walked slowly out of his sight, then ran out the back door.

Mr. Ackley didn't trust anybody. He'd just sent Miss McCormack to the back. She watched me as I ran down the stairs and past her through the yard. "He's running away!" she called out.

I caught up with Ryan and Jill at our favorite hideout, a large tree in a neighbor's yard.

Ryan was standing on one foot crying. Not a sound from him really, just silent tears rolling down his face.

"What's wrong?"

"He wet his pants," Jill said.

I looked. She was right.

"He was scared about being thrown in jail," she said. "That's all."

It was a mark against his manhood, and we all knew it.

"Sure. Hey, Ryan, it's okay."

He shook his head slowly.

"No, really, Ryan, it's okay," Jill said. "We understand. We're scared too. Hey, don't cry, Ryan."

"Are you cold?" I asked him.

He shook his head.

"It's warm now, but it'll get cold," I said. "Hey, Ryan, c'mon. It's no big thing. You gotta quit crying now, okay?"

We stood there for a while, telling Ryan it was okay. It started to snow again. Ryan started to shiver and we had nowhere to go. We were beaten and we knew it.

We walked to Kevin's back door and knocked. His mother answered the door and invited us in. Inside the house everything seemed so ordinary. It seemed a miracle that some people could live like that.

I went to Kevin privately and told him about Ryan. He gave us an old pair of jeans and some underwear for him to wear. TV cartoons were on. We sat down to watch. Kevin's mother asked if we'd like some pancakes.

At breakfast his parents didn't ask questions, and we didn't say much of anything. We just ate and ate. But when Kevin's mother put the second load of pancakes on Ryan's plate, she touched his shoulder the way mothers do. I was sorry she'd done it, because he broke down and started crying.

He cried a long time. After a while, we got the story out clear enough so they could understand. Kevin's dad called the bishop. The bishop came and took me to his office at church, and left Ryan and Jill at Kevin's so they could watch Saturday cartoons.

I told the bishop everything; then he got on the

phone and made five or six phone calls. By the time the morning was over, I'd talked to Mr. Ackley and Miss McCormack. The bishop made me apologize.

The bishop asked if we'd like to stay with Kevin's parents for a while. He said it was okay with Miss McCormack.

"It'll just be for a little while," I told Ryan and Jill, "just till Dad gets back."

"He's not coming back," Jill later said just to me, "and you know it."

CHAPTER TWO

        After Hank phoned, I stewed for a couple of days and then called Jill in Burley, Idaho.

    "Hank called me. He wants to see us."

    She paused. "Who's Hank?"

    "Our father."

    "Daddy phoned?" she asked excitedly. "Where is he?"

    "Buffalo, Wyoming."

    "How does he sound?"

    "All right, I guess."

    "Jimmy, do you want to see him?"

    "No."

    "Why not?"

    There was a long silence, and then I said, "I'm afraid."

    "But we have to, don't we?" she said.

    "Do we?"

    "He's our father. We have to see him when he asks us. Maybe he's sick or something."

    I sighed. "Okay."

    We made plans. I would fly from Los Angeles to Idaho, and then we'd drive their family car to Buffalo.

    "Jill, I'll need some help with this."

    "We'll have time to get our heads on straight during the drive."

    "If we wait for me to get my head on straight, we'll end up taking a ferry across the Bering Strait."

    We said good-bye. Just before I was about to make my plane reservations, the phone rang. It was a reporter from the "National Inquirer," wanting to do an article about me.

    "What kind of article?" I asked.

"About your growing up. We'll talk to high school friends, get their impressions of what you were like. Talk to your parents, you know, human interest."

"I've seen some of the garbage you write. I'm not interested."

"Look, we're going to do the article one way or the other. It'd be better if you cooperated."

I hung up, my forehead beaded with sweat. What if they find out about my father?

We stayed with Kevin's family for a few weeks, then they were transferred to Alaska by the Air Force. The bishop tried to get someone in the ward to take us, but he didn't have much luck—because they knew us. Finally he got permission to send us to Idaho as extras to the Lamanite placement program.

"But we're not Indians," I said.

"Sometimes we send a few special cases to Idaho."

The bus trip to Idaho was a grand adventure for us. They'd given us money, and we bought a large supply of junk food to eat along the way.

I remember our night on the bus. It was late, and everyone was asleep but Jill and me. I was just opening a large bag of Krunchies while she looked thoughtfully out the window.

"Whataya thinking about, Jillsy?"

"Look at the stars," she said.

I leaned over and looked. "Yeah—what about 'em?"

"There's so many."

"Sure are—want any Krunchies?"

"You're hopeless," she said.

"What's wrong?"

"You don't understand anything."

"Understand what? That there's a lot of stars? Cripes, Jillsy, everybody knows that."

She turned away from me. "You're too immature to understand."

"I'm as mature as you are any day. Go ahead, tell me what you're thinking about."

"It was a feeling I had, looking at the stars. It's like they're trying to say something."

I took a large handful of Krunchies, stuffed them into my mouth, then leaned over and stared out the window. "Yeah? What are they saying to you, Jillsy?"

"Just forget it, okay?" she said.

"Sure thing—want any Krunchies?"

"You're about as deep thinking as a mouse."

"Well, if you'd quit talking in riddles. Why don't you quit beating around the bush?"

"You're such a retard. Haven't you ever looked at the stars at night and got goose bumps just thinking about, well, life?"

"Life?" I teased. "You're thinking about life? What's there to think about?"

"Things like—I wonder where Mom is."

"She's dead."

"But where is she? I don't mean her body. Where is she?"

"How should I know? What I'd like to know is, where's Dad?"

"I dreamed about us once, you and me and Ryan."

She was serious. I stopped a handful of Krunchies midway to my mouth as a token of respect for deep thought.

"What happened in your dream?"

"We died. At least I think we were dead."

"How did we die? In a gunfight, I bet. The first famous brother-sister gang in history. I can see it now. The Pepper Gang. Take that, POW, and that, BANG. Ahhh! They got me, Jillsy!" I fell limp on her shoulder, gasping, my tongue hanging out. Then I sprang up. "How about it? Shall we get off the bus and hitchhike to California and steal avocados?"

She smiled, but only a little. "I sort of want to be good," she confessed.

"A religious girl?" I teased her.

"What's so bad about that?"

"Like Kevin and his family? All they do is pray. Pray in the morning, pray at night, pray whenever they eat. What are they so scared about they got to pray all the time? I say don't bother God until things are really scuzzy, then go to it."

"Did you see the way Kevin's father treated his wife?"

"Yeah, what about it?"

"He really loves her."

"So maybe he does. She's not too bad."

"He respects her."

"Ah, come on. I suppose he's your ideal man? I bet he wears a tie in the shower. Anyway, tell me your dream."

"We were walking in a forest, and we came upon a clearing and there he was."

"Who was?"

"God, I think."

I paused, then asked quietly, "Yeah? What'd He say?"

"Nothing."

"Nothing? He sounds like that school librarian who knew everything, but every time you asked a question, he'd say, 'You can look that up yourself.'"

"Don't make fun of my dream," she said. I backed off and tried to look serious while she continued. "It was more of a feeling I got. A feeling that God cares. That's all that happened—a strong feeling that God cares about us."

I took another handful of Krunchies. "Sure, why not? If He cares about the sparrows, like they say in church, then He's got to care about us. For one thing, we're a lot bigger than a stupid sparrow."

She turned away. "Why do you always have to make fun of everything? We used to be able to talk about serious things."

"It's not me that's changing, you know. It's you. You're changing. You're getting so moody."

She stared silently out the window as shadows of the

night passed us by. I sat and philosophically munched Krunchies.

Suddenly she started crying. When she was younger and did that, I could get away with putting my arm around her shoulder and giving her a hug. But somewhere lately we'd come to a time when we couldn't do that. Now we hardly touched each other at all except when she slugged me. "They're going to break us up, Jimmy. I know they will. We're not going to be a family anymore."

"I won't let 'em break us up. I promise."

"They'll do whatever they want to."

"Look, Jillsy, I've been thinking. Okay, we stay in Idaho a few weeks, but then, whataya say, we run away for California—you and me and Ryan. I'll get a job and make good money, and we'll get a place by the ocean, like on TV, and everything'll be fine. I'll take care of you and Ryan."

"That'd be nice. You're so much fun to be with— sometimes."

"It never gets cold in California, and if you want any fruit, you just go outside and pick it. And it never snows, so you don't have to buy coats."

"You're not just talking like Daddy used to, are you?"

"No, I promise it'll happen. I'll take care of you."

She seemed better after that, and soon she went to sleep. Her head lay on my shoulder, and even though I was awake and had to go to the bathroom in the back of the bus, I didn't move for a long time.

The next morning we both woke up at the same time. She stretched and looked over at me. I was still holding the half-eaten bag. "Hey, don't hog all the Krunchies," she said with a mischievous grin, grabbing for the bag.

It was our last tickling contest.

The bus driver made us pick up all the Krunchies we spilled.

* * * * * * * * * * * * *

Jill was right about one thing—they split us up.

The man from LDS Social Services who picked us up at the bus station, Brother Bateman, explained they were going to put us in three different homes. We would end up in towns strung along the Snake River, Jill in Twin Falls, me fifty miles to the east in Burley, and Ryan sixty miles from me, in American Falls.

They took us to an office and asked us a lot of questions; then they took us to a doctor and made us wait in a sitting room, and then made us wait in separate rooms. At first they kept saying the doctor would see us right away, but later they said there was an emergency at the hospital and the doctor had to leave, so we were each sitting there in our underwear in three different rooms, waiting. After fifteen minutes, I decided I'd had it, so I put on my clothes and started knocking on doors with a special code we had. I found Jill and told her to get dressed, and then we found Ryan. We started to walk out of the office, but the nurse told us we couldn't leave, so we went back into Ryan's room and started rummaging through the medical supplies.

Ryan was very quiet that day. I worried the most about him. For his benefit more than anything else I had us sit down on the floor, and I found a sharp knife and made a small cut on my thumb.

"Now you do it," I said, handing the knife to Jill.

"What for?"

"It's a ceremony," I said.

She made a cut. I touched my thumb to hers.

"Now, Ryan, you make a cut."

I was surprised, but he did it.

I took his thumb and touched it to ours.

"This means they'll never separate us. We did it on the thumb because that's what you use when you hitchhike. We're in a special club now, just the three of us. Ryan, I know you might get scared being alone, but we got common blood, and no matter what they do to us, we'll be together. This is a real serious promise we're making. What we're promising is that if it really gets too bad for one of us, then the one who's hurting has to write the other two and tell 'em, and we'll come and, if we have to, we'll run away again, all three of us. Agreed?"

Ryan solemnly nodded his head.

"Don't be so quiet all the time, Ryan. Say it."

"I agree."

"Jill?"

"I agree."

"Okay. Now, Ryan, I got to talk to you. You keep things inside. You got to let 'em out once in a while. All the time you're trying to be good, and that's okay I guess, but if you feel bad, let it out. Look, it's all right once in a while to go turn over somebody's garbage can, or put soap on their car windows, or just let somebody know you feel rotten. Don't let them box you in. If you hurt, let somebody know it. You know, like me. I know you don't like the way I mouth off sometimes, but it feels good to let it out. And if it gets too bad, just call me and I'll come and we'll all go to California and live. Okay?"

He swallowed hard, fought back the tears, and silently nodded.

I knew it was a corny thing to do, and cutting our thumbs didn't really change a thing, and besides I'd read it in *Tom Sawyer* anyway, but Ryan needed something, and it was the only thing I could think of at the time.

A few minutes later a nurse came in and gasped, seeing us sitting on the floor with blood on us and me holding a scalpel. When she finally realized we were all right, she chewed us out. She got Brother Bateman, and he came and told us he was ashamed of us. I didn't care what he thought. The important thing was to help Ryan.

The doctor eventually came back and gave us the exam. Then we were driven back to LDS Social Services, where they split us up into three different cars to be driven to our foster homes.

Poor Ryan. He looked dazed and alone in the parking lot just before we left. I walked up to him and showed him my thumb with the cut. "Remember now, anytime you can't stand it, just let me know."

He nodded and started crying. I hugged him and told him it was going to be all right.

Even Jill let me hug her before they split us up.

I was assigned to Logan and Zinia Larsen, sober people past middle-age with their family all grown up and away from home.

Brother Bateman delivered me to their home about two in the afternoon. It was a small house, stuck in the country a few miles from Burley. The Snake River ran through their farm. They grew mostly potatoes. Many years ago their house had been smaller, but year after year as their family grew it had been added on, so now one walked through a series of small dark rooms that wound out like tentacles from an octopus. The whole house was like a maze.

Brother Bateman introduced me to Zinia Larsen, a thin woman with steel gray eyes and dull brown hair done up in a tight bun. She wore thick, dark horn-rimmed glasses. Her face was bony and creased with deep lines, untouched with makeup. From the conversation with the social worker, I gathered she had several Indian kids stay there before me. She showed me to my room. It was small and square and sparse.

The three of us returned to the kitchen, and she served us each a slice of homemade bread and a glass of milk. It was the best bread I'd ever eaten in my life, home baked and fresh from the oven.

Brother Bateman kept praising her, thanking her for being willing to take in foster kids, but she parried each compliment and turned it away, so none of it reached her. I was to learn that Zinia did not accept praise. For her, it was enough to do something out of duty.

Then Brother Bateman left, and I was all alone. We spent the first afternoon in what Zinia called orientation. "This is the bathroom," she said slowly and carefully as if I'd never seen one before. "Do you know the proper way to use a toilet?"

I started to laugh, but one severe look from her shut me up.

She advanced to the toilet. "Number one: lift up the seat. Number two: use the facility. Number three: put the seat down. Number four: do not use too much paper. Number five: flush. Number six: wash hands with soap and water. Number seven: don't dawdle in the bath-room. Others may be waiting to use it. Those are the seven steps to using the toilet."

I stared in disbelief as she presented her lecture. She turned to face the bathroom door, on which was fastened a poster. "These seven steps will always be listed here. Each time you come in, you should go through the list until it becomes second nature to you. Now, let's turn our attention to the shower."

There was a list of six things for the shower, also posted.

"When we finish our showers, we don't leave our dirty clothes in the bathroom, do we?"

"No," I said.

"Why don't we?"

She answered her own question. "Because that'd make somebody else clean it up. In our family, everyone takes care of his own things. Now this is what we do after we take a shower. First, we turn off the water very tight, because if the water drips it wastes energy. Next we get out and dry ourselves thoroughly but quickly. And again, we don't dawdle in the bathroom, do we. Then we take the soap tray and dump any excess water that might've fallen into it. That will keep the soap from dis-solving. Next we take our towel and hang it up."

She turned around quickly and nearly knocked me

off my feet as she headed to the wall. "Do you see this hook?"

I nodded my head.

"This is your hook."

Oh boy, I thought sarcastically, I get my own hook.

"This hook is where you will hang your towel. I've even written your name on the hook. This is a special place for your towel. It shouldn't be found anywhere but here."

I was getting a headache keeping my jokes to myself.

"Now let's go to your room."

The bedroom lists were posted on the inside of the closet, giving instructions about matching my dirty socks before I put them in the hamper so she wouldn't have to match them after they were washed. Instructions about making the bed every morning before breakfast except on Monday, when I should take the sheets off the bed and deposit them in the hamper for washing. Instructions on what to do with soil-caked jeans. Instructions and lists.

At six her husband, Logan, came home. I was in the kitchen helping her peel carrots when he entered. He was a large, raw-boned man. He took off his boots and overalls in a room off the kitchen, put on another pair of pants and shoes, and came in.

"Supper'll be ready in a minute," Zinia said.

He nodded his head, stared silently at me, shook his head, and went into the bathroom.

She directed me to put the food on the table. We sat down and waited for her husband. He came in and sat down, bowed his head, and offered the blessing on the food. We ate silently, except for me slurping my soup.

"His name is Jimmy," she said.

"He's not Indian."

"No."

"They don't send whites out here unless something's wrong with 'em."

"He's okay. He'll work around the place."

"You always say that, and it always ends up costing me more, what with them losing my tools, and breaking my equipment, and forgetting their chores. I'd be better off without 'em." He turned to me. "What's wrong with you?"

I looked up, uncertain of what to say.

"He was abandoned, he and his brother and sister."

Turning to me again, he asked, "You know anything about farming?"

"No," I said.

"That's what I figured."

Our meal was soup and bread and carrot sticks. I would have liked another bowl but was too timid to ask. She soon whisked the food off the table and had me help with the dishes. Logan went to the living room to read the paper.

After I finished helping, she said I could do whatever I wanted for forty-five minutes, before we went through the countdown for bed. I asked if I could go outside for a while. Permission was granted. She showed me the large bell she'd ring when it was time for me to come in again.

Finally freed from prison, I ran from the house along a path lit by the light from the moon. There was a large tree a few minutes away. I climbed it and sat on a branch. From there I could see the gray metallic reflection of the moon off the Snake River.

I figured I was alone. I practiced mimicking Zinia's instructions about using the bathroom. Then I looked down. A guy my age, wearing a sweat shirt and baggy sweat pants, was looking up at me.

"Nice talk," he said.

"I didn't think anybody'd hear."

"God hears," he said. "He hears what everybody says, even swearing."

"Then He ought to be used to it after all these years," I countered.

"You're an Indian, aren't you, and you're staying with the Larsens."

"I'm not an Indian."

"Why do you think they call it the Indian placement program? You got to be an Indian to come here."

"I'm not an Indian."

"What are you then?"

"I'm a special case."

He guffawed. "Special case—sure thing, Chief," he said, chuckling to himself.

"Don't call me chief."

"What grade you in?"

"I'm a freshman in high school."

"We don't have freshmen here. Freshmen are ninth graders. And ninth graders go to junior high school. Don't say you're a freshman. Say you're a ninth grader, 'cause that's what you are."

"And what are you, a fifth grader?"

"I'm a freshman too."

I jumped out of the tree to get a closer look. He was shorter than me, had a smart-aleck look I liked. "Do you always wear your pajamas outdoors?" I asked.

"Pajamas!" he roared. "That's all you know. This is my uniform. I run cross-country and track."

"You're too fat to run. I can outrun you any day. Indians run like the wind. Everybody knows that."

"I thought you weren't an Indian."

I grinned. "It comes and goes. When I run, I'm an Indian, and I run on wing-éd feet."

"Wing-éd feet!" He laughed.

"It's true."

"Want to race?" he asked.

"Sure, why not? But not tonight. I'm not ready. When I run, I have to wear sunglasses as a heat shield. See, I run so fast there's a red glow around me."

He laughed. "You're really a cornball, you know that?"

"How far you want to go? How about if we run to Twin Falls and back?"

"What's so great about Twin Falls?"

"That's where my sister is."

"An Indian maiden," he said.

"Nobody makes wisecracks about my sister while I'm around."

"Okay, okay."

"Anyway," I said, "it'll take me that far to get warmed up. I hate short distances."

"Listen to the wind blow," he howled. "On wing-éd feet."

"What's it like at school?" I asked.

He laughed. "It's the pits. Some of my teachers taught my parents when *they* were in school. Teachers get brittle when they get old—like dried-out twigs. If they fall down, they snap in two and break. All my teachers are like that. You'll hate it, believe me."

"I believe it."

"All the girls are ugly—the farmers send their pigs to school and keep their daughters at home. What's your sister like?"

"She wouldn't be interested in you," I said.

"Why not?"

"She's got good taste."

Off in the distance I heard the cowbell. It was Zinia's signal.

"I gotta go. Tell me your name."

"Scott Allison. And yours?"

"Jimmy Pepper." I started running away.

"Are you sure it isn't Iron Cloud or Broken Arrow?" he shouted.

I stopped to call back. "Hey, tomorrow night at this same time, you be here and we'll run that race, okay?"

Zinia rang the bell again. I ran home.

"James," she said unhappily as I came puffing into the yard, "do you know how many times I rang the bell?"

"Three times," I said.

"That's right—three times—five minutes apart. I should never have to ring it more than once. You come running when you hear the bell."

"Yes."

"Well, come in now. Bedtime is nine o'clock in this house. But before we go to bed, there are certain steps we take—things that preserve our health and assure us a proper rest." She handed me a list for bed. First she went over it in agonizing detail. She warned me about drinking too much just before bed. She showed me how to brush my teeth, how to squeeze a toothpaste tube from the bottom up, how to put the top back on. She warned me about not reading in bed after nine, and about saying my own prayers just before I climbed into bed. She made me tack the list on the bulletin board above my tiny desk. I looked at that list every night for the next four years, and even now find myself going over it in my head each night.

That first night in bed I felt the cut on my thumb and imagined Ryan and Jill touching theirs. I hoped it helped them get through their first night. I lay awake thinking of how the three of us would soon move to California.

Zinia drove me to school the first day. We walked into the principal's office and she introduced me, then went to his office to talk privately with him.

While I waited, I looked at an old picture hanging on the wall—George Washington crossing the Delaware. The others in the boat probably thought he was stupid to stand up, but he was their boss, so they just couldn't yell at him, "Hey Dumbo, sit down!" They kept their comments to themselves the way I was learning to do around Zinia.

In a few minutes, Zinia left and the principal took me down to the guidance counselor. The halls were long and hollow sounding, and passing each door, we could hear the buzz of education.

The guidance counselor was Miss Crampton. She looked at a piece of paper. "We're in the middle of things now, so it may be a little hard to get you in the classes you want. What classes do you want?"

"Easy classes," I said.

"Like what?"

"Auto repair," I said.

"That's not offered in junior high school."

"Art."

"Full. What else?"

"Wood shop," I said.

"Full."

"Just choose some easy classes for me. I'm just going to be here a short time; then my brother and sister and me are going to California."

A few minutes later, she handed me a schedule.

During lunch, I ate alone.

"Hi, Chief," Scott said, coming up behind me and slapping me on the back.

"Don't call me chief."

He reached over and scooped up the tiny bit of whipped cream on my dessert with his finger and ate it. I pushed his hand away.

"Why don't you join band?"

"Are you in it?"

"In it? I'm the star!"

I held back a grin. "That's one reason for not joining."

"I'm serious. It's a lot of fun. You can play the drums. Indians are good with drums, right?" He reached over to grab my cake.

I picked up the knife on my tray and pointed it at him. "They're also good with knives."

He backed off about my dessert. "Sorry, but hey, I'm serious about band. You and me, we'd have a good time.

Think about it. A band with forty girls and fifteen guys.
And most of the guys are strange—the kind that only talk
about math homework. They all think they're going into
the space program. So we got two or three normal guys to
forty girls. And we don't have homework, and you get to
make noise, and with that many people, the director can't
know who's serious about music and who's just messing
around, so he gives an automatic B to everybody. And
sometimes we go on trips. Hey, whataya say? I don't ask
just anybody to join band, you know."

I enrolled in band.

Starting over in a new school was a lonely experience.
To make matters worse, Scott wasn't in any of my classes
except for band.

On my second day of class, the teacher gave us a reading assignment, but everyone was visiting with everyone
else. She looked up from her book and warned, "Quiet
down, class. I don't want to hear another peep from
you."

They quieted down. In a tiny voice, I gave my impression of a baby chicken. "Peep."

The whole class started laughing. The teacher looked
sternly over at me, and then her frown broke, and she
started laughing too.

I looked at the cute girl who sat next to me. She was
smiling at me. I winked at her. She winked back.

"I think our new student is a comedian," the teacher
said. "Jimmy, we must have it quiet now. But you know,
the school is having a talent show soon. Why don't you try
out for it?"

They were all smiling at me.

"Maybe I will," I said, happy for the first time in a long
time.

I spent the next few days stealing jokes from every
place I could think of. I checked out every joke book I

could find in the library and watched as much TV as I could. I read every back issue of *Boys' Life* that Scott had. And then I practiced in front of a mirror in the bathroom, which was not at all pleasing to Zinia. But she seemed to sense it was important to me, although for what purpose she had no idea.

And then came the school talent show. I walked on carrying a stool and sat down. It had been raining all day, so I had decided to start with a rain joke I'd stolen from a joke book. "Hey, how about this rain? You know, we don't usually get this much rain. During the great flood, you know, the one you read about in the Bible, where it rained forty days and forty nights, this area got two-tenths of an inch."

They laughed.

Next a joke I'd stolen from a TV comedian. "Any parents out there have kids who've taken the Iowa tests? Thing I can't figure out is why we in Idaho have to take Iowa tests. Do you people have any idea some of the questions they ask in the Iowa tests?—What's the capital of Iowa? Who's the governor of Iowa? What's the largest city in Iowa? Strange thing is, kids from Iowa do so much better on it than kids from Idaho . . ."

They laughed.

The girls laughed too. I could see them smiling at me, hundreds of them. And guys too—laughing. And parents. It was important to be loved, especially by parents of daughters. And teachers. Teachers were important because they held life and death power over you in school. And they were laughing too.

They loved me.

It was the best feeling in the world. I wanted to be loved by everyone, to make people happy and have them approve of me. It was almost like they were all reaching out and touching me and I was touching them. Each laugh was love and warmth and tenderness.

I decided on my life's work.

I was going to be a comedian.

CHAPTER THREE

Jill and I didn't plan on leaving her home until she'd gotten her kids in bed after supper.

Just before we were ready, the phone rang. It was for me. "Alan Becker—I talked to you in L.A. about doing an article about you. A friend of mine and I are out here. Tomorrow we'll start talking to some locals about your background. I was wondering if I could come out and talk to you and your sister."

I hung up. An hour later we left for Wyoming. We drove for a couple of hours, then stopped for a snack in a nearly empty roadside cafe.

"They're going to find out about Hank's prison record," I said.

"So what? It was a long time ago."

"You don't know the way they can twist things. Maybe you shouldn't even be going there with me."

Jill shrugged. "I think you're being paranoid."

I bought an issue of the "National Inquirer" for her when I got gas.

"I see why you're worried," she said, a few minutes later.

We took off again. Jill fell asleep before very long. Like an owl, I came alive late at night. It was only me and the road and late-night radio.

And my thoughts.

Before that first year in Idaho, Christmas had been a time of great anticipation because my father, although he was often away from home driving, felt guilty enough at Christmas to overcompensate by giving too many toys and candy.

Seeing the preparations in the Larsen home, I naturally thought it'd be the same. Starting right after I arrived, Zinia turned out fruitcakes by the dozens.

Gradually I learned that none of it was for us. The
fruitcakes were given to friends. After I'd tasted one, I
wondered why she went to all the trouble. It was full of
bitter-tasting fruit rinds dyed unnaturally ugly. One slice
was all anyone should ever have in his entire life. The
cookies were reserved for her grandchildren because
they were too honest, and if you gave them a piece of
fruitcake, they'd spit it out and say it was awful. And, of
course, it was.

Two days before Christmas, the Larsen family members began to arrive. Fred was the oldest boy. He was at
that time in his early thirties, with his hair nearly gone,
especially along the top of his head, leaving only a few
strands along the sides. He was already getting a paunch.
He had graduated as an accountant and now worked for
a firm in Denver. He liked telling people what was wrong
with the government.

His wife's name was Margaret, and she always looked
tired. They had three children in diapers. Their family
took over my room, forcing me to sleep on the floor in
the living room. Whenever I went to my room during the
day to get some clothes, it smelled of diapers.

Logan and Zinia's next oldest was a daughter named
Ruth. She stood six foot two and weighed a ton. Her husband was smaller than she was. He was one of the few An-
drews in the world that nobody called Andy. He taught
math in high school in Montana. He liked to talk about
how low the salaries were and how little people valued
teachers. Ruth pretty much ran Andrew. He changed
the diapers of their two kids quite often.

The last one in the family was Rachel. She was a
sophomore at Brigham Young University, engaged to be
married in the summer. She brought along her future

husband for Christmas. His name was Jeff, and he was from California and was studying to be a lawyer.

Rachel and Jeff were the only ones there who paid much attention to me, and they were the best looking of the lot.

Christmas began at five-thirty in the morning with little kids padding across my sleeping bag to the tree, giggling and laughing and playing with the things Santa had left unwrapped there. An hour later the parents and grandparents were coaxed into the room. Presents were passed around to each one. I had three presents.

There were planes and cars and games and candy—for the children.

I opened a present. It was a white shirt.

"Thanks," I said politely.

"That's for Sunday," Zinia said.

I nodded my head.

There were battery-powered boats for the bathtub and flashlights that glowed red and small puzzles—for the children.

I opened my second present. It was a pair of pajamas.

"Thank you," I said weakly.

"Now you won't have to go to bed in your underwear," Zinia said.

There were toy guns and felt-tipped darts for the dart board. There was what looked like a book but was made up of rolls of Life Savers—for the children.

I opened my third present—five pairs of black socks.

"Thanks," I whispered.

I sat and watched the others play with their toys and eat their Life Savers.

Zinia came out from the kitchen. "I know this will spoil our appetites for breakfast, but it's Christmas, and Christmas only comes once a year. Jimmy, pass around this plate of fruitcake."

Each one took a piece and politely nibbled on it, all except Rachel's fiancé, who, being a stranger to the family and wanting to please, took a hearty bite. After three chews he realized what he'd done. I saw him hide the rest of it under some wrapping.

The children then proceeded to wreck all their toys, while the women retired to the kitchen to fix supper, which was eight hours away. Fred and Andrew sat down and talked about buying up gold. The kids were making a horrible noise. Logan went to his shed to find a screw to fix a kitchen chair. At least that's what he said, but it took him a powerful long time to find one screw.

I sat in the living room and looked at my socks and pajamas and wondered how Jill and Ryan were doing. I went to a small office Logan had where there was a phone. I sat down and called Ryan.

"How's it going?"

"I got a BB gun for Christmas!" he said excitedly. "And a basketball and scout knife!"

"Hey, that's great."

"What did you get?" he asked.

"A lot of neat things too," I lied.

"And they let me drive their neighbors' snowmobile yesterday."

"Hey, that's good."

"I'm a Blazer scout now. I'm trying to earn my second-class rank."

"Good, Ryan. That's real good."

Next I phoned Jill.

"Next year maybe the three of us can spend Christmas by ourselves living in California," I said.

She paused. "Maybe longer than a year. I'd like to graduate from high school first before we go it alone. But then we will, the three of us, just like we talked about."

"If we can talk Ryan into it. You know, he's kind of a pain. He'd be afraid of moving to California because he might miss a scout meeting or something."

I told her how funny I was at the talent assembly. She

made me give my monologue to her on the phone. She giggled all the way through it.

Fred came in the room and grabbed the phone from me and put it up to his ear. "This sounds like long distance. Who are you talking to?"

"My sister."

"It is long distance, isn't it? How long have you been talking to her?"

"Just a few minutes."

"And did you ask permission?" We glared at each other. "That's what I thought—sneaking in here without permission. Well, that's all for you, mister." He hung up. "Get out of here."

My faced burned with anger at his hanging up on Jill.

He followed me out, complaining to Zinia, but secretly delighting in finding me out. "Guess what our little friend's been doing—phoning all over the country, for all we know. I'd sure hate to be getting your phone bill next month. No telling how much it'll be."

"Is that right, Jimmy?" Zinia asked.

"I just talked a few minutes to my sister."

"You could've at least asked," Fred said.

"Okay. Can I phone my brother and sister?"

"Not now you can't. Besides, it's too expensive. I don't phone my parents as a rule on Christmas, so why should you phone anybody?"

"Because I love my brother and sister, and you don't love anybody but yourself," I countered.

"You smart-aleck," Fred said.

"Children, children," Rachel interrupted with a grin. "Jeff and I'll take Jimmy out for a drive until supper's ready."

I sat in the back seat while Jeff drove. Rachel sat close to him and put her arm around him and lightly touched the hair on the nape of his neck. She made him drive by her old schools and told him stories of when she was growing up.

Jeff was good-natured and smiled a lot. He had a small mustache that really looked good on him. Besides, he was from California. That made me like him too.

We stopped at her old grade school, and each of us sat on a swing and tried to see who could get the highest. I won because they started laughing and couldn't concentrate on pumping higher.

Jeff bailed out of the swing and landed on his feet, then turned to Rachel with an exultant, "Ta da!"

She slowed down and bailed out too. He caught her when she landed, and she slipped into his arms and he kissed her. We drove around some more, and I fell asleep. When I woke up, they were talking. I kept my eyes closed so they wouldn't know I was awake.

"Six months," he said.

"Six months? And then what?"

He laughed. "And then you'd better watch out."

"I'll be ready," she said with a smile. "Do you want to know about our reception?"

"Not particularly," he said. "Let's talk about our wedding night."

"C'mon, Jeff, it doesn't help to talk about that. Besides, there's a lot of other details to work out."

"Okay, tell me about the details."

She went into a lot of boring things about who was going to make the wedding cake and about the invitations. It was so bad that I pretended to wake up. They kept talking and joking and touching.

I was so lonely.

The first school year in Idaho passed slowly, unbroken in its tedium only by a bus trip in April that our school band took to Idaho Falls. It was during that trip that Scott and I pulled off our weirdest prank. It was before we learned moderation and good taste.

"Now?" Scott whispered to me as the band bus droned on and on.

I looked over at Tammy Patterson and her seatmate, Barbara Jones, the most straight-arrow girl in town. They were sitting across the aisle from us.

"Now."

I casually picked up a sack and walked to the rest room in the back of the bus. Once I'd locked the door, I opened the sack and took out a can opener and a can of beef stew. I dumped the beef stew into a bag the bus provided for car sickness, then laid it into the brown bag and went back to my place and hid it under the seat.

"I don't feel so good," Scott said so Tammy and Barbara would hear it.

Tammy leaned over. "I have some car-sickness pills," she said.

Scott nodded his head slowly. "I need something."

Just as he was about to take the pills, he started gagging. I handed Scott an empty car sickness bag. He grabbed it and bent down and made terrible sounds. The girls turned away. While he was bent over, he switched bags. When he sat up, he thrust the bag full of beef stew at me and moaned for me to get rid of it.

I looked curiously at the contents of the bag. "Hmmm," I said.

Tammy stared at me with horror as I picked out a chunk of meat from the beef stew and popped it into my mouth. She ran screaming down the aisle to the rest room. I smiled at Barbara, then picked out another chunk of meat and ate it. Barbara ran away also.

As soon as they left, we threw the beef stew out the window and opened our magazines and innocently started reading.

The girls in the back of the bus were gagging and trying to explain what they'd seen.

"Ohhh! Gross!" Barbara cried out.

Mr. Miller, our band teacher, walked back to see what was wrong. In a few seconds he returned. He reached down and pulled me up by the shoulders and shook me hard.

"Pepper, I oughta throw you off the bus!" he yelled.

"What for?" I asked.

"Tammy says Scott threw up and you ate it."

"It was just a joke, Mr. Miller. It was really beef stew."

"A joke?" he shouted. "What kind of joke is that? You go back and apologize to them right now!"

He stormed away.

I walked back to Tammy and Barbara.

"I'm sorry for pulling that joke on you."

"It wasn't funny, Jimmy."

"I know. I'm sorry. I thought it would be. It's hard to know beforehand."

"That's all you care about, isn't it!" Barbara lashed out. "You don't think about whether something's right or wrong, do you! All you care about is if it's funny or not." She left to get away from me.

I sat down with Tammy. "I'm sorry. I really am. I thought it'd be funny."

She smiled just a little. "Well, it sort of was, I guess, in a way."

"Can I sit with you?"

"Okay," she said, giving me a shy yet warm smile.

Two weeks later we attended a ward potluck supper. It was crowded with a long line. Tammy was there. We started talking in the hall.

"Have you ever kissed a girl?" she asked.

"No," I said.

"Would you like to?"

A few minutes later we sauntered into a classroom for my first kiss while everyone else was going through the line piling tuna and noodles on their paper plates.

It wasn't love. It was a long food line and boredom with potluck suppers and curiosity. Lots of people kiss, but we made the mistake of kissing in a classroom at church during a potluck social. We also had the bad luck to be found out by Sister Mills, a lady who had never been married. She was the ward expert on genealogy. To my fifteen-year-old mind it seemed she loved the dead more than the living.

She opened the door quietly during our second kiss, saw us, and gasped, "What's going on here?"

We broke apart. "Nothing," I said quickly. "The line was so long . . . uhh . . . we were just talking."

"Don't lie! I know what you were doing."

Another lady showed up at the door.

"I caught 'em in here kissing," Sister Mills said. "In a classroom, mind you. Can you believe that?"

The other lady looked at me and nodded. "Jimmy Pepper—I might've guessed. Young man, do you realize this is the Lord's classroom?"

"He wasn't using it," I said like a reflex action triggered by any possibility for a joke, whether or not in good taste.

Sister Mills turned beet red. "I ought to slap your face."

By then several persons stood at the doorway, gaping at us. Tammy started to cry and ran out of the room.

Now there was just me and the crowd.

My Sunday School teacher stood in the hall and looked at me. She was about seventy years old. "Jimmy, why would you want to desecrate our church?"

"I don't have a car," I said.

"What'd he say?" someone on the fringe of the crowd asked.

"He said he doesn't have a car."

"What's that got to do with it?"

"If he did, he'd have parked out on some country road with the girl."

"What's happening to our youth?" a woman said.

"He's not ours, you know. He's one of those foster kids."

"It's a case of one bad apple in the barrel," another observed.

"We've got to do something about it," a woman said.

The next morning at breakfast Logan told me he wanted to talk to me in his shed. As we walked out there, I remember wondering how bad he was going to hurt me. He'd built the shed as a place for his tools. It was a small pole barn with rough wood floors and a large workbench with tools hanging from a white painted plywood panel above the workbench. The outline of each tool was painted in red, so you'd know where to put the tool when you were through with it. Every bolt, every nut and washer was located in baby food jars with lids on them. The jars hung from a homemade lazy Susan, with the size and thread of each item printed on the bottle in Logan's writing. A large radial arm saw was in the middle of the room, and on another wall several shovels hung from clamps. Logan serviced his own vehicles and there was a tool chest on wheels full of wrenches.

This was man's domain. I'd never seen Zinia as much as step inside the shed. No curtains hung from the one window, and no little knickknacks cluttered the workbench.

We walked in and he shut the door. There was no place to sit down. He turned to face me. His face was red—he was as embarrassed as I.

"I don't want you fooling around," he said.

"No sir," I said, wishing I could crawl through the cracks in the floor.

"The things that a man and woman do," he said, clearing his throat, "that's reserved for marriage. Do you understand, or do I have to spell it out?"

I'd have died rather than have him spell it out. "I understand," I said quickly.

"And don't go kissing girls in the church anymore. You know better than that."

"Yes sir."

"All right then. Go get your chores done." He turned and walked quickly out the door.

The bishop set up a way for me and Tammy to repent. He talked to her just one time, but I guess he figured I needed more work. We started meeting once a week. Everybody in the ward knew I was meeting with the bishop. I guess they figured it was awful punishment. Actually it wasn't bad at all. Even at that age I'd figured out that if you were in trouble, the best thing to do was to go talk to your bishop.

It was our third interview. The previous week I'd written a letter of apology to Tammy's parents. He helped me write it.

He said he wanted to know if there were any other things I could work on while we were meeting. He gave me a long interview. We spent a long time on being morally clean, then moved on to other things.

"Tell me what being honest means to you," he said.

"Always telling the truth and not stealing anything."

"Do you always tell the truth?"

I paused before answering. "Not always."

"When don't you tell the truth?"

Long silence. Finally I said, "Well, for instance, this interview."

"Do you want to talk about it, Jimmy?"

"I can't," I said miserably.

"Maybe I can help."

"If I tell, you'll never talk to me again."

"I'll always be your friend, no matter what."

Eventually I decided to talk to him. "You asked if there was anything bothering me and I said no, but there is. Once I had a dream. My sister and I were on a bus, but

instead of going here we were going to California, and
she showed me a letter that said she wasn't really my sister—that there'd been a mistake and they'd mixed babies
in the hospital—and so we weren't really related . . ." I
stopped. My forehead was beaded with sweat.

"Have you told her about your dream?"

"I'll never tell her. She'd think I was weird. If you
knew her, bishop—she's ten times neater than any other
girl. Especially the ones in this ward. No offense, but we
really got some dogs in this ward. People think I care for
Tammy, but I don't, not a fig. That's what Zinia is always
saying—not a fig. Well, it's true. I don't care a fig for
Tammy. It was her idea, you know, to go kiss in the classroom."

The bishop wasn't yelling at me. I decided to keep
talking.

"Jill can swim the length of a regular-size pool under
water. You think Tammy can do that? No sir. I bet there's
not a girl in this town who can do that."

"Probably not." He smiled.

"I miss her, bishop. We don't have a mother or father
anymore. It's just the three of us, but they never let me
see 'em. Jill could help me, I know she could help me.
And Ryan—that's my brother—Jill and I'd help him.
Bishop, he's such a worrywart, and it'd be good for him
to be around me. I'd be a help to him. I'd teach him not to
worry about homework. He worries, you know, about
school. I never do. I could help him."

It all started tumbling out now. "Sometimes, I want to
see her so much—and Ryan too." My voice faded away.

He handed me a tissue. I blew my nose.

"Bishop, what if I never know anyone neater than
Jill? What if all the girls I ever meet are dull and ugly and
dumb compared to Jill? What will I do then? It bothers
me a lot."

"You're afraid your sister is the only girl you'll ever
love? And you know you can't marry her. Is that how you
feel?"

It was a relief just to know he understood. "That's right—that's the way I feel."

"Jimmy, somewhere there's a girl growing up, the one you'll marry in the temple. When you find her, she'll even top your sister."

"You think so?"

"I'm sure of it," he said with a wry grin. "I have a sister too."

I left the interview feeling twenty pounds lighter.

Summer came. At least it meant school was over, but I traded one set of duties for another. My duties involved weeding the family garden and helping Logan farm the place.

Some days he wouldn't say more than a dozen extra words to me even when we were working side by side. He wasn't mad at me, he just wasn't a big talker. But he tried to teach me things. In the middle of a field he'd say, "I need a three-eighths socket head wrench." I'd run to the pickup, open the tool box, and wonder what he wanted. I'd pick up everything that looked like a wrench and bring it all to him. Invariably in the time I took, he would have fixed it another way without the wrench. "I don't need it anymore. Take all that stuff back." And I'd dutifully obey.

Sometimes he seemed so melancholy. I had the feeling he knew the tractor'd break down just when he needed it, and he'd have to order parts, but when the parts finally came, they'd be the wrong parts. He knew it, and when it happened, it only confirmed what he knew—that you can't win and you can't even break even. Maybe it was the look of a farmer, that when your crop is destroyed, the prices are good, but when you have a good crop, the price is below the cost of production.

Duty called loudly and consistently in the Larsen home. It called in the fields. A person worked every day on the farm because duty demanded it. And then on

Saturday night, you put away your tools and implements and went into the house to get ready for going home teaching, then came home and laid out your Sunday clothes and went to bed to arise the next morning for a Sabbath day of duty.

I was the wrong boy for that household, because I hated duty and order and neatness. And it was the first time in my life I'd been asked to do something other than what suited my fancy.

Logan knew I was eating more in food than I'd ever be worth to him on the farm, and yet he kept me. I'm not sure why. In the beginning he never talked about his feelings. Steady as a rock, steady as the fact that every morning in the summer we would beat the sun up and work until past the time it set.

Logan never read much other than the scriptures. But I read every science fiction book they had in the library. I was hoping for aliens to come and rescue me.

That summer I went to Rachel and Jeff's wedding reception. They'd been married a couple of days earlier in the Idaho Falls Temple. They looked so good together, so happy, full of jokes and smiles and hugs and winks. Just watching them was better than any lesson in church about chastity.

I went through the reception line, shaking hands with everybody. When I came to Rachel, she leaned over and kissed me on the cheek. Then she whispered in my ear—so loud that everyone could hear—"It was worth the wait."

The conversation in the reception line stopped.

I went through the line blushing, then left to eat all the pecans, almonds, and Brazil nuts from the nut tray, leaving only the peanuts for everyone else.

CHAPTER FOUR

My second Christmas in Idaho came and with it the gathering of Logan and Zinia's family. This time Rachel was pregnant. Jeff was finishing his senior year at BYU and had taken a job in Los Angeles as a junior executive. He'd start in June. Fred and his wife were also there for the holidays, as well as Ruth and Andrew. Fred was unhappy with his job because he wasn't moving up fast enough. Seeing the way he acted around his family, I figured if he wasn't being demoted, he was rising up as fast as possible.

Fred had a new camera and tripod. He made a big production of assembling everybody together for a family portrait, then asked me to take the picture. He took his place standing in the center with one hand laid on Logan's shoulder.

"We need Jimmy in the picture too, don't we?" Rachel asked.

"We just want the *real* family," Fred said. To me he said, "Take the picture now."

I looked through the lens.

"Don't fiddle with the camera," Fred said. When he was mad, as he was then, he spoke in a slow, crisp style, making him sound especially in control. "I've—already—focused it. Just—push—the shutter."

I tried to find the shutter. There were about a thousand knobs and buttons and settings.

The grandchildren were getting restless.

"I can't find the shutter," I said.

"It's—on the top—there—where the shutter—

should be. Kids, get—back—get in place now. Jimmy's
going to take the picture now. Aren't—you—Jimmy?"

One of the grandchildren hit another with a toy
shovel. They started crying.

"Just take the picture, will you!" Fred yelled.

I looked at the camera again. There was a button on
top.

"Do I have to do everything around here?" Just as he
started moving toward me, I pushed the shutter. The
flash went off, getting a wonderful picture of his ample
stomach.

"What did you do that for?" he snapped.

"You said take the picture," I replied.

"Not when I'm walking toward the camera. Don't you
have any sense?"

"Why'd you get a foreign camera anyway? You ever
hear of Kodak?"

The grandchildren were scattering through the
house.

"You used my last flash!" he complained.

"You said take the picture!"

"You people are all alike, aren't you?" Fred exploded.

"Fred, that's enough," Rachel said.

"What people?" I yelled.

"All my life we had foster kids, breaking my stuff,
stealing it too. Poor Homeless Kids, that's all I've heard.
Well, what about me? What about Poor Fred! Having to
put up with people like you. You people steal things.
Don't deny it!"

"Quiet!" Logan demanded.

We became quiet.

"All right, we're through here. Mother, what have
you got planned for us?"

"I thought we could all have some nice fruitcake."

Zinia sliced up a fruitcake and got out cookies for the
children. We all politely nibbled on our assessed portion
of fruitcake.

"It tastes just like last year," Rachel said diplomatically, with only a slight wink in my direction.

"Yes, it's just the way I remember it," Jeff dutifully repeated.

I went outside and threw it into a field and hoped that whatever field mouse ate it wouldn't get too sick.

As a sophomore in high school, I remember spending Friday and Saturday nights, when Scott could get the family car, cruising town, which of course meant driving up and down Main Street, looking for girls. If the girls of America had ever once agreed to stay in one place, there would have been no energy crisis.

This happened on one of those weekends. We were parked at a drive-in having some fries and root beer.

A Corvette drove by.

"Hey, a 'Vette," Scott said.

I looked at it and scowled. "Piece of junk."

"Whataya mean?"

I frowned. "I wouldn't have one if you gave it to me."

"So what's better?"

"A Jaguar XK-E coupe with twin overhead camshafts and four-wheel disc brakes." Of course I'd learned all this from a magazine.

"How much?"

"Six thousand."

He laughed. "You'll never get a Jaguar. Besides, it's not that much better than a 'Vette."

"Whataya talking about? Twin overhead camshaft? You think a 'Vette can top that? You don't know anything."

A car full of girls pulled into the drive-in.

We got out of the car, opened the hood, and leaned over the engine and jiggled wires.

The driver, a girl named Linda, left her car and came toward us.

"Hi, Jimmy." She smiled warmly at me.

"Hey, Linda, how's it going?"

"Hi," Scott said. "What're you doing?"

Nothing. How about you guys?" she said.

I ceremoniously wiped my hands off with a handkerchief. "We were just making a few adjustments."

"On my car," Scott added.

Linda looked at me with admiration. "You understand all about cars, don't you."

Modestly I answered, "Yeah, pretty much everything."

"Both of us do, actually," Scott said.

"It all seems so complicated to me. Can you tell me what the various things are?"

"Oh sure," I beamed.

"And if he makes any mistakes, I'll correct him," Scott said.

"Now this here's the battery," I said. "This particular one happens to be a 12-volt battery. It's very important to know if your car has a 6-volt or a 12-volt battery. Do you know what kind your car has?"

"I always thought a battery was . . . well . . just a battery."

"Oh, gosh no," I said. "There's 12-volt batteries and there's 6-volt batteries. If you were to put a 12-volt battery where it needs a 6-volt battery, it'd wreck your whole car."

"Absolutely ruin it," Scott added.

By this time she was standing close to me, while I pointed to the battery. I could even smell her shampoo.

"Who else is in your car?" Scott asked.

"Well, there's Vicky Colby and Janice Engstrom and, let's see, who else—Carol Smith—and my sister."

Scott went down the list in his head. Just as we would have Jaguars and Corvettes, we were equally discriminating about the girls we'd spend time with at a drive-in on a Friday night. "Do you think your sister would like me to explain about cars?" he asked.

She frowned. "We really need to get home. My parents just sent me out to get a loaf of bread."

They drove away.

"Well, thanks a lot," I grumbled, slamming the hood shut.

"What'd I do?"

"You scared her away, that's what."

"How'd I scare her away?"

"By asking about her sister. She didn't want you with her younger sister. Why didn't you just ask for Carol Smith, for crying out loud?"

"Carol Smith? Are you crazy? You think I'd go out with Carol Smith?"

"They why didn't you just shut up and let me talk to Linda? You realize she leaned into me when I pointed at the battery?"

"What am I supposed to do? Sit and watch you two drool over the battery all night?"

We returned to the car and listened to the radio. The drive-in was momentarily empty.

I hit my fist on the dashboard. "I wonder where everybody is."

"Probably at a party we weren't even invited to," Scott said glumly.

We finally gave up and went to my place to pop some popcorn, and then we went in my room and listened to my radio. He got up to look around. On the dresser was a picture of Jill that she'd sent me a few days before.

He picked it up and looked at it. "This your sister?"

"Yeah."

"Nice."

"Yeah, she's okay."

"Where'd you say she lives?"

"Twin Falls."

He turned around. "Let's go see her."

"Now?"

"Sure."

"It's too late."

"Tomorrow morning then. I can get the car, and I'll pay for the gas."

"What for?"

"Just to see her."

"Okay."

The next morning at ten-thirty we finally pulled up to her address, a white house with a fence near the edge of Twin Falls.

"Is Jill here?" I asked her foster mother. She let us in. The sound of a vacuum cleaner droned on somewhere in the house. Then it stopped, and Jill came running into the living room.

"Jimmy!" she said, throwing her arms around me. It felt good to have her close to me.

"Let me look at you." She stepped back. "Wow, you're becoming a man. Look at those muscles."

"Comes from doing chores," I said, grinning.

"And you must've grown four inches since I saw you last."

I looked at her. "You've grown too—in all the right places."

"Yeah, yeah," she said, laughing it off. But still I could tell she was pleased I'd noticed.

Scott cleared his throat.

"This is my best friend. His name is Scott."

"Hi," he said. "Want to go with us and get a milkshake?"

"Let me finish vacuuming my room first, and I'll be right with you."

The vacuuming took about thirty seconds, but she didn't come out for ten minutes, and when she did, she'd changed her clothes and done something with her hair.

She sat between us as we drove around town. At noon we pulled into a drive-in, and Scott made a big fuss about paying for Jill's order. I'd never seen him behave so strangely. He sounded like an ordinary person. Gone was the belching contest we usually had. He didn't get catsup all over his fingers when he ate his fries, or pretend he'd cut himself, as he usually did. No catcalls to the waitress as she left with our order. He didn't even crack his knuckles.

And Jill was strange too. She agreed with absolutely everything he said. And talk about smiling—I'd never seen her grin nonstop. She looked like a store mannequin—pleasant, neat, and dumb.

I tried to liven things up. "Hey, Scott, let's tell her about the time we took the beef stew on the bus trip."

He looked at me like I was crazy.

"Do you like music?" he politely asked Jill.

"Very much. How about you?"

"Oh yes," Scott said. "I like to get up in the morning and have a song with me the rest of the day."

"I do that too," she said.

"Yeah," I added, "Scott likes the song for the Drano commercial." I sang part of it.

Scott looked at me like I was a five-year-old.

They ignored me. My own sister was being charmed by my best friend—it was hard to take. I couldn't decide how I felt. Was I jealous of him for being able to hustle my sister? Or, seeing the possible end of my closeness with him, was I jealous of her? It was a mixed bag.

"That's so true," she said at some stupid thing he said.

I belched as loudly as I could.

They looked at me like I was the village idiot.

"Do you think you'll go on a mission?" she asked him.

"Oh, sure."

"That's not what you tell me," I said.

"That's great," she said to him.

The waitress walked by my side of the car. "Hey, beauty!" I said, leaning out. "What time do you get off work?"

"Forget it, junior," she said with a scowl.

Now they were talking about poetry.

"I wrote a poem once," Scott said.

"You?" I sneered. "A poem? What kind of poem did you ever write?"

"I'd like to hear it," she said.

Scott began his poem:

> *I want a love,*
> *A love from above.*
> *A beautiful girl*
> *From heaven above.*
> *My own true love.*

I howled and snorted and guffawed.

"What a lovely poem," Jill said.

"Thank you," Scott said.

Finally we finished our food, and Scott started driving around town. He pulled up to a city park, and we all got out, and they started walking together. He put his hand out, and they held hands and talked about poetry. I sat on the hood of his car and practiced seeing how far I could spit.

From then on, a Saturday trip to Twin Falls was a ritual. To keep me occupied, Jill lined me up with a girl named Becky Storm. I dated her every Saturday for a while. I was always in a rotten mood around Scott and Jill.

One night a few weeks later, after a movie, we were outside Jill's home, the four of us. Jill and Scott were having an extended goodnight kiss, and I'd been telling Becky jokes, trying to make her laugh so loud it'd ruin the mood in the front seat and they'd quit kissing. It didn't work.

"Wow, look how late it is," I said as my next ploy.

"Jill," Becky called out, "I need to go home now."

Jill and Scott broke apart.

"What?" Jill called out absently.

"I need to go home now."

"Oh," she said, still a million miles away. "Okay, Becky—good-bye."

"I need a ride home," she said.

"Oh, sure," Jill purred. "Scott, Becky needs a ride home."

It was like watching molasses run to watch them come back to earth.

"A ride home," he repeated. "I have my car—I'll give her a ride home," he said.

"Hey, you two, wake up!" I complained.

"What time is it?" Jill asked.

"Almost midnight," I said.

"I'd better go in," Jill said.

"Not yet," Scott said. "We'll take Becky home first."

Jill's features were softened, her lips open partially, her face flushed.

"Are we ever going to get out of this place?" I demanded. "Becky needs to go home."

We took her home. When I came back from walking her to the door, Scott and Jill were kissing again. I slapped my hand on the door loudly, and they broke apart. I got in front with them.

"What's all this lovey-dovey junk for?" I asked.

"We're in love," Scott said.

"You're both too young to know what true love is."

"Then you're too young to tell us if it is or isn't," Scott said.

"It isn't."

"I don't even think about anybody else anymore," Scott said.

"Me either," Jill said.

I moaned. "C'mon, give me a break. Take me home. I can't stand listening to this garbage anymore."

He walked her to the door and then started kissing her again. I honked the horn a couple of times. Her foster parents came to the door and made Jill go inside.

When Scott came to the car, he was furious at me.

"What's the big deal?" he shouted at me.

"Nothing! Nothing at all. Just drive."

"No, I want to know. What's bugging you?"

"Well, for one thing, I don't like to see you pawing my sister."

"I wasn't pawing her, for crying out loud."

"Just find someone else to hustle. Leave her alone."

He got in the car and drove fast. We didn't say anything until just before we reached my place.

"Find somebody else," I said, "because in a year or two, Jill and I and my brother are going to California. You'll never see her again. So you're just wasting your time."

He stopped and I got out. He said quietly, "I love her."

"She doesn't love you. The only reason she goes out with you is because you're my friend. I mean, if you weren't my friend, she'd never go out with you."

"You're jealous, aren't you. What's the matter? You wish she'd go steady with you?"

I slammed the car door as hard as I could.

He put the car in gear and roared away.

It was the last time we ever double-dated.

But he kept dating Jill.

In August, just before my junior year began, Ryan called to invite Jill and me to his Eagle court of honor. I got permission from Logan to drive his pickup.

On the way Jill made fun of the pickup and called me Farmer Jim. She was full of details about her and Scott and their plans.

"Why don't you like him anymore?" she asked.

"I like him."

"But you two never do things together anymore."

"We will, we will," I said. There was no way I could explain how I felt, since I wasn't even sure myself. I'd just boxed it all up and refused to deal with it.

That night we went to the court of honor. Ryan, the scout-green sash across his chest full of merit badges, stood proudly as his foster mother pinned the award on and kissed him.

Afterwards there was a party at his foster parent's home, with a few girls there from his ward. They looked at Ryan like he was their hero, and he talked with each of them. It didn't seem to matter to him whether or not they were pretty.

After the party was over, Jill and I stayed the night with Ryan. Jill suggested we all sleep out in the backyard, joking how Ryan as an Eagle scout would save us from the bears and lions. There were enough spare sleeping bags in the house, and by eleven o'clock we were lying side by side looking up at the stars. Ryan pointed out the constellations. That interested Jill, but I was bored.

"Let's go steal a watermelon!" I said. "I saw some in a garden about three houses away. They ought to be ripe by now. We'll be back here again in five minutes. C'mon, whataya say?"

Jill giggled. I knew she'd be with me.

"What for?" Ryan asked.

"Just for the heck of it. We'll break it open and eat it right on the lawn."

"That's the Andersons' garden," he said. "I'm not stealing from them."

"Ah, c'mon, Ryan," Jill said. "They've probably got hundreds. They won't miss just one."

"No, it's not right," he said.

"Sometimes you're a real pain, you know that?" I said.

"What's so great about taking something that doesn't belong to us? If you want a watermelon, we'll walk down to a store and buy one."

"That sounds so exciting," I said sarcastically. "What's the matter with you? Afraid of ruining your precious reputation?"

"I'm not going to steal anything."

I got out of the sleeping bag and put on my jeans and a shirt. "Well, I'm going to get a watermelon for Jill and me." I turned to point my finger at Ryan. "You know the trouble with you? You try too hard. You jump through every hoop people tell you to, and you think that'll wash away the past. You want to know what our past is? You ever see a picture of somebody dying from an overdose of drugs? Well, next time you do, remember the stuff might've been brought in the country by dear old dad."

"How do you know that?" he asked.

"It was in the Cheyenne paper. A friend sent it to me. We're the kids of a crook. And it doesn't matter how many badges you pile on that hairless chest of yours, nothing's going to change that."

"Jimmy, shut up!" Jill said.

"Okay, okay. I'll be back in just a minute," I said. "I'm going to get a watermelon."

"Ah, forget it," she said sourly.

Ryan and Jill talked most of the night, with her trying to undo the damage I'd done.

I woke up early in the morning and watched Jill and Ryan asleep. Realizing I'd driven them both away, I tried to think of a way for us to be united again.

"Hey, wake up, you guys." I shook them to get them to wake up.

"You got a knife?" I asked Ryan.

He fumbled in his pocket and gave me his scout knife. I cut my thumb and gave the knife to Jill.

"Do it—like we did before."

She shook her head. "We're too old for that now," she said.

"Ryan?"

"I feel the same way."

"Okay, but hey, no matter what, we've got to stick together. Okay?"

"Okay," they said.

"And sometime soon, we'll all move out to California and live together as a family again. Okay?"

"Maybe," Jill said.

"Maybe," Ryan echoed.

When I drove Jill home and talked about us moving to California, she turned away and looked out the window and didn't say anything.

Almost a year later, in April of my junior year, Logan and Zinia had troubles. It started with Zinia telling Logan he ought to see a doctor. He always said no, but she kept nagging him. Finally she got an appointment and told him he'd have to pay for it whether or not he went. He went.

That night at supper, Logan said the doctor didn't know anything—that no doctors did, and it was just going to cost a lot of money and no good would come of it. I sat and ate and wondered what they were talking about. Eventually I figured out that his doctor wanted him to see a specialist. He didn't want to go, but Zinia finally just told him he was going.

They went the next Saturday morning, and I stayed home and did chores.

When they came home, they got in a big argument. The doctor said Logan had to have surgery, but Logan didn't want to. Zinia blew up at him and said she wanted him alive, and he'd die unless he had the operation. He said he didn't care, that he'd just as soon be dead as to have to live with that.

Zinia won. I knew she would.

The operation was scheduled two weeks later in Salt Lake City. They didn't tell their kids because of some cockeyed idea about not wanting to have their children worry.

I was the only one in the family who knew. The others were away, so it was easy to keep it a secret. They

wouldn't tell me what kind of an operation it was. I asked
Logan once, and he shook his head and walked away.

Just before we left to go to Salt Lake City, Logan left
me with the job of loading suitcases while he went to his
shed. I finished loading the last suitcase, then went to the
shed. He was standing there staring at his tools neatly
hung from their hooks.

"Anything wrong?" I asked.

He turned around and said quietly, "Just thinking
about putting in a cement floor someday."

He walked away.

He didn't fool me. He wasn't thinking about a cement
floor. He was thinking he might die and never come back
to his farm. But he wouldn't ever let on that he was worried. That's just the way he was.

They'd obtained permission for me to get out of
school and go with them. They let me drive most of the
way. I kept the radio on, because they were both so quiet
and I needed something to keep me awake.

It was strange about Logan and Zinia. When we got to
Salt Lake City, they shopped for motels. We'd stop and
Logan would walk into the office and ask the price, then
shake his head and come back out again and we'd drive to
the next one—until finally he found one cheaper than all
the rest.

There's a good reason why some motels are so
cheap—it's because they *are* cheap. Our room was dark
and dingy, with a black and white TV that kept fluttering
no matter what you did with the vertical control. The
walls were paper thin. The couple next to us had a little
baby that cried all night, and if the baby wasn't enough,
we had to listen to them argue about why it was crying.
The guy kept saying for her to do something about it.
Zinia said they ought to put the kid on solids.

I woke up at three in the morning. I was sleeping on a
roll-away that stuck out into the room, so it was almost
wall-to-wall beds. The baby in the next room was asleep,

but I could hear Logan and Zinia talking in low whispers. He was telling her about the stocks and bonds and the will. I looked over and saw him running his finger over the outline of her face.

"Are you my sweet gal?" he asked softly.

"You know that—I'll always be your sweet gal."

"That's right—you're my sweet gal."

I was embarrassed for them because they were so old. I wondered how he could say that to her, because she had wrinkles on her face and her hair was a dull color, and she didn't wear lipstick and never used perfume, and there was just a little bit of mustache beneath her nose, and she had dark plastic glasses that hid her eyes. How could he ask if she was his sweet gal?

I was afraid of hearing anything more, afraid they'd say or do something that'd really embarrass me, thinking I was asleep when I wasn't. They were old people, afraid of death in the morning, their children married and having children themselves—and there they were, old people, him asking if she was his sweet gal.

I couldn't handle it.

I got out of bed and stumbled to the bathroom and made as much noise as I could, flushing the toilet, turning the faucets on and off, brushing my teeth, and even gargling—so they'd know I was awake, and they'd better be careful and not embarrass me. When I returned, they were far apart in bed, facing away from each other at opposite sides.

I was satisfied and went to sleep.

Logan got us up at seven the next morning. After I was dressed, he asked me to help him fold up the roll-away. I told him we could leave it for the maid, but he said it wouldn't kill us to do a little work.

Zinia came out of the bathroom wearing a Sunday dress. Logan brought in from the car a box labeled

"Breakfast." Zinia made up some powdered milk and took out three plastic bowls and spoons and a box of cereal from the box. There were also bananas to have on our cereal.

"This'll be my last meal till after the operation," Logan said.

I thought about that—his last meal maybe in his life. I knew what I'd have done. I'd have gone to a pancake restaurant and had the biggest breakfast on the menu. There's no way I'd bring food from home to eat in a dingy room in the cheapest motel on State Street. But not Logan and Zinia. I figured if she'd been in charge of the Last Supper, they'd have had macaroni and cheese and carrot sticks.

After breakfast we drove to the hospital and Logan checked in. The doctors had to do some tests, and they said Zinia might as well leave the hospital until the afternoon, when she'd be able to see Logan, but she said no, she'd just stay and wait.

We sat in the waiting room and pretended to read magazines. She'd brought some knitting with her so she wouldn't waste time. She was strange that way. I could waste time and never give it a thought, but it made her feel guilty, and so she knitted.

I read all the women's magazines I could stomach. You just don't find *Sports Illustrated* in a hospital waiting room, but there were plenty of *Redbook* and the like. I'd read all the articles that had to do with marriage relationships, and pretty soon they all took on the same pattern. The article would first talk about a problem—any problem, you name it—and then they'd say the problem was only symptomatic of a more serious problem called lack of communication. I decided you could go a long way as a marriage counselor if, no matter what problems people brought, you just said it was a lack of communication.

It was 1973, and I was seventeen. The Vietnam War was over for the United States, but the news magazines in the waiting room dated back quite a ways. They had articles about Vietnam, showing bodies spattered with blood lying on the ground. I wondered if I'd get drafted for some unknown war and end up dead with someone taking a picture of my body for a magazine. Maybe I'd be dead before I had a chance to get married or own a Jaguar.

I decided to go back to the women's magazines.

Finally I got tired of reading. I asked if I could walk around the hospital. Zinia said yes but I was not to get into any trouble. I said I wouldn't.

I walked down the long halls and peeked in each room to see what was happening. In one room an old man was moaning with pain, crying out over and over, "Oh, my leg, my leg." I stopped and looked in. His face was contorted with pain. I watched him for a long time. When I started out again, there was a slight pain in my leg, and I wondered if what he had was contagious. I prayed I wouldn't get it but then felt guilty for only thinking of myself. So I prayed the old man would either get better soon or die.

I moved on. The walkers were out—patients in crumpled white gowns, leaning on aluminum walkers with nurses' aides at their sides. On the maternity floor (a floor I wasn't supposed to be on) young mothers took tender steps down the hall, talking about sitz baths and husbands and weights of babies.

I decided it was pretty much the same with people as it is with animals: if their coat has a nice shine to it, they're healthy. The patients with their hair looking the worst were the sickest.

Zinia and I stayed the night in the same motel. The next morning we got up at four and drove to the hospital. We arrived early enough to go with Logan when he was wheeled to the operating room. After the operation started, we went to the waiting room. Zinia gave me money to eat breakfast in the hospital cafeteria. She said she wasn't hungry.

I ate, then went back. She was sitting there, staring at

the endless patterns of tiles down the hall. She looked worried.

"What's wrong with Logan?" I asked.

"It's a tumor," she said.

"What are they going to do with it?"

"Remove it."

"That doesn't sound so bad."

"It might be malignant," she said.

"What does that mean?"

"Cancer," she said with difficulty.

I raised my eyebrows. "Logan has cancer?"

"We don't know. We'll know in a while."

Instead of making my rounds through the halls as I'd planned, I sat with her. She needed me.

Four hours later, the doctor came out to see us. He sat down and talked calmly about the operation. He said the tumor had been malignant, but it had been localized, and they'd removed it. They'd performed a colostomy. He said he was sure Logan could adapt to it. There were thousands of people in the country who'd had the same operation and adjusted very well. He said there was a lady who dealt with colostomy patients and their families, and he gave us her office number and said if we'd go there, she'd explain things more completely.

Zinia thanked him, and he left us. She sat and watched him leave. There were tears in her eyes. I didn't know what to say. She finally got up and started walking away. She forgot her knitting. I gathered it all in her bag and carried it with me.

The colostomy lady was waiting for us. She took us into another room, where there was a plastic model of a person's insides, with red and blue and green parts that could be taken apart. She explained the operation to us very carefully. For a while I didn't understand what she was saying, but then I finally did.

* * * * * * * * * * * * *

A few days later they released Logan from the hospital and we drove home. Logan was more withdrawn and quieter than usual. When we got home, he went to bed.

They woke me the next morning shouting at each other, or at least Logan was yelling at her. They were both in the bathroom, and the door was closed.

"Just leave me alone," Logan grumbled.

"I want to help," she said.

"I don't want any help! Can't you get it through that thick head of yours? Now just get out of here and leave me alone. Oh, I wish I was dead."

"Well, I don't. No sir, I don't wish that at all."

"Spending my whole life doing this . . . it's gonna take hours—and be a mess."

"No it won't, Logan. Please let me help you."

He blew up. "Get out of here!"

Silence.

His voice was strange. "I don't want you to see me this way. Can't you get that in your head? Now get out."

She came out crying. Logan locked the door after she left. She breezed past my bedroom door to their room.

A few minutes of silence, then sounds of choking and groaning from the bathroom.

Zinia ran to the bathroom door and cried out, "Let me in!"

"Stay away!"

"What happened?"

"It's made me sick, and I threw up."

"Let me clean it up."

"How many times do I have to tell you? I don't want you to see what I've become."

"You think I care about a little mess? Why, land sakes, Logan, I've been cleaning up messes all my life. Now you let me in, or I'm getting Jimmy and he'll figure out a way to break in."

The door opened.

"Take a look," Logan said miserably. "It's all over everything."

"Doesn't matter a bit. This bathroom's seen a lot worse than that. Now you leave this door open while I go get a bucket and a rag."

She returned in a minute with a bucket. I got out of bed and walked quietly to the bathroom and peered in. They didn't notice me. He was standing there, watching, while she, on her hands and knees, vigorously attacked the mess. I saw a plastic tube coming out his side.

"I'm more trouble than I'm worth."

"This doesn't matter," she said. "Doesn't matter at all."

"Aw, Zinia," he moaned.

She looked up. "Logan, I'd clean this up ten times a day just to have you with me. You know I would. So don't fret yourself about it, not at all. You hear me? Not at all."

"Zinia, you're my sweet gal." He reached out and touched her head lightly. She paused, delighted in his touch. Then slowly he removed his hand and she went back to work.

I tiptoed back to my room. It was good for me to know that no matter what, they wouldn't run out on each other when things got tough.

After Logan got home, he asked me to do the farm work he normally did. Every day he'd give me instructions about what to do, and I'd go out to work by myself, trying the best I could to do a good job for him. By then I loved them both and just wanted to make them happy with me. The silent anger had been stilled for a time.

I wanted to be their son.

Sometimes Logan would come out to see me in the fields and look over what I'd done and tell me what was wrong with it. He wasn't all the time dishing out praise, but when he gave it, you knew you'd done a good job, and that he wasn't just being polite.

One day in August he came to the fields. It was a

warm day. He sat in his pickup and watched me work. By this time I knew what to do.

When I was through with that job, he called me over.

"Finish up. We're going camping."

I didn't know that Logan even knew what camping was. It wasn't exactly roughing it. Logan had borrowed a neighbor's camper, so we had beds and a small refrigerator and a stove. We packed some provisions and took off. A few hours later we were in the mountains, beside a mountain stream. We tried fishing but didn't catch anything, but it didn't matter, it was fun anyway. Then we made a campfire and cooked some steaks he'd brought in a cooler. After dark, we sat around and talked.

"You saved my crops this summer," he said. "If it hadn't been for you, I'd have lost it all. My farm is my life, you know." His face clouded. "My kids are all too good for it. Somehow they think they're too good to get down and get a little dirt on 'em. College graduates, too good to farm. So what'll happen to this place after I'm gone? There's nobody in the family to carry on here."

"I can, Logan. I know how."

He put his arm on my shoulder. "Yeah, you could. You know most of what I know now. We'll have to think about that, won't we. Some day soon."

He stared somberly into the glowing ashes.

"The tumor they took out—it had cancer in it."

"But they got it, Logan. I heard the doctor say."

"How could they get it all? What if they just missed one cell? You know how small a cell is? One cell, that's all it takes. One cell to go someplace else and start up again. How can they know if they got it all? It'll come back some-day."

"Maybe not," I said.

"Do you ever think about dying?"

I shook my head.

"No, of course you don't. I never did either when I

was your age. Even in the war, I never thought it'd happen to me. I bet the ones that died thought the same thing. How else could anybody go to war?"

"Where were you in the war?"

"Pacific."

"What was it like?"

"Bad."

I figured that'd be my lesson about the Second World War, but he continued.

"Once we were in Hawaii to rest up after we'd fought to take some islands. We camped on the side of a mountain. It was very green because it rained so much, and the winds came across the mountain all the time. The fighting had been so bad. And we all knew we had to go back. A fella tried to kill himself by jumping off the mountain, but the wind was blowing so much it pinned him against the side of the cliff and he just slid down to the ground. All that happened was he sprained his ankle. I never found out what happened to him after that, but I always wondered if it was like getting another chance at life. Well, it's late. We'd better get some sleep."

The next morning we returned home. He never told me why he'd taken me with him, but I sensed it was to tell me he loved me.

Just before school started, when I came in from chores one day, Logan asked me to go outside with him. I thought he'd be chewing on me for forgetting to do something.

We walked out to where the cars were kept. There was an extra car there, a Mercury.

"Like it?" he asked.

"Sure, why?"

"It's yours."

I shouted and giggled and laughed and almost cried.

My first car. It wasn't just a car, it was a trust. It was saying that I'd done a good job for him, that I was worth something to them. It was love and trust and reward for working.

Logan loved me.

My senior year of high school started out to be the best time but ended up the worst. I settled down in church, became more mature, less of a clown in classes. The bishop asked me to prepare for a mission soon, and Logan and Zinia said they'd support me.

Logan had by then adjusted to slowing down. He and Zinia even had their children home for Christmas, with none of them suspecting anything.

Just before school started, Ryan invited me to go with him to a youth conference held in his stake. We roomed together during the conference, which was held at a college. The amazing thing to me was how much Ryan was liked and respected, even though he was only fifteen.

Earlier that night, before the dance, there were separate meetings for the boys and girls. We went and heard a very serious talk by the stake president about standards. It was one of those talks you try hard not to blush at.

As we got ready for bed that night, I said, "Ryan, you're really something."

"No I'm not."

"Everyone loves you. All I have to do is tell people I'm your brother and they just flip. You've charmed everybody. Ryan Pepper, Eagle Scout; Ryan Pepper, ace student, winner of ninth-grade class officer election; Ryan Pepper, star seminary student, winner of all the scripture chases. What's your secret?"

"What do you mean?" he asked, suddenly on the defensive.

I looked at his expression and could tell he was hiding something. "Is something wrong?"

"I'm not as good as people think," he said.

"Well, it can't be too bad."

"Why can't it?" he snapped.

"Because anyone looking at you can tell you're good. If it were too bad, it'd show. So what's your big problem?"

"I can't tell you. I can't tell anyone."

I sat down on the bed. "Hey, you can't carry something like that alone. Look, take it from a pro—go talk to your bishop. It really helps."

"I can't."

"Why not?"

"I can't tell anyone."

"He'll help you."

"How do you know? You don't even know what my problem is."

"That's right, I don't. But go talk to him—please."

"I'll wait till I've got it under control."

"That's dumb. Sometimes you need help. Everybody does. That's what he's there for, to help people."

"I shouldn't even have this problem. I should be above it."

"But you're not. What's wrong? Afraid to admit you're not perfect?"

Tears filled his eyes. "I can't tell him."

"I know it's tough, but he'll help."

His bishop was one of the chaperons. I knocked on his door and told him Ryan needed to talk. It was one o'clock.

I waited in the hall while they talked. I could hear Ryan crying.

Thirty minutes went by.

The bishop came out with his arm around Ryan's shoulder, telling him he'd work with him. Then he shook my hand and thanked me for talking Ryan into seeing him.

"It's going to be all right now," the bishop said, then left.

Ryan looked sheepishly at me. "You won't tell Jill, will you?"

"No, of course not."

"I want to be good, but lately it's been like I've lost control."

"Hey, look, don't worry about it. Besides, you're the best there is."

"That's what everybody says, but lately whenever they say it, I think if they really knew what I was like, they wouldn't even talk to me. Maybe you're right, maybe I try too hard. Maybe I've got too much of Dad in me."

"No, you're more like Mom. She was good and so are you."

"You think so, even now?"

"Absolutely. Don't worry about it. You're not like Dad at all."

There were tears in his eyes. My little brother, my Gold Star good-guy brother.

"I want to go on a mission. Do you?"

I paused. "I'm not sure."

"Don't you have a testimony?"

"I don't know. Everytime I go to class, instead of listening to the teacher, I spend all my time thinking of jokes."

"You ought to listen."

I yawned. "I guess so. Can we go to sleep now?"

After that I think he was embarrassed that I knew he had a problem once. But actually I guess it made me love him more to know he was human and had to repent like everyone else.

In January of my senior year, Logan began to limp. He said he had a charley horse, but it never went away. By April the pain was bad enough for him to go to a doctor. Nothing the doctor did made things any better. Finally he was admitted to the hospital in Salt Lake City.

High school graduation came the last of May. I remember listening to the commencement speaker tell us enthusiastically this was really the beginning, not the end.

Zinia called the family and asked them to visit their father while they still could. Over the next few weeks they came, entering his room and lying about how good he looked and how he'd be up in no time. And then they'd come out in the living room and cry.

He died quietly in the night near the end of June.

The night before the funeral there was a viewing of the body at the mortuary. At first just the family was there. I looked in the coffin. Logan looked awful, not because he was dead, but because the funeral director had put makeup on him that made his face look pink and chalky. He was dressed in white clothes. Zinia told me that it had something to do with temples and the resurrection.

I looked at him and imagined a graveyard and him popping out one day, looking around, and walking down the road to his place to see how the potatoes were doing. He'd always want to know that, resurrected or not.

The others in the family took their turns staring into the coffin. Some of them remarked how nice he looked. He didn't look nice to me. To me he looked dead.

Rachel hugged me. I started crying, and she said it was all right. I told her I loved Logan, and she said she knew it, and I'd always be part of the family. Jeff hugged me too. They took me outside, and we walked around the garden. I told them how hard I'd worked the previous summer when Logan was recovering from his operation, and how he gave me a car.

When we went back in, there were a lot of people milling around and talking. They ignored him, like he was the centerpiece on a table at a Shaklee convention.

Fred was talking about being laid off in his job, and how nobody did anything right where he used to work, how he was the only one who knew how things should go, and how sorry they'd be someday for firing him.

The next day we gathered in a room at church just before the funeral started. When it was time to go into the chapel, Fred announced that, since he was the oldest, he and his wife Margaret would sit on either side of Zinia, with Ruth and Andrew next to them.

"What about the grandchildren?" Ruth asked.

"I think there'll be room for my Todd and Howard to sit on the first row. The other grandchildren will have to sit on the second row."

"I think it's better if the parents sit with their children," Rachel suggested.

"All right—Margaret and I will sit beside Mom with our kids on the first row, and the rest of you can sit on the second row. Is that all right with everyone?"

"I want to sit near Mom too," Ruth said. "I'm Logan's child too, you know."

Fred scowled. "There's just not room for everyone on the first row. You're delaying the service, Ruth, and frankly, I'm surprised at your attitude. At a time like this I'd hope you wouldn't be so childish as to worry about where you sit. C'mon, Mom, you come with me."

We formed a line. I was the last one.

The speakers said nice things about Logan during the funeral, and as nice as the words were, they weren't as good as they could have been. Logan was the best man I've ever known. I still hear his voice telling me things. I don't always listen, but I still hear it.

After the funeral we went to the cemetery for a graveside service. Fred said a little prayer over the grave, asking that the ground be kept undisturbed until the resurrection. Then we went back to the house. The women from the church had brought in food for the family, and the table was loaded with salads and casseroles and hot rolls and cakes and pies. It was the best meal I'd seen in that house.

I didn't like the way everybody was eating, like it was some big holiday. Fred packed away two big helpings of food, and Ruth—you should see her eat sometime.

Afterwards we all went into the living room. Fred stood up like he was master of ceremonies.

"I don't know if anybody's thought about it," Ruth said, "but I'd like his collection of silver dollars, if that's all right with everyone."

"Oh sure," Rachel said.

"Exactly why do you want it?" Fred asked.

"What do you mean, why?"

"Is it because you like the collection or because you know what it's worth?"

"I resent that, Fred," Andrew said.

Fred took a mint from a candy dish. "All I'm saying is it'd be nice to know how much it's worth. The reasonable thing would be to find out the cost and then decide if Ruth should have it, or if we should sell it and split the money among the children."

"I'd like his tools," Andrew asked.

Zinia sat there, still in shock. Fred was running the show. He continued. "We'll talk about the silver dollar collection and the tools later. Right now, I'd like to present a little plan I've worked on for the property. Mom can't work the farm, and none of us is really that interested in farming, so I was thinking about turning some of the land into a housing development."

I sat there, consigned to the outer fringes with all the little kids. Suddenly tears started down my face. I got up and quietly walked outside. There was work needing to be done, and all I wanted was for everyone to leave so I could go back to doing Logan's chores until the resurrection when he'd come walking toward me in the fields dressed in white, telling me I'd missed a row.

I went in the shed and shut the door. The smell of sawdust and motor oil filled the room. Everything was there just the way he'd left it, the nuts and bolts and

washers labeled in their baby food jars, waiting for someone to walk in looking for a 6-32 bolt. I stood in front of
the radial arm saw. There was just a speck of sawdust on
the floor that'd slipped into the cracks when he was last
sawing.

I picked up his irrigating shovel and started crying
and couldn't stop. There was a strange voice making des-
olate, awful moans, and it was my voice. My tears fell on
the table of the saw and I worried it'd rust, so I took out
my handkerchief and wiped over the surface. But I was
still crying while I wiped, so it never got dry.

I stayed there for a long time. When I returned to the
living room, Zinia reached out and hugged me before I
sat down. Fred was still running the show, going over his
plans. I figure he must have been planning this for a long
time.

Now, years later, I can see that Fred was just doing
what he thought was best. And probably it was. But to me
then, he was wrong because he wanted to change Logan's
farm.

Fred was still talking. "Okay, that's our best ball-park
figure if we decide to develop the land. I'll move back
here and manage things to make sure we get the best
deals. Now if I'm going to be working full time on this, I'll
need to get an extra share of income. That'd only be
fair."

"I don't like the idea of taking the land Dad loved and
turning it into a housing development," Rachel said.

Fred scowled. "Do you and Jeff want to move out
here and learn to grow potatoes?"

"No, but if we sell the land, why not sell it as farm-
land?"

Fred shook his head. "We could, but there's no
money in that. I don't know about you, but my kids need
something to get 'em through college. I think we all need
that. We'll save the house for Mom, and a little land for
her garden, so she won't be out anything, and she'll have

a steady income the rest of her life. Mom, I'm really just trying to look out for you."

"I know, dear," Zinia said quietly.

"I think it's a good idea," Ruth said.

"Well, let's vote then. The only ones who are eligible to vote are me and Ruth and Rachel."

"What about Mom?" Rachel asked. "Doesn't she get a vote?"

"That goes without saying, Rachel. Mom, you vote too."

"It sounds so complicated. The rest of you decide what's right and I'll go along with it," she said.

"All in favor raise your hand."

Ruth and Fred raised their hands.

"All opposed."

Rachel raised her hand.

"The motion carries."

Ruth started up again. "Now can we talk about the silver dollar collection?"

"And the tools," Andrew said.

I ran into the fields and stayed there until night, when I thought they'd all be asleep.

When I came in the house, it was late. Fred was sitting at the kitchen table, poring over pages of calculations strung over the table.

"Where's Zinia?"

"Don't bother her. She's gone to bed. There's nothing you can say now that'd be any help."

"I've got to tell her not to sell the land. Logan doesn't want her to."

"How do you know that?"

"He talked to me about it once."

"Well, you can't talk to her now. She took a sleeping pill. I'll tell her, though, first thing in the morning."

"Where's Rachel?"

"She and Jeff've gone to bed."

"Where?"

"In your room. Don't disturb them. Besides, I need to talk to you. Sit down."

I sat down.

"Dad said good things about you. I think you were very important to him, almost like a son."

I am a son, I thought.

"I guess you realize over the years you've received a lot from my parents. A high school education, a car, clothes, books, food—it all adds up."

He wrote down a number.

"Did he ever tell you the story about the man he knew in World War Two who jumped off a mountain?" I said.

He looked at me strangely. "No, he never did."

"I didn't think he would. He told me though."

"It's all in the past, Jimmy. Time marches on. There has to be progress. I'm in charge now, and a lot of things are going to change. My family'll be moving in this house for a while, until we build our own. We'll be turning the land into a subdivision. This won't be a farm anymore."

"Logan doesn't want that to happen," I said.

He kept punching the buttons on his calculator, looking at the numbers flashing on the screen. I felt sorry for Logan. He must have been disappointed in Fred.

Fred cleared his throat and looked at me for the first time. "I just need to know when you'll be leaving, so we can make plans about using your room."

"Logan said he'd send me on a mission and to college and that I could farm the place someday."

Fred looked at me coldly. "I don't suppose you got that in writing, did you?"

I shook my head.

"I didn't think so. Look, I'm sorry. If you were part of the family, it'd be different, but—and I know this may seem harsh—but you're not, regardless of what he may have said. He was getting old, you know, and sometimes when we get old, our judgment isn't always the best. I'm sure you understand, don't you?"

I stood up to leave, numbly walked a few steps, then turned around. "Logan was in Hawaii, back from fighting, and this guy climbed a mountain to kill himself, but the winds stopped him and slammed him against the rocks, and he slid down the side of the cliff, and it didn't kill him."

Fred didn't bother to look up from his calculator. "Right."

I went to my room. Rachel and Jeff were asleep in my bed. As quietly as I could, I started to pack my clothes into a box.

Rachel woke up.

"Jimmy?" she said quietly.

"Yeah."

"What are you doing?"

"Packing."

"Why?"

"Fred said I had to leave."

She got out of bed and put on a robe. "We'll see about this."

She walked into the kitchen. Fred was still punching numbers.

"What on earth do you think you're doing, telling Jimmy to leave? He's a part of us. Dad loved him. I won't stand for it, Fred."

"Hasn't he bled enough from us already? It's about time he got out on his own instead of freeloading from us all the time."

"Mom loves Jimmy as much as I do. She won't have you telling him he has to leave."

"Mom said she'd go along with anything I decide to do."

"Not this she won't, and you know it, Fred."

I was standing at the edge of the kitchen watching them.

One of Rachel's kids started crying. She turned to me.

"We'll work something out. Let me go take care of my baby, then I'll be right back." She left.

Fred scowled at me. "You think you're gonna just keep sponging off us, don't you. Why don't you grow up and quit being such a leach? I've got an idea. Why don't you go to Mexico and get your dad out of jail and help him smuggle drugs?"

I ran to the shed, took down Logan's shovel from the wall, put it in my car, and drove away.

I drove to American Falls to talk to Ryan. It was a little after one in the morning when I arrived. I knew where his bedroom was, so I drove on the lawn under his window, then got out and stood on top of the car and called through the screen until I woke him up. He came outside, wearing just a pair of jeans and no shirt.

"Get packed—we're going to California tonight. Logan's dead, and I just got kicked out of the house."

He sleepily scratched his head. "You want to leave?"

"Yeah, hurry, we'll pick Jill up on our way."

"Does she know?"

"Not yet. C'mon, hurry."

He yawned. "What'll we do in California?"

"We'll live there. C'mon, we promised each other— remember. You have to come with us."

"I need to finish high school first."

"They've got high schools in California."

He looked at me for a long time, then said, "I can't leave my foster family."

"Why not?"

"I just can't, that's all."

"We all promised that if one of us had to leave, the other two would go with him."

"I need to stay and prepare for my mission. My foster family says they'll help send me."

"They're just saying that. When it comes down to it, they won't help you."

"Yes, they will. Going on a mission is very important to me."

"You think you're so blasted perfect and pure, don't you. Well, you're not, you know."

"I never said I was."

With a mocking tone in my voice, I asked, "Do you still have that problem you used to have?"

"No," he said quietly, "it's all cleared up."

I looked at his eyes and could tell there was nothing he was ashamed about. It scared me.

"Jill won't go to California with you," he said.

"Sure she will. We're as close as a brother and sister can be. Ryan, please go with us."

He sighed. "I can't. I need to stay here."

"You're no brother of mine," I snapped, jumping in the car and driving away.

I arrived at Jill's house about three in the morning. I slept in the car until seven, then rang the bell until her foster father came to the door. "What do you want?" he asked.

"I need to talk to Jill."

"She's sleeping."

"I've got to talk to her."

Jill appeared at the door and said it'd be okay, that we'd just talk quietly in the living room.

She sat down. She was wearing a long pale-blue robe. I told her about Fred, then said, "We're going to California today, just like we always planned. I'll take care of you. Honest I will."

She frowned. "Have you talked to Ryan about it?"

I didn't want to tell her about Ryan.

"We'll go get him after we leave. C'mon, Jillsy. It's what we've always dreamed about, the three of us together, a family again."

She paused. "Scott wouldn't want me to leave him."

"There's plenty of guys in California. Besides, if it's really love, it'll stand the test of time."

"We don't have any money."

"I'll get a job. And I'll put you through school, better schools than they got here, believe me. UCLA or Berkeley."

"My foster parents need me to help out with the twins."

"You're just full of excuses, aren't you. How about considering your family for once?"

She looked at a family picture on the mantel taken the previous summer. She was in the picture. She turned to face me. "This is my family too."

"No! Not them! I'm your family—me and Ryan. I'll take care of you."

She turned on me. "I don't want to be taken care of. Why should I run away from here to go to California with you?"

"Is it too much to expect a little family loyalty once in a while?"

"You call it family, and then you twist it till there's no room for anything else. I can't stand it. You have no right to make me feel guilty for falling in love with Scott. You keep wanting me to choose between him and some weird idea of yours about us as a family. Well, it's not right. Sometimes you just smother me. There's no way I'd ever go to California with you. No way in the world."

I stood up. "Okay then, fine, if that's the way you want it. I've had it up to here with this family."

I left. She followed after me.

Her foster mother, said, "Jill, you can't go outside in just your robe."

But she did.

I got in the car and paused to look at her one last time. I knew I was at a crossroads—that if I'd get out of the car and talk it out, my life would go one way, with the church part of it, but if I drove away and lived without the church, there would be other paths to follow.

For an instant time froze. I looked at Jill as if through a microscope, noticing her eyes and the texture of her face.

Her foster mother stood at the front screen door, watching us. Ten steps between Jill and me. Just ten steps. I couldn't cross that distance. Everyone had a home and family but me.

I started the car.

"Jimmy! Don't go!" she called out as I drove away.

I left her with a breeze moving her robe gently around her feet and the early morning sun on her hair.

"Morning, Ace," the army recruiter in San Francisco said six weeks later. "Want some coffee?"

"Why not?" I said.

He poured me a cup. I took a sip. It tasted strange and bitter, and I wondered why anyone drank it. I'd get used to it. There was no reason now to hold back. I'd be just like everybody else—just like my father.

"I'm out of work, and I need a job."

"What do you do?"

I paused. "I'm a comedian."

"Sit down. Fill out this form. The army's full of comedians."

I sat down and started writing.

It was three months since I'd graduated from high school. The commencement speaker had been wrong.

It was not the beginning.

It was the end.

CHAPTER FIVE

We left from Jill's home in Burley at nine at night and traveled as far as West Yellowstone. The next morning while I packed my suitcase, she came to my room and said a man was sitting in a car watching us. As we walked out the door, he took our picture.

I walked over to him. "What's this all about?"

"Alan Becker, 'The National Inquirer.'"

"She's my sister," I said, realizing what they might do with a picture of me coming out of a motel with someone other than my wife.

He grinned. "I know. Hi there, Jill. How's it going, huh? Is it true your brother calls you Jillsy?"

"Listen to me. I don't want my sister's picture in the 'National Inquirer'."

"Hey, don't worry. I take a lot of pictures on an assignment. Most of 'em I don't use. Let's all just stay cool, okay? I'll be with you for the next few days. Where are we going?"

"None of your business."

"Our readers want to know, and I do too. And I'd like a little information about your family. You were raised by foster parents in Idaho. Why was that? What happened to your parents?"

I hurried to our rooms, tossed our suitcases in the car, and roared away.

He followed us. Once I thought I'd lost him by pulling off the main road and stopping. But when we stopped at Old Faithful for breakfast, he came to our table.

"Sure are a lot of tourists on the road this time of year, huh? Amazing how much a bear can slow down traffic. Say, I notice you aren't taking many pictures of your trip. I'll be happy to

*share some of mine. I got a nice one of the two of you at the Paint
Pots. Took it with a telephoto lens. Should turn out great."*

"Leave us alone!"

*"Hey, I understand. Just tell me a few things and then I'll
quit bothering you. My partner stayed behind in Idaho. He says
the rumor in high school was that your dad spent time in a Mexican prison for running drugs. Any truth to that?"*

"Let's go," I said to Jill.

We left. He ran to his car to follow us.

*"We've got to ditch him before we get to Buffalo," I said,
careening around a curve, nearly colliding with a bear.*

I spent two years in the Army. That's where I developed a drinking problem. After the Army, I returned
to California and tried to be a comedian. At first the only
steady job I could find was being a clown on weekends at
grocery stores, giving away samples of Mity Fine orange
juice. But things opened up a little at a time. Before long,
I could afford to live in a nice apartment and drive a car
that was only two years old.

One rainy night in 1978, Jill phoned. It was just a few
months after she'd married Scott in the Idaho Falls Temple. When I heard her voice I knew something was
wrong. "There's been an accident. Ryan's been hurt bad.
He and his missionary companion were riding their bicycles. Ryan was hit by a car."

"How bad?"

She paused. "He's dead. I'm going to bring him
home." She started crying. "Jimmy, I can't go through
this alone. Will you go with me?"

Ryan was dead. The best of the three of us, and he
was gone. It didn't make any sense.

MasterCard had made the mistake of giving me a
credit card. I drove to the airport and bought a ticket for
Italy.

A plane schedule mix-up forced us to fly separately.

When I saw Jill at the terminal in Italy, I was again amazed how beautiful she is. We hugged each other and she started to cry. I wanted to say something but didn't know what, so I asked about her flight. She said it was fine. I said my flight was fine too. I asked about Scott. She said he was fine. Everything's fine, I thought miserably.

The mission president and his wife met us once we cleared customs. Their last name was Stone. We spent the rest of the day finishing our preparations, then had supper with President and Sister Stone.

After supper, Jill and I took a walk. To some we may have looked like a strangely somber married couple. The fresh ocean breeze, the white sands, the blue of the Mediterranean, the sparkling homes, the music from sidewalk cafes, the steady stream of American tourists in their gaudy shorts and halter tops and cameras and complaining children—it all seemed out of place in our grief.

After a long silence, she said, "He passed his test."

"Sure." I said it quickly so it'd sound like I bought it.

"You don't believe that, do you."

"Why pretend it's part of some grand plan? Ryan wasn't watching where he was going and he ran into a car. What kind of plan is that?"

"You're quite the cynic now, aren't you."

"I call it being realistic."

"And where does religion fit in your realism?"

"You tell me what kind of god raises up a guy like Ryan—good as they come, solid as a rock, not a bad thought in him—then sends him overseas to be bumped off by an Italian driver. Tell me what kind of god would come up with a plan like that."

"Things will work out for Ryan."

"Sure," I said sarcastically. "They've worked out real swell so far, haven't they?"

She let me have it. "What's wrong with you? It's bad enough losing one brother, but now I have to see how messed up you are."

We stopped at a small sidewalk cafe. I ordered a drink. She had nothing.

I took a sip. "Want any? It's very good. It'd be a cultural experience."

"No thanks."

"I won't tell anyone," I taunted.

She looked sadly at me, then shook her head.

"Suit yourself." I took a sip. "Ahh," I sighed.

"Why are you destroying yourself?"

I looked at the glass. "This? It's nothing. I can stop anytime."

"Then why don't you?"

A photographer came and asked if we were on our honeymoon. To avoid saying we came to collect our dead brother's body, I nodded my head. He asked if he could take our picture for a buck. I nodded my head and he stepped back and coaxed us to smile. We didn't. He made a wisecrack about honeymoons.

"Take the stupid picture and get out of here," I muttered. Thirty seconds later he gave me the picture. It was awful. I paid him. He left, no doubt wondering if the marriage would last the weekend.

Jill finally broke our icy silence. "Are you still going with Rebecca or whatever her name is?"

"Not anymore."

"What happened?"

"You don't really care."

"I asked, didn't I?"

"All right, I'll tell you. In the beginning we were really close. But as time passed, a gap developed in our relationship. So we sat down like mature adults and discussed it."

"And what happened from your discussion?"

I sighed. "She left me for a jockey—a small guy, maybe four feet tall. I saw her last week in a grocery store. She said he augments her identity."

"What does that mean?"

"It means she likes being taller than him. It's like Snow White and one dwarf."

She didn't smile. "I assume you and your crowd just reshuffle and deal again."

I ordered another drink. Jill frowned at me. "Do you really need that?"

"Jill, I know what you're gonna say, so don't say it."

"What am I going to say?"

I stared grimly into my glass. "That I should shape up for Ryan's sake."

She touched my arm. "That's not it. Do it for your own sake. What you're doing only brings unhappiness."

I laughed. "Wrong, Jillsy. I'm happy—terrific at parties. Ask anyone in Southern California."

"Jimmy," she pleaded, "please—for my sake then, straighten up your life."

I looked at her. My little sister still loved me. And I loved her. I'd do just about anything for her.

Except change. I shook my head. "Just quit? Now? That'd be real difficult. Sometimes I get lonely, or nervous, or scared, and a drink . . . a drink makes things better."

"If you turn your life around, Heavenly Father will help you find a wife. He's got someone picked out, and He's just waiting for you to get your act together so He can introduce you without having you pass out on the first date."

"That's not kind. I hold my liquor very well."

"Ryan'll help you. I'm sure he will. He always tried to be helpful."

I paid the bill, and we started back.

"I'm pregnant," she said after several minutes of silence.

"You're going to be a mother?"

She looked at me with a slight grin. "It's amazing how fast you pick these things up."

The next morning the missionaries had a memorial

service for Ryan. Jill and I sat on the front row and listened to them talk and sing. After it was over, they came around and shook our hands and said how much they loved Ryan. Looking at them, I suddenly saw them differently than ever before in my life. They were clean and I was not. They had faith and I had none. Sitting there, feeling estranged from the Church, from my sister and my dead brother, I sadly realized—I've come a long way, baby.

We left Italy the same day. After we'd reached our cruising altitude, Jill pulled out a packet of papers and gave them to me.

"What's this?"

"Pedigree sheets. It shows our family line."

"I don't care about that. Save it for your kid."

"I have other copies."

A flight attendant asked if I'd like a drink. Because of Ryan and Jill, I said no.

I looked at the names in pyramid fashion on the pages. "Good grief, Jillsy, this is hard-core genealogy."

She went through the pages name by name, filling in lives as she went. I politely nodded my head until she showed me a picture of my grandmother on her wedding day. You think of grandparents as old, because that's what they are when you come along. But in the picture she was young and beautiful, eighteen years old with a blush in her cheeks (although the black and white picture couldn't bring it out), standing in front of a wedding cake.

"You look like her."

She looked at the picture. "I thought so too."

"She's beautiful. I'd marry a girl who looked like that."

"But she wouldn't marry you, at least not until you shape up."

"For a girl like her, I'd change."

She looked at me with raised eyebrows. "Yeah?"

"I'm serious. I know I have disgusting habits. It's just that right now I'm in my disgusting phase. But I'll change someday."

The flight attendant brought our lunch. I couldn't open the plastic food packets. They're designed so only a gorilla can open them.

"You think of our ancestors as being alive somewhere?" I asked her during dessert.

She nodded. "I think they welcomed Ryan back when he died."

"And they know about us?"

"Especially you."

"Why me?"

"You're the last male in the line who can raise up sons to carry on the family name. Jimmy, they want you to carry on the line."

I looked at her. She was serious.

"I'll think about it, okay?"

"Fair enough. And when I get more information about our ancestors, I'll send it."

I picked up my copy of the family records. "It is kind of interesting."

"Admit it, you're fascinated."

We arrived in Idaho the next day with the casket on the plane with us. Scott met us at the airport. He and Jill kissed enthusiastically; then he shook my hand. He was tanned and his hands were strong, and he wore a Cenex cap and Levi's and a western shirt. He was running his uncle's place while they were on a mission. We drove to their place in a nearly new pickup.

They lived in a farmhouse.

"I'm kind of sleepy," Jill said at nine o'clock.

"Me too," Scott said.

They went to bed. I stayed in the living room and watched TV, dozing off and then coming to during another program.

I wanted a drink in the worst way, but I'd promised

myself I wouldn't drink in their home. Besides, I knew they wouldn't have any around.

About eleven I went to the bathroom to get ready for bed. After going through the same ritual Zinia had taught me, I opened the medicine cabinet. I enjoy looking in people's medicine cabinets. You can learn so much. There was a woman's style razor for shaving legs. Next to it was a bottle of English Leather, recreating the smell I'd caught earlier in the night when Scott came out of the bathroom heading for bed. There were some vitamin pills for pregnancy, two toothbrushes—his would be the tan one, hers light green.

It was late but I couldn't sleep. I wandered around the living room. I found their wedding album on a shelf and looked through it. There were several pictures of them taken outside the Idaho Falls Temple, arm in arm—embracing in front of the temple, a closeup of her looking into his eyes.

I turned a page, and although it was Jill, the picture looked very much like the picture of our grandmother on the day of her wedding—the same high cheekbones, the same long hair and shy smile I'd seen in the picture Jill had shown me on the plane.

Jill and her grandmother were beauties. The pattern had repeated itself from one generation to another.

What about the men in the family? Was I similar to any of them?

Rummaging through the bookshelf, I found several old photo albums. They were of Scott's family. There were lots of pictures of men and women and children, pictures taken many years ago. There was a saucy young couple posing in front of a Model T Ford. I decided it must be Scott's grandparents. Another picture showed them at a miniature village, because the woman, still in her twenties, had an impudent expression as she peeked over the roof of a house.

There was a picture of a baby held by the woman, and after that, with each page, I could see the woman and the husband occasionally shown, grow older. Little by little the children grew. The one was joined by two others in the pictures. The boy would grow up to be Scott's father.

There was another album showing Scott's parents outside the Salt Lake Temple, and then a picture of Scott, chubby, cherubic Scott, growing up.

Some of the later pictures had me and Scott in them. There was a picture of Scott and Jill on the night of the junior-senior prom. More pictures of them and then a picture of Scott in a missionary blue suit outside the missionary training building in Provo. The last page on the album had a wedding announcement for Scott and Jill.

Families moving through time like an endless tide.

Finally I fell asleep watching TV on the couch. When I woke up at seven, I heard voices in the kitchen. Still lying on the couch, I saw Scott sitting at the kitchen table, and Jill, still in an old terry cloth robe, was frying some bacon and eggs. Her hair was still mussed from sleep, and she kept brushing it back out of her eyes. She scooped the food from the pan onto the plate and came around in back of her husband and set it down in front of him, pausing to tousle his hair and hug him. He reached out and held her hand and smiled at her. She kissed him, then asked if he wanted any orange juice.

Seeing Jill in her frayed robe, content with love for her husband, sleepily setting out a dish of bacon and eggs for him, her tummy just beginning to puff out with their future child—I wanted to have a life like theirs.

Life ought to be more than passing strangers in the hall and saying, "Hey, how's it going? How about those Dodgers, hey?"

It suddenly made sense for a man to promise to be faithful to just one woman, and for her to make the same promise to him, and for them to fuse together to produce children, and the children grow up in a stable home where they can be loved, until one day the children leave and start the process all over again.

Ryan's funeral was at ten o'clock. A church leader from Salt Lake City spoke at the funeral and assured us Ryan was all right and his test was over. He said that Ryan had been welcomed by his ancestors on the other side, and that he was happy where he was, and that someday he would be resurrected and live on the earth again.

The strange thing about it was, I believed him.

Later in the day Scott took me for a drive. We drove around looking at the high school and the drive-in. We drove by what had been Logan's place. Now it was a housing development. There was Fred Avenue and Ruth Drive and Rachel Circle.

We stopped at the drive-in for a hamburger and fries. Teenagers played video games inside.

"Make you feel old to be here again?" he asked.

"I guess so."

"Ever play those games?"

"Not much."

"Bet you a milkshake I can beat you."

I grinned. "You're on, cowboy."

Fifteen minutes later it was as if the years had rolled away and we were back together again, punching each other in the shoulder and bragging incessantly.

On the way back he asked, "How do you like my pickup?"

"It's okay to haul pigs around in, but if you want to talk vehicles, let's talk about a Porsche."

"Is that what you drive?"

"No, not yet. But soon."

"The day you drive a Porsche is the day chickens bark."

"It's on order!"

He laughed. "For when? Thirty years from now?"

"You'll see. Someday I'll drive it up here and show you a real car."

We both started laughing.

It felt good to have a friend again.

The next day Scott and Jill drove me to the airport. I had two drinks on the plane. A few hours later I was back in California.

CHAPTER SIX

I lived in a singles complex, complete with swimming pool and volleyball court and coed sauna. The day I arrived home from Idaho, there was a party going on down by the swimming pool. One of the guys was getting married the next day. There were plenty of free drinks. I drank and told jokes. Later I floated on an inner tube in the middle of the pool with a drink cradled carefully in my hand.

Ah, the good life, I thought contentedly.

There was a noise.

I woke up.

Two men in suits were peering down at me.

"Good morning," one of them said brightly.

I looked around. It was daytime. My feet were sprawled out across the sidewalk, and my head was under a rosebush.

"Beautiful day, isn't it?" the other one said.

I moved. My head felt as if someone had carved a jack-o-lantern in it. I moaned.

"We were just dropping by on folks in this neighborhood today, and we saw you there. Did you fall? Are you all right?"

"Trimming the roses," I muttered. "Can you get me up? I seem to have gotten stuck."

They helped me up. I looked at them. They were Mormon missionaries.

"Do you live here?" one of them asked.

I slowly looked around.

"We'd like to share an important message with you. Would it be better out of the sun?"

"Of course. We can go to my apartment."

I was trying to get my bearings. All the apartments looked the same.

"Forget where you live?" one of them asked politely.

"No, of course not. I know where I live."

It was all coming back to me now. I lived on the second floor in number 213. I gingerly moved up the stairs.

"You've got a bad bruise on your leg. How'd you get it?"

I stopped and looked down. The back of my leg was purple. I didn't remember how it'd happened.

"Baseball," I said.

We stood in front of the door. "My roommate's a slob," I said.

I didn't have a roommate, but I knew what shape the room was in.

"That's okay," one of them said.

I fumbled around in my swimsuit pocket looking for a key, then realized the door was unlocked. I opened the door. A dog lunged at me. I shut the door. The dog crashed against the door and barked viciously.

"Good watchdog, I bet," one of the elders said.

I didn't have a dog.

I smiled and nodded my head. "Very good."

A few minutes later, my next-door neighbor, a tall dancer with a slim figure and her hair done into a braided ponytail, came up the stairs with a bag of groceries. Her name was Alicia and she preferred that, but I always called her Ali. I was sitting on the cement walkway holding my head while the two missionaries talked about what a nice day it was. You can always tell out-of-staters that way.

Ali spoke a mile a minute. "Jimmy! I'm so sorry. Oh, I should've told you, but your door was open and you were down by the pool the way you'd been all night, so I thought it'd be okay. See, what happened, Marty, this guy I've been dating, keeps telling me about all the dangers around L.A. Well, last night he gave me a Doberman pinscher, and, well, I had to go out this morning, and I thought if my roommate came in from working the night shift at the hospital and saw the dog, she'd be really scared, so I thought, well, I saw you down by the pool, and I figured you'd be there most of the morning, and your door was open. Boy, I'm really sorry." She looked at my leg. "That was some fall you took off the diving board last night, wasn't it! I'm surprised you can even walk today. Let me look at your leg."

"It's my head that hurts."

She kissed me on my forehead. "Poor Jimmy. Hey, but you were so much fun last night at the party. Well, don't worry about the dog. I'll get it out right away. His name is Spot."

"Spot? A Doberman pinscher doesn't have spots."

"Marty calls him Spot because of what he does to the carpet," she said.

"Spot," she whispered at the door. "Nice doggie. Spot, look, I'm going to open the door now. You be a nice doggie now. I got your food."

She opened the door slowly. Spot was lying down, chewing on a shoe.

"Stupid dog," I muttered.

Spot bared his teeth at me.

"C'mon, Spot, nice doggie," she said sweetly. Spot followed her out.

She left. Strewn all over the floor were the contents of two bags of garbage, courtesy of Spot. Empty beer cans and cardboard pizza containers were scattered everywhere.

"I see what you mean about your roommate," one of the missionaries said.

I asked them to come back later. They said they would.

A few minutes later I knocked on Ali's door again. Spot lunged at the door. "Just a minute," she called out.

"Your dog scattered garbage all over," I said after she finally got the door open.

"Your forehead is sweating. Don't you feel well?"

"I feel lousy."

"Who are the guys in the suits?"

"Ministers. Are you going to clean up the mess or not?"

"Sure. Just a minute. Have you had your garlic yet today?"

She took garlic pills every day. She'd read that garlic helps fight disease. She claimed that as long as she took garlic pills, she never got sick. She did look amazingly healthy. I'd humored her along, and she got me to take some too. After that it became a ritual. Whenever she saw me, she gave me some. When I belched, it was enough to intimidate any germ.

While she cleaned up the garbage, I sat on the couch.

"Ali, are you ever going to get married?" I asked.

"Oh sure, sometime, but not now. I want to be free, to grow at my own pace, to actualize my essence, to be in tune with the rhythm of the times." She looked in the mirror. "Does my stomach look flatter than yesterday?"

"I can't tell."

"Why do you ask about marriage?"

"I don't know. Don't you ever want to be a regular person? You know, a regular married person. Maybe have a garden and raise string beans, or have a baby, or send out a family picture for your Christmas card. And at night you'd sort recipe cards, or something like that. Don't you ever wish that?"

She looked at me strangely. "You're still drunk from last night, aren't you."

I continued. "No, listen to me. You'd have the same man around all the time, and wouldn't be juggling from one to the other. And your husband would have a job, maybe he'd be a member of Kiwanis, and he'd change the oil in your car, and fix leaky faucets, and maybe once a year he'd go hunting. On Saturdays, after he'd mowed the lawn, he'd go down to a small store at the end of your lane, kind of a general store, and he'd just sit around and talk with some of the other men. Maybe they'd talk about the crops, like if there's been a drought, and maybe this is the driest year since 1952, or something like that. And if you got sick, he'd take care of you. And you'd have a robe, kind of an old robe, and flannel pajamas, and you wouldn't spend your life looking in the mirror every fifteen minutes to check out your stomach, because you'd have more important things to do. You ever think about that?"

She sat down next to me and reached over and held my hand. "What's wrong, Tiger?"

"My brother died this week. He was only nineteen years old."

"I'm really sorry. How did he die?"

I told her about his being a missionary, like the two who'd just been there, and that I was a member of the Church too, but not a good one.

"I went to the funeral and saw people with families and mortgages. And they're solid. My sister looks at me with that worried look sisters get. I woke up this morning, hung over, yet still wanting a drink. I'm killing myself. Why am I doing that?"

There was a knock at the door. I had her answer it. It was the missionaries again. I shook my head to indicate I didn't want to see them. She invited them in.

"I'm Elder Farnsworth," one said, shaking her hand as if she'd just won an Oscar.

"And I'm Elder Blake," the less-experienced elder piped up.

"I'm Alicia Alan. I live next door."

They came in.

"Jimmy Pepper," I said weakly, without getting up.

They gave us part of a discussion. She gave the answers while I nursed my head. "If you knew God had called a prophet in our own time, would that make a difference in your life?" Elder Farnsworth asked.

Ali said it would.

They asked if it would make a difference in my life.

I was rummaging through a shirt pocket. "Rats! I'm out of cigarettes."

"Nicotine fit?" Ali teased.

I sat back down. "It's no big thing. I don't need 'em."

Elder Farnsworth was the more experienced of the two missionaries. "I testify that God has sent us today with this message."

"Can I be perfectly honest?" I said. "I don't want His message. I just want Him to leave me alone. And that goes for you two. Now please get out of here."

The elders stood up.

Ali turned to me. "This is what your brother was doing?"

I nodded.

"I'd think you'd want to hear what they have to say."

"I've heard it all," I grumbled.

"Well, I haven't. It's interesting. I want to listen."

"Suit yourself." I started for the kitchen.

Elder Farnsworth wouldn't let me get away gracefully. "We'd like to come back another time when you feel better."

"Elders, you're wasting your time. I'm already a member. So we'll see you around at church sometime, okay?"

"Let me get your name so we can have home teachers visit," Elder Farnsworth said.

I cringed. Soon there'd be a parade of church officials at my door.

Elder Farnsworth had his pen poised. "Let's see, it's Jimmy . . ."

"Pepper," Alicia said with a smile.

"Brother Pepper," the younger elder said, "how do you feel about the Church?"

"Don't call me Brother Pepper," I groaned. "Give it up. Listen, give my regards to the Tabernacle Choir, okay?"

I went to the kitchen and took some aspirin.

Ali continued to meet with the missionaries. They always had their discussions at my place.

In just a short time, she'd made a commitment to quit drinking and smoking, and then the elders gave a lesson about living the ten commandments, one commandment in particular. She committed to live the principle of chastity.

The next night about two in the morning, after I'd returned from doing a bit at the Comedy Store, I passed her door and could hear a guy yelling at her. He sounded very mad.

I let myself into my apartment.

A minute later he put his fist through her large window, stormed off to his car, and drove away.

I went to see her window. She was looking at it too.

"That was Marty. I told him about chastity. He wasn't happy. Sometimes he gets mad when he's disappointed. He says he'll give me a day to think things over."

"And then what?" I asked.

"He didn't say, and I was afraid to ask."

"Anything I can do to help?" I asked.

She kissed me on the cheek lightly. "Jimmy, I sort of think of you like a brother. Don't worry—if I can think of anything, I'll let you know."

* * * * * * * * * * * *

Apparently Ali thought of something, because the next night when I returned, her dog Spot was shut up in my apartment, and there was a note telling me she'd decided to go back to her parents in Kansas, away from Marty. She also said she'd decided to be baptized.

Her note ended with, "Would you please keep Spot for me until Marty comes to get him?"

When Marty came for Spot, he accused me of being responsible for Ali being unavailable to him. Just as he was about to crack my head open with an empty bottle, Spot lunged toward him. Marty jumped quickly away, swore angrily at us, and then left.

"Good dog," I said gratefully.

A while later Ali wrote me and said how much being a member of the Church meant to her.

One morning about eleven o'clock I was sitting at the edge of the bed staring at the floor, holding my aching head, trying to work up enough energy to walk to the window and yell at the garbage men to quit banging the cans around so much. There was a knock at the door.

I forgot about Spot and opened the door. It was Elders Blake and Farnsworth. He rushed toward them, sniffing and growling.

"He doesn't like strangers," I said, grabbing his collar. He snapped at me. I jumped away.

"Strangers?" Elder Blake smiled. "He nearly bit you."

"He has a short memory."

"May we come in?" Elder Farnsworth asked.

"Gee, I don't know. I'm really kind of busy right now."

"Alicia wrote and asked us to see you," Elder Farnsworth said. I let them in. They gave me a letter from her. She asked me to listen to the missionary lessons as a personal favor to her.

I looked up from the letter.

"Just leave me alone," I muttered.

"You are alone," Elder Blake said.

He'd hit it on the head. I was alone.

"Please listen to our message," he said.

My shoulders slumped. "Why bother with me?"

"God hasn't given up on you yet," Elder Blake said, "so why should we?"

I let them give me a lesson.

"Okay, now what?" I asked when it was over.

"You pray and ask God if it's true."

"Anything else?"

"More than that—you need to really pour out your soul in prayer."

I smiled weakly. "There's nothing to pour. Maybe a few dribbles is all there's left."

Elder Blake laughed. Elder Farnsworth did not.

I loved Elder Blake from the first. He had a pimple on his nose. And he'd broken his shoelace and tied it together and was wearing it that way.

"We'd like you to offer the prayer," Elder Blake said.

How could I turn down Elder Blake? We knelt down.

I intended a nice little prayer, tidy and short. After all, I'd been to church as a boy and given little prayers. "Bless us to get something from the lesson, something to use in our everyday lives." That's what I intended for this prayer—but when I started, something happened. Deep inside of me, there was a feeling, something I'd forgotten, that mended and soothed and gave hope that I could return to the Church, to God, and to my family.

Somewhat embarrassed, I wiped my eyes and said amen.

Elder Blake hugged me, and Elder Farnsworth said they would help. They shook my hand vigorously, gave me some pamphlets to read, and then left.

The next day doubt cropped up. A battle raged inside me.

It couldn't be true. It's too wild.

But what if it is?

It isn't.

But what if it is?

It can't be true.

But what if it is?

It's not. If it were, more people would know about it.

But what if it is?

It isn't.

How do you know?

I just know.

How?

What about Fred kicking me out of the house in the middle of the night? He was a member of the Church, wasn't he?

Okay, but what about Rachel and Jeff? You could have stayed with them if you hadn't gotten so mad at Fred that night. You ran away even before letting Zinia know what was wrong. She never would've let you go that night if she'd known. And Logan and Zinia were good people. They believed the Church was true. Jill believes it's true. And Ryan died while teaching the gospel. What about them?

But it can't be true.

But what if it is? What if Christ speaks to mankind again? What if it's true?

I paused. If it's true, then it's important.

You can find out if it's true.

No, I can't. Not for sure.

The elders said you can.

What do they know? Nineteen-year-old kids. Would God trust a message like this to a nineteen-year-old kid?

And then it hit me.

Ryan had been a nineteen-year-old kid.

They gave me other lessons.

They prayed with me and testified to me. Eventually they gave me the lesson that teaches that alcohol and tobacco and coffee and tea are not good for us.

While they talked, I had the feeling that Ryan was in the room. Finally they paused. Elder Farnsworth looked at me steadily. "Will you live this commandment?" he asked. Elder Blake looked hopeful.

Painfully I said it for the first time—the thing that everyone around me was already saying. "I can't stop. I've tried, but it's out of control, and there's nothing I can do to stop."

They brought the bishop of the ward I lived in. He talked with me for a long time.

A day later two others came. They said they were my home teachers. They said they could help me get off booze. I said I didn't believe that. They said they'd once been heavy drinkers too, but they'd changed, and so could I.

They came every day about noon, just as I was getting up. Sometimes at night they'd stop by the Comedy Store and sit with me, three grown men nursing glasses of V-8 Juice.

I started going to church. The first time I entered the building, I felt as if I should have a sign warning that, although I had a tie on and had shaved off my beard, I was unclean.

I met once every Sunday for a few minutes with the bishop. We worked on repentance.

A Sunday sacrament meeting six months later. Two high-school-age boys have broken the bread into bite-size chunks while we've been singing a hymn. One of them kneels and offers a prayer over the bread. Twelve- and thirteen-year-old boys receive the trays of bread. They move quietly to their stations, and the trays are passed from one person to the other down the rows.

A tray comes to me. I pick up a small piece of bread and put it in my mouth.

I am alone with my thoughts. They say we should think about Jesus during this time, about His sacrifice for us. Somehow He took upon Him our sins. It's painful for me to think about that. I added much to His burden.

I'm sorry for my past. The strange thing is, when I was away from the Church, it didn't seem like what I did was so bad. I was basically a nice guy, wasn't I? But as I started back, the realization of how wrong I'd been came on strong.

There's a price we must pay to qualify for forgiveness. The price is a broken heart and a contrite spirit. For the alcoholic the contrite spirit means an admission that he is incapable of doing it alone, that he is helpless alone, that he must rely on higher power.

I made some bad mistakes, and I could make them again if I'm not careful.

The young boys carry the trays back to the table. The second youth kneels down and offers a prayer on the water.

Thanks, God, for making it possible for me to come back.

CHAPTER SEVEN

Months later, at my bishop's suggestion, I attended a three-day regional young adult conference at a college down the coast. Not knowing a soul there, still feeling unsure of myself at church, I registered and got a name-tag and room assignment. I requested and got a single room. I left Spot in my drab brown station wagon. I planned to sneak him into my room after dark.

Sitting at the tiny desk in the dorm room, I looked at the schedule of events. I had already missed the watermelon bust and swimming activity. Right then they were having a pie-eating contest, and after supper, there would be a dance.

Reading the schedule of events depressed me. It was all so lovely and homey—and boring. I slept through supper and part of the dance, then woke up at eight o'clock, thought about taking a shower for the dance, but decided it was too much trouble.

I hung on the fringes of the dance and watched. They were playing the bunny hop. Five hundred feet jumping in unison sounded like the building was about to come down.

A few minutes later I went to the car to give Spot some water and dog food. Then I decided to take him for a walk. Just as I'd put the leash on and was letting him out, I saw a woman in the parking lot doing the same thing with her dog. She was tall and outdoorsy-looking.

Our dogs barked energetically at each other. Spot

pulled at the leash, anxious to maim her small cocker spaniel.

We smiled at each other.

"Walking your dog?" I asked.

"Sorry, I don't have a watch!" she shouted. She was either deaf or didn't hear my question over the noise our dogs were making.

I decided to try again. "We're in a fraternity!" I yelled.

"What?" she shouted.

"Fraternity!" I yelled. "We're in a fraternity!"

"Who is?"

"We are! You and me!"

"Not me!" she shouted above the barking of the two dogs. "Fraternities are too wild!"

"A fraternity of dog owners!" I shouted.

"What?"

Spot was really getting to me. "AH, SHUT UP!" He quieted down. I said calmly to her, "We share common interests."

She looked puzzled. "We do? What are they?"

The dogs started barking again.

"Dogs!" I shouted.

"Oh!" she said. We both laughed. It felt delicious to laugh with her.

Our dogs traded mutual sniffs warily. She and I smiled weakly, trying to ignore them as they went through this strange ritual. In due time, they seemed willing to accept each other.

"We could walk together," I said.

"Fine," she said.

We walked. She looked at the well-kept lawns while I looked at her.

Her name was Amy Malone. I said it over and over in my mind—it fit perfectly—wholesome, all-American Amy Malone.

She was as tall as me, with short cropped blonde hair parted near the crown of her head. The part served as sort of the Continental Divide for hair—strands leaned either to the left or to the right with no deviating curls along the way.

Her thick eyebrows served as a beacon of her moods. Her face didn't appear to have much makeup; she had a scrubbed-clean appearance.

She talked. "They say you can tell a person by the kind of dog he has. A man with a collie would be gentle and wise. And let's see—a man with a Doberman pinscher—" She paused. "I bet you have searchlights on the roof of your house, don't you?"

My mouth dropped open. She has a sense of humor—she's my kind of woman. If a woman can have sensuous teeth, she had 'em. When she laughed, there they were, large, pearly, and white. Her motions were slow and fluid, and although she was walking as fast as I was, she gave the impression that her body was only at half speed, like a well-tuned Porsche slowing at a stoplight.

We left the campus and entered a residential area with large, ample homes and manicured lawns.

Spot started rummaging through somebody's garbage. He ripped open a plastic bag of garbage and began scattering things in the yard. I pulled on his leash, and he turned to snarl at me.

"C'mon, Spot," I pleaded. "Good dog. Spot, be reasonable." He continued scattering garbage. "You numbskull, you stupid dog," I muttered.

The owner of the lawn and the garbage opened his front door and yelled at me to get my dog out of there.

"What do you think I'm trying to do, you yo-yo!"

"I'm calling the cops! They'll lock you and your wolf up." He slammed his door.

I felt like an idiot having a dog I couldn't control. "You go ahead," I said to Amy, not wanting her to be arrested too. "I'll catch up later."

She shook her head. "You've got to show him who's boss."

"I don't blame him—a man hates to have garbage on his lawn."

She grinned. "I meant the dog. May I?" she asked, offering to take the leash from me.

"Don't!" I warned.

"Why not?"

"That dog is an animal."

She laughed. "I understand that."

"I'm serious."

She took the leash and said quietly but with authority, "Heel." Spot sat down beside her.

While she petted Spot, I restored the man's garbage back to some semblance of order. By the time the police arrived, everything was picked up. They let us go.

"What do you do?" she asked.

"I'm a comedian."

"Yeah, but what do you do for a living?"

"I'm a comedian."

She laughed. "Is your dog part of the act?"

"Hardly. What about you?"

"I'm a high school P.E. teacher. I coach girls' basketball."

"How does that work? A male coach tells his boys to go out there and kill the other team. What do you tell your girls?"

"To get more points."

I nodded. "Makes sense."

We continued our walk. She told me she was a convert to the Church of just three months. Nobody else in her family was a member.

After we had returned our dogs to the cars, we both grew silent, uncertain of where our acquaintance was heading.

"Can I walk you to the dance?"

"Okay," she said. We went inside, got some punch and cookies, and sat down to watch the others.

Later we danced. During a slow dance, I put my arms around her and shifted from one foot to the other in time with the music. She melted into my arms. It was very nice.

When the song was over, she asked if I were Italian. I said no. She said she smelled garlic.

I popped a Certs into my mouth. "I take garlic pills."
"What for?"

"They keep me healthy. I'm never sick."

"Sure, sure," she laughed.

We sat down.

"I have a confession to make," I said. "I'm not really a comedian. I'm actually in town on business. I'm starting a new airlines—Generic Airlines. Our planes'll be in plain brown wrappers."

All the women I'd ever known before would have just smiled tolerantly. But not her. She climbed into my fantasy with me. "I've heard of it," she said. "Your motto isn't 'Fly the Friendly Skies.' Your motto is 'So what did you expect at these prices?'"

She says funny things. I loved her already.

"Right," I continued. "Inside the plane, we have no seats, just straps to hold onto, like in a subway. Before the plane takes off, our flight attendant comes on and says, "There are emergency exits on the plane, but we're not telling where they are. If anything goes wrong, the crew want to be the first ones out."

"Yeah," she smiled, "and during the flight, you don't serve a meal. What you do is roll a peanut butter jar down the aisle, and anyone who stops it can eat."

Being with her was like when you go to scout camp and you get on the buddy system, and it turns out your assigned buddy, who you thought would be a nerd, turns out to like to horse around and tell jokes and be a general goof-off—just like you. So even when it's raining and you have to stay in a tent that leaks, you're still trading off stories and jokes to each other as fast as you can.

It's interesting about the big and little decisions in life. It took me four months to decide whether I wanted waxed or unwaxed dental floss, but in half an hour I was positive I'd found the woman I wanted to marry.

We got going on some ad-lib role playing. The first one was a bishop phoning Lot just after his wife was turned into a pillar of salt. I was the bishop and Amy was Lot.

"Hello, Brother Lot, is your wife there?" I said.

"Ah, no, bishop," she said. "Well, that is, she's here, but she's not taking phone calls now."

"Well, I just wanted to thank her for helping with the church supper. You know, your wife is really a pillar in our community."

"Bishop, that's so true."

"She's a rock, your wife."

Amy faked extreme sadness. "I know, I know. Isn't it terrible? She looked back and was turned into a pillar of salt."

"Where is she?" I asked.

"Well, she's just outside here. I can see her from the window. HEY, GET AWAY FROM THERE! . . . Excuse me, bishop, the cows were licking her arm. It's okay now."

"This must've really been a shock to you, Lot."

"Everything happened all at once. First we lose our home to the fire, then we have to leave Sodom. And now this . . ."

"Well, that's the way things go sometimes. When it rains, it pours."

We never finished. We were both laughing too hard.

God had sent me a woman. Or sent her a man. Or

sent us to the dance. Or got our dogs together. One way
or the other I'd found her, and I was never going to let
her go. Think about it, a woman who laughed at my
jokes.

How can I describe the way she made me feel? It was
the way you feel when you're a kid and you go over to
your best friend's house. His mother opens the door, and
you say, "Can Davey come out to play?" And she says yes.
And the moment you see him, you know you're going to
have a great day playing guns or space people, and that
in a while his mom, who's a chubby woman who smiles
even at kids, is going to give you both some fresh-baked
chocolate chip cookies and milk. And later in the afternoon when it's hot out, you and Davey are going to climb
a big oak tree in the backyard and pretend to be a family
of chipmunks and be hidden in the summer leaves.
Davey is your best friend in the whole world.

That's what it was like to be around her.

But that's not all.

It was the feeling that we'd become good friends, and
then fall in love, and then get married. It was the feeling
that changing my rotten habits had been necessary before I could meet her, that God forgave me for all the rotten things I'd done, and to show He loved me, He let me
find a woman like Amy.

In the meantime it was being aware of all the little delicious messages being sent out, watching her smile, feeling the warmth of her hand as I pretended to read her
fortune, enjoying the little pleasures of being around a
terrific-looking woman. Maybe because I knew there
would be only little pleasures for a while, it made me
more sensitive to her. It was knowing that all the delicious senses activated by a man and woman being close to
each other were put there to be enjoyed as long as we
stayed within the proper limits.

"Let's be silly," I said, pulling her into the cultural
hall.

We went to the microphone. It was between dances. "Testing, testing. May I have your attention, please? I'm a dance coach for Universal Studios, and they've asked me to teach you some of the dances featured in upcoming movies. Can we get everyone out on the floor now?"

We waited for couples to come out.

"The first dance we want to teach you is called Sore Toe. It'll be coming out in January with the release of a sequel to *Saturday Night Fever,* called *Monday Morning Headache.* Now what you do is pretend you've just stepped on a nail. You hobble forward two steps, then hobble back two steps, then reach down and touch your foot. My assistant and I will demonstrate it for you. Could we have some music now?"

Someone put on a record, and Amy and I did the Sore Toe.

"Now everybody try it."

Picture several hundred people gimping around to music, and you'll appreciate why Amy had to excuse herself to go laugh in the hall.

A young woman came up to me. "I've got a question. What foot should you pretend is sore?"

"The left," I said with authority. "Always the left in America. In Europe, of course, they do it with the right. But that's called Continental Sore Toe."

"Thank you," she said sincerely.

A few minutes later Amy and I went out on the dance floor and just rocked back and forth and held each other.

The dance was over at twelve-thirty. We had half an hour before we had to be in our dorms. My plan was to see if I could at least kiss her goodnight. But first we had to help each other sneak our dogs into our dorm rooms. Her room was on the first floor of Palmer Hall. She went inside and opened her window, and I handed her dog, Clyde, to her. Then we went to my dorm, and she talked to the guy at the desk while I let Spot chase me up the back stairs.

By the time we finally arrived at her dorm again, it was five minutes to one, and a chaperon was standing at the door, officially clearing her throat.

Amy melted into my arms. Then she sniffed and pulled away. "You smell like a dog," she said.

I scowled. "That's gotta be the least romantic sentence in the world."

We both started laughing. It ruined the mood for the other couples.

"It's exactly 12:58," our chaperon called out, getting ready to lock the doors.

"I was going to try to kiss you," I said as she edged closer to the door as I advanced.

"And I was going to let you," she said.

"Look, if I can find a clothespin within the next two minutes, will you kiss me?"

She laughed and shook her head.

"How about if we hold our noses?"

"I can't kiss and hold my nose at the same time."

"When can I see you again?"

"There's the fireside tomorrow morning," she said.

"Before that."

"I'm going jogging at six in the morning."

"Terrific. I'll meet you here at six. I'll wear a different pair of slacks and take a shower."

"Do you jog?" she asked.

"Every day."

"When did you start?" she asked suspiciously.

"Tomorrow."

The chaperon announced "One o'clock." Amy hurried inside.

"Wait a minute!" I called to her.

"Yes?"

"Suppose Johnny Carson joined the Church and later was called to be a church leader in Salt Lake City. He's giving his first major address in the Tabernacle. Go ahead."

"The world is full of wickedness," she began.

"How wicked is it?" I called out.

She started laughing. "It's so wicked . . . that . . ."

The chaperon closed and locked the door.

The next morning I knew I was in trouble when I saw her with a stopwatch. "What's that for?"

"To time myself. I usually go five miles."

"In a day?"

"I'll go slower today, so we can talk."

She wore lavender sweat pants, a pink sweat shirt with crew neck, and an expensive pair of running shoes. I wore a pair of Hush Puppies, black socks, a pair of jeans whose legs I'd cut off to the knees just a few minutes before, and a torn grease-stained sweat shirt I found in my car during the night.

It was a nice morning, the earliest I'd gotten up since I'd left Idaho. Because I was so slow, she ran circular patterns around me so she wouldn't get too far ahead of me. Soon the only sounds were me gasping wildly for air. She stopped.

"We can walk for a while," she said.

"Sure, go ahead," I gasped, "if you need to."

It took me five minutes to breathe normally again.

"I hope you don't think I'm intimidated by your athletic ability," I said, using my macho voice. "There are some sports that men just naturally do better in than women."

There were fireworks in her eyes. "Yeah? Like what?"

"You ever notice that all the world-class spitters are men? If you want, we can chalk out a line and see who can spit the farthest."

She laughed. "I concede."

While we walked she told me more about herself. She was raised in California and had gone to San Jose State College, where she majored in P.E. She learned about the Church when friends invited her to a church social.

"Being from L.A., you can guess what I thought when they asked me to a potluck. But they seemed like nice people, so I decided to risk it. It was the best thing I ever did."

By Sunday afternoon the conference was over. I helped carry Amy's suitcase to her car, although she was in better shape to do it than I was. Her dog, Clyde, was sitting in the front seat. Spot was in my car, which I'd pulled next to hers.

I put her suitcase in the trunk and closed it.

"So," I said, "the end of a perfect weekend."

"Really," she said with a reserved smile.

"I enjoyed getting to know you," I said.

"Me too," she said. "They say they're having another one of these in three months. Maybe we'll see each other then."

That was depressing. I'd die if I didn't see her before then.

Spot started barking as someone approached the car next to mine.

"Ah, pipe down!" It did no good—it never did. But it made me feel better to yell at him.

She started to get in her car.

"Please don't go," I said, letting my feelings show.

She nodded. "I feel the same way, but I have to leave sometime. I have to work tomorrow."

"Can I see you this weekend?" I asked.

"Friday night?"

"Sure."

"I'll give you my address." She fumbled in her purse for a piece of paper and a pen.

I looked at her. She had a nice nose, and her neck was exceptionally graceful looking. She looked wholesome and streamlined and clean-cut. And she smelled of Dial soap. She was just terrific.

"Does your team do a lot of fast breaks?" I asked.

"Yes, why?"

I smiled. "I just knew you'd be a fast-break kind of coach."

"Come to one of our games when the season starts."

"I will."

"I guess I'd better go." She got into her car.

"Wait!" I said.

"Yes?"

"I didn't get to kiss you last night. Do I get a rain check?"

She looked around. Suddenly the parking lot seemed to be full of church leaders.

She pursed her lips.

"I don't usually do this," she said, getting out of her car.

"I understand."

She stood close to me, her hands at her side, looking vulnerable. "One thing you should know—I don't play games."

I smiled. "Can I trust a coach who says she doesn't play games?"

"You know what I mean," she said.

"Maybe. You don't kiss a guy unless . . ."

She completed the sentence. "Unless I think I'm falling in love with him."

I reached out to hold her hand. "Okay—you don't play games, and I don't kid around."

"A comedian who doesn't kid around," she said quietly.

I kissed her.

When we broke apart, I was dizzy. It was like overdosing on Dial soap.

We kissed again. It was nice kissing someone my own height.

"I'd really better go now," she said, fumbling with the door. She was as spaced out as I was—possibly from the garlic.

Suddenly I realized she was going to leave me. I wouldn't see her for a whole week. It was like being five years old on a beautiful summer morning and you go to your very best friend's house with ideas about playing all day, and you knock on the door and nobody's home, and the next-door neighbor tells you they've gone on vacation for two weeks, and then you realize your best friend is gone, and two weeks seems like an eternity. That was how far away Friday seemed to me.

"So, until Friday," I said glumly.

"Friday," she said, getting in the car. "I want to thank you for a wonderful weekend."

She started to drive away. I watched the car pull out.

Crazily I ran after her down the street. "Amy! Stop!" I shouted.

She pulled over. "What's wrong?"

Out of breath, I gasped, "Can I possibly see you sooner than Friday?"

"How much sooner?" she asked.

"Much sooner."

She parked. I reached out and touched her arm. Clyde started to growl at me. She ordered him to be quiet.

"What do you suggest?" she asked.

I paused briefly to consider how foolish I was becoming, then plunged full speed ahead. "Do your parents happen to have a spare guest bedroom, or a couch that makes up into a bed, or even a sleeping bag, or three extra blankets, or a hammock in the backyard, or an abandoned car with a back seat, or a tree with a large branch . . ."

She was laughing again. "When can you come?"

"Right away," I said. "I'll follow you home. But look, I'll just stay a couple of days and I won't eat much."

"But what about your work?" she asked.

"I'll make arrangements."

* * * * * * * * * * * * *

When we pulled up to her house, she suggested she go in first and tell her parents they were having a house guest. In a few minutes she came out and escorted me in.

It was an old house in what had once been a nice area but was now slowly degenerating. On the front porch by the door was a note pad that read, "If at home you do not find us, leave a note that will remind us." I cringed. She came from one of those knickknack families.

Her father was a fixer of things, a worker, a man you call when your washer goes out, a man you spend twenty minutes with discussing the weather, a man who takes pride in locks locked, a hard day's honest work for a day's pay. A man who listens to Lawrence Welk and then tells people he likes classical music. A factory worker who attends union meetings and reads the monthly newsletter. And his name was Ed.

Ed's wife was a woman who wears an apron, a woman who grows African violets in the windowsills of her home, who saves string, who sends off her entry blank to the *Reader's Digest* sweepstakes every time and after all these years still believes she's going to win, a woman whose greatest hope for her yet unmarried daughter is that she marry somebody who gets a weekly check with time-and-a-half for overtime. She actually attended PTA meetings while her children were in school, a woman who doesn't go to church but who listens faithfully every Sunday on the radio to the sermons and sends in a little money now and then to help them out. And her name was Dotty.

By the time we arrived, it was late. We put Spot and Clyde in the fenced backyard, where they'd be free to run around and ruin the lawn.

Her parents had eaten supper, so we made do with the leftovers. The kitchen was small and tidy with hand-painted yellow cupboards and an old, too-small refrigerator that just had a new compressor put in, because Ed couldn't throw anything away if it still worked. We ate while her parents watched TV, and every once in a while, her mother came in and asked if I'd like some pickles.

On Monday morning I got up to run with Amy before she left for work. I was going to stay another day, but just after she left in the morning, I called my agent.

"Where have you been?" he complained. "I've been trying all weekend to get in touch with you. I've got you a job in Vegas in a lounge. It's for three weeks, and it starts in two days. You're going to have to leave today."

"That's nice," I said calmly.

"What do you mean, nice? This is what we've been waiting for! What better thing you got to do anyway?"

"I'm in love, Bernie."

"Love, shmove. You get to Vegas today, you hear me? That's what's important."

Tuesday I opened. It wasn't one of the headliner acts in the city. Actually it was a lounge, a small bar in a hotel, sort of a poor man's Las Vegas. People liked my act, and by the end of the week I was starting to pull in people due to word of mouth.

I phoned Amy every night and we talked. The Bell system loved our phone calls. When I paid my bill, it allowed them to send up another communications satellite.

Sometimes on the phone we did crazy skits, like we were spies trading coded information.

"The Armenian cow treads amber waves of grain into iron sprockets," I whispered slowly to her.

"Ah," she said knowingly. "The burgomaster carries a bowl of soup on a leash."

"You're too much," I howled.

"You too," she said.

Friday afternoon she called me. I was taking a nap in my room.

A voice whispered, "The burgomaster has arrived."

"You're here?"

"In the lobby with a friend from my ward."

"I'll be right down!"

We had supper, the three of us. Her friend, Sharon, was nice, but a little slow to pick up on Amy and me.

I got them good seats for my monologue. It was as good as I'd ever done, but there was a problem. Some of the material in the monologue was risqué. The audience laughed, but Amy looked uncomfortable. After I finished, I sat down with her. She looked like she was going to cry. I asked if anything was wrong, and she said she had a headache.

After hearing my jokes, Sharon treated me as if I had the plague. She left as soon as she could. Amy and I went outside for a walk.

"Want anything to eat?" I asked.

"No, thanks," she said quietly.

"How about an ice cream cone?"

"No, thanks."

"Mind if I get one?"

"Go ahead."

I bought one and took a bite. She watched me carefully.

"Why are you looking at me like that?"

"To see if you eat with the same mouth you use to tell those jokes."

I quit eating. "It's what they want to hear. It doesn't mean anything. I don't even think about it anymore."

"How can you do this six days a week and then go to church on Sunday? Doesn't your conscience ever bother you?"

I cleared my throat nervously. "It's not permanent. After I get established, I'll change my act so it'll be good enough for church. I promise."

"You know it's wrong though, don't you? I mean, deep inside, you know."

We walked one whole block without talking.

"It's what comedians do in Vegas—they tell that kind of joke."

"Jimmy, there's plenty of decent people in the world who like clean jokes," she said.

"But, Amy, listen to me, they don't go to nightclubs. They go to PTA meetings."

"Somehow I expected more of you than just being like everybody else."

"C'mon, give me a break. It's just like an actor reading his lines. You think they arrest Macbeth for murder every night?"

"It's not the same. It's your monologue. You decide what to say."

I shook my head. "That's not really true. The audience decides. I've got to play to what they want. Please try to understand."

I started to put my arm around her but she pulled away. "Why do you want to hold me? Need more material for the show?"

I wiped my forehead. "Boy, you're really making me feel stress. You want to know something—stress causes sickness. What if I get sick? You think people'll pay to see a man blow his nose? This is my big chance. I can't get sick, and I can't change my act." I reached into my pocket and pulled out a couple of garlic pills and swallowed them. "Want one? You must be feeling stress too, right now."

"There's a difference—my conscience doesn't bother me."

"Let's just walk for a while and not talk, okay?"

"All right."

At least she let me hold her hand. We walked down the Las Vegas Strip, glowing with promises of pleasure. Outside the hotel where I worked was a sign with my name on it. My name in Las Vegas—it was what I'd dreamed about since junior high school.

"I don't have an education or any skills. There's nothing else I can do. If I don't make it here, I don't make it."

Finally she started crying. "I expected more from you."

"You and my sister'd really get along."

We were at the door to her room. This was the girl I wanted to marry, and she was embarrassed because of the one thing in my life I did well. We didn't even kiss goodnight.

I need a drink, I thought, as I left her hotel on foot. Just one to calm my nerves. I deserve it. Just this one time'll be okay. Just to help me get through this.

I can't have a drink, I answered. Never again in my life. No matter what happens. I can never have a drink.

Just one.

I'll take a walk instead.

I spent the night walking, trying to fight the urge to have a drink. By the time the sun came up, I was ten miles outside of town.

Walking back, I found a cafe and had breakfast and phoned my sister and told her about Amy.

"So that's it," I said. "Tell me what to do."

"How bad are the jokes?"

I told her one.

She moaned. "Good grief, Jimmy."

"This is Vegas. That goes over very big here."

"What's worth more to you, Amy or that crummy joke?"

I spent a week trying to work up an act that was clean. I tried it out on a Tuesday night.

After it was over, the manager, a guy named Maury, came up to me. "What's wrong with the old stuff?"

"I decided to leave out the sex jokes."

"Are you crazy? This isn't Sesame Street."

"What about Bill Cosby? His material's clean, and he packs 'em in all the time."

"Cosby made it first with his comedy records. Now he's like a national shrine. People come a thousand miles just to hear him do the old stuff like 'Noah,' or 'Fat Albert.' So he gets away with it. But you can't. Do what everybody else does."

"Maury, work with me. I'll develop enough clean material to do an album. When it sells, you'll have exclusive rights to me in Vegas."

He shook his head. "Let's get something straight here. If you don't use the material you've been using, then you're finished. And not only here. I'll get you blackballed from every club in town. You'll never work again."

We had reached the bottom line. "I'm not going to use the old stuff anymore," I said.

"Then get outa here, hotshot," he grumbled. "Don't even stay for the second show. I'll run stag movies. That's about right for this crowd. Oh yeah, take a good look at Vegas on your way out. It's the last time you'll ever work here."

Half an hour later I left.

Las Vegas looks so beautiful at night.

CHAPTER EIGHT

We checkerboarded county roads for sixty madcap miles before losing the photographer from the 'National Inquirer.' When we arrived in Cody, we rented a pickup truck as a disguise.

"I can't call him Dad," I agonized as we left Worland, one hundred miles from Buffalo.

"What're you going to call him?"

"Hank."

She studied me. "Basically, what's your problem?"

"I hate him, Jill."

After being fired from Las Vegas, I returned to Los Angeles and got a small part in a movie about a giant fly that terrorizes the world. My part was to scream in three languages.

I continued to date Amy.

One night we were kissing in my car outside her house. She liked to kiss as much as I did, but she had better self-control about when it was time to go in.

"I'd better go in now."

"Already?" I complained. "I hate saying goodnight. Whataya say we get married. It'd be good for the dogs. They get lonely during the day. If we were married, they could sit around and chew our shoes while we were gone."

She looked at me quizzically. "Are you serious?"

"About marriage? I've known it from the first day I met you. I love you, wow, a lot. I've just been waiting for you to catch up. Miss Amy Malone, I respectfully request your hand in marriage."

She said she'd prayed about me, having heard of others who'd received special confirmations of whom they'd marry. "But nothing happened," she said, "except I noticed I couldn't stand the thought of *not* being married to you. Finally I decided that was my answer. I'd love to be your wife."

"Yahoo!" I shouted, in a manner befitting a Wyoming native.

We both started giggling like kids. It was a good old time until we saw her mother turn on the porch light and stare out at us.

We sobered up.

"There's a couple of things we need to iron out first," she said.

I smiled. "I'll iron anything."

"Where will we get married?" she asked.

"How long till you're a member a year and can go to the temple?" I asked.

"Six months."

The thought of clenching my teeth for six months was depressing. "Maybe we should think about a civil ceremony first."

Her enthusiasm dampened. "Of course, some people'll be disappointed we aren't getting married in the temple."

"Oh, who?" I asked.

"Me," she said quietly.

"I'd like to get married soon," I complained.

"I understand," she said.

"You do?"

"I teach health, you know."

"Sorry to be a prisoner of my glands," I said.

"I have glands too."

My eyebrows raised. "Yeah?"

She nodded. "We're getting to the place where it'd be more convenient to be married."

"Amy, I've had my quota of mistakes. I can't make any more. If you and I ever did anything wrong—well, we just can't, that's all."

"I know."

I sat and thought. "Maybe, though, if we both worked at it so we didn't get into trouble, maybe I could wait. You know, cold showers and all. It'd be character building, I guess. You ever notice—things that build character are never any fun."

"What would we have to do differently?" she asked.

I paused. "Well, suppose we went to a movie. I'd knock on the door and you'd come out, and you'd drive in your car and I'd drive in my car, and we'd go to the movie, and then if we went to eat, we'd both drive there, and when we came back to your place, we'd walk up to your front door and kiss goodnight using a timer."

Her eyes opened wide. "You're kidding."

"Nope."

We held each other and thought about it.

"Well," she said, "I guess the real question is what does God want us to do?"

We fasted and talked to our bishops and decided God wanted us to take a lot of cold showers and waste gasoline by driving two cars to the movies and using a three-minute timer, and never be alone in a room together, and not see anything but Muppet movies, and for me not to put suntan lotion on her back and legs at the beach even when she asked me to, and a bunch of other dumb things that kept us physically apart.

We decided to prepare for a temple marriage.

Out of respect for her father, she requested that I ask his permission to marry his daughter. I told her nobody does that anymore. She said we do.

So one day, feeling like a fool, I went to the garage to

talk to her father. He was underneath his car draining oil into a bucket.

"I'd like to talk to you, if I might, sir."

He rolled out from underneath the car and looked at me. "What's up?"

"Well, as you know, I've been, that is, Amy and me . . ."

"Excuse me." He rolled back under the car. "Be with you in a minute."

"Take your time, sir."

I stood and waited. A few minutes later he rolled back out and stood up, then proceeded to pour in some new oil. "Go ahead with whatever you were saying."

"Amy and I have been, well, shall we say, close."

He stared quizzically at me. "How close?"

"Not that close. That is, I, well, we'd like to, that is, in a manner of speaking, we, I mean, I . . . would like to ask your permission to marry your daughter . . . Amy, that is. She said I should ask."

We both sighed. "I see. Well . . ."

"So it's okay with you?" I said quickly, hoping for a quick exit.

"I'd like to know more about you. What are your career plans?"

"I'm going to put out a comedy record. Bill Cosby really wasn't a star until after his first record. If you hit it just right, you can make a lot of money with a record."

He opened another can of oil and poured it in, making sure not to waste a drop. "And what if you don't hit it just right?"

I paused. "I'm going to make it big. I just know it. See, making people laugh is important to me. I mean, it's all I've ever wanted to do."

"You're talking marriage. You'll probably have kids. How will you provide for 'em? Have you ever thought about going to college like Amy did?"

"I just want to be a comedian. It's what I do—my profession, I guess you'd say."

"So Amy ends up supporting your family while you putter around telling jokes to American Legion conventions?"

"That won't happen. I promise. If I have to, I'll get a job."

"What do you mean, if you have to."

I paused. "Okay, I'll get a job before we get married and work on my album the other sixteen hours a day."

"Can I be perfectly honest?"

I cringed. "Only if you have to."

He paused briefly. "Don't misunderstand me—I like you. You're good company, fun to be around. And it's clear you've charmed Amy. I've seen her light up when you walk in the room—"

I cut him off. "Thanks for being so honest. Can I go now?"

"I'm not through. You have no education and no trade to fall back on. What happens to comedians who don't make it?"

I sighed. "I can't think about that. I've got to succeed."

"Amy says you lost your job in Vegas because you refused to use dirty jokes anymore. What's that done to your career?"

"I'm on their blacklist. But if my record album does well—"

"Do you ever wish you were still working in Las Vegas?"

I shook my head. "If I were still at Vegas, then I wouldn't have Amy. I really do love her."

He looked strangely at me. "When I first met you, I wondered if there was anything beneath that smooth veneer. But there is, isn't there. It looks to me like you've got character."

"If I can marry your daughter, I'm sure I'll become a real character. That is, I'll develop real character."

He laughed. "I see why Amy's flipped for you. Go ahead. Marry my daughter."

I ran in to see her. "Let's get married!" I yelled.
"Yahoo!" she shouted.

Amy's father got me a job as a night watchman at the place where he used to work. My job was to watch and make sure only mice scurried through a warehouse. I'd get home about seven each morning, sleep until two in the afternoon, then work on material for a comedy record album. Not that any record company wanted me to do an album. My quitting Vegas had gotten around, and nobody wanted me, not even for Bar Mitzvahs.

Sometimes I got discouraged.

"How's it going?" Amy said, greeting me one day as I waited for her on the porch of her parents' house.

"Bad," I mumbled.

She sat down beside me.

"Tell the coach about it."

"Nothing's funny anymore."

We took a walk. Amy tried to prime the funny pump. "What do you see?"

"A man mowing his lawn," I mumbled.

"Why's that funny?"

"It isn't."

"C'mon, work with me." She tried again. "I understand you're the world's greatest bird expert. How would you describe yourself to our listeners?"

She waited.

"Cheap," I answered, almost as a reflex action.

"Doctor, what kind of bird is that on the tree over there?"

"What tree?"

"What do you mean? Can't you see that tree?"

"That? I thought it was a giant rooster."

"Seriously, doctor, is that a pheasant?"

"It's a robin with ring around the collar."

She squeezed my hand and winked. "That's absurd, doctor."

I was feeling better. "No—we're too far west for a surd."

"Look up there. Is that an eagle?"

"That's a robin with a membership to a Jack La Lanne Health Club."

"Frankly, doctor, I seriously doubt your credentials. What would you call a penguin?"

"Harry. It seems to fit, doesn't it?"

"I don't mean that. If you saw a penguin one day, what would you think?"

"I'd missed a turn on the freeway?"

"In your book, what do you call a penguin?"

"A robin with a stuck zipper on his tux."

She started laughing. I'd made her laugh. I fell in love all over again.

I was a basket case without her. As a coach, she spent her whole life telling people they could achieve their goals. She believed it about everyone. She believed it about her tall, slender center who was so nervous and un-coordinated she'd fall down even when nobody was around her, until Amy kept asking her to think of a song and sing it to herself during the game and forget the crowd. She believed it about one of her players built like a tank, great on the basketball court, but no dates off-season until Amy worked with her on hair and complex-ion. And she believed it about me—that I'd succeed.

Her face was like a gentle sea breeze to me. She brought hope and goodness and calm and light.

My very own coach.

We entered a shopping center. I bought us hot dogs and root beer. We browsed. Watching people wash clothes in a Laundromat, she said, "Give me something about Laundromats."

"I love Laundromats. It's like a show-and-tell for

dirty clothes. The dryers at a Laundromat have two set-tings, damp and burnt. Another thing—you can find magazines there you can't get anywhere else—like *Modern Werewolf*, or magazines with strange household hints, like ten uses for toenail clippings."

We walked into a grocery store, past the dairy case. She said, "Buttermilk."

"Have you ever known anyone who actually admitted to liking buttermilk? You ever tasted buttermilk? You know what it is? Sour milk. Every carton of regular milk has a date stamped on it and you're not supposed to buy it after the date stamped on the carton or it'll be bad. You ever notice the dates on a carton of buttermilk? October 13, 2140. I mean, when everything that can possibly go wrong with milk has happened, then they call it butter-milk."

"Cheese," she said.

"When I was a kid, people used to tell me the moon was made of green cheese. I believed 'em, but I used to imagine that, somewhere in the universe, there was a giant cracker in orbit."

I grabbed her hand and we skipped through the mall and nobody noticed. That's L.A. for you. We walked home holding hands.

"You really get to me," she said.

"Tell me all about it, my dear." I rubbed my hands, impersonating a melodrama villain out to get little Nell.

"When I'm with you, with all your joking and kid-ding, I feel like this is the Real World, and that every-thing else in my life is crazy. Like today in faculty meet-ing. We spent forty-five minutes trying to decide if we should have a pop machine in the faculty lounge. You'd have thought it was the United Nations. The worst part was, everybody wanted it. It was a two-minute issue. But no—somebody amends the original motion to strike out the words 'Coke machine' and replace it with 'soda pop machine.' Then we had amendments to amendments.

Somebody kept yelling 'Point of order!' It was insane. So I come home and we pretend that there's a giant cracker in orbit and that a woman on TV washes her face with a dove—and it all makes complete sense to me! Why does the real world seem absolutely bonkers to me?"

I grinned. "Because it is. That's what keeps comedians going—the real world is crazy."

She looked at me. "You know what? I'm hooked on you. Absolutely—your wit, your charm, your silly face."

I frowned. "Ms. Chairperson, I'd like to amend that by striking out the word *silly* and inserting the word *handsome*."

In another accent, I said, "Point of order, point of order."

I continued for a while on that. It really cracked her up.

Amy's parents invited me for supper. Afterwards she and I sat out on her porch. I put my arm around her and started the timer and we kissed. The night breeze brought the smell of flowers to us from the garden. Moonlight softly lit her face.

Holding her in my arms, I whispered quietly, "I'll never forget the first girl I dated, Ima Frog. I picked her up at her house. She'd really gotten dressed up for the occasion—she put new shoelaces in her combat boots. I met her parents. Her mother was in the kitchen writing threatening Christmas cards."

She slugged me. "So help me, Jimmy Pepper, if you ruin a romantic mood like this on our honeymoon, you'll be in big trouble. I mean BIG TROUBLE."

We kissed until the timer went off; then she went inside for the night.

During the time of waiting to go to the temple so we could be married, and waiting to put together enough money to get my comedy album recorded, I got discouraged. One thing helped—Jill sent me information about my great-great-grandfather.

Archibald Pepper was born in Scotland. When he was thirteen years old, he was apprenticed to learn the shoemaking trade. He lived away from his parents in another town. When he was fifteen years old, he heard the missionaries preach. He believed what they said and wrote asking his parents for permission to be baptized. They said if he joined the church, he would never again be welcome in the family.

He was baptized. When he was eighteen, he crossed the Atlantic Ocean in the ship *Samuel Curling* and crossed the plains in Milo Andrus's company. He was separated from his parents when he was young—just like Jill and Ryan and me.

Once Jill sent me the minutes of several church meetings where he had spoken.

June 6, 1895. He told about leaving his homeland as a boy, about the hardships of traveling across the plains, about seeing women bury their husbands and children. At the time he gave the talk, he had been hunted for a year by federal officials pursuing him because of his having entered into plural marriage. He concluded his talk with these words: "We should be willing to make sacrifices for the gospel's sake."

My sacrifice was waiting so that Amy and I could be married worthily in the temple. Maybe it's not as great as crossing the plains, but to me it was a serious challenge.

November 3, 1895. The clerk recorded in his minutes: "Brother Pepper addressed the meeting, spoke of our meeting together and partaking of the sacrament, that we might have the Spirit of the Lord to be with us always that we should not have hard feelings one towards another, but we should have the holy spirit to be with us at all times."

Roots. I have a great-great-grandfather. He gave me a legacy, a lineage, a tradition to uphold.

He was a Mormon pioneer. Do you know what I'm saying? My very own pioneer ancestor.

We spend most of our life just trying to find out who we are. Once we know, we suddenly see that all of us, somewhere down the line, come from noble men and women.

During our engagement, Amy's team made it to the regional basketball tournament. I'd spent time with the team during practices, mainly just waiting for Amy to be finished. Gradually I got to know the members of the team. I'd sit in the empty stands, and they'd come over once in a while, and we'd sort of joke around.

They were an easy group to care about. Nice kids. Very competitive.

I got some of them using garlic.

They asked Amy if I could talk to them just before their first game at the tournament. She thought they'd have wanted the principal, but they wanted me.

After they were ready, Amy escorted me into the dressing room where the team waited, just a few minutes before the game was to begin. They were very nervous and tense.

I began. "First of all, I guess I don't need to tell you how important this game is. You've come a long way to get here—what was it, thirty miles? It wasn't easy getting here either. Mainly because your bus driver lost his way. I knew you were in trouble when he welcomed you to Disneyland. But you're here and that's the important thing."

A few looked up. It sounded almost like the usual before-game speech, but not quite.

"I guess I don't have to tell you this is the most important game of your life, not only to you individually, but to your high school. You will never in your entire life play a more important game. This is it. Don't blow it. If you lose this game, a scarlet tattoo will be placed on your forehead that will read, 'I lost regionals.' You will be forced to wear that for the rest of your life. Not only that, you will be sentenced to live alone in a small cottage outside a tiny village in New England, and tourists will come and pay a quarter to take pictures of you and your forehead standing alongside their nephew Melvin.

"If you lose, your principal and three shop teachers will slash their wrists in a rented hot tub in the parking lot of your high school. If you lose, four hundred unblemished navel oranges and three white Volkswagens will be burned at the stake. Also if you lose, your parents will receive threatening letters from Sesame Street. Mr. Rogers will phone you personally to say you're not special to him. McDonald's will shout in your ears that you don't deserve a break today. That's what'll happen if you lose today.

"But even so—don't be nervous."

One of the girls, named Patrimo, started giggling.

I continued. Pretty soon they were all laughing.

Finally it was time for them to go. Amy, with her clipboard, looked every bit the coach.

I wrapped it up. "Hey, we've had fun, but listen to me. You got an advantage now. The other team's going to be so tight, they'll squeak. Play loose. Enjoy yourselves. In the words of a famous Alpha Beta checkout lady, 'Have a nice day.' Now go out there and play ball! Let's do a cheer. Give me an E . . ."

"E!" they shouted.

"Give me an X!"

"X!"

"Give me a Q!"

"Q!"

"Give me a Z!"

"Z!"

"What does it spell?"

Giggles.

"Okay, so I don't know what it is, but you gotta admit it's a great word for Scrabble."

Laughter.

"Give me a car!"

"Car!"

"Thanks, I needed a car."

"Give me a wife!"

"Wife!"

"All right!" I grabbed Amy and kissed her, much to their delight and Amy's embarrassment. "Now go out there and destroy them!"

When the game started, Amy's team was so loose and the other team so nervous that our kids pulled out to an early ten-point lead.

Watching Amy during the game was good for me. Sometimes a guy gets to thinking of a woman as "my girl," almost as if she were a possession. But as I sat on the sidelines watching her—calling time-outs, bringing the team in for a little lesson on defense, sending them out again, sitting on the bench looking at the clock, wiping a wisp of hair from her eyes, standing up complaining about a bad call, bringing Patrimo out of the game for a few minutes to talk to her about what she was doing wrong, then hugging her before sending her back out again—I realized what a strong person Amy was. She would never be my shadow. I would never swallow her up, or cause her to lose her unique identity. We would share and give and assist and nurture, but she was Amy, and marriage wasn't going to change that.

We were so different from each other. I mean, here I was, about to marry a woman who had her own set of bar-bells. She could do forty pushups in a minute.

During the game there was a bad call. Amy threw her hands in the air and stood up to complain to the referee, her eyes flashing, her expression one of controlled anger.

She argued energetically but, of course, lost. Just as

the referee was about to call a technical, she sat down. I looked at her. She was in full control. The outburst had been staged for her players' benefit, to let them know she cared and to make the referee cautious the next time. I admired her. She was good at what she did.

We won 64 to 58.

I was the team mascot for the rest of the tournament, going with them to eat, spending the pregame time with them, telling jokes when Amy asked me to, warding off boys at night outside their motel rooms.

Two-thirty in the morning, the second night we were there, Amy and I stood guard in a hallway. Two guys had already tried to sneak into one of the girls' rooms—mainly because the girls invited them.

We sleepily leaned on each other in the hall.

She was worried. "The flu's going around, you know. What if somebody gets it? What if Patrimo gets it?"

"Patrimo won't get it," I said confidently.

"How do you know?"

"Patrimo's taking garlic. If garlic'll keep vampires away, it'll certainly stop the flu."

She relaxed. I kissed her.

I whispered in her ear. "Unless, of course, you're attacked by a vampire with the flu . . ."

She was in no mood for humor. "Who else is taking garlic?" she whispered.

"Sullivan."

I kissed an earlobe.

"Patrimo?" she whispered again.

"Patrimo and Sullivan."

She sighed contentedly. "Sullivan too."

"And Myers," I whispered softly in her ear.

She smiled. "I'm glad about Myers."

"Coach?"

"Yes," she said, content to be in my arms.

"I love you. Sometime tell me about b-ball, okay. Like what did you tell Patrimo during that time-out in the second half? You don't have to tell me now—I know you're tired, but sometime teach me about coaching. Okay?"

We kissed again, a slow, luxurious kiss; then she pulled away. "Time-out," she whispered, giving the appropriate signal.

I nodded in agreement. It was time to quit.

"Where will you sleep tonight?" she asked. All the rooms in the cheap motels were booked for the tournament.

"The YMCA. They're full but I'm gonna rent a racquetball court and four towels. If I can keep winning, I'll have a room."

She smiled. "You can't let a joke go by, can you." She started back down the hall. "It's too bad we're not married. My room is really nice."

I groaned. "C'mon, give me a break. Don't talk about your room."

We backed away from each other.

I blew her a kiss. "I've got to get out of here. Goodnight, Amy. I love you."

"Goodnight. Thanks for helping with the team. I appreciate you being so supportive."

She went to her room and closed the door.

I left for the YMCA and another cold shower. By this time in our engagement, I'd taken so many cold showers, I had a rash.

The team made it to the finals, where they lost by two points in the last five seconds. It was a heartbreaker.

I waited around in the hall outside the girls' dressing room after the game.

Amy came out to see me. "The girls want to see you. Can you come in?"

She escorted me in. The girls were just sitting there with their heads down, a couple of them crying.

"Hey, what's wrong with you guys?"

"We let everybody down," Patrimo said, wiping her eyes.

"You're wrong about that. You were terrific. You kept fighting back, even when you were down ten points. You wouldn't give up. Look, I love you guys. I've never been more proud of anybody."

I wiped my eyes.

"Look, anybody'd have trouble with the team you played tonight. Their center, for example. I'm not saying she was tall, but did you notice that she didn't stand at attention for the 'Star-Spangled Banner' until three minutes after the game started? And their other star, Wells, did you notice the coach plugged her into the wall during a time-out?"

In a few minutes they were laughing again.

Amy walked me out to the hall and explained how she had to go home on the bus, and how tired she was, and that she needed some time to catch up on her sleep, and that it might be a couple of days before she was ready to see me again.

I nodded. She kissed me on the forehead.

"You're a lamb," she said.

I nodded. "You notice how good I'm getting at waiting."

"It won't be much longer, you know. One more month and we'll be married in the temple."

I sighed. "It's just a matter of a little self-discipline, right?"

"Right, and you've been super. Just one thing, after we're married, can I wear perfume again?"

Three weeks before the wedding, just after coming back from picking up our announcements, I told Amy about my past.

"But you don't drink now, do you?"

"No, but once an alcoholic, always an alcoholic. I just

want you to know what you're getting yourself into. If I ever started drinking again, it'd be bad news for our family."

I thought she'd say it was all right, that she didn't care about what'd happened in the past, that what was important was I'd repented—but she didn't. She just sat there looking disappointed.

"How long has it been since you had a drink?" she asked.

"Good grief, Amy, do we have to go into every detail?"

"I think we do," she said quietly.

"All right then—it's been a year and a half."

She opened the car door to leave. "I need time to think, okay?"

Early the next day, which was Saturday, she came to my apartment, returned the engagement ring, quickly said it would be better if we broke up, then turned and left me.

I was alone all over again—I needed a drink.

I sat down, my head lowered, my eyes closed, mumbling prayer after prayer as sweat poured off me, fighting to stay in my apartment, willing myself to stay put and not go out for something to drink.

Fifteen minutes passed. It seemed like forever.

I pulled out my genealogy and read about my ancestors, reading aloud over and over the names and dates of birth and marriage and death. How old was he when he got married? How old was his wife? How many children did they have? Where was he born? How old was he when he got married? Where was he born? Over and over again.

I called my home teachers. They came and talked to me. They took me golfing. They kept me walking through eighteen holes. I'd never been golfing in my life. I was so terrible at it. But I got through the day. And at night one of them made me come home with him and

help him put up a swing set for his kids, and stay for supper, and play Pac-Man on his Atari, and watch TV until
late, and then sleep on his couch.

I got up early the next morning, went home, took a
shower, and got ready for church. I arrived there two
hours early and just sat in the chapel, where I was safe. I
helped the custodian set up chairs for a Sunday School
class. I read about the Garden of Gethsemane.

A few minutes before church began, Amy came over
to me. "May I talk to you privately?"

We went into the cultural hall.

"How are you doing?" she asked.

"I'm sober. That's what counts."

She hugged me and started crying. My hands stayed
at my side. We were alone in the center of the basketball
court, and the congregation in the chapel was singing the
opening song.

"My dad's outside in the car. He wants to talk to you."

I went out to see him. It was like the shootout at the
OK Corral, with us facing each other in the middle of the
parking lot.

"I talked Amy into breaking up with you as a test to
see how strong you were. It was just a test."

"A test? You mean to see if I'd stay sober?"

He nodded. "I had to know. By the way, you passed."

I was furious. "You had no right to do that!"

"Probably not."

"With all due respect, sir, I think you're a blockhead."

He smiled grimly. "Probably—but someday you'll
have a daughter too. Then I'll watch you become a
blockhead too."

"So what am I supposed to do? Smile and say it's okay
what you did to me, then go off and marry your daughter?"

"That's what you'll do if you have any sense. She loves
you."

"A test!" I fumed. "Of all the stupid ideas! Playing

with my life for your amusement. If you just knew what you put me through yesterday."

"I know what I put you through," he said quietly.

We stared at each other.

"You do?"

"I know exactly what it was like. So does Amy. She was ten when I quit drinking."

I looked at him as if for the first time.

"So you see, I had to know. She's my daughter. I love her. I couldn't bear for her to go through what her mother went through. Some day you'll have a daughter, and you'll understand. Maybe you'll come up with a test of your own."

"Look, I want an apology," I said.

We stared at each other. "Okay, I'm sorry."

"You should be," I said bitterly.

He shrugged his shoulders and drove away.

I went inside. Amy was waiting for me.

"I'm sorry." She hugged me.

"Why did you do it?" I asked, still feeling betrayed.

"I don't know. My dad . . ."

"Don't listen to him anymore." I put my arms around her and held her close to me. "Amy," I whispered.

"What?"

"Nothing. I just like saying your name."

I held her and we kissed. It was a long kiss. It would have been longer, but we realized the door to the chapel was open, and people in the meeting were staring at us.

We were married in the Los Angeles Temple. Scott and Jill were there with us. The ceremony was sacred. Amy's parents waited outside for us; then there was a reception at the church.

Just before we left on our honeymoon, Scott and Jill walked with us to my car. Scott looked in where we had hung some clothes.

"You ironed your pajamas?" he asked, looking more closely at my clothes hanging from the rack.

I blushed. "Well, yes, I . . ."

He turned to Jill and chuckled. "He ironed his pajamas."

Jill smiled. "Yes, I see he did."

"Well," I stammered, "I often iron my pajamas."

Scott reached in and grabbed the pajamas from the hanger. "Hey, look what we got here!" he shouted.

"Gimme that!"

He sidestepped me and started waving them like a flag. "Look, everybody! Designer PJ's!"

I grabbed them away. Trying to salvage some dignity, I said, "Amy, it's time to go now."

"I never saw designer PJ's before," Scott said. "Jill, did you see the little designer insignia sewn on the back?"

"Goodbye, we're leaving now," I said quickly.

Jill and Amy hugged each other. Scott and I shook hands. He was still grinning like an idiot about my pajamas.

We waved goodbye and drove off—just the two of us, to enjoy our best wedding presents—each other.

Shortly after we were married, I recorded my comedy album. The next job was trying to sell them. I'd take them to music stores and they'd take a few on consignment.

Amy became pregnant four months after we were married. The room that was to be the baby's was stacked with copies of my record album.

I went to radio stations to beg them to play segments from the album. Out of ten stations, two agreed to play it. I even tried selling the records door to door, sort of an Avon Man for comedy.

". . . Now here's Johnny!"

I sat in a room with the other guests. They were all drinking to relax. I went into the bathroom and prayed.

One of the guests had been on the show several times. "Can you tell me what Johnny's really like?" I asked.

He shrugged. "I don't know him that well."

"How about some advice then?"

"Just be yourself," he said, finishing his drink.

"Do I have a choice? Who else can I be?"

"Exactly," he said. "Who else?"

It was a fluke about being invited to appear on the show. The niece of a staff member for Carson bought one of the albums and sent it to her aunt for a gift. The aunt played it the same day and asked her husband to listen to it. After he heard it, he made a mental note to find out more about me, but forgot until one of the regular guests came down with the flu. The staff person suggested me, and the next day he brought the album to work. Carson listened to about three minutes and said for them to get me. A day later I was contacted and asked to come the next day and do one of the routines that was on the record.

That's how I got there that night. I am one of the few people in the world grateful for the flu.

I got a glass of water and had a couple of garlic pills.

"Uppers?" one of the guests asked.

"Garlic," I said.

"Italian?" he asked hopefully.

"Scottish."

"A scotch sounds good to me," another guest said, her voice becoming slurred.

Fifteen minutes before the end of the show, I went on.

"Would you please welcome an up-and-coming new comic, Jimmy Pepper!"

Please, have a sense of humor, I prayed, walking on stage.

The rest is history.

My agent was kept busy the next week.

CHAPTER NINE

We reached Buffalo, Wyoming, about seven at night. After stopping to get directions at a gas station, we found the trailer court. It was on the edge of town. Hank's trailer was old, with some paint beginning to wear off. (I'd given up any hope of calling him Dad.) There was a note on the door telling us that he was at work. He gave us directions and promised us a free car wash if we'd go see him.

It was a coin-operated car wash with eight bays. Hank was in an office the size of a closet listening to a customer complain about losing his money in one of the machines.

"You just can't let the quarter roll in," Hank said. "You gotta push it in. Otherwise it doesn't trigger the mechanism."

"It says insert four quarters. If you gotta throw 'em in, you oughta change your instruction list. Anyway, I put the money in and nothing happened."

Hank walked with him back to his bay to get the machine started.

A few minutes later Hank returned. A shapely coed with a University of Wyoming T-shirt complained that the dollar changer wouldn't take her dollar. Hank turned the dollar bill over and pushed it into the machine. Out came four quarters. She left.

A cattle truck started to pull in the truck bay. Hank rushed after it, shouting. "Hey! You guys are clogging my drains! Take a shovel and clean all that out before you turn on the water! See that barrel? Put it in there."

He returned to us, still watching the guy in the cattle

truck to make sure he got all the manure cleaned out before he turned on the water.

"Cattle trucks," he muttered, then turned to face us.

"Daddy!" Jill cried out, throwing her arms around
him.

He was shorter than me, and wore a baseball cap and
a long-sleeved gray work shirt and slacks. His face was
lean, almost gaunt, yet very tan.

We awkwardly shook hands. "How's it going?" I
asked.

"Can't complain. How about you? How was your
trip?"

"Fine," I said.

Jill told him about the man from the *National Inquirer*.
"Why didn't you talk to him?"

I answered. "He wants to do a story about when I was
growing up."

"You're afraid he'll find out about me?"

"Well, I . . ."

He left to take care of a customer. We waited in the
office for him. There were a pile of magazines and several coffee cups and a tool chest and one chair and an old
radio tuned to a country music station. Jill sat on the stool
and I leaned against the wall.

"Well," Hank said, returning after helping someone.
"It's been a long time."

"Sure has," Jill said.

"A long time," I echoed.

A man appeared at the door. "Excuse me. I need
some advice. We're tourists, see, and about twenty minutes ago our youngest kid threw up all over the back seat.
I thought I'd take off the kid's clothes and spray 'em
down, and maybe wash him off too. So my question is,
what'd be the best setting for my kid—Wash, Rinse, or
Wax?"

We looked at him.

"Well, for a little kid, I don't think I'd use Wax," Hank
said.

"Okay," the man said.

"And I think Wash might be too hot for him. Is it a boy?"

"Yeah."

"I'd say Rinse'd be the best."

"Appreciate it," the man said.

The man pulled into the first stall.

"No! Don't!" a boy shouted. He cried through the whole cycle.

"You meet all kinds here," Hank said.

At ten he closed his office. We followed him home.

Five bags of trash were piled outside his door, evidence he'd worked hard cleaning up the place for us. It was a small trailer with faded linoleum floors and a small black-and-white TV. A couch facing the TV was covered with a large horse blanket to hide the damage to the fabric. In the winter he must have taped clear plastic sheets over the windows to keep the cold out. It was still there on all but two of the windows. Propped next to one window was a large fan, which he turned on as soon as we entered.

"Well, this is home. It's not much, but it's mine."

"It's fine," Jill said.

"Sure is," I repeated.

He opened the refrigerator and pulled out a bucket of Kentucky Fried Chicken, a container of coleslaw, and some doughy white rolls.

"How about this for supper?" he said proudly. "Finger licking good—right?"

"You bet!" I said, sounding too enthusiastic. Either I was very nervous or else I was an actor in a chicken commercial.

"I thought about what I could get to eat, and all of a sudden it hit me. Everybody likes Kentucky Fried Chicken. You want regular or extra crispy?"

"Doesn't matter to me," I said, thinking if I said crispy he'd only have regular. No use rocking the boat.

"Me either," Jill said.

"You can have either one. I got both. What'll it be?"

"Crispy," I said quickly.

"Regular," Jill said.

"Right—one crispy, one regular." He rummaged through the bucket. "Now, let's see, you want a leg, a thigh, or a breast piece?"

"It doesn't matter, Hank," I said.

"Suit yourself," he said. "Have whatever you want. I got legs, thighs, wings, and breasts."

"Well, a leg'd sure be great!" I said, sounding hyper.

"You're sure that's what you want?"

"A leg, sure, a leg'd be great! Boy, it's been a long time since I've had some of the Colonel's chicken! Yessir."

He rummaged through the bucket. "Let's see now, I forgot, you want a regular leg or an extra crispy leg?"

"Extra crispy. Let's go all the way, shall we?" I actually chuckled.

He handed me a leg, and I sat and held it. He had not yet put out plates.

I'd never felt more uncomfortable in my life.

"Jill?"

"A regular wing," she said.

He rummaged through the bucket and then swore. "Wouldn't you know it? Look at that wouldya? I don't got wings in regular. I told the girl too. 'One of each,' I said. But would you look at that—two crispy wings. I should've checked it before I left the store."

"It really doesn't matter," she said.

"No, no—we'll get you what you want. If you want a wing, you can have a wing, but it'll be crispy, or if you want crispy, we got crispy legs, and crispy thighs, and . . ."

"Daddy, I don't really care that much what I have."

". . . or if you'd rather, I'll go back and get you a regular wing. It's just down the street. It was their fault anyway."

"No, really, whatever you've got will be fine," she said.
"You sure?"

"Really, it doesn't make any difference."

"If you're sure." He handed her a crispy leg. "Here you go." He looked around. "Now then—everybody fixed up for chicken? Okay. You know, when I picked it up, I had a choice. I could've got gravy or coleslaw. I decided in the summer nobody wants gravy, so I got the coleslaw. Is that all right with everyone? I guess we could go back and get gravy too, if you want. Chicken gravy's nice sometimes."

"Coleslaw'll be fine," Jill said.

"Actually, I prefer coleslaw to gravy," I echoed.

"You know, me too," he said, dishing up some coleslaw on paper plates. "Must run in the family. Okay, here's your plate of coleslaw. Now, what would you like to drink? I got beer, but I guess you don't want that, do you. That'll be for me. Pepsi, orange soda, Seven-up, orange juice, root beer, and Coke, and, oh yeah, I almost forgot, milk—fresh milk. Got it today. So what'll it be?"

I'd had it. "Are we gonna talk like this all night? It's like living in a TV commercial."

He misunderstood, scowled, stormed to the refrigerator, and pulled out a can of beer for himself, a half gallon of milk, and several cans of soda pop.

"Take what you want," he muttered.

We sat and ate and watched small screen black-and-white TV. TV is wonderful when you don't really want to talk. It gives the appearance of togetherness. After an hour, I had a huge pile of bones on my plate. It was the only thing I could think of doing.

Hank turned off the TV because a presidential news conference was on and it was covered by both stations.

I felt as if someone had taken away my life raft. There was just the three of us together in a small trailer. We would have to say something.

Jill saved me. "Daddy, would you like to see some pictures of your grandchildren?" She handed him a stack of photos. He started through them. "Who's he?" he asked.

"My husband."

"What's his name?"

"Scott."

"Going bald, isn't he?"

She smiled good-naturedly. "We joke about it sometimes."

She leaned over the pictures with him. "The oldest here is Kirk, and our baby is Justen."

"Justen? What kind of a name is that?"

"It was Scott's father's middle name. He's been very helpful."

The sentence dangled in midair. He finished the stack of pictures and turned to me.

"You got any?"

I handed him some pictures from my wallet.

"This your wife?" he asked.

I nodded. "Her name is Amy."

He chuckled. "She's a tall one, isn't she."

"What of it?" I said with just the hint of an edge to my voice.

"Nothing—don't get excited. I just noticed she's tall. If she was short, I'd have said, 'Short, isn't she.' Don't be so touchy."

"She used to be a high school girls' basketball coach. Now she coaches girls' softball during the summer."

He studied the picture. "Taller than you?"

"No," I snapped.

"Close though, I bet."

"What difference does it make?"

"None at all."

He looked at a picture of our baby. "What's his name?"

"Logan."

He paused. "You named your kid after a town?"

"It was the name of my foster father."

It was the wrong thing to say. He quickly laid the picture down. "Well now, we'd better get these things in the refrigerator, and then we gotta figure out sleeping arrangements for tonight. There's only one bed. Jill, you can have that. Jimmy can take the couch here, and I got an air mattress. I'll just put it down on the floor with a sleeping bag."

"We can't let you sleep on the floor," Jill said. "Let me use the sleeping bag."

"No, it'll be fine."

We made arrangements for the bathroom. Jill would be first, me second, and Hank third.

He turned on the TV.

When I came out of the bathroom, Hank went in.

I sat down on the couch near Jill.

"Well?" she asked.

"It was our duty to see him, and we have. But there's no reason to drag it out. When's the soonest we can get out of here? How about tomorrow morning?"

Hank came out of the bathroom. "Guess what I got planned for us tomorrow?" he said brightly. "I'm taking a few days off. I thought we'd go camping. As long as you've come this far, you ought to see the Bighorns. There's a wilderness area you've just got to see."

"What's a wilderness area?"

"Except for a few trails they've built, they've pretty much left things the way they were before the white man."

"Why would they want to do that?" I asked.

"We'll have to hike a few miles. We're going to the Seven Brothers Lakes. I got us backpacks and everything we'll need. Sounds fun, don't it, just the three of us?"

"I have to get back to California," I said.

"Get back? Already?"

Jill looked at me, questioning me with her expression. I finally nodded. "We'll go camping," Jill said.

He turned on TV to Johnny Carson. Jill said good-night and went to bed.

"What's Johnny Carson really like?" he asked.

"I don't know. The only time I was with him was when we were on the air. You know him as well as I do."

"I thought maybe you would've gone out for pizza with him after the show."

"No."

"Well, did he say anything to you after the show?"

"Yes, he said, 'Hey, great to have you.'"

We watched a few more minutes.

"What's Ed McMahon really like?"

"Hank, I just don't know."

"Hank," he muttered, then turned off the TV and rolled out his sleeping bag, blew up his air mattress, and lay down.

"Oh, one thing," he said. "I hope you get to sleep before I do, because people say I snore pretty bad."

I tried to concentrate on going to sleep. It didn't work. Before long, he was asleep and snoring. Sometimes his cigarette cough would wake him up, and he'd quit snoring for a while.

Snoring and coughing and breathing.

I tried to imagine what it'd sound like in a tent.

We got up the next morning and packed. Hank had bought two new packs and sleeping bags and ponchos and fishing outfits just for us.

By ten-thirty we were ready to go. As I stepped outside to load Jill's pack in the pickup, I noticed the *National Inquirer* photographer's car across the street. He was taking pictures of us. As we left town he tailed us as we drove into the Bighorns.

We turned off the highway and followed a narrower road till it ended at a corral. Ahead of us was a bumpy, boulder-strewn road fit only for vehicles with high clearance.

We parked and stepped out of the car. The photographer, Becker, pulled up beside us and got out.

"Get out of here!" I shouted.

Hank looked at me strangely.

"He's the one from the *National Inquirer*."

"You're from the *National Inquirer*?" Hank asked.

"That's right."

"I read it all the time." He shook Becker's hand.

Becker relaxed. "Terrific. We're doing a little article about your son."

"Jimmy's been on Johnny Carson. Did you know that?"

"Yes, sir."

"We're real proud of him. Well, you'd like to take some pictures of us."

"I don't want him taking pictures!" I snapped.

"Nonsense. He came all this way."

"Mr. Pepper, is it true you spent time in a Mexican prison?"

"He doesn't have to answer that!" I shouted. "C'mon, let's go. Don't talk to him, Hank."

"Why are you calling your father Hank?" Becker asked.

"Because that's his name. C'mon, let's go if we're going!"

I started almost pushing Hank ahead of me. Suddenly he stopped, pulled my hand off his shoulder, and turned to confront me. "Are you that ashamed of me?"

Then he walked back to Becker. "Yeah, I did time in prison. It's not something I'm proud of, but it happened. You'll have to forgive Jimmy. He's still bitter."

The two of them talked for a few minutes. Becker asked if he could get a picture of the three of us together before he left. Hank said yes.

"Jimmy, can I get you to move a little closer to your father?"

Grudgingly I moved in. "Becker, what kind of story are you going to write?"

"A good one, I bet," Hank said. "You think Jimmy'll be on the cover?"

"Maybe—you never can tell."

Becker left, and we started our hike.

"Who knows what he'll write," I complained to Jill as we struggled up the bumpy, rock-strewn road.

"Maybe just the truth," she said.

"I hope not," I said.

Half an hour later my back and legs were killing me. "Are we almost there?" I asked Hank.

"Oh, no. We got seven more miles to go."

It was terrible. Hank kept saying how beautiful the scenery was, but I never had enough energy to look up. All I saw were rocks.

You ordinarily think a lake would be in a valley. Not these lakes. The Seven Brothers Lakes are on top of a mountain that is surrounded by even higher peaks. The last mile to the lake is murder—up a switchback trail.

Finally we reached the top. I collapsed on the ground, panting. But we were there. We'd made it. I could see the lake just off the trail.

"Well, let's get going again," Hank said after a few minutes.

"Go?" I gasped. "We're already on top of the world."

"Most people stop at the first lake and fish. But the really good fishing is at the seventh lake. It's only another mile."

We started along the trail again. "Shoot me, Jill," I mumbled as we stumbled after Hank.

Finally we arrived at the seventh lake and picked out a camping site. There were no other humans in sight.

It was Hank's show. He set up the tent, fixed our

fishing poles, even baited our hooks, and showed us how
to cast out. We had a small red bobber placed a foot from
the hook and worm. Our job was to watch our bobber
and wait for it to dip down when a fish bit.

"Hey, you kids remember when I took you fishing
one time? It was when we were on a vacation to Glacier
National Park. Jimmy was, let's see, I don't know, must've
been six or seven. You remember?"

"Oh?" Jill said with a puzzled expression on her face.

"Remember we rented a little boat. It was just the
three of us. Your mother wasn't feeling well. She stayed
in the cabin. Just the three of us. Ryan would've been too
young to go with us. Just the two big kids went fishing
with Daddy. Remember now?"

We smiled weakly. Finally Jill lied. "I think I remember—just a little."

"Me too, just a little," I echoed.

He left to fix lunch.

"Is this supposed to be fun?" I complained as I tried
to thread a worm on my hook.

"They say it is," she said.

"I wish there was a phone around here. I bet my agent
is pulling his hair out, trying to get in touch with me. I've
got an offer to do a movie, and another record, and
maybe even some Las Vegas engagements. And what am
I doing? Sitting on a log torturing worms. Suppose we do
catch a fish, what's the market value? A buck? And
another thing, someday we're going to have to hike back.
Think about that."

Half an hour later Hank called us for a late lunch.
He'd fried us some hamburgers over a campfire. He had
everything fixed for us. All we had to do was eat and repeat over and over, "Boy, this is really great!"

"It really is, Daddy," Jill said.

"Nothing special," he replied.

"I guess it's just that food always tastes better outdoors," I said, trying to sound cheerful while carefully
picking pine needles from my hamburger.

"Lookie here, what we got for dessert," he bubbled as he pulled out a package of marshmallows. "On that fishing trip, one night we had a campfire and roasted marshmallows. Jimmy kept setting his on fire. Jill, you remember how I spent ten minutes roasting one for you, golden brown? After that we all called you Goldie Brown. Remember? Now here's some sticks for you both to do your own."

I speared a marshmallow with my stick and stuck it in the fire. It caught on fire.

Hank laughed. "Hey, look at that, would you! Just like when you were a kid."

He watched with delight as I ate it. It tasted like soot.

Of course, Jill had to prepare one that was golden brown, and we all had to remark how times hadn't changed at all.

"Well, this sure brings back memories!" I said, trying to sound enthusiastic.

"Sure does, but don't stop now," he chuckled. "Have another one."

I just couldn't. "No thanks. They're so filling. One marshmallow really fills a fella up."

"There's plenty—I brought two packages."

The moment of truth had arrived. "Actually I guess I don't like 'em that much, not as much as I did when I was a kid."

"Jill?"

She shook her head. "No thanks . . . maybe later. I have to watch my weight all the time now."

It was painful seeing him there awkwardly holding two full bags of marshmallows. He looked disappointed. Finally he threw the marshmallows in the fire, and we sat and watched them burn.

"I'll just get the pans cleaned up," he said quickly. "You two go fish some more."

"Daddy," Jill said, "you don't have to do everything. We can help."

"No, no, this is your trip. You don't have to do a thing.

I'll do it all. Go fishing or take a walk, whatever you want. Just have a nice time."

We walked down by the lake while he cleaned up.

I swatted at a mosquito. Its remains were red with my blood. "You got any more mosquito repellent?"

"What do you mean, any more? I never had any to begin with."

"Let's get out of here. You game? We'll make a break for it tonight while the guards are sleeping."

She smiled but only a little. She wasn't as eager to get into fantasy as Amy.

A minute later she slapped my face.

"Ow!" I cried out.

"There was a mosquito on your face."

I rubbed my cheek where she'd hit me.

"Don't tell me—you missed it."

"Yeah, sorry."

I checked my bobber. No action. The fish were all taking naps.

There were a million flies buzzing around us. "I gotta get out of this place."

"Maybe we could go swimming," she suggested.

I put my hand in the water. It was ice cold because it was fed from snowdrifts.

"Whataya bet he reads bedtime stories to us tonight," I said.

We looked back. He was busily scouring out the frying pan.

A few minutes later I asked, "Where's the bathroom?"

"This is a wilderness area, remember."

I looked around desperately. "Not even an outhouse?"

"Nothing."

I panicked. "What are we supposed to do?"

"Find a nice fallen tree to sit on," she said.

I slapped at a mosquito. "People talk about getting

back to the basics, but let me tell you something—there's such a thing as too basic."

I took a lonely excursion into the woods to find a fallen tree. When I came back, she smiled. "Well?"

"Good grief," I mumbled disgustedly.

She suggested we take a walk along the path around the seventh lake. It was better than fishing, and the path was nearly level, so I agreed.

Part of the seventh lake looks almost as if it's at the bottom of a crater, because it's bounded by high mountain peaks. We found a waterfall fed from snow melting higher up. I'd brought a small cup with me, and we had a drink. It tasted good.

"Jimmy, we need to talk," she said.

We found a huge boulder that jutted out into the water and sat down on it to rest.

"So?"

"Tell me how you feel about Daddy."

"Good grief, how am I supposed to feel? He was the all-time world's worst father, and now he thinks he can barge into our lives and somehow make everything right, and we're all supposed to pretend the past doesn't exist."

"He has to try. We're all he's got."

"Don't give me that. And what about you? How come you can just walk in and kiss him hello after all this time and not miss a beat?"

She pursed her lips. "I love him."

I grumbled.

"I think you're having such a hard time because you were always Daddy's boy. I remember you sitting in that old junk car and playing truck driver by the hour."

"I don't remember that."

"Jimmy, what do you remember?"

"I remember he always had a six-pack in the refrigerator, and I remember he brought that woman into our house after Mom died."

"And you can't forgive him?"

"Why should I forgive him?"

"How can you expect to be forgiven of your mistakes when you can't forgive others?"

"I can forgive others. It's just him I can't forgive."

"How about giving me three good memories of Daddy," she said.

"What is this, Psychoanalyst for a Day?"

"I'm just saying there must have been some good memories too. Give me three. Take your time. I'm going to walk down to that cove and look around."

She left.

Three good memories.

He was never around, but when he was, he was magic. He'd take the three of us downtown to a toy store and let us pick out anything we wanted. One day he bought us three new bikes and one for himself, and we went to a store and bought a bunch of good things to eat—bologna and potato chips and pickles and olives and Twinkies and root beer and cookies. Then we went home and, without Mom's help, formed an assembly line and made sandwiches and put 'em in a pack sack and took off on our bikes. All we did was go to a park, but it all seemed a grand adventure—because he was there. And we ate our lunches on top of a slippery slide, and just for the fun of it, we let our garbage go down the slide, and Ryan thought it was so funny. Every time we did it he just cracked up, and we all giggled until our sides ached.

That's number one.

When we came home from Mom's funeral, he had us sit down on the couch in the living room and he told us Mom wasn't in the casket, she was in heaven, and we should never forget that, and not think of her as dead. She was happy where she was. Sometime we'd see her again.

Later that night I woke up and heard a sound coming from their bedroom. I tiptoed closer and looked through the half-open door and there he was, sitting on the bed, packing her clothes into a box. He looked so lonely. I went in to him and hugged him, and he held me and said it was going to be all right.

He asked me to help. With each dress, he told me a memory of her. There was the dress she was married in, and the dress she bought just to wear to a second-grade class program where I was going to recite a poem. "Old King Cole was a merry old soul, a merry old soul was he . . ." There was a black slip and a blue silk negligee I discovered in a drawer. He took them from me and quickly, almost roughly, shoved them into the box without a word.

We packed everything. Then he walked out of the room and shut the door tightly behind him and lay down on the couch in the living room. I sensed the terror of that night for him, and got my sleeping bag, and returned to sleep on the floor beside the couch, where he lay staring at the ceiling.

That's number two.

The third memory reached way back. It was of a five-year-old boy being boosted up into the cab of Daddy's semitruck. He and I sat up there, and he showed me how everything worked, and then I got to go out for a drive on the highway with Daddy in his big truck. We sat above all the other cars and trucks. It was like being a king of the road.

I was so proud my daddy was king of the road.

That's number three.

Jill came back. "Did you think of three good memories?"

"Yes."

"Want to tell me what they are?"

"Not now," I said soberly. "How about you?"

"He called me Princess," she said. "He always called me Princess, and that's the way he made me feel, like a princess."

"One time when we were kids," she said as we walked

back down the trail, "we all went to Primary and we
learned a song, and you said we were going to sing it for
Daddy when he came back from his trip. You made us
practice it every day, even Ryan, who couldn't have been
more than four or five years old. When Daddy came
back, we ran to him and you started us. We all sang, but
Ryan was always about ten seconds behind the rest of us.
I remember the song."

She sang it.

> *I'm so glad when Daddy comes home,*
> *Glad as I can be;*
> *Clap my hands and shout for joy,*
> *Then climb upon his knee;*
> *Put my arms around his neck,*
> *Hug him tight like this;*
> *Pat his cheeks, then give him What?*
> *A great big kiss.*

"You loved him once," she said.
"Maybe I did—once."
We started back.
"The memories don't change anything," I said. "He
still left us."
"I've heard you talk about great-great-grandfather
Archibald, about what a great man he was. What are you
going to do—glory in the dead ancestors you never knew
and dump on the one that's alive and you know best?"
We returned to camp. Hank was fishing. We sat down
with him. Suddenly his pole dipped down sharply and
the line started feeding out.
"I got one!" he yelled.
He fought against the fish. He kept reeling in, but
when the fish pulled too hard, the automatic drag allowed the line to feed out rather than break the line.
The trout jumped out of the water.
After a few minutes the fish tired out. Hank reeled it
in and dragged it onto the shore.

"Would you look at that?" Hank said proudly.

I picked up a large rock and knelt down to kill it so it wouldn't suffer.

"No! Let it go! Put it back in the water!" he said.

I grabbed the fish by the gills. The hook was deep inside the fish's mouth.

"I can't get it out."

"Hurry up then and cut the line!"

The trout twisted violently in my hands. Jill took a knife and cut the line, and the fish twisted away, fell into the water, and shot away. Not until it was gone did I realize that she'd cut the line on the wrong side of the red bobber. The fish had taken it along into the lake.

"What a fish!" Hank said in awe.

After that there seemed no point to continue fishing. We returned to camp.

Clouds started to roll in overhead. Hank set up the one-burner stove while Jill opened two packages of dried soup.

It started to rain.

We withdrew into the tent to get out of the rain. Jill climbed into her sleeping bag to stay warm. A few minutes later we brought the food in the tent and ate.

"This won't last," Hank said. "In Wyoming, they say if you don't like the weather, just wait five minutes and it'll change."

We listened to the steady patter of rain on our tent.

"Actually the fishing's best when it's raining. Maybe I'll go out and try it. Anyone want to come along?"

We shook our heads.

He went outside to get his fishing rod. A minute later, he opened the flap and looked in. "Where's my bobber?"

"When Jill cut the line, she cut on the wrong side. I guess the fish took it with him."

"My fish is dragging a bobber around with him?"

"Maybe it's come off by now," I said.

"Do you know how much that's gonna hurt when he goes down deep?"

"I'm sorry, Daddy," Jill said.

"Maybe I can cast out and snag the bobber and take it off."

Jill and I sat in the growing darkness and listened to the rain fall on the tent. We could hear him casting out time and time again and reeling in.

"Get him back before he catches pneumonia," Jill said.

I put on my poncho and ran down to him. The dull gray clouds now covered the entire sky. He stood alone in the rain, his baseball cap dripping, his fingers starting to get clumsy from the cold water. It was hopeless to try to cast out and hook the bobber and reel the fish back in. Why didn't he know it was hopeless?

"There he is." The red bobber moved steadily along the surface. He cast out toward the bobber but missed.

"Hank, we need to get back in or we'll catch a cold."

He watched the bobber move away from us.

"I'm just trying to help. I guess he don't know that."

"Give it up. He'll be all right."

We returned to the tent. His shirt and slacks were soaked.

"Daddy," Jill said, "take off your wet things and get in your sleeping bag."

He did neither. Instead he sat down on his sleeping bag and lit up a cigarette and worried about the fish.

I took off my wet sweatshirt and slacks and crawled into my sleeping bag.

"Daddy," Jill said, "you've got to get out of your wet things."

"Everytime he tries to eat, everytime he swallows, the hook'll be there, tearing away at him, hurting him."

"Will you shut up about that stupid fish?" I snapped.

"Jimmy," Jill cautioned.

I blew up. "You spend more time worrying about some dumb fish than you've ever spent on us. Why don't you ever ask about Ryan? He's dead. Why don't you care about him? Why don't you ever ask what he was like? And what about Jill? Not even a crummy birthday card for her all those years! And you worry about a fish! And what about me? I wasted half my life because of you! You're a fool to think that roasting marshmallows is going to make it all better! Let me tell you something, it won't. Nothing on earth will do that."

I quit.

He sat still, his expression frozen in time.

Half an hour later Jill finally talked him into getting out of his wet clothes and into his sleeping bag. We lay there in the tent, silently listening to each other breathe and the rain falling on the tent. Side by side, in the darkness of night, each sensing the icy presence of the others, each pretending to be asleep. It was the worst of tortures. My stomach tied itself into knots. But eventually I fell asleep.

The next thing I remember was Jill touching me on my head. "Jimmy, he's gone."

I sat up.

"What's wrong?" I said sleepily.

"He left the tent a minute ago. Go find out where he's gone. I'm worried."

The tent was pitch-black, and he'd taken the only flashlight. I rummaged around for my jeans and shoes and got dressed, then stepped outside.

It had quit raining. He was standing by the side of the lake. He shone the flashlight over the surface and then stopped. He'd seen the bobber. It was moving slowly.

I walked carefully from one large granite boulder to the next, trying to get out to where he was.

"Be careful," I warned.

I took a step—and fell in. The water was so cold I couldn't even yell.

A second later he was in the water with me, trying to save me.

"Leave me alone!" I said.

"Let me help you!"

"I don't need your help!"

We pulled and pushed each other up onto dry land.

After we got out of our wet things, we sat around the fire to warm up.

"How do you feel now?" Jill asked Hank.

He shrugged his shoulders. "Takes more than a little water to hurt a Pepper."

He made himself a cup of coffee and had a cigarette. Jill and I had hot chocolate.

With his head down, not looking at us, he started to talk. "After I moved back to Wyoming, I took up fishing on my days off. At first it was just something to do. But once I saw a man and his boy up here fishing. The kid had freckles and a baseball cap and tennis shoes. After a while the man got mad because his kid got the fishing line all messed up—looked just like a bird's nest. He had to untangle it for his kid."

He stopped.

When he started again, he spoke with a strange hoarseness to his voice. "I watched 'em together, just a man and his boy. Nothing special really, but I'd have given anything to have my kid mess up his fishing line for me to fix."

He didn't look at me. He looked into the fire. He couldn't look at me.

"After that I came up here a lot, I guess, in the back of my mind thinking someday I'd bring my kids, or maybe even my grandkids, here. But it's not the same. Time's passed me by. When I should've been with you, I wasn't."

He took a long draw on his cigarette. "There's nothing anybody can do to bring time back. It's just gone."

He tossed the cigarette in the fire.

"It was a dumb idea to bring the two of you up here."

Jill sat beside him and hugged him and told him she loved him.

But I didn't budge. Not me. Stone-faced, staring at dead ashes.

"The fire's down," he said. "I'll go get some more wood." He walked away.

Jill looked at me. "You know he's hurting."

"I know."

"Then help him."

"What can I do?"

"Tell him you love him."

Miserably I whispered, "I can't do that."

He brought back a log and laid it in the fire. He finally looked at me. "You think I didn't want to see you two after I got out? I did—you'll never know how much. But I was sure you'd both hate me, and I was too afraid to find out."

His face, reflected by the wavering flames, was full of shadows and light, tortured, old, and lonely.

He continued. "What I did was wrong. I know that. But you don't know what it was like for me when your mother died. You don't know what she was to me. She was the one who knew what was right. Without her, I was lost. After she died, I fell apart for a while. They said all I had to do was to go to Mexico and pick up a small package. They paid me five thousand dollars every trip. I was going to buy a ranch, and our family'd live there. I just needed to make a few more trips, and I'd be able to make a down payment on the place I wanted. But I was caught, and that was the end of that.

"When I got out of prison, the social workers in Cheyenne told me the three of you had gone to Idaho to live. I hitchhiked there. I talked to some people. They told me about Ryan. It was years after it'd happened. I went to Burley. They said Jimmy'd gone to California. Jill, I went to where you and your husband were living. I walked by the place and saw you there in the garden with your kid, maybe a year old, near you in a baby swing. I hid by a tree all afternoon watching the house. I guess I fell asleep, because when I woke up, I heard you saying to your kid, 'Grampa's coming!' Your kid started laughing. 'Grampa! Grampa!' you said over and over again. I couldn't believe my ears. I stood up, just about to walk into the yard, feeling like a new man. Then I saw a man get out of his car, a man with gray hair and a suit. He bent over and picked up your kid and kissed him, and then you all went inside, and I heard you ask if he wanted some lemonade, and then you shut the door. Your kid already had a grampa, a man who drove a nice car and wore suits. And what was I? A bum. I hitchhiked to Wyoming the same day."

"Daddy, oh, Daddy." She put her arm around his shoulder. "There was nothing in the whole world I wanted more than to see you again. Didn't you know that?"

"No."

He'd said his piece. It was all he'd say to try to mend things. Jill had managed it, but not me. It was my last chance.

He took one last sip of coffee and stood up, grabbed the flashlight, and walked into the darkness.

"Jimmy, please," Jill pleaded.

I shook my head. "I can't. I just can't."

She shook her head and stepped inside the tent to get ready for bed.

I stayed by the fire and waited for him to come back.

I was no longer a fifteen-year-old boy seeing the world in harshly drawn outlines. I've made mistakes in my life, but at least for every one, I can point to reasons why it happened. I'm willing to pay the price for my mistakes as long as someone understands there were underlying reasons.

There are reasons for me. And there were reasons for him.

Take Amy from me and what would I do? He did the best he could.

He returned to the campfire and glanced quickly at me, then turned away. "It's getting late. We'd better turn in. If you want, we can pack up and leave tomorrow. I know you got important things to do in California."

"Dad?"

It was the first time in eleven years I'd called him that.

"Yeah?"

I wanted to say that I knew it was hard when Mom died, and that it was hard for us to talk because we were so much alike, and that I'd made some mistakes in my life too but I'd found the Church, and it was important to me, and that he could do the same thing and go to the temple and have his marriage continue even after death so he could be with Mom someday, and that even Ryan, as good as he was, had had to repent, but then he moved beyond his mistakes, and how great a man he was at nineteen, and how much God must have needed him to take him so young, and about my little sister Jill, my little shepherd, how much I loved her, how important she'd been in my life. And I wanted to tell him about Amy, that when I was around her, everything was better. And about my son, still so small, and how it was to hold him and know I was his father, and that he needed me. I wanted to tell him that the past isn't as important as what we do from now on.

You were my hero. You were what men are supposed to be. You were what I wanted to become. Why did you leave me when all I wanted in life was to be like you, my dad, my king of the road?

King of the road.

King of the road.

My dad was king of the road.

There were layers to it that needed to be folded back, layers of feelings hidden for so long that needed to be exposed to sunshine.

There were so many things to tell him. But I didn't say any of it—not one word.

He started slowly for the tent.

In my mind it was as if time had slowed down, and that I was seeing a movie run one frame at a time.

I cleared my throat. ". . . Uh . . . I just . . . wanted to say . . ."

He stopped.

"Yeah?"

The seconds ticked by.

"I like it up here . . . in the wilderness."

He looked closely at me. "Yeah?"

"Yeah, it's so . . . basic. What would you think? . . . That is, can we do this again sometime, maybe in a few weeks, just the two of us?"

His Adam's apple moved laboriously as he swallowed. "You want to come up here again . . . with me?"

I nodded. "Yeah, well . . . we already got the backpacks. Might as well use 'em."

"Sure . . . might as well."

We could hear Jill in the tent break down, her sobs coming like huge gulps of emotion spilling out.

We listened to her crying.

"Women," Dad said, wiping his face with a sleeve.

"I know—they're such bawl babies," I said, turning so he wouldn't see my face.

Jill ran from the tent, barefoot, wearing a pair of Dad's long johns for pajamas, crazily hopping because of the rocks. She threw her arms around me and kissed me hard on the cheek, then rushed to Dad to hug and kiss him, then as quickly hopped back to the tent and into her sleeping bag.

"When do you want to go?" he asked, wiping his eyes.

"How about the fourth week in August?"

He nodded his head. "Sounds good. I think I'd like to try Misty Moon Lake. Of course, you don't get there from here."

"No?"

"Oh no—you go further on the highway out of Buffalo before you turn off. Nice thing about Misty Moon is it's not that far to hike. And I'll tell you one thing—at

Misty Moon when they're taking lures, it's out of this world. There's a spinner called a Panther Martin. They say it sends sonar waves that drive fish crazy. At Misty Moon one time I had five strikes on one cast with a Panther Martin. And late August, when it cools down, it oughta be real good."

By morning the clouds had gone. Jill and I cooked breakfast. Dad got dressed and, before anything else, walked down to the lake. The bobber was floating motionless in the water.

"It came off," Dad said. "During the night. The fish'll be all right now."

"Sure," I agreed. "It'll be okay."

We stayed longer than we'd planned. Actually it was my idea.

It's strange how you can get used to anything. The first day we washed the pans with soap and boiling water. The second day I just walked out to the lake and swished the pan through the water a couple of times to let the bigger chunks fall off.

The third day, after we came back from fishing, Jill asked me to make her a cup of hot chocolate. I took the billy can and poured some hot water in her cup, but I was too tired to go hunting through our backpacks for a spoon. "Let's see," I said, looking on the ground, "what we need right now is a sterile stick. Aha, there's one." I picked up a stick and stirred the hot chocolate and gave it to her. She took it and drank without batting an eye.

On the fourth day I had to wash my jeans because they had fish blood all over them. After I'd borrowed a pair of Dad's jeans, I walked out to the lake, set my jeans in the water, put a stone on them, and came back to the camp.

"That's all you're gonna do?" Jill asked.

"I'll tell you how it works. I leave 'em in there overnight and just let the rotation of the earth swirl 'em
clean."

The last evening there we ate up our food supply so
we wouldn't have to carry it out. It was a banquet. We had
strawberry Jell-O made by mixing the hot water and
gelatin in a Zip-lock bag, then laying it in the lake. We
made biscuits by wrapping Bisquick around a stick and
heating it above hot coals. And we had macaroni and
cheese and fish. For dessert Dad had a surprise. We took
snow that still lay in occasional patches and mixed fruit
punch mix with it. It tasted better than any snowcone you
can buy.

We sat by the fire again and watched the patterns of
light changing on the mountain peaks surrounding us.

The next day we packed and started down the trail.

"Daddy," Jill said, "after you and Jimmy go camping
again, Scott and I want you to stay with us for a while."

"Yeah," I laughed. "Spoil their kids rotten."

"How about if I teach 'em how to fish?" he said.

"They'd love that," she said.

"And then after that, come down to California. I'll see
if I can have you meet Ed McMahon or Doc."

"I don't care about that," he said. "I just want to meet
Amy and your kid Provo."

I cleared my throat. Jill was smiling. "It's Logan,
Dad."

"Logan, Provo, whatever."

We kept walking.

"Wonder when the *National Inquirer* will come out
with the article about you," Dad said.

"You might even be on the cover," Jill teased.

"Hey, Jillsy, you think I'd make a good cover boy?"

She laughed, pausing on the trail to look at my crazy pose. The sweat beading up on her face was beginning to streak the protective layer of grime we'd all built up during our stay.

"Why not?" Dad said, so much more relaxed than when we first met him. "E.T. made it on a magazine cover. Jimmy looks at least that good."

Jill hooted. "All right! Way to go, Daddy!"

"Think you'd ever use that on Johnny Carson?" he asked me.

"Maybe so, Dad."

He smiled proudly. "How about that!"

We continued down the trail. I stumbled on a rock and nearly fell the rest of the way down the mountain. The backpack was rubbing on my sunburn. A swarm of mosquitoes was dogging me down the trail, treating my skin like a Whitman sampler.

My feet were killing me. Each rock on the trail dug at me through my now worn-out tennis shoes. I vowed if we ever got back to civilization I'd buy the best pair of boots they make, something that will last a few years.

For as long as my dad wants to lead me into the wilderness at Misty Moon.

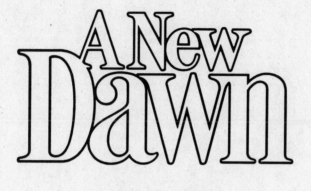

A New Dawn

JACK WEYLAND

Deseret Book
Salt Lake City, Utah

CHAPTER ONE

It was Saturday night, and Lisa Salinger had a problem.

Actually three problems. The first was her graduate research project assigned by Dr. Owens, her adviser at Princeton University. She'd already spent three months on it and had gotten nowhere. It was no wonder—Einstein spent the last twenty years of his life searching for a solution to the same problem, and he never found the answer either.

Her second problem was that she wasn't going home for Christmas. Dr. Owens had asked her to stay in New Jersey over the holidays so they could get some research done.

To top it all off, her roommate Kimberly Brown was coming up the stairs with Hal. Lisa couldn't stand him.

She wrapped the old sheepskin coat tightly around her in case Hal came in. She'd picked up the knee-length coat the previous summer at a garage sale in her hometown of Fargo, North Dakota. She wore the coat over her flannel nightgown to keep warm against the damp winter nights.

She looked at the clock. It was eleven-thirty. She'd have to go to bed soon, or she'd be too tired to sing in church the next morning. She enjoyed singing in the choir of the First Methodist Church.

Hal and Kimberly were talking just outside the door. "Thanks again, Hal. The movie was a lot of fun. See you tomorrow for lunch, okay?"

"Wait, don't go in yet. It's still early. Let me come in for a few minutes. We could listen to records or watch TV." There was a pause, which meant he was kissing Kimberly. "Sometimes I get to feeling so lonely. Just for a while, okay?"

Kimberly sighed. "I'll ask, but you know what a bear she is."

The door opened. Lisa frantically began scribbling equations in hopes of discouraging Kimberly.

"I'm back," Kimberly called out. "Gee, you look busy."

"I am busy," Lisa said abruptly, breaking the point on her pencil for emphasis. She grabbed another pencil and continued.

Kimberly paused. "Hal wants to come in and play records for a while. He says he's lonely."

"If he's lonely, buy him a gerbil for Christmas," Lisa snapped.

"We'll keep the volume way down so you can study."

"I can't study with him around."

"Why not?"

"Because he's a jerk."

Kimberly paused. "Well, how about if you go to the storeroom for a while, like you do when I have a party."

Lisa turned to face Kimberly. "Why do I pay rent here? I spend all my time in the storeroom—your whole life is one party after another."

"You sound just like my mother. By the way, if she ever calls, don't tell her about the parties. She thinks I'm studying this semester."

"Just once I'd like to get some work done in my own apartment."

"Lisa, be reasonable. You've had four hours to study while we've been gone. Isn't that enough? C'mon, just for half an hour."

A minute later Lisa opened the door of the apartment on her way to the storeroom.

"Hi, Lisa," Hal said. "Busy on a term paper, huh?"

She gave him what she hoped was a withering stare. It didn't faze him.

"You work too hard. Me, I buy all my term papers. There's this company . . . I've got the catalog if you want to look at it sometime. It'd save you a lot of work." He flexed his arms. "Hey, how do you like my biceps now? Coming right along, huh? My roommate got me started. We go four times a week. You've probably noticed the difference in my arms and chest lately. Give me three months, and the girls are gonna go crazy." He flexed his muscles again. "How about that? Speaking as a woman, how is it to look at a Real Man?"

"I'll let you know if I ever see one." She turned and walked away.

On the way to the storeroom, she passed a pay phone in the hall. She decided to call home, using the telephone credit card she'd received in the mail a few weeks earlier.

As the phone rang, Lisa imagined the small apartment in Fargo where her mother and sister lived. They hadn't always been in an apartment. Up until she was in the seventh grade, they'd lived on a small farm, but after her parents' divorce, they'd moved into town.

Her mother answered.

"Hi, Mom."

"Lisa, is anything wrong?"

"Everything's fine—I just wanted to wish you a merry Christmas."

"The same to you. Oh, we got your package today. Thanks, but are you sure you can't come?"

"I'd better not. My research adviser wants me to stay and work."

"How's school going?"

"It's okay."

"Well, if you ever decide it's too much, you can always come home."

"I know, Mom."

"I wrote you a letter today. We've got big news back here. Karen's getting married."

Karen was her eighteen-year-old sister, three years younger than Lisa.

"She is? Who to?"

"A young man named David Passey. They met at work. It looks like it might be in May, but they keep moving it up."

"Karen's getting married?" Lisa said, trying not to sound threatened that her baby sister was getting married first.

"Well, I say she's too young, but you know how it is when a girl meets Mr. Wonderful."

"Can I talk to her now?"

"She's out on a date, but I'll tell her you called."

"Tell her I'm very happy for her."

"I will, dear."

There was a long pause. "Well, I guess I'd better hang up now. 'Bye, Mom."

As she started for the storeroom, she saw Mike Anderson coming down the hall. He was a graduate student from Utah, working toward a master's degree. She wrapped the sheepskin coat around her and hoped he'd just nod and pass by.

"Hi, Lisa," he said, stopping. "Kimberly having another party?"

"Not really—she and Hal are playing records, but I can't study with him around."

"I got a letter from Val today," he said, referring to his fiancée. "I told her you had some questions about BYU. She sent you a catalog."

Lisa shrugged her shoulders. "She didn't need to go to all that trouble. I was just curious about their physics program."

"Well, I've got the catalog, if you want to take it now."

She walked with him to his apartment. He let her in

and went to try to find the catalog. She said hello to his roommate.

Once she'd been in Hal's apartment with Kimberly. After seeing that, the most remarkable thing to her about Mike's apartment was that there were no centerfold posters on the wall, no pyramid of empty beer cans, and no stolen road signs.

He gave her the catalog and showed her a new picture of Val.

A few minutes later she shuffled downstairs in her old slippers to the storeroom and opened the door. The room was full of suitcases, trunks, and junk left by generations of previous tenants—a pair of long wooden skis, a lawnmower, three broken bicycles. It smelled of dust and mildew, and it was cold. A dim lightbulb in the center of the ceiling lit up the room just enough to emphasize its ugliness.

Lisa unzipped the sleeping bag on the old cot and crawled in. She wanted to sleep, but it was useless.

Her baby sister was getting married.

The next morning as she got ready for church, Lisa paused to study her image in the bathroom mirror. More than anything she looked efficient. Her short brown hair was styled to reduce the time spent fussing over it. Her wire-frame glasses made her look intellectual and a little bored with life. She wore no makeup, and there was a perpetual frown on her face.

I used to smile, she thought. *Where did it go?*

As a child she'd been happy enough. On the farm in North Dakota, there were trees to climb and always a litter of kittens to play with. In the summer, the sweet smell of alfalfa filled the air. A small pond across the road was stocked with enough fish to make it worth the time spent sitting on the bank watching a red plastic bobber in the water. A girl Lisa's age lived on the farm next to them, and she had a horse. Sometimes she let Lisa ride it.

Yes, she had smiled often enough when she was young.

But then one day in the seventh grade, her father announced he didn't love his wife anymore. He'd met someone else, someone younger.

The divorce proceedings became a war of accusations and legal maneuvers. The farm was sold, and her mother moved the family into a small apartment in Fargo and got a job in a hardware store.

After that, the three of them scrimped by. There was little money; kids at school made fun of Lisa because the clothes her mother bought for her at garage sales were made for short mature women and not for a seventh grader. They looked baggy and awful on her.

Sometimes being thirteen years old seemed like a prison sentence. A growth spurt suddenly turned her body into a war zone. Almost overnight she grew taller and her movements became awkward. Her face broke out. She became moody and spent days sulking in the bedroom shared unwillingly with Karen.

Just before school started the next year, her mother said, "If you want to go to college, you'll have to do it on your own, because I can't help you. Maybe if you study hard and get good grades from now on, you'll be able to get a scholarship."

Realizing the alternative to college might be spending life like her mother, sorting nuts and bolts into bins in a hardware store, Lisa focused her attention on school. Sometime in the process she discovered she was smart, especially in mathematics. Some boys seemed to resent how quickly she learned, but she didn't care.

She fell into the role of being the achiever, and her sister became lovable and sweet. Both were survival tactics.

Lisa looked critically at her reflection in the mirror. So what if Karen got married? It didn't matter. Lisa had a career to think about.

That Sunday before Christmas, Lisa enjoyed church because the choir sang four selections from Handel's *Messiah*. It was her favorite music. She'd read that when Handel wrote it, he stayed in his room for days in a surge of creative energy. What a thrill it'd be to create something that could stand the test of time.

When she returned from church, she found Kimberly and Hal having lunch. She opened the refrigerator, took out an apple, a carton of yogurt, and a pile of wheat sprouts.

"Hey, Lisa," Hal asked, "you got any games for your computer?"

"Oh, good grief," she mumbled. "Hal, this isn't an arcade."

She realized she was scowling again. She did that a lot around men. It was another of her defense mechanisms. Once at a roller skating rink when she was fifteen, she'd smiled at an older boy as he skated past her. A minute later he started skating with her. He was a good skater, and she was pleased he'd chosen her out of all the girls at the rink. They skated for a while, and then it was time to go. He offered to give her a ride home, and she accepted.

He drove out in the country and parked the car, then scooted over and tried to put his arm around her. She moved away.

And then he gave her a look she never forgot. It was as if she weren't really a person—as if she were only an obstacle to be overcome. She panicked and opened the door and jumped out.

He demanded to know what was the matter, saying that he hadn't even touched her.

She couldn't answer—she was too scared to make the words heard.

He accused her of leading him on.

She didn't understand how accepting an offer of a ride home could be misread to mean anything other than that she wanted a ride home.

He got out of the car and started walking toward her.

"What's wrong with you anyway? I'm not gonna hurt you." He was getting closer.

She turned and ran away. He swore at her, then got in his car and roared away, leaving her stranded. She had to walk home.

From then on, she adopted a perpetual frown because she believed that to smile around guys was inviting trouble.

"So, what do you use your computer for if you don't play games on it?" Hal said.

"It's a computer, Hal. I use it to compute," she said.

"And I suppose it'd be too much trouble to buy a couple of games for your friends to use on it once in a while?"

"Friends? You mean you, Hal?"

He laughed. "I know why you're so uptight all the time. You need a man in your life."

"That's the last thing I need."

To avoid being around Hal, she took her food to the storeroom, sat on the cot, and ate. Afterwards she decided to take a nap.

An hour later she woke up to the sound of gentle scratching. She looked down and saw a mouse finishing what she'd left in the yogurt container.

"Hello," she whispered.

The mouse froze.

"It's all right. You can eat it. I'm through."

The mouse stared at her, then cautiously moved toward the yogurt container.

"What's your name?" she asked gently.

He ran away and hid behind a suitcase.

"I know why you're afraid. You're two inches tall, and I'm sixty-six inches tall. So it'd be the same as if I came across a monster thirty-three times taller than me. Let's see . . . that'd be . . . about 180 feet high. I can understand your reluctance to come out while I'm here, but I mean no harm. I think I'll call you Maynard. Maynard Mouse. How does that sound?"

She could see him peeking from around a suitcase.
Kimberly opened the door. Maynard disappeared.
"Hal's gone now."
"Good."
"Were you talking to someone?"
"A mouse. We ate lunch together."
Kimberly laughed. "You've got to get out more. How about meeting one of Hal's roommates?"
"Not if he's like Hal."
"It beats talking to mice," Kimberly said.
"It's the same thing," she answered.

Monday morning Lisa took her research notebook to Dr. Owens's office for their weekly research meeting. Because it was Christmas vacation, the building was nearly empty. Just before entering his office, she reached down and pulled out of her book bag what looked like a textbook. Actually it was a book cover glued onto a cigar box. Inside the box was a small tape recorder. She used it to tape lectures and research meetings. She did it secretly because some professors wouldn't want what they said in class to be recorded. She'd never told anyone about the tape recorder.

Dr. Owens opened the door. He looked surprised to see her.

"If it's not convenient, I'll come back later."

"No, no, come in."

She sat down.

"Well, what have you got this week?" he asked.

The phone rang. He answered it. ". . . What does she want? . . . The house . . . What else? . . . How much per month? . . . That's out of the question. What's she trying to do, bankrupt me? I won't pay it . . . Well, you're the lawyer, you work it out."

A minute later he hung up the phone. "Women," he muttered.

The phone rang again.

"Hello," he said angrily. Then his voice softened. "Sorry, Sugar, I just got off the phone with my lawyer. My wife's trying to break me . . . She wants everything. Sugar Doll, I got our tickets . . . We'll be staying at a condo on Maui . . . It'll be great to be with you too . . . Look, I can't talk now, there's someone in my office . . . No, just a graduate student . . . Yes, it's a she . . ." He laughed. "Believe me, you have nothing to worry about . . . All right, see you tonight."

He hung up. None of it was news to Lisa. All the graduate students knew he was leaving his wife for a nineteen-year-old drama student named Sugar Lee.

Lisa opened her notebook and in a dry monotone reported what research attempts she'd tried since the last time they'd met. While he listened, he glanced at a travel brochure about Hawaii.

Finally he interrupted. "Look, don't tell me about your failures. Have you come up with anything positive?"

"Not really. Do you have any suggestions?"

He sighed. "No, just keep at it. Oh, by the way, I won't be in until the tenth of January."

Her mouth dropped open. "What?" she said tensely. "You told me to stay here over the vacation. You said we were going to work on the project together."

"Oh, so I did, didn't I." He put the brochure down. "Hmmm. Well, something's come up. But we'll get together right after school starts in January."

"What am I supposed to do?" she snapped. "I already bought Christmas presents with all the money I was saving for a plane ticket."

"You've got plenty of work to do over the vacation without me. When I come back, we'll get together."

"You're always too busy to see me."

"Look, I'm going to Hawaii on business and I won't be back for three weeks. I'm sorry, but that's the way it is."

"I understand perfectly," she said, staring angrily at him.

"Do you have anything else today?" he asked, glancing impatiently at his watch.

"No," she mumbled, trying to control her anger.

"Can we cut this short then? I've got a million things to do."

Lisa paused at the door.

He looked up. "What are you standing there for?"

She blurted out, "Look, I know it's none of my business, but don't leave your wife and kids for Sugar Lee. Okay, so you're infatuated with her looks, but if you'll just take time to think about what you're doing to your family. Good grief, Dr. Owens, you're at least twenty years older than Sugar Lee. And, good grief, she's such a dummy. I mean, what do you two ever talk about?"

Dr. Owens turned crimson. He stood up. "Worry about your own life, Salinger, not mine! Worry about whether I'll remember this conversation when you take your oral exams. Who are you to tell me what to do? Do you know what you are? You're average, run of the mill. At best you're marginal. I'm not sure I even want my name associated with anything you turn out. I've tried to work with you because I believe women should have equal opportunities, and I've supported the women's movement for years."

"Does that support extend to your wife too, or just to Sugar Lee?"

"Get out!" he yelled.

In the hall she turned off her tape recorder. She decided to save the tape.

Lisa worked steadily on research all week, even spending much of Christmas day stewing over it, trying to fit the pieces together.

Kimberly had gone home with Hal for Christmas, so Lisa was alone. Each day she got up, ate a bowl of Cream of Wheat, put on her jeans and hooded sweatshirt, sat down at her desk, and worked until noon. Then she went to the gym and jogged three miles. After a shower, she ate lunch, then took a nap for a couple of hours before starting to work again, finishing at midnight.

Sometime during that week she realized she was happy to be alone, trying to find the answer to the puzzle of how the universe was put together. But no matter how hard she worked, the equations got worse instead of better. Hundreds of pages of worthless attempts filled her wastepaper basket.

After a week of being alone, wrapped up in her own world of equations representing force fields, hardly ever talking to anyone, she went to church on Sunday. She noticed people were finishing sentences for her. They'd say, "How about this weather?" And she'd stammer, "Yes, it's really . . ." And they'd wait until they could stand the silence no longer, then suggest, "You mean nice?" And she'd slowly nod her head, and they'd leave as fast as they could.

December 29.

She'd worked all day but to no avail. At six o'clock she made herself supper—another can of soup, a packet of Ry-Krisp, two apples, and a cup of coffee. She realized the kitchen was a mess, but it didn't much matter to her.

She ate in the bedroom. Dirty clothes were strewn over the floor, wherever they'd landed when she'd taken them off each night. She looked in her drawer. It was empty. She was out of everything. She'd have to wash clothes before tomorrow.

She filled her laundry bag, went to the basement, put her clothes in a coin-operated washing machine, inserted three quarters, and sat down to wait. It was better not to leave clothes unattended, because they might be stolen.

She was in a tired daze, watching the clothes slosh around, dozing off and then waking up a minute later.

After a while she took her things out of the washer and put them in the dryer.

A girl who lived on the first floor came to wash. To be polite, Lisa said, "How about this weather?"

The girl looked at her. "What about it?"

Lisa didn't know what to say. She hadn't noticed the weather. "I don't know," she finally admitted.

The girl shook her head.

Lisa drowsily stared at the clothes spinning in the dryer, still slipping in and out of consciousness.

Then it happened.

Out of nowhere, on the edge of sleep, she saw a mathematical term jump into place in one of the equations she'd been agonizing over. Suddenly she realized she had the answer that'd eluded Einstein. She knew how to unify all the forces in the universe into one set of equations. She'd found a mathematical quantity that, like a key, opened the universe.

"I've got it," she mumbled, still in a daze. "I never thought I'd get it, but I finally did. Now I've got it."

The girl eyed her suspiciously. "No kidding. It's not contagious, is it?" She moved two chairs away.

"It's so beautiful," Lisa said reverently, her eyes still staring at the clothes bouncing in the dryer while her mind focused on the equations.

The girl looked at where Lisa was looking. "Hey, what are you on?"

Lisa looked around for paper and pencil, but she'd left everything upstairs.

"Do you have any paper?" she asked the girl.

"No, why?"

"I've got to capture it before it leaves."

The girl looked at Lisa's dryer. "It's bolted down—it's not gonna leave."

Lisa opened the dryer and took out two white sheets. "Do you have a pen or pencil?"

"No."

"Do you have lipstick in your purse?"

"What shade?"

"It doesn't matter."

"Well . . . I usually don't lend it out. You wouldn't believe what some people do to the point."

"Lend me your lipstick!"

"All right, all right. You don't have to shout."

The girl handed it over. Lisa fell to the floor and tried to write on the sheet with it.

"I swear, the weirdos they got in this place . . ."

The lipstick broke in two.

"Somehow I knew you'd do that."

"What else have you got?"

The girl looked through her purse and came up with a Magic Marker. Lisa grabbed it, knelt on the floor, and began writing on the sheet.

"Hey! You just can't go around using people's Magic Markers."

"I have to get it down while it's fresh."

"While what's fresh? The sheet? You don't write on dirty sheets, is that it?"

Lisa kept writing.

"I hope you know that's not going to come out," the girl said.

Lisa filled one sheet and then started on the other. In a few minutes, it was full too. She grabbed a blouse from the dryer and began writing on it. When she finished with that, she looked over at the girl's clothes swishing in the washing machine.

"Oh no, you don't!" The girl pulled her soaking wet clothes out of the washer and ran out of the room.

Lisa grabbed the sheets and blouse and hurried to her apartment. Once inside, she rushed to her desk and began transcribing the equations from the sheets onto paper. The equations proceeded in logical order, each one leading to the other. Tears streamed down her face. The equations revealed order and harmony in the universe.

She thought how surprised Dr. Owens would be— and how he'd apologize for putting her down. But then she pictured him in Hawaii, perhaps at that very moment on the beach rubbing suntan oil on Sugar Lee's back while his ex-wife struggled at home in New Jersey, fighting the snow and the cold.

She decided she didn't want to share her discovery with him. It was too good for him.

She phoned home. "Mom, I've done it!" she burst out when her mother answered.

"You found someone to marry?" her mother asked hopefully.

"Mom, listen to me! I understand how everything fits together."

"What do you mean by everything?"

"The entire universe!"

"That's nice, dear," her mother said pleasantly.

"Mom, you don't understand. I've done something that not even Albert Einstein was able to do."

"Are you sure?" her mother asked. "He was a very smart man. I saw a thing about him on TV."

"I can't describe to you how magnificent it is. I'm just overwhelmed that I should be the one to come up with this."

"Good for you. I'll tell Karen. Oh, before you hang up, do you want any details of her wedding?"

A few minutes later she hung up. She wanted to celebrate. She decided to take a bubble bath and then go out for a pizza.

In a bathtub piled high with suds from Kimberly's bubble bath crystals, Lisa stretched out in the tub, lay back, and relaxed. Her eyes were half closed, but every once in a while she'd giggle with delight.

She'd done it! She'd accomplished what scientists had been trying to do ever since Einstein. She was the one who'd come up with the answer. She'd succeeded where hundreds had failed.

She lifted both arms high over her head in victory and shouted. "All right!" She laughed ecstatically, then laid her head back against the bathroom wall and rested her tired eyes.

She was warm and comfortable and very, very happy.

Another thought lazily drifted into place. Even at this very moment, scientists were still working to discover what she'd just discovered.

Suddenly she sat up, now very much awake. What if somebody came up with her result and published it before she did?

She jumped out of the tub and hastily dried herself. Wrapping the towel around her, she ran to the bedroom and scurried around looking for something to wear. All her clean clothes were downstairs in the dryer. She returned to the bathroom. The clothes she'd taken off before her bath were lying in a sodden heap on the bathroom floor. Finally she ran to the living room, put on the marked-up blouse, then wrapped the two sheets covered with writing around her and pinned them securely. She put on the sheepskin coat and the old pair of bunny slippers she'd had since the seventh grade. She put Kimberly's ski cap over her head because her hair was still wet and she didn't want to catch a cold.

She sat at her desk. She had to get her theory typed up and sent to a science journal before someone beat her to it.

At ten-thirty that night, Kimberly returned from her vacation trip. "All right, what's been going on here?"

"I can't talk to you now," Lisa said, typing away.

"What're you wearing under that coat?"

"Two sheets."

"Bed sheets? Let me look. Good grief, there's strange writing all over them. You wrote on your sheets. Why would anyone do that?"

No answer.

Kimberly cocked her head sideways. "Why can't I read a word of it?"

"It's Greek symbols. I put 'em on with a Magic Marker."

She frowned. "So—you wrote Greek on your bed sheets and then dressed up in them?"

No answer from Lisa.

"Why?" she asked calmly.

"I can't explain now."

"Answer me this—were you alone when you wrote on your sheets?"

"Of course I was alone!"

"All right, don't get mad—I'm just trying to recreate how it was. Okay, you're sitting around, all alone, when suddenly you think, 'Gee, I think I'll go get a Magic Marker and write strange Greek symbols all over my bed sheets, and then I'll wrap the Magic Sheets around me, pin 'em up, and wear 'em.' And I bet that was so much fun that you decided to pull my ski cap over your face, and to wear those silly little bunny slippers you've hung onto since you were a little girl. Is that the way it was?" She paused, then continued. "I'm your friend, and I understand how a person could become, shall we say, temporarily unstable, especially if that person was all alone over Christmas. But there's one thing I've got to know. Please tell me you haven't gone outside like that."

No answer.

"Lisa, have you ever had any professional counseling for this—this little problem of yours?"

"I can't talk now."

"I give up. You're really strange."

Kimberly walked into the kitchen and then came right back out. "I guess you know the kitchen is absolutely disgusting. Didn't you ever take health in high school?"

"I'm too busy to talk to you now."

She wandered into the bedroom, screamed, and came running out again. "What have you been doing in there? There're thousands of dead spiders on the floor!"

"No there aren't—I just dropped a plate of wheat sprouts a few days ago, and I never cleaned it up."

Kimberly shook her head. "You are so weird! Look, I'll make a deal with you. Get out of your Greek sheets, put on some real clothes, help me clean up this place—

and I won't tell anyone about what you've been doing while I've been away."

"All my clothes are downstairs in the dryer."

Next Kimberly tried to be a calm voice of reason. She spoke very slowly. "Then what you need to do is go down and get them from the dryer, and then you'll have them to wear."

Lisa kept typing. "I'm too busy."

"Too busy to get your clothes? Believe me, nobody is that busy!"

"I can't talk to you."

"Look, Hal's waiting in the hall. He wants to come in and listen to a record he got me for Christmas. It's a new group called the Cardiac Arrest."

"I'm not moving."

"Well, aren't we in a rotten mood!"

"Don't talk."

"I'll talk if I want—this is a free country."

Hal knocked on the door. Kimberly opened it. They gossiped for a few minutes, then Hal left. She came back. "Hal's gone for a pizza. When he comes back, we're going to listen to my record. I think you should get dressed and throw away all the garbage you've scattered around the place. I'll help you, and when we're all through, you can have some pizza with us."

"I'm not moving till I've finished."

"How long will that be?"

"It might take all night."

Kimberly slammed a bowl of limp sprouts down on the end table. "Go ahead then—stay crazy! But I'm letting Hal in, and he's going to see you, and then he's gonna go out and tell the whole campus how spooky you are!" She fought to stay calm. "So if you don't want him to see you this way . . ."

"I'm not moving."

Kimberly stormed off to the kitchen and then came right back, yelling. "If anybody wants to start a mold museum, tell 'em they can start here!"

She stayed in the kitchen for only a short time before storming back out again. "The least you can do is get decent for Hal."

"I am decent."

"Wearing bed sheets is not decent."

"It's a blouse, then two sheets and a coat. Besides, who are you to talk to me about being decent? I'm completely covered, which is more than we can say about you in that red dress you wore last month."

Kimberly paused, then said, "All right, I'll admit you're decent."

"Fine." Lisa started to work again.

"Decent yes, but let's face it—very, very tacky. Extremely tacky. The sheet's bad enough—but a grown person wearing bunny slippers? How many college students in the United States do you suppose still wear bunny slippers?"

Lisa whirled around. "Can't you see I'm busy?"

"Yes, I can see that! But why are you so busy? I don't understand that. This is Christmas break."

"I know you don't understand!" Lisa shouted back.

That infuriated Kimberly. "Is that right? Well, listen to me, I understand a good deal more than you give me credit for. At least I've never written on my bed sheets with a Magic Marker! And I'm smart enough not to leave soup on simmer in a covered pan for a week. Good grief, Lisa, I hope you know it's fermented. I took it off the stove fifteen minutes ago and it's still bubbling. Go ahead, tell me why you're so busy. Believe me, I'll understand."

"All right, I'll tell you! I've just discovered the Secret of the Universe."

Kimberly threw up her hands. "Oh sure! And I'm Joan of Arc."

Hal knocked on the door. She went to answer it. He came in. "I got something new. It's called Chinese pizza. Hi, Lisa. Going to a toga party?"

"Ignore her," Kimberly said.

"Sure thing."

Kimberly brought in some plates and a bottle of wine. Hal opened the pizza container, and a rich smell filled the room. Kimberly put on the Cardiac Arrest record and turned the volume up, trying to drive Lisa to the storeroom. The record sounded like someone kicking a set of drums down the steps of the Washington Monument.

"Turn it down!" Lisa yelled.

"It's my apartment too, you know."

Lisa suffered through one more song, then jumped up and broke the record in two with her bare hands.

"That was my Christmas present from Hal you just destroyed!"

"I'll pay for it! Believe me, it was worth it." She tossed her purse at Kimberly and sat down again.

"What's wrong with her?" Hal asked.

"Who knows? She gets spookier by the day. Did I tell you she talks to mice now when she's in the storeroom?"

Lisa kept typing.

Kimberly continued. "She could be attractive and popular, like me, but no, she doesn't try. And her clothes—why does she always have to look like a refugee? And why does she only wear drab colors?"

"Beats me. Why's she so paranoid tonight?"

"Listen to this," Kimberly grumbled. "She says she's come up with the secret of the universe. Whatever it is, it can't be important enough to sit in front of us wearing two bed sheets marked all over with Magic Marker, a ski cap, and those infantile slippers. And the mess she left the bathroom in—I'd be embarrassed for you to see it. Not to mention the fact she used up an entire bottle of my bubble bath."

"She's found the secret of the universe?" Hal said. "That could be important. Did she say what it is?"

"Of course not. Even if she did, who'd ever understand a word she'd say?"

Hal rubbed his chin thoughtfully. "You know what I

think the secret of the universe is? I think it's this—go
with the flow, stay loose, and look for opportunities.
There's opportunities all around, sometimes under our
very noses. Take the dimpled golf ball, for instance. Did
you know they used to make golf balls perfectly round,
but in a tournament the pro golfers would use all their
old knicked-up balls because they found out they
traveled farther? And then one guy started making them
dimpled. Now there was an opportunity right under
somebody's nose, but just one person saw it. It's something to think about, right?"

Lisa heard them talking but couldn't stop to react.
She had to keep working. Suddenly she sneezed. She
jumped up, ran to the refrigerator, pulled out a carton of
yogurt, dumped the contents into a glass, poured milk
over it, stirred it, picked up an empty glass, returned to
her desk, took a mouthful of yogurt, gargled, and spit
into the other glass.

"Good grief, what is she doing?" Hal asked.

"Gargling yogurt," Kimberly said. "She does it
whenever she thinks she's getting sick—but watching her
do it makes me sick."

"Does she always wear that coat to bed?"

"Every night since November."

"Sheepskin pajamas," Hal said. "That's got to be a
first. I wonder why. Must be some deep-seated psycho-
logical need—like maybe she has a crush on the
Marlboro man."

Lisa turned around and yelled, "Would you two shut
up?"

"Sorry, your highness," Kimberly said sarcastically.

A few minutes later, the pizza and wine were gone.
Hal started for the bathroom, but Kimberly stopped him
and made him wait until she cleaned it up.

While he waited, he stood over Lisa and watched.
"What are all those little squiggles on the paper for?"

She turned to glare at him.

He shrugged his shoulders. "Just asking—no need to

get mad. You think you're so great, don't you. Well look, I'm smart too. Oh sure, I'm not into mathematics like you are. I'm more philosophical. Did I ever tell you my philosophy of life? I got it from seeing *South Pacific*. It's this: 'Happy thoughts, keep thinking happy thoughts, think about things you'd like to do. You gotta have a dream, if you don't have a dream, how you gonna make a dream come true?' That's it. That's my philosophy of life."

Kimberly came out of the bathroom. "It's okay to use now," she said. He left.

Kimberly put the pizza container in the garbage, then returned. "Are you almost through?"

"No," Lisa said.

"How much longer is it gonna be?"

"It might be all night."

Hal returned a minute later.

"How am I supposed to sleep with her banging away on that typewriter all night?" Kimberly complained.

"Hey, Lisa," Hal said, "if it'll help out, I'll move the typewriter down to the storeroom for you. Then you can be with Mickey Mouse and all your other little friends."

Lisa stood up and shouted, pointing to the door, "The both of you—get out of here!"

"You see what I put up with?" Kimberly complained.

Lisa ran to her purse and took all the money she had and gave it to Kimberly. "Take it! Just get out! Go to a movie or go bowling or to an arcade—just get out of here and let me work!"

"We don't want your money," Kimberly said self-righteously.

"Hey, wait a minute," Hal said. "Let's not be hasty. How much did she give you?"

Kimberly counted. "Thirty-seven dollars and fifty-four cents."

He reached for the money. "Well, if she offered it, I say let's take it."

They left with the money.

CHAPTER TWO

The night slipped by. Lisa finished the first draft, then started on the second. When she finished that, she went through every equation again to make sure there were no errors. Then she typed the final version. By the time she was finally done, it was six-thirty in the morning.

All that remained to do was the title page. She tried several, then decided on "THE DESCRIPTION OF ALL THE FORCES IN THE UNIVERSE IN TERMS OF A GRAND UNIFIED FIELD THEORY."

For the author of the paper, she first tried *by Lisa Salinger and James Owens, Princeton University.* But then she wondered if an editor might discount the paper because it was written by a woman. Also, the name Lisa seemed too folksy for the most important result in physics in the last half of the twentieth century. She changed it to *L. Salinger and J. Owens, Princeton University.*

Then she pictured Dr. Owens and Sugar in Hawaii strolling on the beach together. Hadn't he said he didn't want his name on any paper she'd write?

She retyped the title page to read *by L. Salinger, Princeton University.*

Seven o'clock—one hour until the post office opened. She went to the kitchen and opened a can of soup and ate it cold out of the can. While she ate, she stood beside her desk and read what she'd written. It was good.

At seven-thirty, she put the manuscript into an envelope and sealed it, then went downstairs to get her clothes from the dryer. She was still wearing the sheets and slippers.

While she was there the girl from the night before came in to finish her laundry. She took one look at Lisa in the sheet, swore, then said, "That's it. I'm moving back on campus."

Upstairs in her apartment Lisa threw the clean clothes on her bed, then picked through the pile to find what she needed to get dressed. While she dressed, she noticed orange splotches on her body from wearing the marked sheet. Ten minutes later, wearing jeans and a hooded sweatshirt, she looked in the mirror. A few orange marks were still visible on her neck.

At eight o'clock she put on her down-filled parka and jogged to the post office. She imagined a distinguished-looking scientist somewhere with his version of her theory putting his manuscript into an envelope and driving leisurely to the post office near his home. She had to beat him.

When she got to the post office, she looked in her purse and remembered she'd given all her money to Kimberly.

No problem, she thought. *I'll cash a check.*

She got in line. In a few minutes, it was her turn. "I need to write a check so I can Xerox something and then mail it."

"We don't accept checks."

"The post office in Fargo, North Dakota, accepts checks."

"Then I suggest you go there. Next?"

"It's just for five dollars."

"Sorry. Next."

"Look, this is very important. I've got to mail this right away."

"Next."

She wandered around the post office, trying to decide what to do. She imagined the distinguished-looking scientist dropping his manuscript into a mail chute. He was going to beat her out unless she did something fast.

She walked up to a man who'd just come in.

"Excuse me. I need five dollars."

"What for?"

"I have to send a paper I wrote to a science journal, and I don't have any money because I gave it all to my roommate and her boyfriend to get them out of the apartment last night so I could finish writing it."

The man laughed and walked away.

A woman came in. Lisa approached her. "I need five dollars. I'll pay you back."

The woman glared at her. "Are you a student?"

"Yes, I am."

"You ought to be ashamed of yourself for panhandling."

Lisa smiled. "It was just a joke. I'm pledging a sorority, and they made me do it."

The woman smiled. "Of course." She walked away.

More people came in. Lisa began sizing them up, looking for an easy touch.

She walked up to a sincere-looking man. "I need five dollars to get food for my baby."

"You have a baby?"

"Yes. Please help me. My husband left me, and there's no food. Please, just a few dollars'll buy formula for my baby."

"Why don't you get a job?"

"I have a rare disease." Lisa showed him her orange-splotched neck.

"Oh, that looks bad," the man said, backing away.

He stopped and reached in his wallet.

"Is the baby all right?"

"So far he is—if I can just get him some medicine too."

"Of course." He gave her ten dollars.

Lisa took the money. "Give me your name, and I'll return the money to you in a couple of days."

She took the money, ran across the street, and waited for him to leave the post office. As soon as he did, she ran back, got change, and Xeroxed her manuscript.

Five minutes later her article was on its way to the editorial office of *Physical Review Letters*.

As she leisurely walked back to her apartment, she smiled and thought about her panhandling in the post office. For a minute someone believed she really did have a child who needed food.

Where was her husband? He worked for the CIA and was away on a dangerous mission. He was ruggedly handsome and yet sensitive too. How had she met him? He'd seen her at a party. He'd been attracted to her from the start. "I love your dress," he'd said. "You look so good in gray."

Those were his very words.

She found it strangely exciting to be someone else.

A month after the new semester began, she received a letter from *Physical Review Letters* containing several suggestions for improving the manuscript. It took her a week to revise it; then she sent it off again. Two weeks later she was advised the paper had been accepted for publication. Because of the importance of her work, they were going to move up the publication date.

There were no more research meetings with Dr. Owens. He ignored her and she avoided him. The rumor on campus was that the divorce was final and that he'd moved in with Sugar Lee.

Her paper was published in May. The day it came out, Dr. Owens and the chairman of the Physics Department, Dr. Remick, burst into a class she was attending and demanded to see her privately. When they got in the hall, Dr. Owens pointed to the article she'd written. "What is the meaning of this?" he snapped.

"Oh, that's just a paper I wrote over Christmas break."

"You had no right to submit this without my approval!" he protested. "We should've worked it out together and then submitted it with my name listed as coauthor."

"You didn't do anything on it. And if you'll remember, you said you didn't want your name on any paper I'd write. Besides, I wanted to get it published before anyone else beat me to it. If you'll recall, you weren't available over Christmas."

"And you didn't have the common courtesy to wait till I got back?"

"I was afraid someone'd get it published before I did."

"You've embarrassed Princeton in front of the whole world."

"Why's that?"

"Because it has Princeton's name on it, that's why," he grumbled. "Besides that, your whole approach is ridiculous."

"The people who reviewed it didn't think so," she said.

Dr. Owens leaned into her. "Apparently you don't understand the ethics of university research. I'm filing a complaint with the graduate dean. When I'm through with you, young lady, you'll be lucky to still be in school."

Dr. Remick added, "This is very serious. We're having a staff meeting today to decide what to do. I'd like you to wait in another room in case we need to speak to you."

During the meeting, she was forced to sit in an office next door, like a naughty child awaiting punishment. An hour later, Dr. Remick came to see her. "We want you to send a letter to the editor, stating that the paper was sent prematurely and that it's currently undergoing revision, under the direction of Dr. Owens. Then when it's resubmitted for publication, we'd like it to have Dr. Owens's name as a co-author."

"The paper doesn't need revision," she said.

"Your scholarship hangs in the balance. And unless you cooperate, we'll have no choice but to terminate you as a student."

"I'll think about it. Give me a little time."

"All right. See me tomorrow morning at eight o'clock sharp."

That night on the Johnny Carson show, a famous astronomer was a guest. "Johnny, you might be interested that a search for unity in the universe, which has been going on since man first looked into the night sky, might be over. Recently a paper was published by a physicist at Princeton that shows that all the forces in the universe can be represented by one set of equations. If the theory proves correct, then we will, for the first time, be able to say that we really do understand the universe in which we live."

"Who came up with this theory?"

"I can't remember the name, but if he's from Princeton, he must be very good."

Johnny grinned. "I'd like to meet him. If he understands the universe, maybe he can help me find a place to park in the NBC lot."

The next morning when she entered the physics building, she noticed a TV crew standing in the hall near the graduate carrels.

The interviewer walked up to her. "One of the students says you're L. Salinger."

"Yes."

"You're a woman," he said.

She stared back at him. "That's right."

As he interviewed her on camera, a crowd of graduate students and faculty began to gather.

"As I understand it, what you've done is to bring harmony to the universe. Is that right?"

"Well, in a mathematical sense, that's true. I've developed a set of interlocking equations that unify all the forces in the universe. All that we see, from the very small to the very large, is now part of an elegant pattern predicted by these equations."

"Is it true that Einstein spent many years of his life searching for the very thing you've come up with?"

She smiled. "Yes, that's true."

"Where exactly were you when you made your discovery?"

"I was in a laundry room washing clothes."

"A laundry room?"

"That's right. I was watching the clothes bounce around in the dryer. I guess I dozed off, and when I woke up I had the answer."

"I hope you don't mind me saying this, but you look too young to be the successor to Albert Einstein."

"Well, Einstein was only twenty-eight years old when he came up with his theory of relativity."

"And how old are you?"

"I'm twenty-one."

"I notice you brought a sack with you this morning. What's in the sack?"

"My lunch."

"And what does the successor to Einstein have for lunch?"

She shrugged. "I really don't think anyone cares about that."

"I think you'll find people will want to know a great deal about you now."

She started pulling things out of the sack. "Well, for lunch I always have an apple . . . and some yogurt . . . and in this Tupperware container is my wheat and alfalfa sprouts." She pulled out what looked like a bird's nest.

"You eat that for lunch?" the interviewer asked.

"Oh yes. Every day."

"I see. Tell me, is there a man in your life?"

"No."

"If there was one, I wonder what he'd think about

your discovery. How does a man deal with a woman who's smarter than Albert Einstein?"

"I can't answer that question."

"Dr. Salinger . . ."

Out of the corner of her eye, she saw Dr. Owens come to the edge of the crowd.

"I'm not really a doctor. I'm a graduate student."

"What can we call you then?" the interviewer asked.

"Lisa, I guess."

"Lisa, is there anyone who should share in your discovery?"

"Well, in a discovery like this, one always stands on the shoulders of giants. There's been much work done previously that helped me arrive at my equations."

"Is there anyone here at Princeton you would consider directly responsible for helping make possible your discovery?"

She paused. "Well yes, there really is." She glanced over to Dr. Owens, who was self-consciously straightening his tie.

"And who might that be?"

She could feel the anticipation of the faculty.

"Sugar Lee."

Dr. Owens stormed away.

A few minutes later the faculty began another emergency session.

An hour later Dr. Remick visited her again. "You've got to give Dr. Owens some credit for your work."

"Why? He said the paper's wrong."

"We went over your paper carefully in our meeting. It may have some merit, although we still maintain it could have been greatly improved if you'd only worked with us on it."

"I like it the way it is."

"What's wrong with you?" he asked impatiently.

"Dr. Owens didn't have anything to do with what I put in that paper. He was off frolicking on the beach with his Sugar Baby while his wife and family struggled through the worst Christmas of their lives. It's the same thing my father did to our family. Dr. Owens deserted his family. Why should I reward him for that?"

"That's a personal matter. We can't have graduate students publishing independently."

"I won't anymore."

"We'll give you two days to think about it, and then you're through here."

She spent the rest of the day in the library. As she walked home for supper, she noticed a van from a TV station outside the apartment. Through the open door of her apartment, she saw a woman interviewing Kimberly. She continued walking quietly past her apartment to the storeroom, where she lay down on the cot. She looked at a large cobweb in the corner and listened to the sounds of people in apartments preparing supper.

She fell asleep.

Suddenly the door opened. "And this is the storeroom where she sometimes works," Kimberly announced cheerily. Bright lights flooded the room. Lisa sat up and faced a TV camera.

"Oh, here she is now," Kimberly said proudly.

"Dr. Salinger, could we have a word with you?"

A woman sat beside her on the cot and touched her on the shoulder. "We're so proud of you!"

Lisa yawned. "Who is?"

"The women of America. We want to thank you for showing that a woman can be as great a genius as any man."

"You're welcome," she mumbled, still not quite awake.

"Your roommate says you come here sometimes. Exactly why do you spend time here?" The camera loomed above them.

Kimberly, off-camera, vigorously shook her head, mouthing the words *my mother*.

Lisa understood. "I come here to meditate," she said.

"And does it help to be here among all this?" The

camera panned the suitcases and trunks and ancient ironing boards and broken bicycles.

"Oh, yes, it matches the Karma of the universe," Lisa said, intentionally sounding mysterious.

"Do you think it significant that a woman should come up with a theory that dwarfs what even Albert Einstein did?"

She paused. "I don't understand the question."

"In light of the women's movement, I mean."

"The universe has no gender," Lisa said.

The interviewer started to gush. "*The universe has no gender.* That is *so* profound. I know you're going to be an inspiration to every woman in America who aspires to greatness. You may not know it now, but you're going to be a symbol to women everywhere. Lisa, what would you like to say to the sixty million people who will watch this?"

"Sixty million people?" She nervously tried to adjust her hair with her fingers.

The woman stopped her. "It's okay, you're fine the way you are. Lisa, what do you have to say to the housewife in Schenectady, to the flight attendant in Los Angeles, to the business woman on her way home in New York City, to the teenager studying around the TV . . . what would you like to say to the women of America?"

"Well, uh, I don't know. I mean, I guess I'd say . . . hang in there . . ."

"Lisa, do you have a philosophy of life?"

"A philosophy of life?" she stammered.

"Yes."

She nervously bit her lip. "Well, sure, I guess so."

"Tell us what it is."

"Well . . . I guess it's . . ." She paused, trying desperately to think of something. "Well, it's . . . You gotta have a dream, if you don't have a dream, how you gonna make a dream come true?"

The interviewer hugged her. "*You gotta have a dream*—what a message of hope. I want to thank you for showing us what we can become. You've given us hope, and, as a woman I'd like to thank you from the bottom of my heart."

"Okay, sure, you bet," Lisa said.

The phone rang all night. Lisa had an offer from the American Yogurt Institute to do TV commercials. She had a call from Phil Donahue's staff inviting her to appear on his show. She was invited to give a paper at the meeting of the American Physical Society next month. Two writers called and offered to do her life story.

Hal sat and watched all this happening. "We're sitting on a gold mine! This is definitely bigger than dimpled golf balls."

At eleven-thirty, the vice-president of Princeton called. "I strongly suggest that you credit Dr. Owens as your co-author."

"I won't do it. He didn't help me write the paper."

"Get yourself a good lawyer then."

"Why?"

"Tonight Dr. Owens showed me proof that you stole his ideas and published them as your own. He's willing to carry this through the courts. You'll need a lawyer."

"I can't afford a lawyer."

"Then cooperate with Dr. Owens. Is it so much to ask for you to include him as a co-author?"

"Yes, it is. It's not his paper. He didn't have a thing to do with it. And why did he wait until now to say they were his equations?"

"He said he was trying to protect you, but now that he sees you mean to take full credit for it, he has to protect his rights."

"He's lying!"

"That will be for the ethics committee to decide. We're having a hearing next week."

CHAPTER THREE

The next week in *Time* and *Newsweek*, the controversy between Lisa and Dr. Owens was discussed. But the disagreement really came to a head at the ethics committee meeting, which the major news networks covered.

Dr. Owens was called as a witness. He showed a November entry in his notebook containing Lisa's equations.

"Dr. Owens," a member of the ethics committee asked politely, "what you're saying is that Ms. Salinger took your equations and published them as her own."

"Yes, I'm afraid that's exactly what she did."

Lisa jumped up. "That's a bold-faced lie!"

"Ms. Salinger, please sit down. You'll have your chance later." He turned to Dr. Owens. "How would she get access to these equations?"

"We talked about them in our weekly research meetings."

"And so she knew about your equations as early as November?"

"That's right. My intention was that we'd work on them together and get the bugs out, so to speak, before sending a paper off for publication. But she must've seen their value and gone ahead, trying to claim all the credit for herself. In a way I feel sorry for her. She's young, and she made a mistake in judgment. I hold nothing against her personally. I just want the record set straight about where the equations actually came from."

Lisa gritted her teeth.

She was called next.

"Ms. Salinger, you claim the ideas in your paper were completely original with you, and that Dr. Owens had no part in them?"

"That's right."

"But you just saw the equations in his research notebook, dated November 4 of last year."

"Yes."

"How do you explain that?"

"Simple—he copied them in his notebook after my paper came out."

"That's a serious accusation. Did Dr. Owens ever discuss these equations with you in your research meetings?"

"Of course not."

"I see. Was there anyone else in those meetings besides the two of you?"

"No."

"Dr. Owens has a fine record here at Princeton. It's hard for me to believe he'd resort to something as unethical as you're suggesting. How will we ever be able to decide if your allegation is true?"

Lisa paused. "I haven't told anyone about this before, but the fact is I tape recorded all our research meetings."

Dr. Owens momentarily winced but then recovered. "She's lying—she never taped anything."

"How could you tape a meeting without Dr. Owens knowing?"

Lisa picked up the book in her lap and opened it to show the hidden tape recorder.

Dr. Owens and his lawyer had a private conference. A reporter for the *New York Times* ran out to phone her newspaper. Lisa looked vacantly into the TV camera and smiled smugly in what was later described as a Mona Lisa look—very understated.

Dr. Owens's lawyer stood up. "We can't allow the playing of any tape-recorded evidence until it's first been verified by audio experts that the tape has not been altered by Ms. Salinger. A test like that might take several months."

The ethics committee members stared at each other, at a loss to know what to do.

Lisa didn't wait—she started the tape running. It was Dr. Owens's voice. "Have you come up with anything positive?"

"Not really. Do you have any suggestions?"

"No, just keep at it."

As the tape played, Dr. Owens's lawyer complained loudly. It was difficult to hear anything over the noise. Lisa backed the tape up again, placed the recorder next to a microphone, and started it over again. Now it bellowed out across the room.

Dr. Owens's lawyer shouted, "If you allow her to play this, we'll bring a lawsuit against each member of this committee for defamation of character."

The chairman gave up. "Ms. Salinger, turn off the tape please."

Lisa shouted, "What's wrong with you people? You said you wanted proof. Well, here it is. Listen to it!"

The chairman, realizing that Princeton now had a scandal being covered by the networks, suddenly turned on her. "You're out of order! Please return to your seat."

She blew up. "What do you mean, I'm out of order?" She pointed an accusing finger at Dr. Owens. "He's accused me of lying and cheating and being dishonest! But that's exactly what he's done! And I've got proof! So why am I out of order?"

Dr. Owens's lawyer protested. "She's already said enough for us to sue her. If you want to protect her, as well as this committee, from further lawsuits, as well as save Princeton further embarrassment, I suggest you dismiss this hearing immediately. This matter should be tried in a court of law, not in an ethics committee meeting."

The chairman declared the meeting closed.

"WHY AREN'T THERE ANY WOMEN ON THIS COMMITTEE?" Lisa raged.

That week Lisa Salinger and Sugar Lee made the cover of *National Enquirer.* Sugar was shown posing in her dancing leotards, while Lisa was pictured shouting at the committee chairman. The article was titled "The Restless Women in Dr. Owens's Life."

During the summer Lisa tried to resume her graduate studies, but it was nearly impossible.

The faculty, still angry about Dr. Owens being humiliated, treated her with icy scorn. No matter what she did, it was wrong. If she tried to be inconspicuous, they told her they expected more from her. When she became assertive, they interpreted it as an attempt to undermine their position as professors. Every physics question she asked in class sent fear through her teachers, since they assumed she knew the answer and was only trying to trap them.

Advised by his attorney that the best defense is a good offense, Dr. Owens brought a lawsuit against Lisa for defamation of character. That meant she had to get herself a lawyer. Her lawyer, a woman, suggested that Lisa initiate a countersuit against Dr. Owens. The tape was sent to a lab in Washington, D.C., to be analyzed.

As long as the case pended, Dr. Owens's job and reputation were preserved. Therefore, to Lisa the case seemed to drag on forever. In order to pay for the ever-mounting legal fees, she was forced to go on the lecture circuit on weekends, much to the delight of Hal and Kimberly, who began functioning as her agents.

As much as she disliked Hal, Lisa found him a good

manager of money. Most of all, with him and Kimberly helping, she didn't have to worry about any travel or business details.

She spoke nearly every weekend. Because of her accomplishments in science and also the publicity resulting from the Salinger-Owens confrontation, she spoke to many feminist groups throughout the country.

Because of Hal's eagerness for them to get the forty thousand dollars she had been offered, she became the TV spokesperson for yogurt, doing three sixty-second spots for national TV.

Hal and Kimberly kept on the lookout for peripheral money-making concepts. "We've contacted the Mattel people about a Lisa doll," Kimberly reported one day as the three of them rode a plane to Chicago, where Lisa was scheduled to speak. "They like the concept—it'll be the industry's first feminist doll. They figure it'll start a whole new trend. Barbie dolls are out anyway—they're sexist, and besides, nobody looks like that anyway. With the Lisa doll, the clothes aren't that splashy, but where they'll make their money is in Phase Two sales—the Lisa doll traveling in a space shuttle, the Lisa doll presiding over a corporate board meeting, the Lisa doll picketing a nuclear reactor, the Lisa doll sitting in the oval office. What do you think?"

She looked up from a physics paper she was writing. "I don't care. Do anything you want—just don't bother me about it."

Hal grinned. "We're talking big bucks here, kid. Just stick with us, and we'll make you rich."

"How about this?" Kimberly said. "A designer dress with your equations on it."

"Sure, whatever you say," she mumbled, wishing she were already in her hotel room so she could be alone to work.

"If you'd like, we can have it done in gray for you," Kimberly said.

The auditorium was filled with ten thousand women. Lisa stood in the wings waiting to be introduced. Hal and Kimberly were next to her.

"Just read it the way I wrote it, and you won't have any trouble," Kimberly said.

They heard the introduction booming over the auditorium. "Our next speaker needs no introduction. She's a distinguished scientist. She recently published a landmark paper in which she unified all the forces in the universe into one set of equations. Not only has she contributed to science, she is also becoming a leading spokesperson for the women's movement. It was she who first coined the now famous line 'The universe has no gender.' It is now my pleasure to introduce the recently named winner of the American Physical Society's Halverson-Smith Award for outstanding theoretical research, Ms. Lisa Salinger."

They gave her a standing ovation as she walked onstage.

"You're all very kind," she said when the noise died down. "It's wonderful to be here and feel your warmth and love, and to know that in a real sense, whether we come from north or south, east or west, we are all sisters . . .

"The human mind escapes any efforts to be limited. Any human mind is a national resource, and the minds and courage of women everywhere must be recognized for the great potential we possess to alter the world in which we live. Excellence, like the universe, has no gender."

She continued for several minutes.

". . . In conclusion, let me close with something that has meant a great deal to me. During those dark days when I wrestled to find the secret of the forces in the universe, this thought buoyed me up. It's from the musical *South Pacific*. It goes like this, 'Happy thoughts, keep thinking happy thoughts, think about things you'd like to do. You gotta have a dream, if you don't got a dream, how you gonna make a dream come true?' Thank you very much."

She started offstage, but the applause was deafening. She paused and lifted up her arms into a V. The image was captured by Hal and Kimberly. They made plans to market it on T-shirts.

At the January meeting of the American Physical Society she chaired a session dealing with the Salinger theory. During that same meeting she proposed several experiments that might be used to validate her theory.

In May the lawsuit between her and Dr. Owens finally went to court. The trial made national news. Dr. Owens's lawyers managed to have Lisa's tape thrown out as evidence. The only thing that saved her was the appearance of the girl who'd loaned her a Magic Marker in the laundry room, as well as Hal and Kimberly's testimony.

In the end Lisa's name was cleared of all charges. The next day Dr. Owens's lawyer called to ask if Lisa's countersuit might be settled out of court. Dr. Owens and Lisa, along with their lawyers, scheduled a meeting.

"I've just been fired at Princeton," Dr. Owens said bitterly. "Sugar left me to go to California because a movie producer saw her picture in the *National Enquirer* and wants to make her a star. My ex-wife won't talk to me, and my kids hate me. So what else do you want from me?"

"Five hundred thousand dollars," she said coolly.

He blanched.

His lawyer cleared his throat. "My client has no income and no assets. I think you're being unreasonable."

"Maybe you're right," Lisa said. "Tell you what—I'm such an old softie, I'll settle for two hundred and fifty thousand dollars."

She enjoyed watching Dr. Owens squirm. But ten minutes later, she realized how tired she was of legal battles, and she dropped all legal action against Dr. Owens.

In June a physicist from Japan who two years earlier had won a Nobel Prize published a paper reporting experimental results that agreed with predictions made from Lisa's theory. A few days later she was named a recipient of the Sullivan Award from the American Association for the Advancement of Science.

One morning she was wakened by a bright flash of light. She looked up to see Kimberly standing over her with a camera.

"What are you doing?" Lisa complained.

"I'm taking a class in photography, and I needed to take some pictures. You looked so cute there sleeping. I hope you don't mind."

"I mind, Kimberly. You woke me up."

"Sorry."

A few days later she was in her robe eating breakfast. Kimberly called out her name. She turned around and Kimberly took another picture.

For the next week every time she turned around, Kimberly was taking a picture.

The last straw was when she sat on the edge of the bathtub, her hair dripping wet, wearing a tattered bathrobe, clipping her toenails. Kimberly opened the door and took a picture.

"Kimberly, that's it! Any more pictures and I'm breaking your camera!"

"That was the last one—I promise."

Two months later, in August, Brent Peters, a graduate student, approached her as she studied in the library. "Hey, how's our cover girl?" he asked.

"What?"

He tossed a copy of *People* magazine on her desk. There, on the cover, was Lisa Salinger mopping the kitchen floor. Below the picture it read, "The Woman Who Topped Einstein: A Fascinating Account by Her Roommate."

Self-consciously she placed a textbook over the magazine to cover up her picture.

He laughed. "I'm afraid that won't do the trick. There's thousands of copies on newsstands all over the country."

She stared in shock at her picture.

"The article's not so bad," he said. "I'll show you—okay?"

She grimly nodded her head.

He opened the magazine to the first picture, showing her asleep on the cot in the storeroom. The caption read: "Lisa often comes to the storeroom and meditates. Sometimes she talks to mice. (The mice are not shown.)"

The second picture showed the broken Cardiac Arrest record. "When she's working, she has a violent temper. Once when I had a few friends in for popcorn after a basketball game, Lisa stomped in, broke the record we were playing, then marched back to the storeroom. I guess she prefers the company of mice."

The third picture was of the bed sheets covered with equations. The caption began, "In coming up with her theory, she first wrote her equations on two sheets, then wore them for days at a time. Nobody knows why she did this."

The fourth picture showed Lisa wearing her sheepskin coat. "She wears this coat to bed when it's cold."

The fifth picture looked as if she had a bird's nest in her mouth. The caption read: "Lisa likes health food. This is what it's like sitting across from her at supper."

Lisa closed the magazine. Tears ran down her cheeks.

"Hey, take it easy," Brent said. "It's not the end of the world. In seven days, there'll be another issue, and nobody'll remember you anymore."

He reached out and took her hand. "Hey, cheer up.

How about if I take you out for a movie tonight? It'd give us both a chance to relax. How about it?"

He seemed sincere. She gratefully accepted the invitation.

After the movie he took her to his place to show her his computer. She sat down and turned it on.

"Would you like a drink?" he asked.

"Just some coffee, if you have any."

"You sure you don't want any wine?"

"No, thanks."

He put on soft music. In a few minutes he returned with her coffee. He sat next to her and tried to put his arm around her. She moved away.

He smiled. "Hey, loosen up, girl. Don't be so tense."

"I don't like a guy to assume I'm his property just because I go out with him once."

"I understand. Hey look, Lisa, I've been watching you for quite a while. You know, you really are pretty. Hey, how about looking at me when I talk? Here, let me turn this off." He turned off the computer. "That's better. Now come over and sit down and let's talk."

"I'd rather talk here."

"Lisa, do you ever get lonely?"

She jumped up. "I really have to go home now."

"What's your hurry? Answer my question—do you ever get lonely?"

"Sure, so what?"

"There's no point in both of us being lonely, is there?"

"Do you have a phone? I need to call a taxi."

"Don't go. I won't bite you."

"You make me nervous."

"Hey, relax. Sit down. We'll talk physics. I'll stay clear over here."

She sat down again.

"I need some help," he said.

"With what?"

"I flunked my graduate comprehensive exam."

"Okay, I'll help you study for it next time."

"That's not what I had in mind. I was just a few points below passing. Talk the department into saying I passed."

"How?"

"Threaten to leave if they don't pass me. You're important now, because of all the good publicity you're giving the department. Everyone wants to go to Princeton because of you. The administration doesn't want you to go someplace else. Look, all I'm asking is just to mention that you'd be unhappy if I wasn't allowed to continue toward my Ph.D."

"Is that the reason you asked me out tonight?"

"Of course not. I just want us to be good friends."

"I'm sorry, but I can't ask them to pass you."

He tried to kiss her, but she pulled away. "No."

He stopped acting. "All right. Forget it. I'll get your coat."

A minute later he tossed the coat on the couch. "The phone's over there," he said. "Call yourself a taxi."

"Our friendship's over so soon?" she asked sarcastically.

"What did you expect? You think anybody's gonna be nice to you now unless they want something? Face it, Lisa, you're a commodity now, like toothpaste. You're billed as the next Einstein. That's going to haunt you for the rest of your life. Get used to people exploiting you."

She phoned for a cab, then put on her coat.

"Don't go away feeling so smug," he said. "The only reason you rejected me was because I'm not smooth enough at it, but there'll be others looking for science favors, and they'll get whatever they want from you. From now on, every smile you get will have a hook attached to it."

A few minutes later she got out of the cab and walked up the stairs to her apartment. Nobody was home. She put on her nightgown and went to bed.

After she'd been asleep for an hour, the door to the

apartment flew open. Kimberly and Hal bounced in, followed by four others. "She's here!"

They'd all been drinking. They were standing over her grinning.

"Hey, I saw you in *People* magazine! I loved all those crazy pictures."

"Hal, get these idiots out of here!"

A girl went to the closet and pulled out one of Lisa's dresses. "Can you believe this?" she laughed.

"It's so awful!" another girl agreed.

"Hal! Kimberly! I don't want them in here!"

"Does she have her sheepskin pajamas on?" a guy asked.

"In August?" a girl replied. "Are you crazy?"

"Well, what does she wear in the summer?"

"Get out of here!" Lisa yelled, pulling the sheets up to her chin.

One of them laughed. "Boy, she does have a temper, doesn't she!"

"Hal, get 'em out of here!" she shouted.

"Sure, Hon, just a minute . . ."

She jumped out of bed, grabbed her pillow, and began hitting Hal as hard as she could with it. "Don't you ever call me 'Hon' again!" she yelled at him. Then she ran out of the apartment.

A minute later she sat on the cot in the storeroom, still breathing hard, trying to control her anger. She wiped the perspiration off her face and tried to calm down. She lay down. She could still hear her heart beating. She concentrated on taking deep breaths. In a few minutes she calmed down. She lay there staring at the dark ceiling.

And then she realized she was hearing other people breathe too. Terrified, she sat up and looked around.

There sitting cross-legged on the floor were two men and a woman, all of them staring at the pile of junk that filled the room.

"How long you gotta stare at this stuff before you get feeling good?" one of them asked.

Lisa screamed and ran out.

A minute later she knocked on Mike Anderson's door. It was late at night. He came to the door.

"Can I come in?" she begged.

"Sure." He opened the door. "Here, sit down."

She sat down woodenly.

"What's wrong?"

She broke down crying. He sat by her and waited as the tears tumbled out. A few minutes later she was composed enough to tell him what had happened.

After she finished, he and his roommate left to go run everyone out of the storeroom.

In a few minutes they returned. "They're gone now. You can go back if you want. Be sure and lock the door."

"Thanks."

"Anytime."

"What am I going to do? Everyone's using me. I don't like it."

"Have you thought about transferring to BYU?"

"It'd be the same there."

"Look, here's last year's yearbook. Look it over. See what you think. If you decide to go, we can write my cousin. She works in records there, and she could tell you what you have to do to get enrolled. I'll give you her name and address. You never know, Lisa. It might turn out okay for you there. And it's just about time for fall semester to start."

Lisa sat in the apartment and looked at the BYU yearbook while Mike and his roommate studied. She felt at home with them, comfortable and safe.

Of course, she couldn't go to BYU. She couldn't go anywhere, because it was true what Brent said—she was now a commodity to be marketed. She was a brand-name person. No matter where Lisa Salinger went, people would eventually impose on her privacy.

And then the most ridiculous idea popped into her mind.

The next morning, after Kimberly left for school, Lisa made reservations for a flight to Salt Lake City, then packed two suitcases. She sat in front of her bookshelf trying to decide which books to take but eventually realized she couldn't take any of them, because they all had her name on the inside cover. She needed to leave Lisa Salinger behind when she left the apartment.

She sat in front of her computer and turned it on. It was four years old, ancient now compared to the new models, but it had a certain charm. It was like an old friend. And in a short time it was going to help buy her freedom. She packed the computer in two boxes.

She called a taxi, then sat down to type a note.

Kimberly,
  I'm going away for a while. You won't be able to find me, but I'll be all right. Tell people I need time to be by myself.

Lisa

She left the note taped on the refrigerator.

There was a knock on the door. It was the cab driver. She opened the door for him. He picked up her things and headed downstairs.

On her way out, she saw Mike's BYU yearbook on the table. She took it with her to study on the plane.

Six hours later she landed in Utah.

I've seen your face some-
where before," Mike's cousin Tanya said. They sat in an
office cubicle in the administration building at Brigham
Young University.

Lisa turned to shield her face. "I look like a lot of
people."

"And you're a friend of Mike's?"

"Yes, I met him in New Jersey. I told him I was going
west, and he said to be sure and look up his favorite
cousin, so here I am."

"What're you doing out here in Utah?"

"Just passing through. How about if we have lunch
together? My treat."

"Sounds great, but I've still got half an hour to work
before lunch."

"I'll wait. Is that a computer?"

"Well, it's a computer terminal. We use computers so
much these days."

"How interesting. Suppose a student sends in an
application form, how would the information be pro-
cessed?"

"I'll show you. First I have to enter the access code."

Lisa's pleasant expression momentarily fell away as
she concentrated on memorizing the access code.

An application form flashed on the screen.

"My, my," Lisa said with a deceptively innocent smile.

That afternoon Lisa used her computer and the phone to connect herself with a computer at BYU. She entered the proper access codes, and in a few minutes she was looking at the form for new students.

She felt giddy. She was about to create a person.

Who hasn't wondered what might have happened if, at certain of life's crossroads, they'd taken a different path? For Lisa in high school, the path had been calculus, physics, and chemistry. There was no time for boys, or parties, or being young.

This time it would be different. It had to be. If she kept the same personality, sooner or later she'd be discovered.

LAST NAME:

Her theory had introduced something now called the Salinger Field. She decided to adopt the name Fields.

LAST NAME: FIELDS

FIRST NAME:

Her middle name was Dawn, and she'd always liked the name. She decided to become Dawn Lisa.

FIRST NAME: DAWN

MIDDLE NAME: LISA

DATE OF BIRTH:

She was twenty-two years old. Since she'd never had a chance to enjoy being a teenager, why not try it again? She giggled and entered a date that would make her nineteen years old.

ADDRESS:

Dawn couldn't come from North Dakota too. She picked up a motel map, closed her eyes, and placed a finger on the map. When she opened her eyes, her finger was resting on Grand Island, Nebraska. She called long distance to get the phone number and address of a Burger King drive-in, which she listed as her home address.

HIGH SCHOOL TRANSCRIPT:

Dawn Fields had taken chorus, social studies, typing,

and some business-related courses. No science for Dawn, and only the barest minimum of math. She'd been in drama club, and one year she had been chosen as the homecoming queen.

MAJOR COURSE OF STUDY:

She closed her eyes and pictured Dawn in high school. Dawn loved music. Some said that Dawn always had a song in her heart.

MAJOR COURSE OF STUDY: MUSIC EDUCATION

CHURCH AFFILIATION: (CHECK ONE)
LDS   OTHER

She noticed it was cheaper to be LDS, so she checked that.

Bit by bit she created a Dawn.

The next day she registered at BYU as Dawn Fields. She spent the afternoon at the Provo Public Library reading about the Mormon church and also about Grand Island, Nebraska, in the *Encyclopedia Britannica.* She'd always had great faith in the *Encyclopedia Britannica,* and after she'd studied what it had to say, she felt more than adequately prepared.

That afternoon she took a cab to Robison Hall, where she'd assigned herself from the list of last-minute vacancies provided by the computer.

She found her apartment and knocked.

"It's open!" someone yelled.

She walked in. There was a long hall with bedrooms going off on either side. A girl wearing a robe stuck her head out of the bathroom. "All right, who used up all my shampoo?" She wiped the water off her face with a towel.

Nobody answered.

"C'mon, somebody did."

"You can use mine," another girl called out.

"I can't use yours! I need mine. Mine has flex conditioners. You all know I need flex conditioners. Last night there was just enough for today. So which one of you used it and left an empty bottle for me?"

No response.

"I just got out of the shower. Will one of you go to the store and get me a new bottle?"

Someone turned on a stereo loud enough to cover up her voice.

"All right! This is the last time I leave my shampoo in the bathroom! And you just see if I ever let any of you use anything of mine again. Do you hear me? Now I have to dry myself off, get dressed, walk all the way to the store, buy a shampoo with flex conditioners, which I shouldn't have to buy at all, mind you, if somebody hadn't used it, then come back and shampoo my hair. Isn't anybody listening? Doesn't anybody care about me?"

"I'll go to the store for you," Lisa said from the shadows of the hall.

The girl jumped. "Where did you come from?"

"Grand Island, Nebraska."

"I mean what are you doing here?"

"They said you have a vacancy."

"You gave me such a scare. I didn't see you standing there."

"I don't mind being unnoticed."

"My room's the one with the vacancy, so I guess you'll be rooming with me. My name's Natalie Foster."

"My name is Dawn Fields." It was the first time she'd said it in conversation.

"You're kidding."

Dawn frowned. "How did you know?"

"I just meant I have a sister named Dawn."

"Oh."

"Look, could you really get me some shampoo? I need French Mist Balsam with Flex Conditioners for Normal Hair. Make sure you get the right kind. The bottle is kind of a light green."

"Sure."

"What a pal. I'll shave my legs while you're gone."

As Dawn walked to the store, a girl passed her on the sidewalk. "Hi," the girl said pleasantly.

Dawn looked around to see if the girl was talking to her or somebody else.

The girl passed by.

Twenty steps later Dawn yelled back, "Hello!"

The girl stopped and turned around. "Hello."

"Hello," Dawn called out again.

The girl shrugged and continued on her way.

Strange people, Dawn thought.

She entered the store with its colorful variety of homemade signs advertising weekly specials. While she was there, she decided to buy some things she needed. She got a cart and started down the aisle.

A tall, muscular athlete was standing in the aisle. She passed him.

"Hi," he said.

She decided he was talking to her. "Hi," she said.

"Decisions, decisions," he said, looking at three shelves of cereal.

She decided he meant he was having a hard time picking a brand of cereal. She named her favorite kind of cereal. "Cream of Wheat."

He nodded his head knowingly. "That's so true— Word of Wisdom."

She wondered what that meant.

He placed the Cream of Wheat in his cart. "Wheat for man, corn for the ox," he said, continuing down the aisle.

She paused and tried to figure it out. How few oxen you see these days, she thought to herself.

She was disappointed in the *Encyclopedia Britannica.* They were usually so thorough, and yet in discussing the Mormons they'd never mentioned oxen.

A few minutes later she approached the checkout stand with the shampoo as well as some sprouts and seven containers of yogurt.

A girl stood in line in front of her, talking to her

roommate. ". . . so Alan invited me to the dance on Friday night, but I couldn't go because I had this date set up with Greg, but I really like Alan, and I didn't want to discourage him, so I asked him if we could get together on Saturday, but then I remembered I had a date with Chet that night, but it was okay because Alan was busy then too, so we decided Alan'd come by for me Saturday morning and we'd go water skiing. But the only trouble was I've never gone water skiing before, and so I asked Dave if he'd take me out tomorrow and teach me. So it's working out all right."

Dawn gazed in awe at the girl. She was tall and had long brown hair. Her face was perfect, and yet her beauty seemed so effortless.

A guy walked up to the girl. "Hi, Shauna."

"Dave! We were just talking about you."

"You were, huh? What about?"

"Wouldn't you like to know?" Shauna said.

Dawn leaned forward intently. The conversation wasn't much, but it was spectacular to see how Shauna used her face. It was like a neon sign flashing, "Hey, everybody! Here I am!"

Shauna tilted her head and smiled. Dawn decided it was the teeth and the eyes. What did she do with her eyes to make them so appealing?

Dawn looked at Dave. He lit up being around Shauna.

"Well, I wouldn't be too sure about that," Shauna said, flashing her appealing smile again.

"Oh, you wouldn't, huh?" Dave teased.

Dawn wondered how many calories Shauna used in a day just to keep her face running.

"Well, you'll just have to wait and see," Shauna said, lowering her eyes and then looking up with a sly grin.

"Okay for you," Dave said with a smile.

Dawn leaned forward, entirely engrossed by the interplay of words and body language. She accidentally bumped her cart into Shauna's cart. Shauna turned around, smiled at Dawn, then turned her attention back to Dave.

When Shauna left, it was like someone turned out all the lights in the store.

Dawn advanced to the checkout stand. There on the cover of *Time* was a picture of Lisa Salinger. The caption read "Lisa Salinger—Einstein's Successor?"

Dawn casually picked up a copy of *Seventeen* and placed it over the stack of *Time* magazines.

She was next in line. "Hi there," the man at the check-out counter said. "Trying the Salinger Diet?"

"What?" she mumbled.

"You know that gal who's smarter than Einstein? Well, she lives on yogurt and sprouts. You ought to read about her in *Time* this week. You know, you look a little bit like her."

"I'm not Lisa Salinger."

"Oh sure, I know that—she'd never come here. It's just that you look a little bit like her, the way you do your hair, and your glasses. But they say she's wacko, not like you at all."

"Thank you," she said, grateful to Hal and Kimberly for having created a cartoon character out of Lisa Salinger. "I think I've changed my mind about the yogurt and sprouts." She took it all back and picked up donuts, potato chips, and apples.

Returning to the apartment, she knocked on the bathroom door.

Natalie let her in. "Where have you been?"

"I picked up a few things of my own."

Natalie took the shampoo. "Well, anyway, thanks for going. I'll be out in a few minutes to help you get settled. Our room is the second one on the left."

Dawn unpacked, then went to the kitchen to put her groceries away. Two girls, dressed in warm-up suits, were sitting at the table, talking.

"Are you a new roommate?"

"Yes, I'm Dawn Fields."

"Hey, great. I'm Tami Randall." She was an energetic blonde with her hair in a ponytail.

The other girl's name was Jan Roberts. She had vivid red hair and freckles.

They talked for a few minutes. Tami was a sophomore majoring in drama. She was from Stillwater, Oklahoma. Talking to her was like watching a fireworks display. Her creative mind started on one thought and then suddenly exploded into a hundred peripheral ideas. Dawn wondered if, as a child, she'd been hyperactive. In five minutes, she did three impersonations: Mr. T, Margaret Thatcher, ending up with Joan Rivers, "Can we talk?"

Jan was a sophomore in psychology. She might be overlooked in a crowd, especially in any group containing Tami, but she was good-natured and friendly.

Dawn noticed Jan watching her carefully. She wondered if she was being analyzed the way psychology majors often do to their friends.

In a few minutes the two roommates left to go jogging. Dawn sat at the kitchen table and ate an apple.

A girl came in with a pizza. She had short brown hair and was several pounds overweight.

"Hi, I'm Dawn Fields. I'll be rooming with Natalie."

The girl smiled. "Welcome aboard. I'm Robyn. Want any pizza?"

"No, thanks."

"I can't eat it all, that's for sure. I should've got a small, but they were having a special on family size."

"Sure."

"I've been on a diet. This is the first meal I've had for two days."

"Then you must be hungry."

"A little." She took a large bite.

Dawn left the kitchen. It was the last anyone saw of the pizza.

On her left was an open bedroom. A girl was practicing Spanish to herself. Dawn walked in. The room looked like a museum, with a bright red Indian blanket on the wall, as well as several copper plates.

"Hi," Dawn said.

"I'm sorry. I didn't see you. Are you Natalie's new roommate?"

"Yes. I'm Dawn Fields. I'm from Grand Island, Nebraska."

"I'm Paula Clauson."

"You must like copper," she said.

"Oh, those? I went on a mission to Chile, and they're just some of the things I picked up while I was down there."

Dawn imagined a quaint Spanish mission in a small village where Catholic fathers had a little gift shop and sold homemade craft items. "You went to a mission and bought all this? The monks must've been very grateful to you for giving them the business."

Paula looked at her with a puzzled expression. Finally she said, "I didn't go *to* a mission, I went *on* a mission."

Dawn paused. "On the roof?"

Paula laughed. "That's very funny."

Dawn smiled. She realized she was giving herself away. She would have to be more careful from now on.

"It was the happiest eighteen months of my life," Paula said.

Dawn couldn't imagine how it could possibly take eighteen months to buy two blankets and three copper platters, but she didn't mention it. "Sure," she said, trying to be as vague as possible.

"You should think about going."

"For eighteen months?"

"Of course."

Dawn wondered why she couldn't just order the souvenirs by mail instead.

She returned to her room and finished unpacking. A few minutes later Natalie came in wearing a robe.

"What's that?" Natalie asked.

"A computer."

"It looks so educational. Would you mind if I sewed a little cover to put over it when it's not being used?"

"No, go ahead."

"Not that I personally object, mind you. In fact, my fiancé—his name is David—he's a graduate student in chemistry, and he uses computers all the time. He could show you plenty about computers. Do you know what he calls computer programs? He calls them software. Isn't that a hoot? Software. It sounds like a type of clothing, doesn't it?"

"Yes."

"Well, tell me about yourself."

"I'm from Grand Island, Nebraska."

"Really? Do you know Angie Martin?"

Dawn frowned. "No."

"How many high schools are there in Grand Island?"

"Two," she guessed, becoming increasingly annoyed with the *Encyclopedia Britannica* for not having complete information.

"I'm surprised you don't know her."

"Oh sure! Angie—I remember her now."

In time Dawn learned that given any five Mormons drawn at random from anywhere in the world and getting together for the first time, at least three of the five will know somebody in common. She heard many conversations at BYU where the first fifteen minutes were devoted to discussing common friends. "Do you know . . ." is probably the question most often asked at BYU. In time she lived in constant fear of actually meeting someone from Grand Island, Nebraska.

Natalie checked her hair in the mirror. "Well, this'll have to do. David'll be here any minute now. We're getting together with all the graduate students and chemistry department faculty. What do you think I should wear?"

"A dress," Dawn said.

"Right, but which one?" She opened her closet. "As you can see, I'm a Spring," Natalie said.

"So—you think you're a spring?" She pictured springs on cars and buses.

"Yes. What are you?"

She vowed to send a scathing letter to the editors of the *Encyclopedia Britannica.*

"Are you Spring, Summer, Autumn, or Winter?"

Dawn shook her head. "I don't know."

"I'd say you're Autumn, but let me see your wardrobe." She opened Dawn's closet. "Oh, my," she said sadly.

"Is something wrong?"

"I've never seen so much gray in my life."

"It always seemed like such an official color to me."

"If you wear those clothes on campus, nobody'll pay any attention to you."

"I hope you're right."

"You're not fooling me, you know."

"I'm not?"

"You're afraid to let people know how much you long to meet a nice guy and fall in love."

"I do?"

There was a knock at the apartment door.

"That's David. Can you keep him occupied while I finish getting ready?"

David was tall and wore thick horn-rimmed glasses, but the most noteworthy thing was that he smelled like rotten eggs.

"Natalie said she'd be just a minute," Dawn said.

"Typical," David said. "Who're you?"

"I'm Dawn Fields. I'm from Grand Island, Nebraska."

"What are you majoring in?"

"Music education."

He scoffed. "So you came to college to learn to sing songs, huh?"

Dawn forced herself to smile.

"Just kidding. I'm sure it's a good major for a girl. You'll be able to teach your kids nursery songs. Me, I'm a graduate student in chemistry."

"Imagine that," Dawn said with appropriate awe.

"Do you know anything about science?"

"Oh no, not me."

"Well, let me tell you something. Life, as we know it, revolves around chemical reactions. Remember that, it's very important. In fact, when I look at you, I don't see a person."

"You don't?"

"Oh, no. What I see is a small biochemical factory. I see stomach acids processing the food you ate. I see hemoglobin picking up oxygen and transporting it throughout your body."

"You mean that life is really just chemistry," Dawn said as naively as she could.

"Very good—you know, there's nothing as challenging as doing research in chemistry. My graduate research project involves a lot of mathematics. Of course, I wouldn't expect you to understand it."

"Oh my no," she gushed. "I wouldn't understand anything as complicated as that. What kind of research are you doing?"

"We're attempting to determine the effect of high pressure on certain chemical reactions."

"By any chance would your research involve sulfur?" she asked, backing away from the smell.

"How'd you guess?"

"Just lucky."

Natalie came out. "Sorry I'm late."

"Typical," David said. They left.

Dawn returned to her room. In a few minutes Robyn came in. "If you want, I'll show you where to store your suitcases."

They walked downstairs. There, in a cage that ran nearly the length of the building, were storage racks for suitcases and skis. And a few feet beyond that was the laundry room with washers and dryers.

"You never saw a storage room before?" Robyn asked.

"What?"

"The way you're staring at all that junk."

"Sorry, I was thinking about something else."

They went upstairs again.

"Want an orange?" Robyn asked. "My dad brought me a case. He's a trucker on a coast-to-coast run. He comes through here about twice a month, and he likes me to eat healthy food. He always says, 'You'll never gain weight eating fruit and vegetables.'"

Dawn took the orange. "Say, when he comes through again, do you suppose he could mail some letters for me? Maybe he could mail 'em from California or wherever he's going. This friend of mine and I have this little game where we post our letters away from where we actually live. Do you ever play that game?"

"No, but I'm sure my dad'll be willing to help."

"Do you want to make a cake or something?" Robyn asked.

"No, thanks."

"It gets so quiet around here at night sometimes."

"I know—isn't it wonderful?" Dawn said.

"What are you going to do tonight?" Robyn asked.

"Either read or hack."

"Hack?"

"That means to program a computer. It's my hobby."

"Sounds better than what I'm going to do, which is to sit around by myself."

"If you want to go out, then go out."

"You mean alone?"

"Of course. Go to a movie or bowling or whatever you want."

"It'd be too obvious."

"What would?"

"That I was alone."

"But you *are* alone."

"I know, but I don't want to advertise it."

"Suit yourself. I'm going to enjoy the quiet."

"I won't bother you. I think I'll bake a cake." She paused. "Do you want any?"

"No, thanks."

"I hate to make it just for myself."

"Then don't make it."

"But I want a cake," she said, wandering off down the hall toward the kitchen.

When school began, she was swallowed up in the large introductory classes. She was relieved that except for an occasional "Hi," nobody talked to her at all on the first day.

On Sunday she went to church with girls in her apartment. They met in one of the classrooms on campus. She wore her gray dress and didn't say much.

A girl gave a talk. "Last year my grampa died. He and Gramma lived on a farm, and a few times a year we'd go visit them. When I was a kid, there was this tall tree swing, and I'd sit on it and swing hour after hour, and sometimes Grampa, when he was going from the tool shed to the house, he'd pass by and give me a giant swing, and laugh when I giggled at going so high in the air. I loved to have him hug me, because he always smelled like the outdoors. And one time my favorite horse, Checkers, died, and Grampa took me aside and told me that God lives, and that He'd taken Checkers to another pasture.

"I remember every morning on the farm when we were visiting I'd wake up before my parents were up, and I'd go in the kitchen and there would be Grampa, sitting at the kitchen table, reading the scriptures. He never said much, but he loved God, and now he's with Checkers too, and with God."

Dawn studied the girl's face. There was no doubt about her sincerity.

". . . I know that God lives, and that Jesus is the Christ, and that this is the Church of Jesus Christ. In the name of Jesus Christ. Amen."

The girl sat down.

The *Encyclopedia Britannica* had failed to mention a peaceful feeling Dawn experienced during the meeting.

After church the feeling left.

She was surprised Sunday night when the six of them knelt for family prayer. Never before in her life had she knelt in prayer with a group, and it seemed peculiar and strange. After the prayer everyone hugged everyone else. They even hugged her.

Lisa Salinger was not affectionate. She felt uncomfortable being hugged, but she didn't say anything about it.

Between classes on Monday she went to the Wilkinson Center. There sitting behind a table were two young men in suits. On the table were several pamphlets about the Church. She began looking at them.

"You're welcome to take some if you want."

"Thanks." She put one of each in her notebook.

She wandered the halls at the Wilkinson Center. One door was marked "The Daily Universe." It was the name of the campus newspaper. It seemed to her an overly optimistic estimate of the paper's coverage.

That night a group of guys from another apartment came over for what they called family home evening. One of them took charge. "Next Saturday our ward's doing baptisms for the dead."

Dawn looked around. Nobody was batting an eye.

"I think it'd be nice if all of us went. What do you say?"

They all nodded their heads.

A series of bizarre pictures passed through Dawn's

mind as she pictured what baptizing the dead might be like.

The guy in charge continued. "One other thing—how many of you have finished your four-generation sheets?"

Dawn pictured an ancient bed sheet passed from generation to generation, from mother to daughter, perhaps on her wedding day.

Paula raised her hand. "Have I ever told you the difficulties in doing the sheets in Chile?"

Dawn pictured the peasants gathered at the side of a river, beating the age-old sheets against the rocks, trying in vain to get them clean.

Strangely enough, though, Paula talked about parish records.

"Oh, one other announcement. We've got meetings coming up in two weeks for anyone in a leadership position."

Dawn wondered how one got into a leadership position. Was it like yoga? Did one practice a few minutes each day getting one's body into a leadership position and chanting "Mmmmmmmm"?

She decided she'd never recommend the *Encyclopedia Britannica* to anyone ever again.

"Well, Tami and Jan have the lesson tonight. I'll turn the time over to them."

"Well, this being the first of the school year, we thought it'd be good for everyone to introduce themselves. I guess we'll start with me. I'm Tami, and I'm a sophomore from Stillwater, Oklahoma. My hobbies are dancing and drama and sports, especially tennis and jogging. I play the piano, and I like to cook and sew. Let's see, what else? Oh, my goals—my first goal is to graduate. After that, I want to go to Hollywood and act for a while, and then, of course, eventually get married in the temple and settle down and raise a family."

Jan was next. "I'm Jan Roberts, and I'm from Seattle, Washington. I'm majoring in psychology, and so if we ever get stranded out in the wilderness, I'll be the one with no survival skills, but I'll go around asking 'And how are you feeling today?' If everything goes right, I'd eventually like to go into family counseling.

"Tami and I are roommates again this year. I'm sort of the voice of reason for us, and she saves me from having a dull life. I love her a lot, and I'm going to be sorry when we graduate or get married and can't room together anymore. We do a lot of dumb stuff together, like last year we went to *Swamp Thing* with green avocado dip on our face."

The two of them started laughing. "It was her idea!" Tami said, pointing at Jan.

"Nobody'll believe that," Jan countered.

To Dawn it seemed strange for a girl to tell her roommate she loved her. Roommates were to be endured, not loved. Like Kimberly and Lisa.

She realized the only person she'd ever told she loved was her mother, and that was several years ago.

"Natalie, I guess you're next."

Natalie stood up. "I'm Natalie. I guess you all know I'm engaged to David. He isn't here tonight because he had to finish up some important research work. He's getting a master's degree in chemistry, so that tells you how smart he is. He'll get out in April, and then we'll get married in June, and then I don't know where we'll end up. I guess that's about all for me."

"Dawn here is brand new to BYU. Dawn?"

She stood up. "My name is Dawn Fields, and I'm from Grand Island, Nebraska. I'm majoring in music education. Grand Island is situated on the Platte River in central Nebraska. It's the business and shopping center of an agricultural district that produces wheat, corn, and other grains."

One of the guys laughed. "You sound like you memorized that from an encyclopedia."

She blushed. She had memorized it from an encyclopedia.

"What are your hobbies?" Tami asked.

"Hacking."

"Like in hacksaw?" Natalie asked.

"It means writing software for my computer."

"You've got a computer?" a guy asked enthusiastically. "Can I come over sometime and see it?"

"Sure."

"What do you do with a computer?" Robyn asked.

"Well, fun things. I have a program that'll generate all the prime numbers from one to a thousand."

"What's a prime number?" Robyn asked.

Tami broke in. "Let me guess! Is it a really special number? You know, like the year you graduated from high school?"

"No, a prime number is a number exactly divisible by 1 or by itself. For instance, 3 is a prime number, 7 is a prime number, 11 is a prime number."

"What do they use 'em for?" Robyn asked.

"They don't use 'em for anything."

"Then why bother going to all the trouble of finding 'em?"

"Just for fun."

They were looking at her strangely.

Tami broke the spell. "We haven't heard from Paula yet. Paula?"

Paula stood up. "I'm Paula, and I returned from a mission to Chile two months ago. My mission was the best experience of my life. I learned to love the people of Chile so much. I'm majoring in Spanish, and I hope someday I can go back there."

"Robyn, you're next."

Robyn stood up. "I'm Robyn, and I'm majoring in home economics, and my hobbies are reading and sewing." She sat down.

"Gary."

"I'm Gary, and I'm from Nampa, Idaho. I'm majoring in . . ."

Dawn studied Gary as he spoke. He wore clothes

from Penney's or Sears, no designer T-shirts like Hal wore, no chain hanging around his neck. She could almost smell the Idaho sagebrush and see him as a boy helping his dad on the farm or ranch. She felt good being around him—it was more like he was a brother.

The other guys introduced themselves. She was impressed with them, not that they were all that handsome, but they seemed calmer and more mature than any other men their age she'd ever known.

Tami continued with the lesson. "Tonight, I thought we'd work on getting in better shape. We're all going to do aerobic dancing tonight. Jan and I'll lead, so if you'll all stand up and watch us, we'll show you the various steps. Jan, will you start the record?"

Everyone watched Tami and Jan dance to the music. Dawn smiled. She realized Tami had planned it so the guys would watch her dance.

Clever, she thought to herself. I never would've thought of that.

Every day she studied the pamphlets about the Church. It seemed incredible reading about an angel coming to a boy in his bedroom, telling him about gold plates buried in a hill. It all seemed like a version of Dungeons and Dragons.

On Saturday, while her roommates went to the temple to do baptisms for the dead, she pleaded a headache and stayed in her room and did research.

A week later she found a safe way to ask questions about the Church without giving herself away. In another apartment in Robison Hall was a nonmember named Rebecca who'd just started taking the lessons from the missionaries. In Relief Society they asked for volunteers to sit in on the discussions and to do something they called fellowshipping. Lisa learned they just wanted someone to be a friend with Rebecca.

From then on, all she had to do was talk to Rebecca

just before a missionary discussion. "Rebecca, have you ever wondered about this?" When the missionaries came to teach, Rebecca would ask the question. In the process of answering it, the missionaries also taught Dawn about the Church. From then on, she seldom said anything that would indicate she wasn't actually a member.

Three weeks later she was surprised to be invited to Rebecca's baptism. She went just to see what it was like. During the service, she felt that same feeling of calm she'd experienced before. She tried to forget it.

Another Friday night. It was quiet in the dorm. Dawn went to her room and closed the door. She was writing a paper extending her original theory. She had found that the theory could be more elegantly expressed in a six-dimensional formulation using a special mathematical term called a tensor.

While she wrote, she could smell the pleasant aroma of a cake Robyn was baking. She thought about having a piece of it later.

She lost track of time. She loved to work. Her theory now had an existence of its own, apart from her. She had given it birth, but it had moved out into the world, finding both critics and supporters.

Some time later she took a break. When she walked into the kitchen the cake was eaten. She grabbed an apple and returned to her room.

Around midnight she heard the outer door to the apartment open. She crammed her research papers into a notebook and picked up a history textbook.

Natalie burst in the room. "We had a great time at the dance. You should've been there."

"I was fine here," she said.

Natalie sat down next to her. "You need to get out more. All you do is stay in your room."

"I like being in my room."

"Why?"

"I like peace and quiet."

"But nobody's getting to know you."

"That's okay."

"But you're just fading into the walls. Before you get asked out, you've got to be noticed. The competition is tough here, and the girl who doesn't try will surely be overlooked."

"I want to be overlooked," she said.

"Don't just shrug your shoulders and give up. You could be more presentable if you'd just put a little time and effort into it. Let me help you. It'll make life here much more interesting."

"No, thanks."

"You know what David said to me the other night? He said you look like that woman they're saying is the next Einstein. You know, the one who eats eagle's nests and soaks her feet in yogurt. Well anyway, she's suddenly dropped out of sight. Some think the Russians have kidnapped her. David says you look just like her. Have you seen pictures of her in *Time?* She looks absolutely awful. Do you want people saying that about you?"

"Of course not!" she said emphatically.

"Okay then—let me help you."

Dawn nodded her head. "Yes, you're right. I need to change my appearance."

Natalie smiled. "Well, I'm glad you finally agree. We'll get started right away. First of all, do you have any money?"

"I've got plenty."

"That makes it easy. First we'll get you contact lenses, then a whole new wardrobe. No more grays. You're an Autumn, and autumns look good in orange and gold and peach and dark brown. You need warm colors with gold undertones. And your hair style is too short. Your hair is such a beautiful golden brown, so why hide it? Let it grow out. And I bet you don't even use conditioner, do you? You need a shampoo with flex conditioners to make it glow. It's gonna be so much fun to see you blossom. And, Dawn, after we get through, we'll have you meet guys, and then life'll be more fun for you. I'm free Monday after three. Let's go shopping for clothes and makeup and accessories, and you'll be on your way."

Within a week she'd bought contact lenses and gone shopping with Natalie and bought five hundred dollars worth of clothes, makeup, and accessories.

Saturday afternoon when they came home from the beautician, Natalie insisted she go to the dance that night at the Wilkinson Center.

While Natalie fussed over her, Dawn sat in front of her computer and ran programs, not really paying much attention to what was being done to her.

"Okay, I'm done," Natalie finally said. "Now get dressed in this stuff I've laid out on the bed, and then let's take a good look at yourself in the mirror in the bathroom."

While she dressed, she concentrated on what was happening on the computer terminal and not what was happening to her.

She slipped the dress on, put on her shoes, and walked into the bathroom.

Natalie was waiting for her. "Well, what do you think?"

She looked in the mirror. There was a stranger standing there.

"It's not me," she said.

"Of course it's you."

"No, it's the wrong face."

"It's you, Dawn."

She was wearing a pumpkin-colored dress. Natalie was placing a brown silk scarf around her neck, and then put on two small gold earrings. But the most fascinating feature of her face was her eyes. She'd never used eye makeup before, but now with eye shadow and liner, her eyes seemed to take over her face. Every emotion seemed to come more alive. She was like the girl she'd seen in Carson's Market the first day.

"What do you think?" Natalie asked.

"I can't go anywhere looking like this."

"Why not?"

"It's not me."

And yet she was fascinated by her reflection in the mirror.

"C'mon, let's go. I told David we'd meet him at the dance. The whole apartment is going to see you make your debut."

A few minutes later the six of them started for the Wilkinson Center.

"Can I make a suggestion?" Tami asked.

"Okay."

"When you walk, don't look down like you're doing an ant census. And one other thing—can we see a smile?"

She tried to smile.

Tami laughed. "Is that the best you can do?"

"I feel so foolish dressed like this. People will laugh at me."

"Why?"

"Because it's not me."

"They don't know that. Besides, it'll be you as soon as you get used to it."

A few minutes later they arrived at the dance. Dawn was relieved to see that not all the girls were dancing. Some of them stood along the sidelines and watched. Standing on the sidelines was what she wanted most from the evening.

Almost immediately Tami was escorted out on the floor. Natalie left with David to go dance before he had to go back to the lab. Jan was the next to go.

Soon there was just Robyn standing next to her.

"Quit looking down. Look up," Robyn coached. "See that guy over there? He's looking at you. Smile at him."

"No."

"Why not?"

"I don't like this, Robyn. I feel like a roast on sale."

The guy walked over to her. "Want to dance?"

"Not really," she said.

"Sure she does," Robyn said quickly, pushing her toward him.

The guy walked her out onto the floor. The music started. Dawn stood there. He started moving around to the music. Dawn stood like a statue and felt out of place. Her partner had a polite but curious smile on his face.

Robyn came out on the floor. "Dance with him!"

"I don't know how."

"It's easy. You just move around to the music."

"What if he touches me?"

"For crying out loud, Dawn, it's just dancing." Robyn started to dance to the music. The guy looked bewildered dancing with two girls at the same time.

Tami came over. "What's wrong?"

"She won't dance!" Robyn shouted over the music.

"Dawn, watch me. It's easy. Move those feet!"

Now three girls were dancing with the same guy.

The music stopped. The guy saw a chance to escape. "Well, thanks a lot."

Tami started her Mr. T. imitation. "I pity the fool who walks away from this girl in the middle of a dance!"

He stopped in his tracks. The music started again.

"Dance with her!" Tami ordered.

He started toward Dawn to begin dancing.

"What's he going to do?" Dawn asked.

"He's going to dance with you."

"I don't want to dance with him!"

"Try it! It's fun."

He put one arm around her waist and held her other hand. She knew her hands were sweating badly. The roommates left her alone.

"Who are those girls?" he asked.

"My roommates."

"Kind of pushy, aren't they?"

Tami and Robyn were asked to dance. As soon as Dawn was out of their sight, she left her partner and fled the Wilkinson Center.

A few minutes later she walked into the bathroom and looked at herself in the mirror. It was all wrong. She had always felt unattractive, and no matter what they draped around her, she knew it wouldn't make any difference about the way she felt inside about herself.

In the past her mind had accepted her body only because it needed to be carried around from place to place. Now it seemed alien to her.

But still, she had to admit that the woman in the mirror was strangely attractive.

"I wouldn't be too sure about that," she said brightly, imitating the girl in Carson's Market. She smiled at some imaginary guy. "Oh sure, you bet," she laughed. "I'd love to dance with you."

She stopped, suddenly realizing she could carry it off if she wanted to. She could fit in and go on dates and meet guys and master the patter of small talk. But she also realized that for Lisa Salinger, feeling bad about her appearance had fueled the drive to scientific accomplishments. Take that away and she might lose it all.

There was only one thing in her life that really mattered. It was her Grand Unified Field Theory, and whatever followed from it. That was more important than life itself, because it would continue even after she died. She couldn't afford to jeopardize the possibility that she might be able to come up with another equally significant discovery.

She frowned. That attractive woman in the mirror might be her enemy. She would have to be careful these girls didn't make her cheerful.

She vigorously scrubbed off the makeup and, for the first time in Utah, put on her sheepskin jacket over her nightgown and went to bed.

A week passed. No matter how much the girls in the apartment tried to coax her, she quit wearing her contact lenses and went back to her old clothes. She spent her

time secretly working on extending her theoretical results.

Sunday in Relief Society, a week later, Dawn was paying very little attention. She was very tired, having
worked late the night before.

The girl giving the lesson was from Southern Utah
and had a rural accent. Because she seemed so cheerful
and friendly, and because she had the habit of ending
every statement with "Okay?", Dawn found it easy to discount everything she said.

"I found this really neat scripture in the lesson," the
girl drawled, "and I just think we should all listen real
good and try to make it a part of our everyday life. Okay?
Well, I'll just read it for you.

"'*And again, verily I say unto you, he hath given a law unto
all things, by which they move in their times and their seasons;
and their courses are fixed, even the courses of the heavens and
the earth, which comprehend the earth and all the planets. . . .
The earth rolls upon her wings, and the sun giveth his light by
day, and the moon giveth her light by night, and the stars also
give their light, as they roll upon their wings in their glory, in the
midst of the power of God.*

"'*Unto what shall I liken these kingdoms, that ye may understand? Behold, all these are kingdoms, and any man who hath
seen any or the least of these hath seen God moving in his majesty
and power. . . . Then shall ye know that ye have seen me, that I
am, and that I am the true light that is in you, and that you are in
me; otherwise ye could not abound.*'"

Dawn was suddenly awake. It seemed completely out-
of-place, this girl with honey-blonde hair casually tossing
off something so remarkable. She had never heard anything approaching it from any of her reading.

"I just think that's so neat," the girl said. "Oh, here's
another one that's good too: '*There is no such a thing as im-
material matter. All spirit is matter, but it is more fine or pure,
and can only be discerned by purer eyes.*' I think it's so special
that we have these things to tell us about, you know, the
universe and everything. Okay?"

Dawn raised her hand. "What you just read, it might be true."

"Oh, I know it's true," the girl said.

Suddenly Lisa was speaking, and not Dawn. "One of the current theories in physics is the existence of matter more fine than neutrons or protons. They themselves are composed of finer matter, called quarks. Maybe that's what it's referring to when it said finer matter. Or it could have reference to neutrinos. Some scientists feel that neutrinos may make up the major mass contribution to the universe. Tell me, when was that written?"

"Gee, I don't know, a long time ago."

Paula looked it up. "It was in 1843."

Dawn shook her head in amazement. "That's impossible. How could anyone know that in 1843?"

"God knew," the girl giving the lesson said, "and He told a prophet, and the prophet told us, so now we know too."

Although the words were tossed off casually, there was no doubt the girl believed what she was saying.

All at once everything seemed turned upside down. Lisa Salinger was accustomed to truth being wrestled from nature in bits and pieces. Here it seemed to come with no work, and sometimes with little appreciation.

After Relief Society, the girl who'd taught the lesson came up to Dawn. "Thanks for your comments."

"Is it true what you said today?" Dawn asked.

"I know it's true," the girl said with conviction.

There was that same peaceful feeling associated with what the girl said.

It was the first time Dawn ever considered that the Church might possibly become important in her own life.

The next day she nervously stopped for a minute in the lobby of the Eyring Center and watched the Foucault pendulum swing.

She knew she was taking a chance coming to the Physics Department.

On the bulletin board was information about how physics could be a useful major for a girl. There was a copy of the article about Lisa Salinger that had appeared in *Time*.

She fled to the women's rest room and examined her appearance in the mirror. That morning she'd asked Tami and Natalie to help her get ready. They were delighted she was at last taking an interest in herself. By the time they finished, she looked nothing like Lisa Salinger. On the way over she had even practiced talking with a Utah accent.

A girl came in the rest room wearing a spattered lab coat. She started to wash an oily steel rod.

Dawn smiled at the girl. "Are you in physics?"

"Yes, I'm getting a master's degree, that is, if I can ever get the equipment working."

Dawn laughed. "I know, I know. Nothing ever works, does it?"

The girl looked at her strangely. "Are you in physics? I don't remember ever seeing you around here before."

Dawn shook her head. "No, I'm in music education."

"That's probably more practical."

"No, stay in physics. It's a wonderful discipline, and there're so many opportunities in it right now for a woman."

"You mean because of Lisa Salinger?"

"You know about her?"

"Oh, sure. Every girl in physics knows about her. She's our hero, but I'm still not sure I understand her theory."

"It's not that hard if you put it in a six-dimensional tensor notation."

The girl looked at her with a puzzled expression. "I'll remember that." The girl left.

Dawn morosely looked at her reflection in the mirror. More than anything else she wanted to go to the graduate carrels and show the girl the elegance of her theory in tensor notation. But if she did and someone found out who she was, the whole rat race would start up again.

She gave one last practice smile, then continued on her way to the office of Dr. J. K. Merrill, a theoretical physicist like herself.

She knocked on the door. Dr. Merrill answered it. "Yes?"

"I'm Dawn Fields. I talked to you this morning on the phone."

"Oh yes, come in."

The office was cluttered with homework papers and physics journals. He cleared aside a chair for her to sit on.

"You said you had a few questions."

"I know you're busy, so I won't take long."

"What are you majoring in?"

"I'm a sophomore in music education."

"I see. Professor Haines teaches the course in acoustics. Maybe he's the one you need to talk to."

"I'd prefer to talk to you, if I might."

"Okay, go ahead."

She began. "My roommates and I were talking about this the other night—you know how roommates are. Well, we couldn't agree, so I got elected to come and ask you. It's just a little question we have about science and religion."

He smiled politely. "Sure, go ahead. What's your question?"

She made an effort to sound breezy and cheerful. "As I understand it, entropy is a measure of the disorder of a system. Of course, from the Second Law of Thermodynamics we know that isolated systems tend to become more disordered with time. Some, trying to argue for a creation, have argued that the formation of a complex system, such as a human being, could not be brought about by natural selection because it forces a system to go from disorder to a more ordered state. They argue that such a transition would violate the Second

Law of Thermodynamics, and that therefore the earth and its inhabitants were created by God and not by natural evolutionary processes."

Dr. Merrill's mouth dropped open in astonishment. She flashed him her best smile and continued.

"However, it seems to me that those proposing such an argument don't fully understand the Second Law of Thermodynamics. It is perfectly allowable for a system that is not energetically isolated to become more ordered in time. For instance, water freezes into ice, and, of course, water as ice is more ordered than water as a liquid. Therefore, I reject an entropy argument as any kind of proof of there being a God. Furthermore, it seems to me quite possible that worlds could evolve by natural processes, and, in fact, as Carl Sagan has suggested, there could be millions of earths in our galaxy alone that support life. What does the Church say about that?"

He cleared his throat. "You're a sophomore in music education?"

"Yes, sir."

He scratched his head. "I've got to get over there more often. Is that where you learned about entropy?"

She smiled. "Oh no, I have a subscription to *Scientific American*."

He reached across his desk to a bookshelf and pulled down a book, opened it to a certain page, and handed it to her. The heading at the top of the page said "Moses." "Read the part outlined in red there."

She began. "*And worlds without number have I created; and I also created them for mine own purpose; and by the Son I created them, which is mine Only Begotten. And the first man of all men have I called Adam, which is many. But only an account of this earth, and the inhabitants thereof, give I unto you. For behold, there are many worlds that have passed away by the word of my power. And there are many that now stand, and innumerable are they unto man; but all things are numbered unto me, for they are mine and I know them. . . . The heavens, they are many, and they cannot be numbered unto man; but they are numbered unto me, for they are mine. And as one earth shall pass away, and the heavens thereof even so shall another come; and there is no end to my works, neither to my words.'"*

"I think that answers your question," Dr. Merrill said. "There are many worlds with life. There is a continual process in which worlds come into being, exist, support life, and then pass away."

She frowned. Somehow he had countered her question. "But how do they come into existence? By creation or by evolution?"

Dr. Merrill leaned back and put his hands behind his head. "Let me ask a question. How do you define evolution?"

"Well, a natural process."

"And creation?"

"God just creating something instantly out of nothing by the wave of the hand."

"I see," Dr. Merrill smiled. "There's another possibility. What if God understands natural laws? And what if he uses those laws in organizing matter, which already existed, into an earth like ours? What would that be, creation or evolution?"

It was like a chess game. She smiled politely. "But if the laws of nature existed before God, and if matter also existed beforehand, would that not tend to place God in a secondary role?"

"Not in my mind," Dr. Merrill said.

"Then you don't believe God can create something out of nothing?"

"That's right. Let me have you read something else." He flipped the pages to another section and handed it back to her. She began reading. "*'Man was also in the beginning with God. Intelligence, or the light of truth, was not created or made, neither indeed can be. All truth is independent in that sphere in which God has placed it, to act for itself. . . . The elements are eternal, and spirit and element, inseparably connected, receive a fulness of joy.'"*

"Is this from Joseph Smith too?" she asked.

"Yes."

"Dr. Merrill, you're an educated man. Exactly how do you regard Joseph Smith?"

He smiled. "I regard him as a prophet of God."

She frowned. "How can you blindly accept that he was a prophet of God? Where is the proof?"

He leaned toward her. "The evidence is the Book of Mormon. When I was your age, I had many questions too. I decided to take him at his word—read the Book of Mormon, then pray and ask God if it was true. The same test will work for you too."

As he spoke, that comforting feeling she had experienced before returned.

She shook it off. "I'll read the book, then I'll be back." *To tear it apart*, she thought as she left.

Finally, at the constant badgering of her roommates, she went on her first date. A guy named Greg asked her for a date for Friday to go to a movie called *Cyber Death*. Because of her interest in science fiction, she accepted.

For the next few days, Tami went through the halls doing scenes from *The Glass Menagerie*, rambling on in a Southern accent about "gentlemen callers."

On the day of her date, Dawn reluctantly let the girls get her fixed up. Before the afternoon was over, she felt like a Barbie doll being dressed by a mob of girls.

Finally she looked in the mirror again at the stranger who was taking over her life.

Jan came in and closed the door. "How do you feel?"

"Terrible."

"I know. Everybody does before a blind date. Just talk about his interests and things'll go okay. Do you want to have a prayer before you leave?"

"No," she said flatly.

Finally Greg came, and she was launched on her date.

"It's hard to keep my eyes off you while I'm driving," he said as he drove downtown.

She thought he was joking. "Sure," she laughed.

"I'm serious."

It was odd the way he was looking at her.

"Tell me, Greg, what are you majoring in?"

"Biology. I wish I had a camera to catch your face in dim light. I bet you're terrific near a candle."

Nervously she cleared her throat. "When you graduate, what kind of a job do you want?"

"I want to be a fisheries biologist."

"Tell me, Greg, what did you think of 'Jaws.' Could a shark really become a killer like that?"

"I like your hair too. It shines."

She felt like a new car in a showroom.

He was staring at her. Nobody had ever looked at her like that before. She started to blush. "Greg, what kinds of fish are the most interesting to you?"

"Carp."

"Why carp?"

"In Japan carp is an important fish for food. Carp can eat garbage. Think of all the garbage we've got in America." He pulled up to a parking space. They were half a block from the movie theater, and they could see a line waiting to get into the movie.

"Why don't we sit in the car and talk till the line goes down?" he said.

"Okay."

"Your lips are so inviting," he said.

"You've been spending a lot of time around carp lately, haven't you."

"You're different from all the others."

She frowned. "I don't want to be different. I want to be the same."

He casually put his arm around the top of the seat, which according to Tami was often the first step to a guy putting his arm around a girl.

She backed away. "Let's go see the movie now, okay?"

"I understand. You don't kiss on the first date. I admire that."

"Good," she said with a sigh of relief.

He paused, then asked, "What date do you kiss on?"

"What?" The sound was muffled, because she was holding one hand over her mouth as she spoke.

"Some girls don't kiss on the first date, but they'll kiss on the second or third date. So what date do you kiss on?"

"This is a joke, right? I bet Tami put you up to this." She laughed.

"I love your name. And when you look at me with those eyes, I see uncertainty, wisdom, mystery, and romance."

She moved the rearview mirror and looked at herself. "Where do you see that? All I see is eye shadow, eye liner, and mascara."

"I love the way you smell."

"It's perfume—it comes in bottles. If you bought some and dabbed it on a dead carp, it'd smell like that too."

"And the way your hair shines."

"It's the flex conditioners. Greg, is it asking too much if we could go to the movie now?"

"Why don't you like me? Is it my lisp?"

"What lisp?"

"I don't say some words right."

She paused. "You do lisp a little bit, don't you. Look Greg, I know you're sincere, and in a way I'm sure this is a compliment, but really . . . look, if you really want to make me happy, please take me to *Cyber Death*. If you can't afford it, I'll pay for both tickets."

He was still sulking. "Just forget it."

"Sure thing. Can we go to the movie now?"

Just as she stepped out, while she was still a little off balance, he kissed her on the cheek.

"Greg, cut it out."

"I'm sorry. I don't know what got into me. It's difficult for me to be around you. I like the way you look."

"But it's not me, not really."

He had a pleading look, like a cocker spaniel.

"Greg, quit looking at me like that. Underneath all this gunk, I'm plain and ordinary."

He tried to kiss her again. "No!" she yelled. She hit him in the stomach. He doubled over, gasping for breath. Two couples walked by and looked curiously at them.

"Are you hurt?" she asked.

He was still gasping for breath.

"I guess I'm not used to guys. Sorry. Can you straighten up any?"

"Aaaah," he moaned, still doubled over.

"I bet I hit you in the solar plexis, huh?"

"Aaah."

She looked in the rearview mirror of the car next to them. "You really think I look okay, huh?"

"Aaaah," he groaned, bent over but nodding his head.

She helped him get in the car. He put his head on the steering wheel and fought to get his breath. Finally he spoke. It sounded as if he was about to cry. "I'm so ashamed. I don't know what got into me."

"Hey, forget it. Can we go see the movie now? There's nothing like a little science fiction to take your mind off your worries."

"Will you ever forgive me?" he groaned, holding his head in his hands. "You probably think I go around try-ing to kiss every girl on the first date. But this is the first time in my life anything like this has ever happened. I'm ashamed."

"It's all right. Now let's go see the movie, okay?"

He wouldn't look at her. "You'll never respect me now."

"That's not true, Greg. I respect you."

"No you don't—not really. I don't blame you. You'll go tell your roommates, and by tomorrow it'll be all over the school. But it's my fault. I've nobody to blame but me."

"I promise I won't tell anyone. Can we go see *Cyber Death* now? Look, there's nobody in the line now."

"It was all my fault. You can't help the way you appeal to men."

"I think cyber stands for cybernetics."

"Every time you see me on campus, you'll think, 'There's that animal.'"

"I promise I won't think that. Can we go see the movie now?"

"What will you think?"

"I'll probably think, 'Oh, look, there's Greg.'"

"You can say that, but I know you'll never respect me again. But what's worse, every time I see you, I'll be thinking, she thinks I'm an animal. Even now I feel so guilty being around you."

"Hey, it's nothing a little *Cyber Death* can't fix."

"What do you mean it's nothing? I showed myself for what I am—a fraud, a guy with no consideration for a girl's feelings, a person with no self-control. It's more than just a little thing."

"Well, it's a little like when a horsefly lands on you—it doesn't hurt, but you're afraid of what might happen."

"You think of me as a horsefly?"

"Greg, don't be so tough on yourself."

"Why not? The damage is done."

"I don't think there's any damage, Greg. So you kissed me. Big deal. It meant absolutely nothing to me. Honest."

"It's not entirely my fault, you know. You looked at me with those eyes—so you're partly to blame too."

She frowned. "They're the only eyes I have. I think maybe the movie's started now, so if we're going to see it . . ."

"I'm so ashamed of myself. I can't be with you anymore. I'm taking you home."

She looked out the back of the car as the sign for *Cyber Death* faded in the distance.

A few minutes later they stood on the steps just outside the dorm. "Sometimes I get so lonely," he said softly, putting his arm around her.

It was the same thing Hal was always saying to Kimberly.

She shoved him away. Unfortunately, someone was leaving the dorm just then. The edge of the door caught Greg in the mouth, cutting his lip and chipping a tooth.

After they'd stopped the bleeding and sent him home, Dawn went into the bathroom, locked the door, and looked at herself in the mirror. She smiled at Dawn's image in the mirror, then went in her bedroom and put on a long white nightgown and slipped into bed. She fell asleep remembering how it had been when she was high school homecoming queen in Nebraska.

"This is not good," Natalie said the next morning at breakfast.

"I'm sorry."

"You can't go around knocking your date's teeth out. Eventually the word's gonna get around."

"I just pushed him a little bit, and he stumbled into the door."

"Was he getting fresh?" Robyn asked.

"Well, he tried to put his arm around me, and he told me he was lonely."

"You beat him up for saying he was lonely?" Tami asked.

"I guess maybe I misunderstood."

"Who's ever going to ask you out once this gets around campus?" Natalie asked.

"It's not important."

"Not important? How can you say that after all the work we've sunk into you? How are you ever going to get married?"

"I don't care about that. Marriage isn't important to me."

"Marriage—not important?"

"There're more girls than guys on this campus. Not all of them can get married while they're here. Why can't I be one of the ones who don't?"

"Are you crazy? Everyone wants to get married."

"What for?"

"God wants people to get married," Natalie said.

Dawn shrugged. "Then let Him worry about it."

"You've got to do your part, and believe me, beating up your dates is not the way to do it." Natalie stormed out of the kitchen.

"Anybody want any more pancakes?" Robyn asked.

"No, thanks."

"Well, there's just a little batter left. Maybe I'll finish it off."

Jan and Tami sat down next to Dawn. "We'll help you. First of all, when you're in the library, where do you study?"

"In a carrel down in the science section."

Tami shook her head. "Why do you study there? It's so quiet."

A few minutes later Robyn sat down to another stack of pancakes.

CHAPTER SIX

It was a Sunday dinner. David and two other guys, boyfriends of Tami and Jan, were eating with them.

"Have you heard this one?" David asked. "If you get a BYU coed and a U of U coed on top of the Marriott Center, which will fall first?"

Nobody said anything.

"The Marriott Center," David chortled. The other guys laughed too.

Robyn put her silverware down and quit eating.

"I've got a million of 'em," David said. "Here's another one . . ."

A few minutes later Robyn excused herself. Dawn scowled at David and left also. She found Robyn in her room, sitting on her bed, her arms folded neatly in her lap. She was staring into space.

"Are you okay?" Dawn asked.

"Oh sure," she said, snapping out of it. "Why do you ask?"

"Robyn, David's a jerk. You realize that, don't you?"

"That isn't a very kind thing to say about your roommate's fiancé."

"Hey, I'm just getting started. He's also insensitive and pompous."

"'Let us oft speak kind words to each other . . .'"

"Robyn, how about if we take a walk together?"

"Okay."

They walked toward the temple grounds.

"Robyn, if there's anything bothering you, I'm a good listener."

"There's nothing bothering me," Robyn said lightly.

They walked another block. Now they could see the temple better.

"When I was little," Robyn said, "I used to dream about temple marriage. But I don't anymore."

"Why not?"

"Because it's not going to happen," she said, dropping her camouflage of cheerfulness.

"How do you know?"

"I've only had one date in the last two years."

Dawn could see tears in her eyes.

"It's funny in a way," Robyn continued. "The summer before I enrolled here, when I told my friends I was going to the Y, they all kidded me. They said, 'Oh, you'll be married after one semester.' And I'd smile and say no, but secretly I wondered if they were right. But then I got here, and nothing happened. All around me girls were dating, but nobody noticed me. Some mornings now I can't come up with a reason to even brush my hair. What's the use? I can't compete with these girls. Sometimes I get so depressed. Have you ever walked behind a guy on campus and watched him? He scans the crowd, his eyes flitting from one girl to another, like he was in a factory grading potatoes as they go by on a conveyor belt. He's looking for beautiful girls. When he sees one, he'll focus his attention on her until she passes by. Guys spend ninety percent of their time looking at ten percent of the girls. Do you know what it's like to have a guy look at you with absolutely no interest? Like you're a bush or a pillar. On campus it's like I'm invisible. And I'm the one they're making fun of when they tell jokes about fat BYU coeds."

"I hate those jokes," Dawn said angrily. "They're

cruel and demeaning. What right do guys have to criticize? Are their bodies perfect?"

"No."

"So what right have they got to expect ours to be? Hey, who needs a perfect body anyway? Not me. Because if I had one, I'd spend all my time worrying that someday it'd become less than perfect. I'd probably be weighing myself three or four times a day just to make sure I hadn't gained any weight. Is that any way to live? What a trap. And what keeps this going? On TV now we've got twelve- and thirteen-year-old models showing us what we're supposed to look like. Hey, let's face it, Robyn, we're women now, and we can't look twelve years old anymore."

"Still, though, I am overweight," she said.

"You think my friendship depends on what you weigh? You think your future husband's going to weigh you every day and if you gain a pound, he's going to get a divorce? You think happiness means going through life looking ideal? Looking ideal is like putting plastic wrap on a salad. It looks nice, but it's not good for anything. Give me a few scars on a guy, or a few clumps of cellulite on a woman. It all adds character."

"If that's true, guys aren't interested in character."

"Why do we sit by while David, who smells like a sewer, insults us?"

She laughed. "You're a fighter, aren't you."

"Lady, you ain't seen nothing yet. I'm tough as nails."

"Thanks for talking to me. I feel better now."

Dawn broke through her natural reserve and hugged Robyn. "I care about you."

"Thanks, I love you too. Still though, I wish I were thin."

"Fine, go jogging with Tami and Jan. They have a two-mile route around the boys' dorms."

"My thighs'll gross out the guys."

Dawn laughed. "Not after a month they won't. By

then, you'll have strong legs without much fat. Besides, that's what they invented baggy jogging suits for."

She thought about it. "Maybe I will."

"One thing, though, we've got to stop coed jokes. It's not good for girls to be ridiculed like that."

Robyn nodded. "When I was a freshman I knew this girl. She was overweight, like me, but she couldn't stand it, and there's so much of a push to be thin here that she became anorexic. She ended up looking like a prisoner of war. She got so she'd wear only jogging sweats, not to hide the fat, but because she didn't want us to see how thin she was. But no matter how thin she got, she kept thinking of herself as fat. One day climbing some stairs, she fainted and fell all the way to the bottom, and they put her in the hospital. It was her heart. It had been weakened by her compulsive dieting. When she got out, her parents came and took her home, and she's never come back. But nobody cares—not really. Oh sure, we sent her a get-well card, but life here marches on. And there's so many girls here. There's always another to fill the place of the ones who drop by the wayside."

"We'll fight back! We'll unite as women to protest against coed jokes."

"Nobody'll join. Nobody cares. The thin girls tell coed jokes themselves, and the ones like me are too self-conscious to say anything."

"We don't need very many," Dawn said.

The first meeting was held the next week. Four girls attended. They called their group COEDS, which stood for Coeds Outraged by Excessively Derogatory Stories.

"I nominate Dawn Fields as president."

"I can't accept."

"Why not? COEDS was your whole idea."

"I can't be in any position where there might be publicity."

"Why not?"

"I just can't. I'll work behind the scenes, but I can't be in any office."

"Well, okay. I nominate Jan then."

The group's first act was to issue a formal complaint that coed jokes not be printed in the school paper. A week later they met with the dean of students and with Gary Doyle, an assistant editor of the *BYU Daily Universe.* It had been his idea to have a daily column of coed jokes.

"This is an attempt at censorship, plain and simple," Doyle said. "Those jokes are perfectly harmless."

"Well, we don't think it's fair to girls to print those jokes," Jan said.

Doyle smiled. "Hey, if you want, you can come up with jokes about guys. We'll feature one from each side. It'll generate lots of interest."

"We just don't think you should print any jokes that make fun of people," Jan said.

It was clear to Dawn that pleading for fairness would get nowhere with Doyle. She had learned at least something from the lawsuit against Lisa Salinger—people fear being sued.

She broke in. "Listen, Doyle, your newspaper is supported by student funds, and at least half those funds are provided by girls, and yet these jokes are an insult to every girl on campus. If you insist on continuing, we'll take legal action against you."

His mouth dropped. "Who are you?"

She smiled sweetly at him. "Why, my dear, I'm a coed."

He shot back, "What a big mouth you have, coed dear."

The dean of students tried to stop the shoot-out. "I think if we just . . ."

"The better to sue you for ten thousand dollars, my dear," Dawn countered.

He frowned. "You're not overweight, so what's your big gripe about coed jokes?"

She walked over to him. "You're losing your hair, aren't you? I mean it's pretty obvious, isn't it?" She moved aside some carefully placed hair on his head to reveal a bald spot. "I see you try to brush it so the hair covers the bald spot, but we can tell. Girls, look here at Doyle's bald spot. It's kind of funny, isn't it." She laughed and the others reluctantly joined in. "Tell me, Doyle, do you ever worry that nobody'll want to marry you? Just think—another six months and you're gonna have less hair than my grandfather. Doesn't that ever bother you? Girls, let's all laugh again at Doyle's nearly bald head, shall we?"

They laughed.

His face turned bright red. His hand went to his head, and he protectively brushed some hair back over the bald spots.

She sat down. "And that, Doyle, is what's wrong with coed jokes."

The dean of students interrupted their confrontation. "I'm sure we can work this out. We're brothers and sisters in the gospel. There should never be any need for lawsuits. Dawn, I doubt if you're aware of how expensive a lawsuit can be."

"I have twenty thousand dollars in my checking account, and I'm willing to spend it all on a lawsuit. I assume Mr. Doyle has a similar amount he's willing to spend to defend what he believes is his right to insult women on this campus."

Doyle blanched.

"We can't have lawsuits at BYU," the dean of students said.

Dawn pointed her finger at Doyle. "Then get him to quit printing those insulting jokes in the paper, or he's going to be sued. It's very simple. If we get no agreement here today, my attorney will start proceedings tomorrow morning."

The dean turned to Doyle. "I think she's right—those jokes aren't fair. I think you should agree not to publish them anymore."

"All right!" Doyle snapped.

"I'd also like an apology from Doyle in the paper," Dawn said.

"No," he squirmed.

Dawn smiled. "Do you mind if I use your phone? I need to phone my lawyer."

The formal apology appeared in Monday's paper.

But Doyle was not a good loser.

That week an article appeared in *Time* on Lisa Salinger's disappearance. Kimberly and Hal and several of the faculty at Princeton had been interviewed. Kimberly had apparently sold the last of her pictures to *Time*.

The magazine also had a picture of the grade school in Fargo she'd attended, as well as the high school physics classroom. The reporters had talked to her high school friends and teachers. They'd also interviewed her mother. "I hear from her once in a while," she'd said. "She must be doing a lot of traveling, because the letters come from all over the country. I don't know where she is."

Dawn continued to go to the library at least once a week. She would sneak into the area where physics journals were kept and read anything she could find relating to the Salinger Grand Unified Field Theory. In early November she read that two researchers from Europe had reported experimental results that agreed with her predictions.

Also that week she found out that Lisa Salinger had been chosen the winner of the Einstein Prize, presented yearly by Princeton University to a former student. Unfortunately Lisa would not be there to receive the medallion.

However, there was still quite a bit of controversy about her first paper. She read one day that a scientist from Russia had recently criticized her theory. She decided to answer his attack.

Monday night after family home evening she announced she was going to do laundry.

"This late at night?" Natalie asked.

"It'll be all right. I've got some studying to do anyway."

She took her typewriter downstairs and plugged it in, setting it on the table used to fold laundry.

The night rushed by. At four-thirty in the morning she was finished. She put the pages into an envelope. She would have Robyn's father mail it from California next week when he came through town in his truck. She took her clothes from the dryer and then sleepily went upstairs to bed.

"Good morning, sunshine!" Natalie said at seven-thirty, opening the curtains, letting the light stream in.

"Let me sleep," Dawn moaned.

"We can't have you skipping classes now, can we? You'll never amount to anything sleeping. Come on, you old sleepyhead."

The covers were pulled away. Dawn sat up. "What time is it?"

"Time to get up. You're going to look a wreck unless you get up and do your hair and face. Now, come on. Studies are important, you know. You're going to flunk out if you don't start paying more attention to school. Come on, get up. You can sleep after your classes. While you get ready, I need to talk to you. I'm going to help you with your social life. I've already set it up. Next Saturday we're inviting David and his cousin to dinner. Now, quit scowling. It's not going to kill you."

Dawn lay back again and plopped a pillow over her head.

Natalie spent the next few days trying to coach her.

David's cousin was named Cody Wells. Dawn hoped smelling bad didn't run in the family. She was assured that her date was not a chemistry major. He was a civil engineering student who had brought fame to the school by designing, building, and racing a cement canoe against those of other Western universities.

By the time Saturday arrived, Dawn was decked out like a battleship. She was wearing Tami's skirt, Jan's blouse, Robyn's earrings, and a necklace from Chile loaned to her by Paula. At six-thirty there was a knock on the door. Dawn hid in her room and let Natalie get it. As she heard the conversation move from the door into the kitchen, she looked longingly at her computer hidden under its flowered pink cover.

Natalie came in the room. "They're here."

"I know."

"Don't look sad. Be happy. Guys like a girl who's happy."

"I'm happy," she said dully.

"Good—now tell your face. Let's go."

The smell of sulfur dioxide was in the air.

"Hello, David," Dawn said.

"Cody," Natalie said, "this is my roommate, Dawn Fields."

Her eyes opened wide. Cody was sandy-haired, with boyish freckles over a still-deep tan. She thought he was named appropriately because she could imagine him on the jacket of a Louis L'Amour novel.

Dawn smiled. "Hi, Cody."

He smiled back. "Hi."

David smirked. "Dawn here is majoring in . . . what is it, Dawn?"

"Music education," she said.

"Right!" David chortled. "She came to college to play games and sing songs and learn to use a pitchpipe." He chuckled at his own joke.

"Actually," Dawn said evenly, fighting to maintain a pleasant smile, which Natalie stressed was a necessity for the evening, "it's a difficult discipline."

"Oh sure," David chortled. "You have to learn all the verses to the 'Star-Spangled Banner,' right?"

"I'm sure there must be more to it than that," Cody said.

Instantly she liked him for rescuing her from David's superiority complex. She leaned toward him just a little. He smelled good.

"Yes, there is," she said.

"I'd like to know more about it," he said.

He seemed quite at ease with her.

"Oh, there's not much to tell really," she said. "Besides, I'm dying to hear about your cement canoe. Natalie says your canoe beat all the others."

He smiled. "If we're going to be friends, don't call it a cement canoe."

"Why not?"

"Cement is the powdery stuff. If you put any kind of aggregate in, like gravel, then it's called concrete."

Dawn liked the small dimple that appeared like magic when he smiled. And he liked to smile.

He asked what she was doing in her classes. She went to her room and returned with a tuba mouthpiece. She handed it to him.

"Where did you get this?" he asked.

"Brass workshop," she said.

His eyes widened in astonishment. "You made this in a brass workshop?"

"No," she laughed, "a brass instrument workshop. I have to learn to play every instrument, and right now it's the tuba."

She showed him how to hold his lips for the mouthpiece. She blew it, producing the same sound horses make on the trail.

"Dawn, dear, may I talk with you in private please?" Natalie said sweetly.

As they entered their room, Natalie turned sour. "I should think it'd be obvious that noises like that are inappropriate in mixed company. If you could've seen your lips just now! A guy'll never kiss lips he's seen puckered like that." Natalie took the mouthpiece and put it on a table. "Now I know you're new at dating, so let's just leave this here."

They went back. "Dawn, please check the spaghetti while I pour water into the glasses."

They'd rehearsed it all beforehand. It was to make Dawn seem domestic. Checking spaghetti is easy enough to do. One merely sticks a fork into it to see if it's limp. She looked at the spaghetti and said, "Just a couple more minutes." She sat down next to Cody again. He smiled at her and she smiled back.

"I've always wanted to play the tuba," he said.

"Sure you have," she said with a smile.

"No, it's true. Bring it out here, and we'll give it a go."

"Well," she said slowly, looking at Natalie buzzing around the kitchen, "I really shouldn't . . . but . . . I did bring it home this weekend."

"Where is it?"

"In the bathtub."

He laughed. "A tuba in the bathtub? I don't feel so bad now about my battery-powered submarine."

She giggled. "We didn't want you seeing it in my room. Natalie says a girl shouldn't have a tuba in her bedroom."

"Right," he said. "What might I conclude if I happened to see a tuba in a girl's bedroom?"

"I don't know—something horrible, I suppose."

"Probably that she played the tuba. What do you say, let's go get it."

"Okay. I'll get the mouthpiece and you get the tuba."

A minute later they returned with the tuba.

"What's that?" David asked with a scowl.

"It's a tuba," Dawn said.

"I know that. What I meant is, what's it doing here? Aren't there rules against tubas in the dorms?"

Cody and Dawn laughed and sat down next to each other with the tuba on Cody's lap.

Natalie scowled. "Dawn, the spaghetti needs checking again."

Dawn sighed. "The spaghetti is just fine, Natalie."

"I'd like you to check it now," she said tensely.

"Play me a song first," Cody asked.

Dawn got the tuba up to playing position and blew into the instrument. It made a sound like a fog horn.

"Welcome to Mystery Theatre," Cody announced soberly.

"Good grief," Natalie said with a sigh, looking to heaven for help.

"For my first selection I will play 'Mary Had a Little Lamb,'" Dawn said.

It was awful. Cody started snickering and couldn't stop. Natlie started banging pans around loudly. Finally Dawn broke up too.

By then Cody was laughing so hard it was difficult for him to talk. "So you've got this . . . two-ton lamb, and he's going around the countryside . . . maiming wolves . . ."

Dawn roared with laughter. It wasn't delicate and refined. It was a gut laugh, coming from deep inside her, past Dawn, past Lisa, into the deep recesses of her mind. It was the way children laugh, open, free, uninhibited, natural, full of joy.

She played a single note, and they both burst out laughing again.

Natalie was not amused. "Dawn, I'd appreciate it if you'd show a little responsibility for this meal and check the spaghetti!"

Suddenly she felt vulnerable. For a frenzied minute, she'd forgotten who she was, whether she was Dawn or Lisa. She put the tuba down and checked the spaghetti. "Just right," she said quietly.

"Now could I have a word with you in private?" Natalie mumbled.

When they got inside their room, Natalie nearly started crying. "Do you honestly think a guy'll ever fall in love with a tuba player?"

"We're having fun."

"Oh sure, he'll let you make a fool of yourself, but

when it comes to taking a girl home to meet his parents, do you think it'll be the girl with the tuba? No sir! Never the girl with the tuba."

"Why not?"

"Are you serious? I should think the answer'd be obvious. Tubas aren't feminine."

Dawn's eyes got big. "You mean there's boy instruments and girl instruments?"

"Go ahead, make fun, but if you ever want to see him again, pay attention. You can play the piano or the violin or clarinet or flute, but the girl who plays the tuba will never go steady. Now, do you care about him or not?"

"Yes, I like him."

"Okay then, you'll just have to do what I tell you. You've pretty much messed things up already, but I think we can undo some of the damage. So listen to me. I'll go in and ask you to drain the spaghetti, and David and I'll leave to borrow some dessert goblets. You say, 'Cody, this pot is so heavy. Can I get you to lift it from the stove and help drain it?' And after he does, you tell him how strong he is. He'll love it."

"Will he wonder how I put the pot on the stove before he came?"

"No, he won't think about that. Guys need to feel strong and masculine now that they've been replaced by electricity."

A few minutes later, with Natalie and David purposely gone, Cody lifted the large pot off the stove and set it on the counter next to the sink.

"You're strong, aren't you," she said. She dumped several pitchers of cold water on the spaghetti to rinse it off, then asked him to tip the pot again so the water would run out.

"How's that look?" he asked.

"Just a little more."

He tipped it too much, causing the spaghetti to suddenly rush out, filling up the kitchen sink, at the same time spilling lukewarm water all over their shoes.

"Are you all right?" he asked. "I hope you didn't get burned."

"I'm fine. I'll get us something else to wear."

She went to her room and changed into a slacks outfit and sneakers. The only thing she could find for him to wear was a pair of gym socks and her old bunny slippers.

He laughed when she brought them in, but put them on anyway.

After they'd scooped most of the spaghetti back into the pot, they noticed the stopper had been left out previously and spaghetti had slid into the drainpipe.

David and Natalie returned with the dessert goblets.

"We're back!" Natalie bubbled, motioning for David to set down the goblets.

"Why are you both looking down the drain?" Natalie asked.

"It's clogged," Cody said.

"Let me take a look," David said, scooting Cody and Dawn out of the way. He looked down the drain, then scowled. "I can see your problem. You got spaghetti in your drain, which means somebody forgot to put the stopper in the drain."

"I *always* put the stopper in the drain," Natalie said, staring at Dawn.

"Well, somebody forgot," David said. "If the stopper had been where it belongs, the drainpipe wouldn't be full of spaghetti now."

Cody tried taking a long knife and reaching down the drain to cut the spaghetti up.

David brushed him aside.

"Let me do it. If you're going to do a job, you might as well do it properly. First we've got to remove the trap down below. Natalie, you'd better watch this, because when we're married, you never know when this'll come in handy."

With a dramatic motion, David opened the cupboard below the sink and pointed. "You see that bend in the pipe there? That's what they call the trap. You see it there, Natalie?"

"Oh, sure!" Natalie bubbled. "There it is. How did you ever know about that? You're so smart. What did you say they call it?"

"The trap," he repeated.

"Why do they call it that?"

"Because it acts as a trap for things that shouldn't be there in the first place if someone had remembered to put in the stopper."

David and Natalie looked at the trap with respect.

"Now what we have to do is remove the trap," David said.

"I've got a pair of pliers in the car," Cody said.

David was shocked. "Pliers? Pliers'd be the absolutely worst thing to use. In plumbing, if you use the wrong tool, you'll wreck your threads. You'd be surprised how many people end up buying new fixtures because they've harmed their threads."

Dawn started giggling at the production David was making out of this. Cody also snickered a couple of times but then tried to be serious again.

David continued. "It's a good thing I carry a complete set of tools in my car. You never know when you'll need 'em. Natalie, here's my keys. Go out to the car, open the trunk, and bring me a pipe wrench."

"I'll get it for you," Cody offered.

"No, you see, Natalie and I are a team. And while she's gone, I'll clear away this junk down below."

When Natalie returned, David, lying on his back with his head in the cupboard, pushed himself out, looked at the wrench, and scowled. "No, dear," he said, "you've brought a crescent wrench. What I need is a pipe wrench. Go out again and bring me a pipe wrench."

Natalie smiled sheepishly.

"It's the biggest wrench in the toolbox."

Natalie didn't move.

"What's wrong?"

"I left the keys in the trunk."

David slid out, sat up, and glared at her. "You did what?"

"Well, I must've set the keys down while I was going through the tool chest and—"

"You locked my keys in the trunk?"

"I'm sorry, dear," she said.

"Sorry isn't going to open the trunk, now is it?"

"I guess not."

He stood up and wiped his hands and glared. "Well, we'll have to get the keys before we do anything else. I've got to go to the lab in an hour and take some measurements, and I need my keys."

"I'm sorry," she said.

"I have to watch you like a hawk all the time, don't I," David said.

Natalie looked as though she was going to cry.

"Now don't start that," David warned. "Just let this be a lesson to you. Next time make sure you have the keys before you close the trunk."

"Yes, dear."

He shrugged his shoulders. "It's water under the bridge now anyway. What we have to do now is remove the back seat, crawl in, and get the keys. We might as well get going. I wish I had my tools."

"I'll lend you my pliers," Cody said with a silly grin.

David nodded and left.

"Are you two going to help us?" Natalie asked.

"What for?" Dawn said. "All we'll do is stand around and watch Mr. Wonderful fix everything."

"The least you can do is show some interest," Natalie said. "It's not his fault the drain was clogged."

Cody agreed. "He might need some help. Besides, I need to get him my tools."

"All right," Dawn said with a shrug. "We'll all go out."

Cody left.

Dawn walked over to her tuba.

"You're not planning to take that outside, are you?" Natalie warned.

"I am."

"You'll never get a husband," Natalie muttered.

"Good."

Cody lent his tools to David and offered to help, but David said he didn't need any help.

A minute later, Dawn burst out of the dorm marching to "Mary Had a Little Lamb."

David gave Natalie a running commentary on his every move as he worked. Every few minutes, Natalie would look up from her respectful attention to David's work and give Dawn a withering stare because she wasn't paying sufficient homage to David. "You don't have the slightest interest in what David's doing for us, do you," she finally said.

Dawn stared back with the same cold glance she was being given. "That's right."

"Just like a woman," David grumbled.

Suddenly Lisa, not Dawn, went on the warpath. She leaned into the car and glared at David, who was on his back unloosening a bolt. "Hey, Mush-for-Brains! Don't you ever play high-and-mighty male around me again! And if I ever hear you put down Natalie again, I'm going to turn the hose on you. Maybe it'll get rid of that wretched body odor of yours."

David jumped out of the car. "I'm not the one who practically ruined the plumbing in there!"

She glared back at him, then stormed off, stopped, and stomped back to Cody, who'd been practicing the tuba. "I don't know how to crochet, knit, garden, make my own clothes, or can food. My life's not going to end if I can't be a wife and mother. I can lift pots of spaghetti without a man's help. I'm not helpless, dependent, or sweet, and I'm certainly not domestic. So that about wraps it up for the entire evening for us, right?" She grabbed the tuba from him and angrily started for the dorm.

"Hold it right there!" Cody called out.

She turned around. "What?" she yelled back.

"You forgot to say that you're impressed with how fast I'm learning the tuba." He smiled at her.

She stopped.

He smiled again.

She smiled back.

Suddenly the mood changed. She faked serious contemplation. "Well, maybe . . . But there're a lot of flash-in-the-pan tuba players. Oh, sure, maybe at first they manage a few good oompah-pahs, but when it comes down to the long haul, they give up. It takes real character to master the tuba."

"Give me a chance," he said.

"Okay," she said softly.

David opened the trunk. "Well, I'm done. Now I need to go to the lab and take another reading. Nat, you want to go with me?"

"Sure."

They left.

Cody grinned at her. "Isn't anybody going to feed me tonight?" he asked.

"Sure. C'mon, let's go inside."

They went in the kitchen. She dished out some spaghetti, and they sat across from each other and ate.

"You've got the most interesting eyes."

She looked away self-consciously.

"But you don't maintain eye contact very long. What's wrong, afraid to look me in the eye?"

"Not at all. I'll prove it. You want to have a staring contest?"

"Sure. The first one to look away loses."

They leaned across the table and stared. He had blue eyes and a wonderful smile, and she felt vulnerable staring into them.

"We forgot to decide the prize for the winner," he said.

"How about an all-expense trip to David's lab and a year's supply of sulfur."

He laughed. "No, I want the prize to be worth something. The winner takes the loser to a dance, and after the dance the loser buys the winner a banana milkshake."

"I don't like banana milkshakes," she said.

"I do, and I'm going to win."

"Oh, yeah?" Without breaking eye contact, she picked up a single strand of spaghetti with her fork, brought it to her lips, and slowly sucked it in, the way she'd done when she was six years old.

He laughed but didn't break eye contact.

Next he slowly reached across the table and pinched her nose. "Beep," he said.

She knew it was juvenile, like kids having lunch together, but she loved it. It had been a long time since she'd allowed herself to be a child.

He reached out and held her hand.

She was blushing. "That's distracting."

"For me too." He let go. "I find you fascinating, and I want to get to know you better, but first I'd better tell you something. There's this girl. Her name is Allison. Right now she's on a mission. We've talked about getting married when she comes back."

She looked away.

"You won," she said quietly. "I'll get us some dessert."

He followed her to the refrigerator. "I was serious about wanting to know you better, that is, if you realize we can't expect too much to come from it except friendship. Allison'll be home in August. So, if you understand . . . well, I do want to be friends."

"Sure, why not?"

She dished him a bowl of ice cream.

"This is a picture, isn't it," Cody said contentedly. "Me here in bunny slippers, you playing songs on the tuba, us sharing a dish of ice cream. Very domestic. I could do this forever."

"That won't be possible," she said. "Next Wednesday I have to turn the tuba in."

"And then what?" he asked.

She smiled. "The trombone."

"One of my favorites. We have to get together for the trombone."

Robyn came into the kitchen. "Anything left to eat?"

"Sure, help yourself."

Dawn introduced Cody.

Robyn ladled out an ample portion of spaghetti and sat down. "Another weekend," she said.

Dawn nodded.

"What does that mean?" Cody asked.

"Sometimes I overeat on weekends," Robyn said.

"Why's that?"

"There's nothing else to do."

"Robyn doesn't date much."

"The truth is, not at all."

"I can change that. Robyn, how about a date?"

Robyn treated it as a joke.

"I'm serious."

"Well, you and Dawn—you know—I don't want to get in the way. Besides, you don't want to go out with me."

"Why not? How about tomorrow night? Isn't there a fireside? I'll take you."

Robyn quit eating. "Dawn, I know you don't want me to go out with him."

"It's okay," Dawn said. "Cody's waiting for a missionary anyway, so we're going to be just friends. Go ahead."

"Okay, I will. Thanks."

Sunday night while Cody was out with Robyn, Dawn spent time reading the Book of Mormon.

The next day after classes, Cody walked her back to the dorm. While he waited in the lobby, she went in to change clothes. He was going to take her to one of the civil engineering labs and show her how to make concrete.

She saw Paula in bed and went in to investigate.

"What's wrong?"

"I'm sick. I want a priesthood blessing. Is Cody here?"

"Yes."

"Ask him."

She went out to the lobby. "Paula's sick. She says she wants a priesthood blessing."

"Sure. I'll get my roommate and be right back."

A few minutes later, with Paula in a robe sitting on a chair in the kitchen, Cody and his roommate solemnly placed their hands on her head. Cody sealed the anointing. "By the power of the priesthood, we seal this anointing, and give you a priesthood blessing . . ."

Dawn looked at Cody. His eyes were closed, his hands gently resting on Paula's head, his words gentle and kind and calm. There was that calm feeling again in her heart.

Tears crept down her face. She had never known a man could be tender, compassionate, and caring.

A few minutes later they were in the civil engineering lab up to their elbows in concrete.

"Thanks for taking Robyn out Sunday. It really helped her."

"Glad to do it. She's a nice girl."

"You care about people, don't you."

"I guess so."

"I haven't known guys who cared about anything but themselves. I find it very—well—attractive."

And then he did something else very appealing to her—he blushed. "Thank you."

That night she dreamed about him.

The next day after classes, because it was a warm day for November, they hauled last year's concrete canoe out to Utah Lake. She brought along her trombone.

He paddled a ways out. She put the trombone together and played for him.

"How romantic," he said when she finished. "A girl playing love songs for me."

"'Twinkle, twinkle, little star'—not much of a love song."

"But it was played with deep feeling," he said.

"Maybe." She smiled.

This is flirting, she thought, *and I love it.*

"I like you," he said.

"Is it me, or my access to musical instruments?" she teased.

"It's you, Dawn," he said, suddenly serious.

She looked away.

"There you go again. Are you hiding something?"

"Why do you ask?"

"Your eyes. Is there someone else in your life?"

She paused. "I guess there is."

"That explains it. I guess the most we can hope for, for both of us, is friendship."

"I guess so. The other person in my life is very demanding of my allegiance." She didn't tell him the other person in her life was Lisa Salinger.

But even as she said it, she realized, almost sadly, that she was falling in love with him.

"You came back," Dr. Merrill said as she walked into his office. "Just a minute." He picked up the phone. "Send Donna Satter to my office, will you please?" He hung up and turned his full attention on Dawn. "Have you read the Book of Mormon?"

"Yes."

"And have you prayed and asked God if it's true?"

"No, I haven't."

"Why not?"

She paused; then with half a smile she said, "I'm afraid I might get an answer."

"What's the worst thing that could happen if you found out the Church is true?"

"If I was sure it was true, I'd have to get baptized."

"You're not a member then?"

"No, sir."

"And it would be so terrible to be baptized?"

"So far I've only had one major goal in my life."

"And what's that?"

"To achieve excellence. If I joined the Church, then there'd be two goals. I like the way things are now. And that's why I haven't asked the question."

"You're afraid of the answer?"

"I guess I am."

"You're extremely intelligent, aren't you."

"Yes, sir."

"That's a gift of God too, you know. Don't pit one gift of God in your life against another. He knows you by name, and He's pleased with what you've accomplished in science."

She tensed up. "Science? What do you mean? I'm a music education major."

"Something interesting happened the first day you visited me. One of our graduate students told me she'd talked to a girl that same day. This mysterious stranger told her that the Grand Unified Field Theory is best understood in six-dimensional tensor notation. Later my graduate student asked me what that meant. I told her I didn't know."

The girl Dawn had talked to suddenly appeared in the hall outside his office.

"Donna, is this the girl you were telling me about?"

"Yes, it is."

"Thanks, Donna."

The girl left. Dr. Merrill continued. "I didn't think anything more about it until a few days ago, when I received my latest copy of *Physical Review Letters*. It has a paper by Lisa Salinger outlining her theory in a new six-dimensional tensor notation. The question is, how did a music education major know something about Salinger's theory that hadn't even been published yet? You want to

know what I think? I think you're Lisa Salinger. I admire
you a great deal. Let me be the first to welcome you to
BYU."

She turned crimson.

"Don't worry, I won't tell anyone you're on campus.
And Donna doesn't know who you are. Your secret is still
safe."

Dawn nodded and quickly left.

CHAPTER SEVEN

After finals in December, she told everyone she was going home for Christmas. But instead of going home, she flew to California and spent three weeks at UCLA writing another paper. She phoned her mother Christmas morning.

"Some reporters have been here this week asking about you. What shall I tell them?"

"Tell them I called from California."

Classes began the first week in January. She went on a date with Cody on Friday night. He told her that while he was home for the holidays, he'd spent a few hours talking to Allison's parents about her mission. Dawn listened, a polite smile frozen on her lips.

Early Saturday morning the phone rang. Tami answered it and knocked on her bedroom door. "Dawn, it's for you. It's a guy."

She padded out in her slippers and answered it.

It was Cody. "I'll be by in half an hour. Wear warm clothes—long underwear, if you've got it. Don't bother to eat breakfast. Any questions?"

"Just one," she said. "Who is this?"

"Very funny," he said, hanging up.

She had planned to spend the day in the library reading physics journals, but suddenly that didn't seem very important.

Half an hour later he picked her up.

"You're supposed to ask for a date well in advance," she teased.

"You look beautiful in the morning."

She softened. "I just don't want to give you the impression that all you have to do is whistle and I'll come running."

"I didn't whistle. I phoned."

"Okay, it's all right then," she said with a smile.

At a stop light, they were lost to the world looking at each other.

"Where are we going anyway?" she asked.

"I'm not sure. I'm really getting confused," he said.

"Roadwise, I mean."

"You'll see."

A few miles into Provo Canyon, he made a turn and started up a steep road heading into the mountains. A few minutes later they pulled into a campground. He opened his trunk and pulled out a Coleman stove, a sack of groceries, and a large frying pan.

"You make the flapjacks, and I'll build us a fire to keep warm."

He scooted the snow off the picnic bench and put down a blanket for them to sit on.

"I love it out here, don't you?" he asked.

"Yes, it's really nice," she said enthusiastically, only partially deceiving him. It was nice, but her feet were cold.

"I can't stand to be locked up inside. I have to be outdoors. That's why I got into civil engineering. Are you warm enough?"

"I'm fine."

She was grateful that he made a blazing fire, using wood from the trunk of his car. She mixed up the pancake mix while he laid a tablecloth on the table.

She cooked a pound of link sausage first, then turned out pancakes until they both were full.

He brought out two sets of snowshoes from the car.

"Let's go." They trudged through the forest. The snow was four feet deep in places. Nobody else had been there all winter, so every step they made on snowshoes was the first mark.

A few minutes later they stood on top of a hill looking down on a snowy world below them.

"It's beautiful," she said.

"I'm glad you like it. I wanted to share it with you. These woods, and the snow, even the cold, even the wind when it cuts through you, all of it, all of nature—there's nothing phony about it."

She recited the poem "Stopping by Woods on a Snowy Evening" by Robert Frost.

"When did you learn that?"

"High school."

"I wish I'd known you then."

"Why?" she asked cautiously.

"Just to have a friend. But I probably would've had to stand in line. I bet you had lots of boyfriends in high school, didn't you."

"Not really."

"I don't believe that. Dawn, you're . . . my best friend."

"Oh."

"I don't know how to say this, or even what I should say, but these past few weeks—I've never felt so happy being around a girl. Dawn, I like you a lot," he said, softly touching her cheek.

"This is dumb, you know," she said, trying not to be captured by the magic.

"You mean being up here on snowshoes?"

"No, that part's all right. It's just that I keep thinking about Allison. Tell me again what a wonderful person she is, and when she gets off her mission."

She'd spoiled it.

"We'd better get back down," he said soberly.

They walked to the car and took off their snowshoes. Before getting into the car, she picked up a pile of snow and tossed it playfully in his face. He yelled as the snow hit him and then started chasing her. She ran away laughing. When he caught her, he gently pushed her into a snowdrift.

Suddenly the snow wasn't cold anymore. It was a wonderful playground. When he reached over to pull her out, she pushed him down and threw snow in his face.

He chased her. They both were laughing so hard they couldn't finish their sentences, and the words came out between gulps of laughter.

When he caught her, he reached down and scooped up a pile of snow. He was going to throw it, but he made the mistake of gazing into her eyes. He dropped the snow, and they embraced and kissed.

He had his arm around her waist as they walked back to the car.

"When I saw you come busting out of the dorm playing the tuba, I said to myself, there's the girl for me, someone who's happy just being herself—somebody who doesn't go around putting up a phony image."

"Oh," she said, turning away so he wouldn't see the guilt in her eyes.

After that, they spent most of their free time together. Because he was her first romance, she deeply meant every one of the goodnight kisses they shared.

Her only frustration was how he could continue seeing her without writing Allison and breaking up with her. Somehow he was able to compartmentalize Allison and Dawn into separate places in his mind. Perhaps, she thought one day, it was the same way she compartmentalized Dawn and Lisa. She wasn't exactly sure how Lisa felt about Cody.

As time passed, the tension she experienced also grew.

The end of March came like a lion. Dawn, Robyn, Paula, and Cody sat on the edge of the indoor swimming pool on campus, dangling their feet in the water. It was Cody's idea to invite Robyn and Paula. They'd just finished a game of water basketball, the three girls against Cody.

Paula told a story about her mission.

"Is there life after a mission?" Cody teased when she finished.

Paula smiled. "You're right—that's all I ever talk about. It's just that everything else seems so unimportant."

"Sure, a mission's important. But once it's over, a person needs to start thinking about other goals in life."

Dawn smoldered inside. At first it had seemed all right for her and Cody to do things with her roommates, but lately she resented their hanging around.

"Nobody's noticed it, but I lost two pounds last week," Robyn said.

"Way to go, Robyn!" Cody encouraged.

"I've been jogging with Tami. She's like honey around flies when we get around the boys' dorms. They always stop and talk to us. I've met at least a dozen really neat guys. It's so much fun to talk to 'em. I love it. No more late-night cakes for me."

"You can do anything you want to," Cody said.

"You started it all by asking me out."

"Hey, we had fun that night, didn't we."

Dawn dove into the water and swam as fast as she could to the other side. *I'm jealous,* she thought. *How stupid. It's impossible for me to fall in love here. I'm not one of them and I never will be.*

She stopped at the other end and glared at them.

Cody pushed off and swam toward her. His strong arms carried him easily through the water.

She didn't want to talk to him.

When he reached the other end, he looked around and saw that she'd moved. He headed toward her. She swam away, but he pursued. A short time later he came up behind her and grabbed her legs. She quit swimming. They treaded water.

"Hi," he said. "Want to play tag? You, me, Robyn, and Paula."

"I'm tired of playing games."

"Let's touch the bottom with our feet, okay?" He put his arms on her waist. "One . . . two . . . three!" They descended. She opened her eyes underwater. He was smiling at her, and bubbles were streaming from his mouth. They touched bottom, and he kissed her. She was furious with him and shot to the top for air, then swam away.

He thought it was a game, and he chased and caught her again, laughing and playful. "Let's do that again!"

"Get away from me! I'm not your water playmate!" she shouted. "Why don't you wait for Allison to come back, and then you can maul her underwater all you want? You've strung me along when you know you're never going to get serious. But it's my emotions you're playing with. Well, I've had it!"

She stopped and looked around. Everyone in the pool was staring at her. She stormed into the women's dressing area.

In the shower, her tears mingled with the water streaming down her face. She didn't want to share him with anyone, not with Paula, not with Robyn, and especially not with Allison.

He drove them all back to the dorm and parked the car in the parking lot. Robyn and Paula, feeling the tension in the car, quickly escaped.

Dawn started to get out too.

"Wait," he said, "we need to talk. What's wrong?"

"When does Allison get off her mission?"

He sighed. "The first part of August."

"Will you be on campus then?"

"No, I'll be working on a highway crew for the summer. What about you?"

"I'm going to summer school."

"How about if I come up and see you on the weekends."

"You mean before Allison gets home?"

"Yes."

"And what about after?"

"We'll have to wait and see." He cleared his throat. "Dawn, let me explain. You caught me off balance. I didn't expect—" he paused, "we'd become so close."

"You just needed someone to fill in for her. I mean, with her gone, you were lonely, weren't you."

"Yes."

"Okay, now it's my turn to be lonely. Cody, I don't want to ever see you again." She made it to her room before she broke down. She was glad he hadn't seen her cry.

"It was the tuba," Natalie said quietly. "I could've told you."

"I hate him," she said.

"Next time do what I say, okay? I know about these things."

"There won't be a next time."

"There's always a next time."

The semester ended in April. Cody went away for the summer. Dawn took summer classes.

To help time pass, she got a job at the Wilkinson Center snack bar.

In June Natalie and David were married in the temple. Dawn attended the reception. She was relieved that at least for that occasion David smelled like a normal person.

That summer she read the Bible, the Doctrine and Covenants, the Pearl of Great Price, the Book of Mormon, *A Marvelous Work and a Wonder, Articles of Faith,* and *Jesus the Christ.* She found on campus a scholar in ancient languages. She took a class from him. He was incredibly intelligent and yet possessed a strong testimony. By the time the class was over, she had enough intellectual confidence in the teachings of the Church to allow herself to fast and pray for an answer.

The answer came with a renewal of those same feelings of peace and calm she'd felt from the very first time she attended a sacrament meeting.

She decided to get baptized. The only problem was that her roommates already thought she was a member. To admit she hadn't been a member before might jeopardize her existence as Dawn Fields. She decided to get baptized off campus.

The next Sunday she drove a rented car to Brigham City, some ninety miles north of Provo, and went to church. During sacrament meeting she looked around the congregation to make sure she didn't know anyone there. After the service, she saw two missionaries. She walked up to them and said, "I want to be baptized."

They both grinned. "How much do you know about the Church?"

"I know quite a bit." She told them the books she'd read during the summer.

"Where do you live?"

"Just a couple of blocks from here," she lied. "I just moved in."

"Give us the address, and we'll come and give you the lessons."

"I don't want the lessons. I want to be baptized."

"We're supposed to give you the lessons."

"Give them to me here at church then. Today, if possible. I'm living with my father, and he doesn't want to have anything to do with the Church."

Ten minutes later they started on the lessons, but it soon became apparent she knew a great deal about the Church. "Okay, when would you like to be baptized?"

"Today would be good for me."

"Is it okay if we interview you first to make sure you're living the right way?"

"Sure. Go ahead."

"I need to ask a few questions. First of all, do you believe in God and in Jesus Christ?"

"Yes."

"Do you understand that when you're baptized, you enter into a covenant with God to do his will? You'll be taking upon you the name of Jesus Christ. Are you willing to do that?"

"Yes."

"Do you believe that Joseph Smith was a prophet of God?"

"Yes, I do."

"Do you sustain the president of The Church of Jesus Christ of Latter-day Saints as a prophet, seer, and revelator?"

"Yes."

"We've been told by revelation that certain things aren't good for our bodies, things such as smoking, or using alcoholic beverages, or drinking coffee or tea. Do you live that principle?"

"Yes."

"We've been asked by the Lord to share ten percent of our income with him by paying tithing. Are you willing to be obedient to that commandment?"

"Yes."

"God has reserved sex for marriage. Are you living within those guidelines?"

"Yes, I'm morally clean."

"God expects us to be completely honest with our fellowmen. I assume you always tell the truth."

Suddenly her shoulders slumped and her confidence vanished.

"Is anything wrong?"

She realized she couldn't go through with it. Dawn Fields was a fraud. She didn't really exist. What good would it do to enter a covenant with God under a false identity?

She stood up, tears filling her eyes. "I'm sorry for troubling you, but I can't be baptized."

She drove back to BYU.

Eventually fall semester began. With Natalie married, Dawn roomed with Robyn. Over the summer she'd firmed her body by eating regular meals, cutting out sweets late at night, and regular exercise. Tami and Jan were still together. Paula's new roommate was a freshman from California named Kelly O'Dougherty. She was very tan. They guessed that her family was rich, because her wardrobe came UPS in five shipments.

Dawn now felt comfortable in the clothes and makeup Natalie had suggested. Her hair had grown long enough to require putting it up every day. She'd even dated a little over the summer, but nothing serious.

Seeing her on campus, even with a photograph of Lisa Salinger in your hand, one would never be able to pick her out of the sea of thousands of other well-groomed coed faces.

The first night the roommates were together again they stayed up late talking and snacking. Tami talked them all into going to an apartment of guys in their ward they'd known the year before and serenading them with songs from *Sesame Street*. Afterwards they were invited in to play charades.

Back in the dorm again, they moved their mattresses in the large kitchen so they could be together all night.

Sometime during that night, with Tami and Paula doing ad lib TV commercials, Robyn doing aerobic exercises in the hall, and Jan quietly analyzing everyone else, Dawn looked around and realized she loved her roommates.

At eleven o'clock they ordered two pizzas to be delivered.

When they came, Robyn had a small piece of pizza and an orange.

After school started, Cody didn't phone. Once Dawn saw a girl walking with him. It was Allison. She was very pretty.

Dawn continued to work at the snack bar in the Wilkinson Center. Once a day she saw Doyle in the supper line. He was the editor of the *Daily Universe* that year. "Sometime this fall we want to do an article about you. Don't worry, I won't write it. I'll have a reporter come and talk to you."

"Don't bother. I lead a very boring life."

"It wasn't my idea. The girls on the staff say they'll quit unless we do a story about you."

After that, someone named Cindy Dyer began leaving phone messages, but Dawn never answered them.

She was taking a music class called Essentials in Conducting. Once a week students got a chance to conduct the orchestra for a few minutes. Because her last name was Fields, her chance came early on in the semester. On that day she was second in line.

The first conductor, a girl named Pam, started the orchestra. They made a mistake, and she stopped them. She smiled. "Now you're doing real good, okay? But I think there might have been just a tiny little mistake back there at G. Let's play it again at G, okay?"

They played it again and continued to make the same mistake.

She stopped them again. "Gee, I hope you don't mind me stopping you all the time, but it still doesn't sound right to me. I know you can do it better, okay? So let's all work really hard this time and see if we can do it even better. Okay?"

"Time," the teacher called. "Fields, you're next."

She took her place in front of the orchestra. "Take it at G," she said crisply.

They murdered it again.

She blew up. "What are you people doing?" Someone laughed. She glared at the offender. He quit. She pointed at the first-chair French-horn player. "What's your name?"

"Alan."

"Alan what?"

"Parker."

"Parker, play it at G."

He played it badly.

She pointed to the second-chair person. "What's your name?"

"Williamson."

"Play it at G."

He played it right.

"Parker, you now play second chair. Change places with Williamson. He'll play first chair."

Parker smirked. "You can't do that."

She slammed the baton against the music stand. "For the next four minutes and thirty seconds I'm the conductor of this orchestra. And while I am, I'll do anything I please. Now move!"

Parker looked to the instructor for a reprieve. Finding none, he grumpily moved to second chair.

They played it again at G. This time it was right.

There was a critique afterwards.

They loved Pam.

They hated her.

She fumed about it all that night. Finally she complained to Jan. "If I'm sweet and docile, then I'm seen as feminine but ineffective. But if I assert myself and try to be professional, then I'm seen as domineering but not feminine. I can't win. All I want is to be feminine and professional. Why does that seem to be impossible around here?"

"Would you like to know a few things I've noticed about you?" Jan said.

She tensed up. "Why not? That's the price we pay for having a psychology major rooming with us."

"Most of the time you're mild and pleasant, but at other times, something sets you off, and you become almost militant. I noticed it first when you talked to Doyle about coed jokes. Is there any reason why you'd have a split personality?"

She tried to make light of it. "C'mon Jan, it's me. Don't try analyzing your roommates. I mean, isn't everyone a little crazy? Sure I get mad at times, but that's all there is to it."

Jan looked at her, smiled, and backed down. "Sure, I must've been mistaken."

In October Cody came to see her at the snack bar while she was working.

"I've been thinking about you."

Keep it breezy and light, she told herself. "They say if your ears are itching, that means someone's thinking about you. My ears were itching yesterday. Were you thinking about me at six-thirty last night?"

"I can't remember the exact time," he said.

"Of course, it may just be my shampoo. I think I'm allergic to flex conditioners."

"I'm sorry I didn't come by sooner."

"Oh, my, don't apologize. I've met so many nice guys since you dumped me."

"You're the one who refused to see me anymore."

"And how is good old Allison?" she asked with a plastic smile covering the tension she felt.

"Fine."

"I bet you're both real busy what with wedding plans and such." Another pleasant smile.

"Not exactly."

"Why not?"

"I can't get you out of my mind. Allison considers that a real drawback in our relationship. She told me to decide once and for all."

She noticed that her voice was getting shrill. "I'll make it easy for Allison. Forget me. I'm not real. I belong in a magic bottle. I lived there hundreds of years until some poor soul opened the top. I'm somebody else, so don't love me." Another smile.

Now he'll leave me again, she thought miserably, *and go back to Allison.*

"Excuse me," a girl said, reaching past Cody for a tossed salad.

"You're blocking my customers," Dawn scolded.

"I'm a customer too, you know."

"You're only a customer if you buy something."

"Okay, I'll take a banana." He reached for one on the mechanical lazy Susan.

"Sure—it figures," she said bitterly, realizing she'd just lost "breezy and light."

"What does?" he asked.

"That you'd want a banana."

"What do you mean by that?"

"Go ahead, take the banana, get your satisfaction out of it, then just toss aside the peel. That's what you do, isn't it? That's what all the guys around here do."

He grinned. "You want me to eat the banana peel."

"Do whatever you want. Do what every guy on this campus does."

"Which is?"

"Date a girl until her expectations are up, let her knock herself out baking bread and inviting him to supper, and then dump her for somebody else. You think we like making bread?" She couldn't help sounding bitter.

"When did you ever bake me bread?"

"Plenty of times. I just never gave any of it to you."

"Why not?"

"It tasted awful."

He laughed. "If I wanted bread, I'd go to a bakery."

"Excuse me," a guy said, reaching for a chef's salad.

"You're in the way again," she said. "Let my customers get the food they want."

"Miss, I'd like a Jell-O, please," Cody called out.

"There's none on the counter."

"Okay—where have you hidden it?"

"You want me to get you some, is that it?"

"That's what you're paid to do, isn't it?"

She left and in a short time returned with his Jell-O. "Here."

"Thanks."

"Don't mention it. Like you said, I'm paid to do it."

"I'd like to start going out with you again," he said.

"What for?"

"I can't get you out of my mind."

"Forget me," she said. She bumped a chef's salad with her elbow, and it fell on the floor. "Now look at what you made me do."

She knelt down and quickly scooped the salad back onto the plate. He leaned over the counter to watch her. "You're wound tighter than a drum. What's wrong?"

"It's hard for me to be around you," she admitted. When she stood up, she hit her head on the counter.

"Are you okay?"

"I'm fine," she answered tensely, rubbing her head.

"Why is it hard to be around me?"

"I'd rather not say."

"If you don't want to say it, maybe you'd be willing to write it in whipped cream on top of my Jell-O."

"Very funny."

"I thought so."

"I'm sure you did."

"Meaning what?"

"It fits your level of maturity," she said, still rubbing her head.

"And you're way above that, right?"

"Listen, I'm smarter than you've ever given me credit

for. If you like me, then you have to like my mind too. It's a package deal."

"I like your mind. I enjoy the challenge of talking to you. You think I'd stand here and watch my Jell-O warm up with just anyone?"

"Why can't you ever frown once in a while? To you everything's a game. The whole trouble with our relationship was that we never talked about substantative issues."

"Substantative issues," he mocked. "Like what?"

"Like acid rain. Trees are dying every day, but do you care? No, of course not."

"I'm sorry they're dying, but what can I do about it?"

A girl going through the food line stopped to watch them.

"Besides, what have you ever done for a tree?" he asked.

"Excuse me, I've got to work."

She concentrated on putting out trays of desserts. A minute later he stood next to her, helping her work.

"This is a restricted area. It's just for Food Service employees."

"They just hired me. You're supposed to train me. Go ahead and work. I'll pick it up as we go along. We were talking about trees."

She turned to glare at him. "We weren't talking about trees. We were talking about our past relationship. It was superficial, just as this conversation is superficial."

He saw a white apron and put it on. "Hey, don't knock this. I'm enjoying every minute. The thing I missed most about you was the challenge of trying to figure you out. And we had good times together. Remember the time we cooked our breakfast in the snow."

She dropped a dish of butterscotch pudding on her shoe.

"Don't worry," he said. "I'll clean it up."

"I never drop things," she tried to explain. "It's just because you're here."

"It's all right. I understand."

He took a towel and wiped it up. "There, I got most of it."

"You liked the time we spent together?" she asked hopefully.

"Best time I ever had."

"But it was all superficial. We'd go to a movie or a dance, maybe have a treat, then pull up to the dorm, and talk. And maybe we'd kiss. Is that all there is to a meaningful relationship? I'm more than just a pretty face."

He followed her into the food preparation area, where she picked up a tray of chef's salads from a large refrigerator.

"Are you saying that nobody fully appreciates your splendor?"

He carried the tray to the food counter for her. They put the salads on the lazy Susan. "I'm saying there's a part of me that nobody here at BYU knows."

"Okay, show me."

She paused. "I can't show you here."

He looked at her strangely. "Why not?"

"It's not something I show, it's something I explain."

"Okay, after you get off work, tell me." He started on his Jell-O.

"I'd better warn you, it's going to be a serious discussion."

"Terrific."

"It won't be easy, but I'll tell you everything."

"Okay."

"But you've got to promise not to tell anyone."

"I won't."

She scowled at him. "Do you have to eat Jell-O while I'm talking serious?"

"Seriously," he said triumphantly. "It's an adverb."

"I quit work at ten o'clock."

"I'll meet you here then."

"And we'll talk," she said.

"Fine."

"Our discussion will be frank and open."

"And afterwards we'll issue a joint communiqué."

"And we won't make jokes. This is serious."

"Right. Can I have another Jell-O?"

At fifteen to ten Cody showed up and bought a small bowl of grapes and sat at a booth while he waited for her to finish work.

A few minutes later she sat down with him. "Want to know what I did this summer?" he asked.

"Sure."

"I worked for a highway construction company in Nevada. Here, I'll show you where I was." He started laying grapes down on the table. "Okay, this grape is the northeast corner of Nevada, and this grape is the northwest corner, and this grape is about where Reno is, where the boundary bends to make the left branch of its V-shape. Okay? And this grape is the southernmost point of the state. You got it so far? This grape is Las Vegas. Okay now, this grape goes where I worked this summer." He placed it carefully on the table. "It was near Winnemucca. We were building twenty miles of new road."

While he enthusiastically explained some of the details of his summer job, she absentmindedly reached down and picked up a grape from the table and popped it in her mouth.

"Oh, no!" he moaned. "You just ate Las Vegas."

Giggling together, they then proceeded to eat the entire state of Nevada.

"Where do you want to talk?" he asked later, as they walked outside.

"Anywhere—it doesn't matter."

"How about in the parking lot outside your dorm?"

"No, not there," she said.

"You said anywhere."

"I meant anywhere but there."

"Why not there?"

"Because that's where we always ended up after a date."

"And that's bad?"

"It's not bad—it's just that this isn't that kind of a date. This is a discussion date."

He shrugged his shoulders. "Where do people go for discussion dates?"

"I don't know. I've never had one either."

"The library?"

"It's closed," she said. "I know—how about the Eyring Science Center by the Foucault pendulum."

He nodded. "Right—this is going to be a pendulum kind of date."

They walked to the science center. The back doors were locked.

"There're always graduate students around a place like this," she said. "Can we walk around and look for lights that are on?"

They started walking. "There's a moon out tonight," he said, reaching for her hand.

She pulled away. "This isn't that kind of a date."

"It's not my fault the moon's out. I had nothing to do with it. Honest, it just came out on its own."

They walked to the front door and peered in. It was locked.

They turned around. They were facing a statue of Dr. Eyring. "Think of all that science has given the world," she said.

"I am," he said, putting his arms around her. She momentarily allowed herself to relax in his arms. He was about to kiss her.

She broke away. "This is supposed to be a discussion date, and you're ruining it."

"It takes two to ruin," he said.

"Cody, we've got to discuss something very important tonight."

"All right, all right. Discuss."

A sleepy graduate student opened the door to leave

the building. Cody grabbed the door before it closed, and they went in. The lobby was dimly lit. She asked him to stand opposite her across the twenty-foot circular framework for the Foucault pendulum.

"Women have come a long way in our time," she said. Her voice echoed in the large, dark room. The red light from the exit sign made them just visible to each other. "In the fields of literature, business, law, and science, women are now making their presence felt."

"Excuse me," he called out, "but should I be taking notes?"

"That's just like a man," she fumed. "You don't treat what I say with the least degree of respect. And you don't respect women. Women are just as capable of doing great things as men. They're just as smart, just as creative, and just as capable. In some cases, they're more capable. It's not right to limit a woman in any way."

"I'm not."

"Society does, and you're part of society. Have you ever heard of a right-hand woman? No. Why not? I'll tell you why, because we live in a male-biased society. That's why." Her voice was rising. "Listen to me. When I chew out that idiot French horn player because he can't carry a tune in a bucket, I'm still feminine. Feminine doesn't always have to be sweet, does it? Of course not! Sometimes feminine is angry! Why can't that idiot play what's written at G?"

He was looking at her strangely. She realized she'd been shouting.

She paused to gain her composure, cleared her throat nervously, and then continued in a lecture style. "Of course, it's true that women have babies, and that in itself makes them unique, but we should never overlook their other attributes."

"I never do," he said, smiling broadly.

She scowled. "You had to say that, didn't you. Well, anyway, take Lisa Salinger as an example."

"Who's Lisa Salinger?"

"She's the one who discovered the Grand Unified Field theory."

"Oh yeah—isn't she the one who sleeps on a roof and eats lawn clippings?"

"It's a storeroom where she sleeps, and it's not lawn clippings she eats. It's wheat and alfalfa sprouts."

"Well, that certainly sheds a new light on things. I have a completely different picture of her now. Oh, I also read she talks to rats, wears sheepskin pajamas, and gargles yogurt."

"She doesn't talk to rats! Well, okay, once she talked to a mouse, but good grief, it was just one mouse. And she doesn't have sheepskin pajamas. She has an old sheepskin coat that occasionally, on very cold winter nights, she wears over her nightgown. And she only gargles yogurt when she has a cold. Mostly her roommate made up those lies."

"What makes you such an authority on her?"

Dawn paused. "I wrote a report about her for a summer class."

"Okay, she's not quite as crazy as people think she is. So what?"

"She's a woman."

"Right—that's what you'd expect from someone named Lisa."

"Lisa Salinger did something that not even Albert Einstein was able to do."

"Okay, fine. She's the next Einstein. So what?"

"I want you to learn to like her."

"Why? I'll never meet her."

She paused, fighting for the right way to let him know who she was. "Let me say this another way. Before our relationship gets too serious, you need to understand something about me."

"And what's that?"

She wiped her damp brow. "It's kind of hard to explain."

"Well, go ahead and try."

Her hand was tugging nervously at a strand of hair. "Maybe if I give you an example. Two trains are approaching each other, each going forty miles an hour. When they start they're two hundred miles apart. There's a bird that can fly one hundred miles an hour. When the two trains begin, the bird starts at train A and flies to train B, then turns around and flies back to train A. He keeps doing this, going back and forth. Question: How far does the bird fly before the trains collide?"

He paused. "Is this important?"

"It's very important."

He shrugged his shoulders. "I don't know how far the bird goes. I can see that the distance he has to travel keeps getting shorter as the trains approach each other."

"That's right."

"I'd need some time to work on it."

"You don't know the answer, but I do. How does that make you feel?"

"It's your problem—I'd expect you to know the answer."

"But what if I gave you ten minutes to work on the problem, and you couldn't work it. How would that make you feel?"

"I could figure it out if I really wanted to."

"Maybe. But what if you couldn't, and what if I told you I can do the problem in my head. How would that make you feel then?"

"Hey, no problem," he said with his hands up for emphasis.

"You wouldn't be threatened by that?"

"No."

"The answer is two hundred and fifty miles. It doesn't threaten you that I can work it in my head?"

"Why should it? Just because you can work a dumb problem about a bird? You think that bothers me? It doesn't matter, really."

"It's very possible that I'm smarter than you are."

"In some things maybe, but I'm smarter than you are

in other areas. When it comes to doing anything outdoors I'm better. I can hike better, fish better, hunt better, and run a survey crew better."

"But what if I'm really good in math? I mean super
good."

"Fine."

"You wouldn't be at all threatened by that?"

"No. Why should I be?"

"You're sure?"

"Of course. I'm very open-minded."

She sighed. "That's good."

"So you know how far the bird flies. Is that your secret?"

"That's not all. Listen to me—I want to tell you something I've never told anyone before at BYU."

"I'm listening."

"You've got to promise not to tell this to anyone."

"I promise."

"Okay." She looked around to make sure nobody else
was listening. "There are four basic forces in the universe: the gravitational force, the electromagnetic force,
the strong nuclear force that binds protons and neutrons
inside the nucleus, and the nuclear weak force. The electromagnetic, strong, and weak forces have all been described by quantum theories, which says that the force is
carried by small packets of energy. For instance, in the
case of light, the force carriers are called photons. For a
long time scientists had hoped that the four different
forces might be manifestations of a single underlying
law. The problem was that the gravitational force refused to fall into line, until Lisa Salinger came up with the
Grand Unified Field Theory."

He paused. "That's cute. Where'd you memorize that
from?"

"Cody, my secret is I'm a genius."

"Hey, no problem. It doesn't change anything."

"Do you mean that?" Her expression suddenly
brightened.

"Sure. So you're a genius. I can handle that."

"All right! Cody, I now declare this discussion date to be over!" She ran into his arms.

A minute later they started toward the door. "It was so hard for me to tell you. I was afraid you'd be intimidated."

He put his arm around her and hugged her. "My little genius," he said.

She scowled and backed away. "You don't really believe me, do you."

"Why do you say that?"

"The term 'my little genius' is demeaning."

"What's demeaning about it?"

"*Little*. It's like 'the little woman.'"

"What do you want—my big genius?"

"I'm not big."

"Okay, how about my genius then."

"That's better—except I'm not yours in the sense of property, as in 'my car.'"

"How about saying, a genius who—I mean whom—I love."

"That's okay."

He breathed a sigh of relief. "Terrific—I got it right. Let's go celebrate. How about buying enough grapes to map out the entire continental United States?"

They walked to his car. "So your big secret is you can do bird and train problems. Is that it?"

She hadn't actually told him she was Lisa Salinger. *I'll save that for later,* she thought. *First let him get used to me being a genius.* "That's right."

"I thought it was something serious."

"Nothing very serious," she said lightly. "Can you come over for supper Sunday?"

"Sure."

"I'll bake some bread for you. I learned how last summer."

A few minutes later they walked up to the dorm.

"Crazy lady, I'm pretty sure I love you. Hey, I've got a bizarre idea. Why don't we get engaged tonight?"

She giggled. "Really? Are you serious?"

"But it's only because you have a cute nose." He kissed her nose.

"Give me a good reason why our getting married would be a good idea," she said, trying to be objective.

"I love you. That's reason number one."

She suddenly moved away. "You love Dawn."

"Right. That's your name, isn't it?"

"I have two names. You know only one."

"Is this another problem, like the one about three missionaries and three cannibals, and they have to row across a river on a boat that will only take two people, but if you ever have two cannibals and one missionary together, the cannibals will eat the missionaries? Okay, I give up. What's your other name?"

"Lisa," she said.

"That's your middle name?"

"Yes."

"That's the same as your weird friend."

"She's no weirder than I am."

"If you say so. Dawn Lisa, will you marry me in the temple in about three months?"

"In the temple?" she asked.

"Sure. Is there any other way?"

She still wasn't a member of the Church yet, though everyone thought she was, thanks to her access to the school's computer files. "There may be one or two things we need to talk about before then."

"You want to talk about them now?" He looked into her eyes, holding both her hands.

She shook her head wearily. "No way. This is plenty for one night."

Cody invited her to spend the next weekend at his parents' home in Ogden. The entire family was getting together. As they drove there Saturday afternoon, enjoying the beauty of the fall, he described his family to her. His older brother, Darin, was married to Gail. They had four children, the oldest being seven years old. He also had a sister two years younger than he. Her name was Dianna. She was married to Kirk and had two children, a girl two years old and a boy six months old. There was also a seventeen-year-old sister, Heidi. She was a junior in high school. Next came fifteen-year-old Alan, and then eleven-year-old Josie.

She met the members of the family all at once, and it took a while to get them all straight in her mind.

The family lived in an older brick home in an established part of town. It was not a large home, considering the size of the family, but it did have a certain charm. In the backyard was a treehouse for the children, as well as a garden that was still producing a large variety of vegetables.

Cody's father was a building contractor. Like his son, he was full of jokes. He loved to play with his grandchildren, and he spent much of Saturday giving rides on the tree swing. Sometimes, with a magician's wave of his hand, he'd find a piece of candy hidden in one of their ears.

Cody's mother had gray-blue eyes and ash-brown hair, flecked with strands of gray. Worry lines had begun to mark her face, but she was still beautiful. She hugged her grandchildren every time they got close enough to her.

To Dawn it seemed like a circus, with kids and dogs and bowls of snacking popcorn together in the small living room.

Cody's father, seeing her experiencing culture shock, came up to her and said quietly, "Come on outside with me. I want to show you something."

They walked through a small kitchen full of good smells and out the back door. On his way out, he picked up a salt shaker.

He showed her his tomato patch. "Pick a couple of tomatoes for us."

"It's a wonderful garden." She carefully pulled off two large tomatoes.

"Smell your hands," he said. "Isn't that wonderful? You get it anytime you work around tomato plants." He gave her the salt shaker. "We'll have to be careful we don't get seeds on our clothes. We wouldn't want to give ourselves away. Spoiling our supper, that's what my wife calls it. I don't know why—eating before supper never hurt my appetite."

She took a bite of tomato. The warm tomato juice seemed to explode in her mouth. She sprinkled some salt in the open part of the tomato.

He took a bite and grinned. "We're rich, you know that? Anytime you can walk out in your garden and eat a whole tomato from the vine, you're rich as Rockefeller."

"It's delicious."

Cody was in the front yard teasing his nieces and nephews. He galloped into the backyard with one on his back and others chasing him.

Noticing that their grandfather was outside, the children came around and begged for a ride on the tree swing. They kept him busy.

Alan, the fifteen-year-old, came out looking for her. "Cody says you like math. Want to see my computer?"

They went to Alan's room. He turned on his computer and the TV monitor. "I bought this with money from my paper route. Last summer I spent about five hours a day programming it. I'm working on a game program. I want to enter it in a contest Atari sponsors and see if I can start getting royalties from it. Want to see it work?"

"Sure."

A few minutes later they went over the program step by step, trying to rewrite it so it'd run faster. "If that's still not fast enough," Dawn said, "I'd suggest you switch to machine language. Initially it'll be a pain to program, but it'll speed things up. I'll send you a book that might help."

"Thanks. Oh, by the way, I'm glad Cody's going to marry you."

"Thank you."

She went into the living room. The men were sitting around talking.

"Dawn, the women are all in the kitchen helping get supper ready," Cody said.

At first she didn't understand what he meant, but then she realized he wanted her to go out there too. She wanted to stay in the living room with the men, who were talking about building ultralight planes from a kit. She was worried that if she went into the kitchen, she might be asked to do something she didn't know how to do. Cooking had never been of much interest to her. All the time she was growing up, feminist leaders were encouraging girls to escape the drudgery of housework and do something significant with their lives. She had gladly followed the advice.

That's why she liked canned soup.

But she could see that Cody wanted her to help out in

the kitchen, so she decided to go see what homemakers do.

"Can I help?" she asked weakly when she entered the kitchen.

"We never turn down offers to help," Cody's mother said. "What would you like to do?"

She paused, not knowing what to say.

"You can take my job," Dianna volunteered. "I've got to go nurse my baby."

"Oh, don't go, Dianna," Cody's mother said. "You can nurse in here. We'll just tell the men and boys to stay out."

Dianna showed Dawn how to make a radish look like a flower, then picked up her baby, put a shawl over her and the baby, and started nursing.

As she worked on the relish tray, Dawn often looked up to watch Dianna. It was the first time in her life she'd ever seen a woman nurse. In fact, she didn't know people did that anymore. She was both curious and a little embarrassed. Dianna, however, seemed quite at ease.

The women were cheerful. They didn't seem to mind doing all the work to prepare the meal. And she had to admit a certain pride in each radish flower she turned out.

Dianna stopped for a minute to burp her baby. A large noise erupted, and she laughed. "That's my boy," she said. He laughed. "Are you my lunch mouth?" she asked. The baby laughed again. A pattern developed. Each time she made a funny face and asked if he was her lunch mouth, he laughed.

The laugh began in his toes and rumbled and tumbled through his body until it rushed out. Dawn felt a tugging at her heart, a yearning to have her own baby.

"Okay, kid, the fun's over," Dianna said. "Lunch time again." She looked up and noticed Dawn watching. She smiled. "I love doing this for my baby."

"Was it hard at first? I'd have no idea how to even start."

"Nature does most of the work. The rest is just patience."

"Dawn, you've been so quiet. Tell us all about yourself," Cody's mother asked.

She told the things she'd invented about Dawn Fields. They seemed willing to accept it, even though, she painfully reminded herself, it was all a lie. She was an imposter in their home.

They trust me, she thought. *But I'm not Dawn Fields, and I'm not a member of the Church, and I can't be married to their son in a temple.*

"Well, I think we're almost ready," Cody's mother said a few minutes later. "Let's dish out the children's plates first. They'll eat on the picnic table outside."

A few minutes later the family knelt in family prayer around the kitchen table. Cody's father offered the prayer. He thanked God that the family was all together again; then he prayed for a blessing on the food.

Suppertime was full of old jokes and good food and kids running in and out of the house, asking for more food or reporting who pulled whose hair or which cousin dumped his beans in the garden.

Afterwards the men volunteered to clean up, and the women sat in the living room and wondered how many plates would get broken before the job was finished.

"Can I hold your baby?" Dawn asked Dianna.

"Sure. Put this shawl over you in case he spits up."

She held the baby in her arms. He was sleepy and warm and cuddly. He gently tugged at her hair. After a few minutes, he fell asleep.

"I can lay him down if you want," Dianna said, picking him up and taking him away.

They decided to have family home evening. It was held in a mammoth tree with huge branches, set on a hillside near the house. The tree was easy to climb by approaching it from the uphill side.

"This is our family tree," Cody's father joked as he

boosted Dawn up on a branch next to Cody. Children and parents were strung all along the lower branches.

"How come we can't be on that branch?" one of the kids complained.

"Because you can't," his cousin said.

"It's not fair. They got the best branch."

The parents tried to stop the bickering.

Cody's father laughed. "Family home evening is the only argument that begins and ends with prayer."

They sang a song. The sound boomed over the valley. Then one of the grandchildren offered a prayer.

"And now the Wells Grandkid Choir will sing some songs for you."

"I don't want to sing," a slacker complained.

Dianna led them in singing "Pioneer Children." The voices came in scattered formation with the younger kids always a little late, one older kid always out of tune, one trying to sing as loud as he could, one hanging back, another just standing there resentful of the whole idea. When it was finished, their grandfather praised them and gave each one a stick of gum.

"We're happy to have you all here tonight," Cody's father began, "especially to have Dawn here with us. We're delighted Cody's found such a lovely girl to be his bride."

"Relieved is closer to the truth," Darin joked.

"Well, anyway," Cody's father continued, "I want all of you to know there's nothing in my life that's given me more joy than my family. I love you all. Dawn, we'd like to hear from you now."

They helped her out of the tree so she could stand and talk to them. "I've enjoyed being here. The food was delicious. Oh, I hope you all liked your radish flowers Dianna and I made. It's been a lot of fun. Seeing Cody's family, I can see why he's such a special person."

"What temple will you two be getting married in?"

Suddenly she felt terrible.

Cody helped her out. "I think probably the Provo Temple, because we see it every time we go on a date. That'll always be our temple."

"Are you all right?" Cody's mother asked Dawn, whose face was flushed.

"It must've been the hike up here to the tree," she said, wiping the perspiration from her face and sitting down on a large rock to rest.

At the request of the grandchildren, the entire family played Hide and Seek until it got too dark. Then they went inside and had ice cream and raspberries from the garden.

Finally it was bedtime. Darin and Gail wandered around the house trying to find scattered shoes or socks or sweaters before they left for their home in Logan. Dianna and Kirk, who lived in California and were out for a visit, bedded down their family.

Dawn was to sleep in seventeen-year-old Heidi's room. Because she was a guest, she was given first chance at the bathroom. When she finished, she returned to the room and looked around. Track medallions and ribbons hung from Heidi's bulletin board, and a certificate naming her the most-improved choir singer in her sophomore year hung on the wall. There were also two pictures of boys. A poster of the Ogden Temple hung over the bed, and a copy of the scriptures lay on a nearby table. Dawn picked up the Bible. Certain passages throughout were marked in red.

On a dresser she saw a beautiful booklet, apparently used by girls in the Church to set their goals in life. A girl was encouraged to set a goal in each of several areas of importance. She wanted to see what goals Heidi had set but decided it would be an invasion of privacy. She put the booklet back.

There was a knock on the door. She opened it, and Cody's mother entered.

"How are you feeling now?"

"A lot better, thank you."

"Here's an extra blanket if you need it."

"Poor Heidi. I feel bad about kicking her out of her bedroom. Where's she sleeping tonight?"

"Oh, don't worry about her. She'll be sleeping in our camper. I think she prefers it there anyway."

"I'll thank her in the morning."

"Fine. Oh, do you have a minute? I want to show you something."

They walked downstairs. In a corner of the basement, Cody's mother turned on a bank of lights. There on an easel was a watercolor painting.

"This is what I do to keep my sanity. Over there is a stack of the ones I've finished."

Dawn went through them one by one, mostly landscapes but also a few portraits.

"I like them very much," Dawn said.

"It's good therapy. Sometimes when I get in the mood, I come down and paint and just forget about all the have-to's in my life. I work down here for a day or two, and then I'm okay and can go back and take care of my responsibilities again."

"You're really happy with your life, aren't you," Dawn said.

"Very much, and you will be too."

"Do you ever wish you had a career?"

"Well, of course, I have worked. I had a job while Cody was on his mission. I was good at it, and sure, there was satisfaction in earning money, but my career is being a wife and mother. It's what I most enjoy doing. I love it when my kids run in the house and yell, 'Mom, guess what happened?' And I enjoy it when my husband comes home from work and tells me how his day has been. I just love what I do. Sure, I know that sometimes mothers have to get jobs out of economic necessity, but I'm glad we've been able to manage most of the time on what my husband earns. All in all, I guess I'm about as fulfilled as I want to be."

Dawn nodded. "I admire you."

"What about you? Will you work after you're married?"

"I don't know yet," Dawn admitted. "I'm having a little trouble sorting out my life."

"It'll come. Don't worry, you'll do just fine. You know, I've prayed for Cody's future wife since he was born. I've prayed that she'd be true to the gospel and worthy to be married in the temple, and now look, here you are."

Dawn turned away, feeling miserable again. "I'd better get some sleep now."

"Of course. Good night."

Dawn went to her room, crawled into bed, and cried quietly so that nobody would hear.

After church and lunch on Sunday, they returned to BYU. As Cody drove, Dawn put her head on his shoulder. She had to tell him that she wasn't Dawn Fields and that she wasn't even a member of the Church.

More than ever, she wanted to be baptized. But when she was baptized, it'd have to be as Lisa Salinger. She wouldn't lie to enter the kingdom of God.

She decided she'd just have to admit to the world her real identity, and then nothing could stop her from being baptized. Of course, it'd put her in the public eye again, but maybe the news media would leave her alone. There hadn't been much interest in Lisa Salinger lately.

She wondered if Cody would accept her as Lisa Salinger. He said he didn't mind if she was good at math. Now all he had to do was accept her as Lisa Salinger. She had it all worked out: She'd tell him who she was, and then she'd be baptized, and then they'd go to the temple and get married.

As they kissed at the door, she decided to tell him the next day.

She entered her room and found that Robyn was still at her parents' place. As she got ready for bed, she daydreamed about Cody. She recalled how that morning at his parents' home she'd been awakened by his gentle knock on her door. Knowing that he was just outside in the hall, she wanted to ask him to come in. It would've seemed natural for him to come in, sit down on her bed, and give her a good-morning kiss.

She decided she was ready for marriage.

She thought it would be nice to have some dreamy music to go to sleep to. Maybe she'd dream about Cody.

She turned on the radio. The news was on. ". . . unique in several ways. First of all, it represents only the third time the Nobel Prize in physics has been given to a woman. Some have suggested that the committee was under considerable pressure to award at least one of the Nobel Prizes this year to a woman. Secondly, this year's winner, Lisa Salinger, has for the past year completely dropped out of sight. It is believed that she is living somewhere in California under an assumed name. The Nobel committee was unable to contact her to let her know of her selection. It isn't clear at this time whether she'll even appear in Sweden in December to accept the award.

"Salinger will be remembered by the publicity she received two years ago when a professor at Princeton with whom she had been working charged that she had stolen his ideas and published them. In subsequent hearings, it was determined that the charges were false.

"Salinger takes on the image of Albert Einstein with this award, since Einstein spent several of his last years trying to come up with the same theory. In addition, although Einstein did not receive the Nobel Prize until he was forty-two, most of the work for which he received the prize was done while he was still in his twenties. Salinger at twenty-four will be the youngest recipient in history, beating William Lawrence Bragg, who in 1915 received the award in physics at age twenty-five for the study of crystal structure by means of X rays.

"In the past the Nobel judges have been extremely conservative, usually waiting at least ten years after significant research is published before considering a scientist for such a high honor. In contrast, Salinger's work was published just two years ago. A spokesman for the Nobel Foundation has indicated that the reason for the lack of delay in Salinger's case is that recent experimental work from several areas of research has verified the predictions made from her Grand Unified Field Theory.

"The awards will be presented December 10 in Stockholm, Sweden. Other winners this year include . . ."

In a daze she walked barefooted in her nightgown down to the storeroom. She sat on a trunk and stared at the darkened shadows of suitcases. It was quiet in the dorm. All the good little girls upstairs were asleep in their beds.

And she was a Nobel Prize Laureate.

CHAPTER NINE

The next day Dawn skipped classes and took a long walk on the foothills near campus.

At noon she phoned her mother at the hardware store.

"Lisa, did you hear the news?" her mother cried out. "You won a Nobel Prize!"

"I know, Mom."

"All last night the phone kept on ringing. Reporters want to know where you are. They want to interview you. What shall I tell 'em?"

"Tell 'em I'm coming home. I'll be there tomorrow night."

She made plane reservations to Minneapolis. She planned to rent a car there and then drive to Fargo.

After supper Cody picked her up and they went to the library. She stared mindlessly at the same page for half an hour, then finally shut the book. "I don't want to study," she said.

"What do you want to do?"

"I want you to hold me."

"Nice idea, but I've got all this homework to do."

"What are you working on?"

"Statics and mechanics."

"How long will you be?"

"I don't know. I've been working on one problem for two hours and still haven't got anywhere."

"Mind if I look at it?"

He shrugged his shoulders. "Be my guest."

She read the problem. A few minutes later she wrote down several equations. "May I use your calculator?"

A short time later she handed him the answer. "Now will you hold me?"

He looked in amazement at her equations. "How did you do this?"

"It's like the train problem. There's a hard way and an easy way. I always try to do things the easy way. Now can we leave?"

"Good grief," he said quietly.

He drove her to the parking lot outside the dorm.

"I've got to go away tomorrow for a few days," she said.

"What for?"

"My aunt's sick. She asked me to come and help out. It shouldn't be very long. Cody, please hold me. I want to be in your arms again."

He put his arms around her. She started crying. "You must really be worried about your aunt," he said.

The next day she flew to Minneapolis, took a cab to a motel, checked in under a fictitious name, changed her identity back to Lisa, took a cab to the airport, put a suitcase with Dawn's clothes in a locker, left twenty dollars in the locker in order to reserve it for more than twenty-four hours, rented a car under Lisa's name, then started for North Dakota.

Lisa Salinger's hair had been short, but in the two years she'd been at BYU as Dawn, she'd let it grow out. The day before she returned to North Dakota, she'd bought a short wig to preserve the Lisa look.

Four hours later she arrived in Fargo. When she approached the apartment her mother lived in, she continued on without stopping because the entire block was filled with cars and TV crews. She took the car to a service station and asked if she could leave it there for a couple of days, then took a cab to the apartment and bravely stepped out.

"There she is!" someone yelled.

She met her mother on the landing. They hugged each other. A crowd of reporters took their picture. Her sister Karen, now six months pregnant, was also there. The three of them hurried upstairs with reporters following close by. Finally they reached her mother's apartment, went inside, and slammed the door shut.

A representative of the media knocked on the door and requested a news conference. Lisa agreed. Arrangements were made for it to be held at her old grade school in an hour. TV crews hurried over to set up.

Lisa went to her room and looked at herself in the mirror. With the glasses, the wig, and the gray dress, she didn't look anything like Dawn. She had to protect Dawn and Cody because all this would destroy what they had together. In a way she was grateful to Kimberly for creating a distorted image of her. Kimberly had created a monster, and all Lisa had to do for the next few days was to be that monster.

At the news conference her grade-school principal took charge, introducing her mother and sister to the media and pointing out that they were in the same school where Lisa had first shown promise in science. Then he turned the time over to Lisa.

She began with a statement to the press, which she read. ". . . I'm pleased to be chosen for this honor. There are many others who paved the way for me to come up with the Grand Unified Field Theory. I would like to thank the faculty of Princeton University for their part in this. Thank you."

Ten hands shot up, and everyone started asking questions at once. The principal, used to unruly classes, stepped in. "Not all at once! Okay, you first."

"What does this award mean to the women's movement?" a reporter asked.

"I believe it shows that women can compete with men in any arena."

A man interrupted. "Some say the only reason you received this is because of political pressure exerted by feminist groups to have more women recognized. As you know, during the week the Nobel committee was meeting, women were outside picketing in the streets. Don't you think this might have affected their decision? Also, why should a woman be given this award on work done only two years ago, when typically everyone else receives the prize for work done ten or twenty years ago?"

Lisa answered. "The experimental verification by Tanaka in Japan and by the CERN group in Europe have been important to the validation of my work. That may explain why the Nobel committee felt justified in giving the award after only two years. As to the first part of your question, I would hope my work was judged on its own merits and with no regard to my being a woman."

"If you were married, would you take a back seat to your husband?"

"How do you mean?"

"Would you ever give up your work as a scientist to be a full-time wife and mother?"

"Let me answer your question using a symmetry argument. Symmetry is an important concept in science. You ask if I could combine my career with marriage, and yet very seldom is the same question asked of a man. That shows a lack of symmetry. Question: Is this lack of symmetry imposed by cultural differences or by nature itself? It seems to many that it has been imposed by tradition. Symmetry considerations alone would lead us to believe it worthwhile for both husband and wife to share more equally the burdens of family and the challenges of professional development." She turned to the man who asked the question. "Let me impose this concept of symmetry and ask you a question: When was the last time you hugged your kids?"

There was an awkward silence.

Another question filled the void. "Is it true you have a sheepskin nightgown, and that you gargle yogurt?"

"Yes, that's all true."

Another reporter: "Is it true that while you were coming up with your theory, you worked in a storeroom and talked to mice?"

"Just one mouse. It wasn't a long conversation."

"Can you tell us where you're living now?" someone else asked.

"I can, but I won't."

"Why not?"

"Because I want to be spared future question-and-answer sessions like this from the media."

She smiled faintly at their laughter.

At the conclusion of the press conference, the women in the audience applauded. Her argument about symmetry was used over and over again. In fact, *Ms Magazine* made her their Woman of the Year.

A few minutes later she left the room, surrounded by reporters. She went home with her mother and her sister. They shut and locked the door, but the reporters stayed in the hall and on the stairs.

At five Karen left to go fix supper for her husband.

At eleven that night several reporters were still waiting outside, hoping for an exclusive interview. Her mother went to bed. Lisa turned on "Nightline."

". . . Salinger seems to have rejected most of the things women traditionally are interested in—marriage, children, nurturing. Frankly, I find that significant."

"Why's that, Dr. Warner?"

"Well, I think it's obvious—she thinks like a man. That's why she's made such progress in her research."

Lisa angrily threw a pillow at the TV.

"We also have in the studio Kimberly Brown. Kim-

berly, welcome to 'Nightline.' I understand you were Lisa
Salinger's roommate at Princeton during the time she
was developing her theory. Tell us what she's like."

"Well, she was just a terrifically hard worker. I remember one Christmas when she didn't leave the room
for three weeks. We tried to get her to join in caroling
with us but she absolutely refused. I guess that's what you
need if you're going to get a Nobel Prize."

"You knew her well. Did she show any interest in men
while she roomed with you?"

"None at all. In fact, she seems to be generally resentful of men. I tried to line up dates for her, but she always
refused."

"Do you have any idea why?"

"Well, as you know, I just finished a biography of her.
It's called *Woman of Destiny*. It'll be coming out in a
month. When I was doing research for the book, I found
out that when Lisa was in junior high, her parents were
divorced. Her mother ended up with nothing, and they
had to scrape by on very little. That might have caused a
lot of the resentment Lisa now feels toward men."

"Some have accused you of exploiting your
friendship with Lisa."

"Oh, I don't think of it that way at all. I just want to
share some interesting details about a truly great indi-
vidual."

Lisa felt sick. She went to bed.

She woke up at six in the morning and looked outside. Some media people were still on the lawn. She went
back to bed and daydreamed about Cody for another
hour until her mother got up.

During the day the apartment was a prison. Her
mother went to work at nine. A TV news team hounded
her at work, interviewing her boss and the customers
who came in the hardware store.

The phone rang all morning with offers. Someone
called and asked if Lisa'd like to pose for a men's

magazine. She hung up on them and left the phone off the hook for the rest of the day.

Just before noon there was a knock on the door.

"Go away," she said through the closed door.

"Lisa, it's Kimberly and Hal. Please let us in."

She opened the door. Kimberly lingered in the doorway and smiled at the reporters and hyped the book she'd written about Lisa. She smiled for several pictures, then closed the door. "I hate all this publicity, don't you?" Kimberly said with a grin.

Hal put his arm around Lisa. "Well, well—how's our little Nobel Prize winner, hey?"

"Do you mind?" she said, removing his arm from around her.

"Same old Lisa, right? Listen, I hope you're not mad at us for trying to make you a rich woman. Remind me to show you your savings account balance before we leave."

"Mad?" she asked. "Why should I be mad? You've lied and distorted everything about me, so that unless I walk down the street with sprouts hanging from my teeth and rats following me, nobody recognizes me."

"You are mad, aren't you," Kimberly said.

She calmed down. "In a way I guess maybe it's worked out for the best."

Hal patted her on the back. "Good girl. We can work together. Look, there's money to be made. We need to get in now while we can. You're hot now, but in two months you'll be as dead as disco. How many times do you figure you could lecture a month? We'll charge five thousand a shot. Think of it, ten thousand a weekend if we just schedule things right."

"I'm not giving any talks."

"You're tossing away forty thousand a month," Hal said. "Kimberly, tell her about the dress."

"It's coming out next month—the Lisa Salinger designer dress. It has all your equations on it."

"And the sheepskin pajamas," Hal added. "A whole

new line. Oh, the sheep industry asked me to say thanks. Also, they were wondering how you feel about leg of lamb."

"Look, I just want to be left alone."

"I love it," Kimberly said. "I think it works for you. I mean it's so Greta Garbo."

Hal nodded his head. "Go ahead, stay hidden for a few weeks. Just tell us where you are. We won't tell a soul."

"It'll be our little secret," Kimberly said.

"I'm not telling you where I'm living. Now please leave."

"Sure, we'll go," Kimberly said. "But can I use your bathroom for a minute first?"

Kimberly left for the bathroom.

Hal flexed his muscles. "See the improvement? I added an inch to my biceps."

"Terrific," she droned.

Hal showed her how much she'd made in the last six months. A few minutes later, she happened to look back. Kimberly was in her bedroom going through her suitcase. "Get out of there!" she screamed, running to stop her.

Kimberly slammed the suitcase shut.

"Did you find anything?" Hal asked.

"Lipstick, eye shadow, a contact-lens case. Lisa, when did you start using eye shadow, and why don't you have any on now?"

"I want you out of here!"

"I've got it!" Hal said. "She's disguising herself as a normal person."

"I'm calling the police unless you leave!" Lisa shouted.

"We're going. Hey, don't worry, your secret is safe with us," Kimberly promised.

They left.

Lisa hurried to see if there was anything else Kimberly might have found. She went through the suitcase carefully. She couldn't find anything to connect her to Dawn. Dawn's clothes were in a locker in the Minneapolis airport.

Her mother came home at five. "What a day," she said, falling exhaustedly onto the sofa. "I spent the entire time talking to news people. My boss made them each buy something. He had good business. I had a lousy day. You want to know what they asked me? 'How does it feel to be the mother of a Nobel Prize winner?' Try answering that twenty times in a row. 'Why does she hide from the world? Will she ever get married?' I'm tired of questions."

"Sorry, Mom."

"How long are you planning on staying here? I'd like to have some peace and quiet again."

"I'll leave as soon as I can travel without being followed."

"Where are you living?"

"I can't tell you."

"You can't tell your own mother?"

"Mom, if they found out, I'd never have a minute's rest."

"Okay, okay."

They went in the kitchen to fix supper.

"I have a friend," her mother said. "His name is Roy Arnold. He runs an upholstery shop. He's been divorced too. We go to the dog track together sometimes. I wanted you to meet him before you go. He's coming over for supper."

Half an hour later there was a knock on the window. Lisa looked out. There was a man standing on a ladder. She let him in through the window.

"Lisa, this is Mr. Arnold. You two sit down and visit while I cook some hamburgers."

"You can call me Roy. Quite a crowd outside, isn't there? I had the ladder in my truck anyway and figured it'd be a way to get in without having to answer a lot of questions."

"Mom says you have an upholstery business. What kind of upholstery do you do?"

"I do a lot of cars. You get a car about three years old and your upholstery starts to fall apart. Unless you want it to look bad, you need to get new seat covers. Oh sure, you can always get something at K-Mart for next to nothing, but if a person wants quality, he has to pay for it."

"Sure," she said.

"My work's guaranteed too," he said.

Her mother brought in the food. They sat down and started eating.

"Had an interesting thing happen to me today after work," Roy said. "Two Mormon missionaries came by. They go door to door, you know."

"I never let 'em in," her mother said.

"Oh, me either. I told 'em I wasn't interested. Sent 'em on their way in short order."

Her mother nodded her head. "The thing I can't understand is why that religion hasn't died out yet. Sure, they could pull the wool over people's eyes a hundred years ago, but today people are more educated."

Lisa couldn't let that pass. "Mom, you don't know what you're talking about. Brigham Young University is one of the best schools in the country. And there're plenty of scholars and scientists who belong to the Church."

"Maybe so, but they're wrong. I know that," her mother said.

"How do you know if you've never listened to them?"

"Oh, I know. I've heard about their gold bible."

"You mean the Book of Mormon? How can you decide about a book you've never read?"

"Don't need to read it. I know they're wrong. That's all I need to know."

The subject was closed.

Her mother brought in some ice cream.

"Are you going to tell her?" Roy asked.

"Lisa, Roy and I—we've decided to get married. We thought you'd want to know."

"Oh," she said.

"I'll be moving in with him," her mother said.

"But you're welcome to stay anytime you want to drop by," Mr. Arnold said. "We've got an extra bedroom, and if you'll give us a few days' notice so I can get my upholstery supplies out of it, you're welcome anytime."

"Thank you."

They watched TV for an hour before Roy climbed back down the ladder. Just as he touched the ground, a reporter saw him. Roy grabbed the ladder, ran to his truck, and pulled away. As it turned, the lettering on the side of the truck became visible. The reporter stopped and jotted something in his notebook.

Her mother looked out the window and then turned to Lisa. "I'll understand if you can't make it to my wedding."

That night Lisa phoned Cody.

"I miss you," he said. "When are you coming back?"

"Soon," she said.

"How soon?"

"As soon as I can."

"I want to marry you," he said.

"Cody, there's something I need to tell you."

"What is it?"

"I'll tell you when I get back."

Two days later she decided to make a run for it.

She got up at two in the morning and walked through backyards until she got to the gas station where her car was. She drove to the Minneapolis airport, turned in the car, picked up her other suitcase from the locker, took a taxi to a motel, checked in, changed back to Dawn, took another taxi to the airport, and took a plane to Salt Lake City and then a limousine van to Provo.

By the time she got to her apartment, it was eight at
night. She phoned Cody.

"I'm home."

"I'll be right over."

She waited in the lobby for him. As soon as she saw
him coming up the walk, she ran outside and threw her
arms around him.

"I love you," she said.

"Lady, I've been dying to hear you say that again. I
love you too. What is it you want to tell me?"

"Not now."

"I've got a present for you from my mother. It's in the
car. I'll go get it."

He returned with a portrait of Dawn. The face was
full of light and cheer and hope. It was Dawn.

It made her cry to see the painting.

Monday morning when she came out of class, a girl
approached her. "Are you Dawn Fields?"

"Yes."

"The *Universe* wants to do a story about you."

"I don't want a story done about me."

"Just a human-interest feature. You know, where you
went to high school, what you're majoring in, how you
got the idea of starting COEDS, things like that."

"Please, no story."

"I've done some research on you. Do you have a minute?"

They sat in an empty lecture room.

"Your student information form says you're a member of the Church from Grand Island, Nebraska. Well, I
know a guy from there, and he says he's never heard of
you. That's the first question. Are you really from Nebraska?"

"My parents moved there from Fargo, North Dakota,
a few weeks before I left for BYU. That's why nobody
there knows who I am."

"Well, that explains it then," the girl said with a re-assuring smile.

Dawn smiled back.

"But you are a member of the Church, right?"

"Yes, of course."

"So there's a bishop in Fargo who knows you?"

"Yes," she lied.

"Who would that be?"

"They just changed bishops. I don't know who the new one is."

"Who was it when you were in high school?"

"Look, I need to get to class or I'll be late."

"Okay. I'll call you tonight. I thought I'd talk to my cousin too. He's dating a girl from some place in North Dakota. It's either Fargo or Bismarck."

Dawn left. *They're getting closer,* she thought. *How many days do I have before this whole thing blows up in my face?*

Saturday they went for a hike. It was late fall, and there was snow on the top of the mountains. Cody kept telling her how beautiful it all was.

Partway up, they stopped to rest. She sat down on a large boulder. He sat beside her.

"How much farther are we going?" she asked.

"To the top."

She sighed. "Is this my punishment for leaving you last week?"

He laughed.

"Hold me," she said.

"Okay."

"Don't let go."

"They'll find us next spring locked in each other's arms—two giant ice cubes."

"Good," she said contentedly.

"You're ruining my plans," he whispered in her ear.

"What plans?"

"We were supposed to get to the top before I gave you

this." He reached into his pocket and pulled out an engagement ring. He slipped it on her finger. It was too big.

"We'll get it adjusted, but anyway, you get the idea. It would've been much more impressive on top of the mountain, don't you think? Also if we were on top of the mountain, we'd be able to see the temple where we'll be married."

He kissed her.

I'll tell him when he takes me back to the dorm, she thought. But she didn't. He asked her about going to the movie on campus that night. She agreed.

I'll tell him before the movie.

She went back to her room and took a long shower and then did her hair.

Tami came in the bathroom, also in the process of getting ready for a date.

"Can I talk to you?" Dawn asked.

"Sure. What's up?"

"I'm not really a member of the Church."

"You aren't? Why not? You live like you are."

"I want to be. It's a long story. Cody doesn't know yet. I'm going to tell him tonight, and if he's understanding, then I'll get baptized and we'll be able to get married in the temple."

"I guess you know about the required year's waiting period between the time you're baptized and when you can go to the temple."

"A year?"

"Yes. The reason I know is because my brother-in-law had to wait that long before he and my sister went to the temple."

Dawn went in her room and closed the door and cried.

The movie was a comedy.

I'll tell him when he takes me home.

They went to the snack area and had a cherry lime.

Gary Doyle came up to them. "Your roommate said I might find you here." He sat down in the same booth. "I had an interesting phone call the other day from a reporter for the *Washington Post.* He was calling from North Dakota. It seems he talked to a man at an upholstery shop . . . let's see . . ." He looked down at his notebook. "Oh, yes, Roy Arnold. Arnold said he'd had dinner with Lisa Salinger, the Nobel Prize winner, and her mom a few days ago, and Salinger had defended the Mormons and BYU. So the reporter called me to ask if there was any chance that Lisa Salinger might be hiding out at BYU. Well, I thought that was really a long shot. I was about to forget the whole thing when Cindy Dyer came in complaining that she can never get to talk to you. And some things you tell her just don't add up. For instance, nobody in the Church in Nebraska or North Dakota has ever heard of Dawn Fields. And the home address you gave in Nebraska is a Burger King. This morning we phoned Grand Island High School and asked about you. They have no record of a Dawn Fields ever being there, and yet your transcript shows you as a student there. Strange, right? Today I went to the Physics Department and nosed around. I met a graduate student. She said she talked to this girl once, a music education major, who told her, out of the blue, that the Salinger theory is best understood in, let's see what she said . . ." He glanced at his notebook again. "Oh, yes, 'best understood in tensor notation.' I showed her a picture of Dawn Fields and she said, 'Yes, that's the girl.' Finally we checked the days you've missed class. Guess what? They coincide with the days Lisa Salinger was in North Dakota."

He stopped.

Dawn was crying.

"So guess what we concluded? Dr. Salinger, let me be the first to welcome you to BYU. And thanks for the story. It comes out tomorrow in both the *Washington Post* and the *BYU Daily Universe.*" He turned to Cody. "How does it feel to be dating a Nobel Prize winner?"

Cody sat there stunned.

"Well, I've taken enough of your time already. Enjoy your cherry lime. Oh, before I go, let me lighten things up by telling you this coed joke I heard the other day."

Then he noticed the tears streaming down Dawn's face. "Well, maybe not now," he said quietly, then left.

"You're Lisa Salinger?" Cody asked.

"Yes."

"You're not even a member of the Church?"

She shook her head. "Listen to me, I can join now. Don't you see, I couldn't be baptized before. Not as Dawn. Cody, please, you've got to let me explain why I did what I did. You don't know what it was like as Lisa Salinger. I had to get away. That's why I came to the Y."

"Who's Dawn Fields?"

She wiped the tears from her face. "I made her up."

He stared at the tabletop in front of him. Finally he looked up. "In other words, you've lied to me from the very beginning, haven't you."

"Yes."

"That's the way I figure it too." He stood up, took one last look at her, and walked away.

CHAPTER TEN

T he radio alarm went off precisely at 7:00 A.M. She groaned, then sleepily stumbled to the dresser to turn it off. It was September, ten months since she'd left BYU—ten months since she'd last seen Cody.

Much had happened in that time.

On December 10 she had stood in the Concert Hall in Stockholm, surrounded by other Nobel Prize recipients, the royal family, the Swedish cabinet, and members of the Nobel family, as the King of Sweden presented her the Nobel Prize in physics.

She sat on the edge of the bed and tried to wake up.

She lived in an expensive high-security apartment within walking distance of the Princeton University campus. Nobody could get inside unless they rang up first and got permission from a tenant. Hal and Kimberly had picked the apartment for her. The object was to keep away the line of would-be inventors with ideas for perpetual-motion machines, earnest people with petitions for her to sign, and parents of grade-school children who needed help on their science-fair projects. "You gotta be protected from the general riff-raff now," Hal had explained.

Hal and Kimberly arranged all her speaking tours. Except for public appearances, she was left alone so she'd have time to work. In January, she'd begin as a faculty member in the Physics Department at Princeton.

She yawned. She'd been up late the night before working on a paper she would give next month to the American Association for the Advancement of Science.

The building was designed so noises from other tenants were deadened by sound-absorbing walls. She listened. It was quiet.

A few minutes later in the bathroom, she found herself staring at her reflection in the mirror. It was Lisa all right. Lisa always frowned. Lisa was never satisfied. Lisa had to keep working. Lisa had to stay ahead. Lisa had to be independent, because relationships slowed you down and kept you from reaching your goals.

She looked terrible. It wasn't just because her hair needed shampooing, or because she'd quit wearing makeup. Her face reflected a general disappointment, a feeling that there should be more to life than what she had.

She went to the kitchen, poured a glass of orange juice, sat down at the kitchen table, and reread an old letter from Robyn. ". . . Cody phoned a few days ago. He graduated in April, and now he's working on a road construction crew in New Mexico. He asked if I'd heard from you. He said he guessed he should start looking for someone else. He said he needs someone who doesn't mind living in a hot and dusty trailer, a hundred miles from nowhere."

She downed her juice, then went to the window and looked down. Three floors below a man and woman came running out of the apartment and drove away. She wondered where they were going in such a hurry.

Across the street she saw two young girls in a park playing hopscotch. It seemed an eternity since she'd played hopscotch. If she tried now, she felt she'd snap in two like a dried-out twig.

The mother of the two girls crossed the street, took

each one by the hand, and escorted them back to the apartment building next door.

It must be time for school, she thought. *I wonder what they'll have for lunch. I hope it's not tuna casserole. I always hated that. I hope it's pizza and carrot sticks and chocolate pudding. That was my favorite. Girls, I wish you pizza.*

She lay down on the rumpled bed. In her mind she was nine years old, getting ready for school in North Dakota.

I should get dressed, she thought a while later. *I can't just lie around in my nightgown all day.*

She and Hal had developed a work schedule designed to maximize production from her mind. Think of yourself as a factory, Hal had told her.

She heard a baby crying as it was carried down the hall. She frowned. They said she wouldn't hear sounds from the other tenants.

Her sister, Karen, had a baby girl, and a few weeks ago Lisa had held it for a few minutes at the Minneapolis airport. It felt good to have a baby in her arms, but then her plane was called, and she'd had to go.

She turned on her new computer. It was the latest model with all the features money can buy. She put two diskettes into the computer's disk drive. A few seconds later a calendar appeared on the screen with all her appointments for the month. She noticed she was speaking in California that weekend.

The talks were always the same. She was whisked in, gave her talk, and then she was rushed out again—like a circus elephant doing the same trick over and over again. Sometimes she gave three talks in a week, all in different states.

She shouldn't complain. She had everything she'd ever wanted from life—money in the bank, respect from her colleagues. She was fulfilling her destiny. She was the envy of thousands of women and a role model for young girls.

When she next looked at the clock, an hour had passed. She was still in her nightgown, way behind schedule. She'd make it up by working late at night. Lisa always gets the work done. Always, always, always.

While she was looking for clothes in her drawer, she saw her Nobel Prize medallion. She hung it from her neck.

Recently she'd read a biography of Alfred Nobel, the inventor who set up the trust making Nobel Prizes possible. She picked up the book and read a passage that had been haunting her for days. It was from a letter Nobel had written to his brother's wife. "I am disgusted with myself, without rudder or compass, like a purposeless, fate-stricken wreck, without any bright recollections of the past, . . . without a family, which is the only life we may expect beyond the present one, without friends for healthy development of the heart . . ."

Family . . . friends. Suddenly she was remembering her weekend with Cody's family, and especially her conversations with his mother. The Mormons are so naive, she thought, so out of touch with their archaic traditional viewpoint of a woman's role. To teach that a traditional marriage can fulfill a woman these days. Why do they teach it? Don't they know the statistics? Forty-three million women in the work force, triple the number just prior to World War II. Sixty percent of all women between the ages of eighteen and sixty-four are working. Nine million families in the United States where a woman is the only breadwinner.

She looked in her closet, trying to decide what to wear. In the back of the closet she saw a flash of color. She moved aside some clothes and pulled out the pumpkin-colored dress Natalie had once helped her pick out. She'd given away her other Provo clothes except this one dress. It looked completely out of place among the dreary wardrobe surrounding it.

This was Dawn's dress, she thought. She remembered feeling beautiful in it.

Dawn was beautiful.

But Lisa isn't.

She draped the dress in front of her and looked in the mirror. She frowned. It didn't look right.

What would it feel like to be Dawn again?

From a closet she retrieved the painting Cody's mother had done of Dawn.

Dawn, full of light, positive and faithful.

I want to be Dawn again, she thought, at least for a few minutes.

She took a shower and shampooed her hair. It was quite long now. She hadn't the heart to cut it after all the time it had taken to grow. To cut down on the time to keep it fixed, she often wore her wig.

She spent a long time fussing over her hair and putting on makeup. She took off her glasses and put on Dawn's contact lenses, then slipped on the dress.

She looked in the mirror again. There was Dawn. She smiled the way Dawn smiled. It was warm and friendly.

Good grief, she thought, *I'm cracking up.*

The intercom phone was buzzing. She picked it up.

"Are you ready?" Hal asked impatiently.

"Ready?" she mumbled, looking at the clock. It was eleven-thirty.

"You didn't forget the luncheon with the women's faculty club, did you? You're the guest speaker. Get decent—Kimberly and I'll be right up. Buzz the buzzer."

"I'm tired of giving speeches."

"Push the button. We'll come up and talk about it."

She hung up but didn't touch the security release button. A second later the buzzer sounded again. She placed a towel over it.

She picked up the phone and dialed. A few seconds later, Tami Randall in Provo picked up the phone.

"This is Dawn Fields—I mean Lisa Salinger."

"Hey! It's Dawn! She's on the phone!"

Suddenly there were three girls on the phone, all talking at once.

"Quiet!" Tami shouted. "We'll take turns. Let me go first. Dawn, are you still there? We're all just about to go to class. Hey, guess what? I'm taking Introduction to Physics this semester. It's fun."

She let them talk about the details of their life, then she said, "I need to ask a question. What's the most significant thing you feel about yourself?"

The question was passed to the others. They talked among themselves and then Tami came back on the line. "We all pretty much came up with the same answer."

"What is it?"

"That God is our Father. He loves us and wants the best for us. He wants us to be happy and to develop our talents." There was a pause. "Look, can you call back? Maybe tonight. If we don't go now, we're all going to be late for class."

"Sure, I'll call back later."

"Thanks. Dawn, we love you."

She said good-bye and hung up.

She thought it much too simplistic to picture God as a Heavenly Father. Besides, why can't God be female? Or why not just an Essence of All Truth? Why must he be a Father?

She vaguely remembered a song they sing. Something about how in heaven parents aren't single. Truth is reason, truth eternal, tells me I've a Mother there.

A Mother in heaven, she thought. Suppose there are gender differences in heaven—does that mean there are role differences also? And if there are role differences between men and women in heaven, and if heaven represents an ideal existence, then those role differences in heaven, whatever they are, must lead to the greatest happiness for both sexes, even on earth.

If that's true, is it wise to try and remove all role differences on the earth?

Interesting, she thought. If you picture God as an essence, or if you believe there is no God, then you might view all role differences between men and women on earth to be bad. You might support any movement whose purpose is to do away with role differences between men and women, with your goal to make men and women not only equal but, except for childbearing, also identical.

On the other hand, if you believe God is a Father and that there is a Mother in heaven for each of us, then you might decide that some role differences between men and women should be maintained on earth.

She found herself deep in thought, standing in front of an open refrigerator door. She grabbed a carrot and started munching, then went back to a chair overlooking the window and sat down.

Lisa Salinger proved to the world that, given any field, a woman can succeed in it as well as a man. But is that enough for either a man or a woman? Is business or professional success enough to give purpose and dimension to a life?

It wasn't for Alfred Nobel. Professional success isn't enough. People need love and friendship.

The phone rang. It was Hal. He made an effort to be calm and reasonable. "Lisa, let us come up. Okay, you don't want to speak to the women faculty today. Fine. What I'm really worried about is Sunday. You're supposed to be speaking in Los Angeles, and they're expecting you there. This isn't going to last forever, you know. We've got to get in and make it while we can—"

She interrupted him. "Hal, I just need some time to myself. Look, I'll give your talk in California, but after that, you and Kimberly are on your own. I can't support you both the rest of my life. Get a job, Hal—an honest job, okay?"

Suddenly desperate, he yelled into the phone, "Wait! Whatever you do, don't hang up!"

She hung up, then took the receiver off the hook.

She went to a bookshelf and picked up her copy of *The Second Stage* by Betty Friedan, a leader of the women's movement. She talked about how, in the begin-

ning of the women's movement, because of their rage at
the inequalities they suffered, women were encouraged
to escape the confines of marriage and family life in
order to seek success in a career. Now several years later
Friedan looked at the results. Lisa turned to a page in the
book and read it again. *"The women's movement has come to a
dead end. . . . Our failure was our blind spot about the family. . . .*

*"For us equality and the personhood of women [should]
never [have] meant destruction of the family, repudiation of
marriage and parenthood, or implacable sexual war with men."*

She put the book down and looked at the clock. Lisa is
behind schedule today, and there's work to be done. Putting on costume dresses and lounging around all day is
not productive. Lisa expects results.

She frowned, thinking how much a bore Lisa was
sometimes.

She realized she'd never met her neighbors. She decided to go visiting. At the apartment next to hers she
read the nameplate on the door: A. McPherson. *Who is A.
McPherson? Have I ever seen A. in the elevator? Is A an Alice
or an Arnold? I hope for Alice,* she thought.

She knocked. There was no answer.

Alice was not home. Alice was working hard somewhere so she could earn enough money to continue to afford her privacy in that apartment.

Dawn went to the apartment on the other side of
hers. The nameplate indicated that T. Howard Ellison
lived there. She knocked loudly. No answer.

"Anybody there? Howard, how do you get in at
night? Why haven't I ever seen you? We're neighbors,
and I think we should have a brunch for all the other tenants. Howard?"

No answer.

Howard was at work, perhaps in an office cubicle,
alone in front of a screen watching green blips that come
and go with the speed of light.

She walked to every apartment on her floor and knocked.

Nobody was home, not on the entire floor. She was the only one.

Then she had a frightening insight into the future.

If you teach that people should be free, emancipated, and self-fulfilled, what will eventually happen?

Emancipation will be interpreted as the breaking of family bonds. Eventually society will reach a condition in which an entire civilization lives as individuals in voluntary solitary confinement. Men and women will pursue careers and shun family responsibilities. Neither sex will have any need for the other, except for brief pairings motivated by a search for pleasure. Couples will live together for only brief spans—a night, a month, perhaps a few years, but eventually they'll break up when one or the other wants more freedom.

The children resulting from these brief couplings will be dropped off in the morning and picked up at night—the same as with laundry.

People will end up living alone, spending their lives in self-centered activities—individuals alone frantically doing aerobic exercises in front of a TV set.

Feeling extremely depressed, she returned to her apartment and closed the door. *I've got to talk to another human being,* she thought.

She glanced again at the painting of Dawn Fields done by Cody's mother. Now there's a woman, she thought to herself. A minute later the phone rang at the Wells home in Utah. "Hello," Heidi answered.

"Heidi, this is Dawn Fields—I mean Lisa Salinger. Is your mother home?"

"Sure, just a minute."

A pause and then, "Lisa, is that really you?"

"I hope this isn't a bad time, but I was just looking at the painting you did of me, and I started thinking about things, and I just wanted to talk, if that's okay with you."

"Sure—you know I love to talk. Can you hold on a minute? We're just in the middle of canning pickles, and I need to give Heidi some directions."

Lisa could faintly hear voices in the background: ". . . one tablespoon salt, one bit of dill, and one piece of garlic . . . Okay, I'm back. Where are you calling from?"

"New Jersey."

"I'm glad you called. I've been thinking about you lately."

"I need to apologize for deceiving you and your family."

"No need for that."

"Sister Wells . . ."

"Good grief, Lisa, call me Margaret."

"Okay. Margaret, when I stayed with you, you seemed satisfied with your life. I don't understand that, because you don't have much time for yourself, and your children take up so much of your day. I know you like to paint, but you can't have much time for that. I must really seem incoherent, but, well, I need to know, are you really happy?"

"Oh my yes. I'm very happy with my life. I feel fulfilled as a woman. Just a minute . . . Heidi, there's more garlic in that sack . . . Okay, I'm back again."

"But don't you ever feel boxed in? I mean you seem to always follow your husband. That to me isn't right. I don't understand how a woman can play second fiddle to a man."

"Lisa, the ideal is this: The husband follows the Savior and His teachings, and the woman honors and sustains her husband. Think about the way Jesus treated the women in his life. Any woman would feel comfortable with a man who treated her that way. A man like that wouldn't be a tyrant. He'd be patient, slow to anger, sensitive to a woman's feelings, compassionate and gentle. He'd want his wife to develop her God-given talents."

Lisa paused and then confided, "I've got a problem

with that. First of all, why can't the wife follow the Savior all by herself without her husband being the middle-man?"

"She can. In fact, she should. But in a family some-body has to have the final say, and God's established that as the role of the husband."

"It's not fair."

"If the husband cares about the Savior, it's fair then."

Another interruption. Heidi had run out of dill.

While she waited for Margaret to come back on the line, Lisa thought about something Betty Friedan had written, that what was needed in the women's movement now was a new order, where men and women could both be free to develop their potential. What if the new order is already in place? What if it's the gospel of Jesus Christ?

"I'm back again. Any other questions?"

"I don't think so. Thanks. Oh, I hope your pickles turn out."

"They will. It's hard to ruin dill pickles." She paused. "Lisa, Cody still talks about you."

"Tell him not to swear."

Margaret laughed. "Not that way."

"Well, I wouldn't blame him if he was still mad. The facts are that I lied to him."

"We talked about it," Margaret said. "I think he un-derstands now how it was for you and why you went to BYU in the first place. You want to know what he won-ders most about? Your feelings about the Church. He'd like to find someone who has the same religious beliefs he does. Lisa, how do you feel about the Church?"

"Well, after the news about me broke and I left Utah, there was the possibility that BYU would press charges against me for breaking into their computer files. It didn't seem like a good idea to be baptized with that hanging over me. Finally they decided to drop charges. But by then I'd been giving all those talks at women's con-ferences, and, well, some women are bitter that the

Church opposed ERA, and, I don't know, I just never started going to church again. It just seemed easier to stay away."

"That's not what I'm asking. Do you believe the Savior is speaking to a prophet today?"

There was a long pause, and then, "I don't know."

"Before we hang up, let me tell you how I feel about it. I know it's true, and every day of my life adds to that testimony."

"Thanks for telling me that," she said.

"Sure. There's another thing that's worried Cody, and that's how a famous Nobel Prize physicist could ever be content being married to an engineer whose only goal in life is to spend his life outdoors building highways."

"I guess if we ever got together again, we'd just have to try and work it out."

"Sure, like everybody else has to. Maybe I shouldn't be saying this, but I think he still loves you."

"After all I've done to hurt him?"

"Why don't you ask him yourself?"

"Maybe I will."

A few minutes later they hung up. She sat down in front of the window and looked out.

I used to feel that the Book of Mormon is true. What about now?

A sudden fantasy sprang up in her mind in which Cody baptized her and then they got married in the temple.

No, she thought, stopping the dream. *The decision to get baptized has to be based on whether or not I'm willing to live the teachings of the Church. It can't be based on trying to impress Cody. To join the Church just for Cody would be wrong.*

Besides, if the Church is true, it's true for singles, and not just for families. If the Church strives to help families, it also has a mandate to help singles.

And I'd better face it—I may be single the rest of my life.

What does it boil down to? Did Jesus Christ give revelation to Joseph Smith or didn't he? Is the Book of Mormon a second witness for Jesus Christ or isn't it?

Strangely enough, she knew the answer. She'd known for a long time, ever since she'd prayerfully read the Book of Mormon. But other things had gotten in the way.

It's true.

Then I should get baptized. And in order to prove to myself that I'm doing it for the right reason, I won't tell anyone. I won't tell Cody about it. And I won't tell my roommates at BYU.

She paused. *But they're my friends. They'll want to know. Okay, I'll tell them.*

She looked at the clock. It was three-thirty in the afternoon, Eastern time. Only one-thirty in Provo. Too early to phone.

She walked to the window and looked down. The girls who'd played hopscotch in the morning had returned to their sidewalk across the street.

Five minutes later she was outside wearing jeans, a BYU T-shirt, and tennis shoes. "May I play?" she asked the girls.

They looked at her strangely. "Do you know how?" one of them asked.

She smiled. "Well, it's been a long time, but sure I do."

They were much better at it than she was. After flubbing up two times in a row, she started giggling. Then she left them and walked further into the park.

It was a beautiful Indian summer day. The sun felt warm on her face. She walked across the lawn and found a spot and lay down in the sun and closed her eyes. Memories of girlhood drifted into her mind, of being with grade-school friends at the Fargo city swimming pool—how they'd jump in the water and get wet, then jump out again and lie on the hot concrete, their wet bodies making damp shapes on the sidewalk where they lay. She remembered the way the wet concrete and the chlorine in the pool smelled. Sometimes she'd have money for a candy bar, and she'd lie on the warm sidewalk and take a bite and hand it to her friend. At first they'd be shivering, but gradually the sun dried them off. Sometimes they watched high-school girls and privately wondered if their own matchstick bodies would ever turn them into women.

Mostly they hated boys. Boys pushed girls in the water when they weren't ready, and ran on the wet concrete, which was against the rules, and always made the lifeguard blow the whistle. Boys made terrible sounds that girls would never even think of. But sometimes when they were tired of girl talk, she'd purposely linger by the side of the pool hoping to be pushed in by a certain boy with blond hair and blue eyes.

Well, it happened, she thought. *I grew up and became a woman, and yet I'm still waiting to find out what I'm going to be when I grow up.*

What is it that Tami said? The most important thing she feels about herself is that she's a daughter of God, that He's her Father, and loves her, and wants the best for her.

Okay, I'll try it out. I'm a daughter of God. I existed as a woman even before my birth. I'll exist as a woman after my death. I'm important to God because I'm his daughter, and He wants me to improve and progress while on earth.

I need all of me. There's no part of me I can toss away. I need the Child, ready to play and joke and laugh. I need the Adult, the list maker, the achiever. I need the Mother who loves to cuddle a baby. I need the part of me that knows that God lives. I need the Fighter, the one who goes to battle over coed jokes and unfair demeaning attitudes toward women. And I need the Woman who loves being in Cody's arms.

I need Lisa.

I need Dawn.

Not just one, but both. Together as one—fulfilling my destiny.

A fly was buzzing around her face. She sat up and opened her eyes. *I'll go back and make a list,* she thought.

That's what Lisa always does. A list of things I like about both Lisa and Dawn.

She looked around. Across the way a rotating sprinkler was shooting a spray of water across the lawn. She got up and ran as fast as she could toward it. Suddenly drops of water hit like small bombs of awareness on her arms and forehead. She continued running, shouting and giggling in icy delight as the coldness bombarded her body. She forced herself to stand close to the spray as water showered her. She laughed and giggled and shouted at the top of her voice.

The two girls who'd been playing hopscotch were standing by, silently watching her make a fool of herself.

She tried a cartwheel and ended up falling down on the grass.

The girls looked at each other. She was the silliest adult they'd ever seen.

A minute later she retrieved her adult dignity and started home. She reached the sidewalk. Her tennis shoes squished water with each step.

The girls watched her as she passed them.

"Hello again," she said primly.

Back in her apartment, wearing a robe and drying her hair with a towel, she sat down at her desk, turned on the computer and typed on the screen "The Unification of Lisa Dawn." When she finished the two-page list, she printed out three copies to post around the apartment.

At six-thirty she phoned the bishop of the local ward near Princeton. "My name is Lisa Dawn Salinger, and I'd like to be interviewed for baptism."

An hour later she returned from the bishop's office. She felt good. The peaceful feeling had returned. She hoped it would never leave.

She decided to phone Utah again. Robyn answered. "Hello."

"This is Lisa Dawn. Robyn, guess what? I'm going to be baptized."

Robyn screamed excitedly and ran to get everyone else. A minute later, with everyone talking at once, she was welcomed into the Church.

"You've got to tell Cody about it," Robyn said, after everyone else had left.

"Do you have a number for him?"

"Well, he called about a month ago from his company phone in Albuquerque. He spends most of his time in the boondocks, building a highway, so I don't know how you can reach him. But I'll give you the number in Albuquerque. He really sounded lonely when he called me. He's in this dinky little trailer off the side of a highway they're building. He kept talking about how dusty it is, and how he's not sure he could ever ask any woman to live there."

A minute later she phoned the number in Albuquerque and asked to speak to Cody Wells. They said it was impossible. She assured them it wasn't. They said he was a hundred miles away in an area with no phones. She asked how they'd get hold of him if there was an emergency. There was a long pause, then the company president came on the line. He said that if there was an emergency, they'd patch the phone call through onto short wave radio. She asked them to do that.

"Are you sure this is an emergency?"

"It is for me."

"We'll work on it. Give me your number, and we'll call when we're ready."

She sat down and waited.

A few minutes later the phone rang. She picked it up. It was Hal. "We need you to do the TV ad for the Lisa doll next week. It could really be a big number for Christmas."

"Hal, not now. I'll see you and Kimberly this weekend when we go to California, but until then, quit bothering me. 'Bye."

The phone rang again.

"Will you quit bugging me about that stupid doll!" she snapped.

After an awkward pause, the company president said, "I've got Cody on the line, but you'll have to speak loud."

"Cody, is that you?" she shouted. "This is Dawn!"

"Dawn! It's great to hear your voice. I'd better warn you that the whole crew is standing around listening to us."

"I'll remember. Cody, guess what? I'm getting baptized tomorrow."

"That's terrific!"

"I thought you'd want to know. I've had a great day today. I ran through the sprinkler, and played hopscotch with two grade-school girls, and missed an appointment to speak to faculty wives, and talked to a bishop about being baptized, and now I'm talking to you. Oh, I also talked to your mother. She suggested I talk to you. First of all, I want to apologize for misleading you about who I was."

"I've been doing a lot of reading about you. I think I know Lisa almost as well as I knew Dawn."

"Call me Lisa Dawn now, okay? I'm the best of both. Hey, can I come and see you next week? I'll be in California over the weekend, so it wouldn't be that much out of my way. Is it too pushy of me to ask?"

"Not at all! I'd really like to see you again. There's a motel about twenty miles down the road where you can stay. During the day you can come with me, and I'll show you how to build highways." He paused. "Lisa Dawn, I'd better warn you though, things are really primitive here. I mean, the dust is everywhere."

"Hey, I love dust!"

"No kidding?"

"Absolutely! And I like little trailers off the side of highway construction projects—especially trailers that get hot as an oven on a summer day."

Somebody began loudly and ineptly singing the wedding march.

Cody laughed. "Did you hear that?"

"Yeah, I heard."

"What did you think about it?" he asked.

"It was really bad singing."

"It was the wedding march," Cody said.

"I know."

"What do you think about it?" he asked.

"It's a nice song."

He laughed. "You know what I mean."

"I'd like to consider it as a possible option. How about you?"

"Me too. I'd also like to consider it as an option." Suddenly he burst into laughter. "I can't believe this conversation. It sounds like we're about to buy mutual funds. Oh, one other thing about this place—the TV reception is lousy."

"So if we were married, there wouldn't be very much to do at night?" she asked.

"Right."

"We'd keep busy," she said.

"Woooo—eeeeee!" someone on the crew yelled.

"C'mon, guys," Cody pleaded good-naturedly, "Lisa Dawn, we have an electrical generator, so you could use your computer. If we were married, you'd still have a lot of time during the day to work."

"But not at night!" someone teased.

"C'mon guys, give us a break."

The president of the company, listening in Albuquerque, broke in. "And that's an order!" he barked.

A few seconds later it was strangely quiet.

"Lisa Dawn? They all left. Look, if you ever needed to go away for a science meeting, I'd understand."

"I'm sorry for lying to you before. Except for creating Dawn Fields, I'm a very honest person. I won't ever lie to you again."

"I wanted to phone you for such a long time, but I figured you wouldn't be interested in me, not after receiving a Nobel Prize."

"It's nice, but it's not the most important thing in life."

"During the winter, I'll be working in the office at Albuquerque. There's a university there if you wanted to teach or do research."

"Look, don't worry about me. I can do my work almost anywhere. Cody, I'd try and be a good wife and mother. I'd read books about it and talk to your mother. I like her very much."

"Are we really talking marriage as a possible option?"

"I think we are," she said. "But look, don't hang up and panic and think you've just signed your life away. Nothing's official. When we get together, we'll just see how things go."

"You sure you could stand living here? You're not going to believe the trailer."

"Don't worry—I'll make drapes."

He laughed. "You'd make drapes?"

"How hard can it be? I'll read a drape book. Besides, the trailer doesn't matter. Just to be with you, even with both of us covered with layers of dust, would still be heaven as far as I'm concerned."

"Wooo—eeee!" the company president cheered.

THE UNDERSTUDY

JACK WEYLAND

THE UNDERSTUDY

A NOVEL

Deseret Book

Salt Lake City, Utah

CHAPTER ONE

A cabin in the woods is good for a boy growing up, but sometimes he doesn't realize it until later in life.

The cabin from my boyhood sits in northwestern Montana, the last cabin on the dirt road that runs past Grizzly Gulch Lake. It sits on a hill, partially hidden by pine trees, but from the front steps you can see the clear blue water of the lake. It was made from lumber taken from a condemned building torn down when I was about six years old. My dad and a friend of his bid on the job and got it. Every night after work they removed boards and threw them in the pickup. They even tried to save the nails, but most of them came out bent.

With that lumber and the money they earned from demolishing the building, they put up two cabins by the lake. Ours was the second one built. By then they were running out of materials, so it ended up a hodgepodge of mismatched, odd-shaped, and warped boards. As a boy it was easy for me to imagine, especially during thunderstorms, that instead of being built, our cabin had been conjured by the spell of a demented witch.

Dad tried to get me to help with the cabin, but after a few minutes I'd get bored and complain until finally he'd let me run off to play. My favorite activity then was catching frogs to terrify my older sister, Beth.

That all seems so long ago now.

The cabin has always been there for us, in the good times and even in the bad.

* * * * *

Three summers ago, when the doctor released my father from the hospital, it was to send him home to die. The cancer was widespread, and there wasn't much that could be done.

1

I flew in from Los Angeles a week after Dad had been sent home. My sister, Beth, met me at the Kalispell airport. As soon as I saw her, I could tell she was still mad because I hadn't come right after she'd called to tell me he was failing fast.

"Hello, Beth," I said as I entered the terminal building.

"Hello, Michael," she said curtly. "How nice you could come."

Unless you know her, you might not realize that "How nice you could come" was her version of a slap in the face.

"Beth, I couldn't just walk out. I had to finish the movie I was doing."

"Of course," she said with an angry toss of her head. "We can't all be Hollywood stars, now can we?"

I sighed. "I'm not a Hollywood star. I'm just an actor who needs the work."

"Yes, and that's all you'll ever be, too."

I had a carry-on bag so we didn't have to wait for luggage. We walked outside.

"Pamela didn't come?" she asked.

"This is finals week at USC. She has exams. She'll come later."

"I would certainly hope so," she replied sullenly.

A few minutes later we were in Beth's pickup, driving home.

"How's Dad?" I finally asked.

"Why don't you tell me how you think he is?"

"All right, Beth, lay off. I know how he is."

"Well, you don't act like it. I've had to carry everything on my shoulders while you've wasted your time being an actor. What kind of a job is that, pretending you're somebody else? You think I don't dream of being somebody else? Sure I do. Lots of times. It's no picnic around here, I'll tell you. But at least I stick to what needs to be done. I'm not like you, Michael. We can't depend on you for anything when it comes to this family. It's always up to good old Beth. Well, I'm sick and tired of it."

"I know it's been hard on you, what with Dad and Wally." Wally was her husband.

She had tears in her eyes, but we didn't say anything about it. In our family we never did.

A minute later she said bitterly, "Dad keeps asking for you." She shook her head. "It's not fair. I do all the work, and he asks for you."

I thought about hugging her, but it would have been awkward. We've never hugged much in our family, and at a stoplight in a '62 Chevy pickup with a tricky clutch is probably not the place to begin.

"Do you want to see Wally?" she asked.

"Sure, Beth."

"Might as well. We need some gas anyway."

We pulled into Gas for Less, a run-down station on the edge of town. We both got out to run the self-service pump. "I can do it," she said. "You go talk to Wally."

When I got to the office, I saw a hand-scrawled note on the door that read "Out for lunch. Be right back."

I turned around. Beth was standing there, her head bowed, her hand to her face. "The pump's turned off," she said, sounding like it was the end of the world.

"There's a note that says he's out for lunch."

She sighed. "We both know where he is."

She drove us to the Stockade Bar.

The place had been built a long time ago, when people could still afford wood. The long mahogany bar was solid and dark and smelled of stale beer. A pool table sat in the middle of the room. On a wooden plank on the wall were all the local livestock brands. There was a dart board on another wall, and a wagon wheel with a clock in its center. And behind the bar, whiskey bottles were arranged in neat, orderly rows.

Wally was the only customer. He was sitting at the bar watching a British-Norwegian soccer game on a satellite sports channel. As soon as he saw Beth, he tossed his money down. "Well, gotta be going now, Frank," he said to the bartender. "Time to get back to work, you know."

"Yeah, well, don't work too hard," the bartender said.

Wally saw me in the doorway. "Well, well, look who's here!" he said with a wide grin. "Hey, Michael, how's it going?"

"Fine, Wally. How're things with you?" We shook hands and stepped outside.

"Can't complain. Of course, wouldn't do any good if I did, right?"

We chuckled. "Right," I said.

Beth exploded. "Wally, you said you'd quit leaving the station unattended anymore."

"Well, gosh, can't a man even have a little lunch around here?"

"I packed you a lunch," she grumbled.

He acted surprised. "You did?"

"Don't give me that! You know I did. You were just looking for an excuse to go drink."

"One beer is all I had. Look, ask the bartender if you don't believe me."

"When have you ever given me a reason to believe anything you say? And how can you sit there drinking all afternoon when we don't even have enough food to put on the table to feed our kids? And what are they supposed to do about school clothes in the fall?"

"Oh, I don't know," he muttered. "You always figure out something."

"If you were a real man, you'd take care of your family and not leave it up to me. I have no respect for a man who won't provide for his family." With a quick glance, she also tossed that barb in my direction.

A man can take only so much. "All right, you can stop now. I'm going back to work." Wally jumped in his pickup and roared away.

Beth drove us home.

When we pulled up, Mom came out to greet me.

It's hard to describe my mother the way she is now. But I can tell how it was when I was growing up.

We had a garden every year. She made me help with it. I hated string beans the worst. They just kept producing until I hated to look at another bean.

In high school she waited up for me after every date, and asked the same question night after night, "Did you treat your date with respect?"

I never saw my parents kiss each other, although I assume they must have once in a while. Ours was a no-nonsense household with chores to be done. As I grew up, I came to cringe whenever Mom called out, "Michael, what are you doing?" There would be a long pause, and finally I'd answer, "Watching TV." And she'd say, "Get in here and help out."

Mom had one weakness though. She liked to read paperback romances. In contrast, I never saw my father read anything but the newspaper. I think Mom could relate to my interest in fantasy. She shamed my father into going to all the high school plays I was in. And after graduation, she was the only one in our family who didn't discourage me from becoming an actor.

Shortly after graduation, when I went to California to seek fame and fortune as a Hollywood star, she bragged to the neighbors about every little part I got. But as the months dragged by, it must have finally dawned on her that the great success we'd hoped for wasn't going to be. As time went on, the scrapbook she'd kept for me since grade school required fewer and fewer entries.

Mom centered her life around her family. I've never asked if it was worth it, maybe because I'm afraid of the answer.

That day when I saw her, she looked very tired. We hugged. "Pamela and Jimmy didn't come with you?" she asked as we continued up the walk. My son Jimmy was nine years old.

"Pamela has final exams. She'll come later."

"And how's Jimmy?"

"He's fine, Mom."

"I thought at least he'd be coming with you."

"No, Mom. He'll come later with Pamela."

Beth couldn't leave it alone. "I can't believe the real reason she didn't come was because of exams. Wouldn't a teacher excuse her if she told him that her father-in-law was dying?"

"You just won't lay off, will you. All right, the real reason she didn't come is that she knows she'll have to come for the funeral anyway, and she doesn't want to make two trips in such a short time. She says we can't afford it."

Beth grumbled under her breath.

Mom and I continued up the walk. "We haven't told your father anything about what he has" Mom explained. "We think it's better this way."

In our family we'd quit saying the word *cancer*.

"Okay."

We continued inside. Mom went with me into the bedroom. It was dimly lit and smelled of pain. The bedstand groaned with glasses and bottles of pills.

"Dale," she said quietly, "Michael's here."

He opened his eyes and looked up at me.

"Leave us alone," he said to Mom. She left.

"Can I open the shades and let some light in?" I asked.

"I don't care. Do whatever you want."

I opened the curtains and turned around to see my father bathed in sunlight. His face was gaunt, and his strength was gone.

"Did Pamela or Jimmy come with you?"

"No, they'll come later."

"You mean for the funeral? What good is that going to do me?"

I smiled optimistically. "What are you talking about? You'll be up in no time."

"Have I ever lied to you?" he asked.

"No."

"Then don't lie to me. I'm dying, aren't I?"

I felt my throat clamp shut.

I tried stumbling again through "being up in no time."

"Don't give me that. Tell me the truth. Am I dying?"

It took a while, but finally I answered him. "Yes, Dad, you are."

He sighed. "That's what I thought."

When I returned to the living room, Beth, who'd listened in through the partially open door, was furious that I'd told Dad the truth.

Over the next few days, my father somehow willed himself to get strong enough to make all the necessary preparations. He called in a lawyer and made out his will, gathered all the insurance forms together, and picked a reasonably priced casket and burial site.

Then he lay back and waited to die.

But death, like sleep, does not always come when invited. He even seemed to improve a little.

One warm June day, he looked out his window and said, "I want to go up to the lake."

Of course, it was impossible. That's what my mother said. That's what Beth and Wally said.

But the doctor didn't agree. "If he feels up to it and somebody goes along and does most of the work, why not?"

"Well, I'm not taking him up there," Beth said. "He needs to be in town so that if an emergency happens, we'll be able to get him to the hospital."

"At this point I don't see what difference it makes," I said.

Beth glared at me.

And so I volunteered to take Dad for one last trip to our cabin. After a flurry of planning and buying groceries and stocking up on pills and going through my mother's long and detailed instructions of how to care for him, one morning I dropped the last box in the back of Dad's pickup and returned to the living room for him. He sat on the couch, still exhausted just from the effort of getting dressed.

I helped him down the front stairs. A minute later I had him inside the pickup. I closed the door and went in to get his sunglasses.

Beth confronted me in the living room. "I just want you to know that I think it's a terrible mistake for him to go traipsing off like this," she said.

"Beth, he doesn't love me more than he does you. It's just that I'm his son."

She went into the bathroom and locked the door. I could hear her crying even though she kept running water in the basin so we wouldn't know.

As I drove up the canyon, Dad looked out the window at the twisting mountain stream running alongside the road.

"I'd forgotten how nice it is up here," he said, looking

strangely out of place in his old, but now much too large, sweater that Mom had insisted he wear.

This is his last trip up here, I thought.

He pointed out the window. "See there, where the river goes under that railroad bridge? Right there on that point of land is a good place to fish. The water's fast, so you'll need about eight split-shot weights maybe two feet from the hook. Try it and you'll always get two or three nice trout."

"You always make it sound easy."

"Well, I've spent the past twenty years fishing around here. I've learned things that nobody else knows. I should write it all down. Somebody ought to benefit from all I know about this river."

We drove in silence for several miles while Dad studied each fishing hole.

I never did like fishing. When I was little, I was always scolded for throwing rocks in the water. And even after I got older, it got worse. To Dad fishing was a religion, and to not keep your rod up while reeling in was a sin.

The last time I went fishing with Dad was when I was thirteen. After that I was always able to find an excuse.

As we drove, he continued to fill me in on the fishing strategy for the best places on the river. None of it was of much interest to me.

We're strangers, I thought, as we continued up the canyon.

After we arrived at the cabin, I made several trips back and forth from the pickup with our supplies. Then we ate the lunch that Mom and Beth had prepared for us.

After lunch he took his pills and lay down for a nap. Three hours later he woke up and said he felt good enough to go fishing.

I carried two lawn chairs down to the lake, and then the fishing equipment, and after that a sunshade Mom had made me promise I'd set up for Dad. After everything was set up, I helped him down the trail to the lake.

I cast out and handed him the rod to hold, and then I sat down and waited. A short time later the bobber dipped.

"Gotcha," he said, setting the hook.

He reeled in and I netted the fish. Then, at his request, I released it again back into the lake.

A short time later he caught another.

A father and his son who were fishing nearby came over and asked what Dad's secret was. Dad gave them the complete history of fishing on the lake for the past twenty years.

The longer he fished, the more optimistic he became.

"This is just great," he said.

"I'm glad you're having a good time."

"Are you sure you don't want to fish?" he asked.

"No, I'm enjoying watching you. How are you feeling?"

"I haven't felt this good in months."

I cast out again for him.

"I've been thinking," he said, "how'd you like to go to Mexico with me for a few weeks? There's a hospital there where they treat people with diseases like mine. They say they can cure people even worse off than me."

I knew about private sanitoriums in Mexico where the very rich went in desperation, hoping for a miracle cure. They often died there.

He continued. "We don't have to just sit around and accept things, do we? We can fight back. We'll leave next week, just you and me. And when I'm all cured, then we'll have Mom and Beth fly down and we'll show them Mexico. Maybe we'll even take a boat through the Panama Canal. How does that sound?"

"Sure, Dad, whatever you say."

He kept talking about getting well and the whole family taking a boat through the Panama Canal, and how we'd stand at the railing and look out and maybe we'd even see wild animals in the jungle.

An hour later he was tired. I made the several trips necessary to get him and our baggage back to the cabin.

Just before we ate supper, he took his pills.

After supper, dark clouds rolled in, and by dusk we were in the middle of a storm. Looking out the window, I watched the wind drive sheets of rain across the lake in sporadic patterns. Lightning lit up the sky around us.

Suddenly Dad looked very sick. His forehead was dotted with

perspiration. He slowly got into his pajamas and took his arsenal of pills and crawled into the metal cot we used for beds in the cabin.

I stayed up and read an old Zane Grey paperback I'd found in the cabin. It was about a man who, whenever things got tough, saddled up his horse and headed into the wilderness. I wondered what happened when he ran out of wilderness.

At ten-thirty, I went to bed.

At midnight Dad woke up gagging. He vomited his supper.

I turned on the light. He was sitting up, his feet on the floor, his body hunched over with pain.

I got a pan of water and a towel and began to clean up the mess on the floor.

"I'm sorry," he said. "It must've been the pills."

"Don't worry about it. It's no problem."

I wiped up the floor and then cleaned him up as best as I could. I got him out of his pajamas and into a pair of old pants and a shirt. He was afraid to take any more pills because he might throw up again. So he sat on the edge of the bed and rocked back and forth, his head down, his teeth clenched, fighting against his invisible enemy.

Finally, at one-thirty, with the pain unbearable, he asked for a slice of bread, a glass of water, and his pills.

I helped him with his pills and then turned off the light.

The night was still being besieged with ragged flashes of lightning and the crash of thunder.

"Forget what I said about Mexico," Dad said in the darkness.

I ached for him. Mexico, his last hope for survival, had just slipped away in the harsh reality of that night.

"Besides, who wants to see the Panama Canal anyway?" he said. "You probably can't see any jungle animals from the boats."

There was a long agonizing silence and then he said, "You know, except for the movies, I've never seen lions running free."

Like a school of teasing dolphins, his boyhood dreams were

surfacing one last time before they slipped forever beneath a dull gray sea.

I wondered how old he'd been when he first dreamed about seeing lions running free? All the years I'd known him he'd never mentioned it, all the time we'd spent together fixing things around the house, taking care of things—while time rushed by without my ever knowing that my dad used to dream about seeing lions running free.

Now it was too late for lions.

* * * * *

The next morning was overcast and the rain continued in a steady drizzle.

Dad was barely able to get out of bed. He asked if we could go home.

A while later when we got in the pickup to leave, he said, "I want you to have the cabin when I'm gone. If I give it to Beth, she'll just sell it. I want it to stay in the family."

I nodded my head.

He slept most of the way back. The rocky rapids and deep holes of his river slipped past him for the last time as we made our way down the twisted mountain road.

Three weeks later he died.

CHAPTER TWO

His funeral was held at the First Methodist Church in Kalispell.

The minister was new to the area and had never even met my father. He knew my mother because she attended church once in a while. "I'm told that the deceased was a good husband and father and worked hard for his family. He was a devoted sportsman, and because of that, perhaps he didn't go to church as often, as he might have otherwise."

"Why is he saying that?" Beth complained to me.

Mary Ellen Ferguson sang. She has a singing voice that is only heard at funerals.

After the funeral we had a family lunch. Some of the food was brought by the women's auxiliary of the Elks Club that Dad belonged to. One of his best friends came to the lunch. He smoked a cigar. A few minutes later Pamela announced she had to go outside or she was going to be sick because of that wretched smell.

I went with her and told her it was rude to say that to one of dad's friends. She said it wasn't rude, it was just being self-assertive.

Jimmy was playing on a neighbor's swing set.

"Get him back here," she grumbled. "He has no business there."

I shrugged my shoulders. "He's not doing any harm."

"It's always up to me, isn't it?" she said. "You never discipline him. With you in the house, it's like having two boys instead of just one." She turned to Jimmy and yelled, "You get out of there before I take a stick to you! One! . . . Two! . . ."

The rules were that if you know what's good for you, never let your mother get to three.

Jimmy didn't budge. "Dad, do I have to?"

"No, it's okay. You can stay there."

She turned and glared at me.

"Pamela, let it be. He's okay. The neighbors don't mind."

"I've got to get out of here. I'm taking a walk."

"I'll go with you."

We started walking. "Mom was wondering how long you'll be staying," I said.

"I'm going back tomorrow."

"What for? I thought you were all through with classes."

She hesitated. "Michael, I've been accepted to medical school, and I need to make arrangements for the fall."

"When did this happen? I didn't know you'd even applied to med school."

"You knew I was majoring in pre-med, didn't you? Well after pre-med comes med."

"But I thought you were just taking classes for fun. You're not really serious about all this, are you?"

"I'm not surprised you don't know about my plans. You've never known anything that happens in this family. I nearly had to send you a birth announcement when Jimmy was born."

Every time we argued she brought it up. The day Jimmy was born, I was on location in a secluded area doing a film. A few days later when I got back in town, she was already home from the hospital. She never forgave me for not being there.

"What med school are you going to?" I asked.

She paused. "It's in Boston."

My mouth dropped open. "Boston? How can you go to med school in Boston when we live in L.A?"

She stopped walking. "Michael, I know this isn't a good time for you. And I wasn't going to bring it up until we got back home, but I might as well tell you now that I've decided to get a divorce. The papers are already prepared. If I thought about it, I could've brought 'em up with me on the plane and saved postage."

I was stunned. "You want a divorce? Why?"

"Don't take it personally. It's just that I want a career. Is that asking too much? Look, if you're worried about losing Jimmy, don't be. Because I'm giving him to you. I had him the first nine years of his life while you ran around pursuing what we laughingly called an acting career. So now it's my turn. You can have him the next nine years. I've decided that what I really want out of life is to become a gynecologist.''

"A divorce? There must be med schools in California. Can't we work something out?''

"Boston is very highly rated. I'd be foolish to turn it down. I leave next week. I brought all of Jimmy's clothes with me, in case you want to stay up here for a while. Also, I assume you'll want me to have the car and the stereo because I paid for them with the money I earned.''

"I can't believe this!" I yelled. "You're divorcing me because Boston is highly rated? That doesn't make sense.''

"No, there's a lot more. I wasn't going to say it, but the truth is, I can't stand to live with you anymore.''

"Why not?''

"Some months you work and we have enough to get by, but then weeks pass with you sitting home all day watching TV soaps and yelling at the actors, 'I can do better than that!' You know the thing that really gets me? There's no guarantee that it'd ever be any different. I look ten years down the line, and I see us living in the same crummy apartment. And another thing— I've raised Jimmy nearly singlehanded. All you've ever done is, once in a while, go outside and throw a ball with him. Everything else is up to me. Maybe if we'd shared responsibilities more—maybe if you'd had a regular job and we could've depended on a steady income—maybe if you'd have looked at me like a partner instead of your slave—maybe then the marriage would've worked. But it's too late now. Besides, I've changed. When we got married, I was just out of high school. I depended on you for everything, but now I'm older. And going to college has shown me that I've got a good mind. I just can't stand to let it go to seed. I've thought about it quite a bit, and I really think this is the best way for both of us.''

She ended it by telling me she thought it best under the circumstances that we didn't sleep in the same house that night. She said she'd already made arrangements to stay at Beth's.

Later Beth told me the two of them stayed up very late that night talking, no doubt trading off stories about how rotten their husbands were. She said she admired Pamela for being able to realize she'd made a mistake in her marriage, and then moving on with the rest of her life. She said she hoped to be able to do that someday too.

The next day Beth drove Pamela to the airport. When she came back, she said she wanted to make one thing clear. I'm sure it was something Pamela had warned her about. "Don't go thinking that I'm going to baby-sit your kid while you run back to Hollywood. He's your responsibility now, and it's time you grow up and face it. So what are you going to do? Get a job?"

"No, I guess I'll go back up to the cabin."

"What about Jimmy?"

"I'll take him with me."

"I think we should sell the cabin—not that it's worth that much. But there is the land. I had a real estate man look at it recently, and he said he thought we could probably get forty thousand for it. We could give Mom half and then split the other half between us."

"I don't want to sell it."

"Why not? You never liked it up there anyway. If I had that money, I could start going to college. Pamela said it'd be good for me."

"We're not selling the cabin, Beth, so just forget it."

That made her mad. "Don't Mom and I even have a say in this?"

"Dad gave the cabin to me."

"When did he do that?"

"When we were up there."

"I'm not saying I believe you, but even if he did, it was probably because he was delirious."

"You and Wally can use it anytime you want, but we're not selling it. It'll always be in our family."

"You want to know something? I think Pamela's doing the

right thing in divorcing you. She deserves better than you. Anybody deserves better than you."

Two days later I had Wally drive Jimmy and me up to the cabin.

*   *   *   *   *

It was a difficult time for me, trying to cope with losing a father and a wife in one week, and, almost as bad, gaining a full-time son.

Fishing was perfect for the way I felt. If a man goes to a shopping mall and spends hours staring at the people shuffling by, sooner or later he'll be suspected of either being a deviate or a bum. But take the same man and put him on the shore of a lake with a fishing pole in his hand, and he can sit there for weeks, never speaking to anyone, not shaving or washing or even eating much—and the entire world will look upon him as an outstanding person, a friend of nature.

Of course, actually catching a fish would have ruined everything, because then we'd have to worry about what to do with it—cleaning, filleting, frying, and then telling ourselves how good it tasted.

What I needed was some time to think, to try and sort out my life. It was as if, with Dad alive, there was a cushion of one generation to protect me from my own mortality. But with him gone, I was the next to go.

My father worked all his life as a surveyor for the state highway department. And yet who in the highway department would remember him in ten years?

Days slipped by while I wrestled with the parade of whys that marched through my mind.

One night I dreamed I was at the cabin and Dad walked up to me and said, "I've seen the lions running free." I looked around and saw hundreds of jungle animals around him, and in particular, a large lion lying on the cabin porch. Dad walked up and scratched it behind the ears.

I woke up and spent the rest of the night wondering what it could mean.

He was a good father. When I got to be about ten years old, he began teaching me the things that were important to him. He'd say, "The car needs work. I need you to help me." So I'd go out to the garage with him. "Hold the light," he'd say, and that'd keep me there until he finished.

He never talked much while he worked, but once in a while he'd shake his head and say, "That's what I thought."

"What?"

"See there. That's the problem. Hold the light closer and let's see if we can get to it."

We fixed cars and did plumbing and house wiring and helped neighbors with carpentry, and once we even learned upholstery when we couldn't afford a new couch.

In some ways I didn't mind the time it took me away from my school friends. It was nice to know that out of all the men in town he could get to help, my dad wanted me.

The only time I ever saw him lose his temper was one time when I was fifteen and Mom was on me for something, and I sassed her back. He came over and jerked me out of the chair and said, "Don't you ever let me hear you talking like that to your mother again!"

He never understood why I wanted to be an actor. "Why waste your time when you could do something useful with your life? You've got the hands to become a carpenter or a plumber or a mechanic. Look, if you want, I'll even send you to college, and you can become an engineer."

"I know, Dad, but I want to be an actor."

He looked at me for a long time and then slowly shrugged his shoulders. "Well, I guess a man has to do what's in his heart."

When I left home, he and I stood there, watching the bus driver load my suitcase. Mom and I had already kissed each other goodbye. Beth had nodded goodbye to me.

I think Dad wanted to hug me. But he didn't. It just wasn't his style. Instead he stuck out his hand. "Whatever you do, do your best at it."

"I will, Dad." We shook hands awkwardly, and then I turned and eagerly jumped on the bus, believing that I was going off to a life of fame and fortune, and never for a moment considering what I was leaving behind.

I still love him very much.

He was my dad.

*   *   *   *   *

In addition to losing my father, I felt bad for having failed in my marriage. Where had I gone wrong with Pamela?

We'd married young. She was eighteen and I was eighteen and a half.

We met at a cut-rate acting school in Los Angeles. She was from Michigan. As a senior she'd been in a school play, playing Anne in *The Diary of Anne Frank*. Everyone in school said she could be a big star, and so after graduation she came to Hollywood to seek fame and fortune.

At any time in L.A. there must be hundreds of eighteen-year-old girls from all over the country who starred in their high school production of *The Diary of Anne Frank*. They come right after graduation, hoping to become famous. Instead they end up working at Jack-in-the-Box.

Just after I met her, I got a decent part in a movie. It paid good money. Thinking this was just the beginning of great success, I put a down payment on a new car and got a better apartment and asked Pamela to marry me.

Suddenly I was a grown-up person doing grown-up things—like marrying hastily and going into debt.

We were married by a justice of the peace. None of our family was there, mainly because we didn't tell them until it was done.

Just after we got married I tried out for a stage play. I wanted the lead, but I didn't get it. They gave me a small part and asked me to be the understudy for the lead role. And so every night I went on stage, gave my few lines, then spent the rest of the night offstage watching the lead actor until I knew by heart his every word and gesture.

I used to laughingly tell people that I was only a heartbeat away from being a big star.

One time the lead got stuck in traffic, and another time he went to the beach and fell asleep under the sun and got such a bad sunburn that he couldn't go on for two days, but mostly he was very healthy. And so my chance for instant stardom passed me by. The play ran three months, and then folded, and suddenly for the first time in California I was out of work.

To tide us over, Pamela got a job working at a dry cleaners and I scoured the city looking for bit parts. I did some TV ads. I became Grape Man for all the Fruit of the Loom commercials. It went very well, actually. I think I added a great deal to the role.

Then Pamela got pregnant, and eventually, because of morning sickness, she had to quit work.

Because we needed money to pay for the baby, I got a job working for the phone company, checking telephone poles to see if they were rotting away in the ground. We walked along rural phone lines. It was an easy job. I'd walk up to a pole, bury my hatchet into it, and shake it as hard as I could. If it broke, it was not a good pole.

A few months after Jimmy was born, Pamela's father sent her some money, and she started taking college courses.

At the lake I wondered if education was the thing that destroyed our marriage. I remember a reception we went to for honor students. Pamela didn't want me to go, but I insisted, since the invitation clearly said students and their parents or spouses.

We were standing in a crowd. A professor came up to us. "Pamela, who is this handsome guy with you?"

"Oh, he's my husband."

We shook hands. "What's your major?" he asked me.

"I'm not in college."

"Oh. What do you do?"

"I'm an actor."

"Is there anything you've done that I might have seen?"

"Well, do you watch TV?"

"Once in a while."

"Have you ever seen any Fruit of the Loom commercials? I'm Grape Man."

He turned to Pamela. "This is a joke, right?" he asked.

She shook her head.

He moved on to someone more promising.

That's why, when I heard about the Carl Sandburg part for a movie funded by the National Institute of Humanities, I tried out for the part and got it. It didn't pay all that much, but it was something you could tell a college professor without having him look at you like you were the village idiot.

It took Pamela several years, but finally she graduated.

*   *   *   *   *

"Dad?" Jimmy said to me one night just after we'd finished our supper of a can of pork and beans.

"What?"

"You never talk to me."

"I'm sorry. I've been thinking about a lot of things."

"Are you mad at me?"

"No. Why should I be mad at you?"

He looked away and barely whispered. "Because it was my fault that Mom got a divorce."

"It didn't have anything to do with you."

"I tried to keep my room clean and do my own clothes right there at the last, but I think she just got tired of me."

"That's not true, Jimmy. She loves you."

"Then why did she leave me?"

I sighed. "It was my fault, not yours. She left because I wasn't the kind of husband and father I should've been."

"Alan Cramer's father gets drunk all the time and beats up Alan's mother. You're better than that."

"Thanks."

"And Bobbie Elliott's dad ran off with his secretary. You never did that."

"No."

"Of course, you don't have a secretary."

"But even if I did, I'd never do a thing like that."

"So you're not that bad," he said.

I paused. "What are some of the things I could've done better as a dad?"

He paused, "You never came to my classroom and met my teachers."

"Anything else?"

"You were always gone. You missed my birthday last year."

"Anything else?"

"I wish you'd have made Mom happier, so she wouldn't have left us."

"Right," I said glumly.

"Dad, how many acting parts have you had?"

"Quite a few."

"What parts have you played?"

"Well, I was Grape Man . . . I was a police lieutenant in *Chainsaw Beach Party* . . . I was the poet Carl Sandburg in *Hog Butcher of the World* . . . I was an army officer in *Sunset over Saigon* . . ."

"But have you ever played the part of just a regular dad?"

A long pause. "No, I never have."

"I didn't think so."

That made me feel rotten.

"Did you have a good dad?" Jimmy asked.

"Yeah, he was real good."

"What was he like?"

We'd taken Jimmy to Montana a few times, but he was too young then to remember my parents.

"Dad was good at fixing things. We spent a lot of time working together. Did you know he built this cabin? The only time he left town was when he took us on a vacation. And whenever I was in anything at school, like a play or for a football game, he was always there with my mom."

"Dad, d'you think you could learn to be more like your dad?"

"I don't know. Maybe. I guess I can try."

We each got into our sleeping bags and lay down on our cots.

"You won't ever get tired of me and leave, will you?" he asked.

"Never."

"That's good, because I think I'm too young to get a job, aren't I?"

"Yeah, I think so."

*   *   *   *   *

I tried to be a better father, but it wasn't easy.

"How long are we going to stay here?" Jimmy asked as we sat and fished. It seemed like we'd been there forever, but it had only been two weeks.

"Just as long as you'd like," I said.

"Good, then let's leave today, because I don't like it up here."

"Some boys would think it was great to spend the summer at a cabin on the lake."

"I don't know why. There's nothing to do up here."

"What do you mean? We go fishing and take hikes, and in the afternoons we go swimming."

"Yeah, but there's no TV," he grumbled.

"It's not good to watch TV all the time."

"Also I don't like what we eat."

"What's wrong with what we eat?"

"All we have is pork and beans."

"That's not true. We have soup. We have bread. We have peanut butter and jelly. We have potatoes. And we have hamburger when I get a check in the mail."

"But there's no McDonald's or Burger King or video arcades or MTV."

"We don't need that. We're mountain men."

"Also, Dad, I think I should have milk to drink."

"What for? Coffee's cheaper. Besides, mountain men don't drink milk."

"But a boy my age needs calcium for his bones."

"What are you talking about? You've got as many bones as any kid who drinks milk. Anyway, who told you that about milk?"

"I read it in that Boy Scout manual I found in the cabin."

"I wish you'd throw that thing away," I grumbled. "It's caused nothing but trouble since we came here. We go on a hike and you spend all your time complaining that I'm leading you through poison ivy."

"But you were, Dad."

I frowned. "Well, yeah, but just that one time."

"You think we'll ever catch a fish?" he asked.

"Sure we will. Someday. You'll see."

"But how come everyone else catches fish except us?"

"Maybe there just aren't any fish where we happen to be fishing."

"But it doesn't matter where we go. We still never catch any."

"We will. You'll see."

"You think Mom'll ever come back to us?"

"She might. Sure, why not?"

"I don't think she'd ever come to the lake though, do you?"

"No, I don't think so."

"So shouldn't we go back to California just in case she changes her mind about leaving us?"

"She'll contact us if she wants to come back."

He sighed. "How much longer do we have to fish today?"

"I'll tell you what. I've still got some money left. How about if we go to the general store on the other side of the lake and split a Fudgsicle?"

He shrugged his shoulders. "What's a Fudgsicle?"

"You don't know what a Fudgsicle is? It's like a Popsicle except I think maybe it's got some milk in it."

"I guess so."

We reeled in. He scowled at me. "Dad, you forgot to put worms on the hooks."

He was right. On purpose I hadn't put any worms on the hooks.

"I was just testing you to see if you'd notice. Let this be a lesson to you, always put a worm on the hook."

"Oh, Dad," he moaned.

* * * * *

Within the month Mom moved to Arizona to live with her sister, who lived in a trailer park near Phoenix.

Beth came out once to see if we were still alive.

"Do you have to wear that awful beard?" she asked, scowling at me.

"Hey, we're mountain men, right, Jimmy?"

"Aunt Beth, can I please go back to town with you?"

I chuckled. "He's just kidding. He loves it out here. Yesterday he caught our first fish."

"Dad made me eat it," he complained.

"You caught it, so you had to eat it. That's our rule. Tell Aunt Beth how delicious it was."

"It was full of bones," Jimmy complained.

"Yeah, but tell her how I gave you a dime for every bone you found."

"You said you would, but you haven't given me anything yet."

I frowned at him. "I will. Just give me a few weeks until I get another check."

"Aunt Beth, do you make your kids drink coffee, or do you buy them milk for their bones even though it costs more money?"

"What's this?" she asked me. "You're not giving him milk to drink?"

"Don't listen to him. Yesterday I bought a package of powdered milk, but he won't drink it."

"It tastes like chalk."

"Look around. Do you see any cows anywhere?"

Beth turned to me. "How long are you two staying up here?"

"All summer."

"And then what?"

I shrugged my shoulders. "Maybe we'll stay here in the winter too."

Jimmy objected. "Dad, I have to go to school."

"I can teach you here."

"What grade is he going to be in?" Beth asked me.

I turned to Jimmy. "Tell Aunt Beth what grade you'll be in."

"Fourth grade."

"That's right," I said, faking it. Pamela always took care of details like remembering what grade Jimmy was in.

"Michael, are you ever going to get a job and be normal?" Beth asked.

"I don't know. It's cheap living here, and I still have some money coming in from the movies I've done."

"Not much money from that, I'll bet. How many people would go see a movie about a hog butcher?"

"Beth," I grumbled, "I've told you before. It wasn't about a hog butcher. It was about Carl Sandburg, the poet who wrote 'Hog Butcher of the World.'"

She shrugged her shoulders. "Hog butcher, poet—what difference does it make? I still wouldn't go see it."

"Look, we knew when we filmed it that it wasn't going to be another *Star Wars*."

"That's for sure. I've never even met anyone who's seen it."

"It was very big in Chicago."

"Why don't you settle down and get a job?"

"Like what?"

"You can work for Wally."

"You mean baby-sit him, don't you? Look, I know you mean well, but pumping gas just isn't right for me."

"That's your trouble—nothing's right for you."

"By the way, how's Wally doing these days?"

"About like you. I still think we should sell the cabin so I can get my divorce sooner."

"We'll never sell the cabin."

She angrily got up to leave.

"Aunt Beth, please take me home with you," Jimmy pleaded.

"No, not today."

"Tomorrow then?" he asked hopefully.

I played my ace card. "Jimmy, don't forget that tomorrow we're going to take a hike to Meadowlark Springs."

"Please, Aunt Beth," he pleaded. "I'll wash dishes for you and empty the garbage and make my own bed. I won't be any trouble."

Beth left. Jimmy pouted about it all day.

*   *   *   *   *

One night we roasted marshmallows in a campfire we'd made in front of the cabin.

"See all those stars?" I said. "It makes you think, doesn't it?"

"What about?"

"It makes you think there must be a God, doesn't it?"

"Is there, Dad?"

I paused. "I think so."

"Is God like us, or is he different?"

I cleared my throat. "Well, in some ways he's like us and in other ways he's, uh, different."

"You don't know very much about God, do you?"

"No, not much."

*   *   *   *   *

In mid-July we had another visitor. He wandered around the lake and eventually made his way to where we were fishing. He had gray hair and looked distinguished. "I'm looking for someone named Michael Hill."

"That's me."

We shook hands.

"I'm Ben Jansen with the Atlantis Group. We're an independent movie company headquartered in Utah. We saw your portrayal of Carl Sandburg, and we were very impressed with the depth and sensitivity you gave to the role. I came all the way from Utah to see if we could interest you in doing a film for us."

"We're interested," Jimmy said quickly.

I smiled. "He's just kidding. Actually we love it out here among nature."

We walked up the trail to the cabin.

"Jimmy, why don't you pour Mr. Jansen a cup of coffee?"

"No thanks," Mr. Jansen said.

"Well, how about some hot chocolate then?"

"That'd be fine."

"Well, then fix Mr. Jansen a cup of your famous hot chocolate."

Jimmy picked up a cup and examined it. "This cup's got some gunk stuck to the bottom."

"What kind of gunk?"

He held the cup up to the sunlight streaming in the window. "I'm not sure. It's either stuck-on noodles from yesterday or a glob of burnt beans from the day before."

"Aw, that won't hurt anything." Then I noticed Jansen's expression. "Hey, but just to be on the safe side, take the cup down to the lake and rinse it out." I turned to our guest. "The pump's broken now, so we use lake water."

Jimmy started out the door and then stopped. "Do you want me to go to where we cleaned our fish last night? I told you we shouldn't have thrown its guts into the water."

"Better go a few feet from there."

Jansen saw a way out. "I really hate to put you to any trouble. How about if I just pass on the hot chocolate."

"How about a graham cracker?" Jimmy said. "The mice get into most everything, but I think you're pretty safe with an unopened packet of graham crackers."

I'd had it with my son. "While you're at it, Jimmy, why don't you go through your list of one thousand ways to die in the forest." I turned to Ben Jansen. "One tiny mouse gets into a few scraps of food and the kid gets hyper. Ben, take a graham cracker." It almost sounded like an order.

Ben carefully selected a graham cracker and took a small bite and then turned to me. "We're not a big company, and we can't pay you what Universal Studios might, but I think you'll be interested in the role. We're doing a movie about the life of Christ, and we'd like you to play the lead."

"Dad, please take the job. I can't stand it up here anymore."

"Go check our lines and see if we've caught a fish yet."

He came back a minute later, panting hard from having run all the way down the trail and back again. "You haven't told him no yet, have you?"

I turned to Ben. "I'm afraid it's really out of the question," I said. "My father died a few weeks ago, and right after that my wife got a divorce and left me with Jimmy. I've been trying to work it out, but I'm just not sure when I'll be ready to work again."

"We saw you in the Sandburg film and decided you were the one we want for the role. We like the way you project on the screen. Strong but sensitive. Courageous but kind. Bold but caring."

"Dad, is he talking about you?"

"Go wash that cup like I told you," I ordered. "One . . . two . . ."

He went outside and swished the cup in some rainwater and hurried back in again.

"I can't go dragging my boy all the way to Israel. He needs stability in his life now."

"No, I don't," Jimmy butted in. "Just get me away from this place."

"Actually we'll be filming in Utah," Ben said. "Much of the same scenery exists there as can be found in Israel."

"You still don't understand. It's not like I have someone to watch him while I'm doing a movie."

"My cousin takes in children. I'm sure we can work something out. We'll be filming not too far from Orem. You'd see Jimmy every night. And we won't be filming on Sundays."

"I still say the answer's no."

He paused. "May I ask why?"

"Well, besides all the other reasons, I'm not a religious man. I don't know anything about Jesus."

"Did you know anything about Carl Sandburg before you played that role?"

"Well, no, but . . ."

"It's probably the best role in the world. I can't understand why you'd turn it down. I'll be directing the movie, and I've come a long way to find you."

"Dad, please."

I paused. "Well, maybe I'll think about it."

Ben took us to supper. He gave Jimmy five dollars' worth of quarters to play video games at the pizza place we ate at. That won him Jimmy's friendship for life.

He outlined some very good terms for me, so that beside the straight salary, I'd be getting a percentage of the profits from the movie. Also, he phoned his baby-sitting cousin in Utah and had me talk to her. Her name was Kellie. She sounded acceptable enough.

By the end of the evening, with Jimmy threatening to run away if we didn't leave, I agreed to do the movie.

CHAPTER THREE

A few days later Jimmy and I pulled into Orem, Utah. We were driving an old station wagon we'd bought in Montana. It was a piece of junk, but it was all we could afford. It looked like the winner in a rust contest. It had paneling along the side, the kind that looks like real wood but is really just strips of wallpaper. Whenever I wasn't looking, Jimmy was peeling it off the car. I tried to get mad at him but had to admit it was irresistible. It was like after a bad sunburn when you try to see how long a continuous piece of dead skin you can peel off at one time.

"Now this one's a real peach cake," the salesman kept saying when we first looked at it in the used-car lot.

Peach cake, my foot. After we left on our trip, I found that when we went over forty miles an hour, the radiator began to spout steam. We had the only car on the highway that could be mistaken for Moby Dick. In fact, from that time we began to call it Moby Dick.

It was a long trip. We had one blowout and a vapor lock climbing a mountain pass just outside of Butte. We had to stop every hour and put more water in the radiator.

The night before we entered Utah, we slept under the stars at a rest stop on I-15 near Pocatello. Jimmy kept going on all night about the number of people who were mugged each year at rest stops late at night.

The next day, after arriving in Orem, we rented a small house and bought some food, using some money Ben had advanced me. I called his cousin the baby-sitter, and she asked us to come by after all the kids had left. Anytime after six, she said.

At six-fifteen we pulled up to her house. The yard was fenced in, with a swing set in the front yard, and a small hand-lettered sign that read "Peppermint Pals Day Care Center."

We walked up the walk and rang the doorbell.

"Just a minute," a voice called out.

"There's still time to escape," I said to Jimmy.

"It'll be okay, Dad."

A young woman with reddish brown hair and freckles opened the door. Looking at her, I could tell it had been a hard day. She had dried glue stuck to her faded BYU T-shirt, and the place smelled like old diapers.

"I'm Michael Hill. I talked to you on the phone."

"Oh yes, come in," she said, trying to rearrange her hair with her hand.

She opened the screen door. "I'm Kellie Green. Excuse the mess."

We carefully made our way up the toy-strewn steps to her living room. Once inside she focused her attention on Jimmy. "And what's your name?"

"Jim Hill."

"He goes by Jimmy."

"Dad, I've told you before. I don't like the name Jimmy. It's a girl's name."

"You ever hear of Jimmy Stewart?" I countered.

"I don't care. From now on, call me Jim."

"Jim," Kellie said, "I'm glad to meet you."

"Do you have any video games here in your house?" Jim asked.

"No."

He looked discouraged. "Well, do you have anybody my age?"

"How old are you?"

"Nine."

"My son is seven."

"Where is he now?"

"He's taking a violin lesson."

Jimmy, or Jim as he preferred, scowled. "Why?"

"He likes playing the violin."

Jim shook his head. "Why?"

"We'll look someplace else," I told him.

He shrugged his shoulders. "This is all right. After the lake, I can stand anything."

I turned to Kellie "I'd like to look around, if that's all right."

"Of course."

We walked through the house. As far as I could tell, she'd taken low-grade junk and turned it into games and projects for kids. Jim drifted into the backyard to check things out.

Letting her give me the guided tour, I had a chance to study her features without being too obvious. She had avocado green eyes and wore little or no makeup. She'd sewn patches on the knees of her slacks, and that, along with her freckles, made her seem a little bit like a character from Huckleberry Finn.

We passed a storeroom. There were large bags labeled "Wheat" lying on the floor.

"Is anything wrong?" she asked.

"Well," I chuckled, "from here it looks like you've got bags of wheat in your house. So tell me, what's really in the bags?"

"Five hundred pounds of wheat." She looked at me. "You know why, don't you?"

I paused. "Uh, let's see. It's got something to do with your religion, right? Like, is it some kind of an offering to the gods?"

"No, it's for emergencies."

"Oh."

"Is something wrong?" she asked, noticing my confusion.

"Uh, well, I'm just trying to imagine what kind of emergency it'd be where a person would suddenly need five hundred pounds of wheat."

"You're not a member of the church, are you?" she asked.

"You mean, a Mormon? Oh no. Are you?"

"Yes."

"Oh." I paused. "Uh, if I decide to let my son stay here, you're not going to try to brainwash him or anything like that, are you?"

"No, of course not."

"That's good. I just want him to be like me as far as religion goes."

"I understand. What religion are you?"

"Well, I don't actually belong to a church. I guess you could say I'm tolerant and open-minded."

"Would you ever like to learn more about the Mormon church?"

"No thanks."

We continued with the tour.

"Tell me, what does your husband think about you running a day-care center?"

"Didn't Ben tell you? My husband died a few months ago."

"Oh, I'm sorry."

"He left me with no insurance and a son with special needs. Having a child-care center seemed like the best way for me to have an income without leaving home. And what about you?" she asked.

"My wife divorced me in June."

"I see."

"Yeah, she just walked out on me. One day out of the blue she tells me she wants to be a gynecologist. So now she's in med school in Boston. Well, I hope she's happy, because she's going to have to live her whole life knowing she abandoned her family. Now it's up to me to carry on." I knew I was milking the situation for sympathy, but I couldn't stop myself.

"It must be difficult for you. Ben says you're doing a movie for him."

"Yes. It's about the life of Christ."

"That explains why you have a beard then."

"Well, actually I had it up at the lake."

"The lake?"

Jim was outside, so he couldn't bad-mouth me. "Yes, I've spent the last few weeks with my son camping at a lake in Montana."

"You know, there're so few fathers that ever take the time to be with their sons. I go fishing with my boy sometimes, but I'm sure it's not the same as with a father and his son."

"Yes, it was really, uh, special. I don't think either of us will ever forget our experience at the lake. I know I won't."

"What part are you going to play in Ben's movie?"

I cleared my throat. "Jesus."

"Looking at you, I can see why they'd want you to play him."

"You can? Why?"

"You have a gentleness in your face that I associate with him."

That caught me off guard. It made me want to be helpful. "What's your son's name?"

"Russel."

"Maybe sometime I can take him fishing with me and my son."

"I'm sure he'd appreciate that. He needs a man's influence."

The tour was over. I called out the back door for Jimmy to get in the car.

I lingered at her door. It was the first time I'd talked to a single woman since my divorce.

"How much do you want for watching Jimmy?" I asked.

"Eleven dollars a day—that's from seven in the morning to five at night. That includes lunch too."

"Let me pay you fifteen."

She paused. "Why would you want to do that?"

"I don't think you're charging enough."

"You don't have to do that."

"Please let me."

"All right. Thank you very much."

Jimmy was waiting for me at the car.

"She's sort of nice, isn't she," he said when I got in the car.

"Don't slouch, Jimmy."

"Jim," he corrected.

CHAPTER FOUR

The next morning I dropped Jim off at Kellie's and made my way to the Atlantis Group offices in Orem. Ben Jansen wasn't in his office so I waited for him to return. Fifteen minutes later he breezed in. He was a man who gave the impression of always doing important things, but I noticed he had a picture of his large family on the desk.

"Are you all settled in?" he asked.

I nodded. "I've rented a house, and I took my son to Kellie Green this morning, so I guess I'm ready to start work."

He showed me around the office and introduced me to the people who worked there. He explained that Atlantis Group did about five films a year and marketed them to theaters all over the country. Some of the films were sold to cable TV as movies, while others made it into theaters.

"Do you have a completed script for me?" I asked when we were through with the tour.

"Sure, let me get one for you." A minute later he returned with a copy of the script.

"I've got a meeting in a few minutes, but maybe we could just talk through the first part so you'll know where we're coming from."

"Sure."

He sat down at his desk. "Okay, let's start at the beginning. It's morning on the Sea of Galilee. Fishing boats slip quietly toward shore after a long night's work. Seagulls circle overhead looking for a free meal from the fishermen. The camera pans from the shore to the foothills. We see a man taking an early-morning walk. It's the spring of the year. Wildflowers carpet the hills surrounding the lake. The rising sun catches the brightly colored petals. The camera moves to a closeup of the man in the middle of a large field of wildflowers. We see that it's Jesus. He bends over and touches one of the petals and appears to be studying it. As he does so, the camera features one of the flowers in microscopic detail.

"We hear a voice from another existence. 'Let the earth bring forth grass, the herb yielding seed, and the fruit tree yielding fruit after his kind, upon the earth.' "

Ben looked up at me. "What we want here is to show that Jesus was the one given responsibility by God the Father to create this earth. The same sun that in the beginning Jesus commanded to give light now warms his back. He walks on land that he once commanded to be separated from the waters. The sun, the rain, the animals, the flowers and trees and grain—he made them all. And yet here he stands, the son of a mortal woman and an immortal father, picking a bouquet of wildflowers to take home to his mother."

Ben leaned back in his chair. "We've got to make this point, because if we don't, then what is he? A good teacher at best. But he's more than that. He's the Son of God come to earth to show us the way."

I had questions but decided to let it go for now. "Okay, what happens next?"

"The camera follows him as he walks back home. He stops to watch the shepherds, how the sheep from each flock know the voice of their shepherd. All this he'll use in his parables.

"He enters the village of Nazareth and walks down the winding streets, passing small dusty houses. Neighborhood children, seeing him come, eagerly run out to meet him. He kneels down and talks with them and gives each one a flower from his bouquet, and then he continues on his way.

"We see him entering his boyhood home. Next to the cottage is a carpenter's shop. We switch to an interior shot. It's a small, neatly kept household. His mother sits in the sunlight of an open window, doing last-minute touches on a robe she's made. Jesus gives her the flowers he's picked and kisses her.

"Next we see Jesus wearing the robe for the first time. Mary is kneeling to make adjustments on the hem. This is the robe he'll wear throughout his ministry. Mary fusses with the robe. Jesus, full of love, reaches out and touches her head. Mary looks up and suddenly realizes her son is about to leave.

" 'Will you go away now?' " she asks.

"Jesus nods his head. Suddenly she becomes every mother just before her son is about to leave home. Where will he sleep? What will he eat? She promises to prepare his favorite food if he'll stay just a little longer.

"He smiles, shakes his head, and tenderly reminds her he must be about his Father's business.

"Next we see him leaving behind his boyhood home. Things will never be the same again for him or for his mother or for the entire world."

He paused. "I guess I don't have to tell you that the whole movie depends on your portrayal of the Savior."

A few minutes later he had to run off to a meeting. I drove to a park and sat on a picnic table and spent the day reading the script.

*   *   *   *   *

Around six o'clock I went to pick up Jim.

Kellie met me at the door looking frazzled and depressed. "I don't think I can have anybody come tomorrow."

"Why not?"

"The toilet backed up, and I had to send kids over to a neighbor's house all day to use the bathroom, and she just called to tell me that she's definitely not going to be home tomorrow." She had tears in her eyes. "A plumber's going to cost me a fortune."

"Let me look at it, okay?" I said.

After a brief inspection, I said to her, "I know just the thing to fix it. I'll be right back."

A few minutes later I returned from a hardware store with a toilet auger for fishing back through the pipes. In a few minutes I retrieved a diaper that somebody'd flushed down the toilet.

"Where did you learn to do that?"

"My dad taught me a lot of things." I paused. "He died this summer."

"I'm sorry. You really have had a rough summer, haven't you."

I nodded. "I'll leave this here so you can use it the next time it happens."

"How much do I owe you?" she asked.

"Nothing."

"Are you sure?"

"Positive."

"Well, at least stay for supper. It might take a while because I forgot to take the meat out of the freezer, but I'll hurry it along."

"I've got a better idea. Let me take us all out for supper."

"No, that costs too much."

"You've had a hard day. You need to relax. And I need a woman to talk to."

She smiled. "All right, let me change clothes first."

I returned to the living room and waited.

Jim was in the backyard climbing the cherry tree to see if anything was ripe yet.

Her son Russel came into the house and saw me. He was small for his age, and he wore the thickest glasses I'd ever seen in my life. He was awkward. I figured he went through life being in everybody's way. I wondered if he ever really knew what was going on around him.

"Hello," I said. "You must be Russel."

He nodded and left to go talk to his mother.

Poor Russel, I thought. I'll bet kids make fun of him at school.

Kellie returned. She'd made an effort to look clean, but not much effort into looking attractive. No makeup. No lipstick. No jewelry.

We asked the boys where they wanted to go and they said McDonald's.

We took the food to a park and let our kids play on the swings while we talked.

She was younger than me by a year. She'd been raised in Idaho and had met her future husband, Steve, during her first semester at BYU. They'd married in the spring of her freshman year. She'd quit school to help him get through. He never did. He died in an automobile accident. She hadn't dated anyone since then. I asked her why, and she said that she and Steve had been married forever.

I didn't understand that.

Her main goal was to finish her education so she could get a better-paying job. So far she'd saved enough money to take one night course next semester.

Her drive for an education reminded me of Pamela, and that was not particularly good for our relationship.

Steve hadn't carried any life insurance, so it was all up to her now. I admired her for making the best of a difficult situation.

When she smiled, which happened only occasionally, I loved the sunshine of her face. With a little more money for clothes, with makeup, and with time to get over the ache of losing her husband, she could be attractive to men. But I wasn't sure if she'd ever want that again.

CHAPTER FIVE

The next day Ben and I got together in his office to do a read-through of the script. After an hour of mutual frustration, he finally shook his head. "I'm sorry, Michael, but it just isn't right."

"What's wrong with it?"

"I wish I could be more specific. I just know it's not right." He paused. "Before you did Carl Sandburg, did you do any research on him?"

"Yes."

He looked at his calendar. "Look, we've still got time before we start shooting. How about if you do research on Jesus? Take your time and then come back and we'll try it again, okay?"

I went to the library and·spent the afternoon reading some of the books about Jesus. It seemed impossible to read through the large stack I found there. And even if I did, I'd read enough to know that they didn't agree with one another. So how could I know which one was right?

At five I went to pick up Jim. When I got there, I was surprised to notice that Kellie had eye makeup on. She looked much better.

"Do you know anything about Jesus?" I asked her.

"Yes, I do. Why?"

"Ben asked me to find out all I can about him. Any ideas of where to look?"

"What do you want to know?"

"Something to base a characterization on. Try acting the part of someone who's described to you only as glorious. I need something besides superlatives."

"I know a place you can go. It's in Salt Lake. Will you take Russel and me there sometime?"

"How about now? I'll treat us all to supper. How would that be?"

She smiled. "I never turn down an offer for a free supper."

*   *   *   *   *

Our destination was the Visitors Center on Temple Square in Salt Lake City. While I guided Moby Dick down the interstate at forty miles an hour, she looked over the script and gave me some hints.

Jim and Russel sat in the back seat, not even speaking to each other. I think Jim felt Russel was beneath him.

After we found a place to park, we started through the Visitors Center, looking at the posters and listening to the presentations. And then we started up a long sloping ramp. I was busy trying to make sure we had the boys with us, looking back and telling Jim to quit fooling around and catch up with us, all the time walking backwards up the ramp.

Then I turned and there it was, the statue of the *Christus*. His hands seemed to be reaching out to me.

I froze in my tracks.

"Are you all right?" Kellie asked.

I stood there, transfixed by that face. His eyes seemed to be looking directly at me. I felt how totally wrong it was for me to even think about playing the part of Jesus in the movie. What right did I have to represent him? None at all.

"You go ahead," I muttered. "I'll meet you when you're through." I turned and fled.

When I got to the first floor, I sat on a bench and tried to calm down. A few minutes later she came and sat next to me. "I took Jim and Russel to a presentation about the pioneers. Is something wrong?"

"I can't do the movie. Ben'll have to get someone else."

"If you didn't feel a little inadequate, I'd be worried. But don't worry, you'll do okay."

"You don't understand." I looked at my hands. "How can these hands be his hands? It'd be like mocking God. I'm not that good of a person."

"Nobody is, Michael. But he loves us anyway."

She reached over and touched my arm. "Have you ever thought about praying for help?"

"I don't know how to pray."

"I can teach you."

"I'm not sure I want to learn."

"Michael, you can't play the part of Jesus if you don't learn to pray."

I paused. "All right. Can you teach me?"

She talked to a supervisor, who agreed to let us use his office for a few minutes. We rounded up our kids and went in and closed the door. She helped me through my first prayer.

It was the first time in his life that Jim had ever had a kneeling family prayer. He wasn't impressed. "We won't be doing much more of this while we're in Utah, will we?"

After that we all went outside and looked at the flowers.

A young woman ran up to Kellie and cried out, "Kellie, is that you? I haven't seen you since we graduated from high school!"

"Marlis!" Kellie cried out.

They threw their arms around each other. Marlis introduced her husband and then turned to me. "And this must be your husband and your two little kids. They're adorable."

"Oh, he's not my husband," Kellie said. "He's just a friend. My husband died last year."

Her smile vanished. "I'm terribly sorry. I didn't know. Are these your boys?"

"One is mine and one is his," she said.

"Oh."

"I'm his," Jim said so there'd be no mistake.

"My wife left me a few months ago to go to Boston to become a gynecologist," I said.

"Oh." She looked at me with a strange expression. A few minutes later, she and her husband moved away, still full of unanswered questions.

*   *   *   *   *

On the way home, I offered to pay Kellie triple what she usually made in a week if she'd coach me about Jesus.

"Just think of it as a job," I said.

She finally agreed. When we got to her home, she phoned and made arrangements for a friend of hers to fill in for her the next week at the day-care center.

The next morning I picked her up and we drove to the Wilkinson Center at BYU and rented an office room for a week—charging it all to Ben.

We sat down opposite each other across a conference table. She'd brought scriptures and reference books with her.

"All right," I said. "What was Jesus really like? I need details."

"We know that he was a carpenter until he was about thirty years old. I think his hands had calluses from working, and his arms and shoulders were strong and muscular.

"He was the best that a man can be. Physically strong, and yet his feelings ran the full range of human emotion. He showed anger when he threw the moneychangers from the temple. He raged against the hypocrisy of the Pharisees, and yet he openly wept with compassion at other times. He never concealed his emotions. When he was angry, he let it out. When he was impatient with the apostles, he chastised them. But no matter what his emotion, he was always in control."

She turned to one of her books. "Here's a guideline he's given for temperament." She started reading. " 'No power or influence can or ought to be maintained by virtue of the priesthood, only by persuasion, by long-suffering, by gentleness and meekness, and by love unfeigned; by kindness, and pure knowledge, . . . reproving betimes with sharpness, when moved upon by the Holy Ghost; and then showing forth afterwards an increase of love toward him whom thou hast reproved.' "

"Does that describe how he was?" I asked.

"Yes, I think so. We know that he did sometimes reprove with sharpness." She turned to her Bible. "Listen to this. 'Now do ye Pharisees make clean the outside of the cup and the platter; but your inward part is full of ravening and wickedness.' Or

think about when he drove out the moneychangers. Nobody
even tried to stop him. They stood in awe of his manhood and
power and the righteousness of the action."

I took some notes. "Okay, let's move on. One of the first
scenes is Jesus changing water into wine." I thumbed through
my script. "His mother says to him, 'They have no wine.' And
Jesus says, 'Woman, what have I to do with thee? mine hour is
not yet come.' " I read the passage as if Jesus was angry at his
mother for bothering him.

"That's not the way it happened," she said. She turned to
her Bible and read a slightly different passage. But the main difference was how she read it. Instead of angrily as I'd done, she
showed a Jesus who was deeply respectful toward his mother.
" 'Woman, what wilt thou have me do for thee? that will I do; for
mine hour is not yet come.' "

I paused. "How do you know he said it like that?"

"It's from the Joseph Smith Translation," she said.

Even though I'd been through at least part of the Visitors
Center, I still didn't catch on. I figured it was just another
version of the Bible.

We worked until noon and then went to the cafeteria for
lunch. Afterwards we took a walk around campus. We finally
stopped in front of the administration building and sat down by
a fountain.

"I wish I had a camera to catch the sun shining in your hair,"
I said.

She closed her eyes and sadly shook her head.

"Did I say something wrong?"

"It's just that Steve used to say that about my hair—how
good it looked in the sun."

For some reason that annoyed me. "Well, sure he did. Any
guy'd tell you that."

She stared at me as if I'd just slapped her face.

"Look, Kellie, I'm tired of us telling each other we're sorry.
Can we just say it one more time and be done with it? I'm really
sorry your husband died. And I'm sorry my wife divorced me
and that my dad died. But it happened. Now you and I are here

together for the next few days. We're still young and now we're
both single, and if I happen to notice the way your hair shines in
the sun, I'm going to tell you about it. It doesn't mean I'm trying
to romance you. It just means I'm alive. Okay?''

"There's no way you can understand how I feel," she said.

"How do you feel?"

"Like I'm still married to Steve."

"You're not though."

"I was married in the temple."

"I don't care where you were married. You can't be married
to a man who's dead."

"You don't know about our church. In the temple you can
get married for time and eternity."

"You keep saying that, but what does it mean?"

"It means that even after Steve died, I'm still married."

"Are you telling me you can't ever marry anyone else?"

She paused. "No. I can marry again, but my second marriage
will last only until I die."

"All right, if you can get married again, then that means
you're not married now, doesn't it?"

She didn't want to talk about it. "We should get back to
work. An hour lunch break is all I'm used to."

I was furious with her for treating this as an employer-
employee relationship. "And as your employer," I grumbled, "I
certainly respect that. It's so hard to get good help these days."

Even by the time we reached the office, I was still fuming.

"I think we should have a prayer before we start again," she
said.

"No. I'm not paying you to pray."

"Michael, I don't think we can talk about the Savior with all
this tension in the room."

"Tension? What tension? I don't know what you're talking
about. Why should there be tension between us? Go ahead
where you left off."

She opened her Bible, started to read, and then stopped. "I
can't do it."

"Why not?"

"There's a bad feeling between us. I think we should talk about it."

"Why do women have to be so emotional?" I raged. "Look, I don't want to talk about it. You want to know why? Because talking to you is like walking on eggshells."

Then I stormed out of the office.

When I returned a few minutes later, she was patiently waiting for me. "You didn't walk out on me," I said.

"Did you think I would?"

"Women always leave me. Why didn't you?"

She shrugged her shoulders. "I really need the money."

It was such an honest thing to say that it made me smile. "Listen to me. I want us to be friends. It's true I'm paying you for your help, but I don't want you to think of it as a job. That's mainly my gripe, okay?"

She looked at me. "Okay, but I still think we should pray."

She knelt down and closed her eyes.

From then on, we always started each session off with a prayer. The first few times I kept my eyes open so I could gaze at her face. It was nice to look at her without her getting nervous by the attention.

But eventually I too began to close my eyes.

*   *   *   *   *

We continued the next day.

"It says Jesus blessed the little children," I said. "How do you picture that?"

"Mothers brought him their children, but the disciples tried to give him time to rest. Besides, they didn't see any need for Jesus to be involved with children, because they knew that children are free from sin until they reach the age of accountability. But Jesus loved little children, and he asked the disciples to let the mothers come ahead with their little ones.

"I picture him picking up a little boy and setting him on his lap, and asking him what his name was. And maybe the boy would give him a special gift, like an extra-smooth rock he'd found along the way from his home, or a flower picked just for him.

"Then came time for the blessing. Jesus would put his hands on the boy's head and call him by name and bless him to grow up healthy and strong and to love the truth. Maybe he'd tell him to always remember that when he was a boy he'd seen the Kingdom of God come to earth.

"He gave a personal blessing for each boy or girl, and then returned the child back to its mother. It was a sweet time for him and for the children."

"How do you know all this?" I asked.

"Once I had a husband who gave blessings to my boy."

*   *   *   *   *

Each day we went through details of the script. I practiced my lines for her. After work I often took the four of us out to supper or she'd cook something for us.

"Are you going to marry her?" Jimmy asked me one night.

"Of course not." I paused. "But if I did, what would you think about that?"

"I like Mom better."

"Sure, well, don't worry about it. Kellie and I are just friends."

*   *   *   *   *

Kellie asked us if we'd like to go fishing with her and Russel on Saturday.

I said of course, thinking I'd impress her with my expertise.

We drove to a reservoir and rented a boat. We rowed out a ways near where some other boats were anchored. She showed us how Steve used to bait the hooks.

"Russel is such a good fisherman," she said. "He always catches the first fish."

She threw Russel's line into the water first and then fixed the other poles.

Just after she tossed Jim's line in the water, Russel caught the
first fish. We all cheered Russel on while he reeled in. She got up
and netted it by herself.

While we were waiting for some more action, she gave us
cinnamon rolls she'd baked that morning.

Jim caught the second fish. It weighed two pounds.

"This is fun!" he shouted. "Dad and I never caught fish like
this!"

I blushed.

We caught five fish, and then Kellie let Jim try his hand at
rowing.

We quit at eleven. Kellie showed me a quick way to clean
fish, and then we had a picnic lunch of potato salad, lemonade,
fried chicken, and chocolate cake.

After we got home that night, Jim said he couldn't see why
Russel's mom said he was such a great fisherman, when the only
reason he caught the first fish was because his line was in the
water before anyone else's, and he really didn't do anything but
reel in the line anyway.

"Jim, it's important that Russel feel that he's good at something."

"Well, he is good at something."

"What?" I asked.

"Tripping over the cracks in the sidewalk," he said with a
smirk.

*   *   *   *   *

"I want to have an official date with you," I said the next day.
She swallowed. "Oh."

"A dinner and then a movie. What do you say?"

She frowned. "I wouldn't be good company for you."

"It'll just be practice for when some rich guy comes along."

"I don't have anything to wear."

"You wear nice outfits to church, don't you? Wear one of
those."

She paused, then said quietly, "Wait here and I'll show you
what I mean."

A minute later she brought some clothes from her bedroom. She showed me a nice dress.

"Sure, that's fine," I said. "Wear that."

"I wore this the first time on my honeymoon."

"Oh."

She carefully laid it aside and picked up another. "And this one I wore the night Steve proposed to me."

She picked up a black dress. "I wore this to Steve's funeral." She stopped. "Do you see what I mean? I don't have anything to wear."

"Get rid of them, Kellie."

She shook her head. "I can't do that."

"I'll buy you a complete new wardrobe—whatever you want. It's not good for you to have those clothes here. Steve's dead. You've got to move on with your life."

"I'm trying, but it's so hard."

"You believe Steve is somewhere now, don't you?"

"Yes."

"Do you think he wants you torturing yourself this way?"

She looked at me. "No."

"Then let me help you." I walked over to the clothes, bundled them up in my arms, and walked out of her house.

By the time I reached my car she'd figured out what I was going to do. She ran out to stop me. I drove away, leaving her standing in the street, calling after me to stop.

I drove to a Deseret Industries store and donated the clothes to them. Just before leaving, I had a clerk look at the dresses and tell me what sizes I should get for Kellie. Then I went to a woman's clothing store and bought her five new dresses.

An hour later when I went to her house and knocked, she wouldn't answer the door. I left the clothes on her front step and went around to get Jim. He was in the backyard doing chin-ups on the top bar of their swing.

We drove to our house and I fixed supper.

"She cried a lot after you left," he said.

"Eat your beans."

Later that evening she phoned me.

"What did you do with my dresses?" she asked.

"I gave them away."

There was a long painful silence. Then, "I know you were only trying to help."

"That's right."

"I tried on the dresses that you bought me," she said. "They're very nice."

"It's no big deal—they were on sale."

"You shouldn't spend money on me."

"When I have money, I spend it."

"I have one of the dresses on now. Do you want to come over and see me in it?"

"Yes, I'd like that very much."

A few minutes later I knocked on the door of her place. She opened the door. She had put makeup on and was wearing perfume. She was wearing the cream-colored dress with lace at the neck.

"Why are you staring at me?" she asked.

"I didn't know how beautiful you are."

"Thank you."

It was true she was stunning, but it was the beauty of a fragile china doll. I felt that the slightest jar would cause her to break in a million pieces.

We sat down in her living room. The phonograph was playing slow songs.

"Would you like a glass of lemonade?" she asked.

"Yes, thank you."

She brought out two glasses of lemonade from the kitchen.

We were acting out a scene, but the only problem was, I didn't know what part she wanted me to play.

"Let me turn off this overhead light," she said. "It makes the room look so bare when it's on." She turned off the light, leaving just a small lamp on top of the TV to give us light. She sat down beside me, desperately clutching her glass of lemonade.

She looked at me. "I can see why you decided to become an actor."

"Why's that?"

"You're very good-looking." She closed her eyes as if it had been an ordeal even to get the words out.

There was a long silence.

"Thank you," I finally said.

"You probably think I say that to all the guys. But I don't."

"Kellie, I know that."

"Tell me, do you like to dance?" she asked.

"Sure."

"I used to belong to a ballroom dance group at BYU."

"Oh."

"It's good exercise. Do you want to dance now?"

"Okay."

I stood up and put out my hand to help her up, but she suddenly turned away and shook her head. She started turning her wedding band back and forth on her finger. "I'm sorry. I guess I don't want to dance after all. You know, I've never seen it rain so much for this time of year." She paused. "Michael, do you think I'm attractive?" she asked.

"Very."

"Even though I'm a widow?"

"Yes."

"There's a waltz called the 'Merry Widow' waltz, isn't there? That's what I am tonight, isn't it? The merry widow. I wanted to dress up for you so you'd get your money's worth for buying me clothes."

I was embarrassed she'd said that. "Kellie, please, this is turning out all wrong. I think I'd better go home now."

Her voice was thin and high. "I've put on a little weight, but I'm getting down to what I used to weigh before I got married. It's like a boxer trying to make a comeback. Someday I'll be back in the swing of things, going on dates, flirting."

She tried to smile, but the pain on her face made it come out all wrong. "I've read about coping with being a widow. I need to meet new people, make friends, get out of the house, get used to men again. They say it's hard at first, but you just have to do it. Maybe they're right. I'm still young. There's other men, hundreds of them, to replace . . . ."

She stopped, her emotions on the ragged edge, teetering between control and breakdown. ". . . hundreds of men to replace the only man I'll ever love."

The charade was over. She buried her face on the arm of the couch and cried.

I tried to put my arm around her but she shook it off. "Kellie, what can I do for you?"

She turned to face me. Tears were streaming down her face. "You can't do anything. You want to know why? Because I don't care about you, not at all. And I never will."

"I want to help if I can," I said.

"All right, you're an actor. Can you be like Steve? Can you say the things he used to say? Can you smile at me the way he used to? Because if you can't, then you're no use to me. Can't you see? I'm stranded here without him. Why couldn't I have died with him? He's the only man I'll ever love. What am I going to do? Nobody knows how much I miss him."

She ran to her bedroom and closed the door.

Her crying had awakened Russel. He came out, wearing pajamas with pictures of bear clowns. He saw me in the dimly lit living room, still holding my untouched glass of lemonade.

"Sometimes she cries at night," he said. "Don't go away—she'll come out when she feels better."

"Thanks."

He went in to see her. He left the bedroom door open so that from where I sat in the living room, I could see them. She was lying face down on the bed, crying. He sat down on the bed next to her and patted her on the back, the way a mother does to her crying child. This time the roles were reversed.

"Mom, it's okay, don't cry."

It was the first time I'd seen her bedroom because she always kept the door closed in the daytime when I came to get Jimmy. There were still two pillows on the bed. One of them must have been Steve's. A blue bathrobe, too big to be hers, hung on a hook in the closet where maybe Steve had hung it after his shower on the day he died. Several pictures of the two of them were on the wall, and a wedding certificate from a temple hung there too. Library books were stacked on the bedstand. I wondered if she read late at night when she couldn't sleep.

I could see her clothes in the closet, and a bare spot where Steve's clothes had hung.

I knew I was invading her privacy, but I couldn't force myself to look away. I wanted to know every detail of that room.

I thought about going with Russel back to his room and tucking him into bed and then telling him that it was better for his mom to cry than it was to always try and hold it in, and that he could cry too whenever he needed to. And then I'd gently close his door after me and go see Kellie. I wanted to wipe the tears from her cheek and hold her in my arms while she cried. I wanted to tell her that someday things would be better. I wanted to be with her.

But I knew I couldn't go, because there were other emotions besides brotherly concern that would persuade me to enter that room.

She was a beautiful woman.

And so I stayed put and watched the two of them struggling to cope.

A few minutes later he said, "Mom, Michael's waiting for you. You'd better go see him."

She sat up and saw the open door and realized I'd been watching all along. Quietly she asked Russel to close the door.

A few minutes later she came out. "I'm sorry," she said. "I didn't know it would be so hard. It was a mistake. I'm not ready for this yet."

"Maybe not, but don't stop now. You need to start dating again. You can practice on me until somebody better comes along."

"I'm no fun for you."

"It's all right. I'm not in such great shape myself. Besides, what are friends for, right?"

"Well, I'll think about it, but now you'd better go. I need another favor. Can you take that record and get rid of it for me?"

She said it was a record with memories, that sometimes Steve had played it at night for just the two of them after Russel was asleep.

When I got home, I carefully set the record on the curb and stepped on it. It broke into many pieces. I picked them up one by one and threw them as hard as I could into the darkness of that bleak night.

The next day when we returned to our work, she wore what must have been her least attractive skirt and blouse. We didn't talk about what had happened the night before.

We were to the point in our studies where we needed to talk about the crucifixion.

"Tell me how you picture it," I said.

Her voice was subdued. "People often picture it as some epic stage production. It wasn't that. It was an innocent man suffering a cruel and painful death.

"While he was on the cross, the only way he could breathe was by standing on the nail through his feet. He did that until the pain was unbearable and then he'd collapse, which put strain on the wounds in his hands and wrists. But then, in order to breathe again, the whole cycle had to be repeated.

"Think what it must have been like from his point of view, looking down from the cross, seeing the hardened Roman soldiers. For them, inflicting painful death was a skill they prided themselves on. His enemies came and mocked him, saying that if he came down from the cross, they'd believe. And even the few friends who did show up felt in their hearts that he'd failed.

"Think about how he felt as he gazed on his mother's face, knowing full well that she shared his every pain, that his every gasp tore her apart.

"Most of his clothes had been taken by the Roman soldiers. I picture his white skin standing out against the dull dark wood of the cross. Did his mother understand that this was necessary? How could she? All she knew was that her precious son was being tortured to death. I wonder if there were drops of blood falling from his wounds upon the dusty ground, and if his mother watched those drops as they fell. That poor woman must have nearly died from the heartache she felt.

"In my mind I see the nails in his hands and feet, and his chest heaving, and his muscles throbbing in spasms. He ached so much. And he was all alone. There was nobody to share the burden. Even the heavens withdrew. It was his burden alone to bear."

We sat without speaking for several seconds. Then she went on.

"He said a few words while he was on the cross. It wasn't something he said just to fulfill prophecy. All that he said was the natural result of his suffering.

"What I'm trying to say is, focus on details: his face, his hands, his feet, his breathing, the texture of the roughened wood. It was not a religious pageant. It was murder, it was painful, it was humiliating, and nobody in the crowd had any idea that it was necessary. They figured it could've been avoided if he'd just used a little more tact, or if he hadn't come to Jerusalem for the Passover, or if he'd been more polite to the Sanhedrin, or if he'd gotten himself a good lawyer, or if he'd fled from the soldiers who came to arrest him, or any number of things. How could they understand that this was the very reason he came to the earth? To his friends on that terrible day, he was an embarrassment, an agonizing failure."

She reached for her scriptures. "Michael, I added to his suffering on that day."

"How?"

"Because he carried the burden of our sins. Mine and yours too. He suffered for our sins not only on the cross but also in the Garden of Gethsemane."

"Why would he do that?"

"So we won't have to."

"I didn't ask him to."

"I know," she said, "but he did it for us, and we all added to the price he had to pay."

She turned to a passage in one of her books. "Here's what he said years later about his suffering in Gethsemane. 'Which suffering caused myself, even God, the greatest of all, to tremble because of pain, and to bleed at every pore, and to suffer both body and spirit—and would that I might not drink the bitter cup, and shrink. Nevertheless, glory be to the Father, and I partook and finished my preparations unto the children of men.'

"Michael, it's so sad to think of him there on that cross. Can we go just beyond that? I want to tell you what happened the instant after he died. Just a minute while I find it." She turned to one of her books. "Okay, here it is. 'And there were gathered together in one place an innumerable company of the spirits of the just, who had been faithful in the testimony of Jesus while they lived in mortality. . . . I beheld that they were filled with joy and gladness, and were rejoicing because the day of their deliverance was at hand. . . . While this vast multitude waited and conversed, rejoicing in the hour of their deliverance from the chains of death, the Son of God appeared, declaring liberty to the captives who had been faithful.'

"Isn't it good to know that at the same instant his body slumped on the cross, he was welcomed by noble men and women who loved him with all their hearts?"

"I've never heard that before."

"I know." She paused as if she was about to tell me something else, but I interrupted her.

"What about the resurrection?" I asked. "Do you really think that happened?"

"Yes, I know that it did. His body and his spirit were reunited, and he walked out of the tomb with a resurrected body of flesh and bone. He was seen by thousands of people over the course of the next few days, and they all testified to what they had seen."

"But maybe he wasn't really dead, maybe just wounded, and then he regained consciousness and walked out of the tomb and told everybody he had come back to life."

"No, that's not the way it happened."

I could see she wasn't going to back down.

"Everyone who dies will be resurrected. It's a free gift, given to us by Jesus. I think about that now more than ever. I can't wait until I see Steve, alive again. I've dreamed about it ever since the accident—the time when I'll be in Steve's arms again."

"Sounds real nice," I said as enthusiastically as I could.

CHAPTER SEVEN

The next day I took Kellie to dinner at a Japanese restaurant in Salt Lake City. We took off our shoes upon entering the small private bamboo room they gave us. She looked more beautiful than ever before. I told her so, and, almost reluctantly, she thanked me.

I asked her how she knew about the restaurant, and she told me Steve had taken her there once.

The waitress brought us a relish dish and water and a menu and then left.

I asked if this was the same booth she and Steve had had.

She said she wasn't sure, but it might be.

We quit talking.

She said she knew she wasn't any good for me. She said she thought it would be best if I quit seeing her. She said it was too soon after Steve's death for her to be seeing a man. Besides that, maybe it would be better if we didn't see each other so much because I wasn't a member of her church.

I asked if she'd ever marry someone who wasn't a Mormon, and she said no. I asked why she had gone to so much trouble lately looking nice for me if she wasn't interested.

She said she just wanted to show her appreciation for my helping her.

I asked if that's all there was to it.

She said she was sorry if I'd gotten the wrong message, but she would never allow herself to get serious with me.

Allow herself? That's what she said. Allow herself. As if I was some terrible temptation that must be avoided at all costs.

When it came time to order, I sarcastically told her to go ahead and order the same thing she'd had with Steve there before, so she could sit and bawl through the entire meal.

She said she thought I was being insensitive.

I told her I thought she was an emotional cripple, incapable of maintaining any kind of mature adult relationship.

She said if I felt that way, maybe we'd better just end the evening right there and then.

I said that would suit me just fine.

I gave the waitress some money for the carrot sticks and we left.

Outside, the wind rustled wrappers in the gutters as we walked silently back to the car. A storm was coming.

The car wouldn't start. I got out and opened up the hood to see if I could fix it.

The rain started to pour down.

"You should get inside," Kellie said to me from the car.

"Don't tell me what to do! Okay?"

I was getting drenched, though, and so a minute later I swallowed my pride and jumped back in the car.

"Stupid carburetor," I raged, slamming my fist against the steering wheel. "The first thing I'm going to do when I get some money is get me a decent car, and the second thing'll be to find a normal woman to date."

"Good. I think that's exactly what you should do," she said.

I swore and angrily hit the steering wheel with my fist.

While lightning ravaged the sky and the rain rolled in sheets down the windshield, we sat there like stones. I had my arms folded tightly around me and was staring straight ahead.

I'll never know why she did it, but suddenly she leaned over and kissed me on the cheek.

I was shocked. "What did you do that for?"

She smiled. "Just to say thanks. I know this is hard for both of us, but I think it's good we're trying to work through it, don't you?"

Uncertain, I slowly put my hand next to hers on the car seat. She completed the action by putting her hand on mine.

We were actually holding hands. All my pent-up anger seemed to drain away.

I asked if she was still hungry and she said yes, so I took a blanket from the back seat and we held it over our heads while we ran back to the restaurant. They seated us in a different room.

I decided to let her open up about Steve so there wouldn't always be this wall between us. And so while we ate, I asked about him.

She told me how they met, the dates they had at BYU, their wedding in the Provo Temple, and where they went on their honeymoon. She described their first apartment in Provo. She told me how tight things were the first year, and about her getting pregnant when they had the least amount of money, and how Steve said it'd all work out, and how when his uncle died, Steve got enough of an inheritance to allow them to make a down payment on their tiny house.

She told about Russel's birth, and how Steve spent hours playing with his son. And how devastated they'd been when they first realized how bad Russel's eyesight was. She told me how Steve had to quit school for a year and a half to earn money to pay for some of Russel's medical bills. And how long and drawn-out college seemed to them, and how broke they were most of the time.

Steve had to go to school in the day and work at nights, and he never got enough sleep. One night he didn't come home from work on time. And then the phone call, saying that he'd been hurt and could she go to the hospital. When she got there, they said he'd been dead all along, but they hadn't wanted to tell her over the phone.

When we left the restaurant, the car still wouldn't start, but at least the rain had stopped. I opened the hood and had her hold the flashlight while I worked on the carburetor.

"I saw a car the other day," I said while I worked. "It's a Corvette. It's a few years old, but it's in good shape. I've got enough money for the down payment, so this weekend I might go trade in this wreck. How'd you like driving around in a red sports car?"

"That'd be nice," she said. "Where did you learn how to fix cars?"

"From my dad."

"Do you miss him?"

I looked up at her. "Sometimes I talk to him in my mind."

"About what?"

"Oh, I don't know. Little things mostly."

"I talk to Steve sometimes," she admitted.

I smiled. "We're quite a pair, aren't we."

On the way home, she told me how much she had loved being in his arms, how sometimes late at night she cried when the loneliness got too great. She told me it was better to cry in the night because then Russel didn't know.

"He knows," I said. "The night I bought you those dresses, he told me that's what you do."

"Poor Russel."

"Is there anything else you want to tell me about Steve?"

"He was my friend, my sweetheart, my husband, the father of my son, and he was close to God."

Having her tell about him had brought us closer. Now I shared her grief. On the doorstep I held her in my arms. Just as I was about to kiss her, she turned away and said she thought she'd better go in.

*   *   *   *   *

I met with Ben the next day. I read for him again. "I can't believe how much you've improved. There's so much more depth and sensitivity than you had before."

"Kellie's helped me a lot."

"Great."

"Ben, she's your cousin. Was Steve as wonderful as she says?"

"He was very good for her."

"You're a Mormon too, aren't you?" I asked.

"That's right."

"She talks about still being married to him. Is that what your church teaches?"

"She's single now, but after she dies, their marriage will continue. We believe a wedding in one of our temples lasts forever."

"But is it possible for her to remarry?"

"Yes, she can be married again, but she can be married to only one man in the eternities."

"Just for the sake of argument, suppose I joined her church, and we got married—who would have her after we died?"

"She'd have to decide which of the two she'd prefer to have in the hereafter. Why do you ask? Are you really that serious about her?"

I shrugged my shoulders. "Probably not. If I wanted to get married again, which I don't, I'd go out and find someone without so much emotional baggage, and I definitely wouldn't go looking for a Mormon."

"Oh, I don't know," he said with a smile. "We're not so bad."

CHAPTER EIGHT

It's a zoo, I thought, the day before the actual filming began.

For the next few weeks extras would be showing up at five in the morning and staying until sunset; a catering truck would be bringing lunch to feed the cast and crew. On location there were fifty head of sheep, six goats, and a crate of pigeons; two working Galilean fishing boats; the exterior shells of the village of Nazareth; several Roman soldiers with horses, spears, and insignia; a large semitrailer containing a diesel engine to run all the electrical equipment; cables running every which way; and two camels with their drivers.

In other words, a zoo.

*   *   *   *   *

The cameras were rolling. As Jesus, I walked along a dusty road accompanied by a large crowd.

A blind man asked a passerby what the noise was all about. He was told that Jesus of Nazareth was passing. He began to call out for Jesus.

"Hold your peace, you old fool!" one of the crowd warned the man.

If he keeps calling out like that, the man in the crowd thought, then the Master will hear him, and we'll have to stop again. At this rate we'll never get there before nightfall. Who knows how many robbers are waiting up there just around the bend for anyone foolish enough to travel at night. And why do we have to keep stopping for any scum that happens to cry for help?

The man in the crowd wanted to have them all rush past that beggar, but Jesus heard and stopped.

With the cameras going, I looked down at the man. Scabs covered his face and eyes.

I found myself wondering what Jesus saw in that blind beggar. What difference can it make if there's one less blind beggar? None at all. The world doesn't concern itself with blind beggars. It makes no difference.

Why did Jesus do it? He could have just walked past. Nobody would have even thought about it if he had. Maybe it was because he saw something remarkable about the man. But what?

What if it wasn't just this particular beggar—what if it was everyone he met.

"Cut!" Ben called out. "Michael, what's the delay here? You're supposed to touch the man's eyes and heal him."

The next time I did it right. But for that tiny instant I had felt as if I were looking at someone the way Jesus did, with overwhelming, unconditional love.

It was a strange experience.

* * * * *

After work I dropped by Kellie's house to get Jim. When I walked in, I saw Russel practicing the violin in the living room. He was wearing green slacks that were a little too large for him. They must have been given to him by neighbors or church members. One cuff was rolled up, the other wasn't. He stood there with his battered, borrowed violin, his eyes nearly touching the sheet music, straining to see the notes on the page, his foot clumsily tapping out the beat. His eyes appeared larger than normal through his thick glasses.

And then suddenly I was seeing Russel through someone else's eyes—someone who loved him with all his heart.

The way Jesus loved him.

The way Steve loved him.

A number of impressions flashed through my mind. A minute later, I knew I had to talk to Kellie. She was at the front door, just seeing off her last day-care child.

"I've got to talk to you in the backyard," I said.

She followed me.

"Why do you have Russel taking violin lessons?" I asked.

"It's something he can learn."

"He shouldn't be taking violin lessons."

"Why not?"

"Because kids already make fun of him. You think violin lessons help that? Russel should be learning karate, or something physically oriented like that."

"Steve used to talk about that too, but I don't know. You can see he's not very coordinated."

"That's why you pay somebody to give him lessons, so he'll get coordinated. Kellie, we've got to help him."

"I'm doing the best I can. The only reason he can take violin is because I trade off lessons for baby-sitting. I know you mean well, but I don't have money for karate lessons."

"I've got some money. Let me spend some of it on your son."

She looked at me suspiciously. "I thought you were going to buy a sports car with your money."

"Russel is more important."

"Are you saying that just to impress me?"

"No," I said.

"Then why?"

"I looked at Russel just now, and . . ." I stopped.

"What is it?"

"I don't know how to explain it. I want to help. Can't you let me help?"

She sighed. "I'm not proud anymore. I'll be grateful for anything you can do to help Russel."

I paused. "There's more but I'm not sure I should tell you."

"What is it?"

"I had a feeling, you'll think it's crazy . . ."

"Tell me."

"I think Steve wants me to help you with Russel."

She looked at me strangely.

I was embarrassed to even have said it, so I went back inside to talk to Russel.

"What's your name?" I asked him.

"Russel."

"No, I don't think so. You're a Rusty. Rusty Green. Come here, I want to test something." I took a newspaper and folded it in two and held it out for him. "All right, you've seen karate on TV, right? I want you to do a karate chop on this newspaper."

He made an awkward uncertain movement down with his fist. As soon as he made contact, I let the paper fall to the floor.

"All right! You've got talent. We've got to get you taking karate classes. In fact, we'll all start right away."

Rusty, Jim, and I drove to a karate training club and bought white uniforms and enrolled in lessons. What with the uniforms and the initiation fees for the three of us, and prepaying for a month of lessons, by the time we left, my down payment for a car was nearly gone.

Rusty wouldn't take the white karate warm-up suit off the rest of the day. In fact, Kellie told me he even slept in it.

The next day the three of us began our first karate lessons. It wasn't so much fighting as choreographing a dance step. We took lessons twice a week.

I took Rusty to an eye doctor and asked what more could be done for him. The doctor recommended a new lens material that would reduce the thickness of the lenses. We ordered a new pair of glasses. Instead of the sturdy plastic rims Rusty was wearing, I ordered a pair of wire frames that made him look like John Denver as a boy.

Sometimes when we practiced karate I called him Tiger. He seemed to like that.

CHAPTER NINE

Each day I poured everything I had into my portrayal of Jesus.

On Saturday we were filming out by Utah Lake. Ben had planned on shooting only in the morning, but we were delayed getting started. At first the wind was blowing too much, and then it rained. By eleven o'clock we still hadn't shot anything. Shortly before noon the weather improved and the wind died down.

We were about to start when an assistant director came up to Ben. "The extras were told it'd only be till noon."

"Tell 'em to bear with us," Ben said.

"You've got children out there, you've got old men and women, you ought to get 'em fed before very long."

Ben turned to someone else. "So where's the catering trucks?"

"You said we'd be working today just till noon. The trucks aren't coming."

"We've got to shoot this now. I don't want to wait another day."

"Maybe not, but I don't see what else you can do. People are getting hungry."

Ben sighed. "Call everybody together and we'll talk about it."

A minute later he took a portable P.A. system and read about the miracle of the loaves.

"People, we all have some food, don't we? I've got a couple of cans of food and some crackers in the car for emergencies. Some of you may have something else. Now let's see if we can forget our own selfish concerns, and go to our cars or trucks or campers, and take the food we have, and not hold back, and let's bring it all here to this table and see if we have enough to give us all at least something to eat for lunch. Look at that sky. It's perfect for what we need for this shot. Please, let's just see what happens when we open up our hearts the way Jesus taught.''

People began filing off to their cars and trailers.

We watched them come back with their food and lay it on the table. Before long the table was full, and we had more to eat than if we'd had the catering trucks.

A few minutes later Ben asked someone to say a blessing on the food. After everyone had eaten, there was still food left over.

It was our own private miracle.

*　*　*　*　*

A few days later we were filming the scene where Jesus sits in a boat talking to the assembled multitudes on the shore. We'd scattered extras all over a steep hillside near the lake.

While I was speaking, one of the extras lost his footing and fell twenty feet.

''Cut!'' Ben called out.

I jumped off the boat and ran to where the man had fallen. There was a large gash on his head where he'd hit a rock. He was unconscious.

A few minutes later an ambulance arrived and two paramedics came running down the incline to the shoreline to where the man was lying.

We quit for the day. I rode in with Ben to the hospital to see how the man was doing. He was still unconscious. His wife was there. She said they had five kids. Her husband had been laid off from his job at the steel mill, and he'd hired on as an extra hoping to bring in a little money.

A short time later two men showed up at the hospital. She called one of them Bishop, and the other Brother Mattson.

They closed the door. One of them poured a drop of oil on the man's head and then gently placed his hands on his head and said a prayer. Then they both placed their hands on the man's head, and the one called Bishop promised the man that he would recover fully.

It was the way the Savior did it, and, in fact, they did it in the name of Jesus Christ.

Half an hour later the man came out of his coma.

I was stunned.

* * * * *

That night I told Kellie what had happened.

"I don't find that hard to believe."

"Well, I do. Why don't you?"

"Because the power Jesus had to heal the sick has been restored to the earth. It's called priesthood. The men in the church have it."

She told me about the restoration of the priesthood.

"Why didn't you talk to me about this earlier?"

"I didn't think you'd be interested."

"Not interested in the power to heal the sick? Of course I'm interested. But I can't understand why you'd hold back. I thought we were friends."

"I didn't want to push my beliefs on you."

I paused. "Maybe there's another reason. Maybe you wanted an excuse not to get serious with me."

She sighed. "I don't know. Maybe so."

"Listen to me. I'm going to learn about this, and if it's true, then I'm going to join, regardless of what happens between us."

I drove to Ben's home. "I want to learn about your church."

"When?"

"Right now."

He called around for some missionaries who were available to come and teach me. After they finished their first discussion, they got ready to pack up.

"Don't stop," I said.

The missionaries looked at each other. "But it's ten-thirty," one of them said.

"I don't care. Please go on."

They started in again. At eleven-thirty they pleaded with me to let them get some sleep. I gave in, but I made them promise to come to my house and teach me and Jim the next night.

*   *   *   *   *

That Sunday Jim and I went to church with Kellie and Rusty.

First we had church for an hour, then we had church for another hour, and then we had church again, for another hour. Three hours of church.

I started the day admiring the girls and women but ended it studying the men.

They were unusual men, almost apologetic in fulfilling their church responsibilities, feeling that there must be somebody more capable to do the job they'd been asked to do, but they went ahead as best they could.

In priesthood meeting, they asked for and got volunteers to visit the hospital during the week. They needed someone with a pickup who could help a family move on Wednesday. And did anybody know of a job, because Brother Jones was out of work. The softball team was going to practice on Wednesday because Thursday was their last game and they'd lost five in a row. Wasn't there anybody in the group who could pitch?

And then there was a lesson. The teacher told about a time recently when he lost his temper with his wife, and how he had to go back and apologize. Another told about a decision he'd made to cut down long hours at work so he'd have more time to spend with his kids, and that eventually it meant he got passed over for a promotion, but it was okay, he said, because he could get by without the extra money, but he couldn't get by without his kids knowing he loved them.

I found myself thinking that if these men hold God's power as they say they do, then it is a power different than what the world is used to. It is a gentle power, a power that can work only if a man is not trying to look powerful.

As I sat there in priesthood meeting, I had to keep reminding myself that the men in that room claimed to possess the power to heal the sick and raise the dead and give sight to the blind. And yet there wasn't one of them that looked like Charlton Heston as Moses in *The Ten Commandments.*

Yes, I was puzzled by the men I met in priesthood meeting.

"How did you like it?" I asked Jim.

"It was way too long."

"Other than that, how was it?"

"They made us sing dumb songs."

"What was dumb about 'em?"

"They were girl's songs. One of 'em was, 'When I'm helping, I'm happy, and I sing as I go, 'cause I love to help Mother, for we all love her so.' "

"You used to help Mom, didn't you?"

"Sure, but what good did it do? She still left, didn't she?"

*   *   *   *   *

I was fasting the day we shot the crucifixion scene. It was a sobering experience to retrace his agony on the cross.

After we finished for the day, I went by Kellie's to get Jim. She could see I was exhausted, and so she asked if I'd stay for supper.

"I'm not hungry."

"Michael, you've got to eat."

I sat down at the kitchen table while she worked. "They put nails in his hands and feet," I said.

"I know."

"And people came and spit in his face."

"It must have been awful for him."

At supper I looked at the food on my plate and told her I wasn't hungry.

After supper, she asked if I'd like to go for a drive with her.

She drove us up Provo Canyon. After we got back to town, she pulled up to a drive-in, hoping to entice me with a root beer.

A girl came to our car to get our order. Kellie ordered two root beers. The girl left.

"Do you see that girl's face?" I asked.

"What about it?"

"There's something bothering her."

"Maybe she's just having a bad day."

A few minutes later the girl brought the root beer.

I got out of the car and walked over to her. "Something's wrong, isn't it?" I took a step toward her.

She turned to Kellie. "You keep him away or I'm calling the cops."

The girl walked quickly away from me.

I got in the car again.

"Here's your root beer," Kellie said, handing me a frosty mug.

"I'm sure there's something bothering her."

"Michael, you've got to loosen up. You're scaring people."

"But don't you see—Jesus would know what to say, what to tell her."

"But Michael, you aren't him."

"I know, but I want to be like him."

It was the first time I'd admitted it.

I loved him.

*   *   *   *   *

"We've got a slight problem," Ben said a few days later.

"What's that?"

"I've been comparing what we shot earlier with yesterday's footage. There's a difference in the way you're playing the role now. We may have to reshoot some of the earlier scenes. There's so much more depth to what you're doing now. What's going on here?"

"I've been reading the Book of Mormon."

*   *   *   *   *

When I first began to learn about Jesus, I would discover a trait of his and use that to describe him in my mind. For instance, when I first read the parables, I came away thinking, okay, Jesus was a master teacher. We can leave it at that or we can go deeper. We can stay on the surface for an entire lifetime. "Jesus? Oh yes, I know about him, He was a master teacher."

We can leave it at that, or we can go deeper.

Because I wanted so much to make him come alive on the screen, I went deeper. What I found is that there are layers to our understanding of him. And when we first reach the next deeper level, we say, oh yes, now I know what he is really like.

Again, we can leave it at that, or we can go deeper.

But we never come to the end of him, we never make a true measure of the man, because he is like a sky with no horizon. As wonderful as you can imagine him to be, he is a thousand times more wonderful.

I'd spent hours poring over the New Testament, searching for just one more insight about him. And so when I discovered the Book of Mormon, it was like finding a dear friend, because the purpose of the Book of Mormon is to testify about Jesus.

It was in the Book of Mormon where I read that after his resurrection, Jesus came down from heaven to stand before a group of people in the New World. He began by saying, "Behold, I am Jesus Christ, whom the prophets testified shall come into the world. And behold, I am the light and the life of the world; and I have drunk out of that bitter cup which the Father hath given me, and have glorified the Father in taking upon me the sins of the world, in the which I have suffered the will of the Father in all things from the beginning."

The crowd fell to their knees.

" 'Arise and come forth unto me, that ye may thrust your hands into my side, and also that ye may feel the prints of the nails in my hands and in my feet, that ye may know that I am the God of Israel, and the God of the whole earth, and have been slain for the sins of the world.' "

He invited them to come up one by one. They touched the wounds in his hands and the prints of the nails in his feet. And when they had all gone forth, they cried out and fell down at his feet and worshipped him.

The deeper I went, the more I loved him.

A few days later I was ready to be baptized.

"What do you think about the church?" I cautiously asked Jim.

"It's all right, I guess," he mumbled.

"Well, you like the missionaries, don't you?"

"Yeah, I guess so."

"And you liked Cub Scout day camp, right?"

"It was okay," he said.

"Then c'mon, let's both get baptized the same day. Afterwards Kellie's invited us over to her house for some cake and ice cream."

He shook his head. "Dad, you'd better go ahead without me."

I sat down beside him and put my arm around him. "What's wrong?"

"If we become Mormons, then maybe that'll make Mom mad, and she won't ever come back to us."

I sighed. "Jim, she's not coming back."

"She might. She might decide she loves us and come back again. We should be ready in case she does."

"The reason she left was because of me, not you. She still loves you. It's just that she and I don't get along. I can see now that a lot of it was my fault. But it's too late for her and me. She's not coming back. I know that's hard to hear, but you've just got to accept it."

"But people change their minds sometimes, don't they?" he asked.

* * * * *

Ben and his wife invited Kellie and me and our kids over on a Monday night.

It was interesting to see Ben as a father. The man who was always racing off to a meeting—at home he was just another dad. When we arrived at their house, he was outside fixing his boy's bike.

We met his wife, Vicky, an attractive, lively woman with four kids. We had an outdoor barbecue, and afterwards their kids put on a program. The oldest took charge and introduced the rest. Ben sat and watched and smiled proudly and, at the same time, turned the ice-cream maker.

A little later that night, while Kellie and Vicky put the dishes into the dishwasher, I had a chance to talk to Ben about Jim not wanting to join the church.

"Don't force him," he said. "Let him come to the decision by himself."

"I'm not sure I can wait that long," I said. "I'm ready now."

"Then I think you should go ahead and be baptized. Jim will follow when he's ready."

*   *   *   *

The next time the missionaries came, I told them I wanted to be baptized. We set the date, and they made arrangements for me to be interviewed for baptism. Just before they left, they asked if I knew of anybody else who would benefit from the church.

"Well, my mom and my sister would." They suggested I phone and tell them about my joining and ask if they'd like to learn more about it.

So later that night I phoned Kalispell, Montana. "Beth, this is Michael."

There was a long pause at her end.

"You know, your brother Michael?"

"I know who you are," she snapped. "Are you calling to try and borrow some money? Look, we don't have any. We're barely making it ourselves."

"Nothing like that. I want you to know that I'm being baptized this weekend into the Mormon church."

A long silence, and then, "Sure, it figures. I guess you know they're not Christian, don't you?"

"Beth, it's called The Church of Jesus Christ of Latter-day Saints. How can they not be Christian?"

"Have they told you about their gold bible?"

"I've read it. You ought to read it too, Beth. Especially if you love Jesus."

"I've got enough to do just keeping up with my church."

She was through discussing religion.

"I'm filing for divorce next month."

"Have you told Wally yet?"

"Not yet."

"Do the kids know?"

"No. That's the part I dread. But it'll be better this way."

"Can I send you any money for the kids?"

"Do you have a steady job yet?"

"I'm working on a movie. We think it's going to do real well."

She'd heard that before. "Is this a sequel to *Hog Butcher?*"

Next I phoned my mother in Arizona and told her about it.

"That's nice, dear."

"Would you like to know about it too, Mom?"

"No, I don't think so, but you go ahead."

"Mom, I'm dating someone now. She's been married before. She's a Mormon. Her husband died in a car accident about a year ago."

"Do you think you'll marry her?"

"It's too early to tell, but I'll keep you posted."

* * * * *

There was prelude music before the service began. I sat on the first row wearing white baptismal clothes.

I thought about the movie, and how hard it had been to try to be like the Savior for even ten minutes at a time when all I had to do was to repeat the lines I'd memorized.

And now I was about to take upon me his name.

He asked the question once of his disciples, "What manner of men ought ye to be?" His answer was, "Even as I am."

Impossible? Of course. But worth the effort to try.

I was back to being an understudy, but this time it would never end with the closing of a play.

The service began. Ben baptized me, confirmed me, and then
ordained me a priest.

Afterwards we went to Kellie's and had cake and ice cream.
Jim was very quiet that night.

CHAPTER TEN

We finished the movie in October.

I stayed in Utah to be with Kellie. Because my salary from the movie had stopped and the deferred payments would come only after the movie opened in theaters, I was a little low on funds. To tide me over, I got a job at a car wash.

Suddenly I was counting my wealth in the number of times I could get her to smile, or when she'd call up and ask me to come fix something around her house, or when after a date, we'd stand at the door and embrace. She still didn't want to kiss me, but she let me hold her in my arms.

It was a stormy time, though, for both of us. Her moods swung erratically from one extreme to the other. Sometimes she clung to me for support. At other times she'd lash out as if she were trying to destroy everything between us. And it always ended with her saying that maybe we shouldn't see each other anymore.

One night I showed up for a date and she said, "Are you ever going to shave off that beard?"

"I like it."

"Do you know what I think about a man who wears a beard? I think he's hiding something. You don't want people to see the real you, so you put this bush over your face." She went into the bathroom and brought out Steve's razor and handed it to me. "I'm not going out with you again until you shave it off."

It was an ultimatum. She'd given it because she didn't really think I'd do it.

And so I did.

Half an hour later I came out clean-shaven. She took one look at me and said, "I guess I liked you better with the beard."

I was so mad I couldn't even talk. I walked out on her.

A day later when I got home from work, she was sitting on my doorstep. "I came to apologize. I'm sorry for being so rotten. I don't know why I'm so mean sometimes. Actually I think you're very handsome with or without a beard."

Of course we didn't spend every minute together. We each still had meals to cook, clothes to wash, and houses to clean up.

"I've really had it with Jim," I said one night on the phone.

"What's wrong?"

"I fix a nice meal, turkey and mashed potatoes. Jim sits down and scarfs it down in about three seconds and then he just walks away. Not a word of thanks. I mean, what good does it do to knock myself out? Why couldn't he at least tell me he liked it?"

"He probably just forgot," she said.

"It was as good as anything Pamela ever cooked," I grumbled.

"I'm sure it was."

"Except for the gravy," I admitted. "I have a little trouble with gravy."

"Well, maybe I can help. This is the way I do gravy . . ."

I was taking notes as she talked. And then I burst out laughing. "What am I coming to? I'm starting to sound like Harriet Homemaker! This is ridiculous. Before you know it, I'll be making little doilies."

"Hey, what about me? I can walk into a hardware store now and ask for a molly bolt without batting an eye."

"This single parenthood is really getting me down. How about you?"

"I agree. Sometimes I feel so alone, like it's me against the entire world."

"Hey, I've got an idea. How about if we get married?"

She laughed. "Oh, sure, you're just looking for a way out of having to learn to make gravy."

I laughed too, but deep inside I wished she hadn't tossed the idea off so quickly.

*   *   *   *   *

Once she phoned me at twelve-thirty at night. "I can't get to sleep tonight. I need someone to talk to."

"We can talk on the phone if you want."

"Since midnight it's been one year since Steve died."

She told me everything about the day he died. How cheerful he'd been in the morning, how they'd talked about how they were going to meet their bills, about an exam he was going to have that day, and about whether or not they'd be able to go to the next football game.

And then it had all ended so quickly.

"Why did he have to go and die?" she said miserably.

She cried for a long time.

* * * * *

The next time I asked her out she said, "I'm sorry but I already have a date that night."

"What?"

"I think we've been spending too much time together. You should date others too."

"Who are you going out with?"

"I don't think that's any business of yours."

"I want to know. Who is he?"

"He's in law school at the Y. We used to know each other in high school."

I spent the day of her date fixing my car, giving it a tune-up to keep it going a few more miles. If I could just wait until the movie opened, I'd start getting some money and then I'd buy myself a Corvette. No woman was going to stop me from getting the car of my dreams. Women aren't worth it.

At nine that night Kellie came over to my house.

"Your date's over already?" I asked.

She sighed. "It was terrible. First of all, when he showed up at my door, he was wearing enough after-shave to be a fire hazard.

"When I introduced him to Rusty, he asked how old he was, and Rusty told him eight, and he said from Rusty's size he would've guessed maybe five or six. What a stupid thing to say to a boy.

"And then we went out in his car and he had a tape deck and

it was playing soft music—and he draped his arm over the seat. It was like his arm was some vulture just waiting for the right time to pounce on my shoulders.

"But his biggest mistake was when he asked me what was wrong with Rusty. I got mad and asked him what was wrong with his heart. I really told him off and then demanded he take me home. When I got inside the house again, I started to cry. Rusty told me I'd better go see you because you always make me feel better, and so here I am. I'm such a basket case, will you let me stay for a while?"

"Sure, but you might as well know that I'm broke. I spent all my money today on a carburetor kit."

"I don't care," she said. "Just let me hang around here with you, okay?"

We went into the kitchen and had graham crackers and milk. I dunked mine. She didn't.

"Steve liked graham crackers too," she said.

"He and I like a lot of the same things. Graham crackers and you."

"How much did it cost for parts to fix up your car?" she asked.

"About thirty dollars, but if I'd had a garage do it, it would have cost at least a hundred." I reached out and held her hand. "It seems natural to be here like this, doesn't it, just the two of us, talking things over in the kitchen."

She could see what was coming. "I haven't thought about it before."

"But you know I love you, don't you?"

She looked away. "Yes, I guess I do."

"Do you love me?"

She didn't answer.

"Well, I'd better put the milk away," I said abruptly, standing up. "One day last week Jim left a carton out all night. We had to throw it away. Nearly a full half gallon too. And then he wonders why I can't afford to buy him video games."

"Michael, let me explain."

"You don't need to explain. It's all right, really it is. I was out of place to even ask. Do you want any more milk before I put it away?"

"Just forget the milk, okay? Look, let me be honest with you. I'm just not sure how I feel about you, except that I know I need you. Sometimes I feel like I'm drowning and you're the only life raft in my ocean."

I paused. "You need me?"

"Absolutely. All the time."

"That's good. Maybe we should go into the living room."

She was puzzled. "Why the living room?"

"I have a big favor to ask you, and I'm afraid to ask it here in the kitchen."

"What's wrong with the kitchen?"

"We need a place that's kind of romantic."

"What do you want to talk about?"

"I have a big favor to ask."

"What is it?"

"Hold on a minute, okay?"

I rummaged through a cupboard until I found a candle. I lit it and used the drippings to stick it upright on the kitchen table. Then I turned on the radio and found a station playing mood music. I excused myself, hurried into the bathroom, and splashed after-shave on my face and neck, then I remembered what she'd said about her date's after-shave, so I washed it all off again, and then returned and turned off the light so we were bathed in candlelight. I sat down next to her.

I waited through one romantic song and then said, "Kellie, I want you to quit wearing Steve's wedding ring."

"Why?"

"I want you to wear mine. I'm asking you to marry me."

She sighed. "I knew this was coming. Michael, it's too soon. I'm still not over losing Steve."

"I'm not asking you to stop loving him. Just give me a small place in your heart. An upstairs attic, a closet, a storeroom, there must be some place left. That's all I ask."

"I've been through too much to start over as a blushing bride."

I smiled. "It's all right with me if you don't blush."

She fought back a smile. "You know what I mean."

"Sure, but look, we won't be starting out from scratch. We'll have two kids right off the bat."

"Steve and I shared some intimate memories. I'm not sure I want to repeat them with anyone else."

"Did he propose to you in candlelight after you'd both had graham crackers and milk?"

"No."

"See there? The memories won't be the same."

"I'm just not sure I want to go changing horses in the middle of the stream."

"Don't think of it like you're in the middle of the stream. Think of it like you're still in the corral. At first you choose this one horse called Single Mother, but then you see another called Remarried. You ask the man in charge if it'd be all right to change your mind, and he says, 'Go ahead.' So he saddles up the other horse for you. So you see, it's not in the middle of the stream—you're still in the corral."

She laughed. "Do graham crackers always do this to you?"

The mood music stopped. The announcer was introducing a farm specialist who was going to answer questions about the application of fungicides. I switched to another station.

"I think we're ready for the living room now, don't you?" I asked.

I carried the candle in and we sat down on the sofa, which had a horse blanket on it to hide the rip in the cushions. With only a candle for light, it was dark enough to hide the fact that Jim's sneakers and dirty socks were still on the floor where he'd left them that night. It was almost dark enough in the room to be romantic.

I reached out and held her hand. "I think we've gone as far as we can as friends. It's time to move on. I want to be the one you ask to fasten the top button in the back of your Sunday dress when you're getting ready for church. And the one to keep you toasty warm when you're sleeping during those long winter nights." I paused. "Unless we're married, we won't be able to share those experiences together. So why not get married?"

"You realize, don't you, that I can't be your wife after we die."

"Right now I'm worried about getting through next week. I lie awake every night thinking about you. I need my sleep. Besides, there's something you should know about me."

"What?"

"When I was a senior in high school, I was the second-string quarterback for the football team. I didn't play until the final game of our season. In the second half our star quarterback sprained his ankle. There was nobody else available, so the coach had to send me in. I played the entire second half."

"Did your team win?"

"Kellie," I grumbled, "that's not the point"

There was just the glimmer of a smile on her face. "I'm sorry. What's the point?"

"The point is that I've spent a lot of my life in the shadows of better men, sort of filling in for them. Now that Steve's gone, let me do that for you too. I love you and I want you to be my wife."

She sighed. "You really do, don't you."

"Very much. A few weeks from now I want us to be sitting here like this, and you'll yawn, and I'll put out the cat, and just before we go to bed, we'll look in on our boys to make sure they've got their covers on, and everything will be okay, and we won't have to say goodbye at the end of the day anymore."

She got up from the sofa and walked to the window and looked out.

A long time passed and then she turned around. I could just barely see her face in the candlelight. "We don't have a cat."

"We'll get a cat."

"I don't want a cat."

"Me either."

A full minute passed before she said with a sigh, "All right, I accept."

"You mean it?"

"Yes."

"That means we're engaged, doesn't it?"

"Yes, it does."

"May I kiss you?"

She sighed. "I guess there's no reason not to now, is there?"

"I guess not. It'll be our first time."

"I know, but it's all right."

On my way to her on the other side of the room, I tripped on Jim's shoe and twisted my ankle and fell down.

"Are you all right?" she asked.

"No problem!" I cheerfully assured her, getting back up. "It was nothing, really." I hobbled over and kissed her for the first time.

My ankle was killing me. I suggested we sit down on the couch.

After we'd kissed a few times, she tensed up, as if a part of her felt it wasn't right to be kissing me. At my suggestion, we returned to the kitchen and ate graham crackers and made plans.

Although I was glad she'd agreed to marry me, I was a little disappointed she wasn't more excited about it.

*   *   *   *   *   *

The next day she phoned to tell her parents she was going to marry a divorced movie actor who worked at a car wash. They rushed down from Idaho to rescue her.

"You're not as large a man as I pictured," her father told me right after we'd met.

"Why's that?"

"Kellie said you were an actor and that you once played the part of a hog butcher. I just figured you'd be a big man."

"The movie was about Carl Sandburg. He wrote a poem once describing Chicago as the hog butcher of the world."

"Oh. Look, we might as well be honest with each other. I don't like the thought of my daughter marrying someone who's already failed at marriage."

"Daddy," Kellie said, "his first wife left him with their son just because she wanted a career. It wasn't Michael's fault."

"Is that true?" her father asked.

"That's what I told Kellie when I first met her. But now I can see that a good part of it was my fault."

"Can you guarantee a second marriage won't end in divorce too?"

"No, but I do know I've changed since I've come down here. I've played the part of Jesus in a movie, and that's changed me a lot. And I've joined the Mormon church. I promise to try and be the kind of husband Kellie needs. I love her with all my heart."

Kellie looked at her father. "Daddy, he's good to Rusty, and he's considerate of me. I really think it'd be better for all of us if he and I get married."

"Well, if you really think so, I guess that's what you should do then."

She didn't tell her parents that she loved me.

* * * * * *

We were married in November in the Relief Society room at church, with Jim and Rusty standing alongside us during the ceremony. They were our best men, but we jokingly called them our best boys.

Mom had flown in from Arizona for the wedding. She looked good. She'd taken the money from the sale on the house and some savings and had used it on herself. I think it was the first time in her life she'd ever bought anything just because she wanted it. She was just about to go on a package tour to Hawaii. She and Kellie got along well.

There were all sorts of introductions to be made in the reception line that day.

"Michael," Kellie said during the reception, "I'd like you to meet Steve's parents."

"Hi there. Nice to meet you."

"I hope you know what a wonderful girl you're getting," Steve's mother said.

"Oh, yes, I sure do."

"Steve was so happy with Kellie," Steve's father said.

"I'm sure I will be too."

"And this is Steve's younger brother Alan."

"Alan, nice to meet you."

Alan, seventeen years old, was fiercely loyal to Steve. "Steve'll have her after she dies."

Maybe so, I thought with an inward smile, but I have her now. But I didn't say that. "Alan, I know you think that Steve and I are rivals, but I think Steve approves of this, because he loves Kellie and wants her to be as happy as she can now."

Kellie squeezed my hand. It was the right thing to say.

*   *   *   *   *

We stayed in the Hotel Utah our first night together.

When I came out of the bathroom in my pajamas, she was standing at the window wearing a lace nightgown, looking out at the temple across the street.

I was very nervous. "I think it was nice of them to give us shampoo, don't you? I mean, how many hotels give a little packet of free shampoo?"

She turned to look at me, and that made me even more nervous.

"The only trouble was, I couldn't get it open. Finally I used my teeth to rip it open, but that caused some shampoo to squirt into my mouth." I paused awkwardly. "Uh, so if I start frothing at the mouth later tonight, you'll know . . ."

I stopped talking.

She smiled at me. "Let me guess. You're a little nervous?"

I paused. "Actually a lot."

"Me too. Come over and let's look out at the temple."

We stood, arm in arm, looking at the temple I'd never been in.

"Were you and Steve ever inside the Salt Lake Temple?"

"Yes, several times."

"And the Hotel Utah?"

"We ate at the rooftop restaurant once."

"It gets kind of crowded around here sometimes, doesn't it?"

She nodded her head.

I kissed her. For just a second it was very nice, and then she tensed up again and broke away. "I think we should call Jim and Rusty to see how they're doing."

We made the call. Her parents were staying with them that

night. We talked to our boys. And then we said goodnight and hung up.

It was a little awkward. We both looked warily at each other.

I smiled. "I've got an idea. The hotel's given us a bunch of free postcards. How about us sending them to all the kids in our high school graduation classes. And when we get done with that, we'll see if the registration desk'll loan us a deck of cards. Let me guess—I'll bet you're good at playing Old Maid, right?"

She smiled and grabbed my hand. "I've got a better idea."

"What's that?"

"Let's just say our prayers and go to bed."

*   *   *   *   *

A week later she came to me looking worried. "There's something I need to tell you. It's been on my mind since I woke up this morning."

"What is it?"

"I had a dream last night about Steve. He showed up here and said it had all been a mistake, that he hadn't really died after all. He asked me to go with him." She paused. "Michael, in my dream I left you and went with him."

"This was a dream?" I asked.

"Yes."

"Don't worry about it. We can't control our dreams. It's just going to take some time to sort everything out."

She felt so guilty she wouldn't even look at me. "But if he did come back, I'd go with him even though I'm married to you. I'd leave you if he came back."

"Kellie," I said softly, "he's not coming back. So I don't think it's something we need to worry very much about, okay?"

She gave a sigh of relief. "Okay."

"Don't worry about night dreams," I said. "But what about daydreams? Do you ever daydream about Steve?"

"Sometimes," she reluctantly admitted. "Even our first night together, after you'd fallen asleep, I lay awake and thought about him."

Now I couldn't look at her. "Did you think about your honeymoon with him?"

"Yes," she said softly.

I was devastated. All along I'd thought that after we got married I'd be able to give her so much love she'd forget about Steve. For the first time I had to face that I might always come in a poor second to him.

I didn't tell her how bad I felt. "Why shouldn't you think about him? You've got a lot of good memories with him. But listen to me, I'm going to give you some terrific memories too."

I'd taken away her guilt, and she gratefully melted into my arms. "Oh, Michael, you're so good to me. I love you more each day."

Beautiful Lady, I thought, that's what I'm counting on.

CHAPTER ELEVEN

Soon after we returned from our honeymoon, I insisted we see about selling her house because of all the memories she had of Steve there. But after visiting with a real estate agent, I realized we'd be better off financially just to stay put.

There were times those first few weeks when I thought that maybe Kellie had been right, maybe it had been too soon for her to get married again. The problem was Steve. He was never very far from us.

For instance, she came to me with a simple suggestion of how to arrange my side of the closet. "How about having your shirts on the left on wire hangers, and your slacks and suits on the right on wooden hangers. What would you think of that?"

"Is that the way Steve did it?"

"Yes, it is."

"I thought so."

"Don't just toss it aside because of that. It worked out very well."

"For Steve maybe, but I do things my own way. And I'd appreciate it if you'd quit trying to make me into his clone. It's bad enough that I have to sleep on his pillow at night. Now you even want me to hang my clothes up the way he did."

"Do it any way you want then. I'm through giving suggestions to you." She tossed me an angry glare and went into the kitchen.

I stayed in the bedroom and fumed. I was about to go tell her I was sick and tired of hearing Steve this and Steve that. She was my wife now, and she'd better start acting like it. Besides, if Steve was so perfect, like everybody says, why did he let himself fall asleep at the wheel? Anybody knows that if you get sleepy when you're driving, you should pull over and take a nap.

While I crammed my clothes in the closet, purposely making
a mess just to teach her a lesson, a shirt fell on the floor. I
reached down to pick it up. In a box on the floor I saw my script
for the movie about Jesus. I started thumbing through it. My
lines, the things that Jesus said, were underlined in red.

The phrase, *What manner of men ought ye to be,* rang through
my mind.

Jesus again.

A few minutes later I'd cooled down enough to go talk to her.
"I'm sorry for snapping at you."

"No, it was my fault. I had no business telling you how to do
your closet."

"I don't care about the closet. I just need to know that you
love me."

"You know I do."

"Do you love me more than Steve?"

"Michael, that's not fair."

I sighed. "I guess not."

"I love you more each day."

She said that a lot to me at first. I was never sure if it meant
she hadn't loved me very much when we'd gotten married, or if
it was just a way to avoid having to tell me she'd never love me
as much as she did Steve.

But what if it was true? If she loved me more each day, maybe
she'd end up loving me more than she did him. And if she did,
maybe in the hereafter she'd choose me. At least it was a
possibility.

•   •   •   •   •   •   •

One Sunday afternoon after church, Kellie and I lay down for
a nap. The boys were next door playing with friends. When I
woke up, the sun was shining through the bedroom window,
showing dust patterns dancing in the sun. The sunlight caused
the copper-colored strands in her hair to come alive. Her face
was calm in sleep and full of beauty. There I was, her husband,
lying next to her, the luckiest man in the world.

The sun reached her eyes, and she awoke and looked at me and realized I'd been watching her sleep. She smiled and held out her arms and welcomed me even closer.

I loved being near her. Sometimes I tried to tell her what it was like for me to be a part of the beauty and goodness I saw in her, but I don't think she ever really understood what I meant.

I know that it made me want to be better.

* * * * *

Not long after we were married, I had an offer to star in a major Hollywood movie about a mass murderer who'd killed forty-seven women.

"Why did you think of me for the part?" I asked the producer who had phoned me.

"Because you have a face that's easy to trust. That's the way he was. Women trusted him. That's why he got to so many."

"I can't do that."

"Why not?"

"I've just finished a movie where I played the part of Jesus."

"So what? You're an actor. You play the parts that come along. Each one presents a different challenge. We all have good and evil in us. You've played from the good side—now make use of your dark side."

"I can't do a mass murderer."

"What are you going to do," he sneered, "play nice guys from now on?"

I paused. "I know you won't understand this, but once you've played the role of Jesus, you're never the same again."

"Quit acting then and get a job selling shoes if that's the way you feel. Look, think it over. This movie'll make you a rich man."

I talked to Kellie. She knew how much we needed the money. She said she'd understand if I took the part.

A day later I reached a decision. "I'm afraid to do it. What if some of that character rubbed off on me, what if I started looking at women the way he did? No, I can't do it. Besides I can't leave you now."

"Why not?"

"I'd miss you too much."

I turned down the role. The producer was right. The movie made a lot of money. But money isn't everything.

* * * * *

Things seemed to be going fine with us until one Saturday. We were at the breakfast table, and Kellie, still in her robe, put an egg on Jim's plate.

"I'm not going to eat that," he grumbled.

"Why not?"

"It's runny. I hate runny eggs."

"No problem," Kellie said good-naturedly. "I'll cook it a little more."

She scooped up the egg and put it back in the frying pan until it was well done. Then she set it back on Jim's plate.

"Not that way," he griped. "Now it's too hard."

"Eat it anyway," I snapped.

"No."

"That's all right," Kellie said, trying to smooth things over. "I'll eat that one. Jim, would you rather have it scrambled?"

"I just want it the way my Mom fixed it."

"How was that?"

"Forget it, okay? You'll never learn how."

"Just tell me how you want it and I'll try."

"I don't want anything from you. Just leave me alone."

"Don't talk to your mother that way," I scolded.

"She's not my mother!" He got up and ran outside.

I told Kellie it wasn't her fault, and then I went out after Jim. I found him in the garage sitting in the driver's seat of the car. I sat down beside him in the car.

"Dad, why'd you have to wreck everything by getting married again? Now Mom'll never come back to us."

"She never would have come back anyway. I know this is hard on you, but the four of us are a family now, and I need you to try to make this thing work out. You've got a new mom, and a brother too."

"He's not my brother," he scoffed. "What a dumbhead. Last night he forgot where he put his glasses and bumped his head on the door on his way to the bathroom."

"That's not his fault."

"If you ask me, we were better off up at the lake. At least we didn't have them to worry about."

"I want you to go back and apologize to Kellie. She's really trying to be a good mom to you. Can't you meet her half way?"

He paused. "Okay, but I won't eat her dumb eggs."

We went back inside and he halfheartedly apologized. I thought it was over, but that Sunday morning, before church, we had more problems. Rusty had taken a shower, and now it was twenty minutes before church started. He came out of the bathroom with just a towel wrapped around him. "I can't find my glasses."

"Where did you leave them?" Kellie asked.

"On the counter in the bathroom."

"We're going to be late," Kellie said. She went in the bathroom and looked. They weren't there.

We looked all over.

Then I saw Jim outside on the swings with a smirk on his face. I opened the back door. "All right! Where did you put them?"

"Put what?"

"You know what I mean. Where did you put Rusty's glasses?"

He smirked. "In the tree. If he wants them, let him climb it, if he can."

I went over and grabbed his arm and yanked him out of the swing. "You go get them right now!"

He climbed the tree and got the glasses and came down and handed them to me.

"Now get ready for church. We're already going to be late."

"I'm not going," he said.

"You are too."

"It's not my church. It's her church. I'm staying home like we always did before we came to Utah."

"Listen to me. While you're in this house, you'll do what I say."

"You can't make me go to church if I don't want to. It's not my church."

"All right, what church do you want to go to?"

He looked surprised. "What?"

"You're going to church this morning, so tell me what church it is you want me to drop you off at."

"You're just going to leave me at some church I've never been to before?"

"That's right. Now go in, and while you're getting dressed, you decide what church you want, Methodist, Catholic, Baptist, whatever you decide."

He went inside.

Fifteen minutes later we got in the car and started out the driveway.

"Have you decided where you want me to take you?" I asked him.

He paused. "I guess I'll just go with you today," he muttered.

*   *   *   *   *

One day several weeks later, the principal asked me to come to the school. He said Jim was in trouble.

When I arrived, I was told that Jim had been fighting in school. I asked Jim why, and ne said some boys were picking on Rusty.

"At first I didn't care if they hurt him or not, but then a boy hit Rusty in the stomach and started laughing about it. I didn't think that was fair, so I told him to lay off, and he told me to stay out of it, and I said, why don't you pick on somebody your own size, and he tried to hit me, and that got me mad. And so I hit him in the stomach the way he'd hit Rusty, and then some of his friends tried to gang up on us."

The principal said that when a teacher finally came to see what the noise was about, he found Jim and Rusty, back to back, protecting each other, waiting to see if anyone else was going to take them on.

"We can't have fighting in the school," the principal said.

"Then I'd suggest you talk to the boys who started it. My boys don't fight unless they're attacked."

Jim nodded. "And you tell 'em, if they start anything with Rusty, they'll have to fight me too."

The principal tried to make me feel bad that Jim cared enough about his stepbrother to protect him, but it didn't work.

Just before we got home, I told the boys I didn't want them fighting in school, but that I was proud of them for sticking together.

*   *   *   *   *

We still had Moby Dick. It seemed that every time we'd finally get enough money to get something better, the washing machine would break down or the water heater would go out, and we'd end up using the money for that instead of a better car.

One Saturday I showed the boys how to do a tune-up. They hung around on the hood and watched me, much as I'd done around my own dad. When we came in, the boys were still excited about learning how to fix cars.

Kellie smiled at me. "You're becoming quite the dad these days, you know that?"

I smiled. "I was hoping you'd notice."

*   *   *   *   *

After the next stake conference I was ordained an elder in the church. A few nights later Kellie asked me to give a father's blessing to Rusty because he had a bad cough.

"I'm not sure what to do."

"If you want, I can tell you how Steve did it." Then she caught herself and looked at me to see if that was going to make me mad.

I smiled. "Yes, I'd like to know."

She explained the details, finally ending with, "Just listen to the Spirit."

I felt inadequate. What if the Spirit didn't tell me anything? "Kellie, maybe we'd better call our home teachers."

"No, you're his father now. I want you to do it."

"I'm not Steve."

She came over and touched my face. "I love you very much. I know that you and God will be able to work out a priesthood blessing. Please, Michael."

I nodded. "Give me a few minutes, okay?"

I went into our bedroom and prayed. A few minutes later I returned. "I'm ready now."

After the blessing, she hugged me and said it was just right.

Jim, who'd watched the whole thing, said no when I asked if he wanted a father's blessing too.

*   *   *   *   *

It began with a phone call in the early summer of the next year.

I was outside putting our camping gear into the trunk of the car. Rusty and Jim and I were going up to Strawberry Reservoir to be there for the opening day of fishing season.

"Hey, guys, look what I got." I showed them three packages of frozen strawberries and two jars of roasted peanuts. "Okay now, when your friends ask you what we lived on while we were camping, you tell 'em we survived on berries and nuts, okay?"

"The phone's for you," Kellie called out from the house.

"You guys finish packing, and I'll be right back."

I walked inside. "It's a woman," Kellie said.

I picked up the phone and said hello.

It was long distance. "Michael, is that you? This is Pamela."

"Pamela, hello."

"Did you hear about me getting married again?" she asked.

"No, I didn't, Pamela."

"It was three weeks ago. We just got back from our honeymoon. We went to Bermuda. It was wonderful there."

"I got married too, Pamela."

"I know. Jimmy wrote and told me about it." She paused. "He didn't sound very happy about it."

"It'll work out. It will just take some time. Who did you marry?"

"A surgeon. I met him at the hospital where I was working. His name is Whittaker Alceister."

"Sounds like a good name for you, Pamela."

"Now that I can afford to travel, we'd like to come out and see Jimmy."

I was secretly glad she was still calling him Jimmy.

"Gosh, I hate to have you go to that much trouble. How about if I just send you some snapshots?"

"Whittaker has a conference in Utah. We're flying out next week. We'll be there next Friday. We'd like to spend a few days with Jimmy."

"Gosh, ordinarily that'd be fine, but we're planning a camping trip then."

"Michael, don't play games with me. I have the right to see my own son, don't I?"

I sighed. "All right. Next Friday, you say? How long do you want to see him?"

"Three days," she said. "We'll have him back on Monday night."

A week later they came in a rented Lincoln Continental. Whittaker was what you would expect from a brain surgeon. Polished, bright, witty, handsome, rich, and smart. Pamela looked good in the clothes he could afford for her.

Whittaker and I verbally dueled out in the driveway while we waited for Pamela and Kellie to quit talking.

"Pamela tells me you're sort of an actor."

"That's right."

"Would I have seen you in anything?"

"Are you a fan of Carl Sandburg?"

"Not really."

"Then I doubt if you've seen me. But then again, I doubt I've met any brains you've sawed into either."

We both chuckled pleasantly.

He looked at Moby Dick parked in the driveway. "Does that

actually run, or is it just being stored until someone has time to haul it to the junkyard?''

"It runs fine.''

He paused. "Well, tell me what movie you're working on now.''

I paused. "I'm between movies.''

"What does that mean?''

"It means I did a movie, and now I'm waiting to do another one.''

"Oh, I see. You're out of work. Well, I guess that explains the car then, doesn't it?''

"What are you and Pamela planning on doing with Jimmy this weekend?'' I asked. I hoped they'd call him Jimmy all the time they were with him.

"Well, knowing boys, I thought first we'd take him to a video arcade, and then I've arranged for him to have his first flying lesson.'' He paused and then smiled faintly. "Also, we thought it'd be fun for us all to learn how to windsurf.''

"I'm not sure if it's warm enough for that yet.''

"We were thinking more of California. We're going there tomorrow anyway to see Disneyland.''

I scowled. "Oh.''

Jim came out with his mother and made a fool of himself drooling over their car. Whittaker promised to let him drive.

When they left, Jim didn't even wave goodbye to me.

That night, from the way I was tossing and turning, it was obvious I couldn't get to sleep.

Kellie turned on the light. "Do you want to talk about it?''

"They're going to take him away from me. I know they are.''

"They said it was just for a few days.''

"You don't know Pamela like I do. She's devious, and now she's got Whittaker to pay the bills.''

When Jim returned from the weekend, all he could talk about was how neat Whittaker was, and how much money they'd spent, and how they'd let him do anything he wanted.

I offered to go out and buy him and Rusty an ice cream cone, but he said he was sick of ice cream. He'd had too much of it in California.

"What did they ask about us?" I asked.

"They wanted to know if I ever went to bed hungry."

"What did you tell them?"

"I told them that sometimes I did."

"Are you crazy? Why did you say that? We're feeding you three good meals a day, aren't we?"

"Sometimes I want a snack before I go to bed, and you tell me it's too late."

"Look, if anybody ever asks you again, you tell them you get good nourishing meals. What else did they ask you?"

"They asked where you bought my clothes. I told them about how Kellie goes to garage sales and buys us old clothes that nobody else wants."

"Oh yeah? Well, what about that pair of jeans we bought you in Sears last month?"

"That was my birthday present. I told them about that."

"What else did they want to know?"

"If you have a job."

"What did you tell them?"

"That you work in a car wash."

"What did they say?"

"Whittaker said that the next time they came to see me, maybe he'd go by while you're working and have you wash his car."

"What else did they say?"

"They told me a lot about Boston and asked if I'd ever like to come out and see it."

"Listen to me," I warned. "People in Boston have to eat codfish and baked beans every day."

He looked worried.

"Tell me, does Whittaker drink?"

"A little. He had some wine after dinner one night."

"Did he ever get drunk while you were there?"

"No."

"There's a lot of stress on a man like him. He's probably on his way to becoming an alcoholic, just like your uncle Wally."

"Stress?"

"That means he worries a lot."

"Why should he worry? He's got money. I think Kellie worries the most of anybody. You hardly give her anything to buy food with."

"We get by, don't we? And another thing—I'd like you to start calling her Mom."

"She's not my mom."

"I know that, but is it going to kill you to call her Mom?"

"Then I'd have two moms. Besides, Kellie said it's okay if I call her Kellie."

"What else did they talk about?"

"Mom asked if I knew there was a clause in the divorce agreement that anytime she wanted, she could request a hearing to get me back again."

My mouth dropped open. "What?"

I'd never looked at the divorce papers. All I'd done was sign them.

*   *   *   *   *

A month passed and nothing happened. I started to relax and think maybe I'd just imagined Pamela was out to get custody of Jim. Kellie and I kept waiting for him to say he wanted to be baptized, but he still seemed reluctant.

Our first big check from the deferred payments for the movie finally arrived. We spent several days shopping and finally picked out a used station wagon in good condition. We'd be able to put down over half the money for the car and handle the rest with monthly payments.

And then it happened. I got an official-looking letter from California announcing a reconvening of the court to determine my suitability as a parent.

Our extra money went to hire an attorney in California, where the hearing would be held. Our lawyer was just out of law school. He had long hair and wore a turtleneck sweater and corduroy slacks.

Their lawyer wore a suit with a vest and had gray hair.

"Mr. Hill, can you tell us what your present employment is?" their attorney began.

"Well, right now I'm between movies."

"Are you saying you are presently unemployed?"

"No, I work part time at a car wash."

"In what capacity?"

"Finishing," I said.

"Could you tell us exactly what you do?"

"As a car goes by, I wipe off excess water on the left-hand side and the front bumper. The other guys get the rest."

"How much does that pay?"

"Two ninety-five per hour, but I'm due a raise next month."

"How much does that bring in during the course of a month?"

"Well, during an average month, maybe about five hundred dollars."

"Do you find that adequate to run a family of four on?"

"No, but I have other income, of course. For instance, on the movie I did about Carl Sandburg I made twenty thousand dollars."

"I see. Well, let's go into that. Over the past ten years, can you tell us how much you've made from acting?"

I paused. "I don't have all the figures right here at my disposal."

"Just an estimate. Take your time. We'll wait."

I took a pencil and figured. A minute later I looked up. "About fifty thousand dollars."

"In ten years? Let's see, that's about five thousand dollars a year, isn't it?"

"Hey, since when does a man's value as a father depend on how much he makes? My son and I do things together. That's worth a lot."

Pamela's attorney played a phone-recorded statement from Beth. She talked about visiting us at the lake right after my divorce. "Jimmy begged me to let him come to my house and live," she'd said.

"I see," the lawyer had replied. "What exactly was inadequate about the way Mr. Hill was providing for his son?"

"Well, for one thing, he made Jimmy drink coffee because he said he couldn't afford milk. And while they were there, the water pump went out and they had to drink lake water. I wouldn't be surprised but that there's raw sewage going into that lake. It's a wonder they didn't come down with something."

"Did Mr. Hill have any kind of a job while he was there at the lake?"

"No. I offered to have him come and work for my husband. But holding down a job is something my brother just can't seem to manage. If you ask me, he's just plain lazy. I've always said that about him."

And then she started in about me joining a non-Christian cult.

I'd had enough by then. "I'd like to answer that," I said.

They stopped the tape, and the judge let me talk. I told them how I'd changed because of the movie, and how that in everything I did now, I tried to let Jesus be my example.

Next Pamela's attorney asked permission to talk to Jim.

"What do you think of the Mormon church?"

Jim shrugged. "It's all right, I guess."

"Is there anything that bothers you about it?"

He paused. "Well, the main thing I don't like about it is Sundays. We go to church at nine and we don't get out until noon."

"You think that's too long?"

"Sure, don't you?"

"Is there anything else you don't like about that church?"

"I don't like singing time in Primary."

"Why not?"

"Because I don't like singing songs about blossoms on apricot trees, like they're supposed to look like popcorn. To me blossoms are one thing and popcorn is another. I never get the two mixed up."

The attorney decided to change the subject. "If you could change anything about your father, what would it be?"

Our lawyer objected to the question, but I stopped him because I wanted to hear what Jim would say.

"Well, if he could get a regular job like other dads, and maybe have an office. I have a friend John, and his brother works with Dad in the car wash. He says everybody working there is younger than Dad. They all make fun of him behind his back.''

Pamela was called to testify. She told in detail how much I'd neglected Jim before the divorce.

Our lawyer, in cross-examining her, hammered away at the fact that she was the one who left Jim.

The day ended with Pamela on the stand sobbing, saying how much she missed Jimmy and how much better Whittaker and she could provide for his needs than I could.

We adjourned at five. The judge told us we would reconvene in the morning.

On our way out of the building, our lawyer told us that our judge had a reputation for always giving children to the mother. He asked if I had any knowledge of Pamela committing adultery while we were married. I said no. He said that was too bad, because it would help us if we could prove she'd been stepping out on me before we separated. I angrily told him we didn't need a lawyer with a gutter-mind. He asked if that meant I'd like him to leave the case, and I said yes, and he left.

"Are you sure it was a good idea to do that?" Kellie asked quietly.

"What difference does it make? We've already lost."

We walked outside. The boys were on the lawn throwing a ball.

Suddenly I had a plan to keep my son. "Hey guys, whataya say we take off for Yellowstone National Park now?"

"No kidding?" Jim asked.

"You bet. C'mon, I'll race you both to the car."

They took off. I started to jog after them.

"Michael!" Kellie called out after me.

I stopped.

"You're not planning on running away with Jim, are you?"

"Yes. That's exactly what I'm planning."

"You know that's wrong."

"Since when is it wrong for a father to be with his boy?"

"He's her boy too."

"She doesn't want a boy. She wants a table decoration—
somebody to show off when company comes. He wouldn't be
happy in Boston."

We all got in the car. I stopped to get gas and some food, and
we took off.

Four hours later we were still heading north. The boys were
asleep in the backseat.

"You're not very talkative tonight," I said.

"You know how I feel about what you're doing."

"If you don't like it, then why are you going along with me?"

"Because you're my husband."

"Blind obedience?"

"The man I married won't break the law. I'm just waiting for
you to come to your senses. Tell me, have you thought about
what you're doing? In the eyes of the law, it's kidnapping. Besides, what will you do to keep from getting caught?"

"We'll change our names, and I'll get a job some place."

"I wonder what the judge'll think tomorrow about your little
sermon about how much Jesus means in your life when he
realizes you've skipped the state."

"What difference does it make what he thinks?"

"Michael, please don't disappoint me. You're one of the few
heroes left in my life."

That hurt. "Don't you see?" I said miserably. "If I don't
leave with him tonight, they'll take him away from me."

"Even if they do, he'll come back. I know he will."

"Sure," I grumbled, "for two weeks every year."

"No, longer. You're very important to him now. He may not
even realize yet how much he needs you. Besides, how much
respect for the law is he going to have if you do this? And do you
suppose he'll ever join the church if his father is a fugitive from
the law?"

I pulled over to the side of the road and grabbed the steering
wheel and tried to be a silent rock.

"Maybe if we talked about it," Kellie said.

We could hear the sound of crickets in the summer air. "I
wasn't a very good father when he was little, but I really think
I've gotten better at it."

She came to me and laid her head on my shoulder. "A boy couldn't have a better dad than you. I really think Rusty's going to turn out all right now. You're a wonderful father."

"If I'm so good at it, then why am I losing Jim?"

"Things'll work out."

"But what if they don't?"

"We'll try and work inside the law." She looked up at me. "Do you want me to drive part way on our way back?"

Slowly I nodded my head. "If you just turn the car around— that'll be the hardest part."

The next day Pamela and Whittaker won custody of Jim.

A week later, they returned to Utah in a rented Cadillac to take my son away from me. I made sure Jim took the tent and sleeping bag and hiking boots I'd bought him the day before. I asked him if he wanted to take any fishing equipment with him, but he said no.

Right after they left, I went in the garage and found his fishing reel and oiled it for him, so it would be ready for him when he came back.

He's not coming back, I thought.

I stayed in the garage for a long time, holding his reel in my hand, remembering our days at Grizzly Gulch.

At one point I looked up and noticed Rusty standing there.

"Can't you see I'm busy?" I said brusquely.

"It's okay if you don't like me anymore," he mumbled.

I set Jim's reel down.

Rusty's head was down. "I'm not as good at things like Jim."

Seconds passed. All I wanted to do was to think about Jim. I remember thinking, Rusty isn't really mine. Let Kellie worry about him.

Then in my mind appeared an image of a blind beggar who had asked Jesus for his eyesight.

Nobody would have minded if Jesus had just walked by. Nobody, that is, except the millions of us, beggars too, who have come along since then. And if a blind beggar is important to God, how about an awkward little boy with bad eyesight?

"Tiger," I said quietly, "come here. I need a hug."

He ran and threw his arms around me.

I gave him my reel, identical to Jim's, and told him that the
next time we went fishing, I'd teach him how to cast.

"Saturday?" he asked.

"I promise."

"I'm glad you're my dad," he said.

"Me too," I answered, mussing his hair as we went in the
house.

CHAPTER TWELVE

Two months later Pamela phoned from Boston. "Jim's right here next to me," she said, sounding frustrated. "I want you to tell him that all churches are good and that he doesn't have to ride his bicycle ten miles down busy streets to attend a Mormon church when he can go with us to our church. Here he is. Tell him."

"Jim, how's it going?"

"All right."

"Pamela says you're going to a Mormon church there."

"Yeah, it's a long ways away so I have to leave real early."

"Wouldn't you rather just go to church with your mom and Whittaker?"

"I don't like their church."

"Why not?"

"It's too quiet. If you drop a book or something, everybody gets bent out of shape like it was the end of the world. And in their church, after it's over, people just go home. They don't stand around and talk like they do in Provo." He paused. "And they don't have the Book of Mormon. I took one there one time, and this lady saw it and got real mad and told me it was the work of the devil. After that I brought it every time. And I always made sure that lady saw me with it."

I smiled because he was a lot like me.

He continued. "And then I decided I'd better read it, just in case she asked me what was in it." He paused. "It's not too bad, Dad. That's when I started riding my bike to the Mormon church every Sunday."

I asked him to call the bishop and make arrangements for someone in the church to pick him up on their way, so he wouldn't have to ride his bike. It worked out fine.

Two weeks later Jim phoned me. "They won't let me join the church."

"I can't do anything about that," I said.

"Yeah, but I want to join."

"I'm sorry, you'll just have to wait."

"For how long?"

"Until they let you. I'm sorry, but that's the way it is."

In December Pamela phoned me again. "Here's your son. It was bad enough he slept in our backyard all summer, but he can't sleep outside when there's a foot of snow on the ground. He's your son. Talk to him."

"Hi, Jim," I said.

"Hi, Dad."

"Your mom's worried you'll get sick if you camp in the snow."

"The Boy Scout handbook says snow is a good insulator. I've been thinking about building an igloo. What do you think?"

"Look, I really think you'd better sleep in your bedroom until spring comes. I'm just sure your Mom won't feel real comfortable with you out in the snow living in an igloo. I'd say go ahead and build it, and maybe once in a while you can go out there and stay in it, but probably not all night. You gotta realize they're not used to having a mountain man living with them. Okay?"

He was disappointed. "Okay."

Three weeks later she phoned me again. "I just want you to know your son's facing a lawsuit and it's all your fault."

"Why?"

"Some boys in his gym class tried to beat him up. Jim fought back until the teacher stopped the fight. One of the boys has a large bruise on his face where Jim kicked him with his foot. I just got off the phone with the boy's mother. She's talking lawsuit. Now I know you're the one who paid for his karate lessons, so you talk to him. Tell him never to fight again."

"Hi, Jim," I said a minute later.

"Dad, the karate really works."

"I hope you went easy on 'em."

"Yeah, sure. I just wanted to teach them some respect."

"Did it work?"

"I think so. Kids were awfully nice to me afterwards."

For Christmas I sent him a jar of peanuts and a jar of strawberry jam. I told him to tell his friends that when we spent that summer in the cabin in Montana, we lived on nuts and berries. It was our private joke.

Pamela didn't appreciate mountain-man humor. She told me that over Christmas vacation, since she wouldn't let him sleep in his igloo, he got back at her by setting up a tent in his bedroom and sleeping on the floor every night.

I phoned him on Christmas day. He told me that Whittaker had given him a computer, but the only software he got was called Stock Market Trends.

He asked if I had steady work yet, and I said it looked like I might have a part in a Robert Redford movie in the spring. I was hoping he'd think that Robert Redford and I were just like that.

* * * * *

In March we learned that Kellie was pregnant.

"Don't look so smug," she said with a smile, knowing how proud I was to have her carrying our child.

The New Testament movie was shown on TV the week before Easter. It played two nights during Easter week.

As I realized that people across the country were seeing it, I had a feeling that I had a responsibility to live right.

I decided to repent.

I'd been holding a grudge against Beth since the custody hearings because she'd spoken out against me, but then I got to wondering how she was doing after her divorce. I called her on Good Friday, and we talked, and she told me how tough it had been for her. I offered to send her a little money each month, and although she couldn't bring herself to thank me, she said she wouldn't turn the money down if I sent it.

* * * * *

In April Jim phoned me. "I don't like it here."

"Why not?"

"I tried to talk Whittaker and Mom into having a blessing on the food. Whittaker said people prayed over their food in Bible times, but we didn't need to do that anymore because that's why we have federal meat inspectors." He paused. "Dad, can I come out this summer and stay with you?"

I asked to speak to Pamela. She told me she didn't see how they could work it in, because they were going to Europe for most of the summer. She said that maybe he could come for a few days near the end of August—if, she said with a note of superiority, I could afford the ticket.

*   *   *   *   *

Late one afternoon in June Pamela called from Boston.

"Jimmy is missing. Do you know where he is?"

"I haven't heard from him."

"We were just about to leave on our trip to Europe. Whittaker thought you might've kidnapped him."

"No."

"We dropped him off this morning at his day camp, and when we went back at six to pick him up, they told us he hadn't been there all day."

"Maybe he just played hooky."

"Couldn't he have at least told us?" she asked.

"Pamela, you don't tell your parents when you're going to play hooky. Look, just relax and have supper. He'll be home by dark, so don't worry."

But he didn't come home.

A day passed. Still no word.

I called Whittaker and offered to go out there and help, but he said he doubted if I could do better than the best detective agency in Boston.

That made up my mind. I flew out the next day.

*   *   *   *   *

They lived in a large two-story brick home in Wellesley Hills. I paid for the taxi and took my suitcase up to the front door. I rang the doorbell. It had chimes that played a one-minute melody.

And it took Pamela about that long to walk from her kitchen to the front door. She looked rich and worried.

"Has Jim shown up yet?" I asked.

"No."

"I came to help."

She scowled. "Oh."

"Don't worry, I won't stay here."

"No, that's okay. You'd better. We have plenty of room, and maybe I can give you some ideas of where to look for him."

"Well, okay. Thanks. My funds are a little tight right now."

That was no surprise to her. "Come in."

I followed her inside. There was a dining room off to the left, and large living room to the right, a set of stairs directly in front of the door, and a hallway next to it that led to the other rooms on that floor.

"The guest bedroom is up here."

I followed her upstairs to where I'd be staying. I was pleased with how polite and courteous we both had become.

"I'll put out some guest towels for you."

"Thank you. You're doing very well here, aren't you," I commented.

"We've been very happy."

"I'm glad for you."

"What will you need me to help you with?"

"I'd like to use your telephone, and maybe a list of his friends, school contacts, anything you can think of."

I spent the rest of the afternoon on the phone talking to people on the list Pamela gave me.

Whittaker came home at seven. When he walked in, I was on the phone.

Pamela kissed him hello and then took him to the kitchen for some tomato juice and crackers and an explanation of what I was doing there.

After I finished my call, I went into the kitchen. It was larger than our entire house in Provo.

Whittaker and I shook hands. "You didn't need to come. The detective agency has already made all the contacts you did today."

"Maybe so, but for them it's just a job. With me, it's my son."

"Supper'll be ready in fifteen minutes," Pamela said.

"I can't stay. I'll be leaving in a minute."

"Do you want to use one of our cars?" she asked.

"If I could, that'd be very helpful."

"You do have a valid license, don't you?" Whittaker asked.

"Of course."

"Traffic out here is worse than you're used to in Utah," he said.

"Look, Whittaker, if it's any problem, just forget the car."

"No, no, go right ahead, if that's what Pamela wants."

*   *   *   *   *

Within a day I'd exhausted every possible lead, talked to every teacher, met with every friend. Nobody knew where Jim had gone.

I went into Boston and walked the streets looking for my boy. I had his picture with me, and I'd walk up to people and say, "Excuse me, I'm looking for a lost child. Have you seen anyone that looks like this?"

"No."

A few more feet and then I'd repeat the question.

Day after day I continued. I started in the center of town and worked out. At night I drove back to Pamela's and ate and went to bed.

It was endless, and probably futile. But I had to do something.

Every day I saw thousands of people on the street. Faces in a crowd. Strangers in a hurry. Their sorrow and disappointment and loneliness etched on their faces.

A young teenage girl, trying hard to look a worldly twenty, stood on the corner, watching me come down the street.

"Looking for a good time?" she asked with a strange leer.

I stopped to look at her face. She was chewing gum energetically and avoided looking me in the eye. She wore tight-fitting black pants and a purple shirt buttoned as little as possible. Somehow I knew she was a runaway.

"Your mother cries every time she passes your empty bedroom," I said.

"How do you know?"

"Because my son is missing. This is what he looks like. Have you seen him?"

She looked at the picture and shook her head. "How old is he?"

"Eleven years old."

Her tough-girl expression softened. "I hope you find him."

"Where are you from?" I asked.

She got street-wise again. "It's none of your business."

"You want to know something?"

"What?"

"God loves you," I said.

She unleashed a string of profanity at me.

I moved on.

* * * * *

I called Kellie every night to see if he'd turned up in Utah. I also phoned Beth and asked her to go out to the cabin and see if he was there. The next day she phoned while I was gone and told Pamela the cabin was empty.

A day later when I came back after searching, Pamela met me at the door. She looked terrible. "The police just called."

"What is it?" I asked, feeling an awful gloom come over me.

"They found a body of a boy about Jim's age. They want someone to go down and see—" she could barely say the words —"if it's Jim."

"I'll go," I said.

She gave a sigh of relief. "I knew I couldn't face it. I'll drive you there."

After a few minutes of silence, she asked, "What will we do if he's dead?"

"I don't know."

"I'm not sure I'd ever get over it," she said.

I nodded. "It'd be very hard."

She pulled in front of the police station. There were no parking places. I told her I'd run in and then meet her there in a few minutes.

A short time later I was walking to the morgue with a police officer.

"How did the boy die?" I asked.

"Stab wounds."

"Who did it?"

"A street gang maybe. We're not sure."

We entered a cold-storage room. He rolled out a metal slab from the wall. A sheet covered the body. "Are you ready?" he asked.

"Yes, go ahead."

He pulled back the sheet. The cold naked body of a boy lay there, his face battered, stab marks in his stomach, a three-inch-long cut across his face. His legs and thighs and lower stomach were black and blue where they'd kicked him over and over again after he'd fallen to the ground.

It wasn't Jim.

I shook my head so the police officer would know it wasn't my son, and then I started gagging. I barely made it to a restroom before I threw up.

A few minutes later, my face drenched in sweat, I walked outside. Pamela's car was double-parked. I got in.

"It wasn't him."

"Thank God."

"Don't thank him too much, Pamela."

"Why not?"

"He was somebody's son."

*   *   *   *   *

The next day I decided I'd done all I could. It was time to return to Utah.

"There's something I want to tell you," Pamela said as she drove me to the airport.

"What?"

"I never had much respect for you before, but now I do. You've become the man I always hoped you'd be."

"Thanks."

At the Salt Lake Airport, when I came into the terminal, Rusty called out my name and ran to hug me. "Dad! Hi! Did you find Jim?"

"No, not yet."

I stood up and hugged Kellie. Being in her arms again made me realize how much I loved her.

We drove back home. Rusty sat next to me, as close as he could.

"Rusty has something to ask you," Kellie said.

"What is it, Tiger?"

"Dad, can I start taking violin lessons again. I like the violin. Is that all right with you? If it isn't, I won't."

I smiled. "I'd be proud to have a violin player in our family. If that's your dream, go for it."

Kellie smiled at him. "I told you that's what he'd say."

The next day I went into the mountains alone and spent the day in fasting and prayer.

That night I woke up suddenly. I'd been dreaming about when Jim and I were at the cabin. I couldn't sleep after that.

I waited until seven in the morning and then called Beth. After hearing her complain about how early it was, I asked her to go out to the cabin again and see if Jim was there.

"Again? I told you before, he's not there. What makes you think he'd be there anyway? He hated it all the time he was there with you."

"Just check it out for me, okay?"

At noon she called back.

"There's nobody there."

"Are you absolutely sure?"

"Look," she said, "I went inside and looked around.

Nobody's living there, I tell you. How many times do I have to
drive up there?''

The next night I dreamed again about being at the lake. Was
it inspiration or was it nothing? He probably wasn't at the lake,
but I had to know for sure.

As soon as it started to get light outside, I got up and dressed.
Kellie was still sleeping. I made peanut butter and jelly sand-
wiches and then went out to the car. I was checking the oil when
I looked up and saw Rusty coming outside in his pajamas.

"What are you doing up so early?'' he asked.

"I have to go to our cabin in Montana and see if Jim's there.''
I slammed the hood of the car shut.

"Are you going all by yourself?''

I nodded. "Yeah. Your mom has kids to baby-sit.''

"You'd better let me go with you then,'' he said.

"Why?''

"I can keep you awake so you won't fall asleep while you're
driving.''

Then it hit me—he'd thought about it before, that if he'd
been in the car that fateful night his father would still be alive.
And I remembered my dad saying he needed me to help him
and how much that meant to me now.

"You're right,'' I said softly. "I need a partner. Let's go wake
your mom and tell her we're going.''

* * * * *

On our first day the water pump in the car went out. After a
gas station fixed it, the manager informed me they didn't take
checks.

No matter what I said, he wouldn't budge.

"Then keep the car,'' I muttered angrily, starting out to the
road to hitchhike.

Rusty followed after me, doing his best to look as disgusted
as I was.

"Hey!'' the owner yelled at me.

"What?''

"Is that your kid?"

"Yeah."

He looked at Rusty. "I guess we'll make an exception and take your check."

Early the next afternoon, I turned off the highway onto the dirt road leading to Grizzly Gulch. After what seemed an eternity we came to the lake. I parked the car in front of the cabin.

The door was locked. I found my key and opened it up.

We went inside.

There was nobody there. Suddenly I gave in to the gloom that had hovered around me for days. In my mind I pictured my son being taken and tortured and then slowly killed.

I told Rusty that I wanted to be alone for a while and suggested that he go explore down by the lake. After he left, I looked around the place. There was the same Western paperback I'd read so long ago, and the cot where Dad had stayed the last time. Here is where he'd reached the end of the line, where all his bubbles burst, where he had to give up on lions and the Panama Canal and the miracle cures.

Dad, I miss you so much even now. If you were here, I know you'd help me. We used to fix things, didn't we? A neighbor'd call about a problem and you'd say, Okay, we'll come and take a look at it. And you and me'd go over and fix it. There wasn't anything we couldn't fix, was there. Dad, can you hear me? I need you to help me fix this. I need you to help me find my son. Is he dead? If he's dead, then at least he's with you. Tell him I love him. I don't think I told him enough.

I realized I was sitting on the cot where Jim had slept the summer we were together, and suddenly I hated the cabin and every nail Dad had driven to build it. I had to get away. There were too many memories here.

I stumbled out the door. Rusty was down by the lake skipping rocks across the water. I called for him to come up right away.

"It's nice here," he said as he rounded the top of the trail a minute later. "Are we staying tonight?"

"No, we'll stay with your Aunt Beth. I've decided to sell this old place. It's no good to anyone now. Get in the car. Let's go."

As I turned to get in the car, out of the corner of my eye I saw
something move.

"Jim!"

We ran and threw our arms around each other. Rusty joined
in, and the three of us hugged and cried.

We returned to the cabin, and he told us how he'd saved the
allowance money Whittaker gave him until he had enough for a
bus ticket to Montana. The first time Beth came to look for him,
he was in the cabin at the time, but she didn't go inside. She just
looked in from the window. Jim was just inside the door. After
that, he got up each morning and took everything that looked
like someone was staying there and hid them in the woods, and
each night he crept back. Because of that, the second time she
came, she didn't suspect anything.

Jim was thinner than I'd ever seen him. I asked him what
he'd been eating while he'd been here, and he grinned and said
nuts and berries.

"But why did you come here?" I asked.

"What I really wanted was to go stay with you in Utah, but I
knew you'd call Mom and she'd make you send me back again.
So I came here."

"But you hated it before, didn't you?"

"I know." He paused as if he wasn't sure if he dare say it.
"But this place reminds me of you, Dad. That's why I came,
because it was the closest I could get to you."

I knew what he meant.

We drove to the store by the lake and phoned Pamela, but
there was no answer. I bought us lunch. I'd never seen a boy eat
so much.

After we'd finished eating, I phoned again. Still no answer.
We decided to go fishing. Jim's bobber dropped below the
surface, and he set the hook. A large trout cleared the water.

"All right! What a whale!" I shouted.

Jim reeled, but the fish continued to pull line off the reel.

"Don't let him get to those logs!" I cautioned.

Jim moved up the lakeshore to get away from the sunken
timber.

I ran to the cabin for the big net. By the time I got back, Jim had the fish nearly to the shore. I dipped the net into the water and lifted it out.

"Look at this, everybody!" I yelled, proudly showing it off to the fishermen on the lake. "My son caught this!"

We drove back to the general store. "Dad, do we have to tell Mom right away?"

"Yeah, we do. She's really been worried about you."

At the store Jim and Rusty sat on the dock while I phoned Pamela on the outdoor pay phone. This time she answered.

I told her all about Jim. "I don't understand that at all," she said. "If he wanted to go to camp, why didn't he just tell us? After all Whittaker and I've done for him, and this is the way he treats us."

I didn't want to delay what I knew had to be done. "How do you want me to send him back to you, air freight or parcel post?"

"Just a minute. Let me have you talk to Whittaker."

Whittaker came on the line. "Thanks for finding the boy. Pamela says he's at a lake. Do they have structured camp activities there? If they do, maybe he could stay there for the summer. I mean, if that's what he wants. We just want him to have whatever he wants. The only thing is, we're never sure what he wants. He's a very difficult boy, you know. He would've slept in the snow all winter if we'd let him. There's no figuring him out."

"Whittaker, I'd be willing to take him off your hands."

He paused. "For how long?"

"Forever."

"You're saying you'd like to get back custody of the boy?"

"That's right."

"Hang on."

There was a long silence. Then Pamela said, "Let me talk to Jimmy."

I yelled for Jim. "Mom wants to talk to you."

He came up from the lake and I handed him the phone. "Hi, Mom."

A long silence at our end. "I'm sorry you worried so much

. . . I don't like it in Boston . . . I don't want to go to Europe . . .
I like it out here . . . I don't care if he is poor, he's still my
dad . . . All right, I love you too . . .''

He handed back the phone and went down to the dock to be
with Rusty.

Pamela was crying. "It was so much easier when he was
little," she sobbed.

"I know."

"And if you hadn't completely warped his mind when he was
with you, it'd be a whole lot easier for Whittaker and me to
handle him now."

"You're probably right."

"And now he's about to enter puberty," she said. "Who
knows what he'll be like then?"

"You're right. It could be trouble no matter who has him."

She paused. "I guess it'd be okay if you take custody, provided you'll let him come visit us a few times a year."

"Pamela, don't talk about this unless you're serious. I don't
think I could stand to lose him twice."

She sighed. "Well, it's what Jim wants, so I guess that's what
we should do. I'll have our lawyer draw up the papers."

"Pamela, you know what this means to me. All I can say is
thanks. I promise to take good care of our boy."

"I know you will, Michael. You've changed a lot lately. I'm
curious though. What's made the difference?"

I thought about Jesus and my dad and Kellie and even Steve.
"I've had good examples to follow."

We said our goodbyes and hung up.

Jim and Rusty were standing on the dock. I ran toward them,
yelling *Geronimo!* at the top of my voice. When I got to the edge
of the dock, I grabbed one in each arm and jumped off the dock.

The three of us sailed through the air.

And landed with a splash in the cold water of our mountain
lake.

We were home at last.

BRENDA
AT THE PROM

JACK WEYLAND

Deseret Book Company
Salt Lake City, Utah

Kade began each day of his freshman year in high school waiting for Brenda to take him to early-morning seminary. They lived about fifteen miles from the small farming community of Shelby, Montana.

Even though Kade's family lived in a farmhouse, they weren't farmers. His father, Paul Ellis, worked for a regional bank whose headquarters were in Chicago. They had moved from Illinois just that summer and were renting a farmhouse from the agri-corporation that had bought the farm after the owner went bankrupt.

Brenda Sloan was two years older than Kade, a junior in high school. On the first day of school, as she pulled in front of the house, Kade grabbed his school supplies, ran out to her battered yellow pickup, and climbed in. "Hi," he called out cheerfully. "Nice day, isn't it?"

"I suppose," she said, making it sound like "I spose."

Kade got in and looked around. A beat-up radio, missing a plastic knob, blared out a country-western song. A horse blanket was draped over the seat to cover the rips in the black vinyl upholstery. He tried to shut the door on his side, but the lock wouldn't catch.

"You have to really slam it," she said.

He tried it again. Still no luck.

"Put some muscle into it."

He pulled as hard as he could, but it still wouldn't lock.

"Here, let me do it." She reached over him and slammed the door with a mighty thud. This time it stayed shut.

Brenda shifted into first gear and let out the clutch. Nothing happened. She grabbed a hammer from under the seat, stepped outside, crawled underneath the frame, hit something, then got back in again. "Linkage," she said.

"You fixed it?"

"Yeah, for now."

Kade was impressed—he'd never fixed anything in his life.

As they traveled along the graveled county road, he studied her features. She had a very straight, but not too long, nose, dark bushy eyebrows, full lips, and a long neck, which made her sandy-brown hair seem shorter than it actually was. She wore a faded Levi jacket and jeans. From where he sat he couldn't tell the color of her eyes, but from having seen her in church, he knew they were a muted green.

"Thanks for agreeing to take me to seminary," he said.

She shrugged. "It's no big deal. Besides, your dad offered to help pay for the gas. I sure wasn't about to turn that down. Money's hard enough to come by these days."

"I'm kind of nervous," he said, "this being my first day at school and all."

"I s'pose," she said, not very interested in his problems.

He sighed. "I wish I was wearing contact lenses today instead of these dumb glasses. I've almost got enough money saved for them. My parents can't understand why I want 'em though. They say I look okay with glasses." He removed his glasses. "I think I look better this way, don't you?"

The song on the radio had put her in another world. She glanced over at him. "What?"

He put his glasses back on. "Never mind, it wasn't important. I don't usually talk this much. I guess I'm kinda hyper today. I just don't know what to expect in school. You're about the only one I'll know." He paused. "Any chance I could eat lunch with you?"

"Forget it. I don't want some little ninth grader tagging after me."

"Oh."

She looked over at him. "Look, it's nothing personal. You'll feel the same way when you're my age."

"But you're the only one I know. If you could just let me eat at your table until I get to know someone else . . . just for one day even."

"I said no, didn't I?"

"Yes."

"Then just drop it, okay?"

"Okay."

"Good. Now just be quiet and listen to the radio."

"How about turning to another station?" he asked.

"What for?"

"I don't like cowboy music."

"Then plug your ears."

He didn't talk the rest of the way into town.

Seminary was held at the home of the teacher, Sister Simmons, with Kade and Brenda and Sister Simmons's daughter Melissa, who was a year younger than Brenda. This year they would be studying the Old Testament.

After seminary the two girls and Kade went out to the pickup.

"Melissa, you want to ride shotgun?" Brenda asked.

"Sure." Melissa turned to Kade as if she expected

him to do something. "I'm riding shotgun," she said to him.

He was still confused. "What does that mean?"

"Where you from, anyway?"

"Illinois."

"It figures. Get in. You're riding in the middle."

On the way to school, they treated him as if he weren't even there except for the fact that every time Brenda had to shift gears, he had to move his legs to get out of her way.

When they reached the school parking lot, Brenda turned to Kade. "I'm leaving at three o'clock sharp. If you're not here then, I'll go without you."

"I'll be here."

Kade went to the principal's office. A woman helped him fill out the necessary forms. By the time he finished, it was nearly ten.

The first class he made it to was gym. The class didn't have to suit up the first day. They were all sitting around on bleachers in the gym when the gym teacher, Coach Brannigan, who was also the football coach, walked in. "All right, girls, pipe down," he called out.

Kade hated it when a man called a group of boys "girls."

After taking roll, the coach went over class rules with them, peppering his comments with stories about boys who'd messed up in past years. Near the end of the period, he went to a thick manila rope hanging from the ceiling. "If any of you want more than a C out of this course, you'll have to climb this to the ceiling and lower yourself back down again. Any of you think you're man enough to do that?"

Several boys raised their hands. Kade looked at how high the ceiling was and decided to settle for a C.

After class Kade went up to Coach Brannigan. "Do you happen to know if there's a soccer league in town?"

The coach smirked. "The girls' gym classes play soccer. Maybe you ought to see if they'll let you join 'em."

Kade was sorry he'd asked. Marvin Mudlin, a large boy with huge arms and shoulders, had overheard. "I bet they'd let him play too, wouldn't they, coach?"

Kade turned to leave.

"Ellis," the coach called out.

Kade turned around. "What?"

"Why did you ask about soccer anyway?"

"I used to play on a team before we moved here."

"Where are you from?"

"Illinois."

"You're in Montana now. This is football country. There's no soccer here."

"Except for girls. Right, coach?" Marvin Mudlin smirked.

What a bunch of jerks, Kade thought as he made his way to his next class.

At three o'clock, he hurried to his locker, then went outside. Brenda's pickup was easy to spot in the parking lot. It had once been yellow, but since then the worst rust spots had been primed with a rust inhibitor, creating a patchwork hodgepodge of browns and yellows. Brenda showed up and they left for home. A short section of pipe in the bed of the pickup rolled back and forth everytime they started or stopped.

Brenda listened to cowboy songs all the way home and didn't even ask him how school had gone.

Every school day began with an early morning ride to town and ended with an afternoon ride back home. Because of the difference in their ages, Brenda didn't talk to him much, which meant he had nearly an hour a day to be with a girl who treated him as if he weren't even there. Even if he stared directly at her, it didn't seem to faze her.

Kade wasn't sure how it began, but he soon found himself fascinated with her face. Because she didn't use much makeup, she sometimes seemed plain, but in the morning as they traveled east toward town, the sun would often catch the highlights in her hair. The interplay between light and shadow accentuated her high cheekbones. For an instant she became more beautiful than any girl he'd ever seen.

Kade's room on the second floor of the farmhouse his family lived in had been converted from the attic by the original owners. The room was long and narrow, with sloping walls matching the roofline on two sides and a small window at each end. The room had a hardwood floor, with a throw-rug next to his bed so he wouldn't freeze his feet when he got up in the morning. To heat the room, the original owner had cut a hole in the floor big enough for a heating vent. Kade found that if he sat near the vent, he could sometimes hear what was being said downstairs.

One day after school, he sat at the desk in his room and began drawing a picture of Brenda. It was a straight front view that focused on her eyes. For some strange reason, perhaps because her distinctive eyebrows made her seem strong-willed and aloof, he turned her into a storybook princess. A veil covered her hair completely, creating a sense of mystery. Perhaps she was traveling at night through dark cobblestoned streets and needed the veil to hide her identity. And yet her very gaze, bold and uncompromising, would give her away as nobility to anyone who looked at her closely enough.

When he finished the sketch, he was fascinated with what he had created. After that he drew pictures of Brenda nearly every day.

Sometimes when Kade was drawing in his room upstairs, he could hear his mother in the living room below, practicing her violin. He had grown up listening to her play the violin. In Illinois, she had been in a symphony orchestra, but there wasn't one in Shelby.

Kade found that it wasn't just Brenda that inspired the artist in him. It was also the area where he was living, just sixty miles east of Glacier Park. Each day on his way home he saw the snowcapped mountains, while in the fields nearby was the brown and tan stubble left after the harvest, as well as the tender green shoots of winter wheat that depended on the snow to come like a blanket and protect it from the bitter winds that would soon come roaring down from Canada. Sometimes he wondered if anyone else saw the world the way he did. And if they did, how could they stand it? How could people live near those mountains and stop looking at them long enough to get any work done? It was all so magnificent.

Before long Kade needed a place to hide the growing stack of drawings. He went to his closet and pulled down from a shelf the box for his Monopoly game. He set the drawings in the box and returned the box to the closet.

As the days passed, he felt himself slipping deeper into another world, a place within himself where things could be created and brought to life. Sometimes he had to fight to come out of that world long enough to do his homework. So far Kade's parents were unaware that much of the time he spent in his room was taken up drawing pictures of Brenda. They assumed he was studying. He felt certain his father wouldn't approve. To Kade, his father was a well-oiled machine, someone who went to work each day in a three-piece suit, came home at night and asked how school was going, discussed finances and bills and budgets with his wife, settled in his favorite chair after dinner and read the *Wall Street Journal* until time for TV news, then went to bed.

Sometimes at night his father worked at his computer. Once he showed Kade a spread-sheet software

package he had just purchased, which allowed a person
to create endless rows and columns of numbers. "This
might be useful to you someday," he had said. Kade
felt certain that would never happen because even if you
could fill all the rows and columns with numbers, what
had you gained? They were still just numbers.

Kade wondered what his parents would say if they
found the sketches of Brenda. They might think he was
in love with her. But that wasn't it at all. What he loved
were the images he created of her. As time went on, he
found himself increasingly in awe of the creative process
itself. Somewhere inside him was a reservoir that never
ran dry.

Each day along the gravel road, he studied Brenda.
Sometimes she seemed lonely, almost sullen, but at
other times, especially after she got used to having him
around, she sang along with the radio to her favorite
western songs. And he, mostly ignored by her, sat and
watched and listened.

And when he got home he drew.

One day in gym, the boys suited up and played touch
football outside. After class, as Kade was coming out of
the shower, someone snapped him from behind with a
towel. He turned around to see Marvin Mudlin standing
there holding one end of a wet towel.

"Knock it off," Kade complained.

Marvin smirked and snapped the towel at him again.
Kade jumped back to avoid being hit.

"I mean it."

"Hey, what're you gonna do if I don't stop?"

Kade knew that to fight Marvin would be suicide.
"I'll tell the coach."

"What's the matter? Can't you fight your own
battles?" Marvin flicked the towel at him again, catching
him just above the kneecap.

"I said knock it off!"

The coach came into the room. "What's going on?"

"Nothing," Marvin said. "We were just having some fun."

"You two get dressed and quit horsing around."

Kade went to his locker and put his clothes on as fast as he could.

That afternoon on the way home Kade waited until they were out of town before reaching over and clicking off Brenda's radio.

"Hey, leave it where it was."

"I need to talk to you," he said.

"What for?"

"I just do. Look, it's not going to kill you to talk to me, is it? We're out here where nobody can see us, in case you're worried someone might find out you actually broke down and talked to me."

She raised her eyebrows. "What's got into you anyway?"

"Do girls ever snap each other with towels in the locker room after a shower?"

She shook her head. "You are really weird."

"Guys do sometimes."

"Kade, I don't really care what happens in the boys' locker room, okay?"

"Today a guy snapped me with a towel."

"So?"

"What do you think I should've done?"

She shrugged. "I don't know—snapped him back, I guess."

"It was Marvin Mudlin. He must outweigh me by a hundred pounds."

"You can't let people walk all over you. Sometimes you've got to fight for your rights."

"If I'd have fought him, he would've killed me."

"He might've hit you a couple of times, but he'd

never mess with you again because he'd know you'd always fight back."

He paused. "I've never fought anybody in my whole life."

"Why not?"

"My parents say it's not right to fight."

"Sure, that's easy for them to say—nobody's snapping them with a towel whenever they get out of a shower. Look, Kade, if you don't fight back, Marvin's going to keep hassling you. So make up your mind." Having given him the benefit of her advice, she turned the radio back on.

That night Kade came up with his own plan: he wouldn't take showers after gym anymore. While everyone else was showering, he would hurry up and get dressed and be gone before Marvin could get to him.

He tried it the next time he had gym, and it worked fine. However, on the way home Brenda rolled down her window. "Good grief, Kade, is that you?"

"What?"

"Something in here smells real bad. You got a problem?"

He blushed. "Maybe so. I didn't take a shower after gym today."

She shook her head. "Kade, you can't let people push you around."

"Nobody pushed me around today."

"Sure, that's because you turned tail and ran."

"I didn't run. I just didn't take a shower, that's all."

"And so after gym you went to all your classes smelling like that?"

"It's not that bad."

"Not that bad? How can you say that? You smell like something that's been dead for two weeks."

"I couldn't think of anything else to do about Marvin."

"You have to learn to stand up for yourself. Fight him if you have to."

"I don't know how to fight."

"You can learn."

"How? There's not even a YMCA in this dumb town."

"What do you need a YMCA for?"

"To take boxing lessons."

"I can't believe you said that. You don't need boxing lessons. Just start fighting. You'll pick it up fast enough."

"Sure, except by the time I learn I'll be dead. His arms are at least twice as big as mine. Forget it. I'm not fighting him."

"What if you wait until he turns his back to you and then you hit him from behind and tackle him?"

"This happens right after we've taken a shower."

"So?"

"So we don't have any clothes on."

"I understand showers, okay? So what's the problem?"

"I don't want to be wrestling some guy when neither one of us is dressed."

"Have you got a plan?"

"Yeah, sort of."

"What is it?"

"I was thinking of maybe putting poison ivy on his soap so he'll get this really bad rash and have to be out of school for a long time."

She shook her head. "You're hopeless."

It was mainly because of wanting Brenda's approval that Kade finally decided to fight Marvin. After the next gym class, as he was drying himself off by his locker, Marvin came and snapped him again with a towel. When he turned to walk away, Kade lunged at him. Because the floor was slick, Marvin fell down and hit his head on one of the benches. At first Kade worried he'd killed Marvin, but then Marvin slowly sat up, gingerly touched his head with his hand, and got up. The other boys gathered around, eager to see a fight.

"You'll pay for this," Marvin threatened.

Marvin shoved Kade backwards against the lockers and then hit him twice in the face and once in the stomach. Kade doubled over and fell to the floor, gasping for breath.

Marvin loomed over him. "Get up, you little twerp. I'm not done with you yet."

Kade was not about to get up just so he could be knocked down again.

"I'll get you up myself then." Marvin grabbed Kade by the shoulders and hoisted him up and slammed him against a locker. When Kade saw the look on Marvin's face, he knew he'd better do something. He ducked just before the blow got to him, and Marvin's fist hit the locker. It sounded like a gun going off, and he cried out in pain.

The noise brought Coach Brannigan in from the gym. "You two! In my office!"

Once they were in his office, the coach shut the door, then turned to face them. "What's going on here?"

"He kept snapping me with a towel," Kade said. "I told him to lay off, but he wouldn't, so I decided to do something about it."

"Yeah, the little twerp came from behind and knocked me down," Marvin added.

The coach turned to Marvin. "Are you okay?"

"Well, I guess so," Marvin said. "I hit my head against the bench when I fell down, and then later he ducked a punch, and my hand hit the lockers."

"Here, let me take a look." The coach carefully examined Marvin's injuries. "I think you'll be okay by Friday."

"Hey, what's the deal here?" Kade complained. "This ape nearly kills me and you're worrying he might've hurt his precious hand." Suddenly the light dawned. "Oh, I get it. King Kong here is on the football team, right?"

"What of it?" Marvin shot back.

"I should've known. It's the same wherever you go. You look for the biggest jerks in school and they're always on the football team." He turned to the coach. "You're not even going to punish him, are you? Of course not. Football players always get special treatment, don't they? Well, that stinks, if you ask me. It's not fair."

"Not fair?" the coach raged. "Not fair? I'll tell you what's not fair!" He went into a long tirade about trying to field a football team with not enough funds, equipment, and personnel. He ended up facing off at Kade. "You report to my office after school."

"I can't."

"What do you mean, you can't?"

"I live out of town, and my ride goes home right after school."

"When I tell someone to report after school, I expect them to do it and not give me a bunch of flimsy excuses why they can't."

"If I stay, how am I going to get home?" Kade knew his father would probably give him a ride home, but he didn't want to mention that to the coach. He wanted to go with Brenda so he could tell her about the fight.

The coach paused long enough to cool down. "Do you have a free period tomorrow?"

"Yeah, at eleven o'clock."

"Report to my office then. Understood?"

"What about him?" Kade asked, glancing at Marvin. "When's he reporting to you?"

"Mudlin, I want you here too," the coach ordered.

"Me? Why me? I didn't do anything."

"You started it," Kade shot back.

"I did not."

"You two—get out of here!" the coach roared.

As the day progressed, Kade looked worse. He had two black-and-blue bruises on his face. He also had a headache and had to go to the office and ask for a couple of aspirin.

Strangely enough, though, fighting Marvin had made him a celebrity. In English class, Whitney Lindquist, the best-looking freshman girl in school, came up to him. "Weren't you scared of fighting Marvin? He's so big."

"Not so big he can't be knocked off his perch," Kade said, trying to sound as macho as possible.

Whitney was standing closer to him than any girl had ever done before. He realized he was breathing some of the very air she was exhaling. "I'm glad somebody finally stood up to him," she said. "He used to pick on my cousin all the time."

"If he ever bothers your cousin again, just let me know. I'll take care of him for you."

"Thanks. Well, I'll be seeing you." She paused. "Kade, if you want to call me tonight, it'd be okay."

He couldn't believe his ears but tried to be nonchalant about it. "Well, yeah, I might call you—if I'm not too busy, that is."

After school Kade got to the pickup before Brenda. It was unlocked, so he climbed in and waited. When she came, she took one look at his face. "Gosh, Kade, you okay?"

"Yeah, I'm all right. I fought Marvin, just the way we talked about. I tackled him from behind when he wasn't looking. Then he got up and hit me. He hurt his fist real bad when I ducked a punch and he hit the lockers, and then the coach came in and stopped the whole thing."

"All right, Kade! You showed him! Are you glad you did it?"

"Yeah, I am. It was great afterwards. Whitney Lundquist came up and talked to me. She's glad I fought

Marvin because he used to pick on her cousin. You should've seen her. I'm not kidding—she was practically hanging all over me. She pretty much begged me to call her up tonight."

Brenda smiled. "So, do you like being a hero to all the little ninth-grade girls?"

He grinned. "Sure, why not?" He paused. "Thanks for telling me what to do."

It was no surprise that his parents didn't approve of his fighting Marvin. They said there are other ways to settle a dispute. But Kade knew that none of their ways would have resulted in Whitney Lundquist coming up and asking him to phone her. He decided the next time he had a problem, he would go to Brenda for advice.

That night, because he wanted privacy, he took the phone into the bathroom, shut the door, and dialed Whitney's number. She answered.

"Whitney, this is Kade."

"Oh, hi. How are you doing?"

"Okay. Of course, my folks got mad at me for fighting." He paused. "But sometimes a guy has to do what a guy has to do."

"I know. Kade, are you going with anyone?"

"No."

"Would you like to go with me?"

Kade paused. He wasn't even supposed to date until he was sixteen. But, hey, no use worrying about technicalities at a time like this. "Sure, why not?"

"Okay. Are you going to the dance Friday night?"

"I suppose."

"Would you like to take me?"

"Yeah, might as well—since we're going together. I'll meet you there."

"Aren't you going to pick me up?"

"You mean, like in a car?"

"Yes, of course."

"I don't have a driver's license."

"You don't?" she said. "I do."

"You do?" His voice cracked as he said it.

"Sure. In Montana you can get a permit to drive when you turn fourteen."

"In Illinois you have to be sixteen."

"You're not in Illinois anymore, Kade."

"I asked my parents about it when we moved here, and they said they wanted me to wait until I at least turned fifteen."

"Are you saying you don't even know how to drive?" she asked.

He tried to get back his fading confidence. "Well, no, but how hard can it be?"

"I guess maybe the guys I usually go out with are older than you."

He cleared his throat. "You've dated other guys?"

"Sure. Last summer I dated a college student."

Kade gulped. "But you're only fourteen, aren't you?"

"I'm almost fifteen. Besides, I'm very mature for my age."

"Some people I know don't actually start dating until they're sixteen."

"Why would anyone want to wait that long?" she asked.

"I'm just telling you what some people do, that's all."

"If you can't drive, I guess I could meet you at the dance. What do you want to do after the dance?"

"I don't know. Go home, I guess."

"I know where there's a party we can go to. Are you a party animal?" she asked.

"Well, sure, I guess so. I've been to parties."

"I'm talking about parties where everyone gets wasted."

"Wasted?" His voice cracked as he said it.

"One time I was so out of it that when I woke up the next morning I couldn't remember where I was or anything that happened the night before. Has that ever happened to you?"

There was a long silence. "No, but sometimes I can't remember where I put things."

"Kade, tell me the truth, have you ever got drunk?"

"Well, no, not actually."

"Have you ever even tried it?"

"No."

"Why not?"

"I just never wanted to."

"You ought to try it at least once. How can you be sure you don't like it unless you try it?"

It didn't seem fair. This was his one chance to go with the best-looking girl his age in school. He had purposely avoided mentioning the Church just so she'd accept him, but it wasn't working out the way he wanted.

"You want me to help you get started, Kade?" she asked.

This was a big decision—he was afraid it would cost him Whitney's friendship. He sighed. "I guess not. Thanks anyway, though."

"How come you won't even try it?"

There was no escaping. "The reason I don't drink is because that's what my church teaches."

There was a long pause. "You belong to a church?"

"Yeah."

"And you go to church every Sunday?"

"Yeah."

"Gosh, Kade, that's nice and all, but the thing is, I guess I'm looking for a guy who's more of a real man."

To Kade this was the ultimate insult.

"I think we'd better hang up," she said. "My mom needs to use the phone."

"Are we still going together?" he asked.

"I don't think so. Look, I'll see you around, okay?"

"Yeah, okay. 'Bye." Kade hung up the phone and came out of the bathroom.

"Kade," his mother called, "be sure and put your dirty clothes in the hamper tonight before you go to bed."

"I wish everyone would quit treating me like a little kid," he grumbled before stomping up the stairs to his room.

"What does a guy have to do to become a real man?" Kade asked Brenda when she picked him up the next morning.

"How should I know? Ask your dad."

"He'd tell me not to worry about it."

"Why are you worrying about it?"

"Whitney broke up with me last night."

"I didn't know you were even going with her."

"We were for about three minutes. Then she broke up because she said I wasn't man enough for her."

"Kade, you're fourteen, right? You're not supposed to be a man at fourteen."

"I just wish people would quit treating me like a little kid."

"The fact is, to someone my age, you *are* a little kid. There's probably nothing you can do about it. Look, if you want to know the truth, being sixteen is no picnic either." She paused. "I don't have any real close friends in school."

"What about Melissa?"

"She's okay, I guess, but she and I are a lot different. And sometimes she really gets on my nerves." She sighed. "Most everybody my age parties every weekend."

"Whitney wanted me to go drinking with her but I said no. That's why she broke up with me."

"Drinking is a dumb thing to do."

"I know, but still, I wish I hadn't lost her."

She shrugged. "That's life." And with that she turned on the radio.

"Why do we always have to listen to cowboy songs?" he complained.

"Simple—because it's my rig."

At eleven o'clock Kade reported to Coach Brannigan. "The way I figure it," the coach said, "you've got two hours of detention coming for what you did yesterday. You can either sit in a chair or you can make yourself useful. What'll it be?"

"I'd rather do something than just sit around."

The coach led him into a room containing a large washing machine and a clothes dryer—and a huge stack of dirty uniforms. He told Kade exactly what to do. "You got that?"

"I think so."

"Good. I've got a class now, but I'll come back when I can to see how you're doing."

"Who usually does this?" Kade asked.

"We had a student equipment manager, but last week he up and quit on me. I guess it wasn't glamorous enough for him. I've been doing it myself until I can find someone else to help out."

"You shouldn't have to do this."

"Tell me about it." With that, the coach left.

Kade enjoyed the challenge of doing the laundry exactly the way the coach had told him. He separated everything into three piles, each waiting its turn to be thrown into the washing machine.

He was sitting at the folding table reading a magazine for high school coaches when Marvin walked in the room. "How's it going?" he said.

Kade was wary, even though Marvin seemed friendly. "Okay."

"Looks like the coach put you to work, huh?"

"Yeah."

"I just talked to him. He told me to come in here and help out."

"There's not much to do right now."

"Is it all right if I stick around?" Marvin asked.

"I guess so."

"You're kind of a spunky kid, aren't you."

"Not usually."

"You were yesterday, that's for sure."

"I don't like to be pushed around."

"I understand. Hey, I was way out of line. My dad got really mad when he found out what I'd been doing. He said I could've done some permanent damage to you." He paused. "I didn't, did I?"

"No."

"Good. He said I had to come and apologize."

"Oh."

It was an awkward moment. They stared at each other. "Well, I guess that's taken care of," Marvin said.

"I guess so."

"How come you don't mind washing our sweaty outfits?"

Kade shrugged. "It's no big deal."

"Maybe you should become the equipment manager."

"What would I have to do?"

"Well, keep up with the wash. And during a game you'd be in charge of giving players water and making sure the first-aid kit is on the field. That's about it. Why don't you talk to the coach about it?"

"Maybe I will."

"Tell me something," Marvin said. "Is it hard moving to a new town?"

"Yeah, it kinda is."

"My dad says if things don't get better, we'll have to move to where he can make a decent living. I'd hate to leave here though. Look, I'm sorry for giving you a hard time. I'll say one thing for you, you've got a lot of nerve for someone so small."

"I'm not small. I looked it up in a book. I'm average for my age." He paused. "Maybe you're just extra big. You ever think about that?"

"I'm older than most guys in the ninth grade. I was held back a year."

"Oh."

"Not because I'm dumb though. I just got sick, that's all."

"Why did you decide to pick on me?"

"I don't know. You just looked like someone it'd be fun to pick on."

"Was it because of my glasses?"

"I don't think so. Why?"

"I hate 'em. As soon as I can, I'm going to get me a pair of contacts."

"I've got a cousin who wears contacts. She likes them a lot. She got 'em in Great Falls. Got a really good buy, too. I'll see if I can get the name of the place."

"That'd be good. I'm not ready to get 'em right now because I still have to save up a little more money. My parents won't help me out any. They say I look good enough with glasses. I don't care though. I'm getting 'em anyway."

"How come you want contacts? To impress the girls?" Marvin teased.

"Not really."

"I bet that's the reason, all right."

"No way."

"Have you ever gone with a girl?"

"No."

"You didn't have one in Illinois?"

"No."

"Have you got yourself one picked out here yet?"

"I thought I'd just play the field for a while."

Marvin laughed. "That means you can't find anyone either, right?"

"Right."

"Me neither." He looked at the clock. "Well, I guess I should go."

"Yeah, sure. See you in gym class."

"Don't worry about being hassled anymore. And if anyone ever gives you a hard time, just let me know, okay?"

"Yeah, thanks."

"No problem. Well, see you around." Marvin left.

The washing machine stopped, and Kade made the transfer of clothes into the dryer. He picked up the next pile and dumped it into the washing machine, then started both machines and sat down.

The coach came in. "Looks like you're doing a real fine job."

To receive praise from the coach made Kade feel good. "If you want, I can help out all the time."

"You mean be my equipment manager?"

"Yeah." He paused. "There's just one problem—would I have to stay after school?"

"Well, we could use you after school, but I know you've got to catch your ride home. I think we can pretty much take care of things during the practices if you can keep caught up on the laundry, and, of course, we'd need you for the games. Most of 'em are on Friday night."

"That's no problem. I could come every day during this period and wash the things from the night before."

"That'd be great. There's funguses that grow in sweaty clothes that can make an athlete's life miserable. So what you'll be doing to keep things clean is very important to the team."

"I'd like to do it."

"Well, how about that? You've made my day, I'll tell

you." He looked at the clock on the wall. "I guess I'd better get to my next class."

As Kade worked, he realized he was whistling one of the cowboy songs he'd heard that morning in Brenda's pickup.

After school Kade could hardly wait to tell Brenda. "Guess what? I'm going to be helping out the football team."

"You mean you're on the team?"

"Not exactly. I'm going to be the equipment manager."

"What does the equipment manager do?"

Kade hesitated. "He takes care of the equipment."

"Yeah, sure, but what exactly do you do?"

He paused. "I wash towels and dirty uniforms." He watched for her reaction. He hoped she wouldn't make fun of him.

"Oh," she said. "Well, that's nice, Kade."

"It's also important. The coach told me that if they don't have clean uniforms, they could get this really bad fungus. If they got that, it'd be pretty bad. They'd all be standing around scratching themselves instead of concentrating on the game."

"That'd be awful, not only for the team but also for the people who come to watch. What else does an equipment manager do?"

"I'm responsible for the first-aid kit."

"That's important."

"And I make sure they get water if they're thirsty."

"I'll bet they appreciate that. I know I would if I were a football player."

"So in a way, it's like I'm helping them win. And I get to stand around on the sidelines during a game. I think they might even let me buy a team jacket. And another thing, I'll get to know all the players. So if you or any of your friends ever want me to put in a good word to one of them, just let me know."

She smiled. "I can see you're an important guy to know."

That night after supper Kade told his parents.

"It sounds to me like just an excuse to get you to do their dirty work," his mother said.

"Not at all," his father said. "Every football team has to have people who can help. I think it'll be good for Kade. He'll be helping the team out, and he'll make new friends. Kade, if that's what you want to do, then I'd say go for it."

And so Kade became the new equipment manager for the team.

CHAPTER 2

The next day at work Paul Ellis got a phone call from Dwight Allen, a corporate vice-president of the bank in Chicago. Dwight had been the one who had asked Paul to move to Montana to run the Shelby bank.

"Paul, I was thinking about you this morning. How are things going out there in the Wild West?"

"Not too bad."

"How's Denise doing?"

"She's missed being in the symphony this year, but other than that, I'd say she's adjusting to life in a small town."

"Paul, look, something's come up that I need to talk to you about. When we first talked about you going to Montana, I mentioned we didn't anticipate that this'd be a long assignment. We've had our eyes on you for some time, and we've just been waiting for the time when we can put you in place as one of our regional managers. But with this farm crisis and the problems the manager you replaced created for us, we needed someone with your objectivity who could go in and set things right."

25

"I'm working on it."

"I'm sure you are. My main reason for calling is that an opening has come up a little sooner than we anticipated. One of our regional managers had a heart attack last night. To be honest, we don't think he's going to make it, and even if he does, I doubt he'll be able to return to work. So if you can wrap up what you've got to do in, say, about a month, then we could move you into our Indiana region. It would be a very good career move for you."

Paul was pleased. "Sounds good."

"Great. Of course, we'd like you to clear up things there in Shelby first."

"To tell you the truth, I don't enjoy very much being the bank's hatchet man."

"Nobody does, but sometimes it has to be done. So finish up so we can get you out of there soon. From what I've heard, you don't want to be there in the winter."

On Friday night Shelby High School had a home game. Kade stayed after school to prepare everything. His parents dutifully came to watch him perform as equipment manager.

One of the players loaned him a letter jacket so he'd look the part. It was too big for him, but he liked the way it made him feel to wear it.

When the players came off the field, he made sure there were towels to wipe the sweat off their faces and cups of water if they wanted some.

They lost 14 to 6, but Kade took consolation in the fact that the team, at least during the first quarter, looked clean.

The Mormon church was still struggling for survival in that part of Montana. There was a small branch in Shelby, which was part of the Great Falls Stake. The

stake center was nearly a hundred miles away. Each
Sunday Kade and his family went to church at the Odd
Fellows Hall on Main Street, above the hardware store.
They could usually count on about twenty people mak-
ing it out to church on Sunday.

The branch had been in existence for five years, and
for all that time the branch president had been Otis
Cummings. On Saturday night President Mathesen, the
stake president, phoned to ask Paul to meet him the
next morning before church.

On Sunday President Mathesen asked Paul to serve
as the next branch president. Paul said he wasn't sure
how much longer he'd be in the area, but President
Mathesen asked him to take the assignment for however
long it was. Paul accepted the calling, and they talked
about possible counselors. The list of candidates was not
long. Brother Arnold, who had been the branch clerk
since the branch was organized, said that was job
enough for any man, and he didn't want anything else
to do. Brother Aldrich, who was in his late sixties and
had a hearing loss, refused any church callings that required talking to people. Sister Simmons's husband was
not a member, and Brenda's father, although a member,
seldom attended.

"Someone may turn up later," President Mathesen
said.

After church Paul was set apart.

Kade soon learned what it meant to have his father
serving as branch president. It meant the family went
to church early, gathered up smelly ashtrays and empty
beer bottles left there from the night before, opened the
windows to air out the place, and set up folding chairs.
Kade was the only active Aaronic Priesthood holder in
the branch, so he set up and passed the sacrament every
week.

After church Kade helped put the chairs back again.
Then he and his mother usually went home while his

dad and Brother Arnold counted donations and made out a deposit slip.

Paul's main goal as branch president was to find a replacement for himself when he left. He visited almost every family that first week and tried to encourage everyone to start coming out to church. He often wondered what would happen to the branch after he left. It appeared there was nobody else who could step in as branch president.

Once a month the early-morning seminary students from the small branches and wards in the stake met for a Super Saturday, which consisted of a seminary lesson taught by the seminary coordinator for the region, followed by an activity.

The first Super Saturday for the school year was held the next Saturday. Kade and Brenda rode to the stake center with Sister Simmons and Melissa. Brenda and Melissa sat in back and for the most part carried on their own private conversation, leaving Sister Simmons and Kade trying to think of what to say to each other.

"Kade, what's exciting in your life these days?" Sister Simmons asked.

"I'm the equipment manager for the football team."

"That's wonderful."

"It sounds wonderful until you find out what he does," Melissa said. "He washes the team's sweats. Big deal."

"I'll be able to get a letter jacket out of it."

Melissa giggled. "So when someone asks you what you lettered in, what are you going to tell them? Laundry?"

"Melissa," her mother said.

"Sorry, but it's so funny. Gosh, Kade, I wonder if there's an Olympic laundry team."

"Knock it off."

"Sorry. Gee whiz, you don't have to be so sensitive about everything."

A while later Sister Simmons asked what hobbies he had.

It was the first time he'd ever admitted it. "I like to draw."

"Are you taking an art class in school?"

"No."

"Do you draw very much?"

"Almost every day."

"What do you draw?"

Kade didn't want anyone to know that most of the pictures he drew were of Brenda. "Nothing much."

Brenda leaned forward. "I didn't know you liked art."

"I just got started in it."

"Sometime let me see what you've done," Brenda said.

"I'd like to see it too, Kade," Sister Simmons said.

"Sometime maybe."

"How about tomorrow after church?" Brenda asked.

"No. I don't want to show it to anyone yet."

"Well think about it, and when you're ready to let us see it, just let us know. Now there's donuts in a bag in the back seat, Melissa, if you want to get them out and pass them around. Oh, and there's orange juice too."

It took them two hours to get into the stake center in Great Falls, but it was worth it. For Kade it was fun to be with a large group of members his age. In Shelby the Church was so small that it was easy to believe he was the only guy in the world who didn't drink. That was all anyone in school talked about. Sometimes he felt as if he'd never fit in, no matter how hard he tried.

He met Linda Cooper, a girl his age, when they played volleyball in the gym after the lesson. She had short blond hair and a nice smile, and she liked to talk a lot, which was good for Kade because it put less pressure on him.

He also met lots of boys at Super Saturday. It was a comfort for him to be with them—some strong, some tall, some funny, some chubby, but all trying to live the way they'd been taught.

While he was playing volleyball, Kade saw Brenda walk out of the cultural hall with Jason Pasco. He wondered what that was all about.

After the activity, on their way out of town, Sister Simmons stopped at McDonald's. They went through the drive-through and ordered an early supper. It was her treat.

"Well, how was it today?" Sister Simmons asked as they cruised down I-15 for home.

"Brenda did okay for herself," Melissa teased. "She met Jason Pasco. *Oo la la!* Big time romance, hey, Brenda?"

"He's okay."

"Your mouth says okay but your eyes say wow," Melissa teased.

Brenda fought back a smile. "We just talked, that's all. It's no big deal."

"I saw the two of you standing in the hall, drooling over each other."

"Is Jason new?" Sister Simmons asked.

"Yes," Brenda said. "His family moved to Great Falls during the summer. His dad is the new superintendent of schools."

"What year is he in school?" Sister Simmons asked.

"He's a senior."

"What's he going to do after he graduates?"

"Marry Brenda," Melissa teased.

"He's going to work for a year and then go on a mission." Brenda paused. "He has a girl in the town where he came from. He's still interested in her."

"That won't last long, not with Brenda on the prowl."

"Melissa, I'm sure Brenda doesn't appreciate you talking like that," Sister Simmons said.

"All right, let's turn our attention to Kade then," Melissa said. "What a mover with the girls he's turned out to be."

"What are you talking about?" Kade said.

"Don't give me that. I saw you playing up to Linda Cooper."

"We were on the same team in volleyball. I was just talking strategy with her."

"I saw strategy out there all right, but it didn't have anything to do with volleyball. Did you know your voice dropped about an octave around her? And I noticed you took off your glasses. What for? So she could see your eyes? And that one time she got hit by the ball, there you were, giving her the big sympathy treatment. The way you were fussing over her, you'd think she'd been run over by a truck."

Surprisingly, Brenda took over where Melissa left off. "Look out, girls, 'cause Kade's hit town. And with his dark eyes and brown hair and sheepish grin, no heart is safe."

Kade denied Brenda's description of him, but he secretly wished it were true. It also made him wonder what it would be like if he and Brenda were the same age.

On the second Saturday in October the stake scheduled the first of a series of monthly stake youth dances in Great Falls. At first Sister Simmons was going to take the kids from Shelby in her car, but the night before she called to say she'd come down with a bad cold and wouldn't be able to go. And so it looked impossible for Kade and Brenda to go until Saturday afternoon, when

Brenda phoned and said she'd gotten permission to
drive to the dance. If Kade was willing to share in the
cost of the gas, he could go along with her. He quickly
agreed.

Because of long travel from the outlying branches,
the dance was scheduled to begin at seven and end at
eleven. Brenda picked Kade up at five. She was wearing
a dress. It was the only time he'd seen her in a dress
except for Sundays. "You look nice," he said.

"I feel a little foolish, if you want to know the truth.
Going to all this trouble for most likely nothing."

"You smell good too."

"My mom let me use some of her perfume. She's
had it a long time but doesn't use it much anymore."
She looked at Kade. "You look good too."

"It's no big deal."

"The weather report says it might snow tonight, so
we'll have to be careful. This rig doesn't have much
traction in the snow unless you put some weight in the
back end, but then the gas mileage goes way down, so
we try to hold off doing that until we absolutely have
to. Money's real tight in our family this winter."

"How come?"

"Grasshoppers got a lot of our crop last year. You
don't pay attention to things like that, do you?"

"Why should I? I'm not a farmer."

Thirty miles from Great Falls it started to snow and
the wind picked up. It was a relief when they finally
pulled into the parking lot at the stake center. They
walked into the building together.

"I'm going to fix myself up before I go in," she said,
"so I'll see you in there."

Kade wandered into the cultural hall and looked
around. He walked over to one of the guys from town.
"Where's Jason?"

"I don't know. He hasn't shown up. See that girl
over there? That's his sister. Go ask her."

He walked up to her. "Where's Jason?"

"At home."

"Phone him and tell him he's got to come to the church. Brenda Sloan came all the way from Shelby just to see him."

"He can't come. He's got the flu."

"But we came all the way down here to see him."

"Look, I'm not making this up, you know. He's been throwing up all day. He can't even keep ginger ale down."

Kade saw Linda Cooper dancing with another guy. She looked over at Kade and smiled. He nodded back.

Brenda came in the gym. Kade went over to talk to her. "I asked around," he said. "Jason's got the flu."

She tried not to show her disappointment. "It's no big deal."

"Don't give me that. We came all the way down here for you to be with him. The least he could have done was called and told you he was sick."

"It's not his fault. He didn't know I was coming." She looked around. "Well, it's not a complete loss. I see Linda's here. Go dance with her."

"She's already dancing with someone."

"Wait until she isn't and then go ask her."

"What will you do?"

"Don't worry about me. I'll be okay."

Kade went over and asked Linda to dance.

"You came down from Shelby in a snowstorm?" she asked while they danced.

Kade tried to sound macho. "I'm not afraid of a little snow."

"Did Brenda drive?"

"Yeah."

"Why do you keep looking back at her?"

"I want somebody to ask her to dance, that's all. We came all this way so she could dance with Jason Pasco, but he had to ruin everything by getting the flu."

"You like Brenda?"

He didn't know what to say.

"Kade, you're blushing."

"No I'm not."

"Yes you are. Go look in a mirror if you don't believe me. Your face is a bright red."

"That doesn't mean I'm blushing."

"What else could it mean?"

"I just came in from the cold, that's all."

"It happened when I asked if you liked Brenda."

"You don't know anything, Linda, not anything at all."

"I don't see why you're so sensitive about this."

A couple dancing next to them horned in. "What are you two arguing about?" the guy asked.

"I think Kade here has a crush on Brenda Sloan."

"Brenda?" the girl said. "You're kidding. She's a junior, isn't she?" The girl turned to Kade. "What are you?"

"Kade's in the ninth grade, like me," Linda said.

The guy smirked. "Well hey, if you can't get her to go out with you, maybe you can pay her to be your babysitter."

Kade walked off the dance floor and went over to Brenda. "Let's get out of here."

"What's wrong?"

"I just want to get out of here, that's all."

"What about Linda?"

"Forget her. Let's leave this stupid dance."

She thought about it. "Actually, that might not be a bad idea. It's really starting to come down. We'll be better off if we start back before it gets much worse. I brought some other clothes. How about if I go change? You can move the pickup closer to the door if you want. I'll be out in a minute."

"I don't know how to drive, remember?" Kade grumbled. "I'm just the little kid you haul around."

"What's got into you anyway?"

"Go change, will you? I just want to get out of this place."

While he waited for Brenda to finish changing, Linda came over to see him. "Kade, I'm sorry for what happened."

"You and your friends had no right to make fun of me."

"I know that. I'm really sorry. I'll treat you better next time you come to town, okay?"

"Okay."

A minute later Brenda showed up wearing jeans and a Shelby Coyotes sweatshirt. After brushing snow off the windshield, they were on their way again.

Soon they found themselves in the middle of a major winter storm. Snow completely blanketed the road. An hour out of Great Falls, Brenda pulled over and stopped. "We're going to have to get out and put on chains," she said.

"I don't know how."

"I'll show you."

He felt useless. "How come you know everything?"

"Because I'm older." She reached under the seat and pulled out a flashlight. "I need you to come hold the flashlight so I can see what I'm doing. You'd better bundle up. That wind's pretty bad. If it gets too cold, we'll come in and warm up."

Outside, as the storm raged around them, they got into the back of the pickup. He shined the flashlight into the tool compartment while she rummaged around looking for the chains. Her hair was blowing wildly in the wind. The image became imbedded in his mind, and he felt himself slipping into his private world. He knew he would draw a picture of this someday. She found the chains and began pulling them out of the tool compartment. To his vivid imagination they were not chains but the cold brains of a dead metallic monster. She dropped the chains on the ground beside each rear tire.

"Let's go warm up," she yelled above the wind.

They climbed back into the pickup. While they warmed up, he turned on the flashlight so he could see her face more clearly. Her cheeks were flushed, her hair still windblown. The way she looked fascinated him.

"Kade, don't waste the batteries, okay?" she said.

He turned off the flashlight and tried to come back to the real world.

A short time later they went outside. She laid out each chain in the snow just behind the rear tires.

"I need you to start the pickup and back up until I tell you to stop!" she yelled above the roar of the wind.

"I don't know how to drive!" he yelled back.

"This is ridiculous. The next chance I get, I'm teaching you how to drive. All right, I'll go do it. Yell when it rolls this far, okay?"

Okay."

While he waited, he huddled close to the pickup. She started up the motor, and the pickup started rolling back slowly. "Okay!" he shouted.

She got out and knelt down to finish hooking up the chains on the tire. From out of nowhere a large semitruck roared past, scattering in its wake a fury of swirling snow. In an instant it was gone, swallowed up by the thick snow.

"Let's warm up before we do the other tire," she called out.

They climbed in again.

"I'm no good at anything," he said.

She looked over at him. "Hey, it's okay. I had an advantage growing up on a farm. Stick with me, and I'll teach you all I know."

"Thanks for putting up with me."

"No problem. You're a good little guy, Kade."

He wished she hadn't called him little.

A short time later they managed to get the chains on the other tire and then they started off again. They had to go slow because the visibility was so poor. At times they had a difficult time even knowing where the road was.

"This wind is blowing us all over the place," she said. "We need some weight in the back end." She thought about it. "We haven't passed Dutton yet, have we?"

"How should I know? I can't see anything. Why do you want to know?"

"On the way down I noticed the state highway department had a gravel pile next to the road just north of Dutton. We could borrow some and put it in the back end. That'd give us a lot better traction. Of course, we could use snow, but gravel is heavier, and that pile should be close enough to us when we pass by. Keep your eyes peeled for Dutton, okay?"

Half an hour later he saw the sign.

"Okay, it's not much further," she said.

Because he wasn't sure exactly what he was looking for, she spotted it before he did. She slowed down and parked, leaving her lights on in case a car happened to come upon them.

"C'mon, I've got two shovels in the back."

"Isn't this stealing?" Kade asked.

"Look, if we don't get some weight in the rear end, we may not be alive by the time the storm's over. I think the highway department'll understand. C'mon, Mr. Purity of Conscience, let's go to work. You've got to do your share of the work on this job. Don't go telling me you don't know how to use a shovel either."

Because of the bitter winds they had to stop three times to warm up. Finally she said they'd hauled enough, so they threw the shovels in the back and took off again. "This is a lot better," she said.

The storm continued to rage. The drifts in some

places got up to a foot deep. They'd hit the big drifts and slow down, then finally break free again.

"What if we get stuck?" Kade asked.

"Then we dig ourselves out."

"What if it's too deep to dig out?"

"Then we wait until morning, when a snowplow'll come. Whatever happens, there's always a way."

"I wish I were more like you," he said.

She shrugged. "Don't be so hard on yourself. Give yourself some time. I'll teach you all I know, so don't worry about it, okay? You're going to be quite the guy when you grow up."

That made Kade feel better.

Paul and Denise Ellis looked outside at the raging storm. It was snowing so hard they could hardly see the yard light near the barn. And the wind! Paul had never seen a wind like this one tonight, so wild and full of vengeance. He turned to her. "I'll phone the stake center and tell Brenda and Kade to stay in Great Falls at a member's home until the morning."

"That sounds like a good idea."

Nobody answered at the church. Paul called the stake Young Women's president and found out that because of the weather, the leaders had closed the dance and sent everyone home. Those from out of town had gone to members' homes for the night. The Young Women's president called around town for half an hour before she finally found out from Linda Cooper that Brenda and Kade had left for home not long after the dance started. She called Paul and told him.

Paul took the message, then hung up and told Denise.

"So they're out on the road?" she said.

"I guess so."

"We never should have let them go," Denise said.

"I'll call Brenda's parents and see what they say."

Emmet Sloan didn't seem worried. "Brenda knows how to survive in bad weather," he said. "She'll do the right thing. Tell you what, though—I've got a friend who works for the highway department. I'll give him a call and see what he can find out, and then I'll get back to you."

Paul hung up. "He's going to call the highway department and see what he can find out."

"What do you think about Emmet?" she asked.

"He seems okay."

"Since you've been branch president, you've visited most of the families in the branch, but you haven't visited him, have you?"

"No, not yet."

"Why haven't you visited him?"

No answer.

"Is it because he's one of the farmers in trouble with the bank?"

"I can't talk about that."

"I know you can't. I like Susan a lot. She's tried to help me get used to living here. And I think Brenda is good for Kade, even though they are so far apart in age. Emmet is a hard worker, too. They just don't seem like people who should be in financial trouble."

"I really don't want to talk about this."

They waited twenty minutes. Paul was about to phone again when they heard a vehicle pull up into their driveway and stop. Paul went to the door and opened it. Emmet Sloan was stomping his feet on the steps to shake off the snow from his boots and pants. "Think it'll snow?"

They went into the kitchen. "Let me tell you what I found out," Emmet said. "They say the worst of it is just outside of Great Falls. They just closed the road north of Great Falls, but the road crews out of Shelby and Conrad are still working, so there's a good chance

Brenda and Kade will make it through all right. Best thing for us to do is to just stay put and wait."

The pickup was the only vehicle on the road, and their world extended only as far as the headlights reached in the thick, swirling snowstorm. Kade felt abandoned and alone, but also he felt tired. He tried to stay awake but finally fell asleep.

When he woke up, he looked over at Brenda. "I'm sorry I fell asleep," he said.

"Don't worry about it. Hey, guess what, it's getting better. I think there must be a snowplow ahead of us."

A few minutes later they came up behind a snow-plow.

"All right!" Brenda exclaimed. "All we've got to do is follow this guy into Shelby. It might be slow, but at least it'll be safe."

They both relaxed. "I'll bet this is more than you bargained for," she said.

"That's for sure."

"Well, we did it. Looks like you're becoming my number one sidekick these days, right?"

"I guess so."

"Do you know what time it is?" she asked.

"No."

"It's after midnight. I'll bet our folks are getting worried."

"I suppose."

"Well, it's almost over. We'll be home before long."

The pressure was off, so they could talk about other things. "You never told me what happened between you and Linda at the dance," she said. "You were talking with her, and then all of a sudden you just walked off and left her standing there. How come?"

"No reason."

"C'mon, Kade, level with me."

He paused. "She and some of her friends were saying I had a crush on you."

"I hope you set 'em right."

"I did."

"Good."

He paused. "I've been thinking about it, though. In a way I guess it might be true."

"It might?"

"A little. But don't worry. I know I'm too young for you."

"That's right, you are."

"There's something I need to tell you, though."

"What?"

"I really like to look at you." He hesitated. "You're very beautiful. In fact, to me you're the most beautiful girl in the world."

She seemed worried. "Kade," she began.

"Don't worry. It's not like I'm in love with you or anything like that. I know I'm too young for you. It's just that I like to look at you. Every day after school I draw a picture of you. I've kept about ten. I just thought you should know."

"Can I see them?"

"I've never shown them to anyone. To tell the truth, I'm kind of embarrassed about all this."

"Why?"

"Sometimes I think there's something wrong with me. I can't seem to stop drawing your face." He cleared his throat. "And I imagine things . . . like one time I drew you as a princess escaping some danger. It was late at night and you were hurrying down a narrow street in England—I guess in the olden times—and you had a veil over your head so nobody would know it was you." He paused. "It sounds like I'm crazy, doesn't it? I don't know what's wrong with me. Sometimes I wish I were more like other people. One thing for sure, I'm not much like the guys on the football team."

"Do you want to be like them?"

"Not really. They're kind of foul-mouthed sometimes. So if they're the way a guy is supposed to be,
then there's something wrong with me."

"Don't worry about it. You're ten times better than
those guys. I'd rather spend time with you than with
any of them."

"No kidding?"

"Absolutely."

"And you're not mad at me for drawing your picture?"

"No, of course not."

"Can I ask another question?"

"Sure."

"Are we friends now?" he asked.

"Yeah, I guess we are. That's kind of a surprise in
a way, isn't it? I mean, let's face it, you're only a ninth
grader. But even so, yeah, I'd say we were friends."

Kade felt terrific.

Paul was amazed at how much confidence Emmet
had in Brenda that he could sit there and drink hot
chocolate and talk about things other than the storm.

"I should've brought Susan over here with me, but
she thought she should stay at home in case Brenda
phoned. But since we're neighbors, let's get together
sometime."

"Sounds like a good idea," Denise said.

"Great, we'll do it then. Paul, let me ask you a question. You don't look like a man who would have chosen
Shelby as a place to work. In fact, neither of you strikes
me as a rural type."

"That's right, we're not," Paul said.

"You never knew Clayton Jones, did you?" Emmet
asked. "He was the bank manager before you came."

"No, can't say I did."

"Clayton fit in real good around here. My, but that man loved to loan money. He'd come out every spring and look around the place and make some suggestions of what improvements he thought we should make. We'd say, 'But Clayton, we don't have the money.' And Clayton'd say, 'Hey, no problem. All I've got is time and money.' And so he'd talk us into one thing or another. And then all of a sudden, the bottom dropped out of the farm economy. Clayton retired and moved away, and then you showed up. We were talking about you the other day, Paul. A few of us get together at Pat's Diner some mornings in the winter. Well, we got to talking about the fact that all you do is sit in your office and stare at your computer. We wonder what it is you're doing here in Shelby. We noticed you haven't bought a home yet. Kind of curious, isn't it?"

Paul felt his face getting red. "I didn't think anybody noticed me."

"That's one thing about living in a small town—people notice what you do. As far as any of us can tell, you haven't gone out of your way to make friends with any of us. It makes us wonder what you're up to. I guess we're all a little edgy these days, what with the price of land dropping so low. So when our banker won't talk to us, we get worried. Paul, why don't you get away from your desk one of these days and get to know us a little better."

"That's good advice. I'll do it."

"Good."

"Now can I give you some advice?" Paul asked.

"I suppose."

"We could use you in church on Sundays."

"One of these days when I'm not so busy."

The phone rang. Paul answered. "Emmet, it's for you."

Emmet talked for a while, then hung up. "Good news."

"What?"

"The man running the snowplow south of here radioed in to say Brenda's pickup is following him into town. They should be here in another hour."

"Thank heavens," Denise said.

"When they get to town, he's going to let him stay at his place until morning because the county road out this way hasn't been plowed yet."

Just before they got to town, Brenda asked, "When are you going to let me see the drawings you did of me?"

"There's one thing you gotta understand. My parents don't know about the drawings. I don't want 'em to know either."

"I promise I won't tell anyone about the drawings."

"All right. I'll show them to you whenever you want."

"Thanks."

He didn't want to talk about the drawings anymore. "Turn on the radio," he said. "Let's hear some cowboy music."

"It's growing on you, isn't it," she teased.

"Maybe."

"It is, I can tell. We're going to make a mountain man out of you yet, Kade. You just see if we don't."

"I guess I wouldn't mind that."

"We had ourselves a pretty wild time tonight, didn't we?" she said.

"That's for sure," he said.

As they pulled into Shelby, the operator of the snowplow stopped in the middle of the road and flagged them down. "Brenda?" he asked as she rolled down her window.

"Hi, Mr. Gallagher. So you're the one we've been following all this time, huh?"

"That's right. Say, your dad phoned our dispatcher asking about you, so when I saw your pickup come up behind me, I radioed ahead to let your folks know you were okay. You two'll have to stay the night with my family because the county road isn't plowed yet. Follow me. It's not far."

A few minutes later Brenda and Kade gratefully slipped into sleeping bags in the living room of a small house, Brenda on the couch and Kade on the floor nearby.

Mr. Gallagher went to explain to his wife what was happening. Then he bundled up and left to go back to work.

"Well, pardner, looks like we made it," Brenda said in the dark.

"Yeah, looks like it. Thanks to you." He paused. "Brenda, I've never known anyone like you before."

"My dad says there aren't any more like me. He says they broke the mold after they did me."

"He's right about that."

"I was just joking," she said. "I'm nothing special."

"Don't say that. I didn't even know girls like you existed. You can do just about anything you set your mind to, and you live the way you're supposed to, and you're really good looking." He paused. "If you only knew how you look in the morning when the sun first shines on your face . . . "

She felt uncomfortable hearing him talk like that. "Kade, it's late. We really need to go to sleep now, okay?"

"Okay."

A few minutes later they were both asleep.

By morning there was blue sky and sunshine. The sun reflecting off the snow was so bright it was hard to see.

Mrs. Gallagher made pancakes for her three children and two unexpected guests. Afterwards Kade and Brenda phoned home. Kade's father told him they had cancelled church because of the roads. When Brenda talked to Emmet, he said he would call her back as soon as the county road was plowed.

The morning passed slowly. Kade and Brenda offered to wash the dishes, but Mrs. Gallagher said no. Kade found a pad of paper and drew a picture of each of the children and gave it to them as a present. The youngest girl brought her doll to him and asked him to draw it too. He was just finishing the picture when Emmet called to say the county road had been plowed. Kade and Brenda thanked Mrs. Gallagher, said goodbye, and then left for home.

"You did a good job drawing those pictures," Brenda said.

"Thanks."

"It makes me want to see the ones you've done of me. When can I?"

"We have to be someplace where we can be alone," he said.

"You could come over to my place this afternoon. I'll tell my mom I'm helping you with your homework, and we could go into my mom's sewing room and look at them there. How about if I pick you up around three?"

"Okay. I could bring my books along to make it look like you really are helping me in school."

"Good idea."

A little before three that afternoon he went to the living room, where his mother was practicing the violin. His dad was somewhere doing church work. "I'm going over to Brenda's. We're going to study."

"You and Brenda?" his mother asked.

"What's wrong with that?"

"I would think she'd want to find someone her own age to study with, that's all."

That made Kade mad, but he knew if he made a big fuss she might not let him go at all. "It's just for one assignment."

"All right then."

He went to his closet and pulled down the Monopoly box and put it in his book bag and covered it with a sweatshirt. When Brenda honked for him, he hurried down the stairs, yelled goodbye, then ran through the snow to her pickup.

A few minutes later they entered Brenda's house. "Mom, Kade's here," she called out.

They went into the kitchen, where Brenda's mother was just taking a sheet of chocolate chip cookies out of the oven.

"Kade, you're just in time," she said. "As soon as they cool, I'll have some for you and Brenda."

"Thanks a lot."

Brenda glanced at Kade. "Well, I guess we'd better get started."

They went in the sewing room and Brenda closed the door. "Whenever you're ready."

They sat down. He handed her the Monopoly box. She opened it and took each drawing from the box and looked at it. When she finished, she glanced up at him. "Kade, they're really good. I just wish I was like the girl in these drawings."

He noticed that her eyes were brimming with tears. "You're the most beautiful girl in the world, Brenda. Gosh, don't you know that yet?"

She looked again at one of the drawings. "I think you must be some kind of artistic genius."

"No, not me."

"I'm serious. We need to show these to somebody, a professional artist or a teacher or somebody like that."

"No."

"Why not?"

He thought about what members of the football team might say if they knew about the drawings. "I just don't want anyone to know, that's all."

"All right, if that's the way you feel."

"I'd better go home now."

"Before you go, please have some cookies. My mom baked 'em just for you."

"All right."

They went to the kitchen and sat around the old oak kitchen table and had cookies and milk. A pickup pulled into the place, and Brenda looked out the window. "It's my dad," she said.

Her father came inside. He was in a hurry.

"What's up?" Brenda asked.

"Some of us have decided to go hunt coyotes." He unlocked his gun cabinet and took out a rifle and a box of shells. As he turned around, he looked at the two of them and smiled. "Kind of robbing the cradle there, aren't you, Brenda?"

"I'm just helping Kade with his homework."

"You don't say. Well, I got to go. Brenda, you want to come? It'll be a lot of fun."

"I guess not."

"Doug Albers and his dad'll be there."

"I think I'll stay here with Kade."

"Suit yourself. Oh, since you'll be here anyway, you might as well get something useful done. Do me a favor and hook up the battery charger to your mom's car. When I tried to start it this morning, the battery seemed shot. It's got to last us through the winter."

"Kade and I'll get right to it."

Emmet looked at them and grinned. "A banker's son, huh? I take back what I said before. You marry this kid as soon as he makes it through puberty. We could use a banker in the family."

"Dad, don't be such a tease."

He put a box of shells in his coat pocket and tucked the gun under one arm. "Well, I'm on my way. Doug's going to be real disappointed you're not coming." He left.

"Sorry," she said to Kade. "My dad likes to kid around a lot."

"That's okay."

"Do you want to help me hook up the battery charger for the pickup?"

"I don't know how."

"I'll show you what to do."

"Okay."

They used her pickup to push her mother's car into the barn. A minute later they had the hood open. "Okay," she said, "the first thing we have to do is decide which is the hot side and which is ground."

He was puzzled. "Ground is what we're standing on."

She smiled. "It's something else when it comes to electricity."

As they worked, he asked her why she hadn't gone

with her dad when she knew Doug Albers would be there too.

"What's so special about Doug Albers?" she asked.

"He's one of the best players on the football team. He'll probably get a big football scholarship when he goes to college next year. He's got a great build, and he's good looking too. After a game there's always girls waiting around for him outside the locker room. How come you're not impressed with him?"

"Doug and I used to be friends, but we're not anymore."

They went back to the house, and she showed him several family scrapbooks, going back to when her dad was a boy living in the same house. "Our family's been on this land since the area was first opened up for homesteading in 1910," she said. "The first house burned up in 1940, so this place was built. My dad was even born in this house. After high school he joined the Navy. That's where he met my mother. She was a member of the Church living in San Diego with her parents. They weren't too happy about her going with a nonmember. She had him take the lessons, and he got baptized before they got married. After he got out of the service, they moved back here and helped out until my grandparents retired and moved away. Then my dad took over the place."

"So are you going to take over someday?" he asked.

She paused. "I'm not sure. My mom wants me to go to BYU before I decide."

She gave him a ride home a little before six o'clock. His parents had eaten without him. He went to his room and put the Monopoly box containing the drawings back on the shelf of his closet, then went downstairs.

His mother put his supper in the microwave for him. "Did you have a nice time at Brenda's?" she asked.

"Yeah, she showed me how to hook up a battery charger."

"I hope you got your schoolwork done too."

"Oh, yeah, that too." After he finished eating, he said, "I'm going up to my room to study."

"I've never seen you spend so much time alone in your room before."

"It's a hard year for me."

She gave him a strange look. "Yes, I think it must be."

After school on Monday, as soon as they turned onto the county road, Brenda pulled over and stopped. "You ready to learn how to drive? There's not much traffic here usually."

"Really?"

"Sure, no problem."

They traded places. "Okay," she said, "that's the clutch over there and the brake next to it, and that's the gas. You push that when you want to go faster."

"I know all that."

"Good. Shifting gears is the tricky part. What you have to do is shove the clutch down to the floor, put it in the gear you want, and then take the clutch out at the same time you give it more gas. Okay, now you try it."

He tried it but killed the engine.

"No problem. Try it again."

He killed it again.

After five tries, he managed to keep the engine going. They started moving slowly down the road.

"All right, Kade! You did it."

He felt terrific. He was actually driving.

"You want to put it in second now?" she asked a few seconds later.

"No, this is okay."

She paused. "But we're only going ten miles an hour. We could do a lot better in second."

"Is second going to be as hard as first?"

"No, not really."

He thought about it. "I guess I'll try then."

She put her hand over his on the gear-shift rod and helped him shift into second. Now they were going twenty miles an hour. Kade hadn't felt so excited since he was little on Christmas morning.

She helped him shift into third.

He spotted a pickup coming toward them fast. He slowed down and pulled to the right, nearly off the road.

"We're allowed half the road, Kade. Don't pull over so far. And either give it more gas or shift into second. The engine's lugging down."

Kade overdid it and pulled into the center of the road. The driver of the pickup frantically honked for them to get out of his way. They narrowly missed having a collision.

"Well, I think maybe that's enough for today," she said, relieved to still be alive.

Kade slowed down and killed the engine.

"Thanks a lot," he said.

"No problem."

After that she let him drive partway home every day. He didn't dare drive all the way because his parents didn't want him driving until he turned fifteen.

From the beginning Paul Ellis had known what needed to be done. There were certain guidelines the bank had adopted to help in its decisions. One was that when a person's outstanding loans exceeded 50 percent of his equity, he became a bad risk for the bank. It was a simple policy, not open to much interpretation.

Up until last year the country had been in an inflationary spiral. Many experts felt that it made sense to borrow during a time of inflation because you always paid back your loan with cheaper money. Besides that, the land kept increasing in value every year, so your equity continued to grow. Since it made sense to borrow, lending institutions found themselves competing with each other for loans. Clayton Jones, the man Paul replaced as bank manager, had gone out of his way to talk farmers into borrowing money for new equipment and improvements.

And then suddenly, within one year, the value of land dropped dramatically nationwide. Some farmers saw the value of their land drop to half of what it had been. This meant a farmer might find that almost overnight he had become a bad risk to his lenders. Strangely enough, it had nothing to do with his skill as a farmer.

A less thorough man than Paul might have shown up in Shelby and within a week taken steps to reduce the bank's bad loans. But Paul couldn't do that. He felt a responsibility to see what he could to help those who had been doing business with the bank for many years.

He took Emmet's suggestion and started visiting families who had large loans with the bank. He found himself impressed with these people. They were hard-working and honest and valued their families. For the most part their farms had been in the same family for generations.

One day when he got back to his office after spending the morning out talking to people, there was a message on his desk that Dwight Allen from the corporate office had called. He sat down at his desk and punched the phone number.

A minute later Dwight came on the line. "Paul, I was beginning to wonder if you'd been eaten by a bear. I haven't heard from you lately."

"Sorry. I've been visiting some of the farms in the area."

"I haven't seen much paperwork coming from your office. What's the delay?"

"It's more complicated than I thought."

"Look, Paul, you're too late for the regional manager slot in Indiana. It's already filled. Finish up there. Let's see some action from you, okay?"

"These are good, hardworking people," Paul said. "Their whole lives are in farming. It goes back from father to son for generations."

"We run a business, not a historical society. I'm worried about you. Don't let them turn you into another Clayton Jones."

"I'll do what's best for the bank, but not until I have all the facts."

"Don't take too much time, or you'll find yourself stranded in Montana for the rest of your career."

Kade enjoyed being equipment manager for the football team. He liked spending his free periods in the laundry room. It gave him a place to study as well as let him do something useful at the same time. The team accepted him. Most of them would at least nod when they saw him in the hall. The coach appreciated Kade's dependability. One time at a pep rally he introduced him as the best equipment manager the team ever had.

Sometimes Marvin Mudlin would come in the laundry room and they'd talk. One time he brought in a soccer ball used in the girls' gym classes. "Show me what you can do."

Kade put on a show, moving the ball with just his feet.

"That's good, Kade. Too bad it's worthless out here in Montana."

"Yeah, too bad."

The buzzer on the dryer went off. Kade took some things out and then sat down again. He took off his glasses. "Do you think I'll look better with contacts?"

"Sure you will."

"I hope I look older, too."

"How old you want to look?"

"I dunno. Sixteen, I guess."

"Why sixteen?"

He thought about saying how much he was beginning to like Brenda, but didn't because he was afraid it would get back to her. "No reason. I wish I could get contacts now. My parents won't help pay for 'em because they say there's nothing wrong with my glasses. I wish they'd change their minds."

"Hey, my parents don't pay for things I want," Marvin said. "I have to earn it all or go without. I figure that's part of being a man."

After that, Kade quit bothering his parents about contact lenses. He just kept saving his money.

In November Brenda asked Kade if he wanted to go deer hunting with her and Emmet on Saturday.

"I've never gone hunting before."

"It doesn't matter."

"All right, I'll go then."

The night before they left, Kade set his alarm for five o'clock. When the alarm went off, he got up immediately and took a shower. When he came out of the bathroom, his father was in the kitchen reading. "You took a shower before going hunting?" his father asked with a smile.

"Yeah, so?"

His father smiled. "Nothing."

After he got dressed, Kade sat down at the kitchen table and had breakfast.

"I've never taken you hunting before," Paul said.

"That's because you don't hunt."

"Do you wish I did?"

"Not really."

"We don't do much together like we used to, do we."

"We set up chairs for church on Sundays."

"That's true. It's just that time is going so fast. I always thought that we'd be closer at this time in your life than we are."

"Most of the things that interest you I don't care about. Like investments and loans."

"I didn't always used to be interested in those things."

Kade heard the sound of someone pulling into the driveway. He shoved a spoonful of cereal into his mouth, then stood up. "I'd better go brush my teeth."

"Of course. You don't want to offend the deer with bad breath, do you," his dad said with a smile.

It was still cold and dark as Kade trudged through the snow to the pickup.

"How's the mighty hunter today?" Emmet said.

Because Kade was shorter than Brenda, he had to sit in the middle, dodging the gearshift lever. "Mr. Sloan, I really want to thank you for taking me along."

"Hey, no problem. And just call me Emmet. That's my name."

"I think I'll call you Emmet too," Brenda said.

"Hey, you call me honorable father."

She smiled. "Oh sure, like I'm really going to do that."

They drove for a long time. Kade fell asleep. When he woke up, he realized his head had been resting on Brenda's shoulder.

"Well, Mountain Man, you all done with your nappy pooh?" Emmet said. He sang the first line of "Put Your Head on My Shoulder."

Kade blushed and looked over at Brenda. She didn't seem bothered about it one way or the other.

It was a gray, cloudy day. The pickup climbed through the mountains on a gravel road, with Emmet balancing a mug of coffee in his hand while he drove. "We're almost there," he said.

It started raining, and the wipers flapped back and forth across the windshield. As they continued to climb, the rain turned to snow.

Brenda pulled out a package of donuts and passed them around.

"You've never been hunting before, is that right, Kade?" Emmet asked.

"Yes."

"Well, we have kind of a tradition in our family. The first buck we get, when we're cleaning it out, we cut off a slice of deer heart, and each hunter takes a piece and eats it raw. That wouldn't bother you any, would it? I mean, you're not afraid of eating a piece of raw deer heart, are you?"

There was a long silence and then Kade gulped. "I guess not."

"What if it's still beating?" Emmet asked.

"Dad, you quit your teasing. I mean it, too."

Emmet was laughing. "He fell for it."

"I knew you were kidding."

"Sure you did," Emmet said.

A few minutes later he stopped to let Brenda and Kade out. "Brenda, you know what to do, don't you?"

"Sure, no problem."

She turned and removed her rifle from the gun rack.

"Be careful," Emmet called out. "Make some noise so bears can hear you coming. This is grizzly country."

Kade gulped.

"Kade, you're not afraid of a grizzly bear, are you?" Emmet said.

Kade smiled faintly.

Emmet drove off, leaving them standing there in the snow.

"Don't let my dad get to you."

"Was he kidding about this being grizzly country?"

"No, but don't worry, we won't see any. What we're going to do now is hike up that ridge. My dad'll be waiting on top. The idea is that we chase the deer toward him. C'mon, let's go."

There was about two inches of new snow on the trail. Kade imagined a bear behind every bush and tree along the way.

"I think my dad likes you, Kade."

"He has a strange way of showing it."

"Oh, that's just him. You'll get used to it." She paused. "I had a little brother who died when he was just a couple of weeks old. I think you and he would be about the same age. After that my mom couldn't have any more kids. Dad's sort of raised me like a son, but still, I think he wishes he had one for real. I think that's why he's kind of taken to you."

"I don't see how he could want anybody else, seeing how he's got you."

"That's nice of you to say. Thanks."

He paused. "There's a lot of other things I could say about you."

"Like what?"

He paused, not knowing whether to say it or not. Finally he decided to say it. "I've thought a lot about it lately, and I think I love you."

She stopped walking. "Look, Kade, don't try to make our friendship into something it can't ever be, or this'll turn sour on us and I'll have to quit seeing you. Okay?"

"But I think about you all the time. The way you look in the morning when the sun is on your face. Sometimes when you sing along to a song on the radio, I pretend you're singing it to me."

"Stop it, Kade. I really mean it. You can't go talking like that. It's not right."

"Why isn't it right?"

"Because you're just a kid." She glanced at him. He looked devastated. "You're not going to cry, are you?" she asked.

"You had to say that, didn't you?"

"I'm sorry. I shouldn't have said that."

They walked for a long time without saying anything. And then she said, "I think we should sing a song. It'll let the bears know we're coming. What do you want to sing?"

"I don't feel like singing."

"Well, how about 'We Thank Thee, O God, for a Prophet.' " She started out.

He tried to sing an octave lower to show her how low his voice was, but then decided it wouldn't make any difference to her anyway, so he sang in unison with her.

Four deer, startled by their noise, ran out of the woods into a clearing. Kade stopped to watch them. They were so graceful. There was a fence in front of them. They jumped over it in one graceful leap.

He took in the scene—the deer, the snowy field, Brenda with a red hunting vest over her coat, her face flushed from their exercise, snow gathering on her hat, her eyes somber, her expression subdued and a little sad.

A short time later they heard three shots. Each shot came in multiple echoes to their ears.

"That was my dad. C'mon, let's go see how he did."

They hurried to where the sound had come from. When they made it to the top of the ridge, they saw three deer on the ground. Emmet was bending over one of them, slicing its throat. The blood from each of the other deer stained the snow.

"Good shooting, Dad!" Brenda called out.

"Sure, what'd you expect?" Emmet said. He stood up. "Well, Kade, one of these is yours. Which one do you want?"

"It doesn't matter."

"Why don't you take that one over there?"

"Okay."

"You know how to clean a deer?"

"No."

"Brenda, why don't you show him?"

"Sure. Come here, Kade, and watch me do mine."

Kade knelt beside her as she dressed out the deer. "Do you want to save the heart?" Brenda called out to her father.

"No, leave it for the bears, or else give it to Kade."

She laughed. "If you don't quit your teasing, Kade'll never come anywhere with us again."

Brenda finished her deer, then helped him do his. Afterwards she said, "Dad, Kade did a good job, for his first time."

"Well, that's just great."

Kade got home by noon. His parents were at stake leadership meeting in Great Falls. Emmet helped him hang the deer in the garage, and then they left.

Kade fixed himself some soup and a couple of sandwiches. After he finished eating, he took a shower and then went to his room and sat down and drew a picture of Brenda the way she had looked when they were hiking. But it was no good, and he ended up throwing it away.

He wandered out to the garage and stood in front of the deer as it hung from the rafters. He remembered how it had been when it was running and jumped the fence. Even though he had enjoyed his first hunting trip, he felt bad to have had a part in killing something so beautiful.

The next week Brenda went out of her way to be nice to Kade because she wanted him to understand that she did enjoy having him as a friend, even though that's all it could ever be between them.

On Saturday her mother asked her to go to town to buy groceries. She asked Kade if he wanted to go along for the ride. He said yes.

Though it was still cold and the ground was covered
with snow, the wind wasn't blowing, so if you stood in
the sun long enough it would warm your face.

In the grocery story Kade helped her find the things
she needed. By the time they were finished, they'd filled
two shopping carts. After they were done, she suggested
they drop by Pat's Diner and have some hot chocolate.
He offered to pay for hers, but she said she had enough
money.

The place was crowded with farm families who'd
come to town. The booths were all full, but they managed to find a couple of seats at the counter. The place
smelled of hotcakes and bacon and sausage.

While they sipped their hot chocolate, Doug Albers
came over. "Hey, Brenda, you want to go bowling?"

"Now?"

"Sure, why not?"

"We just got groceries."

"So?"

"The milk'll freeze if I leave it in the pickup very
long."

"We can put it inside."

"Then the ice cream'll melt. Besides I need to get
Kade home."

"How about tonight then?"

She hesitated. "I don't know."

"Come on, Brenda. You never do anything anymore."

"Will you be getting drunk tonight like you usually
do?" she asked.

"I don't drink that much."

"Just every weekend, that's all."

"Look, I promise not to touch a drop. What do you
say?"

"I'm not going to park with you either, so you can
just get that out of your mind too."

"Now why would you even bring that up?"

"I heard about you and Traci Hunter after the homecoming game."

"What'd you hear?"

"That she had to slap your face to get you to back off."

"Look, I had too much to drink. I didn't know what I was doing. It'll never happen again."

"You've got to respect the way I believe, Doug."

"I do, honest. C'mon, Brenda, you need a man in your life, not some twerp who tags around after you like a puppy dog."

"Don't pick on Kade. He's okay. He's more of a man than you are."

Doug smirked. "Get serious. C'mon, how about it? I'll pick you up at seven. We'll go bowling and then go and get a pizza and a pitcher of root beer. No drinking and no parking. Whataya say?"

Brenda sighed. "All right, but you'd better watch yourself, Doug, or this'll be the last time I ever go out with you."

"No problem. See you tonight." He went back to the table he'd come from.

They went outside and started back home. Kade was so furious, he could hardly speak.

"It's just bowling," she said after several minutes of silence.

"Why are you going out with him? He's not even a member of the Church."

That made her mad. "Who around here is? Nobody. I think it's okay for church leaders to tell kids in Utah to only date members, but out here, who else have I got to choose from?"

"There's Jason Pasco."

"Jason Pasco," she grumbled. "Forget Jason Pasco. I could wait ten years, and you think he'd ever phone or write me a letter or let me know he cares about me? No way. He's useless to me. What am I supposed to do—go into hibernation until I graduate from high school? Well, I can't. I like guys, Kade. I'm attracted to them. I like being around a guy my age. Is there something wrong with that?"

"What about me?"

She sighed. "Look, we've gone through this before. I like you and all, and you're really a nice guy, but it's just not the same."

He turned away and pouted.

A few minutes later she said, "Gosh, Kade, I wish you wouldn't be so sensitive all the time. Look, I'm sorry if I hurt your feelings, but I have to let you know how it is for me."

As soon as she pulled in front of his house, he jumped out and hurried inside.

The next day was Sunday. Kade was curious to know how her date with Doug had been but he was still so mad that he snubbed her at church.

On Monday she picked him up for seminary. They didn't talk much. She tried to get some kind of conversation going, but he wouldn't cooperate. During the seminary lesson Sister Simmons said that members of the Church should only date members. Kade turned around to glare at Brenda.

After seminary Kade had to ride to school with Brenda and Melissa, but he refused to sit in the middle again. "It's my turn to ride shotgun today," he declared. He got his way.

When they pulled into the school parking lot, he noticed Doug getting out of his Ford Bronco. He started over to see Brenda.

Kade and Melissa left before Doug got there. Once they were inside the building, Kade looked back. Doug had his arm draped around Brenda.

"What's the matter, Kade? Are you jealous?" Melissa said.

"Why do you have to be such a witch all the time?" Kade grumbled. He turned to leave.

When Kade went out to the parking lot after school, he found Doug and Brenda together in her pickup. Doug was in the driver's seat. Kade was sure they'd been kissing. He got in and shut the door.

"So, Kade, what's this?" Doug said. "You come to watch?"

Kade was furious. He swore at Doug. It was the first time he'd ever sworn in his life.

Doug laughed. "The twerp's got a big mouth, don't he? Kade, maybe I should pound some sense into that pea-brain of yours."

"Anytime you want to try, just let me know."

Doug laughed. "Hey, like I'm really worried."

"Doug, you'd better go," Brenda said. "I need to get home and help my dad."

"All right. I'll call you tonight. See ya." He gave her a quick kiss and left.

Five minutes later they were on the road heading home.

"It sure didn't take him long, did it," Kade said bitterly.

"Back off, Kade. It's none of your business."

"He goes around acting like he owns you. I bet you let him kiss you anytime he wants, don't you."

"Look, after you grow up a little, we'll talk about this, but until then, just back off, okay?"

"What does he think about the Church?"

"It hasn't come up."

"I bet it hasn't."

"What do you mean by that?"

"You're willing to give up everything you've been taught just to please him, aren't you. Well, just make sure you don't get pregnant."

She slammed on the brakes. They came to a sudden stop. "Get out!"

"What?"

"I said get out, and I mean it! Nobody talks to me that way."

"I can't get out here. It's snowing, and it's a long ways home."

"I don't care. I want you out!"

He opened the door and stepped down. "What am I supposed to do out here in the middle of nowhere?"

"It's your choice—either freeze to death or walk home."

He slammed the door as hard as he could, and she drove off. He was alone. The wind was blowing snow in his face, and it was cold. He was suddenly worried.

A quarter mile down the road she stopped and put the pickup in reverse, then backed up to where he was and stopped. She leaned over and opened his door. "Get in," she ordered.

He got in. She took off again, and they rode in silence. "I'm sorry for talking to you the way I did," he said.

"You should be. I can't believe you said that to me. You don't know anything, Kade. Not anything at all."

As soon as they pulled up to his house, he got out and left without even saying goodbye.

For the rest of the week they didn't talk much. Every morning Doug was waiting for her when she pulled into the parking lot.

On Friday night there was a home game played in a snowstorm. Shelby easily won it 42 to 10. In the locker room after the game, as members of the team shouted and punched each other in victory, Kade quietly went about the business of gathering muddy uniforms from team members.

On Saturday night he watched TV until eleven and then went to bed. A little before one o'clock he heard a soft thump on the side of the house.

"Kade," someone called out.

He got out of bed and looked out. Brenda was standing below him in the snow, throwing snowballs at the house. He opened the window. Cold air poured onto his bare toes. "What do you want?" he asked.

"I need to talk to you."

"Okay, just a minute." He got dressed, then tiptoed down the stairs. He grabbed his coat, slipped on his boots, and went outside.

She was standing there waiting for him. "I left my pickup down on the main road so we wouldn't wake your folks. I thought maybe we could drive around for a while."

They walked down the snow-packed driveway to her pickup. She'd left the motor running, so it was warm inside. They took off down the road. "I went out with Doug tonight."

"How was it?"

"Awful. He took me to a party at his friend's house. The parents were gone for the weekend. Someone brought a keg of beer, and everyone was drinking except me. I felt so out of it. I tried to get Doug to stop drinking but he wouldn't. We danced for a while, and then he asked me to go upstairs with him to one of the bedrooms. I told him no. He got mad at me. I told him to stop acting like a fool, but he just kept at it. Finally I made him take me home. When I got home, my dad asked me if I'd had a nice time, and I told him that we'd had an argument. I could tell my dad was disappointed. I think he'd like Doug and me to get married so we can take over the farm someday."

"Did you tell your dad what happened?"

"No, I can't talk to him about things like that." She paused. "I went to bed and tried to sleep, but it was no use, so I got dressed and came over here. I'm sorry for dumping this all on you, but I feel so awful and mixed

up and I don't know who else to talk to. I just don't
know what to do."

"Do you still like Doug?"

"I don't know. Most of the time he's really nice. He
called me every night last week, and he was there every
morning when I got to school. He walked me to my
classes, and we ate lunch together. A couple of nights
ago he came over, and we all just sat around and talked.
Doug and my dad really get along." She sighed. "But
Doug has no interest in the Church and I don't think I
could ever get him to stop drinking." She hesitated.
"There's another thing. Doug says there's nothing
wrong if a couple in high school go ahead and . . . rush
things." She paused. "Do you know what I mean by
that?"

"Yes."

"Kade, what do you think I should do?"

"What do you want to happen?"

"I want Doug to quit drinking and join the Church."

"Do you think that'll ever happen?"

It took a long time before she answered. "No, not
really." She sighed. "Most of the time he's good to me,
and I like being with him. But when he starts drinking,
things get ugly. The thing is, I'm not sure I can go with
Doug and still maintain my standards." She paused. "I
guess that means I'd better break up with him."

"I suppose."

"But it's not fair, Kade. If I decide to only date Mormons, then I won't ever go out because there's nobody
around here for me."

"We could start going to the youth dances in Great
Falls again."

"How can you say that after we nearly got killed the
last time we went to a dance in Great Falls?"

He smiled. "I know, but even so, it was kind of fun."

"So I guess it's just you and me again," she said.

"I guess so. Look, I'm really sorry I'm not . . . " He

paused for a long time. It was painful for him to say it.
" . . . that I can't be what you need."

"Oh gosh, Kade, you're everything a girl could want except for the fact that you're too young for me."

"There's probably not much I can do about that, is there."

"No, but at least we can be friends. You know, if it weren't for you, I'd be all alone."

"Me too," he said. "You're the best friend I've ever had."

"The same for me. Well, I'd better get you back before your parents wake up and wonder where you've gone. Thanks for talking to me."

"Sure, anytime."

Later in his room he couldn't sleep, so he got out of bed and went to his desk and drew a picture of Brenda the way it had been as she drove, her face barely visible by the dashboard lights, the opposites of light and shadow repeatedly playing against each other as she moved her head closer to and then farther away from the light.

C H A P T E R 4

After football practice on Monday, Doug, bitter at having been dropped by Brenda, started bragging about his exploits with her, telling lies about what they'd done on their dates.

Kade had stayed after school to get caught up after Friday night's game. Because it had been such a mess out on the field Friday night, he had to wash some things twice. He overheard what Doug was saying and came out into the locker room. "None of what you're saying about Brenda is true."

"How do you know? You weren't there. You don't know what happened."

"Brenda's not that kind of girl."

"She is now."

"You're lying. Take back what you said."

"No. What I said is all true."

"Take it back, I said."

Doug smiled. "You think you're man enough to make me?" He cuffed Kade on the side of his face, but not hard enough to hurt him—he was just having fun. "Let's see how fast you are. Stop this." He tapped Kade on the mouth. "Here's another one. You ready for it?"

He hit him again, a little harder, this time on the nose. Kade's nose began to bleed.

Kade swung as hard as he could. Doug blocked the punch. "You got to be faster than that. C'mon, try it again. This time I'll close my eyes. Maybe you'll get lucky. See what you can do." Doug dropped his guard and stuck out his chin and closed his eyes. "C'mon, see if you can hit me with my eyes closed."

Kade threw a punch. Doug grabbed his wrist. "Whoops! Not fast enough, even with my eyes closed. What a loser! You're not much good for anything, are you!" He paused. "Oh, there's one thing you're good for, isn't there? Sure there is. You're good at washing clothes. Here, Kade, I've got a little present for you." Doug turned to pick up parts of his practice uniform. Kade, seeing an opportunity, lunged and caught him off balance. Doug's shoulder hit the lockers. The smile on his face was gone. "You want to play rough? Okay by me. Looks like I gotta teach you a lesson, don't I!" He shoved Kade backwards. Kade managed to stay on his feet, but Doug kept coming.

Suddenly Marvin Mudlin came behind Doug and put a hammerlock on him. As hard as Doug tried, he couldn't break loose. The more he struggled, the more pressure Marvin put on his neck.

"You leave Kade alone, you hear me?" Marvin said.

Doug, desperate for breath, nodded.

Marvin let up some on the hammerlock. "Now take back what you said about Brenda."

Doug spoke softly. "It was all a lie. Nothing happened between us."

"Louder," Marvin said.

"Nothing happened between us. I was lying about everything."

"All right then. Now you listen to me. You ever mess with Kade again and I'll come looking for you. You got that?"

Doug nodded again. Marvin shoved him away, and he hurried to his locker, picked up his things, and walked out.

Marvin walked up to Kade. "You either got to get a whole lot stronger or else learn to back down once in a while. The way you're going, you're not going to make it out of ninth grade."

The football season for Shelby High School ended with the quarter-final state championship playoff game the second weekend in November, held in the field-house at Montana State University in Bozeman. Kade traveled with the team. They went by chartered bus and stayed in a motel. Kade and Marvin roomed together.

It was an exciting game. The score was tied going into the final two minutes. The opposing team ate up the clock with running plays, advancing the ball to the twenty-yard line. With twenty seconds left, they kicked a field goal and won the game.

It was a tough way to end a good season.

On the trip home, Kade and Marvin sat together. "If you ask me, you need to start lifting weights," Marvin said. "You need to put some meat on those bones of yours. Like if your mom ever fixes mashed potatoes, eat as much as you can stand. That's what I did, and look at me."

"What if I don't want to be as big as you?"

"If you were, I think it might change Brenda's mind about you."

Kade blushed. "We're just friends."

"Don't give me that. I've seen the way you look at her in school."

"It's no use, Marvin. She's older than me."

"So what? Let's say you got yourself a set of weights and worked out every day and got, you know, in really good shape. I don't think her being older would matter

then. It can't hurt to try, can it? Ask your folks for a set
of barbells for Christmas."

Kade did ask about getting barbells for Christmas.
His mother said they were too dangerous because he
might get a hernia.

Dwight Allen hadn't called for a while, which made
Paul feel that if he wasn't careful, he might find himself
permanently trapped in a dead-end job in Shelby.

He realized that Denise wasn't very happy living in
Montana. She missed playing in a symphony orchestra,
as she'd done in other towns they'd lived in. But that
wasn't all. In Illinois they'd had season tickets to the
Chicago Symphony, they'd been in a ward with a brand
new building, and when they went shopping, they'd
had more of a choice of what to buy.

As time went on, Paul found himself feeling more
of a victim himself. Because of falling land prices, farmers who would ordinarily be able to weather bad economic times were now in serious trouble. Everything
depended on the loan-to-equity ratio.

He had prepared a list of farmers in trouble. One on
the list was Emmet Sloan, and another was Marvin Mudlin's father.

Paul worried how Kade would take it if the families
of his two closest friends were refused operating loans
for the next growing season.

During the two-week Christmas break, Kade went
over to Brenda's house every day. Sometimes the two
of them went with Emmet into town. Kade liked being
around Emmet because he knew how to do things that
men traditionally do—auto and diesel mechanics, wiring
a home, plumbing, hunting, fishing, football, basketball, baseball.

Brenda's grandparents drove up from Arizona for Christmas. They had farmed in Shelby for forty years until finally they retired and Emmet took over.

When they met Kade, Brenda's grandfather asked him where he lived. He told them. "Oh, that's the Aldrich farm. Whatever happened to them?"

"They went broke and had to sell out," Brenda said.

"Poor management," her grandfather said.

"Not necessarily," Emmet said.

"How else can you explain it? A farm five miles away goes belly up. They have the same soil as us, they grow the same crops, they get the same weather we do. What else can it be except poor management?" With that, the subject was closed.

One day when Brenda was fixing a pie and didn't want to leave until it was done, Kade rode into town with Emmet, just the two of them.

"What's it like being the son of a banker?" Emmet asked as they bounced down the country road.

"It's all right, I guess." Kade paused. "Except my dad's not as much fun to be with as you."

"Why's that?"

"He doesn't know how to do anything useful."

Emmet laughed. "He might not agree with you about that."

"I know, but it's true. Like yesterday when you showed Brenda and me how to weld. My dad never does stuff like that. He pays to have people do things around the house. I've learned more practical things from you and Brenda than I ever have at home."

"But, Kade, you got to realize your dad's a busy man."

"Yeah, sure he is. He's the branch president and he's trying to raise some money to build a church, but first they got to get more people to go to church, so he spends a lot of time going around asking inactives to go to church."

"Like me?"

"Yeah. How come you never go to church?"

"Force of habit, I guess. Maybe I'll start coming out the first of the year."

"My dad'd like that a lot. And it wouldn't hurt if you quit drinking coffee either."

"There's no pleasing you, is there?" Emmet said.

"No, I guess not."

"Kade, you're quite the guy, you know that?"

"Me?"

"Yes, you."

"Not me."

"What do you mean, not you?"

"I wear these stupid glasses."

"It doesn't matter. What matters is what's inside you."

"I've lost every fight I've ever been in."

"Why's that?"

"Because I'm not as big as the guys I fight."

Emmet grinned. "That's easy to fix — pick on smaller guys." He glanced over at Kade. "Look, don't worry about it. One day you'll hit a growth spurt and just shoot up. That's what happened to me."

"I was thinking that if I had a set of barbells and worked out every day . . . " He sighed. "I asked my mom about it, but she said no. She said I'd hurt myself, but I know that'd never happen."

"Maybe Santa Claus'll bring you a set of barbells."

He scoffed. "Yeah, sure."

They stopped at a farm co-op for supplies and then dropped by Pat's Diner. They sat down at a booth with some friends of Emmet.

"What's this, Emmet? You adopt a kid or something?" one asked.

"No, this is our neighbor's boy, Kade Ellis."

"The banker's kid?"

"Yeah."

"You're the one who knocked my son on his can in the locker room, aren't you," one of the men commented.

"Are you Mr. Mudlin?" Kade asked.

"That's right."

"Kade, I haven't heard this story before," Emmet said.

"There's not much to tell," Kade said. "When school started in the fall, Marvin kept snapping me with a towel after gym class. One day I decided I wasn't going to take it any longer. We got into a fight until the gym teacher broke it up."

"You did the right thing," Mr. Mudlin said. "You can't let people push you around."

"I know. Actually it turned out okay. Marvin and I are real good friends now."

"He talks about you sometimes. I think you've been good for him."

The conversation drifted to other topics. Kade quietly drank his hot chocolate and ate his doughnut. He felt like he'd been accepted into a select group of the men who did the most important work in the world. These were men who could make things happen.

Kade's father walked in the cafe with another man, both of them in overcoats and three-piece blue suits. Kade had never seen the other man. He looked like someone who was used to getting his way.

The two men sat at a table near the back of the cafe. Nobody called out to them as they'd done when Emmet walked in. But even so, everyone had their eyes on them, as if they were the enemy. It was something Kade picked up on. Being there with these men made it seem as if he were looking at his father for the first time. Compared to the men he was with, his dad seemed stiff and formal and official.

Emmet put his arm around Kade's shoulder and

leaned over. He spoke confidentially. "Kade, are you going to go over and say hello to your dad?"

It seemed too much to ask, to let everyone know that the man in the three-piece suit was his father.

"No, that's okay. We see each other at home all the time."

"Kade, you've got to go over and say hello."

"What for?"

"Because if he sees you walking out of here, he might think you're ashamed of him."

Kade sighed. "Nobody here likes my dad, do they?"

"It's nothing personal. We're just worried about losing something we've worked for all our lives." Emmet squeezed his shoulder. "Go say hello. C'mon, you've got to do it."

Emmet stood up and let Kade out of the booth. The walk up the aisle seemed to take forever. He felt as though everyone was staring at him. His father looked up from the report the other man was showing him.

"Hi, Dad," Kade said softly.

"Kade, what are you doing in town?"

"Emmet brought me."

"Kade, I'd like you to meet Dwight Allen. He flew in today to help me with my work. He's from the corporate office in Chicago."

"Hello, Mr. Allen."

"Sit down and let me buy you something to eat."

"No, thanks. I've got to go. Emmet's about to leave now."

Dwight smiled. "Your dad says you're a fan of the Chicago Bears."

"That's right."

"If I can ever get your family out to Illinois again, I'll take you over and let you meet some of the team."

"I'd like that. Well, I'd better go now. 'Bye."

"Goodbye, Kade," his father said.

Kade walked back. Emmet had already paid and was

waiting at the door for him. They went outside. Kade looked up at the time-and-temperature sign on the bank. It read ten below zero. They got into the pickup. Emmet started it up. "It was the right thing to do," he said.

"I suppose," Kade said in the same drawl Brenda used.

That evening Dwight Allen offered to take the family out for supper. He asked if there were any really good places to eat in town. Kade's mother suggested the Dixie Inn.

Kade didn't like Mr. Allen because all he did was to brag about how wonderful he was. When the waitress came to take their order, he tried to order in French, until the waitress finally admitted she didn't understand.

"How can you have French cuisine here and not speak French?" Mr. Allen asked.

"Hey, I just bring the food to the table."

After the waitress left, Mr. Allen made fun of her. "She wouldn't last a day in a good restaurant in Chicago."

"She's not in Chicago," Kade mumbled, but not loud enough to be picked up by anyone.

Over dessert, Mr. Allen turned to Denise. "We hope to get you and Paul out of Montana soon. We'll get you back to civilization where there's culture and the arts and a symphony orchestra you can play in."

"Well, that'd be nice," Denise said, "although there are some advantages to living here."

Paul was surprised at her response. "Like what?"

"Well, the people here are friendly and honest and hard-working."

"Kade, you can't possibly be happy here," Mr. Allen said.

"Why's that?"

"Well, for one thing, riding through town today I

didn't see a McDonald's or a Burger King. And I know teenagers can't survive without fast food."

Kade didn't appreciate Mr. Allen thinking he knew everything there was to know.

Mr. Allen continued. "I'm sure you'd like it better in a place where there's more things to do for someone your age."

Kade had had it. "What makes you such an authority on my life?"

His parents were shocked. "Kade, is that any way to talk?" his mother said. "I think you'd better apologize."

"I'm sorry," Kade said, out of respect to his parents but not because he meant it.

"No problem. I like a person who speaks his mind." The next day Dwight Allen returned to Chicago.

Two days before Christmas, just after supper, Kade's father came up to Kade's bedroom and suggested they do something together.

"Like what?"

"I don't know. Maybe a board game." He went to Kade's closet and looked up on the shelf where Kade kept his games. "How about Monopoly?"

Before Kade could react, his father had taken the Monopoly box down from the closet shelf. "I haven't played this for a long time." He sat on the bed and opened the box, then noticed the stack of drawings. "What's this?" he asked.

"Just some drawings I did," Kade said, his face turning bright red.

"Mind if I look at them?"

"No, I guess not."

His father looked at each drawing. "These are all of Brenda, aren't they?"

"Yes."

"Why so many of her?"

"I like the way she looks."

"I can tell you've spent a lot of time on these. They're very good." He paused. "Kade, how do you feel about Brenda?"

Kade's face felt like a furnace. "I love her."

"Does she know that?"

"Yeah, but she doesn't feel the same way about me because of the difference in our ages. She wants us to just be friends."

Kade was waiting to be lectured how wrong it was for him to feel the way he did about Brenda. Instead, his father turned wistful. "You know, when I was in junior high, I felt the same way about a girl in high school. She came twice a week to work in our school library. For a while there I checked out more books than anyone else in school. Sometimes five or six a day, just to watch her stamp the book and hand it back to me. She had the most beautiful red hair I've ever seen."

"Did you ever tell her how you felt?"

"I was too embarrassed to actually say it, so one time when I was returning a library book, I folded a love note into the checkout slip and handed the book to her. I knew she had to take the slip out and take a pencil and cross out the due date. I sat down at a nearby desk and waited. Just then the phone rang. Of all the rotten luck, it was for the girl. She went to take the call, and the head librarian, a crusty woman, came to the desk. She grabbed my book, removed the note, read it, and announced to the entire library, 'Who wrote this horrid note?' I got up and ran out of the library and never went back."

Kade smiled. "So it's not too awful to feel the way I do about Brenda?"

"Not as long as you can keep your feelings under control."

"Brenda makes sure of that. One time she told me she'd quit seeing me if I kept going on about how much

I liked her. So I don't talk about it much anymore. It's kind of hard sometimes, but I guess that's the way it's got to be. Sometimes I dream about her at night. It's a funny thing. In my dreams I'm always the same age as her." He paused. "Other than that, I've pretty much got it under control."

"It's not easy, is it," his dad said.

"No. I'm glad you told me about the girl with red hair."

"You suppose this runs in the family?" his dad said with a smile. He studied the drawings again. "These are exceptionally good. I think you should take art in school so you can develop this talent."

"They're not that good."

"Don't kid yourself. They're excellent."

"You really think so?"

"Absolutely."

"Thanks a lot. Dad, you won't tell Mom about this, will you?"

"Not if you don't want me to."

"I don't want her to worry."

"All right. I won't tell her."

"Thanks."

"I love you, Kade. Don't ever forget that—no matter what happens."

"I won't." It seemed an awkward moment. If Kade had been a little younger, he might have gone to his father for a hug, but now he held back. His father was likewise uncertain of what to do. It was new territory for both of them.

"You still want to play Monopoly?" his dad asked.

"Sure, if you do."

"Let's take this downstairs and see if we can talk your mother into playing with us."

"She always wins though," Kade said.

"This time she won't."

But sure enough, Denise won again.

On Christmas morning they gathered around the Christmas tree to open presents. Kade had a married sister, six years older than he, who lived in Orem, Utah. She sent him a BYU sweatshirt for Christmas. He also got two shirts and a pair of jeans and a watch and some underwear and a Levi jacket just like the one Brenda had and fifty dollars in cash, which could go toward him getting contact lenses. Now he was only thirty dollars from having enough to pay for the examination and lenses and also the insurance that his father insisted he get.

Even though he had received what he'd asked for, he felt a little disappointed there were no surprises. Christmas wasn't the same as it had been when he was little.

At about ten thirty Brenda and Emmet showed up. When Kade answered the door, Emmet smiled, as though he had a joke up his sleeve. "Can you help us? We need some help moving something that's kind of heavy."

"Sure, I can help."

"Come outside and let's get started."

Kade put on his boots and went outside. It was a cold, clear, sunny day, and the snow crunched under their feet. In the bed of Emmet's pickup was a set of homemade barbells, made from large gears from some old farm machinery. Every piece was painted a bright red.

"Oh, great! Barbells! This is just what I wanted!"

"Sure it is. You laid down enough hints," Emmet joked.

"No I didn't."

Emmet turned to Brenda. "Kade says to me, 'Either get me a set of barbells for Christmas or I'll start lifting Brenda over my head.' What was I to do? I knew if he tried that, it'd wreck his back for sure."

"Watch it there," Brenda playfully warned her father.

Kade touched the cold metal. "This is terrific! I can hardly wait to start working out."

"Where do you want us to take 'em?"

"How about up in my room?"

"Whatever you say. Brenda, you're in charge of opening and closing doors. Let's go."

Kade's mother was sitting at the kitchen table when the three of them burst into the house. Kade was the first one in, carrying two large red gears from some ancient machinery.

"Look what Emmet made me!" he called out.

"It's very nice," his mother said. "What is it?"

"A set of barbells."

Emmet was the next one in with a load. "Sorry for busting up your Christmas like this."

"Kade says you made him a set of barbells."

Emmet grinned. "Actually it was a way of getting rid of some of my junk."

Brenda was next. "Merry Christmas."

"Merry Christmas. It looks like you and your dad have made Kade's day."

"It was mostly Dad's idea."

The three of them were now up in Kade's room.

Paul came into the kitchen. "What's going on?" he asked.

"Emmet made Kade a set of barbells for Christmas. They just brought it over. Kade's really excited. You should've seen the look on his face just now. They've taken it all upstairs."

"Every time he sets the weights down, it'll jar the entire house. They should be put in the barn."

"I'd rather put up with a little noise than have him out in that cold barn."

"How can anyone make a set of barbells?" Paul asked.

Upstairs they heard Brenda. "Okay, Macho Man, show us your stuff." Pause. "All right! Look at that, would you? Dad, how many pounds is that?"

"Sixty," Emmet said.

"All right, Kade!"

The barbell crashed down onto the floor above them, making a terrible noise and causing a small piece of ceiling tile to fall down.

"If they keep this up, we're not going to have a ceiling," Paul complained.

A minute later there was another dull thud above their heads. And then Kade, Brenda, and Emmet bounded down the stairs.

"I'm going over to Brenda's," Kade said, grabbing his coat.

On his way out Emmet stopped to talk. "I hope this won't be too awful for you folks. Next time I come I'll bring an old carpet, and we'll lay a few layers on the floor so it won't be so noisy when Kade sets the weights down."

"We appreciate your taking time with Kade," Paul said.

"No problem. I always wanted to have a son, but I guess that wasn't in the cards. Kade's a good boy. You both should be very proud of him. Well, I'd better be going. We're going to try out a new video game I got for Brenda. Christmas is a great time of year, isn't it? Well, Merry Christmas."

"Merry Christmas," they answered back.

A minute later it was quiet again.

"It's hard to compete with that family," Paul said.

Denise shrugged. "That's what happens to kids. They grow up and pull away from their parents."

"I know that."

"Then what's the problem?" Denise asked.

"I don't know."

A few minutes later Kade called to see if he could

stay for lunch. Paul tried to persuade him not to, but Kade said they were having a big video-game tournament, and that if he left now, his team, composed of him and Brenda's mom, would have to forfeit.

"All right."

"Thanks, Dad. 'Bye."

Paul hung up. "Kade's staying over for lunch," he told Denise.

"Is that what you want him to do? This is Christmas, Paul. We can call him back if you want him here with us."

It was painful for him to say it. "I don't stack up very well alongside Emmet, do I?"

"What on earth are you talking about?"

"I mean as far as being the kind of a man a boy wants to spend time with."

"Paul, you're the most wonderful man I know. Someday Kade's going to realize that."

"Maybe so, but we're all in for some tough times real soon. I just hope Kade and I don't drift too far apart in the process."

"What are you talking about?"

Paul sighed. "This may be Emmet's last Christmas on the farm."

The visit by Dwight Allen had not been a social call. By the time he left Paul, they had agreed on a plan. Four farmers in the worst shape financially would be refused operating funds for the upcoming growing season. Dwight knew this might force some of the four to sell out altogether, but with the loans to each of these families being over 60 percent of equity, it would be irresponsible for the bank to continue to advance money to them.

"It's for the best," he told Paul just before getting on his chartered plane.

"Maybe so, but these are good people."

"Do you know them very well?"

"Two of them. Emmet Sloan and Harvey Mudlin."

"How do you know them?"

"The Sloans belong to our church, and the Mudlin boy is one of Kade's friends. Dwight, the thing that bothers me the most about all this is that it isn't entirely their fault."

Dwight shrugged. "Through the years I've noticed that most people who can't pay back their loans have good excuses. In this business, though, excuses don't count for much."

Paul shook his head.

"Something wrong?"

"I was just wondering what all this is going to do to my son."

Kade worked out every day after school. He liked to take his shirt off and look in the mirror for any sign that he was getting stronger. He got tired of tromping down the stairs all the time, so he asked his mother for a mirror in his room.

"What for?"

"So I can look at myself when I'm working out."

"Why on earth would you want to do that?"

"Mom, that's what weight lifters do."

"They must be very conceited then. I certainly don't want you to become like that."

"Oh, Mom," he grumbled.

Kade's birthday was the second week in January. His parents asked if he wanted a birthday party. He said all he wanted was to have Brenda over for cake and ice cream.

"Maybe you should spend with someone else besides Brenda all the time," his dad said.

"What for?"

"I just think it'd be for the best." He thought about it some more. "Oh, never mind. It's your birthday. You go ahead with whatever plans you want to make."

Brenda did come for birthday cake. She gave him a set of watercolor paints and a brush. His parents gave him a shirt, some cash toward the purchase of contact lenses, and a driver's training manual, which meant they'd decided to let him get a license.

"If you want, I can teach Kade how to drive," Brenda said.

"I thought that'd be something I'd do," his dad said.

"Kade'll probably learn real fast," Brenda said. She and Kade tried to keep from laughing.

"What's so funny?" his mother asked.

"Nothing."

After they had cake and ice cream, Kade took Brenda up to his room to watch him lift weights so she'd know how strong he was getting.

"Good job," she said as he lifted a barbell above his head.

He set the weights down. "I'm fifteen now and you're still sixteen," Kade said. "So there's only a year between us."

She smiled. "You think you're catching up with me, is that it?"

"It's not just age. It's everything else. My dad says I'm on a growth spurt. I'll be as tall as you are pretty soon. Stand up and turn around."

They stood back to back. She touched their heads with her hand. "No doubt about it, Kade, you're getting taller," she said.

"Anybody seeing us, like at a movie together, if they didn't know us, might never guess you're older than me."

"That's probably true."

"So I was wondering if you'd go out with me . . . "— he felt awkward saying it— ". . . on a date."

"Kade, c'mon, we've talked about this before."

"I know, but I'm older now."

"You've got me as a friend forever. Isn't that worth something?"

"I suppose."

"Okay then," she said. "Let's leave it at that." She paused. "Are you still drawing pictures of me?"

"Yes."

"Can I see them?"

He pulled down from the closet the box where he

kept her drawings and handed it to her. Then he sat on the floor next to the heater vent. She sat cross-legged on his bed and looked at the drawings.

Kade heard his mother coming up the stairs. Brenda quickly hid the box under the bed.

"Kade, I'm not sure you and Brenda should be up here all alone," his mother said.

"Why not?"

"A girl shouldn't be alone in a young man's bedroom."

"To Brenda this is more like babysitting than anything else."

"That's not true, Kade," Brenda said. "Your mom's probably right. Let's go downstairs."

"We'll be down in a minute," Kade said to his mother. She left.

Brenda looked through the stack of drawings. "You've got to let the art teacher in school see these."

"No."

"Why not?"

"What if she showed them to someone in her class?"

"What if she did?"

"Then everyone would know."

"Would know what?"

He looked away. "That I can't get you out of my mind."

"Look, I'm not so sure it's me. You're a natural-born artist. I think you'd be drawing pictures of any girl you spent as much time with as you do with me. I just happen to be around, that's all. The important thing is you can't just ignore a talent like this." She paused. "I've got an idea. What would you think if I took art with you next fall?"

He grinned. "The two of us in the same class? That'd be great."

"All right then, it's settled."

A week later the stake had a youth dance in Great Falls. Brenda asked Kade to ride with her. Melissa Simmons would have gone too, but she had to go visit her grandparents.

Winter had set in for good, but although it was cold and the countryside was covered with snow, the roads were clear and there was no wind.

Brenda let Kade drive the first little while. He liked being in the driver's seat with her beside him on their way to a dance.

"You think you're pretty hot stuff these days, don't you," she teased.

"What are you talking about?"

"I see you're wearing a short-sleeve shirt tonight. Is that so you can show off your muscles to all the girls?"

He was surprised she'd guessed.

"Let me see how strong your arms are now," she asked.

He gripped the steering wheel hard so his muscles would flex. She touched his upper arm. "It's coming along. I bet you set some girl's heart on fire tonight."

"At least one, maybe two," he said with a smile.

"You know what? I think I've created a monster."

"Who do you want to dance with tonight?" he asked.

"Hey, I'm not particular. Anybody who'll ask me."

"I'm serious."

"I don't know." She paused. "Jason Pasco maybe."

"What do you like about him?"

"He's fun to talk with, and he's got this really good sense of humor, and he's smart, and he tries to live the teachings of the Church." She paused. "And I like his looks . . . a lot."

"What do you like about his looks?"

"Well, he's got the most wonderful face. I don't know if you've noticed it before."

"Not really."

"What about you, Kade? Who do you want to dance with?"

"You."

"Who else?"

"Linda Cooper, I guess."

"Maybe this'll be our lucky night and Jason and Linda'll both be there," she said.

"Yeah, maybe so," he said quietly.

After they arrived at the stake center, they went in the cultural hall and looked around. There were pockets of kids clustered together, watching the braver ones out on the floor dancing.

"There's Linda," Brenda said. "Go ask her to dance."

"Not yet."

"Kade, come on. Don't be bashful."

"I want to stay with you."

"I'm not going to let you do that. Go dance with Linda."

"How about if you and I dance first, just so I'll get used to it."

"All right, one time, but then you have to promise to ask Linda."

"Okay."

He never wanted the dance to end. But it did.

"Now go ask Linda," she said.

"Just one more with you."

"No. C'mon, you promised."

"I'm as tall as you are now."

"That's because I have my shoes off. Go ask Linda."

"And I'm pretty sure I'm going to turn out taller and stronger and better looking than Jason. Especially once I get my contact lenses."

"Kade, I mean it now."

"Please. Just one more dance with you."

"No. Either you dance with Linda or I'm not talking to you anymore tonight."

He finally went and asked Linda to dance.

"You look different," Linda said while they danced.

"In what way?"

"I don't know. You seem more sure of yourself."

"Brenda's been helping me. You know what? The next time they have a stake dance, I'll be wearing contact lenses. I've pretty much got all my money saved. I'm pretty sure they'll make me look older." He glanced over at the sidelines. Jason was talking to Brenda. He watched them together. Things were going okay for her.

The two couples danced nearly every dance after that. Kade kept dancing with Linda because it was easier not to have to go find a new girl every time, and because she seemed to like him.

At eleven o'clock Jason and Brenda came over. "Jason wants to go out for something to eat. Linda, can you come too?"

"As long as we're back by midnight. That's when my mom is coming to pick me up."

"We'll be back by then. Kade and I have a two-hour drive ahead of us."

They had so much fun at McDonald's that they almost stayed too long. When they finally returned to the church parking lot, Linda's mother had already arrived and gone inside to look around. Linda said good night and left to find her mother.

A short time later Kade and Brenda were on the highway heading home.

"I had a good time tonight. What about you?" Brenda asked.

"It was okay."

"I think Linda is great for you."

"I suppose. Do you still like Jason?"

"Yes. Very much. He's a lot like you, except he's older."

"No kidding?"

"I wish I could somehow arrange for him to take me to our school's junior prom. I'm on the decorating committee. I'll be doing all this work on it, so if I possibly can, I want to go to it. But there's no chance anybody at school will ask me, seeing as how I've let it be known I don't want to have anything to do with drinking. And there's no guy in school my age who doesn't drink."

"Why don't you ask Jason to go with you?"

"He's supposed to ask me."

"But he lives so far away. He probably doesn't even know about the prom. If you want, I could phone and tell him about it."

"But what if he doesn't want to come all the way here just to go to a dance with me?"

"Then he won't ask you."

"I'd feel dumb knowing we sort of engineered the whole thing."

"Hey, don't worry. He'll want to take you."

"Well, okay, I guess it's all right if you phone Jason. As long as you do it on your own, and not because I told you to."

"Sure, no problem."

The next day Kade phoned Jason and told him about the junior prom.

"Hey, I'll take her. I'll call her up right now and ask her."

They hung up, and a few minutes later Brenda phoned and excitedly announced that Jason had just asked her to the prom.

On Monday at work Paul Ellis phoned Emmet Sloan. They talked about Kade and Brenda for a while and then Paul said, "I've been looking over your request for operating funds for this next year." He paused. "I was wondering if you and your wife could come in sometime soon so we could talk about it."

"What'd we do? Fill something in wrong again?" Emmet said. "Clayton Jones always used to just cross out my mistakes and write it in the way it was supposed to be."

"I just think it'd be best if we sat down and went over a few things."

"There's nothing wrong, is there?"

"I just think we need to go over a few things. When will you and Susan be in town next?"

"We can come in anytime. When's a good time for you?"

"How about tomorrow morning, say, at eleven o'clock?"

"Sounds good. I'll see you then."

After school that same day, Brenda asked Kade if he'd mind if they stopped at a local dress shop before going home, while she looked for a prom dress.

A few minutes later, in the store, Kade sat in a chair as Brenda came out wearing a low-cut formal.

"What do you think about this one?" she asked.

"Shows too much," he said, then started to blush.

She looked in the mirror. "Gosh, you're right. Sorry."

Soon she came out in another dress. "What about this one?"

"It's better."

"It's the most expensive one."

"How much is it?"

She showed him the price tag. He couldn't believe one dress could cost so much.

"There's another one that isn't as much. I'll go try that one on."

In a few minutes she was back out again, wearing a pastel pink formal. "Well?"

"That's the best one. I really like that color on you."

"I like it too. Well, I think I'll look around a little more, but if I can't find anything better, I'll probably get this one."

Tuesday at eleven Emmet and Susan Sloan showed up at the bank for their appointment.

"Can I get you two anything?" Paul asked. "Some hot chocolate maybe?"

"No thanks. Let's get this taken care of first. I've had such bad luck filling out forms that I've taken to letting Susan do it. She doesn't make many mistakes, but apparently she did this time."

"Actually, the form was filled out correctly."

"Then what's the problem?" Emmet asked.

Paul turned to some figures he'd written down. "I've looked at your overall credit situation. Emmet, your outstanding loans now total 60 percent of equity. We red-flag anything over 50 percent as being in trouble."

"Except for our operating loan, we haven't taken out any new loans the past year," Susan said.

"The problem is that land values have dropped so drastically. Take a case of someone with loans totaling forty-five percent of equity. What happens if the price of land drops to half of what it was? Now that person's loans are ninety percent of equity. A bank can't tolerate that because it becomes doubtful the loan can ever be repaid. Your situation isn't that serious, but it's bad enough that you ought to be thinking of ways to reduce your indebtedness."

"If we're in trouble," Emmet said, "then you people are the ones to blame. Every year Clayton Jones came out and suggested improvements we could make—just so he could loan us some more money."

"Clayton didn't always use his head when it came to making loans."

"And you do?" Susan countered.

"One of the reasons I was sent here was to try and improve the bank's financial situation."

"Are there other people around here in the same boat as me?" Emmet asked.

"Yes."

"Who are they?"

"I can't tell you that."

Susan came to her husband's defense. "Paul, ask anyone and they'll tell you Emmet runs the best operation in this country. Two years ago he was chosen as the county's outstanding farmer."

"I know that."

"So how can you tell him he's suddenly in trouble?"

"What's happened isn't his fault. We base everything on the price of land, and it's dropped a lot lately."

"You must have called us in here for a reason. What is it?" Emmet asked.

"You asked for a larger limit on your operating loan. I'm afraid I can't give you that."

"What are we supposed to do then?" Susan said. "We need money to produce a crop."

"You might lease out your land to someone else, or if worse comes to worst, you could sell off some of your land."

"But you just said the price of land is low," Emmet said. "This'd be the absolute worst time to sell."

"I realize that."

"We can do business with someone else, that's what we can do," Emmet said.

"That's up to you."

"They don't make bankers like they used to, do they," Emmet commented. "At least Clayton Jones had a heart. He knew farming and he believed in the people around here." He shook his head. "I don't go to church much, but Susan is one of the most faithful members you've got. You're her branch president. And so to reward her faithfulness, you're going to refuse us a loan?"

"I have a responsibility to the bank's best interests. You may not believe it, but also I'm doing this for your good too."

"There's one thing I don't understand."

"What's that?"

"How did someone like you produce such a good kid as Kade?" Emmet turned on his heels and walked out.

Susan lingered. "I don't understand this. I thought we were friends. Why are you turning against us?"

"I'm not turning against you. I'm trying to help you both see you've got to make some changes or else you might lose everything."

"I can't believe this is happening to us."

"I'm sorry I had to be the one to tell you."

She left and went out to join Emmet in the pickup. Paul watched them go and then asked his secretary not to disturb him for a while. He closed the door to his office and sat at his desk, his head cupped in his hands.

He had three more farmers to see that day.

The next day after school, Brenda went back with Kade to try on the formal she'd liked the day before.

"I still like this one," she said. "How about you?"

"Yeah. You look great in it."

"I guess I'll take it then."

"How are you going to pay for it?" he asked.

"I've got some money in the bank. And my dad owes me for some work I did for him. It'll all work out."

"Can we go now?" he asked.

"Sure. I'll go change."

The clerk finished up with another customer and then came over to where Kade was sitting. "What did she decide?"

"She decided to buy it."

"Good. I think she looks real nice in it, don't you?"

"She always looks nice."

"Are you the lucky guy who's taking her to the prom?"

"Me? No, I'm just a tag-along."

"Don't believe that," Brenda called out from the dressing room. "Kade's my best friend."

"Who's she going to the prom with?" the clerk asked Kade.

"You wouldn't know him. He's from Great Falls."

"Well, he'll be pleased how nice she'll look in that formal."

"Yes, he will."

Brenda came out of the dressing room carrying the formal. "Can you hold this for a couple of days until I have the money to pay for it?"

"Sure, no problem."

Kade had never seen Brenda so happy. She let him drive. She had him stop at the drive-in and bought them both some hot chocolate, and she talked him into singing along with her to the songs on the radio. He knew that when he got home he would draw a picture of the way she looked, so happy and alive and full of hope.

That night at nine o'clock Brenda phoned him. She sounded upset. "I need to talk to you right away."

"What's wrong?"

"Everything. I'll come and pick you up, okay?"

"Sure."

He went downstairs and put on his coat and waited for Brenda.

"Where do you think you're going?" his mother asked.

"Brenda needs someone to talk to."

"No you don't, young man. This is a school night, and you need your sleep."

"Mom, Brenda needs me. She was practically crying when she talked to me on the phone."

"You talk to your father about leaving."

Paul came into the kitchen. "What's the problem?"

"Kade says he's going out to talk to Brenda. I told him tonight's a school night and he should be going to bed now. He wouldn't listen to me. Paul, you talk to him."

"I think we'd better let him go."

"Why are you taking his side?"

"I think Brenda probably needs someone to talk to."

"I don't understand you at all sometimes, Paul." She turned to Kade. "Don't blame me if you get sick because you don't get enough sleep at night."

Kade saw headlights sweep across the yard. He said goodbye and hurried out so he'd be there when Brenda arrived.

A minute later they were driving toward town.

"What's wrong?" Kade asked.

"Didn't your dad tell you?"

"What?"

"He refused to loan us any more money. Kade, we've got to have operating funds. If we don't get any, we won't be able to farm this summer, so we might end up losing everything."

"There must be some mistake. My dad wouldn't do that."

"I'm not making this up."

"What are you going to do?"

"My dad's going to see if he can find someplace else to get the money." She paused. "We'll just have to wait. One thing for sure. I can't go to the prom now."

"You've got to go. Jason's expecting you."

"How can I? It costs too much money. For all I know, we might end up needing every penny for food."

"Don't call Jason yet about not going."

"Why?"

"Something might turn up."

"What?"

"I don't know. Just hold off before you call him, okay?"

"Okay, but it won't do any good."

They drove in silence for a while and then she said, "I'm sorry it had to be your dad. I think this might make it harder for you and me to be friends."

"We can't let it do that."

She nodded. "I agree. I'd miss having you around to talk to."

They stopped at a cafe and had something to eat and then drove back. It was nearly eleven before Kade walked in the door. He thought his parents were asleep, but as he went into the kitchen he saw his dad. "How's Brenda doing?" he asked Kade.

"Not very good. Is it true what she said about you not loaning them the money they need?"

"Yes, it's true. I can't talk about my reasons. You'll just have to trust that I'm trying to do what's best for them."

"They don't look at it that way."

"I know that."

"How can you do that to a family that belongs to the Church?"

"I have to think of what's best for the bank."

"You don't care what happens to them, do you." Kade's comment was a statement, not a question.

His father sighed, then said, "It's because I do care about them that I'm doing what I'm doing."

Kade looked at him. "I hope I never get to be like you," he said, then went upstairs to his room.

He had just put on his pajamas when his dad appeared at the top of the stairs. "Kade, we need to talk."

They sat down on the bed. "Where do you suppose the money comes from that a bank loans?" Paul asked.

"I don't know."

"In our bank we have the life savings of other farmers in the area. Parents put a few dollars a month into an account for their children's education. Young married couples save for a down payment for their first home. We even have the money you're saving for contact lenses. People trust us with their savings. Don't I have a responsibility to them to make sure their money is safe?"

"I guess so."

Paul stood up. "Well, we'd both better get to bed. It's been a tough day. Do you want me to get the light?"

"Yes, please."

"Good night."

"Good night, Dad."

At school the next morning Kade couldn't stop thinking about Brenda. At nine o'clock he decided he was wasting his time being in class. He left school and walked down to the bank. His dad's car wasn't there, so he went in and withdrew all the money he'd been saving for contact lenses. Then he went to the store where Brenda had picked out a formal.

"What can I do for you?" the clerk asked.

"Brenda Sloan and I were in here yesterday. She had you set aside a formal. I'm here to pay for it."

"Does she know you're doing this?"

"No, it's sort of a surprise." Kade pulled out a roll of bills from his front pocket.

"I'll go get it. Will you be taking it with you now?"

"Yes."

"Will she need a slip or some shoes?"

Kade paused. "She's probably got all that stuff already."

After he paid for the formal, Kade said, "There's just one other thing. The formal is my gift to her, but she might try to return it. If she does, do me a favor and tell her you can't take it back, okay?"

"Why are you doing this?"

"Because she's my friend."

"Why can't she pay for it herself?"

"Her dad's a farmer, and they're going through tough times."

The woman, born and raised in the area, understood.

Kade walked back to school. He put the formal in the pickup, then returned to class.

After school, by the time he made it to the pickup, Brenda was already there looking at the formal.

He climbed in the pickup. "What's that?" he asked.

"It's the formal I picked out. Why is it here?"

"I don't know. Maybe the Prom Elf brought it."

"You did it, didn't you?"

"Me? Do I look like a Prom Elf?"

"I can't let you do it. I'm taking it back right now."

"They won't take it back."

"How do you know?"

"Remember the woman who waited on us the other day? While you were changing, she told me it's their policy. Look, go back to the store and find out for yourself if you don't believe me."

"Kade, where'd you get the money to pay for it?"

"The Prom Elf doesn't need money."

"Was it from the money you've been saving for contacts?"

"You're talking to the wrong person. You should be talking to the Prom Elf."

"You've been saving for so long for contacts. It isn't right for you to do this."

"I'll tell you what's not right. It's not right that your dad should be refused a loan."

"My parents will never let me keep this when they find out you paid for it. We don't take charity."

"Tell them you picked it up at the Salvation Army for a couple of bucks."

"They wouldn't believe that."

"Why not?"

"Kade, you can't pick up a brand-new formal at the Salvation Army."

"Mess it up a little then."

"That'd be deceiving my parents."

"Maybe so, but it'd get you to the prom. Brenda, I'm serious, the store won't take the formal back. So what do you want to do, hang it in your closet or wear it to the prom?"

She thought about it for a long time. "All right, I'll go."

On the way home he folded the dress into a ball and sat on it so it wouldn't look brand new when she showed it to her mother.

"What about your contact lenses?" she asked.

"They probably wouldn't have made me look older anyway."

"You truly are the nicest guy I've ever known in my whole life."

He smiled. "It wasn't me. It was the Prom Elf. Every year the Prom Elf looks for the most beautiful, deserving girl in all the world. This year it just happened to be you."

"Kade," she said, her voice wavering, "I'll never forget this, not if I live to be a hundred."

"Me neither," he said.

The next day at school Marvin Mudlin came up to Kade, his face red with anger. "Tell your dad thanks for everything."

"I'm sorry."

"I try to be friends with you and look what it gets me." With that, Marvin left him.

The few days before the prom were a blur of activity. Together, Kade and Brenda planned every detail.

"Where do you think Jason and I should eat before the prom?"

"Pat's Diner."

"You can't eat there for a prom. It's too ordinary."

"So what? Everything in this town is ordinary." He paused. "You might try the Dixie Inn. I ate there once. It was all right. By the way, where's Jason going to stay when you two finally call it a night?"

"He'll stay at Sister Simmons's."

"Great. That'll make Melissa happy."

"Are you going to start on Melissa?" she asked.

"She's such a witch sometimes. How can someone as nice as Sister Simmons have a daughter like her?"

"She'll grow up one of these days."

"Sure, in about fifty years."

"Kade, don't be so negative all the time."

"I'm sorry, but it's what males do when they develop sexually. They exhibit aggressive characteristics."

Brenda burst out laughing.

"It's true," Kade said. "I read it in the barber shop when I was getting a haircut. Of course, it was about mule deer, but I think the same thing applies to a guy."

"You're so funny sometimes."

"Hey, maybe I wasn't trying to be funny. Did you ever think of that?"

"Oh, gosh, Kade, we have such good times together, don't we?"

"Yeah, that's for sure."

"In a way I wish you could come with Jason and me to the prom."

"I'm sure he wouldn't mind if I sat between you two in the car."

"Why not? I bet the three of us'd have a good time."

"Except when he tried to kiss you."

"Maybe he won't try."

"If he does, are you going to let him?"

She paused. "I don't know. What do you think?"

He thought about it. "I'd say go ahead."

She was surprised. "Really? Why?"

"Because he's laying out a lot of money, and I think he should get something back in return."

"You're awful, you know that?" she said.

"What's awful?"

"I won't kiss a guy just because he's put out money for a date."

"Why not?"

"Because when two people kiss, it's supposed to mean they really like each other."

"Well, you do what you want, but he's going to figure it's a big waste if you don't kiss him at least once."

"How do you know that?"

"I just do."

"You're only fifteen."

"I listen to guys talk in the locker room."

"Jason's not like those guys."

"Maybe not, but he has some of the same male characteristics."

She smiled. "Are you going to talk about mule deer again?"

"I say give the guy a good-night kiss."

"Well, I don't know. I'll think about it."

"Good."

They were in front of his house. "Thanks for the ride," he said.

"Sure. See you tomorrow."

On Saturday, the day of the prom, Brenda asked him over while her mother fixed her hair. When he got there, they were in the kitchen. He sat down and they talked. Emmet came in a while later.

"Come and take a look at your daughter, Emmet."

He took one look and smiled. "You look like a creature from outer space with those rollers in your hair."

"Thanks, Dad," she said. "That really builds my confidence."

"Are you fishing for a compliment? The best thing you've got going for you is that you've got your mother's beauty." He noticed Kade. "Hi, Kade. How's it going? What are you doing, making sure they do it right?"

"Something like that." He paused. "I'm sorry about my dad not loaning you the money you need."

"Don't worry about it. We're working on getting another loan. Things'll work out."

"Speaking of that, Otis Cramer called," Susan said.

"What did he want?"

"He wanted to know when was a good time to come out and look around and help us fill out a loan application."

"Tell him to come anytime it's convenient for him." He looked at the clock on the wall. "Well, I'd better be going."

"Daddy, will you be around at five when Jason comes to pick me up?"

He smiled. "You bet. I thought that'd be a good time to clean my shotgun. Just to let him know what'll happen if he doesn't treat you right."

Brenda laughed. "You would, too, wouldn't you!"

"You bet I would."

"Well, if you promise not to do that, I'll let you see what the finished product looks like. Just so you'll know you really do have a daughter here."

"No kidding? Is that what you are? No wonder you look different in jeans than I do."

She grinned. "Sure. For one thing I don't have a big paunch around my middle like some people I could name."

"Watch it," Emmet said. "You're getting into deep waters now." He glanced at Kade. "Kade, you ever wish you were Brenda's age?"

"Daddy," Brenda objected.

"All the time," Kade said.

"Well, if it's any consolation, age isn't that important once you're out of high school. A lot of people don't know this, but Susan here is five years older than me."

"Such lies," Susan said. "You'll never get anybody to believe that."

"Kade here believes it. Don't you, Kade?"

"Sure. If you said it, it must be true."

"You see there? Kade and me, we stick together. Well, I gotta run."

"Where are you going?" Susan asked.

"Into town. A few of us are getting together at the diner to talk about our options. He looked at Kade. "You probably never figured a dumb farmer like me would use the word options, did you? It's what happens when your back is up against the wall."

After Emmet left, Kade got up to leave. Brenda invited him back at four thirty. "You can see me all fixed up and glamorous."

"I'm going over to Brenda's," Kade said a little before four thirty.

"What for?" his mother asked.

"To see Brenda with her formal on."

"Are you sure they want you over there now?"

"Brenda invited me."

"All right."

"Can I use the car?"

"When will you be back?"

"I don't know. I don't think I'll be very long."

"Your father will be home in an hour."

"Where is he?"

"At his office." She paused. "Kade, he's going through a tough time right now. If you could . . . "

"What?"

"If you could just try and see things from his point of view."

"Mom, he's refusing to loan money to Brenda's father and Mr. Mudlin. It's not fair. They need money to keep things going until their crops get harvested."

"There's some things you don't know. You'll just have to trust that your father is trying to do the right thing."

He sighed. "I just don't see why he has to be so strict all the time."

"Kade, this is a difficult time for everyone, including your father."

A few minutes later Kade sat at the kitchen table in Brenda's home and waited. Her mother came into the room. "Ladies and gentlemen, may I present the most enchanting young woman in the entire world."

Brenda appeared, ready for the prom. Besides being embarrassed that her mother was making such a fuss over her, she radiated something else. It was the realization that somehow in the process of growing up, she had become a beautiful woman.

"What do you think?" she asked.

"Wow," he said softly. "You look great."

"Thank you," she said somewhat formally, not sounding like the girl in jeans he rode to school with every day.

They heard a door slam. Emmet walked in, took one look at Brenda, and stopped in his tracks. "Gosh, gal, you ought to get gussied up more often."

"I couldn't work outside with you if I did that. You still think I should?"

"You got me there all right." He turned to Kade. "We're interested in knowing what a typical teenage boy thinks of the way my daughter looks."

"She's the best-looking girl I've ever seen."

Emmet nodded. "And there you have it, folks."

"Let me get a picture of Brenda and Kade together," Susan said.

"No, not me," Kade objected.

"Oh, sure. Don't go shy on us now. Stand alongside Brenda. Emmet, you get in there too."

Brenda was in the middle with Kade on her left and Emmet on her right. "Talk about your rose among thorns," Brenda said.

"Kade and me think it's the thorn among roses. Right, Kade?"

"You bet."

"And besides, Missy, you're not so dolled up you can't be tickled."

There was a quiet elegance in her bearing that allowed her to take charge. "Not tonight," she said. That was all it took.

"I'm going to go make some punch for when Jason comes," Susan said.

"Dad, you behave yourself when Jason comes, okay?"

"All right, if I have to. Well, I do need to get on the horn and talk to a few people. Come and get me when he shows up. I have a list of one hundred rules I want to read to him before he takes you out."

Kade and Brenda went to the living room and sat down.

"You're kind of quiet tonight," she said.

"Yeah, I guess I am. You look so different."

"I feel different."

"How do you mean?"

"I feel more like a woman."

"Guys who see you at the dance are going to get weak in the knees, and if you happen to smile at them, they won't be able to sleep tonight. Girls are going to hate you because you look better than they do. And Jason is going to feel like he's taking out Miss America."

"And to think I owe it all to the Prom Elf."

He shrugged. "It wasn't that big of a deal."

"Kade, in some ways I wish I were going to the prom with you."

"Me? Why?"

"Because you're the best friend I ever had."

They heard a car pull into the driveway. "That must be Jason," she said.

A few minutes later Jason and Brenda left for the restaurant.

"I'd better be going now," Kade said.

"We thought we'd peek in tonight and see how the dance is going," Emmet said. "You want to ride into town with us about nine?"

"Okay."

Kade went home and ate supper and watched TV until eight thirty and then went to his dad, who was preparing the lesson he would give in priesthood meeting. "Brenda's parents invited me to go into town with them to watch Brenda and Jason dance."

"Are you all ready for church tomorrow?" he asked.

"Pretty much."

"Have you taken a shower and washed your hair?"

"I'll do that in the morning."

"All right. Don't stay out too late."

When they arrived at the school, they went up to the bleachers, where they could look down on the dance-floor without being seen. Jason and Brenda were dancing. They looked good together.

"Our baby is growing up," Susan said.

"And I'm losing the best farmhand I've ever had," Emmet said. He paused and then added, "In fact, I might even be losing the farm."

"Let's forget all that tonight," Susan said.

After watching for a few minutes, they left. "What do you say we stop at the diner and see if anybody's there?" Emmet said.

"You men must spend half your waking life in that place."

"That's our office. Kade, you want a dish of ice cream, don't you?"

"Sure."

"I thought so."

They walked in and sat down in a booth. The waitress came over. "Mary Ellen, what's a good-looking girl like you doing here when you could be over at the dance?"

"You mean the high school dance? Emmet, I'm twenty-nine years old."

"You are? Gosh, you could've fooled me. You look a lot younger than that."

She smiled. "You're just saying that because you want an extra-large piece of pie. Well, you've outdone yourself this time, Emmet. For that compliment I might just give you the whole pie."

Emmet seemed to know everyone who walked in. He'd call out a greeting, and people would come over and talk.

A man and his wife entered the diner and saw Emmet and Susan. They came over, pulled up some chairs, and sat down.

"Emmet, I hear you're in the same boat as me," the man said.

"Yeah, that's right."

"If that idiot over at the bank thinks he can just shut us down, he's got another think coming."

Emmet cleared his throat. "This is Kade. He's Paul Ellis's son."

"Sorry, Kade, but it doesn't change the way I feel. We're not going to put up with the treatment we've been getting from the bank lately."

"I hope you come out on top," Kade said.

"The kid's got more sense than his old man," the man said.

"We'd better go," Susan said to Emmet.

"Yeah, I guess we'd better. We need to get Kade home. You two, don't be strangers. Drop over sometime and we'll play cards like we used to."

"Maybe we will," the man said, "if you promise not to cheat like you usually do."

"Hey, you're the one who taught me how to play the game," Emmet said.

Later that night Kade was awakened when he heard a vehicle coming down the lane. It stopped in front of the house, and a minute later he heard Brenda under his window calling his name. He opened the window and leaned out.

"Kade, I want to talk to you."

He got dressed and went outside and got into the pickup with Brenda.

"I just got home from the dance," she said.

"What time is it?"

"One o'clock."

"How was it?"

"It was the most wonderful night of my life."

"Did you give Jason a good-night kiss?"

"Yes."

"That's nice. For him, I mean."

She smiled. "For me too."

"No kidding?"

"I really like him."

"I'm glad."

"I saved the last dance for you because of what you did to make it so I could go to the prom. Let's go into the barn where it's dry."

She didn't have boots, so he carried her through the snow to the barn. He flipped on the light. The barn was cold and barren. She removed her coat, leaving her bare shoulders exposed to the cold.

"Are you sure you want to do that?" he said. "It's really freezing in here."

"I'll be okay. Dance with me, Kade."

She hummed a song as they danced. There were tears in her eyes. He thought about holding her close to him to try and keep her warm, but he wasn't sure if he should do that or not. Before he could decide, she quit dancing. "Kade, I'll never ever forget what you did for me." She kissed him on the cheek, then turned and reached for her coat and put it on.

He carried her back to the pickup. A minute later she left, and he went inside and went to bed. He couldn't sleep for a long time, though; he could still smell the fragrance of her perfume.

At seven that morning his father came to the foot of the stairs and called for Kade to get up and get ready for church.

The family arrived at the Odd Fellows Hall at eight thirty and started cleaning up, so that by a quarter to nine they were ready to begin. Attendance was way down that Sunday. The people assigned to give talks weren't there. The deacon assigned to bring bread had also not shown up, so Kade was sent out at the last minute to a store to buy some. By the time he returned, it was ten minutes after nine—and yet there was still hardly anyone there.

Kade's father got up to conduct the meeting. "I guess our speakers haven't shown up yet."

"The Aldriches said they weren't coming anymore as long as you were branch president," one of the older women said. "They said they can't see how you can be a branch president and refuse hard-working people loans to run their farms."

Kade wasn't sure if his father would be able to carry on with the meeting. A minute passed. The Simmons's baby began crying, and Sister Simmons took her out to the kitchen.

Finally his father spoke. "I never asked to be branch president." He stopped. "I'm sorry. You didn't come to hear that—you came to partake of the sacrament. Let's at least do that today."

Kade was painfully aware that Jason and Brenda were there. He wondered if Jason would go home and tell everyone how awful church was in Shelby.

After the sacrament, his father stood up again. "Our speakers still haven't shown up. Are there any volunteers?"

"I have a poem I could read," Sister Richardson volunteered.

"Please, that would be wonderful."

She read the poem and then rambled on for about ten minutes. A couple of other people got up and bore their testimonies. And then the meeting ended. Because there were so few people there, the Sunday School classes had to be combined.

After they got home from church, Kade's dad tried to get hold of the stake presidency, but he was told they were traveling to another ward that day and wouldn't be home until much later.

Kade had wanted to go over and see Brenda in the afternoon, but she had told him at church that she was probably going to sleep most of the day, and so he went up to his room and sketched out what it had been like when they danced in the cold and empty barn. With just one overhead light on, the darkness and shadows and harsh cold provided marked contrast to her warmth and beauty.

Around four in the afternoon the phone rang. Kade's father took the call on the kitchen phone. Kade was having a snack, so he could hear his father's end of the conversation.

" . . . President Mathesen, thanks for returning my call . . . You know I work for the bank here in town. I'm sure you're aware the farm economy is in a real slump these days. I've had to refuse loaning any more money to some of the farmers in the area until they do something to improve their financial situation. Well, the word's gotten out. Some of our members are staying away from church because of my being the branch president . . . Well, I'm thinking I might be the wrong man for this calling . . . Maybe if I had counselors, it'd be different . . . No, there's nobody who could be a counselor . . . I have prayed, President. There's nobody . . . All right, I'll try fasting about it too. President

Mathesen, you've got to come up here and see if you need to release me . . . Yes, next Sunday would be great. Thank you. Goodbye." He hung up the phone. "Kade?"

"Yes."

"Get your mother. I'd like to have family council."

A minute later the three of them, sitting around the kitchen table, began family council. Kade was asked to give the prayer.

His father seemed off balance and somber. "I talked to President Mathesen. He'll be visiting our branch next Sunday. I thought I'd fast and pray for help, and I was wondering if my family would be willing to join me."

"Of course we will," his mother answered. "When?"

"We could start after our evening meal today and go until our evening meal tomorrow."

"I have school tomorrow," Kade said.

"If you'd rather not fast, that's all right," his dad said.

"Kade," his mother said, "this is really important to your father."

"I don't like to fast."

"He doesn't have to if he doesn't want to," his father said.

His mother put her hand on Kade's arm. "Won't you do this one thing for your father?"

The way she said it made him feel guilty. "All right." He paused. "Can we pray for Emmet and for Marvin Mudlin's dad and all the others too?"

"Yes, of course," his dad said.

For supper they had split pea soup and tuna sandwiches. Then they went into the living room and knelt down. His dad offered the prayer as they began their fast.

That night Brenda invited him over to study with her. The minute he walked in her house, he knew he was in trouble because of the smell of cinnamon rolls baking in the oven.

After he'd been there for half an hour, Emmet invited Brenda and Kade to the kitchen for a snack.

"I can't eat," Kade said.

"Why not?"

"I'm fasting."

"What for?" Emmet asked.

"Our family is doing it because of my dad. Things aren't going very well for him these days, both at the bank and at church. So we're fasting so he'll know what to do, and also for the farmers in trouble."

Emmet looked at the platter of cinnamon rolls. "Susan, let's have these some other time. It wouldn't be fair for us to eat in front of Kade."

"Does that mean we'll be fasting too?" Susan asked.

Emmet paused. "I guess it does."

"And praying?" Susan said.

Emmet cleared his throat. "I suppose you got to have one with the other, don't you?"

"Yes," Susan said.

"All right, we'll pray too." He turned to Susan. "I'm kind of new at this. You got any suggestions?"

"I think it'd be nice to have family prayer."

"All right."

"Maybe if we knelt down too," Susan said.

Emmet got out of his chair and knelt down.

"We've never prayed before as a family," Brenda said as she and Kade knelt down.

"There's always the first time. Now what?" Emmet asked Susan.

"I think it'd be nice if you said the prayer."

"Me?"

"You're the head of this family."

"But I don't even go to church."

"You're still the head of the family."

"I think you should start going to church," Kade said.

"Why?"

"My dad needs help in church too."

"He and I are on opposite sides these days. It wouldn't make much sense for the two of us to be in church together, would it?"

"Maybe it'd help," Brenda said.

"How?"

"I don't know."

"Me neither. Well, I guess we'd better pray," Emmet's prayer came painfully slow, but he did it.

When Kade got home his mother had gone to bed. His father was in his office, sitting at his desk, reading the scriptures. Kade went in to see him. His father looked up from his reading. "You're home."

"Yes."

"You'd better get to bed so you'll get your rest."

"All right."

His father read for a few seconds and then, not hearing the sound of Kade's footsteps, turned around. "Is anything wrong?"

"No." Kade wanted to do something that would let his dad know what was in his heart. Without knowing exactly why he did it, he went over and put his hand on his dad's shoulder. The two of them froze in place, neither one wanting the experience to end, both hesitant to ask why this gesture of affection was there when it had been absent between them for so long.

"Dad?"

"Yes."

"I know this is a hard time for you. I hope everything turns out okay."

A long time passed, and then his father, his voice husky with emotion, said, "Thank you. I appreciate that."

Kade removed his hand from his father's shoulder. "I guess I'll go to bed now."

"All right. Good night, son."

"Good night, Dad."

The next morning his mother was sitting at the kitchen table when he passed by on his way out of the house to go to seminary. "Kade, you don't have to fast all day if it gets to be too hard. If you feel sick or anything, be sure and have something to eat."

"I will."

"Your father appreciates what you said to him last night."

"Oh."

"I packed you a snack just in case you need it during the day."

"I won't need it."

"It won't hurt to take it along, just in case."

Brenda pulled into the driveway. He took the sack of food his mother had fixed him and left.

As they were pulling onto the county road, he said, "My mom packed a snack in case I decided I need to eat, and so you can have it too, if you need it."

"Do you think you'll need it?" she asked.

"No."

"Have you ever fasted before on a weekday?" she asked.

"No."

"Me neither. Could we get together at lunchtime and go to the library?" she asked.

"Sure."

At lunch they went to the library and talked. It was the first time she'd ever openly associated with him at school. There was an unspoken rule against a junior girl choosing a freshman boy as a friend. But on that day she didn't seem to care. They sat where anybody who came into the library could see them. Once she even put her hand on his arm and left it there for several seconds.

Marvin Mudlin saw them together. He probably would have walked by, but Kade made the first move. "Hi, Marvin."

He stopped. "Hey, Kade, what's this? You chasing older women these days?"

"We're just studying together."

"I don't see why Brenda spends time with you when I'm available."

Kade smiled. "What can I say? Some guys got it and some don't."

Their joking was an uphill battle. It was followed by an awkward silence.

"How's your dad getting along?" Kade finally asked.

"Okay. Right now he's trying to find some other place to get a loan."

"Look, you guys," Kade said, "I'm really sorry about all this."

"We know you are," Brenda said.

Marvin sat down at the table. "Brenda, did you ever hear about the time Kade defended your honor?"

"No. When was that?"

"Just after you broke up with Doug. We were in the locker room after practice, and Doug started mouthing off about his dates with you. We all knew he was lying, but for some reason we let him go on anyway. Except for Kade. He told Doug to shut up. They were just about to fight when I grabbed Doug and made him take back the things he was saying."

"Thanks, Marvin. I'm glad Kade didn't have to fight Doug."

"I should've been the one to tell Doug to quit. I knew he was lying, but I let him go on anyway. Kade was the one who first stepped in. That really impressed me." He paused. "Well, I'd better be going."

After Marvin left, Kade tried to study, but he was

aware that Brenda was staring at him. "What?" he finally asked.

"What am I ever going to do with you?"

"I don't know."

"I don't know either."

That evening before supper, Kade's family had family prayer. After it was over, his father said, "I have an answer about what to do."

"Tell us," Kade said.

"You'll have to wait until Sunday to find out."

On Tuesday night, while Kade was studying, his mother came upstairs. "President Mathesen is going to come and stay with us Saturday night. Would it be okay if we gave him your room and had you sleep on the couch in the living room?"

"Will I have to clean my room?"

"Yes, of course. Kade, it'll be so good for your dad to have President Mathesen here. Can I count on you to help me get ready for him?"

"Okay."

Kade cleaned his room on Saturday morning. As he straightened out his desk, he came across a copy of *Time* that he'd been keeping for a long time. It contained a painting done by a famous artist of a scantily clad woman. Shortly after the magazine had come in the mail, Kade had taken it upstairs to see if he could draw a picture of the woman the way she was in the magazine. While he worked on it, his dad called him down for family prayer. To make matters worse, he was asked to say the prayer. Afterwards he returned to his room and looked at what he had drawn. He felt like a hypocrite. He crumpled up the drawing and promised himself he wouldn't draw any more pictures like that. He crumpled up the paper and took it to school the next morning and dropped it in one of the large wastepaper baskets in the hall. Even if somebody found it, nobody would know that he was the one who had done the drawing.

That seemed like a long time ago. Kade had been true to the promise he'd made himself—but still he kept the magazine in his room. And sometimes he even looked at the picture. Now, knowing that President Mathesen would be staying in his room, he decided it was a good time to get rid of that temptation. He carried the magazine out to the trash incinerator.

Later that day he tried to think if there was anything else in his life that needed throwing out. He wondered what it would be like if the Savior was going to spend the night in his room. What things in his life would he change then? He went inside himself to find the weaknesses he needed to overcome, so that by the time the room was done, he felt clean too.

President Mathesen arrived at about eight o'clock on Saturday night.

"President, Kade will show you up to your room," his mother said. "Be sure and watch your head on the stairs."

Kade led him up the stairs to his room. "This is it."

"I'm sorry to be bumping you out of your room."

"No problem."

"Do you always keep it this clean?"

Kade smiled. "No."

"Good. My sons will be glad to hear that. They hate to be told about boys who keep their rooms clean."

At nine that night Kade took a shower and washed his hair because his mother said they had to leave President Mathesen as much time in the bathroom as he needed in the morning. After Kade's shower, he changed into a pair of pajamas, rolled out his sleeping bag on the couch, shut the door, and turned the TV on low so it wouldn't disturb anyone.

A little while later the doorbell rang. His mother opened the door, and he heard the voices of Brenda's parents and then Brenda herself. His mother took them into the kitchen, and Kade heard President Mathesen greeting them. "I'll need to talk to Brother Sloan alone if I might," President Matheson said.

Suddenly the door to the living room opened and the light went on. Brenda and the two mothers were standing in the doorway.

"Oh, gosh, I forgot about Kade being in here," his mother said.

"It's all right, Mom. I'm not asleep."

They came in. Still in his sleeping bag, he sat up on the couch.

"Hi," he said to Brenda.

"Hi." She sat down in a chair next to the couch.

"How was President Mathesen's trip here?" Brenda's mother asked.

"Not too bad," Kade's mother said. "That storm they were warning us about must have slipped past us."

"Good. We've had enough storms for this winter. I'm looking forward to spring again. You know, my garden catalog arrived the other day. I must have spent an hour just looking at the pictures."

Brenda, bored by the conversation, turned to Kade. "You look like a cute little caterpillar in that sleeping bag."

"Thanks, I've always wanted to be called a caterpillar."

A few minutes later Brenda's mother was called into the room to speak to President Mathesen. Kade's mother excused herself to go finish folding clothes.

"What's going on?" Brenda asked after they left.

"Beats me."

A few minutes later Emmet came in the room and sat down across from Kade and Brenda. "Brenda, something's come up that I need to talk to you about."

"I can leave if you want," Kade said.

"No, that's all right. Maybe you should hear it too." He paused. "President Mathesen has asked me to be a counselor in the branch presidency to help Kade's dad."

Brenda's mouth dropped open. "He asked *you*?"

"Yes."

"But you haven't even been going to church."

"I told him that. I told him everything, about drinking coffee and not paying tithing and swearing once in a while when I'm trying to fix something and hit my thumb with a hammer."

She grinned. "It's more than once in a while, Dad."

"I also told him about Kade's dad refusing us operating funds for next summer. It doesn't make sense for him and me to be working together in a church calling."

"What did he say?"

"He said he felt we could work it out."

"What are you going to do?"

"I told him I'd think about it and let him know in the morning. Let's go home now."

The clock struck one o'clock. Emmet sat alone at the kitchen table. He had gone to bed earlier, but after tossing and turning for more than an hour, he'd finally gotten up so he wouldn't keep Susan awake.

At one thirty Susan got up to see if he was all right.

"I've decided to say no," he said.

"I see."

"It doesn't make sense for me to work with Paul when he's trying to shut us down."

"Is that what he's trying to do?"

"Sure it is."

"Maybe he's really trying to help us."

"He's got a strange way of going about it then."

"Maybe he's right. Maybe we *are* too much in debt. It might not hurt to sell off some of our land."

"We'd take a big loss if we sold now."

"I know, but it'd cut way down on how much we owe."

"Whose side are you on anyway?"

"I haven't been able to sleep either. The question that keeps running through my mind is what if President Mathesen is right. What if this is a call from the Lord?"

"He probably says that to everyone."

"The point is he said it to you."

"It's too much to ask of a man to change his whole life-style overnight. I'd have to quit drinking coffee. I'd have to start going to church. I'd have to start paying tithing."

"Emmet, why haven't we been paying tithing?"

"We can't afford it."

"If you ask me, we can't afford not to."

"You think God will solve our problems if we start paying tithing?"

"No, I don't think that. But I'm pretty sure that paying tithing would help us more than it would hurt us. Emmet, we're in trouble. We could use a little help from God about now, couldn't we? How well have we managed on our own?"

"Someday I'll start paying tithing, but not now."

"Brenda's sixteen now. In a few years she's going to want to get married—in the temple, I hope. I want to be there with her, and I want you with me. Why don't we try doing things the Lord's way for a while and see if things work out any better?"

"You make everything sound so simple."

"Emmet, all our married life I've been waiting for you. Time is running out. My daughter needs a father who honors his priesthood so she'll want that in her home when she's married."

"There's other decent young men in the world besides Mormons. What about Doug? He comes from a good family, and he's got an interest in farming. He'd be a good husband for Brenda."

"You still don't know why she broke up with him, do you."

"No. Why did she?"

"Your precious Doug got drunk and tried to talk Brenda into going to bed with him."

"Did he do anything to her?"

"No, he just suggested it. That's all it took for Brenda. She made him take her home, and the next day she broke up with him."

"That sleazeball."

"That's why she spends so much time with Kade, because there's nobody else in school she trusts."

"Kade's a good boy."

"How can you say that and still not recognize how much the Church has helped to make him the way he is? I get so frustrated being your wife sometimes." She went back to bed.

Now Emmet felt worse than before.

At three o'clock Brenda got up to go to the bathroom. On her way back to bed, she saw him sitting in the kitchen. "Can't sleep, huh, Dad?"

"No."

She went over and began massaging his shoulders. "How's that?"

"Great. That'll probably put me right to sleep. Sit down, Brenda, and let's talk."

She sat down.

"Your mother says Doug tried to talk you into . . . " He cleared his throat. " . . . into going all the way with him."

Brenda blushed. "That's right. Nothing happened

though. Don't get mad at Doug. He was drunk at the time, so he probably didn't know what he was doing."

"That's no excuse."

"I know that."

"Why wasn't I told about it?"

"I don't know. I talked to Mom about it. I guess she didn't tell you because you always say what a great guy Doug is." She paused. "Also, I wasn't sure but what it might've been okay with you if I'd gone along with what Doug wanted."

"Why would you think that?"

"Because it might make it so I'd end up marrying him. That's what you want, isn't it, so that he and I can take over the farm someday? Besides, Mom is the one who talks about chastity. You never do."

"I feel the same way about it as your mother does."

"I guess I didn't know that for sure."

"Your mother says the reason you spend so much time with Kade is because he's the only boy in school you trust. Is that right?"

"Yes. Most of the guys in school my age drink a lot, so I end up with Kade. It's a little strange, him being only in the ninth grade and all. But he's a nice guy, and we're friends." She paused. "Of course, there's no big-time romance between us, but I guess he'll do until I go to BYU and meet—"she got a big grin on her face—"some real men."

"I feel like I don't even know you anymore. Where have I been all the time you've been growing up?"

"You've been busy."

He shook his head. "That's being too busy."

"Are you going to accept the calling, Dad?"

"I don't know. I've got six more hours to decide. You'd better go back to bed. Somebody in this family has to be awake enough tomorrow to drive."

When Susan got up at seven, she found Emmet in the kitchen, staring at a cup of coffee.

She sat down. "Are you going to drink that or what?"

"Coffee has such a wonderful smell, doesn't it? I mean, you will admit that, won't you?"

"Yes, it smells great."

"You walk into any office in town, and the first thing anyone asks is if you'd like a cup of coffee. And you say yes, and they give you a cup and sit around and talk, and it's like you're all good friends. It's great. Especially in the winter when it's forty below. A cup of coffee warms you up all the way down. No doubt about it, it's great to be a coffee drinker."

"Then why aren't you drinking it?"

He sighed. "I can't. Not anymore."

"Why not?"

"Do you know that Brenda thought that it might have been all right with me if she had gone to bed with Doug? She says I've never talked to her about morality. If it weren't for the things you taught her, she might've made a terrible mistake. Kade's done more to help her see what a man should be than I have. There's not much time left, but I've got to do what I can to be a good example for her." He paused. "I've decided to accept the calling in the branch presidency."

The next morning in sacrament meeting, President Mathesen was given time to conduct some business. "It is proposed that we sustain Emmet Sloan as first counselor in the branch presidency of the Shelby Branch. All those who can sustain Brother Sloan in this calling, please indicate by the uplifted hand." He looked over the congregation. "Any opposed? Thank you. It would be most appropriate now for Brother Sloan to come and take his place on the stand. We would like to hear a few words from him and then from his wife."

Emmet, a little uncomfortable in his suit, walked to the podium and nervously cleared his throat. "I was up all night trying to decide whether or not to accept this calling," he finally began. "I've had to do a lot of soul searching." He paused. "When a man looks back on his life and tries to decide what it all means, a lot of things you thought were important fall by the wayside. Sometimes you have to ask yourself, 'What's the most important thing in life?' All the things we own will be left behind when we die. But some things won't ever die. One is the love I have for my wife, Susan, and my daughter, Brenda. This church is important to the two people in my life I care the most about. So if it's important to them, maybe it should be important to me too. I need to learn more about the church. I need to find out how it can turn out a girl like Brenda and a boy like Kade. I don't know much about what exactly I'm supposed to do, but I promise you this—I'll do my very best." He sighed. "No matter what happens to my land."

After church, they gathered in the kitchen of the Odd Fellows hall, and there President Mathesen set apart Emmet.

On Tuesday night the two families got together for a potluck supper. Afterwards the two men went to Paul's office to talk and make plans. Kade and Brenda went into the living room to talk, while their mothers cleaned things up in the kitchen.

"Do you want to listen to some of the music my mom likes?" Kade asked.

"Sure, I guess so."

He put on a record of Beethoven's Fifth Symphony.

"You actually like this?" she asked.

"Yeah, sure, why not? I've been listening to it all my life. Even when I was little, my dad would take my sister and me to hear Mom play in the symphony. At first I had a hard time lasting all the way through it, but then my dad started giving me Lifesavers at the beginning of each concert. The thing I found out is that very few concerts last longer than one roll of Lifesavers. And after a while I actually started to enjoy it. I'll bet if you listened to classical music for a while, you'd learn to like it too."

"Maybe so." She paused. "You know what? You're a strange combination. Are you still lifting weights?"

"Yeah."

"I noticed your arms the other day. You're really turning into a hunk."

"I'm going to be taller and stronger than Jason before long."

"I bet you are too."

"Better looking too."

"Maybe so."

He gave up. "But not older."

"Right, not older."

"How are you and Jason getting along these days?" he asked.

"Good. His parents made him quit calling me because it was too expensive, so now we just write. We'll see each other next week at the youth dance."

"Do you miss him?"

"Yes, a lot. He's fun to be with. I like his sense of humor. He's always saying funny things."

"Like what?"

"Like when we were eating before the prom. He said the Chinese invented noodles and that spaghetti is a Chinese word meaning worms."

He looked at her. "That's not funny."

"Well, not now, but it was then."

"I could tell dumb jokes like that too."

"Kade, back off, okay? You're not in competition with him. I like him in a certain way and I like you in a different way." She paused. "I hate it when you get that puppy-dog look in your eyes."

"I want to go with someone," he said.

"You're not even sixteen. You're not supposed to date yet."

"I can think about it though, can't I?"

"I guess so."

"You've got Jason. Who've I got?"

"Linda."

"I want someone who lives around here."

"There's girls at school who like you."

"Who?"

"Lots of girls. Cynthia Rathlutner, for one."

"Cynthia Rathlutner?" He moaned. "You gotta be kidding."

"What's wrong with her? She's nice."

"Sure, if you like clarinet players."

"What's wrong with clarinet players?"

"Have you ever watched anyone play the clarinet? They sort of curl their bottom lip into their mouth, so it looks like they lost it in a fight with a bear."

"Kade, that's an awful thing to say."

"Then why are you laughing?"

"Because you're so funny sometimes."

"I'm funnier than Jason, that's for sure."

"There you go again."

"We do have good times together though, don't we?" he said.

"The best."

"I wish it could always be this way between us."

"It will be."

"What about when you go to college?"

"We'll still write to each other." She paused. "Besides, you won't always need me."

"How can you say that?"

"I can see it coming. You're like an eagle learning to fly. At first you go just a short distance and then come back to the nest, but one day you'll fly so high that you'll see how big and wonderful the world is, and you'll leave the nest and never come back."

He thought about it and then said, "That's the stupidest thing I've ever heard."

"It's not stupid, it's an analogy. When you get to be a junior, you'll learn about analogies."

"I don't care what it is, it's still dumb. I'm no eagle."

"What are you then?"

"A chipmunk."

"No, Kade, you're an eagle."

"In the first place, you're the one who's going to leave the stupid nest first. So if one of us is an eagle learning to fly, it's you, not me."

She paused. "Maybe we're both like young eagles learning to fly."

"Yeah, right," he scoffed. "You want something to eat? I thought I'd have ice cream, but, hey, since you're an eagle, maybe I can find you a live mouse."

"How dare you make fun of my analogies!" She chased after him, both of them giggling, through the kitchen and out the door.

The next weekend Paul and Emmet needed to go to Great Falls for a bishopric training session.

"How are you coming on getting an operating loan?" Paul asked as they rode along.

"Well, to tell you the truth, it's been a little disappointing. We haven't given up yet. It seems like if you're a poor risk with one bank, you're a poor risk with everybody."

"Maybe I can help. I could contact the places where you've applied and let them know that even though my hands are tied, I'm confident you're going to make it through this okay."

"You'd do that for me?"

"Of course."

"I don't want you to help me unless you do the same for the others." He paused. "How well do you know Harvey Mudlin?"

"Not very well."

"He's an awfully good man. If you just knew him better, I'm pretty sure you'd want to go to bat for him too. The same goes for the others. We can understand

135

you might not be able to loan us any more money, but if you could at least show people you care about 'em, that'd lessen some of the resentment we feel at the way we've been treated lately."

On Monday morning Paul stood at the door of a farmhouse and knocked.

Harvey Mudlin came to the door. "What do you want?"

"I came to see how you were doing."

"How would you be doing if you were in my shoes?"

"Have you found another source for an operating loan yet?"

"Why are you asking? Have you changed your mind about helping us?"

"No."

"Then get off my property."

"Wait, hear me out first. I'd like to see what I can do to help out. I'm willing to put in a good word for you at wherever it is you've applied for a loan."

"Why would you do that?"

"Emmet Sloan and I were talking the other day. He thinks a lot of you. This morning I did some checking. You're one of the top producers in this area. It looks to me like if you go under, there's not much hope for anyone else. Harvey, this area needs you. I just want to do whatever I can to help."

"I guess you'd better come in then."

Two weeks later Paul got a phone call from Dwight Allen.

"Paul, how are things going out there on the frontier? You haven't frozen to death yet, have you?"

"Not yet."

"Good. Look, I just wanted to make sure you've refused operating loans to the four we talked about."

"Yes."

"They can't farm without operating loans. Have any of them decided to sell out?"

"No. They got operating loans from other sources."

Dwight was surprised. "All of them?"

"Yes."

"How did they manage to do that?"

"I helped them."

"You what?"

"I went and talked to the loan officers at the places they applied to for loans."

"Your mind is turning to mush, Paul."

"That's not it."

"How do you explain it then?"

"It doesn't have anything to do with the mind, Dwight. It has to do with the heart."

With Paul Ellis's help, Emmet and the others were able to obtain operating loans for the summer. And so with another season assured, the pressure eased up some. Now all the four farmers had to worry about was if they'd have rain but not hail and if the price of wheat would be high enough so they could make a decent living—or at least break even.

At the end of April Paul and Emmet went to Great Falls for a stake leadership meeting. Kade and Brenda rode along because a home-study seminary Super Saturday lesson and activity were scheduled at the same time. Paul drove, with Emmet in the front seat and Brenda and Kade in the back.

Because she treated Kade like one of the family, Brenda slept for an hour, then woke up and brushed her hair and put on makeup.

"Going all out, are we?" Emmet kidded her. "Poor Jason doesn't stand a chance."

She smiled. "I hope not."

Kade figured Jason would be waiting for Brenda in the foyer of the church when they arrived, but he wasn't. Kade and Brenda walked to the seminary room together. Brenda looked for Jason. He saw her but didn't get up from where he was sitting, which was next to a girl with long blond hair.

"It's time to start now. Everyone take a seat," the teacher in charge announced.

Kade and Brenda found two empty seats and sat down. They had a good view of Jason. He was talking to the other girl.

After an opening song and a prayer and some announcements, the lesson began. Brenda kept her eyes on Jason and the blond girl. She leaned forward and asked the girl in front of her, "What's the name of that girl with Jason?"

"That's Amy. She's going with him."

Brenda's face turned a bright red. "Excuse me," she said. She got up and left the room.

Kade waited for her to come back, but she didn't, so he left to go find her. He walked through the building and went outside. She was standing by the car in the parking lot. He went over and stood beside her.

"I'm sorry," he said.

She nodded. Her eyes were moist but she wasn't crying.

"Are you going to talk to him?" Kade asked.

"No."

"You should. You should tell him what a puke-face he is. That's what I'd do."

"You're not me."

"You can't just let him get away with this. The least he could've done was to phone and tell you he didn't want to go with you anymore."

"We weren't going together."

"I know, but he kissed you. He shouldn't have kissed you unless he wanted to go with you."

"Maybe if I lived here, things would've been different. We only saw each other once a month."

"Why are you taking his side? The guy's a creep, that's all there is to it." He pulled out a set of car keys from his pocket. "You want to go for a ride?"

"Your dad doesn't want you driving around when you're supposed to be in a meeting."

"He'll never know. We can go anywhere you want. Just say the word. You want to go to the mall?"

"No. Let's go back inside."

"But Jason is there with Amy."

"I don't care. Let's go in." She started to walk away.

"Wait a minute."

"What?"

"Let me take over where Jason left off."

She frowned. "It can't ever be like that for us."

"Why not?"

"It just can't."

"I love you."

She closed her eyes as if it were bad news. "I know that."

"I'm taller than you now, and I have a driver's license."

"Kade, will you stop it? I've told you a hundred times how I feel. Why can't you just accept it and quit bothering me all the time?"

She went back inside.

He stewed for a while and then went back to the meeting, but he didn't sit next to her.

On the way home after the meeting, Brenda started reading a paperback novel. Kade, still hurt by her rejection, curled up and eventually went to sleep.

When he woke up, he glanced over at Brenda. She was asleep, the book on her lap. He closed his eyes and tried to go back to sleep, but it was no use.

His dad and Emmet were talking. "You want to know

something?" Emmet said. "I like being in the branch presidency."

"Good. I like having you there."

"If you want to know the truth, I'm a little surprised I can do the job."

"Why?"

"You know what they say, 'You can't teach an old dog new tricks.' "

"You're not exactly old."

"I know, but it's so easy to get in a rut. In leadership meeting today, when they started asking questions, I surprised myself because I knew the answers. It's like I'm discovering a part of me I never knew existed." He paused. "You know when they had us split up into small groups? Well, we got done before the other groups, so I started talking to the bishop of one of the wards in Great Falls. He's in the motel business. You might know him—Dennis McKinnon?"

"Sure, I've met him."

"He got to talking about his job, and all of a sudden I realized he gets paid every week. He pretty much knows how much money he's going to make this year. I thought to myself, isn't that amazing? I bet when he goes home at night, he can devote his energies to his family. I thought how lucky he is not to have a cloud hanging over his head twenty-four hours a day like I do."

"Even that isn't one hundred percent certain. If people quit staying at his motel, he'll lose money."

"Oh sure, but let's say that he does some things so his motel is full every night. He makes more money, right?"

"That's the way it works, all right."

"In farming, if you have a bumper crop, the price drops and you lose income." He paused. "Today I realized how much pressure is on me these days."

"You ready to be a motel manager?" Paul asked.

"No, but you know what? I could be if I wanted to." He sighed. "Of course, my dad would probably never speak to me again if I sold the place and pulled up stakes. He thinks the land has to remain in the family. I used to think that too, but now I'm not so sure. I guess I'm getting tired of all the time saying, 'Next year will be better.' It never is. Besides, who cares about farmers? Nobody."

"The reports that come across my desk predict a bumper grain crop this year," Paul said.

"I hope so. Not just for me, but for everybody. We're hurting these days. We really need a good year."

"Is Kade asleep?" Paul asked.

Emmet turned back. "Yeah. Why?"

"I was wondering if you could give me some advice."

"Advice about Kade? You don't need advice. You and Denise are doing a great job."

"Maybe so, but I've seen the way he lights up when he's around you. You're his favorite adult right now. I was just wondering what your secret is."

"Look, the only thing I've done is to put him to work when he comes around."

"You've done more for him than that. That set of barbells you made was the best Christmas gift he ever received."

"I'm glad to be Kade's friend, but one thing I'm sure of. When he gets older, he's going to see what a great man you are. When that happens, a set of homemade barbells isn't going to amount to a hill of beans."

"I just want to be what Kade needs me to be."

Kade felt the tears coming. Still pretending to be asleep, he turned so nobody could see.

"Emmet, you think that maybe someday you and I and Kade and Brenda could do something together?"

"You want to go camping?"

"Sure, why not?"

"All right. We'll do that real soon."

Kade heard Brenda moving, waking up from her nap. "How much longer?" she asked.

"Two thousand miles. We've decided to go to California," Emmet said.

"Oh, sure. President Ellis, I know you'll tell me the truth. How close are we to Shelby?"

"We'll be there in half an hour."

"And then we're going to California," Emmet added.

On Monday students signed up for the classes they wanted to take in the fall. On the way home after school, Kade asked Brenda if she'd signed up for art.

She paused. "No, I forgot."

"You said you'd take it with me."

She sighed. "I know, but I already have a full schedule."

"But you promised."

"Look, you have to learn to stand on your own two feet. You're the artist, not me. If you want to take an art class, then go ahead, but leave me out of it."

"But you promised."

"Why is it so important I take art with you?"

"I just want to have a class with you."

"Why? So you can pretend you're the same age as me?"

That hurt. "Just forget the whole stupid thing then."

"Are you going to take the class?" she asked.

"No."

"Why not."

"It wouldn't be the same."

"What are you trying to do, punish me? Sometimes you make me so mad. If you acted more grown up, then maybe we'd get along better. The kind of guy who interests me is someone who can stand on his own two feet. Don't go around trying to please me all the time. Decide what you want out of life and then go for it.

After I leave for college, you won't have me around to tell you what to do every step of the way."

When Kade got home, he went to his room to work out. He took off his shirt, picked up the barbell, and did an arm curl. He looked at his reflection in the mirror. He was a lot stronger than he used to be, but he wondered if it made any difference to Brenda. All this time he'd been trying to impress her one way when what she really wanted from him was something else. The only trouble was, he wasn't quite sure what she wanted.

After supper he asked his father if they could take a walk together. "Sure, let me change my shoes first, okay?"

They walked out past the barn. "Dad, I need some advice. I've got this summer and one more year of school before Brenda goes away to college. Before she leaves, I want her to like me the same way I like her. At first I thought it'd happen when I got to be stronger. That's partly why I've been working out. But today she told me some things that made me realize I don't understand her very well."

"What did she say?"

"She wants me not to depend on her so much. Does that make sense?"

"It might. Brenda has a very strong personality. She probably looks for that in others."

"Do you think I'll ever stand a chance with her?"

"I don't know, Kade. She *is* two years older than you. One thing in your favor, though—she chooses to spend time with you over any other guy in school. That must mean something."

"Sure. It means I'm the only guy in school who doesn't drink."

"Is that really true?"

"I don't know. It seems like it."

"I'm glad you haven't gone along with the crowd. I know it must not be easy at times."

"It's all right because of Brenda."

"You're both lucky to have each other. No matter what happens, you'll always be good friends."

"That's not enough." He paused. "I'll try being more independent and see how that works."

At school the next day, Kade set about proving that he could set his own course. First he approached the art teacher. "Mrs. Felton, can I talk to you for a minute?"

"Yes, what is it?"

He pulled out the drawing he'd done of Brenda and him in the barn after the prom. "I drew this."

She looked at it. "It's very good."

"I'm going to take art next year. I just wanted you to know."

"Is that all?" she asked.

"Yes, why?"

"Most people who bring me something ask if they have any talent. You didn't do that. Why not?"

"I already know I have talent."

She smiled. "You'll do fine. I'll look forward to having you in class."

An hour later, as Coach Brannigan ended another boys' gym, Kade approached him in the gym. "Can I talk to you?"

"Sure, Kade, what's up?"

"I've decided to go out for football next fall."

"What position?"

"A kicker."

"We don't have a separate kicker on our team."

"You will next year."

"What makes you think you can kick a football?"

"I played soccer in Illinois."

"Soccer isn't football."

"I'm going to practice all summer. I'm going to help the team win some games next fall, Coach. You'll see."

Kade could tell the coach wasn't convinced. He went to the rope hanging from the ceiling, lifted himself hand over hand to the top, and then lowered himself back down. "Coach, I don't suppose you could change my grade to an A now, could you?"

"What's got into you?"

"I'm just growing up, that's all. Look, I need a favor from you this summer."

"What?"

"I need to borrow some practice footballs. I'll need a supply so I can practice kicking without chasing after one ball all the time."

"I don't loan out school property over the summer."

"Coach, how much did we lose that last game by?"

"By a field goal."

"That's why you need a kicker. Give me a chance to show you what I can do."

The coach thought about it. "All right, come see me the last week of school, and I'll check out some footballs to you."

On the way home from school that day, Kade told Brenda what he'd done. "So, what do you think?" he asked.

She scowled. "I think you just ruined it."

"How?"

"By asking me what I thought. It's like you did it all just to impress me. If you want to play football, then play football, but don't do it just to impress me. It's your life, not mine."

"What do you want from me anyway? You're impossible to talk with anymore."

"Maybe we shouldn't see so much of each other for a while."

"Fine, no problem. I don't need you."

They drove in silence for several miles. "I'd still like to pick you up in the morning though," she finally said.

"Why?"

"Because your dad is helping with the gas and, well, the truth is we need the money, so let me keep picking you up. Okay?"

"There's only three more weeks of school. I guess I can stand it till then."

The next morning when he got in her pickup to ride to seminary, he brought with him a portable tape deck. He turned it on until it was louder than the music coming from her radio.

"What are you doing?" she yelled above the noise.

"Today we're going to listen to what I want."

"It's too noisy in here. Turn it off."

"No. You turn your radio off. You're getting paid to drive me into town, so be a good cab driver and do what I say."

She could see he wasn't going to back down, so she turned off her radio. "Honestly, Kade."

"What?"

"Why don't you grow up?"

"That's what I'm doing. Hey, if you cooperate, maybe I'll have my dad put in a couple of dollars extra at the end of the month. That's all you've cared about all this time anyway, isn't it?"

"You're hopeless."

"Good. That's what I want to be."

They listened to "Night on Bald Mountain." It sounded the way Kade felt—dangerous and a little out of control.

In school he saw Whitney Lundquist in the library. "Mind if I sit down?" he asked.

"No."

"What are you doing?"

"I have to read a book," she said.

"I hate it when that happens," he joked. "So, how are things going for you?"

"Can't complain."

"You want to go out with me sometime?" he asked.

"I'm going with Doug."

"You're kidding."

"No. What's wrong with Doug?"

"Nothing. It's just that I knew a girl who used to go with him, that's all."

"You mean Brenda Sloan?"

"Yeah."

"Doug's told me about her. The way Doug tells it, she should be a nun."

"Do you and Doug get along okay?"

"Yeah, fine. Why?"

"Just wondering. Is he still drinking?"

"Of course. We both are. What else is there to do around here?"

"Not much." He stood up. "Just be careful on the roads, okay?"

She smiled. "You sound like my mom."

He started to leave and then paused. "Brenda and I are Mormons."

"So?"

"I just wanted you to know."

"Why?"

"If things ever get bad for you, promise me you'll look into the Mormon church."

"Things are never going to get bad for me, Kade. I got things figured out."

"I know, but if they ever do."

She looked at him strangely. "You believe in your church, Kade?"

"Yeah, I do."

"And yet you know I like to party and have fun, right? So if you're such a great Mormon, why did you just ask me out?"

"Good question."

"I thought so too."

"I guess I was trying to get back at somebody."

"Who?"

"Brenda."

"Why?"

"I want to go with her."

"She's too old for you."

"Look who's talking. Doug's older than you."

"That's different."

"Why is it different?"

"It just is."

"Brenda's the only girl I'm interested in. I want to go with her, but she just wants me for a friend."

When he met Brenda in the parking lot after school, he said, "I need to talk to you."

"What about?"

"I'm sorry for the way I acted this morning."

"No problem. I figured you'd snap out of it eventually."

"I don't know what happened. Things got really crazy there for a while."

"Things are changing between us, Kade. That's what's making all the fireworks. I'm beginning to think of you as more of, well, an equal. When you don't act the way I think you should, it makes me mad. The fact is, I've been really getting mad at you lately. Sorry."

"I guess a friendship is a growing thing," he said.

"Yeah, I guess so."

On the last day of school, instead of going straight home, they stopped at a grocery store and bought some food and then drove to a lake and had a picnic. They talked about going swimming, but there was a brisk northerly wind and the water was too cold. He was wearing a cowboy hat because when he got up that morning he felt wild and crazy—crazy enough to wear what the locals wore every day.

They sat at a picnic table overlooking the lake. "An-

other year bites the dust," Brenda said, pulling off a
clump of grapes from the bunch they'd brought.

"Yeah, right."

"One more year for me and then I'm off to BYU."

"BYU has too many students," he said.

She smiled. "That's why I'm going there. I want to
be someplace that's crawling with Mormons."

"You mean crawling with Mormon guys."

"What's so bad about that?"

"Nothing. I know you need that."

"You make it sound like a weakness. What's wrong
with me liking guys?"

"Nothing."

"Wait till you get back from your mission. You'll be
singing a different tune then. I'd love to be around to
watch you trying to catch up after two years of not
dating."

"I won't be like that."

"You will so. You'll have five or six dates every weekend. I want to be in the background, laughing at the
way you'll be carrying on."

"By that time you'll be married and have two or three
kids."

"Not me. I'm in no hurry to get married. I'm just
going to play the field."

"No way. You'll marry the first guy you find at BYU
that looks halfway decent."

"Not me."

"You will. You even drool over the missionaries."

"That's not true."

"Don't give me that. I've seen you talking to them
after church."

"You're supposed to talk to people after church, so
they'll feel welcome," she said.

"Oh, they feel welcome around you. Yes sir, no problem there."

"You're not going to rile me this time, so just drop it, okay? You want another sandwich?"

"I suppose."

"Did my dad talk to you yet?" she asked.

"What about?"

"He's going to ask you if you want to work around our place this summer."

"For money?"

"Of course for money. What do you think?"

"I don't know much about farming."

"Much? Let's face it, you don't know beans about farming. It doesn't matter. Dad and I'll teach you all you need to know. What do you say?"

"You wouldn't be my boss, would you?" he asked.

"Why, couldn't you handle that?"

"You're not an easy person to get along with, in case you didn't know."

"Hey, just do what I say and there won't be any problem. When I say jump, you say, 'How high?' Got the picture?"

"I'd rather pick up pop cans along the highway than be under your thumb."

"Just kidding. Actually, my dad'll be the boss."

"That'd be okay."

"It looks like it's going to be good year for us. The winter wheat is looking good. We had plenty of snow this winter so the sub-soil moisture is looking real good."

He smiled.

"What's so funny?" she asked.

"It's so weird to hear you talk like a farmer."

"You ought to hear my Grampa." Her expression grew serious. "He and Gramma are coming back for a visit next week. I hope we can stand it."

"Why do you say that?"

"It's what Grampa does to my dad that I don't like."

"What do you mean?"

"Dad took over the place when Grampa retired, but

the way Grampa talks, it's still his place, and we're just working it for him. He finds fault with every little thing my dad's changed since he left. A lot of the time he treats my dad like he was still a kid."

"That must be tough to take. Life's kind of rough sometimes, isn't it? Even when you're grown up."

"Yeah, it doesn't seem to get any easier," she said. "What do you want to be when you grow up?"

"A football coach. Coach Biff Ellis of the Chicago Bears. It has a nice ring to it, doesn't it?"

She unceremoniously pulled his hat over his head. He chased her but she was too fast for him, so he went back to the table.

A minute later she came up behind him and leaned on his shoulders. "Hey, coach, you ready for dessert now?"

"Sure, why not?"

She got a package of donuts and a carton of milk from the paper sack. "We forgot to get glasses."

"We can trade off drinking from the carton."

"We'll get each other's germs that way."

"I can take it, I've got my cowboy hat on."

"Since it was my fault, you can take the first swig of milk."

While they ate, they watched white puffy clouds race toward them from Canada.

"You know what?" she said. "There's nobody I enjoy talking to more than you."

"It wasn't that way in the beginning."

"Gosh no. You were a real pain when I first started picking you up. There you were, Mr. Goody Two Shoes, with your little angel face, all eager and ready for school. You seemed like such a little kid. I could hardly stand you at first."

"And now look at us," he said, "sharing a carton of milk together and grossing out on donuts."

"No doubt about it, we've come a long ways."

"Just one more year of school and then you'll go off
to college."

"That's right."

"That'll be tough to take, for me anyway."

"For me too. But hey, it's over a year away. No use
talking about it now." She looked at the setting sun. "I
think it's time to go."

On their way back they had several miles to go on
a dirt road before they got to the highway. She gunned
the pickup so they'd have a wild ride.

"Slow down, okay?" he called out.

"What's the matter, cowboy? Can't you take it?"

"I mean it. Slow down before you kill us both."

She slowed down. A minute later she turned on the
radio. He sang along, adding a cowboy twang in his
voice.

They sang all the way home.

CHAPTER 9

A week after Kade started working at the farm Brenda's grandparents arrived. In the afternoon on the third day of their visit, Brenda, Kade, and Emmet were out near the barn trying to fix the tractor when Brenda's grandfather stormed out of the house and over to them. "Susan just told me you're thinking about selling some land."

"That's right. If I can find a buyer," Emmet said.

"You can't be serious."

"I don't have much choice. The bank says I'm way too much in debt."

"What's got into you? You can't sell land that's been in the family for five generations."

"Dad, with due respect, you don't have any say in this. I'm the one who makes the decisions around here now."

"I thought I could trust you to carry on the family heritage."

"It's fine and good to talk about family heritage when times are good, but the truth is we end up losing money every year. I'm not sure how much longer I can keep it up, even for the sake of family heritage. There's other ways to make a living, you know."

"This is a whole lot more than just making a living."

"Dad, it's not that anymore."

"I was able to do okay here. Why can't you?"

"Things are different now."

"Not that different. If that's the way you feel, why don't you just sell off the farm and get a job in some factory?"

"Maybe I will," Emmet said.

"You can't be serious."

"I'm thinking about it. I guess it depends on how well we do this summer. This place is eating us alive. All we do is worry about making payments and whether or not we'll get a loan to get us through the next season. If what you're doing to make a living doesn't pay you to do it, maybe it's time for a change. There's more important things in life than holding onto a parcel of land."

"Like what?"

"Like my family."

"There's no better way to raise a family than on a farm."

"Maybe that was true a few years ago, but I'm not sure it is now."

"I can't believe I'm hearing this from you. I never pegged you as a quitter."

"I've got to live my life the way that's best for me. Maybe I'll stay and maybe I won't, I just don't know. A lot depends on how well we do this summer."

"Brenda, what about you? Do you have any interest in carrying on here after your dad retires?"

"I don't know. Dad and I work so hard and yet we're just barely getting by. I'm not sure I want that."

"In my day people had loyalty to their land." Emmet's father, his face red and his jaws clamped shut, turned and stormed back to the house to talk to his wife.

Brenda's grandparents left as soon as they could get packed. Emmet tried to talk them into staying the night, but his dad, still fuming, said he thought it'd be best if they got a good start before nightfall.

"Well, at least that's over," Emmet said as his parents drove away.

Brenda and Kade didn't always get along as they worked.

"Let me show you," Brenda said when Kade tried to tighten the wire as they mended fence.

"I know what I'm doing."

"I know, but just let me show you."

"I don't want your help."

"Kade, let me do it. You're messing it up."

"No I'm not."

"I'm telling you—you're doing it all wrong."

"All right then, you do it."

"Now watch me. And don't be so pig-headed next time. All right?"

"You're not strong enough to do that. That's man's work."

"You don't have to be strong, you just have to be smart. That's why I can do it and you can't." She finished. "There, how's that?" She popped the hammer on the wire. It was so tight it sang.

"Not bad," he grudgingly admitted.

"Not bad? Face it, Kade, it's perfect. You saw how I did it. You do it that way from now on. You agree my way is better, don't you?"

"Not that much better."

"It's so hard for you to admit a girl is better at some things, isn't it." ⌐

"You have an unfair advantage."

"What's that?"

"Your dad raised you like a son."

"He raised me to work, that's all. I'm better than you at this, and I always will be. You better get used to it. You're going to run into it the rest of your life."

"I'm still better at drawing than you."

"That's for sure. Are you still drawing?"

"Yeah, when I'm not too tired."

"Pictures of me?"

"You're so conceited. You think all I do is daydream about you?"

"Who else have you drawn lately?"

"I did one of your dad. It's a closeup of his face after a long day."

"Have you ever done a picture of your dad?"

"No."

"Why not?"

"I don't know."

"You think you might take him for granted sometimes?"

"Maybe."

"You've got a wonderful dad, Kade."

"I suppose."

"You think you'll turn out to be like him?"

"Probably not."

"I think you will." She paused. "At least I hope you do." She looked out over the fields, then back at Kade. "It's been fun watching you grow up. Your voice has dropped about an octave just lately. And you're getting so tall. I really think you're going to turn out okay. Don't forget I had a part in it. Be sure and tell the girl you marry how much I did to help you turn out halfway decent."

At night after work they sometimes drove to town and cruised Main Street like everybody else their age, but usually after a couple of passes they got bored and did something else. A couple of times a week they went swimming at the city pool. During the day it was full of little kids and mothers, but in the evening, the crowd thinned out and high school youth and college students home for the summer took over.

When Kade and Brenda were together, either lying

down by the side of the pool or bobbing in the water next to each other, other guys would mostly leave her alone, but Brenda knew how to dive and Kade didn't, so sometimes she was practicing diving while he was lying down on the still-warm cement.

One time when they were separated, a college student, working in town for the summer, asked if she wanted to go with him to a party.

"I guess not. Thanks anyway."

"Why not?"

"I already have a date."

"Who?"

"That guy over there."

"Oh. How come he leaves you alone so much of the time."

"He doesn't dive."

"He should pay more attention to you, or he'll lose you."

She smiled. "I'll tell him. Thanks."

Sometimes after swimming, they'd drive over to the high school football field. They'd drive her pickup out onto the cinder track and she'd keep the motor running with the headlights on so they could see in the dark. Then she'd hold the ball for him while he practiced kicking extra points and field goals. After a few weeks Kade got so he could make it from the twenty-yard line about half the time.

"You're getting better, Kade."

"Yeah, too bad you can't hold the ball for me in the games."

"I'd like to do that. You want to ask Coach Brannigan?"

"Not really. He'd say that football is no game for a girl."

"But we know different, don't we," she said with a grin.

One night while they were practicing, another car

drove up and stopped. Two people got out, but Kade couldn't see who they were because they were still behind the light from the headlights.

"Well, look here," a voice said. "It's Kade Ellis, the boy wonder." Doug stepped out into the light. He had Whitney with him. "What are you doing this time of night?"

"Practicing kicking field goals," Kade said. "I'm going out for the football team in the fall."

"You think you're man enough for that?"

"Sure, no problem."

Doug spotted Brenda. "Well, I see you're still chasing little boys."

"Kade's not so little anymore though, is he," she said.

"Hi, Brenda," Whitney said. "How's it going?"

"Can't complain. How about you?"

"Okay. Did you know Doug and I are getting married?" Whitney asked.

"No, I didn't know that. When?"

"As soon as possible," Whitney said.

"Will you still be going to Montana State to play football?" Kade asked Doug.

"No. The football scholarship didn't come through like I thought it would. So I'll be staying here and helping my dad."

"Sounds great."

"It's not."

Kade hesitated and then said, "You don't sound too happy about it."

"Haven't you heard?" Doug said. "Whitney's gone and got herself pregnant."

"You don't have to go around announcing it to the whole world, do you?" Whitney complained.

"People around here can count to nine, so why not just come out and admit it?"

"I'd just like to be treated with a little respect, that's all."

"Seems to me it's a little late for respect."

"Is this how you're going to treat me from now on?"

"If it weren't for you, I'd be going to college in the fall." He turned to Kade. "She refused to get it fixed."

"By getting it fixed, he means getting an abortion," Whitney said.

"You did the right thing," Brenda said to Whitney.

"You women always stick together, don't you," Doug said, sneering.

"Abortions are wrong," Brenda said.

There was an uncomfortable silence. "Well, let's go, Gus," Doug said.

"Don't call me that," Whitney said.

"You're so hard to get along with these days."

Brenda watched them drive away. "That's so sad. Poor Whitney."

They drove home listening to the music on the radio. Just before pulling up to let him out, she said, "Kade, thanks for being my friend."

"Yeah, sure."

She stopped in front of his house. They sat there in the dark. She reached over and tossled his hair. Somehow she seemed different. "You know what?" she asked softly.

"What?"

"You're getting to be one handsome dude."

He wondered if that meant she'd let him kiss her if he tried. Frantically he tried to figure out what to do. Finally he worked out a plan. He would scoot over next to her and then yawn and stretch. With his arms still outstretched, he'd casually put his arm around her shoulder and then lean over and kiss her.

He scooted as close as he could get, but the gear-shift knob was in his way. Even so, he was still within arm's length. He yawned and stretched according to plan.

"Are you tired?" she asked.

It was a difficult question to answer. "Yeah, I guess so."

"I'd better go then so you can get some sleep. We've got a full day tomorrow. See you in the morning."

"Yeah, right." Bewildered, he got out and watched her drive away.

That night he had a hard time sleeping because he kept playing the scene over and over in his mind, trying to decide where he'd gone wrong.

One thing he decided—yawning was definitely not the way to go.

Emmet sat in his pickup on top of a knoll looking out at his land, now ripe with wheat, ready to be harvested.

"You're going to have a good year," Darrell Brekhus, a representative for an agri-business firm, said.

"Looks that way, if it doesn't hail before the combine crews get here."

"I like what you've shown me. Of course, I'll have to make a few phone calls to make it official, but I'm fairly certain we'll take it."

"Great."

"Actually, if you want to know the truth, we'd rather just buy the whole farm."

"Are you serious?"

"Absolutely. We could make you a pretty good offer on the place."

"It'd be tough to just walk away. This place has been in the family a long time."

"When's the last time you had a good crop like this?"

"Three years ago."

"It's hard to make money when you lose money two out of every three tries."

"You're not telling me anything I don't already know."

"Think about it, Emmet. I'll be in town at the Tip Top Motel until tomorrow at noon."

That night Emmet phoned his father.

"Is everyone all right?" his father asked, believing that you don't phone long distance unless there's a death in the family.

"Everyone's fine." Emmet cleared his throat. "Dad, I have an opportunity to sell the place. Susan and I've talked it over. We think it might be for the best. At least we'd leave the place with a little nest egg. That's better than the ones who've ended up losing everything."

"What on earth would you do for a living?"

"I have a friend in Great Falls. He's a member of the Church. He runs a motel. I called him this afternoon to ask his opinion. He told me he's building a ski lodge in Vail, Colorado. He asked me if I'd like to manage it."

"You don't know anything about managing a motel."

"I can learn."

"Sounds like you've already made your decision."

"I guess maybe we have."

"Then why did you call me?"

"To get your blessing."

"You want me to tell you it's all right to give up? You want me to tell you it's all right to sell off a farm that's been in the family for all these years? Well, forget it. I know what you're after. You want me to ease your conscience just because you don't have the gumption to last out a few bad years. Well, forget it. You do what you want, but don't come crying to me when you're out of a job and wish you still had the farm to fall back on." With that, his father hung up.

Emmet slowly put the phone back. "He hung up on me," he told Susan.

She touched his shoulder. "I know this is hard for

him, but he's got to understand we have to live our lives the way we think is best for us."

"Do you think we're doing the right thing?" he asked.

"I don't know. What do you think?"

"It's been a long time since farming was any fun for me."

"Then maybe it's time to move on. Will you miss it?"

"Yes, very much."

"Me too."

"It ought to be possible to make a living farming here, but for some reason it doesn't seem like it is anymore."

She came to him, and he held her in his arms for a long time. Then he sighed, pulled away, and said softly, "We'd better go tell Brenda."

Vehicles were parked all over the yard with the overflow lined up alongside the road. The auctioneer's voice boomed over the PA system. Kade and Brenda stood on the edge of the crowd and watched until it got too painful for her. Then she asked him to take her for a drive.

He was driving his dad's car. He pulled out onto the road and turned the radio to the country-western station she liked. They left a trail of dust behind them as they sped along the gravel road. She looked out her window but didn't say anything.

"Where do you want to go?"

"To town, I guess."

When they got to town, she had him drive past the school once and then down Main Street slowly.

"Do you want to stop anywhere?" he asked.

"No."

He turned onto Interstate 15, heading north in the direction of Canada. He imagined they were running away to start a new life. They'd find an apartment in Calgary and nobody would know where they were. He wanted the dream to stay but reality kept seeping through. He knew it could never be.

"You're kind of quiet," she said.

"Yeah."

"What are you thinking about?"

"Nothing."

"I'm going to miss you, Kade."

"Yeah, sure." He clipped the words short.

"Are you mad at me for leaving?"

"No."

"Kade, this is our last time together."

"So?"

"Tell me what you're thinking."

"That I'll never let myself be hurt like this again."

"I'm hurting too."

"Not like me. You never needed me as much as I needed you."

"That's not true, Kade."

"Yes it is."

"What am I ever going to do with you?" she said.

"Nothing, because it's over."

"It'll never be over. Even though we won't see each other very much from now on, we'll always be in each other's thoughts. We helped each other grow up. You can't just cut me out of your thoughts, because if you do, you'll end up losing a part of yourself."

"I have lost a part of myself, the best part. I've lost you."

Suddenly it was too much for him to hold in, and tears started to come. He was ashamed of having her see him this way, but he couldn't seem to stop. It wasn't safe for him to drive anymore; he pulled over onto the side of the road.

She came to his side, and they threw their arms around each other and cried.

Brenda was right—he never forgot her. She was in his thoughts during the first football game of the season when after two misses he finally kicked his first field goal. He thought of her the first day he walked into art class. When the teacher asked the class why they were taking the course, he said, "I have a friend who saw some drawings I'd done. She told me I should take this class. Actually we were going to take it together."

"Who was it?" someone asked.

"Brenda Sloan. She moved to Colorado."

"She's older than you, isn't she?" a girl next to him asked.

"Yeah, but we were friends anyway."

For weeks after Brenda left, he drew nothing but the barren windswept fields of November; that was how he felt. But then one day he drew a picture of an old Indian man with a weather-beaten face. He had seen the man one day in the hardware store. The next day he drew a picture of the football team practicing on a clear, crisp October afternoon. That opened the floodgate of drawings again.

"Life goes on" is something you hear in small towns from people who have seen their share of disappointment and heartache. Kade heard it often growing up in western Montana. Strangely enough, though, he found it to be true. Life did go on without Brenda.

His family stayed in Shelby through his high school years, even though his father was asked to move to the corporate headquarters in Chicago. Paul turned down what would have been a promotion because he was the branch president and didn't want to leave until he accomplished getting a building finished, and also because he didn't want to move until Kade graduated from high school.

Kade became an important addition to the football team. In his senior year during the final game of the state football championship tournament, he kicked three field goals and two extra-point conversions. Shelby won, 23 to 21. Kade was one of the players the coach singled out for praise when he was interviewed by the Shelby radio station after the game.

During his senior year of high school, Kade and Linda Cooper became close friends. She was the first girl he ever kissed. He wrote to her often his senior year, and went to Great Falls every chance he got to be with her.

After he graduated from high school, he worked at the bank until it was time for his mission. By this time Brenda was at BYU. They wrote once in a while just to let the other know how things were going.

Kade served a mission in Guatemala. While there, his father was promoted to the bank's corporate offices in Chicago, so when Kade returned home from his mission, he didn't go back to Montana.

The day after he arrived home from his mission, he phoned Emmet in Colorado and asked about Brenda. He hadn't heard anything from her for a long time.

"She's at BYU still," Emmet said. "This is her junior year. She dropped out for a while to come help us out at the ski lodge." He paused. "I had an operation and it kind of slowed me down for a while, so we needed her to help us out."

"How are you doing now?" Kade asked.

"As mean and ornery as ever. When are you going to come and visit us?"

"One of these days."

A week later Kade left to start fall semester at Ricks College in Rexburg, Idaho, majoring in business management. He had chosen Ricks because Linda Cooper was there. After their first date, though, she told him she'd found someone else and that he'd asked her to marry him.

"What did you tell him?" Kade asked.

"I told him I had to wait until you got home."

"I'm not ready to get married," he said.

They broke up shortly after that.

During Christmas vacation at his family's new home near Chicago, Kade found the Monopoly box containing the sketches of Brenda. Each one brought back rich memories.

The next semester, just for fun, he decided to take "Introduction to Oil Painting." He enjoyed the course immensely. He'd forgotten how fulfilling art was. He often stayed up late at night and worked. He began to use his earlier drawings of Brenda as a starting place for his paintings.

One day the art instructor suggested that he major in art, but Kade told him he had decided to major in business.

"Why business?"

"Because you can help people if you're in business."

"I've never heard that before."

"That's because you don't know my dad."

"Who's the girl in all your paintings?"

"Just a girl I used to know. Her name is Brenda."

"In this one, she's wearing a formal in an old barn, dancing with a boy who's obviously younger than her. Is that supposed to be symbolic?"

"Not really. It happened just the way I've drawn it. It was after the junior prom."

"Did you take her to the prom?"

"No, I was too young. She came by and woke me up and asked me to come have the last dance with her."

"Why did she do that?"

"It's a long story."

"I think you should enter that painting in a contest BYU is sponsoring."

"What for?"

"More people than just you should see it. How about it?"

"I don't think so, but thanks for suggesting it anyway."

"Would you object if I entered it under your name?"

"It won't win."

"Just let me enter it."

"All right."

The instructor studied the painting. "Were you in love with her?"

"I don't know how to explain the way it was between us. If I said we were in love, you wouldn't understand the way it really was. The closest I can come to what it was like is to say we were best friends."

The painting entitled "Brenda at the Prom" took second place in the contest. Kade was invited to BYU to exhibit his painting and to meet with some of the faculty of the Art Department.

On the opening night of the exhibit, he was asked to stand beside his painting to talk to anyone who might have questions.

A professor came up and looked closely at the painting. "I like this very much. Are you going to major in art?"

"Probably not."

"Why not?"

Kade smiled. "I want a steady income."

"You could have one if you'd keep painting."

A minute later Kade turned around and saw Brenda standing there. It almost took his breath away to see her again. "Hello," he said, feeling awkward again for the first time in years.

"Hello."

"I hope you don't mind," he said, glancing from her to the painting.

"Not at all. I'm honored you'd remember that night." She looked more closely at the painting. "I still have that formal."

He looked at her while she gazed at the painting. He was now three or four inches taller than she. She was still beautiful, but he was a little disappointed that she'd lost much of her country charm. She wore more makeup now than when he'd known her. From what she was wearing—a light orange dress—he realized she was very much aware of what she looked good in. He could see she spent much more time on herself than she had in high school. Somewhere along the way she must have discovered how beautiful she could be if she put forth a little effort.

Kade wondered what it was like for Brenda at BYU. She was someone you couldn't help but notice even if you only passed her on a sidewalk between classes. And yet, for all her beauty, she wasn't the same as she'd been in high school, and for some reason that disappointed him.

She turned to look at him. "I see you finally got those contact lenses you wanted so much."

He blushed, not because he was wearing contacts, but because he realized she was thinking the same thing about him, that he'd changed.

"Yes."

"You were right to get them. You have nice eyes."

He smiled. " 'The better to see you with, my dear.' "

She turned back to the painting. "It's a wonderful painting," she said.

"I've done a couple more of you."

"I'd love to see them."

"Sometime when I come down here, I'll bring them along."

"Do you come down here often?" she asked.

"Yes," he lied.

"Call me up when you get into town the next time," she said. "Maybe we can go practice kicking field goals."

It struck a resonant chord. He realized that even

though they were now both much different from before,
their memories, like deep roots, were the same.

"How're your folks?" he asked.

"They're fine. My dad really likes what he's doing.
I know he'd like to see you again." She paused. "Do
you ski?"

"Not really."

"Show up in Vail sometime, and my dad and I'll
teach you."

"Sounds like a good deal."

She hesitated, then said, "Actually, if you're really
interested, I could teach you here in Utah."

"I'd like that." He smiled. "Seems like you're always
teaching me things, doesn't it?"

"I'm sure there're plenty of things you could teach
me. I'd really like to hear about your mission."

Suddenly he realized that two coeds were standing
next to them, not looking at his painting, but staring at
him and Brenda.

"Is there someplace we can go and be alone?"

"Wow," one of the girls said, "we've got fireworks
here, don't we!"

He tried to ignore the remark but felt his face getting
red. "Just someplace where we can talk and maybe get
something to drink."

Brenda nodded. "I know just the place. It's in the
Wilkinson Center. Can you leave now?"

"Yes."

The faculty member in charge of the exhibit saw them
leaving. "We'd prefer that you stay by your painting
until nine o'clock."

"We won't be long."

They walked out into the cold winter night. It was
snowing.

"Let's see," he said. "I was younger than you the
night of the prom, wasn't I?"

"And you're not now?" she teased.

"Not anymore. Now we're the same age."

She nodded. "I guess I feel that way too."

He reached out and held her hand.

"Kade, do you think we might become good friends again?"

"I hope so."

"Me too. I've really missed having a friend like you."

"I've missed it too."

They got their drinks and then returned to the exhibit until it closed. He drove her home. She invited him in, and he met her roommates. They sat around the kitchen table and talked until midnight. She invited him to come for breakfast in the morning before he headed back to Ricks.

After he returned to the guest housing the university had arranged for him, even though it was late, he took out a piece of paper and drew yet another picture of Brenda.

It felt good to be home again.

KIMBERLY

JACK WEYLAND

Deseret Book Company
Salt Lake City, Utah

1

Ben Fairbanks sat in a music practice room at the University of Utah on a cold January day, waiting for anyone else who might want to try out. He was looking for a female singer who played acoustic guitar and wanted to earn a little extra money on weekends. He fumbled on his guitar for a song that would change the world—or, if not that, at least help pay for college.

He heard what sounded like a cat scratching at the door. Glancing up, he saw a girl struggling to get through the door while balancing two college textbooks and a three-ring binder in one hand, a guitar case in the other. It was a great act, but it only lasted until she got inside. Then the books and binder crashed to the floor.

He hurried to help her. "Thanks for dropping in," he said. She was someone he would have noticed even across a crowded room. As she picked up loose papers that had fallen from her three-ring binder, he was fascinated by how graceful she was. It was as if she moved to a song that no one else could hear. Even though he knew she was embarrassed, she radiated a composure that only added to her beauty.

She turned to him and smiled. "I'm practicing dramatic entrances today. So, how'd I do?"

"Great. You got my attention." Which was true. He was intrigued by the color of her hair. He tried to recall when he'd seen that color before. Finally it dawned on him: he saw it

1

every day at breakfast. It was the color of honey in the morning sun. Her perfume was subtle but unforgettable; it seemed to match her personality.

She held out her hand, palm up. He fantasized that she wanted him to hold it, but then he realized she just wanted her book back. He glanced down at the title. It was a calculus book. He got rid of it really fast.

"Thanks," she said. "I saw a notice on the bulletin board about a tryout here today. Are you the one I should talk to?"

"Yes. I'm Ben Fairbanks."

"Hi. I'm Kimberly Madison." She set her books on a desk, then took her guitar out of its case and began to tune it. "Your notice was sort of sketchy. You want to tell me what this is all about?"

"Yeah, sure. This summer I got off my mission with no money and not much time before fall semester began. I managed to make enough to get registered and buy books, but that's about all. The last part of September I ran into a girl I used to sing with in high school."

"What's her name?"

He cleared his throat. "Julia Alton. Do you know her?"

"No."

He was relieved she didn't know Julia. Maybe she hadn't heard anything. "Well, anyway, we worked up some songs and then went around town trying to find someone who'd pay us to sing. We finally lined up a job for Friday and Saturday nights at an Italian restaurant called Angelo's. Have you ever eaten there?"

"No, but I've heard of it."

"We sang every weekend until Christmas break, but then Julia got married over Christmas and moved away, so now I'm looking for someone to take her place. It's steady work, it pays well, and it doesn't interfere much with school. We put on a twenty-minute show three times a night from seven until ten Friday and Saturday nights. For that and mingling with the customers, and once in a while, when they're really busy, waiting on a few tables, we each get seventy-five dollars a night."

"Sounds good." She tuned her guitar and then asked, "What would you like me to play for you?"

"Anything you want."

"Okay. I'll do a song I wrote and sang for my high school graduation."

"When was that?"

"A year ago last May."

Her hair in the back was in a French braid. He tried to imagine what it would be like to watch her braid it, but then, because of the problems he'd had with Julia and her boyfriend, he reminded himself that he needed to keep things with the new singer on a strictly professional basis. With that in mind, he quit fantasizing about Kimberly's hair.

She started singing. Her voice was clear and natural and vibrant, but it was her song that amazed him most of all.

"What do you think?" she asked when it was over.

"It sounds terrific. Are you majoring in music?"

"No, mechanical engineering. Music is just a hobby."

"Mechanical engineering? Gosh, I'm impressed."

"Don't be. It's just that math has always come easy for me. What are you majoring in?"

"Business. Music is sort of a hobby for me too. Look, I've got some sheet music for some of the songs Julia and I were doing. Why don't you look them over and find one you like, and we'll try singing it and see how it goes."

She picked out a song and they began singing. He was surprised how well they sounded together. When they finished, he said, "I think this might work out. Can you start this Friday?"

"I won't know enough songs by then."

"I know, but if we can get together tomorrow and Thursday, I think we can work up enough to get by."

"Okay, sure."

"After that we'll set up some regular practice sessions."

3

"Anything else I should know?" she asked.

"Just one thing." He paused. "That song you wrote, it's unbelievable. I can't get it out of my mind."

"You really liked it?"

"Absolutely. But even as good as it was, I do have a couple of suggestions for you—if you're interested."

"Okay."

"First of all, it's too good to only be sung once at a high school graduation," he said. "The lyrics need to grab everyone who hears it."

She crinkled up her nose. "Let me guess—you want to turn it into a love song, right?"

"Why not? Most people are either in love or else wish they were."

"I'm not in love and I don't wish I were," she said.

"Me either, but let's face it, we're the exceptions."

"All right, let's try it as a love song."

They changed the words first but that caused a change in part of the melody, so they ended up jockeying back and forth until finally they were both satisfied. "Let's try it together all the way through now, okay?" Ben suggested.

She stepped forward and addressed a large imaginary audience. "I know you'll all recognize this next song because it was our first big hit. We'd like to sing it for you now."

When they finished, she held up her hand to stop the thunderous applause of an imaginary audience. "Thank you, thank you! You've been a wonderful audience! Would you like us to sing it one more time?"

They did it again. For a moment, for them, there really was a sell-out audience shouting their approval.

When they were done, he sat down. "Here's a song I've been working on," he said. He played it, then asked, "So, what do you think?"

"I like it," she said, "but . . . what would you think about this?" She played a variation on his tune. It was better. And

4

then he improved on her idea. And then suddenly it was like they were one person, working together, coming up with ideas for words and music they never could have done alone. It all seemed to take place in about ten minutes, but by the time they looked at the clock, an hour and a half had passed.

"I can't believe it's so late!" she said. "My mom's going to kill me."

"Can I give you a ride home?"

"Yeah, thanks. That would really help. I don't live very far from here."

"What happened just now doesn't happen every day. It's like by myself I'm only half a person, and you're the other half. We've got two great songs finished in just a day. I know we're both busy, but what if, in addition to practicing, we spent a little time each week writing some of our own songs?"

"What for?"

"We could make a tape to sell to the people who eat at Angelo's. Even if we only sell two or three a night, it will bring us in a little extra. And, who knows, someday we might make it big."

She didn't believe him. "Yeah, right."

"Hey, it's not that expensive to record a few songs in a studio. Say it costs four dollars a tape and we sell them for ten dollars — that gives us a profit of six dollars a tape. If we sell five a night, that's an extra thirty dollars a night."

"You're definitely in the right major."

As they pulled into her driveway, he looked at her and said, "Don't go in yet, okay? There's still a lot we need to talk about."

"Let me tell my folks I'm home first."

When she returned, she said, "My mom says you're welcome to come in and eat with me. Everyone else has eaten."

"Can't we just talk in the car?"

"You got something against eating? Look, if we're going to

5

talk, let's at least do it over food. You don't want me passing out from hunger, do you?"

"You're sure I won't be in the way?"

"Not a bit. We'll just be scraping the pan for whatever food my brother Derek left. Derek's my little brother. He's only fifteen, but he's a big guy and he eats a lot. Come on in. Don't be bashful."

"Nice house," he said as they went up the walk to the old two-story frame house.

"Thanks. When we bought it, it needed a lot of work. We fixed it up ourselves, and now it's the pride of the neighborhood. At least that's what my dad always says whenever he shows people around."

"I bet you made some hardware store owner happy when you were fixing it up. The reason I say that is, my dad runs a hardware store in Rock Springs, Wyoming. That's where I'm from."

She took him into the kitchen. "Mom, this is the guy who kidnapped me and wouldn't let me come home for supper. He told me his name is Ben Fairbanks, but of course I don't believe that for an instant."

"Ben, it's nice to meet you," Kimberly's mother, Anne Madison, said, holding out her hand to shake his.

Someone had once told Ben that if he wanted to know what a girl is going to look like someday, he should look at her mother. Ever since then, he had made it a practice to pay attention to the appearance of the mothers of the girls he spent time with. Even though he wasn't looking for a wife in Kimberly, mainly because of what had happened with Julia, he decided it wouldn't be so bad to be married to Kimberly if she looked as good as her mother in twenty years. Anne had brown eyes and brown hair with a little gray mixed in. To Ben she looked quietly competent and totally conscientious.

"Mrs. Madison, I apologize for making Kimberly late. We started working on a song and lost all track of the time."

6

"I'm just glad she's home. Look, there's not a lot of food here, but you're welcome to whatever you can find. As usual, Derek ate most of it." She got them started and then left.

A few minutes later, Derek came in for a snack. He was a big kid who was growing so fast it was hard to keep him in clothes. There was about an inch of open skin between the bottom of his T-shirt and his jeans. He had sandy hair, which his mother always insisted was too long, and an infectious smile that few could resist.

"Derek, this is Ben. He and I are going to be singing together at a pizza place Friday and Saturday nights."

"Bring some pizza home when you're done," Derek said, getting the jar of peanut butter from the cupboard.

"Derek is almost an Eagle scout," Kimberly said.

"That's really great, Derek!" Ben exclaimed.

"I just have to do my Eagle project and then I'll be done. Did you ever get your Eagle?"

"Yeah, just barely. If you need any help, let me know."

"It's mostly my dad who's pushing me to get it. Right now my main goal is to get strong enough to intimidate all the guys my age."

"I'd say you're about there," Ben said.

Derek smiled, then turned to Kimberly. "You'd better listen to this guy. And from now on, quit telling your friends I'm your little brother when I'm bigger than you."

"Derek, you'll always be my little brother. Oh, and tuck in your shirt. People don't like looking at your belly button."

Derek tucked in his shirt, sat down at the table with them, and started to make a peanut butter and jelly sandwich. "I'm not only getting stronger, but I can tell now that I'm going to be really hairy too."

"Oh my gosh, Derek," Kimberly complained, "give us a break. We're trying to eat."

"I wasn't talking to you." He turned to Ben. "Anyway, I'm going to be hairy, but not half as hairy as this guy I saw at the pool last summer. I'm serious. He had so much hair on his chest and his back, he looked like a gorilla. I hope I'm like that someday so that when little kids see me, like at a swimming pool, they'll start bawling and run to their mothers. A guy needs something like that going for him, right?"

"Sure, and a voice like Darth Vader," Ben said.

"Yes! Finally somebody around here understands what things are like for me. Having two sisters is tough. Like you would not believe the things they hang over the shower curtain in the bathroom."

"Derek, isn't there someplace you'd rather be now?" Kimberly cut in.

"No. Hey, Ben, do you think Kimberly's good looking?"

"The first time I saw her, it took my breath away."

"Yeah, well, you ought to see her in the morning when she first gets up—that'd take anybody's breath away." Derek made the desperate sound of someone struggling to breathe. "It's like that one scene from *Swamp Woman*, you know, the one where Swamp Woman comes out of the swamp with all this green crud hanging from her hair and a tour bus in her mouth."

"Derek?" Kimberly muttered.

"What?"

"Go away."

"Why should I?"

"We're busy."

"Oh yeah, right, I can see you're real busy."

"We need to talk about music."

"In a minute, okay? I'm not through with my sandwich yet." He took another bite and then turned to Kimberly. "See if you can talk Mom and Dad into getting us a computer."

"They have computers in school, don't they?" she asked.

"Yeah, but Mrs. Vitali is so afraid of them, she goes crazy when someone tries to use them. Like she comes up and goes, 'Be careful and don't push the wrong button and break it.'

Yeah, right, like somebody at the factory goes, 'Hey, I've got a great idea. Let's put a button on this thing so if anyone pushes it, the whole thing blows up.'" He took a big swig of milk. "People are so dumb. Sometimes I feel like I live in an insane asylum and just down the road is a place where normal people live except I don't know that. Thinking things like that can drive you crazy. But maybe that wouldn't be so bad. At least I'd fit in more. Well, I've got to get back to my room." He stood up to leave.

"I don't suppose you'd consider cleaning up the mess you made here, would you?" she asked.

"What mess?"

"Put away the peanut butter and the jelly. And wash your knife and glass."

"Why should I do that? That's women's work."

"Derek, how would you like me to go to your school and announce your middle name over the P.A. system?"

"You wouldn't do that."

"Not if you clean up."

Derek turned to Ben. "You see what it's like living around here? Take it from me, sisters are a pain."

After a half-hearted attempt to clean up, he spotted a basketball on the floor. He picked it up and became both announcer and player. "The game's tied, Madison has the ball, he races down the court and puts up a lay-up." He tossed the basketball into the kitchen sink. "It's good! The crowd goes wild! Aaaaahh!" He dribbled the ball up the stairs to his room.

"That's my brother Derek," she said.

"Nice guy."

She smiled. "That's easy for you to say. You don't have to live in the same house with him. I'm positive his goal is to make as much noise as possible."

"That's what a guy his age is supposed to do."

"Were you ever like that?"

"Sure, probably worse."

9

"Well, it's good to know there's still hope for him."

"It's fun getting to know your family."

"What's your family like?"

"I'm an only child. The doctors told my mother she'd never have kids, and then I came along—but I was the only one."

Kimberly's twelve-year-old sister Megan walked in. "Oh, I didn't know anyone else was here," she said.

"Megan, this is Ben. He plays the guitar too. We've got a job singing together this semester."

"Hello," Megan said.

"Hi, Megan. Gosh, you're as good-looking as your sister," Ben said, not so much as a compliment as a statement of fact. She had long brown hair and gray-blue eyes; her skin was an elegant ivory tone. She seemed more serious than Kimberly.

Megan, entranced by this tall, dark stranger, sat down.

"Don't you have some homework or something?" Kimberly asked.

"No."

"I bet you get really good grades, right?" Ben said.

Megan smiled. "Yeah, pretty much."

"And I bet there's guys in school wishing they had the courage to come up and talk to you."

"Not really."

"Hey, I'm hardly ever wrong about things like this."

Kimberly realized that Megan felt so comfortable with Ben that she might stay there for a long time. She tried to speed things up. "Megan, Ben and I need to talk."

Megan nodded her head and got up to leave.

"I enjoyed meeting you," Ben said.

"Me too." She left.

"Well, somehow you've managed to impress my family," Kimberly said.

"I really like them."

"We haven't talked much about music yet," she said.

10

"Is there someplace we can go where we won't be disturbed?"

"Downstairs. My dad used to have an office at home. He doesn't use it anymore. We could go there."

They went downstairs. The basement was unfinished, with a room built at one end. The room, which was carpeted, had a small desk, two chairs, and a filing cabinet. Kimberly plugged in a portable electric heater.

Ben moved the two chairs together and they sat down. "The first thing we need to do is work up some songs for Friday. And then after that, we'll need to practice two or three times a week, and if you have the time, it'd be great if we could get together once a week to write new songs. After we've got five or six new songs, we'll put together a tape. How does that sound?"

"Busy. You want to know what I'm taking this quarter? Calculus, chemistry, English, computer programming."

"Give me one hour a day, four days a week, that's all I ask."

"Okay, one hour, but that's all."

"Great. When's a good time for you?" he asked.

"How about four o'clock, Monday through Thursday?"

"Yeah, sure, that'll work." He paused, then cleared his throat. "There's something else we need to talk about."

"What's that?"

"We'll be spending a lot of time together, so it'd be best if we kept everything on a strictly professional basis."

"Are you worried about that?"

"I just don't want some silly romance to come from this. Physical attraction can be really distracting."

She smiled. "You make it sound like a disease." And then she stopped and stared at him. "Why are you telling me this anyway? Did you and Julia have a problem?"

"No, why? What have you heard?"

"What have I heard? What kind of a question is that? I

haven't heard anything, but you'd better level with me now or else get yourself another singer."

"Nothing happened between Julia and me, but the guy she was going with thought there was. I guess because we spent so much time together. Well, anyway, he started secretly following us. One night I invited Julia over to my apartment, just to talk. It was totally innocent. For one thing, I live in my aunt's house in an upstairs apartment. Anyway, Julia and I are in my apartment eating popcorn and watching TV when all of a sudden somebody starts banging on the door and yelling like a crazy man. Of course, my aunt is scared to death and won't even open the door, but it's not locked so he barges in and demands to know where Julia is. My aunt tells him and he runs up the stairs. He sees us together and starts shouting at us and accusing us of a lot of things that weren't true.

"While this is going on, my aunt calls the police. We try to reason with the guy but it's no use. Finally he gets so mad he grabs Julia and starts dragging her across the floor, telling her she's coming with him. But she doesn't want to go with him when he's like that. So anyway, I try to get him to let go of her. And then all of a sudden, it's like something snaps inside his head and he comes after me. We start fighting, and then the police show up. He's yelling at Julia and me as they drag him off to jail. The police let him cool off in a cell overnight. But when he gets out of jail, he goes back on campus and tells everyone a bunch of lies about what kind of a person I am. And then a month later Julia gets married."

"She ended up marrying him?" Kimberly asked.

"No, she married one of the cops who answered the call." He paused. "So you see, after all that, I'd really like to keep things low-key and professional."

He could tell she wasn't totally convinced. "Like you did with Julia, you mean?" she asked.

"Yeah, like I did with Julia. Look, if you have any questions about any of this, I'll give you Julia's phone number or you can talk to my aunt. I've got nothing to hide."

"No, that's okay, I believe you. All right, low-key and professional." She turned away. It gave him a good chance to look at her again.

She turned back to face him. "Why do you keep staring at me?" she asked.

"Was I staring at you?"

"Yes, you were. Why?"

"Well, there's some things about you . . . that I find attractive — but, of course, when we're working together, I won't even notice those things."

"What things won't you notice?" she asked.

"You want me to give you a list?"

"Sure, why not? Our relationship isn't going anywhere, so I don't have to worry about that. But I've always been curious about what guys notice when they see a girl."

"I'd really rather not talk about this," he said.

"I'm just curious, that's all. I promise I won't bring it up again. What did you think when you first saw me?"

"The first thing I noticed was your hair."

"What about it?"

"It's the same color as my honey in the morning."

Her smile vanished. "Oh . . . I see." She cleared her throat and moved her chair six inches farther away from him. "I didn't know. What is . . . your honey's name?"

At first he didn't know what she was talking about, but when he finally did, he gasped, "Oh no, nothing like that. What I meant is the honey I have with my toast in the morning."

They both laughed at the misunderstanding.

"What else?" she asked.

"You get freckles in the summer, don't you? I like that. In Wyoming there's two things we look for in a girl. One is freckles and the other is if she owns a quarter horse."

"One out of two isn't bad, is it? Maybe I should move to Wyoming."

"Sure, why not?"

"Do you want to know what girls find attractive about you?"

"No," he said quickly.

"You do too, Ben, you liar."

"I'm just trying to protect myself. You have someone barge in your house in the middle of the night and accuse you of all sorts of things and then see how anxious you are to get personal with someone you're working with."

"I like the way your hair in the back curls."

"I think we should keep things—"

"I like your strong, rugged jaw."

"—low-key and professional."

"I like your thick eyebrows. It's like two small forests. And I love your voice. You sound like that guy on the radio—what's his name? Tom Bodett, isn't it? 'We'll leave a light on.' You'd leave a light on for me, wouldn't you, Ben?"

For just a second they found themselves staring at each other. He panicked, stood up, and started pacing the floor. "Well, okay, we're finished with that. Now let's get to work. We need to decide where we're going to practice."

"How about right here? Nobody ever uses this room anyway."

"You think it would be okay with your parents?"

"I'm sure it will, but I'll ask my dad."

"I hope I get to meet your dad sometime."

"I hope so too. He's been really busy lately at work. We don't see much of him around here anymore."

"I wondered about that. I saw a bunch of things upstairs that need fixing, you know, things that fathers do on Saturdays. Growing up in the hardware business, I notice things like that."

"Like what?"

"When I washed up for supper, I noticed you have a leaky faucet in the bathroom. And in the kitchen one of the chairs

14

is wobbly. If you want, I can do some repair work after we finish over the next few days."

"My mom would love that. She'll probably want you to stay for supper all the time if you start fixing things around here."

"Sure, no problem. That's what I liked most when I worked for my dad, being able to help people."

"My dad gets around to things like that eventually, but right now he's so busy that . . . " She paused. "He doesn't have time for us."

They practiced Wednesday and Thursday, working up what he thought would be enough songs for Friday and Saturday at Angelo's.

Ben knew they sounded good but wasn't sure if anyone else would notice. Before, when he and Julia sang at the restaurant, people either ignored them or else just stared at them while eating their pizzas. Ben wondered if people knew how strange they looked with cheese dangling from their chins.

On Friday night at Angelo's it was even better than Ben thought it would be. The two of them together had a fresh, new, vibrant sound. Not only that, but for every song they sang, Kimberly acted as if the song had been personally written for her. When they finished all the songs they'd practiced, people started calling for more. "What are we going to do? We don't have any more songs," Kimberly said.

"Let's do your graduation song the way we changed it."

The crowd loved it.

After they finished, Angelo Postrollo, the manager, came up and treated them like they were part of the family. He gave them a pizza to eat while they waited for their next show.

A man came over to their table. "Do you have any tapes of your music for sale?"

"No, not yet, but we will soon. We're working on it," Ben said.

15

Three other people came up and told them they liked their music.

"We could've made an extra fifty dollars tonight if we'd had the tapes to sell," Ben said.

"Okay, I'll give you an extra half hour a day, but that's all I can do, or I'll end up flunking everything."

On the way home that night, he had a difficult time bringing up what was bothering him, but finally he decided to just start. "You're really a good actor," he said.

"How do you mean?"

"On some of the love songs, the way you looked at me, I mean, it was very effective."

She snickered. "Yes, I could tell that—you missed two entrances."

"Yeah, sorry. See, the thing is, Julia and I didn't interact much that way. We just stood up there and sang."

"Must've been pretty boring for the audience, right?"

His shoulders slumped. "Yeah, it was."

"What are you saying, Ben?"

"I don't know. I've never had a girl look at me the way you did tonight."

"I'm just trying to give the folks a good show. Relax, okay? You're safe with me. You're not the only guy in my life. I mean, like, Sunday I'm seeing a guy I used to go with in high school. He just got out of prison but he's really a nice guy. He just made one little mistake."

Ben felt a panic attack coming on. "What kind of mistake?"

"He knifed a guy he caught talking to me in the hallway. We've been writing all the time he's been in jail. I told him about you, and he seemed really interested. He even asked where you live." She looked at his reaction, then burst out laughing. "Just kidding, okay?"

"Don't ever do that again."

"I know, I know. Low-key and professional, that's my middle name."

16

They got together every day at four o'clock and either practiced or wrote songs. Ben was often asked to stay for supper. After they finished eating, while Kimberly studied, he sometimes did repair work around the house. And then around eight he went to his apartment to study.

Having Ben around the house was all right with Derek. He enjoyed having another guy to talk to. Megan also basked in the attention Ben gave her.

Paul Madison, the father of the family, often worked late at his office. When he did come home in time for supper, Ben couldn't help but compare him to his own father. Paul Madison was younger looking than his wife, but as time passed the achievement was taking considerable effort. He seemed obsessed with reducing the fat content of the food he ate. He never had dessert, avoided eating much meat, and didn't even put butter or margarine on the half slice of bread he might have with his meal. Ben couldn't help but wonder whom he was trying to impress.

In contrast, Ben's father, who treated his employees to sweet rolls every morning at the hardware store, had put on several extra pounds over the last few years.

In the home where Ben grew up, after supper his father helped with dishes. It gave his folks time to talk about what had happened during the day. But in Kimberly's family, their father seemed to have very little to do with his wife either before or after supper.

Ben could see there was tension in the family, but he didn't worry about it much because he had learned from his mission that almost every family has a few problems.

One afternoon a week later, Kimberly and Ben were in her father's office in the basement. They had the door closed so the electric heater in the room could keep them warm.

Kimberly's mother, Anne, had just come home from shopping for groceries. They could hear her asking Derek to help her unload the groceries from the car. A minute later she came downstairs to put another load into the washing machine. She must not have realized Kimberly and Ben were in the office writing out a final version of a song they had just composed.

Paul Madison came downstairs. "I'm home but I have to go back again tonight," Ben heard him say.

"Is business that good that you have to be gone four nights a week?" Anne asked.

"You know how it is this time of year."

"Does Gloria work with you when you work nights?"

"Not usually. Why do you ask?"

"Just curious." A long pause. "I took Megan to the dentist today. He says she needs braces."

"How much will that cost?"

"Around three thousand dollars," she said.

"We can't afford it."

"People can never afford braces. It's something parents have to do, one way or the other."

"Maybe she'll grow out of it," he said.

"Look, you're welcome to talk to the dentist yourself."

"What did you tell him?"

"I said I'd get back to him after I talked to you."

"I need some time to figure out where the money's coming from. Let's put it on hold for a while."

"We can't wait too long."

"I know that. What else do we need to talk about?"

"Can you talk to Derek about finishing up his Eagle project?"

"I thought he was working on it."

"He was but it's hard for him. He could use your help in mapping out what he needs to do."

"Can't you do that?"

"Yes, but I think you should. It would give you a reason to spend some time around here. You're never here anymore."

"You know what work is like for me this time of year."

"It's not so much the time you're away. You always work hard, but this year for some reason it's different. Now it's like you're not a part of the family anymore."

"If you want, I'll talk to the dentist about Megan's braces."

After her parents went back up the stairs, Kimberly was silent for a long time. Then she said, "Most of the time my mom and dad get along okay. I guess it's just that he hasn't been home much lately."

"Sure," Ben said, but at the same time he couldn't help but notice how worried Kimberly looked.

2

During supper a week later, Megan was excited because her dad was taking her to the Ice Capades. He wasn't home yet, but he'd promised to pick her up at seven-thirty in order to get there for an eight o'clock performance.

Ben ate supper with the family and then stayed to fix a dripping faucet in the bathroom on the first floor. What should have been a five-minute job was turning into a major project because the faucet was so old. Ben finally suggested to Kimberly's mother that she buy a washerless faucet. She agreed. So after another trip to the hardware store, he was on his back with his head in the bathroom cabinet under the faucet. Kimberly was sitting cross-legged on the floor in jeans and sweatshirt, trying to keep him company while studying chemistry at the same time.

"How's it going?" she asked after hearing him grumble.

"Ever wonder why there's so few happy plumbers?"

"That bad, huh?"

"I've seen worse."

"What a guy. My mom really appreciates this. Last night she told me, 'Any guy can take you to a movie, but a guy who can fix things around the house is worth his weight in gold.' "

A few minutes after seven, Megan stuck her head in the bathroom.

"Use the bathroom upstairs," Kimberly said.

20

"I know. I just want to talk to Ben for a while."

"Hi, Megan!" Ben called out, his head and shoulders still inside the cabinet.

"What are you doing in there?"

"Replacing the faucet."

"Is that hard?"

"Not once I get the old one out." Ben scooted out long enough to get a good look at Megan. The turquoise in her sweater somehow made her eyes come alive. He was certain she had no idea how terrific she looked. "You all ready for your daddy-daughter date?"

"I've been ready for ten minutes. The show starts at eight. I want to be there before it begins. I hate to be late to things."

"Your dad will probably show up any minute now."

"He said he'd be here by seven-fifteen."

"There," Ben said, "the rest will be easy." He slid out, stood up, and lifted out the old faucet.

"I need to phone somebody about an assignment," Kimberly said. "Megan, will you keep Ben company?"

"Sure."

Kimberly left.

"You've got a smudge on your face," Megan said. She got a tissue and wiped his cheek.

"Thank you."

"We have to keep you looking good for Kimberly."

"We do? Why?"

"She talks about you all the time."

"She does?"

"Of course. One night she even dreamed about you."

"Oh? Tell me about it." He tried to sound only mildly interested, but he wanted to know every detail of Kimberly's dream. His heart started beating faster, and he felt as if the room had suddenly become too warm.

"She didn't tell me any of the details, but she did say it was very romantic."

21

He was glad his head was in the cabinet so Megan wouldn't know how red his face was.

Megan went to the kitchen to check on the time and then came back. "How long does it take to get downtown?"

"I don't know—fifteen minutes, I guess."

"If my dad gets here soon, we can still make it in time."

"Sure. Look, Megan, if for some reason your dad doesn't come, as soon as I get this fixed, I'll take you out for ice cream."

"You and Kimberly, you mean."

"No, Kimberly's got to study. Just you and me."

"I'd rather go out with my dad than with you."

"Of course. And he'll be here any second too, I just know he will."

Megan got a kitchen chair and set it in the doorway and watched him work. "This isn't the first time he's been late."

"He's not late now."

"No, not really—he's just later than he said he'd be." She paused. "If he were taking Kimberly, he'd be on time."

"He's not doing this on purpose. Something probably came up."

"I know." She stood up and looked in the mirror. "Do I look okay?"

"You look great. I mean it. Sometimes I wish I was your same age so I could grow up with you. Then we could be friends together in school."

"You're crazy then. Growing up once is bad enough. I'd never want to do it twice."

As the minutes slipped by, Megan quit talking.

"How you doing there, kiddo?" he asked.

"I guess we'll miss the beginning, but that's okay. It's two hours long, so there's plenty to see even if we are a little late."

"If your dad doesn't come, we can go see if they have any tickets left, and if they do, I'll take you."

"No. The main reason I wanted to go was because my dad

asked me." There was a long pause, and then she said, "He doesn't really care that much for me anyway."

"Of course he does."

She didn't answer except to say, several minutes later, "I guess he's not coming. I'm going to go up and change and then finish my homework." She left.

A few minutes later Kimberly returned. "How's it going?"

"You'd better go talk to Megan. She's pretty disappointed."

"I know. I just talked to her. Poor kid."

A short time later Paul Madison burst into the house. "Where's Megan? Is she ready?"

"Megan, your father's here!" Anne called out.

Megan came to the second floor railing and called out, "Just a minute, Daddy, I need to change back to what I was wearing."

"Paul, could I talk with you in here?" Anne asked her husband.

They went into their bedroom, next to the bathroom where Ben was working. The bathroom had two entrances, one from the hall and one from the master bedroom. The door to the hall was open but the door to the master bedroom was shut.

"Where on earth have you been?" he could hear Anne saying. "You told Megan you'd pick her up at seven-fifteen. It's now five minutes to eight. Why do you do this to me and the children time after time?"

Kimberly and Ben could hear what was being said, even through the closed door. Ben continued to work, hoping he could finish and get out before things got too bad.

"I don't do this all the time," Paul said.

"You can take me for granted if you want, but I won't have you taking your children for granted."

"I'm not taking anybody for granted," Paul said. He opened the door to the bathroom from the master bedroom and saw Ben and Kimberly sitting on the floor and the old faucet as well as several tools scattered about. He turned to Anne. "Excuse me, but what is going on here?"

23

"I asked Ben to fix the leak," Anne said.

"To fix a leak, you don't need a whole new faucet."

Ben tried to explain. "Everything was so old and . . . uh . . . well . . . your wife said it kept leaking even after you fixed it, so I thought it'd be better to get a good washerless faucet. Now you won't be bothered by it anymore."

"Listen to me," Paul lectured Ben, "I want you to put everything back the way it was, take the new faucet back to the store, and get your money back. I'm not paying for a new faucet when the old one is perfectly good."

Megan came to the bathroom entrance. "Hi, Daddy, when are we leaving?"

"In just a minute, sweetheart. Go get in the car."

Megan went out to the car.

"My gosh," Anne said, "aren't you even going to apologize to your daughter for being late?"

"I'll take care of it when I'm in the car. What I want to know is who told Ben he could buy a new faucet."

"I did," Anne said.

"Why on earth would you do something like that?"

"How long have I been after you to fix that faucet? Well, it got so bad I couldn't wait any longer. Ben said he'd do it. He suggested we get the kind that doesn't need a washer."

"I realize you don't understand things like this, but I can guarantee that what he's done is a total waste of money. I'm having him pack it all up and take it back."

"You're not doing anything of the kind! That boy has been working on this for over an hour, and you don't have the decency to thank him for trying to help out. He knows what he's doing, and he's willing to do it as a favor to us. When you come back, there will be a new faucet in the bathroom, and that's all there is to it. Now go so you don't miss any more of the show. I mean, it would be nice if you could get there before intermission. If you could have seen how excited Megan was to be going out with her dad and then see how hurt she got

24

as the time passed and you didn't show up. What were you doing that was more important than being on time for your daughter? Now I'm sure you think you can go out there and turn on your charm and sweet-talk her out of her disappointment, but it doesn't work that way. If you were going to be late, why didn't you at least call?"

Paul turned and, without another word, walked out.

The storm was over, but Ben felt exhausted by the tension he'd felt. He picked up his tools and put them back in the tool chest. After turning on the new faucet and letting cold water flow, he sat down to check underneath to make sure there were no leaks.

Kimberly came up from behind, knelt down, and gave him a hug. "Hey, Mister Fix-It Man, I think you're wonderful."

"You do? Thanks."

"I'm really sorry you got put in the middle of this."

"No problem."

She stood up. "I hope Megan has a good time tonight, don't you? It didn't start out very well, but maybe it'll get better once they get there."

"I bet it will."

Anne came in. "You're all done?"

"Sure." He turned the water on and off a couple of times.

"Oh, would you look at that!" Anne exclaimed. "No more leaky faucets. How wonderful! Thank you so much."

"Hey, it's the least I can do for all the meals you've been feeding me lately."

"We enjoy having you here," Anne said. "Ben, I need to apologize for my husband. He's under a lot of pressure at work right now. I'm sure that once things calm down, he'll be really grateful for all you've done for us tonight."

"If he won't pay for the new faucet, I will," he said.

"Thanks for offering, but that won't be necessary."

* * * * *

25

Ben lived in an upstairs apartment in his aunt's house. She had been happily married for twenty-five years, and then four years ago her husband suddenly had a heart attack and died. He sat in his aunt's kitchen that night and told her what had happened at Kimberly's. They stayed up late and talked about marriage and families and the problems that come into people's lives.

3

A few days later Ben phoned Kimberly. "I've got a way for us to make some extra money next Friday night, if you're interested," he said.

She laughed. "Excuse me, but did you say extra money?"

"You'd better hear what it is before you decide. My dad's store is having its annual banquet, and they have some money budgeted for entertainment. My mom just called to ask if we'd be interested in singing. We could drive to Rock Springs Friday afternoon, go to the banquet and perform, then stay the night at my folks' place. We'll come back Saturday and work for Angelo that night. My dad's store will pay us each two hundred dollars. I think it's mainly because my mom wishes I'd come home more often. What do you think?"

"What's Angelo going to say?"

"I already talked to him. He says it's okay. His nephew has a group and keeps bugging Angelo to let them play at the restaurant. It'll work out okay, if you're interested."

"Let's do it," she said.

"Okay, I'll tell them they can count on us." He paused. "Now there's just one thing. You're the first girl I've taken home to meet my parents since my mission. They're both trying to get me married off. If my mom thinks there's anything going on between us, she'll ask if we need any help picking out wedding invitations."

"Well, we'll be honest and let her know we're just friends."

"Honesty? That might work with some parents, but I'm not sure it will with mine."

On Friday afternoon at four-thirty they arrived at his home in Rock Springs. They came with a plan. "Mom, this is, uh, oh gosh, I forgot your name."

"Kimberly."

"Yeah, right, Kimberly . . . Mitchell?"

"It's Madison, actually," Kimberly said.

"Oh yeah, right, Kimberly Madison. She'll be playing guitar and singing with me tonight."

"Kimberly, I'm very happy to meet you. Ben didn't tell me how lovely you are," his mother said.

His father, a big man with a booming voice, gave Kimberly a big hug. He was still wearing his red Ace Hardware vest from work, a vest he hadn't been able to button for years.

"Uh, Kathryn, would you like me to show you to your room?" Ben asked.

"It's Kimberly!" her father and mother both said at the same time.

"Yeah, right. Gosh, I don't know why I can't remember your name."

He carried her suitcase to the guest bedroom. "The bathroom is across the hall. Knowing my mom, there's probably some guest towels on the counter in there. If you need extra blankets during the night, there's some in the closet. I think that's all I'm supposed to say. Anything you need, just let us know."

The banquet was held in the dining hall of a motel. When they entered the room, there was a banner on the wall that read, "Welcome Ace Hardware Employees." They sat at a round table near the front of the hall.

"What are you studying in college?" Mr. Fairbanks asked Kimberly.

"History," Ben answered for her.

28

"No, not history," she said. "I'm majoring in mechanical engineering."

"Oh, right," Ben said. "Another girl I spend time with is majoring in history. It's hard to keep it all straight."

The show they presented was well received. They sang songs the audience would be familiar with, but the last song they sang was the one they'd worked on the first time they got together, her graduation song. When they finished, several in the crowd stood up and shouted their approval. They were asked to do an encore. They did two more songs they'd written together. After they finished, people came up and told them how much they enjoyed the program. And then a country western band started setting up. Ben and Kimberly stayed for a couple of dances and then decided to go back to Ben's house.

When they got there, Ben started a fire in the fireplace while Kimberly fixed them some hot chocolate. It was a cold February night, and the wind was drifting snow across the road they'd just traveled over.

Ben turned off all the lights in the house except the one in the kitchen. They sat in front of the fire and talked and sipped hot chocolate and ate cookies. His fingers picked out snatches of new songs on the guitar while they talked.

"Your parents seem to get along really well," she said.

"Yeah, I guess they do. They argue sometimes, but they're always able to work things out."

"I like them a lot. I can see now why you turned out the way you did. You got your love of music from your mom and your down-to-earth practicality from your dad."

"I never thought about it before, but you're probably right. My mom was the one who made sure I had music lessons when I was a kid. In high school I played trumpet in band, and I was in choir too. My parents always went to our concerts — my mom because she loved music, my dad mainly because I was in it."

"When did you learn to play guitar?" she asked.

"The year after I graduated from high school, while I was working for my dad and saving for a mission." He put another log on the fire. "What do you want to do now? Watch a movie? Play a video game?"

"Oh, let's just talk," she said. "There's a lot about you I don't know, even though we do get together every day."

"It's just that when we're together we have more important things to do. My time with you is the most important part of my day."

"Because of the music, right?"

"Yeah, sure."

"Have you ever been in love?" she asked.

She was sitting close enough to him that it seemed natural for him to put his arm around her shoulder. "In high school I was," he said.

"What happened?"

"I went on a mission. When I came back, she was married. What about you?"

"Not really. Actually, I have no business writing songs about love when I've never experienced it firsthand."

"You do okay."

"For some people this'd be a romantic situation, the two of us sitting in front of a fire, a snowstorm outside, just the two of us here alone with the lights down low."

"A snowy night, a fireplace, the shadows from a fire upon your face."

She set her hot chocolate down just in case he was about to kiss her.

He paused. " 'A snowy night, a fireplace, the shadows from a fire upon your face.' What do you think? It might work. Get your guitar. Let's see if we can get a song out of this. Or how about this — 'A fireplace hearth on a winter night, your face aglow in the firelight.' "

She moved away. "Do we have to do this now? Why can't we watch TV or pop popcorn or do what ordinary people do?"

"I'm sorry. You're right. We need to forget about music for a while. You want to watch a movie?"

"No, not really. I probably should study a little. I've got a chemistry test Monday."

"Yeah, sure, go ahead. You can use the kitchen table if you want. I'll see if I can come up with another song for our tape. Oh, I talked to a friend of mine who has a friend whose uncle has a recording studio in Provo. If we can get with him some night, he'll record all our songs for us for practically nothing. I was thinking about next Friday after we get done at Angelo's. Will that work for you?"

"Yes, I think so."

"Good."

She laid her books on the kitchen table. He sat by the fire with his guitar in his hand, hunting for the rest of the melody and words to the song they would later call "Winter Love."

When he had a first version finished, he went into the kitchen and sang it to her. She adored the sound of his voice. While he was singing, she looked up at him, and for a brief instant, low-key and professional was thrown out, and they were looking at each other like two people in love.

When he finished, they were still staring at each other. "What do you think?" he asked, sounding like he was under a magical spell.

"About what?" she asked.

"I don't know."

"Me neither."

"What's going on?" he asked.

"I don't know."

"Me neither, but something is."

"Yes."

He thought about kissing her, but she was sitting down holding a calculator and he was standing up with a guitar in his hand. It would be a little awkward.

They heard his parents pull into the driveway. Instinctively,

31

she returned to her book and he went into the living room and turned on more lights.

"Hey, you two! Everyone is still talking about how wonderful you sounded together tonight," his mother bubbled as she came in.

"Yes. Everyone told me how much they enjoyed your program," his dad echoed.

His parents challenged Ben and Kimberly to a game of Pictionary. They sat around the kitchen table and played and ate popcorn and laughed and teased each other and gloated when they guessed right.

For Kimberly, along with the fun was a sadness that came from the realization that her parents had long ago quit playing board games on the kitchen table with the family. She felt like she needed to be alone, so she excused herself and went to her room to get ready for bed.

"She's a fine girl," she heard Mr. Fairbanks say as she walked down the hall to the guest room. It was easy to hear him anywhere in the house.

"I know that," Ben said.

"She'd make a good wife."

"I know that too."

"Then what's the problem?"

"We just work together."

"You can say anything you want," Mrs. Fairbanks said, "but when you were up there singing, everyone noticed the way you were staring at each other. I'm sure of one thing—it's not just business with her. And I don't think it is with you either."

"No, not really, but we're trying not to rush into anything. You know the mess I had with Julia and that guy she was going with. I don't want to repeat that again. And besides, I wish I could explain what it's like when we work together writing music. It's magic. I'm afraid of losing that. I think we have a real shot at making it big."

"If you make it big, fine," his father said, "but don't sacrifice your education for some one-in-a-million chance that most likely won't pan out anyway. I'll tell you one thing. There's a lot more hardware store owners and also people with business degrees making it than there are singers and guitar pickers. You get your education first and then worry about this 'making it big' foolishness later."

"Yeah, right. Look, I think I'll go to bed now."

"Let's have family prayer," his mother said.

After family prayer, his father said, "Oh, one thing, the roads are getting worse. You might think about staying until this storm blows over."

"I'll see how it is in the morning."

"I was hoping you'd stay until Sunday after church," his mother said.

"Sorry, Mom, we've got to get back. We're supposed to work at Angelo's tomorrow night."

Kimberly lay in bed wide awake. She heard Ben go down the hall to his room. She realized she was falling in love for the very first time. On the way up from Utah, while he drove, she had studied his face. She could close her eyes now and bring it again to mind—his thick, sandy-colored hair that seemed impossible to muss up (she called it industrial-strength hair), the small, nearly invisible scar on his right cheek caused by a bicycle accident when he was twelve, his long face with prominent cheekbones that somehow reminded her (although she never told him) of a young, beardless, and still cheerful Abraham Lincoln.

His parents finished the leftover hot chocolate. When they passed the guest bedroom on their way down the hall to their room, they danced to the out-of-tune humming of Mr. Fairbanks. "This is our night, kiddo," he said as softly as he could, but with his gravelly voice, he could be heard in every room in the house.

"Is that right?" she teased.

"Absolutely."

They danced into their bedroom and closed the door.

Kimberly started to cry. She was really worried about her parents.

After breakfast Ben and Kimberly said good-bye to his mother and then drove to the hardware store to see his dad.

Ben gave her a tour of the store, which was crammed with merchandise of every kind. A tall girl in her early twenties, with short brown hair and a mischievous smile, breezed past them. She was wearing jeans, a long-sleeved wool shirt, and an Ace Hardware vest. "Better not let the boss catch you making out on company time," she teased Ben as she led a customer to where they kept the axe handles.

"That's Jeni," Ben said. "She's a walking hardware encyclopedia. Anything I can do, she can do better."

Jeni returned a minute later. "Hey, you two, except for the fact it wasn't country western, your singing last night wasn't half bad. Of course, it could've been a lot better," she said, with a broad smile in Ben's direction.

"How could it have been better, Jeni? Please, won't you tell me?" he asked, knowing full well what was coming.

"It would've been better if we hadn't been able to hear you."

"Yeah, yeah. Kimberly, this is Jeni. She's lean and mean, but people come for miles around to ask her advice on how to fix things."

"Hey, somebody around here has to know what's going on. It's for sure Ben doesn't. The only reason he can get a job here every summer is because he's the boss's son."

"That's right, and don't you ever forget it."

"How can I? You bring it up every ten minutes," Jeni said. "Well, not everyone around here can stand around and make eyes at their sweetie. I guess I'd better get back to work."

"Whoa! Did you say you're actually going to work? Wait, let me get my camera."

"Careful, Ben, don't get me riled. Did I ever tell you about the time we put a paper towel in Mel's bologna sandwich? He never even noticed. This summer if your dad makes a mistake and hires you again, you'd better check your lunches. Fair warning." She left to go help another customer.

"As you can see, Jeni and I have this thing going."

"You really like it here, don't you," Kimberly said. It was more of a statement than a question.

"Oh, yeah. This is my second home. This is where I learned to work and where I found out I like serving the customer."

"And that's why you're majoring in business?"

"I think so."

"Are you going to come back and work here after you graduate?"

"I might. It's not a bad life. Our customers are like old friends. For almost anything that breaks down in this town, we're the first ones to know about it. You're probably not impressed by shelves full of bolts and nails, but it's important to the people around here. There's something I've been thinking about lately though. Stores like this are dying out. Before long there won't be people around like Mel or Jeni. I'm wondering if there's a way to use technology so that a customer can have the advantage of talking to someone who can answer their questions. Some sort of a computer data base with all sorts of practical hints. Right now it's just in the dreaming stage." He looked at his watch. "Well, I guess we'd better tell my dad good-bye and then take off."

They found his father helping a man with a bad back decide what kind of snow shovel would be best for him to get. When the man decided and left, Ben said, "Dad, we're going to take off now."

"Have you checked the weather report?"

"Yes."

"And?"

"I think we can make it."

"Famous last words," his father said, resting his large hand on Ben's shoulder. "Look, son, you be careful, and if there's any problem, let us know right away. You got that?"

"Okay, sure."

Mr. Fairbanks turned to Kimberly. "It was an honor for us to have you come visit us. You look like an angel and you sing like one too. Now you make sure Ben doesn't do anything stupid out on that highway." He gave her a hug.

They started to leave.

"Oh, one more thing, there's still some donuts and rolls in the back if you want to take 'em along," his father called out.

"Thanks, Dad, we'll grab a couple on our way out."

They left Rock Springs at eleven in the morning. Though it was still snowing, the wind had died down and the interstate was still open. But the farther they drove, the worse it got. The wind picked up and started laying down drifts across the road. Just before they reached Green River, there was a state highway patrol car parked across the road. The officer told them that the interstate was closed and they should go into Green River and wait out the storm.

"How long will that be?" Ben asked.

"Around here you never know. It could be a couple of days or just a few hours."

"Where do people go while they're waiting?"

"There's probably still some motel rooms in town, but they'll be going fast."

Ben glanced over in Kimberly's direction, then said, "We're not in the market for a motel room."

"Try the high school then. They'll be putting people up during the storm."

They were among the first ones at the high school. They were each assigned an army cot and a blanket.

They decided on a place to set up their temporary home, then phoned their parents and told them where they were. Ben asked his parents to call Angelo and tell him they weren't going to make it that night. Next they found a store and stocked up on junk food. Then they returned to the gym.

They sat on the floor through the long afternoon with an army blanket wrapped around them and watched people file in, truckers unhappy about being shut down, families with children who cried, salesmen unlucky to have been caught on the road during a blizzard.

At seven that night Ben went to his car, got his guitar, and came back in and started playing some songs. Children drifted over to where he was. He taught them several songs and had them sing with him. Then he did silly songs and monster imitations that made the kids shriek. He wrestled with them, carried them on his back, and made them giggle and laugh and beg for more. They clung to his back, wrapped their arms around his legs, tried to tickle him, came up and hugged him. One little boy even fell asleep on his blanket.

And then a woman in a fur coat came over and told him the children were creating too much of a commotion and that Ben was the worst of all. He was told to act his age and let the children calm down so they'd be able to sleep that night.

It was all over. Parents came and took their children, and Ben was forced to turn into an adult again.

"Just when I make up my mind not to like you, you do something wonderful," Kimberly said.

He smiled. "Let's face it, life is unfair."

"How did you get all those kids to love you?"

"I guess there's a part of me that never grew up."

They lay on separate cots, next to each other. They listened to the combined noises of sixty people around them coughing, talking, trying to get to sleep. Somewhere in the dim light a man was snoring loudly.

"It's going to be a long night," she said quietly.

"At least we're together and can talk."

"Remember in kindergarten when you used to take naps in the middle of the day," she said, " and it didn't matter if a girl or a boy was next to you on the floor. Everyone was the same. That's what this reminds me of."

"I wished I'd been in kindergarten with you," he said.

"Why?" she teased. "So we could write songs without that dreaded physical attraction getting in the way?"

"I just wish I'd known you then," he said. "I bet you were a cute kid."

"Of course I was."

"Are you going to dream about me tonight?" he asked.

She sat up. "Who told you about that?"

"Megan."

"What did she say?"

"She told me you had a romantic dream about me. This might be a good time for you to tell me all about it."

"No, go away."

"C'mon, why not? I like bedtime stories."

"It would be too embarrassing."

"Now you've really got my interest."

"Quit talking and let me get to sleep." She turned her back to him, a signal she was through talking for the night.

Strangely enough, he dreamed about her that night. It made him realize how much he cared for her. But also, like her, he didn't want to tell her about his dream either.

In the morning Ben was the first to wake up. Kimberly was facing him but still asleep. It gave him an opportunity to look at her. Her face was relaxed, her breathing slow and even.

She woke up. "Have you been watching me sleep?" she asked.

"Yes."

"Just shows how desperate a person can get when there's no TV."

38

"I'm not complaining."

The road didn't open until one o'clock in the afternoon. And then they were on their way.

"I've been thinking that we both need a little romance in our lives," he said. "So I think we should concentrate on dating after we finish at Angelo's on the weekends."

She was surprised, but delighted. "You do?"

"Yes. If you need any help, I know some guys I can line you up with, so then we can keep working."

Her smile vanished. "Who will you date?"

"Don't worry about me. I've got plenty of girls to choose from. What about you?"

"Same thing with me," she said. "I turn down dates all the time."

"I didn't know that."

"Oh yes, all the time."

From the way she looked at him, he knew she was disappointed, but he didn't know what else to do.

4

The next Friday night after they finished at Angelo's, Ben and Kimberly recorded all their songs at a recording studio belonging to an uncle of a friend of a friend's. It took them until three in the morning before they finally finished. But when they listened to the tape again on Monday, they decided it was worth it.

They duplicated one hundred tapes and put handmade labels on them. At Angelo's the next week they sold four tapes. To them it was sweet success.

On their Wyoming trip Kimberly and Ben had come to an understanding about dating others, which in the beginning made sense but within two weeks had degenerated into a bizarre game.

"I had the most wonderful date last night," Ben said as he stared into Kimberly's eyes during one of their afternoon practices.

"Tell me all about it," she said.

"Her name is Courtney Thomas. She's a model. She's done three covers for *Seventeen*. She's a returned missionary. She speaks three languages. She's majoring in Russian studies too. She's away a lot because when any Russian dignitary comes to the West Coast, they hire her to act as a translator. She's writing a book about foreign policy. The book's going to be published

40

next fall. In her spare time she teaches aerobics and works with the elderly. I couldn't believe how well we got along together. For some reason she was really attracted to me."

"How could you tell?"

"Well, when we were in the theater, she leaned her head on my shoulder and reached out for my hand."

"You mean like this?" Kimberly said, repeating the action.

"Yes, like that."

"How did that make you feel?"

"Well, I felt like she must like me a lot. I think she and I are about to become romantically involved."

"I'm so happy for you. I've also found someone to become romantically involved with. His name is Christopher Monti-leaux. He's a returned missionary. He plays first-chair violin for the Utah Symphony, and he's also a member of the Olympic ski team. He was here with the team this weekend. They were driving by when he saw me downtown. He told the driver to stop, and then he got out and ran up to me. We spent the rest of the day together. So now I too am romantically involved with a wonderful person."

"We're very lucky to both be romantically involved," Ben said.

"Yes, very. Did you kiss Courtney?"

"No. She begged me to kiss her, but I told her it wasn't right on the first date."

"That was very wise."

"Have you kissed what's his name?"

She stood up. "No, but once when he was practicing his violin, I came up behind him like this . . . and put my arms around his neck like this . . . and bent over and blew into his ear like this . . . and asked him how his practicing was going."

"That must have melted his violin."

"Just the rosin."

"We're very fortunate to both be romantically involved," he said.

41

"Yes, we are."

He kissed her. It was not the first time. The last few times they'd gotten together in the basement to learn some new songs, they'd ended up kissing. The only problem was that outside of that room they pretended it had never happened.

This time was different. She held up her hand. "Time out." She brushed back strands of hair. "Look, whatever happened to low-key and professional?"

"Oh, that. Good question."

"We're supposed to be working now, not doing this."

"I know. Sorry. Any suggestions?" he asked.

"I think we need to be honest with each other and face the fact that we have feelings for one another and, no matter how much we try to deny it, they're not going to go away. No more making up people, okay?"

"All right," he said.

"We have to make a separation between working and . . . uh . . . recreation or whatever you call what we were just doing."

"We were kissing."

"Yes, that's right, we were. And another thing. You've got to give me more time to study. I think we should practice from four to five and then you should go back to your aunt's place. We're spending too much time together. I can't study about chemical reactions when you're trying to braid my hair at the same time, because that causes plenty of chemical reactions in me. Also, we can't keep practicing down here in the basement, because it's too isolated. We need to get upstairs where we'll be bothered. We could practice upstairs in the hallway. There's always someone going by there."

They moved their chairs and guitars and music stand to the hallway upstairs.

"What's going on?" Derek asked.

"We're going to work up here for a while."

"What for?"

"Ambience," Kimberly said.

"I don't know what that word means," Derek said.

"That's why I used it," Kimberly said.

"And people say *I'm* weird."

After they finished practicing, Kimberly said, "Go home now, Ben."

A few minutes later, though, they were still lingering at the doorway.

"What happens now?" he asked.

"If you want us to get together socially, then you ask me out. That's how it's done in the real world. Why should we be any different?"

"Look, I'm sorry about how this has turned out. I owe you an apology," he said. "This is what I was trying to avoid by talking about low-key and professional. Guess I didn't do a very good job, did I?"

"It's not totally your fault," she said. "It was just something that happened. But we've got to make a separation or we'll ruin everything—both the singing and our relationship."

"So we're entering a new phase then, is that it?" he asked.

"Yes, that's what it is, a new phase. Good day, sir."

"Will you go out with me this weekend?"

"I'd like that very much."

"Good. It's a deal then. It's a pleasure being professional with you." He shook her hand, wished he could kiss her again, decided against it, and then left.

5

A few days later Kimberly came home early to clean the house before Ben showed up. She hung up her coat. "I'm home!" she called out. No answer. She entered the kitchen but nobody was there. She could hear Derek's video game in the TV room, so she went in to see him. "Where's Mom?" she asked.

"She's in her room. She's got a headache." Derek sounded relieved not to be hassled about after-school chores. "You're supposed to go see her. What I want to know is, who's fixing supper?"

"Is feeding your stomach the only thing you can think about?"

"I'm sorry she's sick, all right? But I'm also hungry."

"Have you done your after-school jobs?" Kimberly asked.

"You're not my mother," he said.

"It won't kill you to help out once in a while. We don't want Dad coming home to a messy house again."

"It doesn't matter. He never comes home anyway," he said.

"This is a busy time of year for him."

"Shut the door when you leave, okay?"

Kimberly knew her mother probably wanted her to fix supper, so she decided to change clothes first. When she entered her bedroom, she found Megan standing in front of the mirror wearing a sweater Kimberly had received last Christmas. "Caught you, didn't I?"

Megan looked at her but didn't smile. "Something's wrong," she said.

"I know. Mom's not feeling well. Derek told me."

"It's more than that. You go talk to her. She always tells you things."

"Okay. What do you have in mind for that sweater of mine?"

"Nothing. I was just trying on some of your things. I wish I was like you."

"Whatever for?"

"People pay attention to you."

"They pay attention to you too."

"Not really. We were reading out loud today in English, and it talked about someone being a plain-looking girl, and I heard one of the guys whisper, 'Yeah, like Megan.' "

"Don't pay attention to guys like that. I'll tell you one thing—I wish I had your face. It's so perfect. I mean it."

"You're just saying that."

Kimberly took Megan's face in her hands and leaned until their foreheads were nearly touching. With each word, she gently bumped her forehead to Megan's. "I . . . love . . . your . . . face."

"Nobody knows I'm even alive," Megan said.

"That's not true."

"It is."

"Don't you know how wonderful you are?"

"I'm not anything."

"I won't listen to you talking like this. Besides, we've got to start supper before Dad gets home. We'll talk later. But look, if you want to wear my sweater tomorrow, go ahead. It's a little big for you but not too bad. Just don't spill anything on it."

Kimberly changed, then went downstairs to her mother's bedroom. She knocked on the door, and her mother told her

45

to come in. "Derek and Megan say you're not feeling well," Kimberly said as she entered. "You want me to fix supper?"

Her mother sat up in bed. "That would be a big help."

"What do you want me to fix?"

"I thought we'd have spaghetti. There's hamburger in the refrigerator you can cook, and some bottles of spaghetti sauce in the storeroom. If you're going to have Ben stay for supper, make a little extra."

"He won't be staying for supper anymore."

"Why not?"

"We just work on music together, that's all. Well, I guess I'd better fix supper before Derek starts chewing on the furniture."

"Don't fix anything for your father. He won't be coming home for supper."

"Is he working late again?"

Her mother didn't answer. Kimberly thought maybe she hadn't heard the question and was about to leave when her mother said, "I don't know what to say about your father."

"What do you mean?"

"He's found someone else."

The only thing Kimberly could think of about her father finding someone else was the time her father had brought home a kitten he'd found near his office. They'd kept it; it was still in the family. To Kimberly it would have made more sense if her mother had said her father had found another kitten or another animal, but saying he had found someone else didn't make any sense at all. "I don't understand."

"Today he told me he wants a divorce."

In the bleak darkness of the room Kimberly heard the muffled sounds from the TV. She tried to imagine that in the TV room none of this existed, only here in her parents' bedroom. She stood there for a long time, numb and confused. "That can't be true."

46

"That's what I thought too at first. I'm going to tell the others after supper."

"Maybe he'll change his mind."

"I don't think so."

"Where is he now?"

"I'm not sure. He came home from work in the middle of the morning, told me he wanted a divorce, then packed a suitcase and left. He said he was going to move to an apartment."

"Did he tell you who the woman was?"

"It's his secretary."

"Gloria?"

"Yes. Do you know her?"

"She typed a term paper of mine last spring, remember? Dad made me send her a thank-you card."

"I'd forgotten you knew her. Well, you'd better get started fixing supper. Ask Megan to help you."

Kimberly started to leave but then stopped. "Mom?"

"What?"

"I'm sorry."

Her mother started crying. Kimberly sat on the bed with her until Derek knocked on the door and asked when supper would be ready.

"You'd better get started," her mother said to Kimberly.

Kimberly went to the kitchen. She didn't want any help, she just wanted to be alone. Derek was making a peanut butter and jelly sandwich. She turned to face him. "Derek?"

"What?"

"Nothing."

"Why'd you call my name then?"

"Mom's going to talk to us tonight."

"It's probably about keeping the bathroom clean again. I don't know why she gets on me all the time. You and Megan are a lot worse than I'll ever be."

"It's not about that."

"What is it then?"

"I'll let her tell you."

"Fine, don't tell me. See if I care." He stood up to leave. "Are you crying?"

"No."

"Yes, you are. What's wrong?"

"Nothing."

"Is it about Ben?"

"No."

"What is it then?"

"I just want to be alone for a while, okay?"

He shrugged his shoulders. "Girls," he said on his way out.

Ben showed up a short time later.

"I can't work with you today. Something's come up," Kimberly said.

"What?"

"Let's go downstairs where we can talk."

They went to the office in the basement.

"Today my dad told my mom that he's in love with his secretary," she said. "He wants a divorce."

"How can he do that?"

"I don't know, but he's doing it. I know I'm not going to be much good to you for a while. I can't write love songs while my family is going through this."

"How about if I come every day for a while just to see if there's anything I can do?"

"I'd like that. Maybe you can help Megan and Derek. I'm really worried about how they're going to take this."

After supper, Megan washed the dishes while Derek, under protest, dried them. Kimberly and Ben sat at the table strangely quiet. Then Anne came out of the bedroom and announced to her children they were going to have a family council.

"You don't look so good," Derek said.

"I know. Ben, can you go in the living room for a few minutes? We need to meet as a family."

"I should go home now anyway," Ben said.

"No, stay," Kimberly said. "You could go down to the practice room." She paused. "Please."

"Sure, no problem."

Anne sat down at the table and gingerly touched her forehead.

"You okay?" Derek asked.

"Just a headache, that's all. Your father told me some things today that you need to know. He still loves you but he's found someone else, another woman, that he'd rather be with."

"Who?" Derek asked.

"His secretary, Gloria."

"She's too young for him," Derek said.

"Where is he now?" Megan asked.

"He moved some things out today. He won't be living here anymore."

"Where will he be staying?"

"He's getting an apartment. For the time being, if we need to get in touch with him, he said we should call him at work. He and I might be able to work things out between us. We'll just have to wait and see what happens."

"How can he be in love with someone else when he's married to you?" Derek asked. "That's not right."

"No, it isn't. He told me he and his secretary haven't done anything wrong."

"If he's in love with her, that's wrong," Megan said.

"I think what he meant is that he hasn't . . . committed adultery." She sighed. "I'm really sorry I have to talk about things like this with you kids."

"Maybe he'll change his mind and come back," Megan said.

"Maybe so."

"Doesn't he love you anymore?" Megan asked.

"I can't answer that, but one thing he wanted me to tell you all is that he still loves you."

"If he loves us, then why did he walk out?" Derek asked.

"It's not that he's unhappy with you kids. It's between him and me."

"Mom, you and Daddy will try to work things out, won't you?" Kimberly asked.

"I'm willing to try, but I'm not sure your father is. I talked to him about us going to a counselor, and he said it was too late for that. His mind seems to be made up. I don't know that there's anything we can do to change it."

"If he did change his mind, would you take him back?" Kimberly asked.

"Not with Gloria around. But with her gone, if he was willing to try and work things out, then I would too."

"There must be something we can do. We can't just sit by and watch our family be torn apart," Kimberly said.

"None of this makes any sense," Derek said.

"I know, but listen, whatever happens we're still a family. We all have to help each other. We're going to make it through this. Problems like this have always been something that happened to other people, and now it's happening to us. We just have to stick together and we'll make it. I love you kids so much. You three are the most important people in my life. And right now I need a hug." Megan was first and then Kimberly. Derek hung back until he was shamed into it by Kimberly.

"Mom, you look like you're in a lot of pain," Kimberly said when they broke up. "Why don't you go back to bed for a while? We'll be okay."

Anne stood up. "All right. My headache should go away if I just lie down and be very still and take another pill." She walked to her room and closed the door.

Derek was practicing trombone upstairs in his bedroom when Kimberly and Ben knocked on the door. He called for them to come in. They entered his room. It was so messy that the only place they could find to sit on was his unmade bed.

"Have these sheets ever been washed?" Kimberly asked.

"I don't know. Why?"

"They smell like old cheese."

"It's a new kind of detergent."

Ben looked up at the ceiling, where several pencils were stuck into the acoustic tile. "After you get the pencils stuck up there, why do you leave them?"

"It's sort of like a trophy."

"How are you doing?" Ben asked.

"Terrific, never better. Nothing fazes me. I'm sitting here playing the trombone part to 'Stars and Stripes Forever' while our family is falling apart. Nothing stops me."

"How are you feeling?" Kimberly asked.

"Hey, I don't have any feelings. That's the best way. That way nothing can hurt me."

"It's okay for a man to have feelings," Ben said.

"Maybe it's okay for some, but it's not okay for me. I don't want to talk about it to either one of you, so why don't you both just leave and let me finish practicing."

"If you ever need someone to talk to, let us know," Kimberly said.

"Yeah, yeah. Get out of here now, okay? I have work to do."

Ben and Kimberly left his room and went to Megan's door. Kimberly knocked and asked if she and Ben could come in. "Just a minute," Megan called out.

A moment later she opened the door and let them in.

Ben sat down at her desk. Her books were neatly stacked with the homework from each class ready for the next day of school. Out of curiosity, he opened her desk drawer. Pencils were stacked neatly in a tray. There was a half-empty roll of Lifesavers in the drawer, but with no extra paper and foil streaming out, the way most people handle their rolls. Her entire room showed that she had things under control.

"You want to talk about anything?" Kimberly asked.

"It's all my fault, isn't it."

"No. Why would you think that?"

She could barely say the words. "Because when we went to the Ice Capades and Daddy was late, they argued, and that started it all."

"Megan, they've been arguing for years."

"It's not only that. I'm the third child."

"What difference does that make?" Kimberly asked.

"I heard Mom tell someone once that they'd had enough money before I was born, but after I came they were always poor. You know how Mom and Dad sometimes argued over money. It must have gotten so bad that Dad couldn't stand it any longer. It's all my fault. If I'd never been born, none of this would have happened." By now tears were streaming down her face.

"It's not your fault, Megan," Kimberly said. "It's between Dad and Mom. It's not because of us."

"You can say what you want, but I know it's my fault." She continued to cry. Kimberly held her and told her again and again it wasn't her fault. When she and Ben left a few minutes later, they realized Megan still felt responsible for her parents' problems.

"Thanks for sticking around tonight," Kimberly said.

"Sure. I'd better go home now, but if anything comes up, give me a call and I'll come back," he said.

"I think we'll be okay now."

Later, as Kimberly brushed her teeth to get ready for bed, Megan came into the bathroom to talk to her. "Can I sleep in your room with you tonight?" she asked.

"Yeah, sure, if you want to."

"Is it okay if I ask Derek too?"

"Why?"

"So we can all be together. He can sleep on the floor in his sleeping bag."

"I guess so."

Megan went to Derek's room. "I'm sleeping in Kimberly's room," she said. "Want to be with us?"

"Not really."

"We'll all be together. It's like when we went camping at Yellowstone. You could sleep next to the bed on the floor in your sleeping bag."

"It's a dumb idea."

"But you'll go along with it because I asked you, right?" Megan said.

"All right."

Derek grabbed his sleeping bag and followed Megan into Kimberly's room. He lay down on the floor next to the bed.

"Derek, you have to clear out of here in the morning when we need to get dressed," Kimberly warned.

"I know that," Derek said.

"Now everybody go to sleep, okay?" Kimberly said.

"If someone has to use the bathroom during the night," Derek said, "be sure and watch where you're walking, because I'm down here."

"What's the matter, Derek?" Kimberly said. "Don't you want a footprint on your face in the morning?"

Megan, in the bed, was just a few inches above Derek on the floor. "Kimberly is fun, isn't she?" she said softly to Derek.

"Yeah."

"You think Dad will miss her?"

"Yeah."

"Enough to make him come back?"

"Probably."

"That's what I think too," Megan said just before she fell asleep.

6

Sunday began cold and cloudy and got worse as the day progressed. It started snowing just before the family left for church. It was the first time they had gone to church as a family without a father.

As they walked into the chapel for the beginning of Sunday School, a counselor in the elders quorum presidency came up and asked Anne where her husband was.

"He won't be here today," she said.

"I wanted to ask him how he's doing on his home teaching. Do you know if he's gone this month yet?"

"No, I don't know."

"I need the report today."

"I can't help you."

"Could you have him call me?"

"I'll give him your message."

"Thanks." He glanced down at a sheet of paper and set off to find someone else.

"Doesn't anybody know about Dad yet?" Kimberly asked her mother.

"Not yet. I have a meeting with the bishop this afternoon."

"Why haven't you told anybody?" Kimberly asked.

"I thought your father might come back."

Later, as they sat together in the chapel before sacrament

meeting started, Derek leaned forward to rest his head on the pew in front of them. Kimberly started touching him on the back. "What are you doing?" he complained.

"Picking lint balls off your sweater."

"Don't. I like 'em there."

"Let's play 'Guess What I'm Writing.' "

It was a game they'd played since they were kids. She would write on his back with her finger and he'd try to guess what she'd written.

She traced out several letters on his back. "Well?" she said.

"I'm too old for this."

"I'll try it again. This time concentrate."

When she was through, he was clueless.

"Give up?"

"Yes."

"It was, 'Get your Eagle.' "

He sat back in the pew so she'd have nothing to write on.

"When are you going to get your Eagle?" she asked.

"Never. That was Dad's idea, and now he's gone."

"You're so close to getting it. You can't quit now."

"Why don't you go pick lint balls off Megan?"

"She doesn't have any."

The bishop stood up and welcomed everyone to sacrament meeting. Kimberly quit talking but did write the word *Eagle* with her finger on Derek's arm.

After church was over, Gina, a sophomore like Derek, came over to talk to him.

"Are you going to the dance after the game at school next Friday?" she asked.

"I don't know."

"If you go, maybe I'll see you there."

"Yeah, maybe," he said with little enthusiasm. It wasn't that he disliked Gina. It was just that, for him then, she seemed a little too sincere. She answered questions in class and stood up and cheered for the school team at pep assemblies. She was elected secretary for student senate in school because everyone knew there wasn't anybody who could take better minutes than Gina. All of this Derek held against her.

"Sometimes people go out for pizza after a dance. What do you think about that?"

He wasn't sure if she was asking him to go with her for pizza after the dance or if she just wanted his opinion about people who eat pizza after a dance. "It's all right, I guess."

"I have money, but we'd need to catch a ride from someone," she said.

He shrugged his shoulders. "Whatever."

After church the family went home and had soup and sandwiches, and then Anne left to go see the bishop to tell him about her husband.

"I'm going upstairs to take a nap," Kimberly said. "Ben's coming over in a while. Wake me up when he comes. And don't mess up the house. Okay?"

After Kimberly left, Derek started wondering where Gloria lived. He went to the kitchen and got the phone book and brought it back to his room, then knocked on Kimberly's door. She mumbled something, so he opened her door. "What's Gloria's last name?"

"Montgomery," she said sleepily. "What are you going to do?"

"Nothing."

"Whatever you're thinking of doing, don't do it."

"I'm not going to do anything. Go back to sleep."

He looked up Gloria's address in the phone book. She lived in an apartment building less than a mile from their home. He memorized her phone number, then went to the phone in the kitchen and punched in her number. When she answered, he hung up. *Let her worry about that for a while,* he thought.

He wanted to know if his father was at her apartment. He looked outside. It was snowing hard, but that didn't bother him. He put on his jacket and gloves. Just as he was about to leave, he saw Ben walking up the sidewalk. He opened the door for him. "Kimberly's taking a nap. Ask Megan to go and wake her up," he said.

"Where are you going?" Ben asked.

"For a walk."

"It's not very good weather for a walk."

"I don't care, I'm still going."

"Do you want me to take you somewhere?"

"No. It's only a few blocks."

"To where?"

"I want to find out if my dad's at Gloria's apartment."

"I need some exercise. Is it okay if I walk with you?"

Derek shrugged. "Whatever."

Walking in the snow made it hard for him to stay mad, especially with Ben along. They had a contest to see who could hit the most stop signs with snowballs.

He was almost feeling good until they came to the apartment building where Gloria lived and he saw his father's car in the parking lot. He wrote "I hate you" in the snow on the hood of the car. Ben stood by and watched.

"Why didn't you try and stop me?" Derek said as they headed toward the entrance of the apartment building.

"You weren't doing any harm."

"I hate him, you know."

They went inside the building, looked at the names on the mailboxes, and found that Gloria lived on the third floor in apartment 317. They took the stairs.

"What are you going to do?" Ben asked.

"I haven't decided yet."

"Don't do anything stupid that'll get you in trouble."

"I don't care anymore."

"If you get in trouble, then I get in trouble too, because I'm with you."

"Leave me then."

"No."

"Why not?"

"Because we're friends."

"We are? That's news to me. Just because you're a friend of Kimberly's doesn't mean you're my friend."

"I'd like to be your friend."

When they got to apartment 317, Derek stopped and put his ear to the door for a while, then continued down the hall.

"What did you hear?"

"The football game on TV. My dad is watching TV on a Sunday. That figures. We could never even watch the Super Bowl, even when it was after church. He's such a hypocrite. From now on I don't have to live by any of the rules he ever gave me. I've been missing out on life all these years. I guess it's time I changed all that. I don't know where to start. Maybe I'll get drunk this weekend, or maybe I'll get in a fight at school, or maybe I'll start smoking. There's so many things to choose from, I don't know where to start. I can do anything I want from now on. But no matter what I do, it won't be half as bad as what my father has done to us." Suddenly he ran down the stairs and out the building. Ben ran after him.

Derek ran to his father's car. The snow that had fallen since they'd gone inside was beginning to cover up his message. He started kicking the tires of the car with his foot and hit the side of the car with his fist, but all it did was hurt his hand, so he looked around for a large rock to throw at his dad's precious car, but everything was covered up with snow.

"C'mon, Derek, we need to go home."

"How can he get away with this? Why doesn't anybody send him to his room? Or take away his privileges? How can he just walk away from us and have nobody stop him? I wish I had a stick of dynamite so I could blow up his stupid car into a million pieces!"

A car pulled into the parking lot.

"Derek, we need to go now."

"No, not until I've paid him back for what he's doing to our family."

The driver of the other car got out and saw them standing there. "You two live here?" he asked.

"No," Ben said.

"Then you don't have any business here. Get out of here or I'm calling the police."

"I don't have to do what you say," Derek shot back. He hit the window of his dad's car with his fist.

"Hey, stop that!" the man shouted.

"Come and make me, you jerk face!"

The man came after Derek but slipped on the ice and fell down.

"What's the matter, can't you even stand up?" Derek shouted.

The man swore at Derek and came after him.

Derek turned and ran away. Ben ran after him. The two of them cut down an alley and then through somebody's yard. They zigzagged from one block to another until they were sure the man was no longer following them. Then they slowed down and walked in the snow.

"I know why God invented snow," Derek said.

"Why?"

"Because he knew how rotten things were going to get and sometimes he can't stand it either, so he just covers everything up, all the garbage cans, all the junked-out cars, all the families that are falling apart, all the husbands in their secretaries' apartments while their wives are bawling their eyes out. I think sometimes God just covers everything up with snow and lets it be nice and white and clean for a little while. That's what I'd do if I were God."

"I think you're probably right."

When they got home, Anne was still gone. The first thing Derek did was turn on the TV as loud as he could. Ben asked Megan to tell Kimberly he was there.

59

Then Anne came home. "Why is the TV on?" she asked.

"It doesn't matter anymore," Derek said. "Those were Dad's rules, and he's gone."

"They're the rules of our family. Turn it off."

"Not until my program is over."

She walked over and turned the TV off.

"That's not fair," he complained.

"What makes you think it isn't fair?"

"Dad was the one who set up the rule, and now he's at Gloria's apartment watching football on TV."

"How do you know that?"

"Ben and I went there and walked by his apartment and stopped and listened."

"Did you go in?"

"No."

"You must never go there unless you're invited."

"Is he living with her?" Derek asked.

"No, he has an apartment."

"That's what he says, but how can we believe anything he says anymore? Do you hate him now?"

"No. I'm just very disappointed in him."

"Well, you can be disappointed if you want; but as for me, I hate him."

"He's still your father."

"Then why isn't he acting like a father?"

"I don't know. I'm sorry you children have to be subjected to this. The bishop is going to try to talk to him and let him know how serious what he's doing is."

"That's all? He falls in love with his secretary and all that happens is the bishop talks to him? That doesn't sound very bad to me. I got a C in math and had all my privileges taken away. He walks away from his family, and all that happens to him is the bishop talks to him."

"If he doesn't change his ways, he may end up losing his

membership in the church and his family and the trust of his children and his marriage."

"I bet he doesn't care about any of that. Gloria must be worth more to him than any of us. In a way I don't blame him."

"What do you mean?"

"All he got from us was problems. Megan has to have braces, Kimberly needs money for college, and you need him to do jobs around the house."

"What do you need?" his mother asked.

"I don't need anything from him or anybody. I don't feel anything, I don't need anything. I just want people to leave me alone." He bounded up the stairs to his room and slammed the door.

Anne focused her attention on Ben. "You went with Derek to Gloria's place?"

"Yes. I wasn't sure what he had in mind so I thought I'd better go along just in case."

Anne nodded. "I appreciate you looking out for my son."

"Sure, no problem."

Wednesday morning when they went out to go to school, the car wouldn't start. Anne tried it several times, but all it did was make a clicking noise.

"I have to be on campus by eight o'clock," Kimberly said.

"I'm doing the best I can," Anne snapped.

"You don't have to bite my head off."

"Sorry, this is just so frustrating, not knowing anything about cars. Your father has always taken care of things like this."

The car still wouldn't start. Finally Anne called a neighbor for rides for Derek and Megan, and Kimberly phoned Ben and asked him for a ride.

Before Derek and Megan left to go next door, Derek asked his mother what she was going to do about the car.

61

"If I call your father, I know he'll come and get it started."

"Don't call him."

"Why not?"

"We don't need him anymore."

"If I call a service station, they'll charge me a fortune."

"It's worth it not to have to see Dad again. I don't ever want to see him again."

She looked at him for a long time without saying anything. "Derek, I know this is hard for you. With all my heart, I wish you didn't have to go through this."

"I'll learn all about cars, and then I'll be able to help out like Dad did."

"I know you will, Derek. You're a good boy. I know I can depend on you to help out."

Every day in study hour Megan took a few minutes to write in her diary. This is what she wrote that day:

Why can't I have a perfect life? I mean my dad is in love with his secretary and probably is going to get a divorce. I feel so sorry for my mom because she is all alone now and she has to try to keep the family together all by herself. I can't imagine walking into school and saying that my dad and mom might get a divorce.

I wish I was more like Kimberly. She's so lucky. She's almost through being a teenager.

That evening at supper, Anne asked Derek if he was going to scouts that night. He said he wasn't. She asked why not. He said he didn't feel like it.

"You'd better finish up so you can get your Eagle."

"I don't care about that anymore."

"You put all that work into it, and you're so close to getting it now. It would be a shame not to get it."

"The only reason I worked on it was because Dad wanted me to, and he's not here anymore."

"I want you to get it," Anne said.

"Don't I have any say in this?"

Kimberly stepped in. "Derek, quit being such a jerk. We all want you to get your Eagle. Do it for the family."

"What family? We don't have a family anymore."

He didn't go to scouts but instead stayed in his room and tried to do homework. Gina phoned him. He talked to her mainly because he felt sorry for her. He decided she must not have many friends to keep calling him all the time when all he did was go "uh-huh" to whatever she said. He realized that he might be the only guy at school who said anything to her. She told him how much she was looking forward to the dance on Friday night at school. He wondered if he'd spend his entire life talking to people nobody else wanted to talk to.

After supper Ben came over to see if he could fix their car. Kimberly went out with him and stood in the cold and held the flashlight for him.

"When a car doesn't start, most of the time it's because of corroded battery terminals," he said. After he finished cleaning the terminals, he tried to start the car. This time it worked.

"Yes! Mr. Hardware to the rescue!" Kimberly cheered, kissing him on the cheek.

He smiled. "I guess I've learned a few things from my dad."

"I should do something to show my appreciation. How about if we work on a new song?"

"Sure, that's always fun."

"But not here. Can we go to your apartment?"

"I'd better call and ask my aunt if it'd be okay. She's still recovering from the last time I had Julia over."

"Tell her I'm not going with anybody who's crazy, deranged, or an escaped convict."

Ben laughed. "She'll be so pleased to hear that."

Fifteen minutes later Ben and Kimberly were on their way.

"What's your aunt like?" she asked.

"Her first name is Elizabeth. She works for the Church.

She has more white blouses than just about anyone I've ever met. She likes music, but her tastes run more toward classical music. We go to concerts together. I think she's trying to give me some culture. She told me that next week she's going to come to Angelo's and hear us sing."

They stopped off at a store to get some grape juice and crackers and then continued on their way to his aunt's place.

When they walked in the house, he made the introductions. "Kimberly, it's so nice to meet you," his aunt said. Then she turned to Ben. "She's a lovely girl, Ben. You can bring her here anytime you want."

Ben led Kimberly up the narrow stairs to his apartment. "One of the rules about having a girl here is that I keep the door to the stairs open. My aunt is very protective of me."

"Good for her."

His apartment was in what was formerly the attic. Two of the walls were slanted to match the roof line. At one end of the small living room was a tiny area for a kitchen. A door at the other end of the living room led to his bedroom. He wouldn't let her go into that room, explaining that he hadn't made the bed that day.

The living room had a couch, a table to eat and study on, an oval throw rug in the middle of the floor, a CD player, Ben's guitar, and some posters of seagulls his aunt had put on the wall before he moved in. He told Kimberly that he didn't much care for the pictures but didn't have the heart to take them down. The best part of the room was a gable that extended out from the window. A built-in platform filled with fluffy pillows allowed a person to sit in the gable and look out at the lights of the city.

He poured them both a glass of grape juice and dumped the crackers into a bowl. Then they sat with crossed legs on the ledge in the gable and sipped their grape juice and munched on the crackers.

"Let's not work on a new song," he said. "Let's just talk."

"Okay."

"I know you're going through a hard time, and I want to be here for you when you need someone."

"Thanks."

"What do you need from me now?"

She handed him her empty glass. "Some more grape juice."

He jumped up and got the pitcher from the refrigerator and filled her glass. "What else do you need?"

"Ben, what do you want me to do? Pour out my soul to you?"

"Okay, what do *you* want to do?" he asked.

"I want to sit here and look out at the lights of the city and listen to some music. Don't ask me how I'm feeling. Don't tell me that other families go through divorces and get through it just fine. Just don't try so hard."

They sat and listened to music and looked out at the city lights and drank grape juice.

After a while she said, "I feel better now."

"I'm glad. I wish I could help you."

"I know you do. You know what? It's a lot harder than I thought it would be. I've had friends who had parents go through a divorce. For the most part I didn't do much to even show I cared about what was happening. And now it's happening to me. Sometimes I wonder why people aren't trying to help us out more, but then I think about what I did when my friends went through it."

He stood up. "Tonight I'm going to take you away from all your troubles."

"How are you going to manage that?"

He took her hand and led her to a throw rug in the entrance to his room. "Sit down. This is a magic carpet. It can take you wherever you want to go, anywhere in time, anywhere in space," he said. He turned off the lights then lit a candle. They sat on his throw rug facing each other.

His aunt called up. "Ben, did the power go out up there?"

"It's okay. We're just talking."

"All right. I'm baking some cookies. I'll bring them up in a few minutes."

"Thanks."

Kimberly smiled. "Everyone should have an aunt like yours."

"I agree. Decide where you want to go on your magic carpet tonight. Just close your eyes and make a wish."

She closed her eyes and said, smiling, "I wish I wasn't with such a goofball tonight."

He tiptoed into the bathroom and closed the door.

She opened her eyes. "It's a miracle!"

When Ben came out, he had a ridiculous-looking green towel with pink floral print wrapped around his head. Kimberly, seeing him, laughed until her sides ached.

"Good evening," he said in a fake accent. "My name is Shammim. I'll be your genie this evening. Make a wish, my lady, and I will take you wherever you wish to be taken."

On another day it might have worked and she would have let Ben take her to a land of make-believe. But there was too much pain and uncertainty in her life now for that.

She sighed. "Take me back to the way it was in our family before my dad met Gloria."

The magic was gone. His shoulders slumped. "I wish I could do that."

"Me too. You want to know what I really would like to do tonight? I want to go talk to my dad. Will you take me there?"

"This is the address my dad gave. It's where he's having his mail forwarded to. But he might not be here," Kimberly said as they climbed the stairs in the apartment building. "He's probably over at Gloria's."

They knocked on the door. After a minute her father opened it. "Kimberly, I didn't expect you."

"You remember Ben, don't you?"

66

"Yes, of course. What can I do for you?"

"I need to talk to you. Is that all right?"

"Yes, of course. Come on in. I was just catching up on some paperwork." He picked up some papers, stuffed them in his briefcase, and turned off the small black and white TV. "Sit down."

Kimberly and Ben sat on a well-worn couch. Her father sat on a kitchen chair.

There was a long, awkward silence. "I'm sorry for what I'm putting the family through," her father finally said. "I know it hasn't been easy on you kids. I still care about you and Derek and Megan."

"If you really cared about us, you wouldn't have fallen in love with Gloria and you wouldn't have left us."

"Someday you'll understand how it was with me."

"I don't think I'll ever understand that."

"As you get older, it gets harder to decide what to do in certain situations."

"It's not hard for a lot of adults to live the right way. Why is it so hard for you?"

"In the beginning I didn't know this was going to happen. Gloria and I haven't done anything wrong."

"Have you ever kissed her?"

His father looked at her strangely. "Why would you ask a question like that?"

"You have kissed her, haven't you? When you kissed her, was it during the time you were supposed to be at work? And if it was, when you came home that day after work, did you act like nothing happened? Did you walk in and kiss Mom the way you usually did? Do you remember what you said to me that night?"

"This is not appropriate for us to discuss."

"I think it is. I just keep wondering if it was one of the nights you encouraged Derek to finish his Eagle project or if it was one of the nights you told me to be careful what kind

67

of guys I spent time with. Or was it one of those nights you told us we were going to be a forever family and that we'd be together even in heaven? Do you remember what you said to us the night you kissed Gloria for the first time?"

"You don't know any of the circumstances surrounding this."

"Maybe I don't, but I also don't understand how you could tell Gloria you loved her and then come home and act like nothing was wrong."

He didn't answer for a long time, and then he said, "I never meant to hurt your mother."

"Well, in case you don't know it, you *have* hurt her."

"I know that, and I'm sorry."

"Sorry enough to come back to us?"

"I can't do that."

"Why not? Because you love Gloria? Well, you loved Mom too once, didn't you? So what's the difference? There's only one of Gloria, so you'll hurt fewer people if you leave her. Besides, you might leave Gloria in a year or two."

"I'm sure that won't happen."

"How can you be so sure of what you will or won't do? If you ask me, you don't seem to have much self-control. I have a lot more of that than you do. At least I'm still living the way you told me to live. And you're not."

"Someday you'll understand this better."

"What is it that I need to understand?"

He sighed. "Okay, I guess you deserve to know the truth. I haven't wanted to tell you, but your mother and I had grown apart over the last few years. Somehow the spark was gone. We were just going through the motions of being happily married. Gloria isn't the villain in all of this."

"Okay, but if things weren't right in your marriage, why didn't you do anything to make it better? Why didn't you go to a counselor? Why just abandon everything and go chasing after Gloria? Don't even try to make me understand this. The way I see it, either a person lives the right way or he doesn't. And now I know you don't. I won't ever understand it because it's wrong what you're doing, and nothing you can ever say is going to change that. What was so awful with Mom anyway? Wasn't she thin enough for you? You could have told her to lose some weight and she would've done it. She would have done anything you asked her. She'd have even dyed her hair to get rid of some of the gray, if that's what you wanted. She would have done anything for you if you'd asked her, but you had to turn to someone else. It's not right and you know it, so don't ever lecture me again about what I do, because whatever I do from now on will never be as awful as what you've done."

Her father glanced at Ben. "I don't think Ben should be listening to this."

"Why not? I tell him everything. Actually, I tell everyone who will listen. I want everyone to know what it's like to have a hypocrite as a father."

"Kimberly, you may not believe this, but the thing that's been the hardest on me is knowing how much this was going to hurt you and Derek and Megan. I am truly sorry for the pain I've caused you kids."

"What about Derek? You were his hero, and now he doesn't have any heroes. I think that's pretty rotten for a boy not to have any heroes."

He sighed. "I am sorry . . . but nothing you can say is going to change the way things are."

"Maybe not, but I had to say it anyway." She stood up. "I've lost all the respect I ever had for you. Good-bye."

She and Ben got back in his car.

"Thank you for going with me." She sounded emotionally drained.

"Yeah, sure."

"Do you think I was too hard on him?"

"No."

"Boy, I could really use that magic carpet of yours now. Let's escape to a tropical island, whattaya say?"

"Do you want to go back to my apartment now?"

"I want to go somewhere and forget everything that's happening in my family. Everything is so messed up." She wiped her eyes. "I guess you'd better take me home. I still have some studying to do."

"Okay." He paused. "Have you met Gloria?"

"Yes. Last year when she typed a paper for me."

"What's she like?"

"She's looks a little like Demi Moore—short hair, a great face, a kind of whispery voice, nice smile. She's okay but she's not that great. I mean, she's not the kind of a woman I'd pick as one that a man would abandon his wife and family for." She looked out the window, then turned back to face him. "I don't think she tried to break up my dad's marriage. She's just not the type. That's just it. I don't know what made my dad do what he did. If it can happen to my dad, maybe it can happen to any man. Maybe you'll do the same thing someday to your wife. I mean, how can anyone predict what's going to happen? When my mom was my age, how could she have known that she shouldn't marry my dad because of what he would do to her someday? How can anyone know for sure who they can trust?"

"I don't have the answer to that," he said.

"I don't think anyone does. Sometimes I'm not so sure I even want to get married."

"Everyone feels that way once in a while."

"Do you?"

"Yes, sometimes," he said.

"Why?"

"Being married is a big responsibility."

"Hey, just living is a big responsibility."

He took her home and then went to his apartment and sat overlooking the city and played their songs. He could still smell traces of her perfume in the alcove where she had been sitting.

7

Friday night Derek went to the basketball game at school. He didn't intend to stay for the dance afterwards, but then some friends talked him into it. The instant he walked out on the floor, Gina was waiting for him like a vulture. She was all smiles, but it didn't do any good because he felt mean.

The two of them stood around and watched people dance. She asked if he wanted to dance and he said no. She asked what he wanted to do. He was about to say "Nothing with you," but then he looked at her, so hopeful, smelling of shampoo and perfume. He knew how much work Kimberly went through when she got ready for a date. He knew Gina had done the same thing, and so all of a sudden he felt sorry for her because he didn't think anyone else would ask her to dance. It wasn't that there was anything really wrong with her—she just tried too hard.

"Gina, you look . . . uh . . . okay tonight."

She smiled like it was the most wonderful thing anybody had ever said to her. He knew he was trapped for the rest of the night. He asked if she wanted to dance. Her smile got bigger, and she said yes.

As they danced, he could tell this was a big deal to her, even though he felt like he was a million miles away. He wondered why she went to all this trouble for a stupid dance.

After they danced for a while, he left her and went out to

71

the hall and found some guys to talk with. It was a lot more fun there, but then they had a girls' choice and Gina found him, so he had to dance with her again. She asked if he was going with Jason and MacKenzie to Pizza Hut after the dance.

"I dunno. Maybe."

After the dance he went with her in Jason's car to Pizza Hut. She turned to him and smiled. That's when he realized she didn't know what he was thinking. He thought that maybe nobody ever knows what anyone else is thinking. Maybe it's the same with adults. He thought, *Maybe Mom thought Dad loved her and would never leave her, but maybe Dad didn't think that at all. Maybe Dad never did love her. Maybe he was just pushed into everything because Mom smiled at him all the time the way Gina smiles at me in that kind of a happy, trusting smile.* He looked out the car window and felt more depressed than ever before in his life.

At Pizza Hut, after they got seated and ordered, Jason wanted to show off how good he was at video games, so everyone crowded around to watch him play. He was good, so the game kept going for a long time. After a while MacKenzie, Gina, and Derek got bored watching and returned to their table.

Gina excused herself to go to the restroom, which left MacKenzie and Derek alone together at the booth. MacKenzie had long blonde hair that cascaded down in bold and brassy curls. She had a great smile, which she was flashing a lot more since she got her braces off. She loved life and being with boys and wasn't afraid to show it.

For a few minutes Derek had more fun with her than with any other girl he'd ever been with. They started talking about what would happen if the pizza came while Jason and Gina were gone and he and MacKenzie ate it all. What would they say when they were asked about it? They each came up with ideas, and most of them were dumb, but they were both in a crazy mood, and they started laughing. Derek loved to make

72

her laugh. He found himself wishing this could go on for the rest of his life. Not only that, but he felt like she must be feeling the same way, so he asked her if she'd go with him, but she said she was going with Jason.

"I know that, but you could always break up with him, couldn't you?"

"Yes, I guess so."

"Then why don't you do it?"

"What about Gina?"

"I don't care about her."

"Why are you going with her then?"

"I'm not. Tonight was her idea. I'd rather go with you."

He reached out and held her hand under the table. She didn't try to pull away from him. He took his fingertips and ran them down the palm of her hand. She closed her eyes, and he knew she liked it a lot.

Jason, still playing the video game, glanced in their direction and called out, "I'm already on Level Nine."

They smiled at each other. "Great, Jason," Derek said, all the while holding MacKenzie's hand under the table. "We are too," he said, softly enough so that only MacKenzie could hear it.

"Stop," she giggled.

"Let's go lock Gina in the restroom."

"You wouldn't want to do that."

"Yes, I would. You're more fun. You like me, don't you?"

"Yes."

"I like you too. I've always liked you. This is fun. Jason doesn't suspect a thing, does he?"

"No. When he's playing a video game, he doesn't think about anything else," she said.

When Gina came back, Derek felt a little guilty because she had only been gone five minutes and he'd already asked another girl to go with him. Because he knew how it was with Kimberly and Megan, he knew that all the time Gina was in the restroom she was probably doing things so that she'd look better for him, and while she was doing that, he was flirting with another girl. He wondered if his mother was like Gina when she was a girl. Gina smiled at him, and that made him feel even worse.

When the pizza was served, Jason quit playing his video game and came back to the booth. "It's too bad you're no good at games, Derek. We could have played partners."

"What am I good at?" Derek asked.

"Nothing that I can think of," Jason teased.

"I can think of something," Derek said, glancing at MacKenzie, who blushed.

After MacKenzie finished eating, she dropped her arm that was closest to him and rested her hand on the seat. Derek dropped his hand too and held hers. She started blushing but didn't move away.

Suddenly Gina cried out, "What are you doing?" One look at her and he knew she'd seen him holding MacKenzie's hand. MacKenzie pulled away.

"I need to go home now," Gina said, standing up quickly. "I'm going to call my mom to come pick me up." She grabbed her coat and started to put it on.

"What's wrong?" Jason asked.

"Derek was fooling around with MacKenzie under the table," she said.

Jason glared at Derek, who protested, "We were just holding hands. It didn't mean anything. The whole thing was just a joke. You don't have to make such a big deal out of it. The only reason I did it was because I was bored." It was the truth, but it was the wrong thing for Gina to hear. She stared at him. "Gina, I didn't mean it that way," he said quickly. "Look, I'm sorry I messed up. I guess I'd better go now."

He walked home. Along the way, he passed a pay phone. He dialed Gloria's number and hung up when she answered it. At home he lay in bed and wondered if he would have any

74

friends on Sunday at church or on Monday at school. He felt worse than he had ever felt before in his life. He wanted to talk to someone, but there was nobody who would understand how he felt. He went to his room and paced the floor. Then he went downstairs and turned on the TV.

Because she had two exams the next Monday, Kimberly had asked Ben to take her home after they played at Angelo's that Friday night. She studied until midnight and then went to bed. But she couldn't sleep, so she went downstairs and saw that Derek was still up. She sat down with him. He told her what had happened after the dance. She suggested that he call and apologize to Gina the next day. He said he didn't want to. She said she'd help him. He reluctantly agreed to try it and then went to bed.

She watched TV for a while and then went to bed, but she still couldn't sleep. Finally, at one-thirty she called Ben. He answered on the first ring.

"Were you asleep?" she asked.

"No. I was just going over some of our songs."

"I can't sleep."

"Me either. You want to drive around for a while?"

"Sure."

He picked her up ten minutes later. "Where do you want to go?" he asked.

"I don't care."

"Did you get any studying done?"

"Some. I still have a little left for tomorrow. What did you get done?"

"I just had a reading assignment for the weekend. I got that done and then went through all our songs."

"What for?" she asked.

"Just something to do." He paused. "Every song reminds me of you. By the time I was done, I was really missing you, so I'm glad you called."

75

"Right now being with you and away from my family is the only good part of my life," she said. "You don't know what it's like for me at home. Sometimes I just want to run away from it all, to have even just a little bit of time when I feel comforted and safe and secure. The only time I feel that way is when I'm with you. Everything is pressing down on me. Suddenly it's like I'm responsible for Derek and Megan, and they're both falling apart a little at a time. I try to help, but it doesn't do any good. Tonight Derek got in trouble with his friends after a dance. And Megan's starting to clam up. I don't know what she's thinking half the time. And my classes are so hard. All my teachers are having a race to see how fast they can cover the material.

"I'm not supposed to have all this dumped on me. I'm not the mother—I'm just one of the kids. On top of that, I don't know how I'm going to pay for books and tuition next quarter. I don't know if my dad will pay for any of it from now on. I've never been more uncertain about my future. Sometimes I get so depressed, I just want to forget all my troubles. See, the thing is, I have to be strong for Megan, and I have to be strong for Derek, and my Mom is doing all she can, so I don't want to bring her down with my problems. Sometimes it gets to be too much for me. Like tonight. You're the only one I can talk to, the only one I can open up to, the only one I can be totally honest with."

"I want to help you any way I can."

"I know you do, and that means a lot to me."

No sooner had they pulled into the driveway an hour later than her mother marched out to the car.

"Oh no, we're in trouble now," Kimberly said, rolling down the window to talk to her mother.

"What is going on here?" Anne asked. "You just walk out of the house in the middle of the night without telling me where you're going?"

"I couldn't sleep."

"Where did you go?"

"We just drove around."

"At this time of night? Good grief, Kimberly, don't I have enough to worry about? I want you inside the house right now." Her mother headed back to the house.

"I'll talk to her so she won't think this was your fault," Kimberly said, kissing him on the cheek. Then she got out of the car and hurried inside.

The next day, Saturday, was as bleak a day as any that had come before it. When Anne came home from looking for a job, she found a carton of milk that had been left out since morning. With money as tight as it was, she called her family together and, with tears in her eyes, lectured them on how much a carton of milk cost.

During supper there were still all kinds of undercurrents of anger and bad feelings. Anne was still upset about Kimberly sneaking out of the house the night before to be with Ben. Kimberly felt that her mother didn't give her credit for taking on many of the responsibilities in the family. Derek was angry with the world because of rumors and gossip going around about him and MacKenzie at Pizza Hut the night before. And Megan could hardly stand the tension brought on by everyone else. She wished she had the courage to tell her mother she wished she could move in with some other family.

Into this hostile environment came, unannounced, visitors. The doorbell rang.

"If that's Ben, tell him you can't go out tonight," Anne said firmly to Kimberly.

"Mother, I'm in college now. Don't you think I'm a little too old for you to ground me?"

"If you live here, you go by the same rules as everyone else."

"Isn't someone going to answer the door?" Megan complained.

"You've got legs, Megan. Answer it yourself," Kimberly snapped.

Megan went to the door. In the kitchen the rest of the family could hear a man with a booming voice. "Hi there, is your mother home?"

Anne, thinking that if it was a salesman she would make short work of him, got up from the table and marched to the door.

It was Robert Hatch, a member of their ward, and Mike Jefferson, a deacon. Brother Hatch was retired. He and his wife had just returned home from a mission. "Sorry, we tried to call, but I kept getting a busy signal. The bishop asked me and Mike here to be your new home teachers. We were in the neighborhood and thought we'd drop by some banana bread. My wife made some today, but she forgot and doubled the recipe like she used to when our kids were around, so Mike and I are going around trying to get people to take it from us before it gets old and stale. It's just out of the oven."

Derek heard the magic words and came out of the kitchen to get the banana bread. It smelled wonderful. He took it into the kitchen, and a minute later, he and Megan went back to the living room, each with a slice of banana bread in their hands. "This is great stuff," Derek said, talking with his mouth full.

"It sure is," Megan agreed.

"Well, good, I'll tell my wife you like it. Look, we can't stay long. I just wanted you to know we'll be coming around, probably more often than you want us, but, you know, I don't have much else to do with my time. Whenever I go home, my wife keeps trying to put me to work." He had a rich, contagious laugh. "You know how that goes."

"Please sit down, won't you?" Anne asked.

Brother Hatch and Mike sat down. Brother Hatch's hair had turned white long ago but it didn't matter—he was still a

78

handsome man. Mike was glad to be going home teaching with a man who treated him to ice cream after every visit.

"Well," Brother Hatch said, "I understand from what the bishop told me that things maybe aren't going the way you'd like in your family. Is that right?" He focused his gaze on Anne, and then on Kimberly, and then on Derek and Megan. He seemed to be looking for clues to how each of them was doing. "I don't have answers for most of what happens in this world," he said. "People do get hurt, innocent people, people who have done nothing to deserve the way life is treating them. I don't know why that is, but I've seen it enough to know that life is not always fair."

He looked again at each of them in turn and then said, "I've had a few disappointments in my life too, things that I couldn't understand why they were happening to me. Some I never did find out why they happened. There is something I have found, though, that I can always count on, and that is prayer. When you feel the worst, you can always go to Heavenly Father and ask him to help you get through the hard times. I've been disappointed by a lot of people, people I thought I could trust, but I've never been disappointed by God." He paused. "Excuse me for asking, but are you folks having family prayer?"

"Most of the time," Anne said.

"Good for you. And what about personal prayer? Kimberly?"

Everyone looked at Kimberly. "Not very much lately," she said slowly.

"What about that, Kimberly? Here you are, going through one of the hardest experiences a son or a daughter can go through, and you're not asking for help from the one person who loves you and can help you more than anyone else."

"Can he bring our dad back home?" she asked.

"He doesn't force people to do what they don't want to do."

"Then how will it help to pray?" Derek asked.

"I don't know for sure, Derek. Why don't you try it and then tell me?"

Next he turned to Megan. "Megan, how are you handling this?"

"There's no problem with Megan," Derek said quickly.

"Somtimes those are the ones you need to worry about the most. Why don't we let Megan tell us how Megan is doing."

"I'm doing okay," Megan said, but with no eye contact.

"Derek, what about you? How are you taking all this?"

"I don't feel a thing."

Brother Hatch reached over and rested his hand on Derek's knee. "Let's talk about that sometime, okay?"

"I don't need to talk about anything."

"Maybe you will sometime though. If you do, I'm always home, getting in my wife's way. Come over anytime."

Derek just shrugged his shoulders.

"Sister Madison, how are things going with you?"

"I'm not sure. Sometimes I'm not a very good mother to my kids. I want to be, but sometimes — well, like today, I jumped all over them because someone left the milk out." Tears began streaming down her face. "Sometimes I'm not sure if they even know how much I love them. I don't say it enough, not like I used to."

"Why don't you say it now?" Brother Hatch said.

She looked at him a moment, then turned toward her family and said, "Kids, I love you a million times more than some silly carton of spoiled milk."

By then everyone was having to deal with tears. Brother Hatch turned to his companion and said, "Well, Mike, we've stayed too long already. Sister Madison, could we have a word of prayer before we leave?"

Anne asked Mike to say the prayer.

"Why are you our home teachers now?" Anne asked as she walked with them to the door.

"Because the bishop asked us," he said. "If he had more time, he'd come here himself to be your home teacher, but he's a pretty busy man, so he sent us. I have a little more time to devote to things like this than a man who has to make a living. I'm all done with that."

"Thank you for coming."

"I meant what I said. Call me anytime you need someone. If Mike's not available, I'll bring my wife. She's better at things like this than I am anyway." He stood up and clasped Anne's hands in his. "You know, our daughter got a divorce a few years ago and she's had to go it alone, so I know a little bit about what you're going through. I know it's not easy to raise a family all by yourself. If you need help, you let us know. I mean it. Here's my phone number. Call me anytime, day or night."

She thanked them for coming, said goodbye at the door, and watched them walk away.

The visit hadn't solved any of her problems, but she was glad Brother Hatch was her home teacher.

8

Megan walked in the door after school on Monday. Compared to Kimberly and Derek, she had always been the one who made the least noise when she entered the house. This time was no exception. Her mother, who was on the phone with her father, didn't hear her come in.

"I don't know why you're saying it's unreasonable," she heard her mother say. "I think it's very reasonable. All I'm asking for is that I get to keep the house and a little child support . . . They're your children too, Paul. What do you want to do, send them out on the street to fend for themselves? . . . You can't be serious. That won't cover even food and the house payment . . . I'll get a lawyer, Paul, you can be sure about that . . . Sell the house? Why should I sell the house? . . . I want all the children . . . Why should I send my children into that kind of an atmosphere?"

Megan had heard enough. She quietly climbed the stairs to her room, went inside, and closed the door. She pulled a blanket off the bed, went into her closet, sat down on the floor, and closed the door. She wrapped the blanket around her. She wished she were dead, but she didn't want to be dead if it caused her family any more grief. She wished that she could just cease to exist, that her name would be suddenly wiped from all the records in the world and nobody would ever remember she had ever existed.

This is all my fault, she thought to herself over and over again. *If I'd never been born, this never would have happened. I wish I were dead.*

She heard the door slam and heavy footsteps as Derek ran up the stairs. She knew he would go in his room, drop off his books, and then come knocking on her door. She didn't want him to see her this way, so she got up and threw the blanket back on the bed and wiped her eyes, then pulled out a book and sat down at the desk.

"Hey, what's going on in there?" he called out, pounding on her door.

"You can come in."

He barged in. "You can't believe what people are saying about me at school today."

"What?"

"That MacKenzie and me were really going at it under the table in Pizza Hut and that I hit Jason in the jaw in a big fight. It's so unfair. How was your day?"

"Okay, I guess."

He flopped down on her bed. "Hey, you didn't make your bed today! Does this mean you're human after all? I can't believe it. One of these days your room will look just like mine."

"You think so?"

"No, not really. To get it that bad takes a special genius. What are you studying?"

She had to look at the book to find out. "American history."

"Ask me any question about American history," he challenged.

"What is Manifest Destiny?"

"Beats me."

"I don't know either," Megan said.

"Oh, wow, what's happening here? I can't believe it. I'm starting to rub off on you. One of these days you'll be known as the rebel of your school."

She wanted to tell him how bad she felt. She was pretty

sure he'd listen to her, but how could she begin to tell him or anyone that she wished she was no longer alive? Besides, she knew she would never try to kill herself, because that's not something she could ever imagine herself doing.

"You think you'd ever get into a fight?" he asked.

"No."

"Well, you never know. Jason still wants to fight me for fooling around with MacKenzie while he played video games. Well, if he does, I'm ready for him. Let me show you what to do if you ever do get into a fight. C'mon, stand up, we'll go a couple of rounds."

"I have to study."

"C'mon, c'mon, this won't take very long. Okay, what's your best friend's name?"

"Jennifer."

"Okay, let's say I'm Jennifer and you decide to punch me out some day. Okay, now, the thing to do is watch the eyes. The eyes telegraph everything the rest of the body is going to do. Okay, put up your dukes."

"I'm never going to fight anybody."

"You never know. I mean, who would have ever thought you wouldn't make your bed one day? Things like that sneak up on you. One day it's not making your bed and the next day you beat up Jennifer and steal her guy. Okay, are you watching my eyes? Okay, try and throw a punch."

She halfheartedly tried to hit him.

"You're not watching my eyes. You got to watch the eyes . . . " He stopped speaking and his mouth dropped open. "You've been crying, haven't you!"

"No, I just got something in my eye on the way home from school."

"Both eyes?"

"No. Oh, Derek, I feel so bad."

She cried a long time. He didn't know what to say, so he

didn't say anything. He just let her cry. He touched her hand though.

"It's all my fault," she said.

"What is?"

"Mom and Dad breaking up. It's all my fault."

"Why is it your fault?"

"Because when I was born, they never had enough money after that."

"It's not your fault. It's not any of us kids' fault. It's Dad's fault because he looked at Gloria too much."

"I heard Mom talking to him. He wants Mom to sell the house and maybe split us up."

"That'll never happen."

"Mom was practically crying when she was talking to him. I felt so bad." She paused. "I wanted to ... to give up."

Derek didn't understand what she meant. "You can't ever give up," he said.

"I know." She dried her eyes. "I'm all right now. Thanks for coming in."

"Hey, I'm always happy to come and bother people. The way I look at it, if I can keep you from studying, then you won't get such good grades, and that'll make me look better."

"I'm glad you stopped in to see me," she said.

"You are? No kidding? I always thought I was pretty much a pain to you."

"Sometimes you are, but not always. Especially not today."

"I did something right today then. Wow, I've gotta go write that down in my journal." He paused at the door. "If I can find my journal, that is."

"I'm glad you're my brother," she said.

He cleared his throat awkwardly and, in a barely audible voice, said, "Thanks." He wiped his eyes. "You're pretty okay too. Now that Dad's gone, we have to stick together. Well, I guess I'll go down and make myself a peanut butter sandwich. See you later."

He paused on the staircase and shouted, "Megan is glad I'm her brother!" And then he thundered down the stairs as usual.

When Kimberly got home from school the next day, her mother was resting on her bed.

"Anything wrong?" Kimberly asked.

"Just a headache, that's all. I tried to find a job again today."

"How'd it go?"

"I should have finished college."

"Why didn't you?"

"I got married young and then got pregnant soon after."

"With me."

"Yes, but that's not the problem. I should have been taking classes every year since then, but at the time I couldn't see any need to graduate. Now I do. Basically I can get the same kind of job now that I could have had when I was a senior in high school. Minimum-wage jobs. One thing's for sure, we're going to have to cut way back on the way we live."

"Dad should pay for everything. It's his fault this is happening anyway."

"He's willing to pay child support, but that won't cover everything."

Ben showed up a few minutes later, and he and Kimberly went downstairs to practice some songs.

"I might not be able to practice as much anymore," she told him.

"Why not?"

"I've got to get a job to help out my family."

"If we want to keep our job at Angelo's, we've got to practice."

"I know that, but maybe not so much."

"What kind of a job do you have in mind?"

"I'm not sure. I think I'll check around campus and see what's available."

86

At two in the morning, Derek got up to go to the bathroom. Then he went downstairs to the kitchen and dialed Gloria's phone number. When she answered, he hung up and went back to his room.

Just as he closed the door to his room, he heard the phone ring. He went to the top of the stairs to listen in. His mother answered it in her room on the first floor. "No, there's nobody up now. Why?" he heard her say.

Derek hopped back in bed. He heard his mother coming up the stairs and then going into the bathroom. A short time later she opened his door. "Derek?" she whispered.

He pretended to be asleep.

"Derek, I need to talk to you." She shook him gently. "Wake up."

"What?"

"Your dad just phoned me. Somebody just called Gloria and hung up when she answered. She was upset so she called your father at his apartment and then he called me, wanting to know if it was any of us. I told him I'd find out. Derek, was it you?"

"No, I've been asleep."

"Are you sure?"

"Yes."

"I heard the toilet flush a few minutes ago. Was that you?"

"No."

"Are you sure? The seat was up so it wasn't Kimberly or Megan. I need to know if it's you that's been calling Gloria and hanging up."

After several seconds, he said, "I might have done it a few times."

"I can understand you being mad at Gloria, but this isn't doing anybody any good."

"It makes me feel better."

"Would you like to tell your father yourself how angry you are at what he's done?"

"No."

"Why not?"

"He'd just give me a lecture."

"What if he promised not to do that? What if he promised just to listen to what you have to say?"

"It wouldn't make any difference. He'd still turn it around so everything is my fault."

"What if I was there to keep him from doing that?"

"Would he let you tell him why you're so mad at him?"

"No, I don't think he'd let me do that."

"Well, if he won't do it for you, then I don't want him to do it for me."

"There's a difference. He may not always be my husband, but he will always be your father."

"I don't want him for a father anymore."

"He still loves you."

"No, he doesn't. He's never liked me very much."

"How can you say that?"

"It's true. He's never been satisfied with anything I've ever done."

"You should have heard him brag to people how smart you were."

"He never told me that."

"I'm sorry he didn't." She touched his sleeve. "He's so proud that you're about to get your Eagle."

"I'm not getting it."

"I understand how you feel, but don't give up on it now." She paused, then said, "Derek, do you know how much I love you?"

"Not really."

She put her hand on his shoulder. "You're the most wonderful son anyone could ever have."

Derek stook up and moved to the window so his mother couldn't see him wiping his eyes. "Thanks, Mom."

She went to him and gave him a big hug. He was no longer her little boy; already he towered over her. "You're getting to be so tall and strong, but it's okay for you to come and talk to me when you feel bad. Okay?"

"Okay." He let her hold him longer than usual and then moved away.

"Well, we'd both better get back to sleep. Good night. No more crank phone calls, okay?"

"Okay."

The next day Anne waited until supper to tell her family what she considered to be good news. "Guess what, kids—I got a job! I start tomorrow."

"Where at?"

"Jiffy Buns Donut Shop. It doesn't pay much, but at least it's a job. I'll work early mornings and whenever someone else can't make it. It means you're all going to have to get ready for school without me. Oh, there's one other thing. Derek, I need to talk to you after supper."

After supper Anne had a private conversation with Derek in her bedroom.

"I talked to your father today. I told him I thought you needed to express your feelings to him. He agreed to come over tonight and let you tell him how you're feeling about all this."

"I'm not talking to him."

"I can understand why you feel that way. Look, if you want I'll be in the same room to make sure he doesn't intimidate you."

"Why do I have to do it if I don't want to?"

"Calling Gloria in the middle of the night and then hanging up is not a very grown-up way of expressing anger."

"Did you tell him about that?" Derek asked.

"Yes, I did. It's better they know it was you rather than worry that it might be some homicidal maniac on the loose."

"I can't talk to him."

"What are you afraid of?"

"That he'll turn it all around and make it out that we were the ones who messed up. I can hear him saying, 'If you kids had only kept the house cleaner, then this would never have happened.'"

"A man doesn't abandon his wife and kids because the house isn't as clean as he'd like it to be."

"He'll end up lecturing me like he always does."

"I'll make sure he doesn't do that. Look, if it's too awful, you can always get up and walk out on him."

He paused. "I can?"

"Yes."

"Okay."

"He said he'd be here at about eight."

A little before eight Derek saw his father's car drive up but his father didn't get out of his car until it was precisely eight o'clock. Anne let him in, then called up the stairs, "Derek, your father is here."

Derek went down to the kitchen, where his father sat at the table. He stood up as Derek came in. "Hello, Derek."

"Hello," Derek said, trying to sound like a computer. They both sat down. His mother was sitting on a bar stool in the corner of the room.

In some ways his father looked like he usually did, except somehow it was different. It was as if somehow he'd lost his authority as a father. "How are you coming on completing your requirements for Eagle?" he began.

Derek couldn't believe it. Later, when he told Kimberly about the interview, he said, "The man leaves his wife for some stupid secretary, and the first thing he does is ask me how close I am to becoming an Eagle scout."

Derek was furious with the question but tried not to show it. "All right."

"When do you think you'll get it?"

"I don't know."

"If you ever need any help on your Eagle project, just let me know."

"Yeah, sure."

"Your mother says you didn't go to scouts last week. You're so close to Eagle now. Don't stop now just because you're mad at me."

"Why do you want me to get it? So you can impress Gloria with what a great dad you are?"

There was a long, awkward silence, and then his father said, "Why don't you go ahead and tell me everything you're feeling about me these days?"

Derek knew his mother had suggested the question, because it was not a question his father had ever asked anybody.

"Not good."

"Why's that?"

"I don't see why you had to leave us."

"That is between your mother and me. Let me assure you that it's not because I suddenly quit loving my children."

"No, it's because you suddenly started loving your secretary."

"What else would you like to share with me?"

"Not a thing."

"Are you sure?"

"Yes. What good would it do anyway?"

His father waited a few seconds and then said, "All right. While we're here, I think we should talk about these crank phone calls you've been making. I hope you realize that what you've been doing is against the law. I could notify the police about this, and I will if it keeps up. In fact, I checked into it. It's actually a federal offense, and the FBI can be involved in cases like these."

Derek was furious. He stood up. "Can I go now? I have to go work on scouting. I want to get my Eagle so I can make you proud of me."

Anne intervened. "Derek, don't leave. We're not done here. Paul, this has been totally unsatisfactory. You waltz in here, barely pay any attention to Derek, and then proceed to tell him you're going to turn him over to the FBI."

"He said he didn't have anything else to say to me. What was I supposed to do? Besides, don't I have any rights in this matter? You don't know how upset Gloria gets every time she answers the phone and nobody's there."

"Why don't you listen to your son for once in your life?"

"All right, Anne, now calm down. If you're not careful, you'll give yourself another migraine."

"Don't be patronizing, Paul."

"I wasn't being patronizing. I was just stating a fact of life. You do get migraines."

"Not since you left." It wasn't true, but she said it just to get back at him.

Paul glanced at his watch. The gesture was not lost on Anne. "Oh dear, Paul, I do hope we're not wasting your valuable time." She looked at him with mock sympathy, then added, "You know, I can't believe you. This is your only son. You do remember that, don't you?"

"If he has something to say, then why doesn't he say it?"

Derek felt like a tennis ball being batted back and forth. He couldn't take it anymore. He stalked out of the room and up the stairs to his room and slammed the door as hard as he could.

He could hear his mother and father downstairs arguing. And then after a while his father left.

Most of that night Megan stayed at her desk, working on a map that was due in the morning. It was to be a map of Utah. Her teacher had given her a list of fifty geographical sites to be included on the map. She had given specific guidelines: rivers were to be blue, interstates red, towns over fifty thousand orange.

Megan felt like she would either get an A or a B on the map. She knew it was important to be neat and accurate. She had been working on the map for several days.

She was just finishing it up when her father came. She opened her door to listen. She could hear the muffled sounds of Derek and her father going after each other, followed by Derek stalking up the stairs and slamming the door. And then her mother and father were yelling at each other in the kitchen.

Megan took out a pair of scissors and folded the map neatly into fourths and cut along the creases. She then took each of the fourths and cut them into fourths. She repeated it again and again until all that was left of the map was dozens of small, precisely cut pieces.

9

Two days later Kimberly announced after supper that she also had found a job.

"Where?" her mother asked.

"Working for one of the professors in my department. He's got a research project, and he needs someone to help out. It's mostly routine things, you know—cleaning up, taking data, things like that—but it pays six dollars an hour."

"When will you work?" Ben asked.

"After classes three days a week. I'll be done by six o'clock. And there's a possibility I might be able to work this summer full-time. Isn't that great?"

"Sounds terrific," her mother said. "Where do I sign on? It's more than I'm making."

"At least I'll be able to help out now."

"They're paying you to do research?" Derek asked. "What a mistake. You'll probably blow up the lab."

"That's really great you've got a job," Ben said.

"Yes, and we can work on music the other two days a week."

Megan finished brushing her teeth and then found herself looking at her reflection in the mirror. She wondered how it was that nobody seemed to know how bad she felt. Sometimes it was okay, sometimes she even felt good, but then, even only a few minutes later, she would descend into a black hole, and there didn't seem to be any way out.

She must have lost track of time, because suddenly she heard Derek banging on the door. "Megan, what's the big delay here? There are other people in this family, you know. What do you want me to do, go outside?"

She opened the door.

"After I leave home, I'll never share a bathroom with another female," Derek complained. "You and Kimberly drive me crazy. Before you get married, I'm going to have a talk with your future husband and tell him how much time you take in here. If he's smart, he'll build himself his own private bathroom. Otherwise he's going to spend his whole life waiting for you to get out of the bathroom."

She smiled. "Oh yeah? Well, I've got one or two things to tell the girl you marry, so you'd better watch out."

"Me? What could you possibly tell about me?"

"Right, I forgot, you're perfect. Goodnight, Derek."

A week later Anne called her family together. "I'm sorry, kids, but there's something else we need to talk about. Even with what Dad will be giving us each month and with me and Kimberly working, there's not going to be enough money coming in. We have to be very careful about how we spend our money from now on."

"Why don't you just ask Dad to give you more?" Megan asked.

"All that has been turned over to our lawyers. My lawyer says that with Dad being willing to give us the house, it might be very hard to get more for child support. If I want to earn more money than what I'm making at Jiffy Buns, I might need to finish college."

"But won't it cost a lot of money to do that?" Megan asked.

"Yes, but after I graduate, I'll be able to make a decent salary, so it'll pay off in the long run. It'll mean taking night classes occasionally, and having to study sometimes when you'd rather have me take you to the mall."

"If we're not making it now, how are you going to pay for college?" Derek asked.

"That's what we need to talk about. I talked it over with your father. He suggested I sell the house. That would give us some extra money. It would also help Kimberly and me pay for college next year. So selling the house has some advantages. What would you think about it?"

"Where would we live?" Derek asked.

"We'd either rent a house or an apartment."

"With a pool?" Megan asked.

"Yes, maybe we could even find an apartment with a pool."

"Just make Dad give us more money," Derek said.

"I wish it were that easy. Kimberly, what do you think?"

"Well, if it would make things easier for us in the long run, maybe we should do it."

"What if we sell the house and end up crammed all together in a tiny apartment?" Derek asked.

"We'd have to make sure that didn't happen. Would you object if we find out how much we can get for our house?"

"I guess not," Derek said.

"Megan?" Anne asked.

"Sure, it won't hurt to find out."

Anne decided to put the house on the market, ask for more than she expected she could get for it, and then take her time to see if that's really what they should do. She announced that on Saturday the entire family would work to get it clean enough to show to buyers.

Ben and Brother Hatch volunteered to put in new linoleum in the upstairs bathroom. On Saturday they showed up at nine and began taking out the old linoleum.

Derek worked for a while, then went across the hall to Megan's room. He sat on her bed and watched her sort through some things in her closet.

"Look what I found," she said, handing him a stuffed bear she'd gotten at Yellowstone Park on vacation the summer before.

"Nice bear. Does it have a name?"

"Buffy."

"Buffy the Bear. Hello, Buffy the Bear."

"Remember we got it at Fishing Bridge? I wanted it but Mom said I already had plenty of stuffed animals. Then Dad said it would be all right and he got it for me."

"What a great dad, right? I wonder if he liked Gloria then. If he did, I bet he could hardly wait to get back to work."

"You don't have to wreck all my memories, do you?"

"Sorry. Are you going to keep Buffy the Bear?"

"No, I guess not."

"So long, Buffy." He slam-dunked the bear into the trash bag.

"Don't treat him so mean." She pulled the bear out of the trash bag.

"I'd better get back to work. Take care of Buffy for me, okay?"

Derek went to Kimberly's room to see how she was doing in cleaning up her room. She was almost done.

"Is it okay if I come in?" he asked.

"Sure. You can even help by carrying this stuff I'm throwing away outside."

She had three large trash bags full of junk. He took them outside. When he returned, he said, "It only took me one trip. Aren't you impressed?"

"I always knew you'd be a good garbage man," she said.

"You'd be the first thing I'd haul away."

"Yeah, yeah."

She had found an old candy bar in a box. "Here, I saved this for you."

"How old is it?"

"At least a year."

"Just right." He tore open the wrapper and took a bite. "So when are you and Ben going to make a million dollars in the music world?"

She smiled. "After we work a million hours."

"If some big recording company wants to do an album, put me on the cover, okay? People will buy it just for the picture of me."

"Do you realize you're the only conceited one in our family?" Kimberly asked.

"Maybe so, but do you realize that I'm the only one in the family who has any reason to be conceited?"

She threw a pillow at him.

After Megan finished with her room, she went to talk to Ben and Brother Hatch. She looked around. The old linoleum had been ripped out and the toilet was in the hall.

"You think we'll ever be able to use this room again?"

"Probably not," Ben joked.

"He's right, Megan," Brother Hatch said. "I hope you're good friends with your neighbors, because we're going to tear into the downstairs bathroom next."

"You'll fix this one first though, won't you?"

"I don't know. What do you think?" Brother Hatch said.

"Fix one before you wreck 'em both."

"Gosh, that's a good idea, Megan. We're glad you came along, aren't we, Ben?"

"Sure, Megan's good to have around, even if she is mean to me," Ben said.

"I'm not mean to you."

"You're supposed to have a crush on me, Megan."

"What for?"

"Because I'm older and wiser."

"Brother Hatch is even older and wiser, and I don't have a crush on him."

"You don't?" Brother Hatch asked in a shocked voice before laughing.

98

"See what I mean?" Ben said. "She's a heartbreaker."

"But we love her all the same, don't we?" Brother Hatch said. "Megan, how are things going with you?"

"In school, you mean?"

"No. With *you*."

"All right, I guess."

"You want to talk about anything?"

"Not really."

"Now's your big chance. Ben and I aren't going anywhere for a while."

She thought for a moment and then said, "I don't understand adults."

"What don't you understand?"

"My dad knew it wasn't right to fall in love with someone else, so why did he do it if he knew it was wrong?"

"Things like this happen a little at a time, and going from one step to the other doesn't usually seem all that bad," Brother Hatch said.

"People keep saying I'm turning into a woman, and I know things are happening, but sometimes I get afraid."

"What are you afraid of?" Ben asked.

"That I'll end up doing things I know are wrong but I won't be able to stop because it'll take over my life. I mean, that's what happened to my dad, isn't it? Something just took over. I'm not sure I want to be an adult. Maybe I won't be able to control myself the way my dad can't control himself. I mean, how else can you explain why he would just walk away from us?"

"Things just don't take over your life unless at some point in the beginning you give them permission," Ben said.

"I don't like it when people tell me how fast I'm growing up." She paused. "Ben, I don't like it when you tell me that if things don't work out with Kimberly, you're going to come for me."

99

"I'm sorry, Megan, I just meant I think you're a wonderful girl. I won't say it anymore."

"I don't want to talk about it anymore either," she said.

She watched them work for a few minutes and then returned to her room. She cleaned a spot on Buffy the Bear and carefully packed him in a box of things to be saved.

On the next Saturday they had a garage sale. Anne had to work, and so she asked Kimberly to be in charge. The sale wasn't supposed to start until eight-thirty, but people started showing up at seven. By eleven o'clock most of the good stuff was gone. It started to rain in the afternoon, but it didn't make any difference because by then they had sold most of it anyway. Megan was in charge of keeping track of the money. She proudly announced they had made $267.23.

On Tuesday of the next week, after supper, the phone rang. It was for Anne. When she got off the phone, she told the family that the realtor was bringing someone over to see the house, so they needed to hurry through the house and pick up everything.

"It's like we have to be this ideal family spending a wonderful evening at home," Derek said.

"We need a dad, though," Kimberly said. "Come with me and we'll get one."

Kimberly, Derek, and Megan went into the attic and found an inflatable clown. Megan blew it up. Derek found one of their father's old hats and put it on top of the clown's head. Then they put the clown on a chair in front of the kitchen table with a newspaper propped up in front of it. They started laughing so hard that Anne came in to see what was going on. She made them put it all away.

Ten minutes later the real estate agent arrived with a man and his wife. They walked through the house like nobody was there, with the man criticizing everything he saw. For every complaint the real estate agent said, "We can take care of that."

After they left, Derek went to his mother to complain. "I don't like people walking through our house. I don't like it at all."

"Nobody does, but it's one of the things you have to put up with when you're trying to sell a house."

"Dad gets a younger woman, and we get strangers walking through our house."

"Here it is," Anne said the next day as they pulled into a parking space next to the brick apartment building.

"This dump?" Derek said.

"I'm not saying we'll take it. It's just one we can look at to see what they're like."

"I don't want to live here," Megan said.

"C'mon, you guys," Kimberly said. "Don't be so negative all the time. The least we can do is look at it."

They got a key from the manager and walked up two flights of stairs. The door to the apartment opened into the kitchen. It had a lonely echo.

"I know it's not as nice as we'd like, but if we worked on it, we could fix it up," their mother said.

"Where would we all sleep?" Megan asked.

"I was thinking Kimberly and Megan could be in one bedroom and Derek in the other."

"What about you?" Kimberly asked.

"We could get a couch that makes into a bed, and I could sleep on it in the living room."

"Why do we have to move anyway?" Derek asked.

"We don't have to. It's just that if we were to sell the house, we'd have more money to live on and pay for school expenses."

"There's a spider in the tub," Megan said, coming out of the bathroom.

"It comes with the apartment," Derek said sarcastically.

"Look, you guys," Kimberly said, "I don't think you should be so negative about everything. Mom's is doing the best she can. If we all work together, we can make things work out."

"You want my opinion?" Derek said. "Okay, here it is. I say we stay in our house and never move."

There was silence, followed by Megan saying, "I don't see why we have to move either."

"If we don't sell the house, I don't see how I can go to college," Anne pointed out.

"I think it's too late for you to go to college," Derek said. "You should have done that when you were Kimberly's age."

Anne sighed. "Let's go home."

That night Megan went into Derek's room. "Did you know that Mom was crying when she drove us home?"

"So?"

"You shouldn't have told her it was too late for her to go to college."

"Hey, she asked, so I told her what I thought. What else am I supposed to do?"

10

The next day there was no school because it was an in-service day for teachers. Anne had to work all day, but she made a list of things that needed to be done by the family before she got home.

Between her classes at the university, Kimberly took charge of getting Megan and Derek to help with the work. It took almost all morning. Just before lunch, she approached Derek. "There's one more thing Mom wanted us to do today."

"What?"

"Go to the scout office and pick up an application for your Eagle service project. Ben's coming over soon to take us there."

"Forget it."

"Derek, you're so close to getting your Eagle. All you have to do is your project and a little paperwork. Don't quit now."

"The only reason I even got started in scouts was because of Dad."

"So now you're going to give up what you've been working on for so long?"

"Yes, that's right. I'm through."

"It's not just that Dad wants you to get it. Mom does and so do I. I've never had a brother who was an Eagle scout before."

"No, I'm done with all that."

"Look, Mom made me promise I'd take you to the scout

office so you could pick up an application. Once we get that done, we're both off the hook and can do whatever we want the rest of the afternoon. So let's get it over with, okay?"

By the time Ben arrived and picked them up, the scout office was closed for the noon hour. "I'd like to go shopping for some clothes over at the mall," Kimberly said. "You two interested?"

"I am," Ben said.

"Not me," Derek said. "I think I'll sit on the grass and listen to a tape MacKenzie lent me."

"All right, we'll meet you back here at one o'clock. Okay?"

"Yeah, sure."

Derek sat on the grass of a park across the street from the scout office and listened to music on a Walkman he'd bought. At ten minutes to one he glanced up and saw a woman opening the door. By the time he crossed the street and entered the building, the woman was on the phone in another office answering a question about the whittling merit badge. Derek stood and waited. On the counter was an Eagle medallion in a felt-covered black box.

If Dad wants an Eagle, maybe I should give him one, he thought. *He could hang it on the wall of his office, and then when people came, he could tell everyone what a wonderful father he was because his son had his Eagle. Yes, I should do this for Dad. He wants me to get an Eagle so much and we don't ever want to disappoint our father even though he disappoints us all the time and then in the end he leaves us all without enough money and no way for any of us to ever climb out of the hole he's left us in.*

He grabbed the box, stuffed it in his shirt, checked to make sure the woman hadn't seen him, looked around to be sure nobody was coming in the office, and slipped quietly out the door and went across the street. Then he opened the box, removed the medallion and stuffed it in the front pocket of his jeans, and hid the black box in his windbreaker. He walked over to a nearby dumpster and got rid of the box, then returned to the park bench.

While he waited for Kimberly and Ben to return, he tried to imagine how he would give the medallion to his father. Maybe he'd hang it on the antenna of his dad's car, or maybe he'd put it under one of the tires so that when his father pulled out, it would give him a flat tire. Or maybe he'd send it to Gloria with a note that read, "You deserve this more than I do." Or maybe he'd nail it to the door of Gloria's apartment so his father would see it the next time he went to her apartment. *If he wants an Eagle,* Derek thought, *then I'll make sure he gets one. We must always do what our father tells us to do, even when our father is a hypocrite and a liar and can't ever be trusted again.*

He knew Kimberly wouldn't let him leave until he'd picked up the application form, so he would have to go back to the office. He would have to be careful what he said. He decided he would need to appear eager to earn his Eagle so they wouldn't suspect him.

The first question Kimberly asked when she and Ben returned was if he'd gotten the application form yet. He yawned and stretched. "No, not yet."

"Well, c'mon, let's get this over with so we can have the rest of the afternoon free."

Just as they approached the door, a man who worked at the scout office returned from lunch and opened it for them. "Can I help you?" he asked.

"My brother needs an application for his Eagle service project," Kimberly responded.

The man was chatty and pleasant. He introduced himself as Art Gulbransen and said he was the local scout executive. He took Derek's name and address and asked about his progress. Derek tried to be positive and cheerful so Mr. Gulbransen would not be suspicious of him when they discovered the medallion was missing.

105

On the way home, Kimberly asked Derek about the change in his attitude when he had been talking to the scout executive.

"I was thinking, maybe you're right. Maybe I should finish when I'm this close," he told her.

"Mom will be so proud of you. And so will I."

"But especially Dad will, right? I mean, we've got to make Dad proud, don't we?"

She looked at him strangely but didn't say anything.

That night Mr. Gulbransen phoned Derek. "I was wondering if you saw anything suspicious this afternoon when you came in to pick up the application form."

Derek's heart raced. "What do you mean by suspicious?"

"I'm not sure. Someone said they saw a boy across the street during the noon hour. Was that you?"

"Yes, that was me."

"How long were you there?"

"About thirty minutes."

"Did you notice anyone going into the scout office during that time?"

"No, but I wasn't watching. And I did take a little walk around the park. Why do you ask?"

"One of our Eagle medallions has turned up missing."

"Could it have been misplaced?"

"That's not likely. We had it set out on the counter for someone to pick up. We noticed it was gone around two o'clock. You don't know what happened to it, do you?"

"No."

"I just thought I'd check to see if you saw anything suspicious. If it were returned right away, we wouldn't contact the police."

"I hope you don't think I took it."

"No, not really. It doesn't make sense for someone as close as you are to Eagle to steal one. But I'm afraid I'm going to have to contact the police about this. Whoever did this needs to learn that crime doesn't pay."

"Scouting teaches that."

"Yes, of course it does. Well, I'm sorry to have bothered you. We're all looking forward to the time when you finish your Eagle project. When will that be?"

"I'll be done in a month."

"Well, good luck with everything. Good night."

Derek hung up the phone. He had difficulty breathing. His forehead was beaded with sweat. He felt that Mr. Gulbransen suspected him but didn't have any evidence that he'd been the one who had stolen the Eagle medallion.

He thought about taking Mr. Gulbransen's offer and admitting that he was the one who'd done it. The only problem with that was that his mother would find out, and Derek wasn't sure she could take that on top of everything else that was happening in the family. Besides, if he didn't tell, there was no way they could ever find out for sure.

He decided that the best way to keep Mr. Gulbransen from suspecting him was to go ahead and finish his requirements for Eagle. He went downstairs to talk to his mother. "I've decided to try and finish up my requirements for Eagle as soon as I can."

She smiled. "That's wonderful, Derek. We're all so proud of you."

He went to his room and closed the door and tried to deal with the guilt that now pressed down on him from every side.

11

Ben sat behind Kimberly with his arms wrapped around her waist as they gazed out at the lights of the city. It was a Saturday night, and they had just come to his apartment from working at Angelo's.

His aunt came up the stairs. "I hope you like lots of butter on your popcorn, because that's the way I fixed it."

"Thanks a lot," Ben said.

"I'll just set it here on the table. Are you two still looking out the window?"

"I never get tired of it," Kimberly said.

"I'll leave the door open, if that's all right," she said as she left.

"It's great having your aunt on duty," Kimberly said with a slight smile.

Ben kissed her on the back of the neck.

"I don't know how you can stand me when I smell like a pizza," Kimberly whispered.

"I like pizza," he said, kissing her neck again.

She laughed. "Yes, I can see that you do."

He untangled himself and went to his desk. "I bought a surprise for you today. Close your eyes." He placed a small box in a sandwich bag, set it in a small bowl, and dumped some popcorn over it. "Okay, you can open your eyes." He handed her the bowl.

"Have some popcorn."

"I'm not really that hungry."

"Please."

She reached in for the popcorn and felt the bag.

"What's going on here?" Inside the box she found an engagement ring.

"Will you marry me?" Ben asked.

"Oh, my gosh! I wasn't expecting this! Are you sure you want to give me this?"

"Kimberly, I love you. I can't stand the thought of not spending the rest of eternity with you. Yes, I'm sure. I talked to my aunt and she said we could stay here so you'd be close to your family, and we could even send them a little money every month. And we could still work at Angelo's on the weekends. We can be married in the temple, and everything will be just the way we want it." He put his arms around her and kissed her. "And one other thing. We'd be here every night, just the two of us. And we'd finally be able to close the door at the bottom of the stairs."

She stood up and walked around the room, turning on all the lights. "I don't know what to say. My mind is racing. We'd stay here? Is it big enough for two of us? What's the bedroom like? Do you mind if I look in?"

"Go ahead. I made the bed today."

She opened the bedroom door. "This is a really small room. We'd need a mirror above my vanity for when I put on makeup. Can you do that?" she asked.

"I'm Mister Hardware Man, remember? I can do anything. I'd just get some quarter-inch-long toggle bolts. Take about two minutes."

She stuck her head out of the bedroom. "Toggle bolts, huh? We'd also need more closet space."

"No problem. With a little planning we can double the amount of closet space available.

She went over to the tiny kitchen area. "We'd need more cupboard space. And one of the burners doesn't work."

"I know. It needs replacing."

"This is fun being domestic!"

"With you it is."

"Ben, there's one thing you need to understand. I really do want to finish college."

"I think you should."

"I still don't know what to say. I think maybe my family might be able to get along without me. I mean, Derek's doing okay—he's getting his Eagle soon. And Megan seems to be doing well. So maybe it would be okay for me to leave. Does this offer of yours have an expiration date?"

"You mean like on a carton of milk? No, not really."

"Just give me some time to think about it, okay?"

"Sure. Do you have any idea how much I love you?" he said.

"I love you too. I really do, but right now, tell me again about the closets."

He held her in his arms and whispered step by step how he was going to double the closet space.

Kimberly woke her mother up when she came in from being with Derek. The first thing she did was tell about Ben's proposal. "What do you think I should do?" she asked.

"What do you want to do?"

"I really love him and I want to marry him."

"Then I think you should. You couldn't find a more wonderful man than Ben."

"I know. He's been so good for me. Do you think I should wait a while before I get married?"

"Oh, I don't know. You're the same age I was when I married your father." There was a long, awkward silence. "I guess that's not such a great recommendation anymore, is it?"

"And what about my leaving the family now? I feel like I should stick around for Derek and Megan."

"You can't live on shoulds. What do *you* want?"

She thought about it. "I want to spend my life with Ben."

"Then why don't you tell him that?"

"I will, but in my own special way next Saturday night."

"Thank you very much," Kimberly said after the two of them finished a song for appreciative patrons in the restaurant on Saturday evening. "Our next song is one we worked on in January but never finished. But as a surprise for Ben, I've finished it. I'd like to dedicate it to him tonight because this is a special night for the two of us. Ben, this is your song."

She did a short introduction on the guitar and then, gazing into his eyes, began singing:

> *A fireplace hearth on a wintry night,*
> *Your face aglow in the firelight.*
> *Do you remember? I really do,*
> *How, for you, in those embers my love grew.*
>
> *An April night, a window for two,*
> *You asked me if I would marry you.*
> *Could you forget? Well, I never will,*
> *For I'll be yours, in love, forever.*

She ended the song, then shouted, "Yes, Ben, I'll marry you!"

The crowd caught on to what was happening before Ben did. Some clapped and yelled. Finally Ben realized what had happened. He threw his arms around Kimberly and kissed her, to the delight of everyone there.

That night after everyone else had gone to bed, Kimberly looked at her mother's wedding pictures. Her mother had been a beautiful bride, standing in front of the Salt Lake Temple with her new husband.

Kimberly suddenly wondered how anyone could have possibly known then that her parents' marriage was going to end in divorce. *I'm not ready for this,* she thought, experiencing a sudden feeling of panic and dread.

12

The next Tuesday, while Derek was studying in his room, the doorbell rang. A minute later his mother called for him. "Derek?"

"What?"

"There's a police officer here who would like to talk to you."

Derek's heart raced and his breathing became labored. His first impulse was to run, but he knew he couldn't do that. He walked down the stairs. An older man in a police uniform stood at the bottom.

"I just need a few minutes of your time," the man said. "I'm looking into the theft of the Eagle medallion from the scout office."

"Don't you have more important things to worry about?"

"Actually, I'm doing this off-duty. You see, I'm an Eagle scout myself. Mr. Gulbransen asked me to do some investigating, not so much because of the value of the medallion, but to see if we can help whoever stole it."

"You think I stole it?"

"Not at all. It's just that, as I understand it, you were at the scout office about the time it was stolen. Is that right?"

Derek felt there was a trap in anything the policeman said. "I have no idea when it was stolen, so I can't say I was there when it was stolen."

"You were across the street before the office opened at one o'clock. Is that right?"

"Yes."

"Why were you there?"

"My sister Kimberly and Ben—he's the guy she's going to marry—brought me, but when we got there, the office was closed. Kimberly wanted to go shopping and I decided to sit in the park. It was a nice day, and I had a new tape I wanted to listen to. So I just waited there until they came back, and then we went and got what I needed."

"Is Kimberly at home now?"

"Yes."

"May I speak to her?"

The policeman spoke privately to Kimberly, then thanked them both and left.

Derek went to his room. Kimberly knocked and asked if she could come in. When she entered, he was pacing the floor. "How long are they going to keep coming back and asking the same questions over and over? I told them I don't know anything about it. Why do they keep coming back if it's not because they think I did it?"

"I think you're overreacting. You didn't do anything wrong, so you don't have anything to worry about. I told the policeman I was absolutely certain that you weren't the one who took it, so relax, okay?"

"I want to finish this stupid Eagle project so they'll know it wasn't me and they won't keep coming back. You've got to help me. I can't seem to get anything done. I can't even make the phone calls I'm supposed to make. I pick up the phone and then I freeze and think, what difference does it make? They already think I'm the one who stole the medallion. They won't ever let me have a moment's peace until I prove to them once and for all that I'm not the one who took the Eagle. Please help me. I can't do this by myself. Please, you've got to help me."

"Take it easy, okay? Sure, I'll help you. And we can get Ben to help too. We can work on it right now, if you want. Let's get this done once and for all."

True to her word, Kimberly and Ben helped Derek finish his Eagle project. It took a great deal of preparation and planning over the next two weeks, but it was completed in a day.

The first week in May, when Derek walked into the Eagle board of review, he was surprised to see Mr. Gulbransen there representing the scout office. Through everyone else's questions, Mr. Gulbransen said nothing. But then after everyone else was satisfied, he asked if he might ask Derek a few questions. "Derek, could you give us the scout law?"

"A scout is trustworthy . . . " He wiped his sweating forehead. He started coughing. Someone gave him a glass of water. "Thank you. . . . Uh, let's see, loyal, helpful, friendly, courteous, kind, obedient, cheerful, thrifty, brave, clean . . . and reverent."

"Very good. Can you tell us what trustworthy means?"

Derek knew his face was a bright red. "It means people can trust you."

"And are you trustworthy, Derek?" Mr. Gulbransen asked softly.

Derek knew that Mr. Gulbransen still suspected him. "Yes, I am."

Mr. Gulbransen looked at him for a long time and then nodded his head. "No other questions."

Derek passed his board of review.

"This is such a luxury," Anne said two days later as she had lunch at a restaurant with Kimberly.

"Thanks for thinking of the idea, Mom."

"I wanted you to know how much I appreciate what you've done to fill in for me the past few weeks. I lost track of a lot of things there for a while. Everything was so hard for me — getting used to working again, suffering from the loss of in-

115

come, having to cope with everything all by ourselves. Sometimes I wouldn't even notice what you were doing for Megan and Derek and me. I guess I was in shock there for a while. Anyway, I just wanted to let you know how much I appreciate what you've done. Thank you for going the extra mile. And now Derek's about to get his Eagle. And Megan seems like she's getting along okay. I'm getting used to my job. Things are looking up again for our family."

Kimberly smiled. She hoped her mother was right.

Derek sat on the stand and looked out into the chapel at the people who had come to see him become an Eagle scout. A Primary teacher from when he was little. A Sunday School teacher. The families who lived next door to them. In the front row were Kimberly and Ben, Megan, and his mother. His father was seated in the last row of the chapel. He had come just before the meeting began.

I've fooled them all, he thought. *I'm not trustworthy, I'm not cheerful, not anymore, not with this to worry about. I'm not brave, because if I was brave I would have told Mister Gulbransen the truth the first time he called. I'm not honest. I'm not clean—most of all I'm not clean.*

Looking at Megan made him feel worst of all because she looked up to him, but now there wasn't anything worth looking up to.

Mr. Gulbransen came and sat on the stand. Then he leaned over and shook Derek's hand. Derek could hardly breathe. It was like a truck was parked on his chest. It did no good to look out into the audience, because everyone was looking at him like he was this wonderful person, and he knew the whole thing was a lie.

What made me think I could go through with this? he thought. *I can't do this. I think I'm going to die.*

During the opening song, he couldn't stand it anymore.

Suddenly he stood up and ran out of the building into the darkness of the night.

At first his family thought Derek would come home when he was tired of walking around. Anne stayed at home in case he called. Kimberly and Ben drove around in Ben's car, trying to find him. Paul took Megan with him, and they too drove around to places they thought Derek might go. Brother Hatch organized members of the high priests quorum into a search party to check the bus stations and shoulders along the interstate in case Derek was hitchhiking.

Ben and Kimberly called home every hour to see if Derek had been found yet. The rest of the time they drove past the homes of some of his friends.

At eleven o'clock, Kimberly turned to Ben. "It's getting late. You can take me home and go get some sleep if you want."

"No, that's okay. I'm not sleepy."

"You've been a good friend to Derek and Megan," she said. "I just want you to know that means a lot to me."

"It does to me too."

"I don't know how I would have made it without your help."

"We're in this together." He backed out of the parking place. "Where do you want to try now?"

"Let's drive by the school one more time."

Derek had walked around for a while and then doubled back to the church. He stayed in the shadows until only one car remained, and then quietly entered the building. He could see a light down the hall in the ward clerk's office. He ducked into a classroom and stayed there in the dark until he heard a car drive away, and then he came out and walked through the building without turning on any lights. The building creaked when the wind blew.

He tried to go into the chapel but it was locked. The doors

to the cultural hall were locked too, so he sat down on a couch in the foyer. The exit lights were the only lights on in the building. He thought about praying but decided against it. He was sure that God didn't want to hear from him again. That part of his life was over. He didn't want to ever come back to this building, didn't want to ever have to look in the faces of the younger scouts and know they were ashamed of him, didn't want to ever see his bishop, his Sunday School teacher, or his scoutmaster.

Since it didn't matter anymore what he did, he phoned MacKenzie from the hall phone. She answered. "This is Derek. I'd like to see you tonight," he said.

"I'm going with Jason."

"You can still go with Jason and see me once in a while too. Jason doesn't have to know. I could come by sometime when your parents aren't around, and we could fool around the way everyone thinks we did anyway. The way I see it, we've got nothing to lose, right?"

"I used to like you, Derek, but I don't anymore."

"Join the club. So, whattaya say, MacKenzie, you want me to come over tomorrow?"

She hung up.

He went back to the couch and sat down again. He felt that he had gone about as low as a person can go. *From now on*, he thought, *I'm on my own.*

He forced himself to think about Kimberly. He wished he never had to see her again, because he didn't want to see how much he had hurt her by living a lie. He knew he could have told her right away that he'd stolen the Eagle, and she would have gone in with him and talked Mr. Gulbransen out of calling the police. He knew she wouldn't have given up on him. The only thing that would make her give up on him was if he lied, and that's what he had done.

He looked around. Then he called out softly, "Hey, God,

here I am. If you want to strike me dead, go ahead. I don't care anymore."

Nothing happened. He felt like sleeping, but he knew he couldn't stay there forever. He had to go somewhere, but he couldn't go back home again. He didn't think he could face his family.

There was only one person he wasn't ashamed of seeing that night.

At about eleven o'clock her father dropped Megan off and then went out looking for Derek again. Her mother was downstairs waiting by the phone in case Derek called. Kimberly and Ben were still out looking.

Megan went up to her room and closed the door. She was certain that Derek had run away from home and would never come back, which meant she wouldn't even have him to talk to anymore.

She sat down at her desk. *I should write a note*, she thought. *You're supposed to write a note.* She opened her top drawer and pulled out two sheets of lined paper and began writing.

Dear Mom and Derek and Kimberly,

When you find this note, it will be too late. I love you all and I'm sorry for everything. Dad, I'm sorry about what happened the night you took me to the Ice Capades. If I'd said no when you first asked me, then our family would still be together. And I'm sorry that after I was born the family never had any money. I'm sorry things are so bad now. Just forget about me and everything will be all right.

Love,
Megan

She folded the note in two and taped it on her mirror. She wondered what it would be like to die. She hoped it would

119

be like going to sleep and never waking up. *That would be the best if it's like that,* she thought. *But if it's like walking from one room into another, like some say, then that wouldn't be so good. I don't want to spend the rest of eternity having to explain why I ended my life. If only I knew what it's like.*

Their cat was scratching at her door. She got up and opened the door and let him in. The cat jumped up onto the bed and plopped himself on Megan's lap.

Tiger was his name. He liked to have his head petted, but nobody else in the family bothered much with that anymore. Megan hadn't done it for a long time, but because this would be her last chance, she did it. Tiger closed his eyes contentedly.

"You want to go outside now?" she asked a few minutes later. She picked Tiger up in her arms and went down the stairs to the back door. When she opened the door, Tiger hurried outside like someone late for an important meeting.

Megan decided to step outside. She wondered where Derek was and if he would ever come home again. It would be just like him to run away and never come back.

But if he comes back, she thought, *the first person he'll want to talk to will be me. I can't think about that. I just want to go to sleep and never wake up.*

She had hoped to see the stars one more time, because she loved to locate the Big Dipper and Orion. Derek had shown her how. But the sky was totally covered with clouds.

She felt a drop of rain land on her face. *I should go in,* she thought. But then she remembered it didn't matter anymore if she got a cold, so she decided to stay there and feel the rain coming down.

She closed her eyes. The rain was like a good friend coming to make things better. *What a wonderful thing for there to be rain,* she thought. *Soft and gentle, quiet and helpful. Instead of a gentle rain, what if God just took a huge bucket and dumped it on the earth? But that would scare the little children.*

This is so quiet that little boys and girls can sleep through it and never wake up.

Raindrops were trickling down her face. She opened her mouth and stuck out her tongue and captured some of the water and tasted it. Nothing had ever tasted so good.

She could see the outline of her rosebush in the family garden. Every year since she could remember, their family always had a garden. Last year they had divided the plot into thirds, and Megan and Kimberly and Derek each had responsibility for a section. They could plant anything they wanted. Derek planted corn and Kimberly planted radishes. But Megan planted a rosebush. It already had a tiny bud on it when they bought it. She had dusted it with rose dust to keep the bugs away, and watched it day after day as the bud unfolded into a beautiful, deep-red rose. Derek had teased her because at least what he was growing could be eaten, but Kimberly came to her rescue by telling him that the beauty of a rose feeds the spirit.

That happened last summer. And now another summer was coming, but she wouldn't be around to see it. She wondered how her rose would do this year. She couldn't imagine Derek or Kimberly or her mother dusting it to keep the bugs away. Everyone was too busy for that. She wondered if the rose would make it without her.

The intensity of the rain increased, and in a few minutes she was drenched. Tears started to come. She knew it didn't matter because her tears just mingled with the rain, and it would all help things grow. She went to her rosebush and knelt down and touched it. It was coming to life again for another summer. She felt the tiniest bud on one of the branches.

She thought about the rosebush, that even though it doesn't know if anyone is going to protect it against the bugs and hail or not getting watered, it still goes on making little buds every spring. And it never gives up, no matter what.

121

Suddenly she knew she didn't want to die, not even if things were bad in her family. They were bad, but the rosebush was still growing buds, and the rain was still coming down, and there would be a summer with hot days and swimming. How could she end her life when there's still rain to stand out in and cats to pet and roses to grow?

Her mother opened the door. "Megan?" she called out. She seemed desperate.

"I'm here, Mom."

"What are you doing?"

"I heard something. I thought it was Derek." Megan walked toward the house. "You're soaking wet."

"I know. Isn't it a wonderful rain?"

"Get out of your wet clothes right away before you catch a cold."

"I will. Have you heard from Derek yet?"

"Not yet."

"He'll come back."

"How do you know?"

"Because he and I need each other. Wake me up when he comes back. I know he'll want to talk. We're going to be all right, Mom, as long as there's rain."

She started up the stairs.

"Megan?"

"What?"

"I saw your note."

"You did?"

"Yes. I didn't know you were hurting so much. I promise you we'll find a way to make it better for you." She started to cry. "Oh, Megan, I couldn't bear to lose you."

Megan ran down the stairs and into her mother's arms.

Derek paused in front of the door to Gloria's apartment. It was past one o'clock in the morning. He knocked on the door for a long time before she opened it.

"Do you remember me? I'm Derek."

She let him in. "Everyone's out looking for you," she said.

"I know."

"Are you all right?"

"Yes."

"Can I fix you something to eat?"

"No."

"I can make some nachos."

"All right."

"And some salsa too?" she asked.

"Yes."

She fixed it, then watched him eat at the kitchen table. "Derek, I need to phone your mother and your father and tell them where you are. They need to know. They're really worried."

"Okay."

She made the phone calls and then came back to be with him.

"Some people don't think very much of you," he said.

"I know that."

"You knew my dad was married when you started liking him, didn't you?"

"Yes."

"Are you going to marry him after he gets divorced?"

"Yes."

"Are you ever going to have a baby?" he asked.

"We've talked about it."

"After you have your baby, will you keep working?"

"No, I'd probably quit work, at least until our child is old enough to be in school."

"So if you're not working, then maybe Dad will have to hire another secretary. Do you ever worry you'll end up like my mother?"

She faced him like a gunfighter unafraid of anything. "I

123

know this was hard for you, but we can't turn back what's already happened. We have to go on and do the best we can."

"That's what my mother is doing. She works at a donut shop. That's the best we can do right now. And here you are in a nice apartment. I'd say your best is better than our best."

"I've had this apartment for a long time. It has nothing to do with your father. I'm the one who pays the rent, not your father."

"How long have you been working for my father?"

"About a year and a half."

"A year and a half. That's all it took. I just don't understand what went wrong. If I could understand, then maybe it'd be better. You want to know something? I'm afraid I'll do the same thing to my wife."

"It's not hereditary, Derek. I wouldn't worry about it if I were you."

"I hope you don't mind my saying this, but you're not that great looking, if you ask me. I mean, you're pretty, but my mom, even though she's a lot older, looks okay when she gets dressed up."

"Yes, she's very attractive." She paused. "I often think about your mother."

"What about?"

"How she's doing. I'm sorry that she and I will probably never be friends."

"Friends? Are you crazy? She hates you. We all hate you. Did you purposely try to get my dad to go for you so he'd leave my mom?"

"No. We became friends first, then fell in love gradually. Do you have any other questions you want to ask me?"

"Would you answer any question I asked?"

"Yes, I think I owe you at least that. We're not going to get anywhere by putting walls up between us, are we?"

He sensed how tough she was, and that made him like her just a little bit more. "I guess I'm a lot like you now."

"How's that?"

"A disappointment to the people who used to respect me. I stole an Eagle medal from the scout office. Kind of a stupid thing to do, right?"

"We all make mistakes."

"I don't want to ever go back to church again," he said.

"Why not?"

"Because everyone is going to know what I did."

"They also will know you feel bad about it."

"Do you have any brothers?" he asked.

"No. Just one sister."

"Kimberly and Megan are my sisters."

"I know."

"Kimberly really helped me a lot with my Eagle project. She even told the police she was sure I wasn't the one who took the Eagle. I guess I fooled her, didn't I? I feel bad about that now. And then there's Megan. I like to go in her room and talk to her. She's always at her desk doing homework or some other dumb project. One time she told me she was glad I was her brother. We're really different though. She's so organized, and yet she likes me and even asks my advice sometimes." He paused. "I really think I'm the most like my dad of any of the kids."

"Why do you say that?"

"I can't be trusted either."

There was a knock on the door. Gloria opened the door, and Derek's father stepped in.

"We've all been worried sick about you," he said.

"Sorry."

Paul looked at his watch. "It's late. I'll take you home."

When Derek walked into the house, his mother ran over and gave him a hug. Kimberly did the same thing. Ben was there and gave him a pat on the back. Megan, hearing the noise, came running down the stairs.

"I stole the Eagle from the scout office."

"Yes, but we still love you," Kimberly said.

That was too much. Tears started down his face. Because he was embarrassed, he turned away.

Anne put her arms around him. Kimberly put her arm around his shoulder. Megan joined him on the other side and they held each other and let the tears come.

The next day Derek stayed home from school. He went with his mother to the scout office and confessed what he had done and gave back the medal he had stolen. Then he spent the afternoon writing letters of apology.

That night Brother Hatch and Mike came home teaching. Their lesson was on how our faith in the Savior can help us get through difficult times.

A day later Anne and her children met for the first time with a counselor in LDS Social Services. It was the first of four visits aimed at helping them communicate better as a family.

13

"Thank you for coming," Kimberly said when she opened the door to Ben two days later. She placed the engagement ring in his hand. "I need to give this back. Things are too crazy here now. I still love you, and everything, but I'm not ready to get married now. Not only that, I've got to be here for Megan and Derek. They need me."

He wouldn't take the ring. "This doesn't make any sense," he said. "When will you be ready? When Derek comes back from his mission? When Megan graduates from high school?"

"I don't know."

"Why is it that everyone else's needs come ahead of mine?"

"It's not only Derek and Megan. Right now marriage seems like a trap that will take over my life and cause me to fulfill everyone else's needs without having time to see to my own. That's what has happened to my mom all these years. I'm just not ready for a commitment like that. Besides, I wouldn't make you very happy if we got married now. Really, it's better this way. I'm not going to end up like my mother. Do you know how much she makes now? A college graduate can earn three or four times more. I have to be prepared to raise my kids if my marriage ends in divorce."

"Your marriage isn't going to end in divorce."

"You don't know that for sure. Who can say what the future

holds? It happens all the time, Ben. Just look around. In three years I'll graduate. Maybe then I'll be ready."

"Three years? Are you out of your mind? I can't wait three years."

"I'd wait for you that long if you asked me to."

"Well, I'm not you."

"What is it with you? If your woman doesn't satisfy your needs, then you dump her and find someone else. Is that how it goes with you? I mean, that's what my dad did, and that's what you're about to do with me. Well, walk out on me and find someone else then. You don't care about me or my feelings. All you care about is getting what you want. So how are you any different from my dad?"

"You have no right to say that."

"Why not? My mom suddenly isn't young enough for him so he dumps her. I tell you I can't marry you right away and so you're about to dump me. I can't see there's much difference between the two of you."

Out of his frustration and anger, Ben hit the wall with his fist and, much to his surprise, put his hand through the plasterboard. They both looked at the caved-in hole in the wall of the living room.

"I can't talk to you now," he said and then left.

"What'll it be?" Anne asked at six o'clock the next morning at Jiffy Buns Donut Shop.

"Donut and orange juice," Ben said, his elbows on the counter, his head in his hands, his eyes nearly closed.

"You're up early this morning."

"Never went to bed," he muttered.

"What kind of a donut do you want?"

"I don't care, any kind."

She set his order down in front of him.

"It's all over between Kimberly and me," he said.

128

"Kimberly said you had an argument, but does that mean it's all over?"

"It's over. That's what she wants." He paused. "I came here to apologize. I'm sorry for putting a hole in your wall. I can fix it today if you want, while Kimberly is on campus."

"There's no hurry."

"I don't know what came over me. I guess you know she broke off our engagement."

"Yes. She told me she needed more time."

"I guess I could have taken that, but then she accused me of being just like her father. That's not fair. I'm not like him. That's when I put my fist through your wall. Sorry."

"What's going to happen now between you and Kimberly?"

"I don't know. I think she wants me out of her life."

"I'm not so sure about that. She was pretty broken up after you left last night."

"Well, that's good news," Ben said with just a hint of a smile.

"And, if it's any consolation, if I could pick anyone to be Kimberly's husband, you'd be my first choice. But, even so, Ben, you've got a lot to learn."

"I do?"

"Yes."

"And Kimberly doesn't?"

"No, Kimberly has a lot to learn too."

"How can anyone eat a donut at this time of day?" he said, pushing the plate away. "What do I need to learn?"

"You need to learn to listen with your heart."

"You sound like one of those articles in a women's magazine my mother buys at the grocery store."

"You read women's magazines?" Anne teased.

"Not really."

"It might do you some good actually."

"I doubt it. What does listening with my heart mean?"

"It means that if Kimberly is upset about something, you

129

don't rush in to solve the problem until she's told you how she feels."

"Give me an example."

"This morning when I came to work, I tried to turn on the dishwasher and nothing happened."

"Did you check the circuit breaker?"

"Sorry, Ben, you just flunked."

"What are you talking about?"

"You jumped in with a solution to my problem."

"What are you talking about? Checking the circuit breaker is the first thing you do when you've lost power."

"Go home and get some sleep, Ben. If you ask me, you should have read more of your mother's home magazines."

"First Kimberly's on my case and now you."

"But don't ever forget I'm on your side, okay?"

He paid for his food, then returned to his apartment and went to bed. He slept until noon, went to his one o'clock class, then came back to his apartment and called Jeni at his dad's store in Rock Springs.

"Jeni, this is Ben. How's it going?"

"Why are you calling me?"

"You're different from other girls. You're more like a man. I really admire that in a woman."

"Have you been drinking? Look, I'm not loaning you any money, no matter what kind of a jam you're in, so you can just forget it."

"I need some advice. You remember Kimberly? Well, she just dumped me."

"Find someone else then. Look, I gotta go. There's a guy here who locked his keys in his pickup, and he's due in court in fifteen minutes."

"That's it? That's your big advice? Find someone else?"

"What other choices are there? If she dumps you, you move on."

"Don't you want to know how I feel?"

"Good grief, man, what's wrong with you? You're not turning mush-brained on us, are you?"

"You didn't even let me explain how I feel."

"Look, Ben, I told you how to fix your problem. What more do you want? But now I've got to go. You're not the only one around here with problems." She hung up.

Ben felt like it had been a mistake to even call Jeni. *She doesn't even care about me,* he thought. *She didn't even listen to me.*

It was then that what Kimberly's mother had said suddenly made sense to him.

Later that afternoon Ben showed up at Kimberly's home to fix the hole he'd put in the wall with his fist. Derek let him in. Ben was all primed to listen to Kimberly's feelings and let her know once and for all how truly sensitive he had recently become.

She didn't come home until he was nearly finished. She walked in the door, saw him, and said, "Hello."

"Hello."

"Doing a little repair work?" she said.

"Yes. How was your day?"

"It was okay."

"You felt good about your day then, is that right?" he asked, trying to apply what he'd learned from her mother.

She looked at him strangely. "I just said that, didn't I?"

"Yes, of course."

"Are we still singing Friday and Saturday night?" she asked.

"How would you feel about it if we did?" he asked.

"The money's good. If we possibly can, let's do it, even if things between us aren't the way they used to be."

"All right then, it's settled."

"I need to give you back some things," she said.

"What things?"

"Some tapes and . . . your ring."

131

Ben panicked. This telling how you feel was harder than it looked. All his life he had grown up with the image of the strong, silent man who takes on the world and never complains, and now, all of a sudden, it seemed like the rules had suddenly changed and he was supposed to be weepy and sentimental.

It was too much to ask in such a short time. "Well, if you're not going to use it, I might as well get it back. It cost me a lot of money."

"I'm sure it did. I'll go get everything and come right back."

While she was gone, he practiced in his mind what he would say to her when she returned. *I feel bad we're breaking up. That's good,* he thought, *because it's honest and it shows I'm a sensitive kind of guy. And I do feel bad we're breaking up, but of course it's mostly Kimberly's fault this is happening anyway.*

I feel like this is mostly your fault, was his second round of feelings, followed by: *I feel like you don't really care about me one way or the other,* followed by: *This is all your fault.*

That's right, he thought.

Kimberly came down the stairs and gave him the ring and tapes.

"I hope you're happy now," he said sarcastically.

He knew he'd blown it, but she made him so mad he couldn't think straight. So much for sensitivity, he thought. He left without another word, the ring in his hand.

The next morning he showed up at Jiffy Buns again.

"It doesn't work."

"What doesn't work?" Anne said.

"Listening with my heart. It doesn't do any good. She didn't want to tell me what was in her heart. All she wanted to do was give me back the ring."

"Did you tell her how you felt?"

"Yeah, sort of."

"What did you say?"

132

"I said, 'I hope you'll be happy now.' " He said it in a sincere voice, much differently than it had sounded when he had said it to Kimberly.

"Are you sure that's what you said?"

"More or less. Oh, what's the use? What I said was, 'I hope you're happy now.' " He said it the way he'd said it to Kimberly.

"My gosh, Ben, where'd you get your sensitivity training— from the National Rifle Association?"

"This isn't easy for me."

"How do you feel about the fact that you and Kimberly have broken off your engagement?"

"I feel like none of this would have happened if she—"

"Stop it, those aren't feelings. Feelings are more basic. People feel sad or angry or giddy or silly. Are you even in touch with your feelings?"

Two construction workers came in for a cup of coffee and a donut. Their presence threw a blanket over Ben's being able to talk about his feelings, because these were the kind of men he'd always looked up to—men who got things done instead of standing around wringing their hands and telling people how they felt.

The men left a few minutes later, but for Ben their influence lingered on.

"This morning when I came to work, I noticed the car was running hot," Anne said. "It kept getting hotter and hotter. I was afraid I wasn't even going to make it here."

"Could be a stuck thermostat," Ben said.

"You failed again, Ben."

"What?"

"You're supposed to say, 'That must have been frustrating.' Learn to listen with your heart."

"How long am I supposed to do that when I'm talking to someone?"

"As long as it takes."

"How am I going to judge that?"

133

She sighed. "All right. Listen with your heart for three minutes, and then you can go ahead and solve their problem for them."

He'd had enough for one day. He paid Anne for his breakfast and started to leave.

"Ben, listen with your heart, but also you need to tell Kimberly what's *in* your heart."

"Yeah, right."

"I know this is hard for you to learn, but it'll be worth it if you can learn it now." She paused. "Is there anything I should be working on, you know, as a mother?"

"You never have fun with your kids."

She gazed at him. He could tell she was thinking, and then she nodded her head. "Thanks. I'll work on that."

That night he wanted to practice on someone, so he called Jeni at home. "Hi, it's me again."

"I could tell."

"I've always liked you, Jeni. Oh sure, we've done pranks on each other, like the time I put a laxative in your hot chocolate, but despite it all, I always knew we were friends. I feel like underneath that hard exterior lies a wonderful human being. And I for one feel good about our friendship."

"You put a laxative in my hot chocolate?"

He hung up.

That night out of frustration he went out to a store and bought a copy of *Woman's Day* magazine. It didn't do him any good, although he did appreciate the helpful suggestions on cooking broccoli.

14

On Friday night, Ben and Kimberly went to Angelo's in separate cars. "I think it would be best if we didn't look at each other during the love songs," Ben said.

"What do you want me to do, look straight ahead?"

"Yes."

"Look, we have to act out a part here or we're both going to end up without a job, and I can't afford that because I really need the money."

"Just don't look at me on the love songs, okay? Nobody will notice."

Angelo noticed. After the first show, he came up to them. "What's going on? It was like a funeral in here. And whose bright idea was it to do 'Feelings' anyway?"

"Mine," Ben said quietly.

Angelo pointed at Ben. "You do that again, Mister, and you're both fired! Feelings, my foot."

"You didn't bring us a pizza," Ben said.

"Hey, you want a pizza, buy it yourself."

They ordered a small pizza and sat in wounded silence in a corner booth. They had forty-five minutes until their next show.

"Is that all you're going to do—play with the salt shaker?" Kimberly asked.

135

"I feel like crud," Ben said, in what he considered a supreme triumph of shared feelings.

"They say something's going around."

"It's not that."

"What is it then?"

He cleared his throat. He felt a rush of emotion, which he fought against, because he was afraid if he told her how he felt, it wouldn't make any difference, and on top of everything, she would think of him as a wimp. But, on the other hand, if he didn't tell her how he felt, then he might lose her, and he couldn't stand for that to happen. He had to do something to let her know how he felt.

"It's probably just a cold," he said.

"Drink plenty of fluids," she said.

"Yeah, sure."

He gave up on the salt shaker and stared at the pepper shaker.

"Oh, for our second show," Kimberly said, "a guy from my math class said he might come by to hear us. His name is Michael. I'll introduce you when he comes."

"Didn't take you long, did it?"

"He's just a friend. He and I are in a collaborative study group."

"Yeah, right."

"Look, from now on, what I do is my business. I don't have to answer to you. And one other thing, since you don't want me looking at you during the slow songs, I might take a microphone out in the audience and sing to Michael . . . just as a gag."

"Hey, sit on his lap, for all I care."

"Excuse me, I've got to get away from you for a while. You're such a grouch tonight."

The second show was a disaster for Ben. On every love song, Kimberly went out into the audience and picked out one of the guys to sing to. The first one she picked was her friend Michael from school. Ben quit singing and just stood there with his mouth open while she sang to Michael one of the songs they had written.

After two songs, Kimberly returned to Ben.

"Now we'd like to sing 'Feelings,'" Ben announced.

Angelo banged two empty pizza pans together to remind Ben what would happen if they sang that.

"No, Ben, we're going to sing, 'You are My Sunshine,' and we'd like everyone to join in," Kimberly said.

"You Are My Sunshine" saved them from being fired, but after the second show, Angelo went up to them and said, "When's the last time you two practiced together?"

"It's been a while."

"Look, either you come back tomorrow night with new material and a little life in your act, or you can go find yourself another restaurant to sabotage."

The next morning they met at nine at Kimberly's house and started practicing. They practiced until noon, and then Kimberly said she had been invited to lunch by Michael. She scheduled another practice for two o'clock and left. Megan and Derek invited Ben to have lunch with them.

"Kimberly still loves you," Megan said as she opened two cans of soup.

"How do you know that?"

"She told me."

"She's got a strange way of showing it."

"You're not much better. Why don't you tell her you love her?"

"Why should he do that?" Derek said. "I say if a woman crosses you once, then you dump her."

"Derek, you don't know a thing," Megan said. "And tuck in your shirt, will you?"

137

Ben and Megan sat silently for a while. Then Megan spoke up. "My bike has a flat tire."

A perfect opportunity, Ben thought, *to practice listening with my heart.* He set his watch to time himself for three minutes.

"That must make you feel really bad," he said.

"It's been like this for months."

"It must be so frustrating not to be able to use your bike when you want to."

"How about fixing it now while you're waiting for Kimberly to get back?"

"A flat tire can be very discouraging, especially when you're all ready to ride your bike and you go out to the garage and it's flat."

"Are you going to fix it or not?" Megan snapped.

Ben looked at his watch. Only forty-five seconds had passed. He couldn't see how anyone could go three minutes with this "listen with your heart" garbage. He gave up. "Sure, I'll fix it for you."

They ended up having to go the hardware store to get another tube. Megan went along with him for company.

"I hope things work out for you and Kimberly," she said in the car.

"Thanks. If they don't, can we still be friends?"

"Sure we can. I like you, Ben. It gives me an idea of what kind of a guy to look for when I get older." She paused. "I am going to get older too. I'm pretty sure about that now."

He looked at her strangely.

"For a while there, I was thinking about killing myself."

"You were? Why?"

"Because everything kept getting worse."

"I'd hate to think of a world without you in it."

"Yeah, I'm pretty sure I'd have ended up regretting it if I'd done it. The trouble with killing yourself is that you keep on existing even after you die."

"If you ever feel that you don't want to live anymore, promise me you'll call me, even if it's in the middle of the night. I'll come over and we'll talk. Okay?"

"Okay."

Ben and Derek and Megan were in the garage working on the bike when Kimberly and Michael returned from lunch. Michael pulled into the driveway. Kimberly stayed in the car and talked to him. They didn't know that twenty feet away Megan was looking out the small window in the garage and describing to Ben what was going on.

"She's smiling at him, like he said something really funny."

"Mister Collaborative Learning Group," Ben grumbled.

"You want me to help you waste this guy?" Derek asked.

"That wouldn't solve anything."

"They're getting out of the car," Megan said. "Now he has his arm around her waist while they're walking to the front door."

Ben was still working on the bicycle. Megan turned to face him. "You've got to do something, Ben, right away, or you're going to lose her," she said.

"Tonight for sure," Derek said.

"What?" Ben asked.

"Kidnap her and tell her you won't let her go until she agrees to marry you," Derek said.

"Is that the best you can do?" Megan said.

"You got something better?" Derek snapped.

"Ben, just let her know how much you love her," Megan said.

"What difference is that going to make?" Derek asked.

"Oh well, sure, Derek, your way is much better."

"I know that."

That night Ben gave Kimberly a ride to Angelo's. "After we finish tonight, could we spend some time together?" he asked.

"Sorry, Michael and I are going to study."

139

"Study, yeah, right."

"It'll be more than just Michael and me. There's two more in the group."

"How come this is the first time I've heard about this group?"

"We used to meet right after class, but one of the guys in the group can't meet then anymore."

"Are you the only girl in the group?"

"Yes."

"It figures."

"It just turned out that way."

Saturday night was always a big night at Angelo's. As they set up to play, Angelo came over. "You understand how important tonight is for you two, don't you? You mess up again like last night and you're finished." He stopped. "But, relax, have a nice time, make the customers happy."

"Are we going to look at each other tonight?" Kimberly asked Ben as they tuned up.

"I guess we'd better."

"I'd say so."

Their first show was a big success. Angelo brought them a pizza and put his hand on Ben's shoulder and said, "That's more like it. Keep it up."

They sat at a small table next to where they performed and ate. While she was eating, he said to her, "I'm always surprised at how beautiful you are. It's like I forget, and then I see you and it's the first time all over again."

Looking at each other again, for just a minute all the barriers were down and it was like the first day they met. But it wasn't their first meeting, and much had happened since then. He could see a sadness in her eyes.

She glanced toward the door and her expression changed, and he knew Michael had just walked in.

"Excuse me, I need to make a phone call," he said, getting up and starting to leave.

"Is it okay if Michael sits with us?" she called after him.

"Yes, of course."

He went to a pay phone in the hall and called Anne. "What's the one thing I can say to Kimberly that will make the biggest difference to her?"

"Can I talk to you before you leave with Michael?" Ben asked Kimberly after they finished performing for the night.

She put her guitar in its case and turned around. "Yeah, sure."

"Can we talk in my car?"

"Fine with me."

They sat in the car for what seemed like a long time before he said anything. Finally he began, somewhat hesitantly. "I know that you've had to go through some hard times lately . . . and . . . I understand that you're not sure if you're ready to get married now."

She sighed. "That's right, I'm not."

He spoke softly but with a little more confidence. "I just want you to know that I love you. There's never going to be anyone else for me except you. I know you need some time, so I've decided to work for my dad this summer at the store. I'll come down to see you whenever I can get away. And I'll be back for school in the fall." He stopped a moment, then went on. "I guess the main thing I wanted to say is, take as much time as you need. It's like this song I heard once. It goes, 'If it takes forever I will wait for you.' Well, that's the way I feel. I guess I'd better let you go study. Michael looks like he's about to fall asleep."

"Ben, thanks for being so understanding," she said.

"Sure, no problem."

She kissed him on the cheek and then left to go study with Michael.

15

That summer Ben's usual pattern was to take off after work on Saturday and drive to Utah. He'd get in late, stay at his aunt's house, go to church with her, and then show up at Kimberly's house for lunch. Then he'd leave Monday morning for Wyoming, arriving in Rock Springs just in time to go to work at one in the afternoon.

"What are you doing after work tonight?" Jeni asked the second Saturday in July.

"Driving to Utah."

"Again? My gosh, Ben, why don't you just buy yourself a bus and take passengers? You're on the road more than Greyhound."

"I suppose."

"Your sweetie still got cold feet about getting hitched?"

"Yeah."

"Can't say I blame her. You'll be lucky if you can find anybody who'll have you."

"Thanks for the vote of confidence, Jeni."

She paused. "Look, I know your weekends are filled up, but . . . look, just forget it, okay?"

"What's on your mind?"

"Well, I'm on a bowling team and one of the guys left town. You interested? It's Wednesday nights. Look, if you're not, it's no big deal. It doesn't matter to me one way or the other."

142

"I'm not much good as a bowler."

"That's okay. We're just in this for laughs anyway."

He smiled. "Sure, why not. Count me in."

The next week he went bowling with Jeni. She teased him unmercifully, but that was what he expected anyway. They ended up having a good time.

When he got home, his mother told him Kimberly had called while he'd been gone. He phoned her right away. He had planned on leaving Friday night because he'd worked at the store on the Fourth of July just so he could get an extra day off later in the summer.

Kimberly told him she'd be working until five on Saturday. She was working in the Mechanical Engineering Department. "Sorry, once we start the experiment we can't stop. You still want to make the trip?"

"Sure, no problem."

"Where were you when I called?" she asked.

"Bowling with Jeni."

"You know she adores you, don't you?"

"Jeni? No way. We're just friends—just like you and Michael are friends. Are you still seeing him every day?"

"We work together, just like you and Jeni do."

Ben drove to his aunt's house Friday night and slept in until noon on Saturday. Then he got up and worked around his aunt's place. At five o'clock he went over to Kimberly's. She wasn't home yet, so he sat around and talked to Megan and Derek and Anne.

"Derek has some good news," Anne said.

"What is it, Derek?"

"They're going to let me have my Eagle," Derek said.

"That's great. What made them change their mind?"

"Brother Hatch went around talking to people. He set up

143

a meeting for us to go to. I told them I was sorry for what I'd done."

"Are you glad you're going to get it?"

"Yeah, I guess so."

Derek stayed a few more minutes, then left to go out with some friends. Anne excused herself to go work in the kitchen.

"I keep telling Kimberly she's crazy for treating you so mean sometimes, but she never listens to me," Megan said. She talked with him for another fifteen minutes and then told him she was going over to a friend's house.

Anne called Kimberly's work number but there was no answer. She waited until eight-thirty and then told him she had to go shopping for groceries, but he was welcome to stay in the house and wait. At nine o'clock Kimberly arrived in Michael's car. She was wearing cut-off jeans and a T-shirt.

"I didn't think you'd still be here," she said as she walked into the house.

"What happened?"

"We finished the experiment early. Michael asked me to go up and see his uncle's cabin."

"Why would he want you to see his uncle's cabin?"

"Because the professor we work for asked Michael and me to be in charge of a party for our research group, and we had to see if it'll be big enough for us to use."

"And then what happened?"

"It was so pretty up there that we decided to take a hike. I guess we lost track of the time."

"Kimberly, thanks a lot. I've been waiting four hours for you to show up."

She didn't seem very concerned. "Sorry."

"Why didn't you at least call to say you'd be late?"

"Why do you keep coming around here anyway? I know it's just a matter of time. You'll end up leaving me sometime, so what difference does it make if it's now or later?"

"I won't ever leave you."

"You will. Everybody breaks up eventually. Since my folks' divorce, I've started noticing how many marriages are ending in divorce. It happens all the time."

"It won't happen to us."

"You want to know the truth about today? I wanted to hurt you," she said. "I wanted to make you so mad you'd quit coming around. It wasn't Michael's fault. He kept saying, 'Shouldn't we go back?' And I'd say, 'No, we have plenty of time.' I'm sorry. I don't know what got into me. All this week I've felt that if I made you mad enough, you'd break up with me and take up with Jeni big time. I just kept thinking it's better for us to break up now instead of after we're married and have two or three kids."

"I'll never leave you."

"You can't say that for sure. If we got married, we'd have problems. Everyone I know has problems in their marriage."

"We'll work out our problems."

"What if we can't?"

"Then we'll go to somebody for counseling."

"I'm not always going to look the way I look today. Someday I'll be old and fat and I'll have wrinkles."

"We'll get old together."

"But you'll always be surrounded by younger women where you work, maybe even your secretary, like with my dad, or someone else you work with." She sighed. "Oh, I'm so messed up. Look, I know what I'm doing to you isn't fair. I think maybe it'd be better if you didn't come to visit me for a while. I need some time by myself to work things out."

He looked at her for a long time and then said, "Whatever you say."

On Wednesday of the next week Kimberly called Ben just to talk. She told him that Brother Hatch had found a better job for her mother in the registrar's office at the university. It paid better, but the main advantage was that her hours allowed her to be home when her children were home. She'd also have more time to be available when prospective buyers came to see the house.

"Anything else happening?" he asked.

There was a long pause and then Kimberly said, "My dad and Gloria are getting married Friday."

"Are you going to the wedding?"

"No." She paused. "I'm really having a hard time with this."

"Why?"

"When my dad called to tell me and Derek and Megan about the wedding, he also told us Gloria is taking the missionary lessons. What if she joins the Church?"

"Would that be so bad?" Ben asked.

"I just don't think it's fair. My dad abandoned us because of Gloria. I don't think she should ever be allowed to join the Church. I keep thinking that in five years, they'll be living in some ward where nobody knows how they got together. When someone finds out he's been married before, they'll ask him about his first marriage and he'll say, 'It just didn't work out.' And nobody will know that it was my dad's fault. He'll make it sound like it was just something that happened, like when the leaves fall off the trees and there's nothing you can do to stop it."

"Maybe it wasn't all your dad's fault."

"I don't know. I don't know much of anything right now. My dad is moving on with his life. It's just the rest of us that are still stuck in the past. I keep thinking things are going to get better for me, but it's not happening yet. Somehow I've got to work this out."

"Your engine sounds like crud," Jeni said as she watched him drive into the parking lot for work one day. "You want me to help you overhaul it?"

"It's okay."

"We could work on it after work."

146

"Jeni, I still love Kimberly."

"And a whole lot of good it does you too, right? Now she won't even let you come down to see her."

"She's trying to work through some things."

"And what about you? The only time you smile anymore is when I'm on your case about something. So, what do you think about us fixing up your car?"

"Okay, thanks."

"Why should I get married when I know that every marriage has problems?" Kimberly asked Brother Hatch the next time he came home teaching.

Brother Hatch thought about it for a minute and then bent down and whispered something to Mike Jefferson, his companion. Mike got up and left without another word. "Mike will be back in a minute with the answer to your question."

"If I could know for sure that my marriage would end up as strong as yours, then I'd go ahead," Kimberly said.

"My wife and I have had our shares of disagreements and hurt feelings, but we never have thought of giving up."

Mike returned a minute later with a rose he'd cut from Brother Hatch's garden. He handed Kimberly the rose. It was a dark red and smelled wonderful.

"That's the answer to your question, Kimberly. You can't have a rose without some thorns."

She kept the rose in her room for days, and every time she saw it, she thought of what he'd said.

But somehow she wanted more assurance than that.

Kimberly woke up at six o'clock on that first Sunday morning in August. She was fasting and wanted plenty of time to be alone before she had to get ready for church.

She turned to the topical guide in her Bible and began looking up scriptures dealing with fasting. She worked her way down the list until she came to one reference that seemed to

147

be exactly what she was looking for. She turned to Alma, chapter 17, which tells about the sons of Mosiah on their way to teach the Lamanites. "And it came to pass that they journeyed many days in the wilderness, and they fasted much and prayed much that the Lord would grant unto them a portion of his Spirit to go with them, and abide with them. . . . And it came to pass that the Lord did visit them with his Spirit, and said unto them: Be comforted. And they were comforted."

Kimberly kept reading until she got to chapter 26, where Ammon summarized their missionary labors among the Lamanites. " . . . we have been cast out, and mocked, and spit upon, and smote upon our cheeks; and we have been stoned, and taken and . . . cast into prison; and through the power and wisdom of God we have been delivered again."

The sons of Mosiah had been comforted by the Spirit to go ahead. And because they had gone ahead, even though they had difficult experiences, their lives had been spared and many people had been blessed.

Kimberly wasn't naive enough to think that there was a "one and only one" for her. There were probably many men whom she would be compatible with if she were married to one of them. And no matter whom she married, she knew problems would come up that both of them would need to work out. She knew there were no guarantees in life.

She had already talked to her bishop about how reluctant she was to get married because of what had happened to her parents. She had read several books about the family, she had talked with Brother and Sister Hatch about their marriage, and she had asked her mother for her opinion about what she should do. But none of what she had learned or heard was enough. She still felt uncertain.

There had been times in her life when she had felt the Spirit give her a feeling of calm when she was worried about something—when she was eight and had to play at a piano recital at her teacher's house; the day before school began when she had to go to a new school; when she had to sing the song she had written for her high school commencement — times when she had prayed and felt a comforting peace of mind.

She was dressed for church, but they didn't need to leave for another half an hour. She closed the door to her room, went to her bed, and knelt down. "Heavenly Father," she began softly.

It was not until sacrament meeting, while she listened to the testimonies of others as they related some of the blessings they had received in facing their problems, that suddenly, like a gentle breeze, she felt a calm spiritual assurance; and then, like the sons of Mosiah before her, she also was comforted.

Kimberly left Monday morning and drove to Rock Springs. She arrived in the early afternoon.

She walked into the hardware store and looked around for Ben. Jeni spotted her and came over. "What are you doing here?"

"I came to see Ben."

Jeni looked at Kimberly for a long time and then shrugged her shoulders. "Sure, it figures."

"What?"

"I just finished overhauling his engine."

"I'm sorry."

"Hey, don't apologize. The truth is, he's a pain. He's been taking up way too much of my time anyway." She stared at Kimberly again. "You've changed your mind, haven't you?"

"Yes."

"I could tell. Well, he's in the back. I'll show you."

In the supply room in the back, Ben was talking to two men about plastic pipe. Another employee was assembling a bicycle. "You got someone here who wants to see you," Jeni said, and then she walked away.

Ben and Kimberly stared at each other. "What are you doing here?" he asked.

She didn't want to open her heart up in front of all these people. "I wonder if you could help me. I'm looking for a monkey wrench."

He excused himself and led her into the main part of the store. "Don't they have hardware stores in Utah?"

"I like personal attention for my hardware needs. I was hoping I could get that here."

"We pride ourselves on personal attention."

"How personal?" she said without thinking, and then started to blush. "Sorry."

He looked at her strangely but didn't say anything. A minute later, in the plumbing supplies section, he said. "These are our monkey wrenches."

She hefted one of the wrenches. "Do the monkeys complain much?"

Their eyes met.

"Ben, what I really want is to marry you."

His mouth dropped open. "Uh . . . well . . . okay, but I have to work until six."

She smiled. "It doesn't have to be today."

The week before Christmas, Kimberly and Ben were married in the Jordan River Temple.

On their wedding night in their honeymoon suite, she waited for him to come out of the bathroom. He'd been in there a long time. She was starting to worry about him. Finally she went to the door. "Ben, is everything okay?"

"Yeah, sure. The toilet won't shut off completely. I thought I'd adjust the float. I'm almost done."

"Ben, listen to me. If you don't come out right away, then when we get back to Wyoming, I'm going to tell all your customers that this is what you did on our honeymoon night."

150

He opened the door immediately. "Maybe I'll just finish it up later."

She sat in a chair with a guitar in her hands. "I'd like to dedicate this song to you," and she sang "A Wintry Night."

When she finished, he clapped. "Very nice. Encore."

"My encore is you, my life is yours, my love is true."

She set down the guitar and came over and kissed him.

"What you said rhymes," he whispered in her ear.

She was kissing his eyelids. "Not now," she said. "Later maybe, but not now."

"It could be the beginning of a new song."

"It is a new song, Ben. This is our song . . . and this is the first verse."

About the Author

Jack Weyland, a native of Butte, Montana, received a B.S. in physics from Montana State University and a Ph.D. in physics from Brigham Young University. He is a professor of physics at Ricks College in Rexburg, Idaho. A popular youth leader and speaker, he has served as a bishop and as a member of a stake presidency in The Church of Jesus Christ of Latter-day Saints. He and his wife, Sheryl, are the parents of five children.

Dr. Weyland has had numerous short stories published in the *New Era*. His books include *A Small Light in the Darkness*, a collection of short stories; *If Talent Were Pizza, You'd Be a Supreme*, a volume for youth on self-esteem; and several best-selling novels: *Charly; Sam; The Reunion; PepperTide; A New Dawn; The Understudy; Last of the Big-time Spenders; Sara, Whenever I Hear Your Name; Brenda at the Prom; Stephanie; Michelle and Debra; Kimberly;* and *Nicole*.